KU-012-481

Harry Bowling was born in Bermondsey, London, and left school at fourteen to supplement the family income as an office boy in a riverside provisions' merchant. Called up for National Service in the 1950s, he has since been variously employed as lorry driver, milkman, meat cutter, carpenter and decorator, and community worker. He now writes full time. He is the author of seven previous novels, *Backstreet Child*, *The Girl from Cotton Lane*, *Gaslight in Page Street*, *Paragon Place*, *Ironmonger's Daughter*, *Tuppence to Tooley Street* and *Conner Street's War*. He is married and lives with his family, dividing his time between Lancashire and Deptford.

'What makes Harry's novels work is their warmth and authenticity. Their spirit comes from the author himself and his abiding memories of family life as it was once lived in the slums of southeast London' *Today*

Pedlar's Row

Harry Bowling

HEADLINE

Copyright © 1994 by Harry Bowling

The right of Harry Bowling to be identified as the Author of
the Work has been asserted by him in accordance with the
Copyright, Designs and Patents Act 1988.

First published in 1994 by
HEADLINE BOOK PUBLISHING

First published in paperback in 1994 by
HEADLINE BOOK PUBLISHING

10 9 8 7 6

All rights reserved. No part of this publication may be
reproduced, stored in a retrieval system, or transmitted,
in any form or by any means without the prior written
permission of the publisher, nor be otherwise circulated
in any form of binding or cover other than that in which
it is published and without a similar condition being
imposed on the subsequent purchaser.

All characters in this publication are fictitious
and any resemblance to real persons, living or dead,
is purely coincidental.

ISBN 0 7472 4520 7

Typeset by
Letterpart Limited, Reigate, Surrey

Printed and bound in Great Britain by
Clays Ltd, St Ives plc

HEADLINE BOOK PUBLISHING
A division of Hodder Headline PLC
338 Euston Road
London NW1 3BH

To Edna and my roving family,
and to the ones who stay at home,
with love

Prologue

For more than a hundred years pedlars had been selling
their wares in the grimy cobbled streets of Bermondsey.
At first they came on foot and on horse-cart, lured by the
vast changes and the chance to make a few coppers. The
riverside borough was rapidly growing from a green and
pleasant village into a cramped, filthy industrial slum;
docks and wharves were being built along the water-
front, and tanneries were beginning to thrive in an area
which was perfectly suited to their needs. There were
many streams flowing through Bermondsey, and an
abundance of oak trees in the surrounding countryside to
supply the bark needed in the dyeing process. There
were also more than enough hides for the taking, for
they had been thrown into nearby pits, as required by an
ancient statute, after the animals had been slaughtered
for food and skinned.

The pedlars watched more and more workers' houses
and tenements being built almost overnight, dark brick
smothering the last vestiges of the green fields, and they
eagerly hawked their wares through the cobbled streets
and up the rickety wooden stairs of the tenement blocks.
They traded from battered suitcases and sacks and from
deep pockets that ran the length of their overcoat
linings, and when they were tired they rested on a small
stretch of greenery beyond a side street off the main
thoroughfare, shaded from the sun by a spreading

chestnut tree. There they ate their cheese sandwiches and drank ale from earthenware jugs, and some smoked strong tobacco in stained clay pipes.

The local children eyed the resting pedlars from a safe distance, for the men were not from their neighbourhood and some of them were swarthy, much like the gypsies who brought the travelling fairs to town. The suitcases that the pedlars carried were very large, large enough to take a child away in, and if for no other reason the children kept their distance. A few of the bigger boys would go near enough to the pedlars to trade obscenities, and they laughed off the terrible curses inflicted on them by one of the pedlars, who was known as Gypsy Joe.

Trade was invariably good for the itinerants in the early industrial years, since collar studs, cottons, needles and pins were always needed, as were candles, tapers and patent medicines, and as the pedlars rested under the spreading chestnut tree after traipsing round the streets and up and down stairs they were contented. Had they been able to peer into the future, however, they would have had cause to worry, but in blithe ignorance they ate their fill, drank the ale, and smoked their evil-smelling clay pipes while they rested.

It did not take the new market at Tower Bridge Road very long to become established, and when the women from the industrial houses and tenements came to buy their fruit and vegetables they realised that they could buy cotton, needles and pins and material too, as well as all the other items that were hawked around the backstreets. Very soon the pedlars started to feel the cold wind of change. A new transport network was opening up through the riverside borough and more travelling traders were now arriving by tram and train, but they did not care very much for what they saw. The Bermondsey street pedlars soon came to realise that for them the halcyon days were over.

In the spring of 1880 workmen came and cut down the chestnut tree and proceeded to dig up the grassy area. They laid pipes in the trenches and soon bricklayers and carpenters were hard at work. The pedlars who had watched the progress of the flourishing street market now had to witness the destruction of their leafy haven of rest, and they were angry. It was said that Gypsy Joe uttered a dark curse upon the spot which had been his old resting place, growling through his beard terrible words to open the very gates of hell, and he damned the workmen too before he shuffled out of the area hunched and sullen, vowing never to return.

The new houses were six in number, two-up two-down properties which were owned at first by a charitable trust and then taken over by the Bermondsey Borough Council. The six houses looked out over the high back wall of Garfield's leather goods factory and backed on to Bolton's tannery, one of many in the immediate area. The space between the front of the houses and the high brick wall was paved and at each end of the paved area there was an iron post set into a concrete base. One end of the walk led off from Weston Street, and the far end turned into Cooper Street, restricted somewhat by the end wall of another tannery.

It would have been quite natural to assume that Pedlar's Row, as it was called by the powers that be, was the first choice of name for the place, but Mrs Martha Bromley knew otherwise, and she smiled knowingly to her neighbour Aggie Carmichael as the two looked up and saw the new street sign for the first time.

'They was gonna call it Sunlight Place, would yer believe,' Martha said disdainfully. 'I read it in the paper. They would 'ave done it too, if it 'adn't 'ave bin fer ole Polly Parker.'

3

'Polly Parker?'

' 'S'right,' Martha went on. 'She's a right superstitious ole gel an' she got really upset when she 'eard about the curse Gypsy Joe was s'posed to 'ave put on the place. She got on to 'er ole man ter see if 'e could do anyfing about it, 'im bein' on the Council.'

'What, the curse, yer mean?'

'Nah, yer silly mare. I mean about gettin' the name changed,' Martha chided her. 'Polly didn't wanna upset ole Gypsy Joe, yer see, an' she reckoned that by callin' the place Pedlar's Row it would pacify 'im.'

Aggie Carmichael snorted as she tucked her hands into her fresh, crisp apron. 'It's a load of ole tosh,' she replied. 'I don't believe in such fings as curses. I've told Gypsy Joe more than once ter peddle 'is wares somewhere else when 'e knocked on my door. Those sort o' people don't worry the likes o' me.'

'Well, Polly Parker got 'er wish anyway,' Martha continued. 'It seems very strange though.'

'What does?'

'That workman gettin' killed the way 'e did when they was buildin' the places.'

Aggie gave her neighbour a quick look of disapproval. 'There was nuffink strange about it, the trench caved in, simple as that,' she countered sharply. 'There's workers gettin' killed nearly all the time, and I bet there's not a week goes by wivout somebody in a factory round 'ere gettin' killed or ruined fer life. It's nuffink ter do wiv curses.'

The six little houses in Pedlar's Row were soon occupied, and less than a year later Martha Bromley was reminded of the curse on the place when the tenant of number six stabbed his wife to death after finding out that she had been carrying on with another man. That winter he was hanged in Pentonville Prison.

4

In 1907 Martha was deeply saddened when her ageing friend Aggie Carmichael fell on the ice while walking through Pedlar's Row and broke her hip; she died of pneumonia in Guy's Hospital later the same week. It seemed to Martha that the ghost of Gypsy Joe was still leering malevolently over the houses, but nothing further happened until the winter of 1918, when the influenza epidemic hit Bermondsey and all five children from number five Pedlar's Row perished.

Older folk remembered the tale of Gypsy Joe, but younger people laughed at the story. They considered that life was for living, and the twenties were difficult, exciting times. The curse of Gypsy Joe the pedlar became quaint folklore and all but forgotten, until almost twenty years later.

The London Blitz was raging at its height, and one winter's night in 1940 a land mine fell on Cooper Street. The full blast travelled into Pedlar's Row and gutted the little houses there. Miraculously, although all the houses were occupied at the time, no one was killed. The next morning an unexploded bomb was found in the leather factory adjacent to the houses, and local folk felt that Lady Luck had surely been keeping her eye on Pedlar's Row that particular night.

Martha Bromley's daughter Clara had been told time and again about the curse of Gypsy Joe, and she knew that, had her mother still been alive, she would not have been talking about their lucky escape, but about the evil that was still glaring down at them, watching. Watching and waiting.

Chapter One

On a bitterly cold Monday morning in January 1946 a removal van drove along Weston Street, Bermondsey, and pulled up at the entrance to Pedlar's Row. The driver cursed loudly as he pulled back on the handbrake and pushed his cap up to scratch his forehead.

'Anuvver bloody fine job 'ere, I can see,' he grumbled to his younger assistant. 'What they wanna go an' put a post there for? If it wasn't fer that bloody fing I could 'ave backed down ter the front door.'

The assistant looked along the row of houses and wondered what his driver was getting so stewed up about. He had heard the nice young lady giving the driver instructions and he distinctly remembered her saying that it was the third house along the row. It was only a few paces to the front door, and after all there wasn't much furniture anyway. Not like the last job, when they had to cart a piano up two flights of stairs, and there wasn't a tip at the end of the job either. Or at least, that was what his driver had told him.

'Well, it's no good sittin' there, yer better get the back opened,' the driver said sharply. 'They'll be along in a minute an' we wanna be away from 'ere by one sharp.'

The young man gave the driver a quick glance and reluctantly got out of the warm cab. As he went round to the back of the van he saw a large woman standing a few yards away, staring at him.

'Are yer comin' in 'ere?' she asked in a loud voice.

'Nah, we can't get in, not wiv that post there,' he replied amiably.

'I know that. What I'm sayin' is, are yer movin' somebody in?' the woman said in a louder voice.

The driver had come round to the back of the van and he stood looking at the large woman who was quizzing his assistant. 'Yeah, 's'right, missus. Number three,' he told her in his official voice.

The young man had pinned back the two doors and was lowering the tailboard.

'Don't drop it right down,' the driver said irritably. 'Put it on the chain.'

The assistant did as he was bid but the woman made no attempt to leave. Instead she came nearer to stare into the van and was rewarded with a blinding look from the driver.

'Yer'll 'ave ter stan' back, missus, in case yer get 'urt,' he said quickly.

Queenie Bromley had seen all she needed to see and without answering the man she turned on her heel, walked into the paved area and pulled on the doorstring of the first house.

'Bloody nosy ole cow,' the driver moaned at the young assistant. 'Yer'd fink they'd 'ave better fings ter do than stand around watchin' people work.'

The young man ignored the comment and jumped up inside the removal van to untie the canvas straps securing the load.

'I 'ope she ain't gonna be too long,' the driver went on. 'She said she'd be 'ere a few minutes after us. I can't 'ang about 'ere all day.'

The young assistant cursed under his breath. When he got the job of furniture porter with Blake's Furniture Removers he had not bargained for being paired up with the most obnoxious driver on the fleet. Well, he wasn't going to put up with it for much longer. They could give him another driver or he would take his cards. After all, there were plenty of jobs going.

'Fank Gawd fer that,' the driver said suddenly.

The assistant looked along the turning to see a young woman hurrying towards them. As she reached the van she turned to the driver and smiled.

'I 'ope I 'aven't kept yer waitin',' she said breathlessly. 'I got delayed at the office. They couldn't find the key.'

The driver's face changed. 'It's all right, luv, we've only just got 'ere,' he said pleasantly. 'If yer'll open up we can get started.'

Queenie Bromley peered through the clean lace curtains of number one Pedlar's Row and eyed the young woman talking to the driver. 'She only looks a bit of a kid,' she remarked to her husband who was sitting beside the fire reading the *Daily Sketch*.

George Bromley grunted, shifting his thin frame in the easy chair. He had been at the call-on that morning but had not been picked for work at the wharf, and he was secretly pleased that trade was slack. He did not relish the thought of slogging away on the jetty while the weather was bitterly cold, and at fifty-three he felt that it was time he took it a little easier anyway.

Queenie had other ideas, however, and she gave him a sideways glance as she stared out into the street. George was getting lazy, she thought. Betty Conway's husband always seemed to get picked for work, and they were going to Margate for two weeks in the summer.

'Why don't yer come away from that winder,' George said as he turned the page of his newspaper. 'They'll fink you're a real nosy ole cow.'

Queenie took no notice as she watched the young woman turn into the row. 'I wonder if she's got any kids,' she mumbled.

George shook his head slowly and turned another page. There was no racing on that day due to the frozen turf and he wondered whether he ought to pay the Sultan a visit to get out of Queenie's way.

His mind was quickly made up for him. 'I 'ope yer not finkin' of goin' up the boozer terday,' Queenie said quickly as she turned away from the window towards him. 'Don't ferget yer promised ter put that paper up in the boys' bedroom.'

Laura Prior hurried into Pedlar's Row and inserted the key into the front door of the third house along. She had viewed the place the previous week and knew what to expect, but as she entered the empty house she sighed. There was so much to do and so little time. Lucy had not been able to get any time off work, and her boys would be home from school at four o'clock.

A shuffling of feet outside spurred the young woman into action and she threw the room doors open wide and showed the men the stairs as they carried the first of the beds into the house. Before she got down to anything else the first job was to get the place warm, she decided. Dad was not very well and he felt the cold.

The removal men seemed to make light work of bringing all the family's belongings in, and very soon the last of the furniture was carried through the door – a heavy oak sideboard, which the men eased into the parlour. Laura signed the sheet of paper that the driver thrust at her, then handed both of the men a half-crown. 'Fanks very much,' she said, smiling.

The driver nodded and touched his cap as he walked out of the house, and the young man gave her a big grin. That's what they should all do, he thought, suspecting that he might not have got his fair share of the tip if the driver had been handed the five shillings.

Laura stood looking around for a few seconds after the men had left. There were plenty of old newspapers in the boxes to use for the fire, but she would need a bag of coal, and a bundle of wood from the oil shop. She buttoned up the warm coat that hid her shapely figure and looked down at her shoes, then ran her fingers quickly over her head. Her hair was long and fair, and she pulled it tightly to the back of her head and fastened it in place with slides behind her small, close ears. Laura was thirty-four years old, five foot two in her stockinged feet and still unmarried, though she was an attractive woman with cornflower-blue eyes in a round face, and full lips above a dimpled chin. Lack of sleep had made her eyes puffy this morning, but she had not bothered to put on any make-up and her face looked pale.

As she let herself out of the house a woman came to the front door of number two and smiled at her. She was tall and thin-faced with thick-lensed spectacles and mousy-coloured hair coiled rigid in a mass of curlers, and she wore a tatty cardigan over her apron.

' 'Ello, luv. I'm Elsie Carmichael,' she said, the grin getting wider.

Laura smiled and nodded. 'I'm Laura, Laura Prior,' she replied. 'I'm just off ter get a bag o' coal ter light the fire.'

'There's no need ter do that, luv,' Elsie told her. 'I got a couple o' shovels o' coal yer can 'ave. Ransome come yesterday.'

'Ransome?'

'Yeah, the coalman. 'E comes twice a week this weavver. 'E'll be 'ere again termorrer. Yer'll be able ter get an 'undredweight then.'

Laura hesitated. 'If yer sure yer can spare it?' she ventured.

'It's no trouble,' Elsie assured her. 'Why don't yer

11

come in fer a minute. I've just made a pot o' tea.'

'I'll need some sticks o' wood though,' Laura said quickly.

Elsie smiled at her, revealing a row of large, protruding white teeth. 'I got plenty o' wood,' she said. 'My Len chopped me a box up last night. 'E's a dear – sometimes,' she added with emphasis.

Laura followed her new neighbour into the house and immediately felt the warmth on her face. The fire in the front parlour was banked high with coke and an iron kettle was spouting steam rings as it sat on a gas ring attached to a length of rubber tubing in the hearth.

'Sit yerself down, luvvy, an' undo yer coat or yer'll roast in 'ere,' Elsie said as she pressed a hand over her curlers. 'My Len likes me ter keep the place warm, yer know. 'E feels the cold, yer see. Suffers terrible wiv rheumatics.'

Laura nodded with a smile and watched while Elsie Carmichael poured the tea from a yellow enamelled teapot into two large mugs which were decorated with Union Jacks.

'Yer take sugar, do yer?' Elsie asked, already spooning sugar into the mugs.

'Just one, please,' Laura replied, intrigued by the amount the thin woman was spooning into her own.

'I like plenty o' sugar. My Len sez it ain't good fer yer, but I don't care,' Elsie went on, adding yet more sugar to her tea. 'I couldn't drink tea wivout sugar. I fink it keeps the cold out. D'yer like the mugs? I 'ad 'em given ter me at the victory party at work. I work at the box factory in Weston Street. I've bin orf sick though. It's me back. I fink I caught a cold in it doin' me washin' in the scullery. It's bleedin' draughty out there.'

Laura was anxious about the time and she glanced up at the large chimer on the mantelshelf over the fire. It said ten minutes past two and she sipped her steaming tea gratefully.

Elsie gulped a mouthful from her own mug then got up quickly. 'While yer drinkin' that I'll get yer a bucket o' coal an' a few sticks o' wood,' she said, pushing her glasses up on to the bridge of her nose. 'Yer must 'ave a lot ter do.'

While Elsie was filling the bucket Laura took the opportunity to glance around the room. Pictures of country scenes in gilt frames covered the walls and on the mantelshelf there were lots of small ornaments. A large aspidistra sat in a china pot in the window space and the lace curtains looked as though they had just been starched. The heavy-looking over-curtains appeared to be freshly laundered too, and red velvet cushions were scattered freely on the flower-patterned settee and armchairs. The room was clean and cosy, notwithstanding the streaks of soot stains on the ceiling.

Elsie returned and set the bucket down by the room door, placing a bundle of sticks on top of the coal. 'That should keep yer goin' till the mornin',' she said cheerily. 'Nuffink worse than a cold 'ouse, I say.'

Laura put down her empty mug. 'I'd better be goin',' she said, buttoning up her coat. 'I'm grateful fer the coal an' wood, an' the tea.'

As Laura carried the bucket of coal to the front door Elsie's expression became serious. ''Ave yer spoke to 'er next door yet?' she asked.

'No, not yet,' Laura replied, shaking her head.

'Well just be careful o' that ole cow,' Elsie warned her. 'She finks she's the big I-Am. Finks everybody's frightened of 'er. Don't tell 'er too much neivver if yer take my advice. That woman can't keep 'er bloody mouth shut. She might scare my Len, but she don't frighten me.'

Laura would have liked to tarry a while and learn a little more about her new neighbours but there was so much to do. 'Well, it's bin very nice meetin' yer, Elsie, an' fanks again fer the coal,' she said as she stepped out into the row carrying the bucket.

'Mind what I said about 'er,' Elsie whispered, jerking her thumb towards the house next door.

'I will,' Laura smiled, taking the key from her coat pocket and letting herself into her new house.

Albert Prior was feeling depressed as he sat beside the fire in Minnie Allerton's flat at Crystal Buildings in Long Lane. Minnie had gone out shopping and left him alone with his thoughts. The woman was a good soul, he had to admit, and she had been a very good friend to the family since they were forced to move into the buildings in 1941 when their house in Leroy Street was destroyed in the bombing, but she was inclined to go on a bit, and she made his head ache.

Albert pulled on his left arm and eased it in front of him. 'Bloody useless,' he mumbled aloud. 'Can't do a fing to 'elp. That poor little cow's gotta do it all.'

As if ashamed of talking to himself Albert coughed and pulled a face. He had never quite come to terms with losing his wife Ada so suddenly that first year of the war. She had suffered with bronchitis for years and in the end it had proved too much for her heart. She had missed the bombing though, that was a blessing, he told himself. Ada couldn't have stood the bombing. She had always been a very nervous woman. The girls had managed well though, especially when he had his stroke. It was funny how it happened, he reflected. No warning, just a sharp pain in the head and then the lights went out. Anyway, it was going to be better living in Pedlar's Row than in these old buildings. At least there would be no stairs for him to climb, and in the summer he'd be able to sit at the

14

front door and chat to the neighbours. I wonder what they'll be like, he thought. I hope they're not a miserable lot.

A piece of coal dropped from the fire and rolled into the hearth. Albert reached out painfully with his foot and kicked it under the grate. 'That woman's gonna set this place alight one o' these days, the way she banks that fire up,' he grumbled to himself.

A few minutes later he heard footsteps on the wooden stairs and a key going into the lock.

'I'm back, luv,' Minnie called out as she stepped into the dark passage. 'It's bleedin' cold out. I fair froze waitin' fer that queue ter go down at the bread shop.'

Albert eased himself back into his chair. 'I wonder 'ow Laura's gettin' on at the 'ouse?' he said. 'I 'ope she didn't stand any lip from that removal man. Cheeky git 'e was. I told 'er not ter go givin' 'em a tip. They get their regular wages.'

Minnie slipped off her coat and walked out into the tiny scullery to put the kettle on. 'I'll make yer a nice cuppa, Albert luv,' she called out to him. 'Me lad's gonna be 'ere soon ter take yer ter the new 'ouse. Don't worry though, I'll come round ter visit yer all when yer get yerselves settled in. I'm gonna miss you an' Laura, an' the kids. Lucy too, though I don't see much of 'er these days.'

Albert nodded to himself and turned his head towards the scullery. 'Lucy's 'ad ter work full time, Minnie,' he called out. 'She's worried about 'er Roy as well. I bin finkin' about that lad. Gawd knows what state 'e'll be in when 'e gets back 'ome.'

'I'm sure 'e'll be fine,' Minnie answered. 'They're givin' those boys the best treatment possible. It was on the news the ovver night. By the time Roy's ship gets 'ere 'e'll be fit as anyfing.'

Albert was not so sure. He had read other things in the

15

newspapers, and he worried for his son-in-law. Roy hadn't been robust even before he went away to the Far East, and some of the pictures in the papers had shocked the old man. The servicemen who had been released from the Japanese prisoner-of-war camps looked like walking skeletons. God knows what Roy would look like, and what mental damage had been done too. It was common knowledge that all of the prisoners had been brutally treated, to say the least. How would he and Lucy fare together once he was home?

Minnie walked in with two cups of tea. 'There yer are, get that down yer, me lad's gonna be 'ere any minute,' she said.

'I don't know 'ow I'm gonna climb up in that motor,' Albert grumbled.

'Don't worry, luv, my Bernie'll give yer a lift up. 'E's strong as an ox,' Minnie told him with a smile.

The two sat quietly drinking their tea. Albert was brooding on the indignity of having to be physically lifted into the cab of Bernie's lorry, while Minnie was thinking over what they had just been talking about. Lucy's husband was going to find it hard settling down in civvy street after his long and terrible captivity on the Burma railway, she reflected, and Lucy would have to make allowances too. She seemed a flighty girl who liked a good time. She hadn't sat at home much in the evenings during the war by all accounts, and there were those men friends of hers. All that would have to stop, now that Roy was coming home.

A knock on the front door interrupted Minnie's thoughts. 'That'll be Bernie now,' she said as she got up quickly.

Albert sat back in his seat and stared straight ahead as the lorry trundled down Weston Street. Bernie was whistling loudly and tapping the wheel, and when he

16

braked and steered his large lorry into the kerb at Pedlar's Row he turned to Albert and gave him a big grin. ' 'Ere we are, Alb. Didn't take five minutes, did it?'

The old man had to agree. It had taken him almost as long to get into the cab, he thought ruefully. Anyway, he had avoided the shame of being bodily lifted into the lorry, even if he had been given a helping hand up by the cheerful young driver.

It was less of a task for Albert to swing his legs round and let himself slide out on to the pavement, and he allowed Bernie to take his arm as he slowly and painfully walked the few steps to the front door of number three, Pedlar's Row. Laura answered her father's knock and her face lit up as she saw him standing there. 'Get yerself in out o' the cold, Dad,' she said, taking his arm. 'Fanks, Bernie, would yer like a quick cuppa?'

The young man shook his head. 'Nah, I've gotta get the lorry back, Laura,' he told her. 'It's gotta be loaded ternight.'

Laura led her father into the parlour and helped him down into a chair beside a flaring fire. 'Well, Pops, welcome to our new 'ome,' she said with a big smile.

Albert looked around the room. He could see that his daughter had started to unpack the boxes and she had even set the table for tea. 'Yer a brick, luv,' he said, suddenly filled with emotion. 'Our Lucy's gonna 'ave ter do a bit when she gets in. I don't want you goin' down wiv a bang.'

Laura patted his head fondly and hurried out into the scullery. Pots were steaming on the gas stove and there was a sausage toad cooking in the oven. The small room was uncomfortably hot and she leaned against the little wooden table as she felt the walls suddenly start to spin. It had been a terrible rush, she told herself as she

17

recovered her composure. Never mind, she'd take it easy tonight.

Albert's voice carried out into the scullery. 'Yer wouldn't like ter do us a favour, luv, would yer? Could yer pop ter the shop fer me? I'm right out o' baccy an' the evenin' papers'll be in now anyway.'

Chapter Two

The cold wind rattled the windowpanes and occasionally smoke blew back down the chimney and into the parlour as the two young women sat talking quietly.

'I wanted ter do what I could, but yer know what my firm's like,' the younger of the Prior sisters said as she filed her long fingernails. 'They're clampin' down on people takin' time off wivout good reason.'

Laura looked away from her sister and picked up the poker to rake the dying fire. 'Yeah, well, never mind. It's all done now,' she replied in a tired voice. 'I can sort the rest out termorrer.'

Lucy Grant studied the manicured nails of her left hand carefully, then set to work on her other hand. She was dark-haired, with large brown eyes set wide apart in her pretty oval face. She was the same height as Laura, although a few pounds lighter, with a trim figure and slim, shapely legs. Lucy took great pains with her appearance and was of the opinion that a girl should always look smart and well groomed, even if it was only to go shopping or pop down to the corner. She tended to criticise her older sister for not making the most of her good looks and figure but Laura ignored her comments, aware that Lucy had always been a little too concerned about the impression she made on other people, even as a very young girl. She had always been able to attract the boys, but even so it had been a surprise when one day out of the blue she announced that she wanted to get married to the young Roy Grant, whom she had only been dating for a very short time.

The sound of coughing from the small bedroom along the passage interrupted Laura's thoughts. 'I 'ope it's warm enough fer Dad in that bedroom,' she said as she hurried out. She was back in a few minutes. ' 'E seems all right,' she pronounced sitting down heavily in the armchair beside the fire.

Lucy uncurled her legs from under her and stretched them out in front of the fire. 'It's gonna be a bit awkward wiv the sleepin' arrangements when Roy comes 'ome,' she said with a sigh.

Laura glanced up at her sister. 'I thought we'd already sorted it out,' she replied quickly. 'You two can 'ave the front bedroom an' I can use the chair-bed down 'ere.'

Lucy pulled a face. 'It's not very comfortable.'

Laura was becoming increasingly irritated by her sister's seemingly heedless attitude towards the household. 'Well, you an' Roy can't share the chair-bed, an' yer can't expect Dad ter sleep in it,' she replied sharply.

Lucy put down the nailfile and spread her hands out in front of her. 'Well, it might not 'ave ter be fer too long,' she said, studying her fingers. 'I'm gonna see if I can find anuvver place. We'll need somewhere of our own. Besides, the boys get on Dad's nerves an' 'e shouts at 'em all the time. It'll be better fer them too.'

Laura leaned forward in her chair, her eyes fixed on her younger sister. 'Yer not still seein' that foreman at work, are yer, Lucy?' she asked quietly.

Lucy avoided her sister's enquiring gaze. 'It's all finished,' she replied.

Instinctively Laura knew that Lucy was lying. She sighed deeply. 'Roy's gonna need yer when 'e gets 'ome, an' you're gonna 'ave ter be patient wiv 'im,' she told her. 'I was listenin' ter this programme on the wireless last night, an' it said that . . . '

'Oh don't go on, Laura,' Lucy retorted angrily as she too leaned forward in her chair. 'I know what's expected of me. I know it won't be easy fer 'im, but it ain't bin easy fer me eivver. Fer the first six months I didn't know if Roy was alive or dead. Then when I got the news that 'e was a prisoner o' war I thought, all right, now I know Roy's alive I can cope wiv the waitin', as long as 'e's safe an' well.'

Laura's expression softened and she reached out to grip Lucy's hand but her younger sister pulled back suddenly, her eyes flaring. 'D'yer realise just 'ow long I've bin waitin', Laura?' she grated, her voice edged with emotion. 'Roy said goodbye ter me an' the kids in June forty-one. Young Terry was only six years old. 'E 'ardly remembers 'is dad. The Japanese war's bin over since August forty-five. It's now January an' I'm still waitin'. That's over four an' 'alf years, Laura. Four an' 'alf years! What was I s'posed ter do? Was I s'posed ter sit in worryin' meself sick every night, wonderin' if 'e was alive or dead? It wouldn't 'ave bin so bad if I'd 'ave got a letter now an' then instead o' those cards every six or eight months.'

'That's all they were allowed ter send, yer knew that,' Laura said quietly, trying to ease her sister's distress.

'There was only enough space ter put all our names, an' just ter say 'e sent 'is love,' Lucy went on, her eyes filling with tears. 'It wasn't enough, not fer me anyway. All right, there was ovvers who didn't go out fer a good time, but I couldn't sit in night after night, Laura. It would 'ave driven me barmy, what wiv the kids, an' worryin' about what 'e must be goin' frew. I couldn't 'ave carried that burden, I needed some comfort – can't yer see that?'

Laura leaned over and forcibly took her sister by the shoulders. 'Now listen ter me, Lucy,' she said with passion. 'I'm not gonna moralise. Anyway, it's all water under the bridge now. Roy's comin' 'ome very soon an' you two 'ave gotta pick up the pieces. Yer'll 'ave ter break off any relationships now, not next week or the week after. Yer gonna 'ave ter be strong, fer both of yer, an' those kids o' yours.'

Lucy's shoulders sagged, then she raised her sad eyes as she reached up and squeezed Laura's upper arms. 'Yer right, Laura. Yer always are,' she said, her voice trembling. 'I don't know what I would 'ave done wivout you. Yer've always bin the strong one, always there fer me an' the kids, an' Dad. I'm gonna change from now on, I promise yer.'

All the anger had gone as Lucy slipped out of her chair on to her knees and threw her arms around her older sister. She felt Laura hold her close and gently pat her back and she did not even try to halt her tears. She had been wrong, so wrong to allow herself to get into those meaningless liaisons, but it had been so hard to face up to what had happened to her life. The constant fear had hovered like a cloud that followed her everywhere, never once leaving her, and she had needed solace so badly. It had been so nice to feel a strong pair of arms around her, a shoulder to lean on, the opportunity to blot out all of her fears and anxieties, and there had been no shortage of available men who found her attractive.

Laura sighed sadly as she gently comforted her younger sister. Lucy was right: she was the strong one, always there for everyone, but she was having to pay a price. Already it seemed that people saw her as the eternal spinster and she had felt wounded by their attitude and assumptions on numerous occasions. Some people had intimated that she was afraid of men and had chosen to bury herself within the family, caring for her ailing father and her sister's children instead of finding herself a good man who could love her, wed her and father her own children. At first she had become angry and resentful, but eventually she had got to the stage where it didn't matter what they thought. Life had dealt her the cards and she was compelled to play the hand. There was no choice. Perhaps one day things would be different. Her father was an old man and at this time in his life he needed her, but it would not be for ever. Lucy and Roy would be together again soon and her sister would be able to take care of her children. There would be time enough then to pick up the pieces of her own life and maybe find a good man. She would not be a budding rose, that was for sure, but she would have the advantage of being ready to care for and cherish the right man, just as she cared for her own family now.

Lucy had composed herself and she sat back on the floor beside the dying fire, her eyes searching. As if reading Laura's thoughts she smiled affectionately and said, 'Yer know, you should find yourself a fella, Laura.'

Her sister sniffed contemptuously. 'Fat lot o' chance I get ter find a fella,' she replied quickly. 'I spend all day shoppin', cookin' an' keepin' the place clean, apart from the two hours every mornin' cleanin' at the pub. I'm drained by the evenin'. Besides, where am I likely ter meet a fella?'

'Yer used ter go dancin' a lot. Yer could start again,' Lucy suggested.

'Oh, an' who would I go wiv?' Laura said dismissively. 'All the gels I used ter go wiv are married wiv kids now. Besides, I just can't find the time these days.'

Lucy got up from the floor and stretched. 'I'll put the kettle on fer a cuppa,' she sighed. 'I need ter get ter bed early, it's bin murder at the factory terday.'

Laura eased back in her chair and yawned. The clock on the mantelshelf was showing ten minutes past ten and the room was starting to get a little colder. This was to be the first night in their new house and she felt pleased with the progress she had made that afternoon. In a few days the family would be settled in nicely and then she could think about doing some decorating in the spring. The upstairs back bedroom, which had been given to the boys, needed brightening up with some different-coloured paint, and the scullery needed lino over that cold stone floor. She would try to get some of the thicker stuff with the canvas backing. The back yard was a mess, with discarded builder's materials still lying around, but that would have to wait until the weather became warmer.

Lucy came back into the room carrying two cups of tea and she yawned widely as she put one of the cups down on the wooden table near Laura. 'I'm off ter bed,' she announced. 'Yer shouldn't be long yerself. Yer must be exhausted.'

Laura raked the fire and then picked up her tea. Tiredness seemed to wash over her and she stifled another yawn. Would they all be happy in their new home? she wondered. How would they all get on with the neighbours? Elsie Carmichael seemed a friendly soul, but she had been quick to warn of the woman next door to her. What were the rest of the neighbours like? Would the boys be happy here? Questions chased each other dreamily through Laura's mind as she slowly sipped her tea. Her eyes felt heavy as lead and she stared thoughtfully into the dying embers of the fire, suddenly reliving old memories.

She was young. Pretty as a picture, Ralph had said, and she twirled around until her lace petticoat lifted the thin summer dress. She was nineteen and wishing for twenty. At twenty a girl was no longer in her teens, and the word 'twenty' sounded so grown-up. Ralph laughed in that boyish way of his and took her hand as they strolled through the scent-filled gardens. In that late Indian summer of 1931 there was little joy for most: the depression was beginning to bite, and while the men hunted down jobs or joined the ever-increasing dole queues, their womenfolk struggled bravely to feed and provide for their families. For Laura, though, it was a magical time, that hot, balmy summer. She recalled the old man playing haunting melodies on his accordion that particular evening in the garden of the country pub beneath a star-studded sky. She and Ralph had spent the whole day in Richmond and as darkness fell they danced in the garden to the strains of 'Moonlight Bay'. When they boarded the riverboat to return to Greenwich and snuggled close on the upper deck, her heart was filled with the love she felt for him. Later that same night, as the full moon climbed high above the cranes and wharves and the dark waters of the Thames washed against the shore, she gave herself to him in the seclusion of the riverside church garden.

The glowing embers in the grate darkened and went out, but Laura remained seated in her chair. It was all so long ago now, but the memories were still so vivid. Ralph had been older than her, with more experience of life; she had been little more than a child. She had never meant to hurt anyone, or to be the cause of such misery. She was madly in love, and they had been so happy. It seemed that they were meant to be together, to spend the rest of their lives with each other. Ralph had told her at the very beginning that he was married but had separated from his wife. He had said that she had fallen for another man, and he had looked so unhappy.

As she sat staring into the dying fire Laura recalled the first time she had seen the young fitter. He had passed her machine at the biscuit factory, and she had noticed how sad he looked. He would often walk by, and finally she found the courage to give him a shy smile. Soon he was stopping to pass the time of day and their friendship developed. There had been a strange closeness between them right from the start. Laura remembered how easy it had been to talk to him, and he seemed to respond naturally. It was inevitable that they would become lovers, and for a brief moment in time love prevailed.

The sound of Lucy turning over in bed roused Laura from her thoughts and she sat up straight in her chair. The room had become cold and the wind was still howling outside. It was wrong to dwell on the past, she told herself. What had been done was done, there was no changing it. Her mother had understood, and her father too, after a while, bless him, but there had been much heartache to bear. To rake it all up again now was only going to cause more pain and anguish. Better let it all stay buried in the dark corners of her mind. Life and time had moved on, and life was for living.

With a deep sigh Laura got up from her chair and looked around once more before climbing the steep wooden stairs to the front bedroom that she shared with Lucy. As she quietly undressed and slipped between the cold sheets she heard Lucy's muffled sobs. Normally she would have gone to her and offered comfort, but tonight she had nothing more to give so she buried her head beneath the bedclothes and closed her eyes.

Chapter Three

Laura refilled the boys' teacups from the enamel teapot and eyed her nephews with a feigned look of horror. 'Now look, you two. I'm 'avin' no arguments roun' the table, understood?'

Reg gave his younger brother a wide grin as he reached for the last piece of toast. 'Pass the marmalade, Tel.'

'Get it yerself, I'm not yer slave,' Terry answered him curtly.

Laura sighed. It was always the same in the mornings. Reg was wide awake and lively as soon as his eyes were open but Terry, the younger of the two, was less ready to joke around and swap banter with his thirteen-year-old brother. It took him longer to pull himself together in the mornings and he was easily riled.

'Fanks fer nuffink,' Reg said as he reached across the table.

'Shut yer trap,' Terry mumbled.

Laura hid a grin as she leaned over the table. 'Right, any more arguin' an' I'm gettin' yer mutton stew fer tea,' she growled.

The boys pulled faces and Reg wiped the back of his hand over his sticky lips. 'It's 'im, Aunt Laura,' he said, giving Terry a blinding look. ' 'E's always miserable in the mornin's.'

'Well, then you should take no notice. Give yer

bruvver time ter wake up,' Laura replied. 'We can't all be as bright as you first thing.'

Terry washed a mouthful of toast down with his tea and scratched his head as he looked around the small parlour. 'I like it 'ere,' he said. 'It's better than the Buildin's. One o' my best mates lives 'ere.'

'Oh, an' who's that?' Laura asked as she started to clear away the breakfast things.

'Charlie Bromley,' Terry replied. ' 'E lives at number one.'

Laura was reminded of Elsie Carmichael's warning about the woman in number one. 'That's nice fer yer,' she told him.

The wind had dropped during the night and a film of frost coated the paving outside. Cold air greeted Laura as she stepped out of the house and watched the two boys march off into Weston Street with their school satchels slung over their shoulders. They were different in looks as well as temperament. Reg at thirteen favoured his father: he was fair-haired and blue-eyed, slightly built with an abundance of energy and growing tall. Terry on the other hand was shorter and dark-haired like his mother. He had her temperament too. Lucy was not the most talkative person in the morning. Terry was the more studious of the two boys and was happy to sit in a corner reading, while Reg was always restless and at his happiest playing football or running the streets. The two lads got on well together, apart from the early-morning arguments, and Reg was always very protective of his younger brother.

Laura waited at the front door until the two boys disappeared from view, then she went back into the house. There were things to do before she left at nine o'clock to go to her cleaning job at the Sultan in Weston Street. Her father would be getting up soon and she wanted the parlour clean and tidy for him to sit in. She had already been to the corner shop for his paper and tobacco but the fire needed stoking. She used the last few knobs of coal from the bucket to feed the meagre flames and then set about sweeping the room. Just before she went out to work she straightened the cushions and left a fresh pot of tea under the cosy.

The thirty shillings Laura earned for cleaning the busy pub helped to supplement the money Lucy put into the housekeeping. That, and her father's pension, was barely enough for the family to survive on. Occasionally Laura was able to utilise her skills as a machinist and made a few extra shillings doing sewing and alterations. Times were hard, but Reg would be leaving school next year and he would be able to help out too.

While Laura mopped the sticky floor in the public bar and then set about polishing the tables she worried over her father. She had used up the last of the coal and he felt the cold since his stroke. He was not able to get about much and she prayed for the warmer weather. At least he would be able to sit outside in the sun.

'Yer look all worried this mornin'.'

Laura looked up to see Jack Murray, the pub manager, staring at her. She had always been very careful not to encourage the publican. He had a dubious reputation where women were concerned and he was always trying to draw her into conversation.

'I'm all right,' she said quickly. 'Dad's not too good an' the movin' took it out of 'im.'

Jack Murray smiled and walked out from behind the counter. 'Yer need a break. Yer need ter get out a bit,' he said, a ghost of a grin playing round the corners of his mouth. 'Why don't yer come 'ere one evenin'? It'll do yer good.'

Laura smiled, not wanting an argument with the man. 'I s'pose it would, but I don't get the time,' she told him.

The publican was aware how Laura looked after her

family and he shook his head. 'Yer need ter fink o' yerself once in a while,' he went on. 'Look, I get the night off Tuesdays. Why don't yer come up West wiv me? I could show yer a good time.'

Laura afforded him a brief smile and shook her head. 'Fanks fer the offer, but . . .'

Jack raised his hands. 'Just fink about it. There's no strings attached,' he said. 'We'll just 'ave a few bevvies an' then we can go to a club. Yer'd enjoy it.'

Laura nodded and dropped her head as she worked away with the duster and polish. The man repulsed her. He was large, middle-aged and lecherous, with dark crinkly hair and a beer belly that threatened to pop the buttons of his shirt. He was managing the Sultan for Archie Westlake, a local villain who had a finger in every devious activity in Bermondsey. Jack Murray was known to be a minder for Westlake, and his face bore the scars. He had one thin white line running down his left cheek and another crescent-shaped scar above his right eye. Word had it that he had been involved in a fracas at a racetrack bar and someone had used a razor on his face. Murray was a hard man by reputation and he kept a tight rein on the Sultan. It was well known that he was separated from his wife and was currently involved with one of the pub's barmaids, though that had done nothing to curb his roving eye.

Laura finished her chores at eleven and while Jack Murray was opening up the pub she slipped on her coat and made to leave, but the publican sidled up to her and smiled crookedly. 'Now don't ferget the offer. Yer'll 'ave a good time, I can promise yer,' he said in his usual gravelly voice.

Laura walked home along Weston Street trying to put the man out of her mind. She would have to be careful not to antagonise him, but it was going to get difficult. He had been coming on to her stronger lately and he could become very nasty. The simple answer would be to find another job, but it wasn't that easy. The hours suited her, and it was local. The money was good too for two hours a day, Monday to Saturday.

Laura turned into Pedlar's Row and was immediately confronted by Queenie Bromley who was standing at her front door with a coat pulled up around her ears against the cold. Queenie eyed Laura up and down, her flattish, round face impassive.

'You're the one who's moved inter number three, ain't yer?' she asked.

Laura nodded. 'We moved in yesterday.'

'Yeah, I saw the van pull up,' Queenie told her. 'It's not bad 'ere, an' the neighbours ain't that bad, apart from the scatty mare next door. She ain't troubled yer, 'as she?'

Laura shook her head and smiled, remembering what Elsie had said.

'Was that yer farvver I see come in yesterday?' Queenie went on with her enquiries.

'Yeah, that was me dad. 'E's not too well at the moment,' Laura replied.

' 'Ad a stroke, 'as 'e?'

'Yeah, early last year.'

'I thought so. Yer can usually tell,' Queenie said, touching the mass of curlers in her blond locks with the flat of her hand.

'Well, I'd better be gettin' in,' Laura said in reply.

'By the way, Ransome the coalman's comin' terday. D'yer want me ter tell 'im ter knock?' Queenie asked. 'I'm lookin' out fer 'im now.'

'I'd be grateful,' Laura said with a smile. 'We're almost out.'

Albert Prior was sitting in the armchair when Laura walked into the parlour and he immediately nodded towards the low fire. 'We're out o' coal,' he said simply.

31

'I'm gettin' some delivered terday, Dad,' Laura replied cheerfully. 'Why didn't yer put yer warm cardigan on?'

'I couldn't find it,' Albert replied.

Laura sighed to herself as she went into the back bedroom and found the cardigan lying over the bedrail. 'Here it is,' she said with a despairing look.

'Where d'yer find it?' he asked.

'Where yer put it last night,' she told him.

Albert stared down at the fire for a while and then looked up at his daughter. 'I 'ope it's gonna be all right 'ere,' he said.

' 'Course it will,' Laura answered brightly. 'Yer'll be a sight better 'ere than stuck in the Buildin's. Jus' wait till the spring. Yer'll be able ter sit outside the front door an' 'ave a chat.'

'Yeah, as long as they're all right,' Albert mumbled.

'What d'yer mean, all right?'

'Well, neighbourly.'

'Well, it cuts both ways, Dad,' Laura told him. 'Yer gotta be neighbourly yerself. It's no good you gettin' all mean an' moody. That way none of 'em are gonna talk ter yer.'

'That couple next door seem a bit dopey ter me,' Albert went on.

'Oh, so yer've met 'em then?' Laura asked, surprised.

'Not exactly, but I 'eard 'em goin' orf at each ovver,' he said.

' 'Avin' a row, yer mean?'

'Not exactly.'

Laura stood in front of her father with her arms akimbo. 'What exactly do yer mean, Dad?' she asked him.

'Well, it takes two ter row. That poor sod didn't get a word in edgeways wiv 'er,' Albert replied, jerking his thumb towards the wall. 'She's bin goin' on ever since I got up, an' I could 'ear every word. She's only jus' stopped. Run out o' steam, I s'pose.'

'What was she on about?' Laura asked, smiling.

Albert shifted his position in his chair and took up his pipe, a sign to Laura that it might well be quite a lengthy tale. 'Well, apparently, 'er ole man was s'posed ter scrub the back yard down this mornin' an' 'e didn't do it,' he began. 'I 'eard the front door go an' then 'er voice started up. Like a bloody fog'orn it was. "Why ain't that yard done?" I 'eard 'er say, then, "Can't find the bucket? What d'yer mean yer can't find the bucket? It's in the karsy where it always is." Then I 'eard 'im tryin' ter pacify 'er, but she was goin' on ten ter the dozen. "Yer bloody useless. Yer must 'ave mislaid it. I know yer game. Yer've 'id it so yer don't 'ave ter do it. Yer just a bone idle, lazy git, that's what you are." I tell yer, gel, if that 'ad bin yer muvver talkin' ter me like that I'd 'ave crowned 'er.'

'Was that it then?' Laura asked him.

'Was that it? Bloody 'ell, no. She never left orf. "Yer don't do anyfing fer me. Yer don't 'elp me one little bit, after all I do fer you." Then she called 'im everyfing from a pig to a dog. I 'eard the front door slam just after that. I don't know if it was 'im or 'er stormed out. If it'd bin me I'd 'ave bin out o' there like a bolt o' lightnin'.'

Laura grinned and pinched her chin. 'Who'd 'ave thought it of 'er? I was talkin' to 'er yesterday mornin' an' she seemed very nice. In fact she was praisin' 'er 'usband ter the skies. She said 'e was very good round the 'ouse. She was 'elpful too. She lent me some coal. Oh no! The bucket!'

'What about the bucket?'

'I've got it.'

'You've got it?'

Laura nodded with a wince. 'Elsie lent me some coal yesterday mornin' – in the bucket.'

Albert raised one of his rare smiles. 'Well, yer'd better take it back right away. Don't ferget ter tell 'er ter say sorry to 'er ole man neivver.'

The rattle of machinery had ceased and the workers filed out of the biscuit factory into the cold winter air. As the others went off to the canteen for their midday meal Lucy Grant tarried on the shop-floor stairway. While she waited she took out the pins holding her factory cap in place and patted her neat dark hair. It had been piled up under the cap and clipped in place on top of her head, but a few strands had come adrift and Lucy pulled them up and used the cap pins to secure them. She could see Patrick making his way up the stairs towards her and she gave him a big smile.

Patrick Harris was a shop-floor foreman, tall and slim, with a clipped moustache and dark hair smoothed down and parted in the middle. He smiled back at her as he reached the landing, exposing a row of even white teeth.

'Canteen?' he asked.

Lucy nodded. 'It's warmer than goin' out,' she replied.

They walked side by side to the canteen, keeping a respectable distance between them but fooling no one. It was common knowledge that they were carrying on and their entrance into the large hall was duly noted.

'Look at those two,' one of the girls remarked to her friend as they stood in the queue. 'Don't it make yer sick?'

The girl's friend smiled. ' 'E could stick 'is shoes under my bed any time,' she replied.

The first girl snorted. 'I dunno what people see in 'im. 'E looks like a walkin' pencil.'

Her friend was not to be dissuaded. 'I reckon 'e's 'andsome,' she sighed. ' 'E reminds me o' Robert Taylor.'

Another girl leaned over the first one's shoulder. 'Did

yer know 'er ole man's on 'is way 'ome from the Far East?' she said.

The two turned to stare wide-eyed at her. 'Is that right?' they chorused.

The girl nodded knowingly and glanced briefly behind her before going on. ' 'Er ole man was on the Burma railway by all accounts, an' now 'e's comin' 'ome,' she whispered. 'The poor bleeder's gonna need lookin' after, that's fer certain. If 'e finds out about the game she's playin' 'e'll be in 'is rights ter give 'er a bloody good 'idin'.'

' 'Im an' all,' the first girl cut in.

'Well, as long as 'e leaves 'is face an' 'is important bits alone,' the second girl said, ' 'cos I might be interested if 'e's goin' spare.'

Lucy sat facing Patrick as they ate their lunch, quiet and nonchalant while other workers shared their table, but as soon as they were alone she broached the subject. 'Roy's gonna be 'ome very soon, Pat,' she said. 'I gotta be careful. Some people are so wicked they'll be out ter make trouble.'

Patrick had had his eye on another of the factory girls for a week or two – a new arrival on the shop-floor who had shown some interest in him – and he was secretly pleased at the news. 'I understand, Lucy,' he said gravely. 'I couldn't expect yer ter continue the way we are, but we can still be good friends.'

Lucy felt anger rising inside her. 'Is that 'ow much yer fink of me?' she grated.

Patrick's face coloured slightly and he looked around quickly to see if anyone had noticed. 'Of course not. I do luv yer, Lucy, but you're a married woman, an' yer man's gonna need yer. I'm tryin' ter let yer see that I understand, that's all.'

'So yer wanna call it quits, then?' Lucy growled in a low voice, her eyes flashing at him.

Patrick felt that now was the time to extricate himself from what, to him, had become a dangerous situation. He was well aware that men returning from the war had little mercy on civilians who stole their wives and girlfriends while they were away, and he had no desire to put himself in any unnecessary peril. 'Maybe we should let fings quieten down a bit,' he said, wincing inside.

Lucy stared hard at him for an instant, then she dropped her eyes to her clasped hands. 'Listen, Patrick,' she began, 'We don't flaunt ourselves. All right, people 'ere are gonna talk, but they don't know anyfing definite about us. They can only guess,' she reassured him quietly, her eyes suddenly coming up to meet his. 'I'll tell yer this much though. If I walk away from yer, it'll be fer good. I'm not gonna share yer wiv any ovver girl yer take a fancy to.'

Patrick Harris shrugged his shoulders and remained silent, not knowing quite what to say, and he breathed a deep sigh of relief when Lucy suddenly got up from the table and walked away without a word. It was for the best, he felt. There were plenty more fish in the sea, and she had been making a lot of demands on him lately.

Lucy held her head high as she left the table, trying to look unconcerned to anyone who might be watching. Patrick's silence had told her that they were finished, and she bit back on her angry tears as she walked resolutely from the canteen.

Chapter Four

At number five the table had been set and Lizzie Cassidy hummed contentedly as she stood in the scullery stirring the beef stew. Steam filled the small room and Lizzie brushed a hand quickly over her forehead. She was a large woman in her late fifties, with a round, happy face, deep-set dark eyes and raven hair pulled into a bun on the top of her head, exposing large and rather prominent ears in which she wore small gold rings. She had on a clean spotted apron tied around her middle, and on her feet were a pair of worn-out slippers that she was loath to get rid of.

Lizzie smiled to herself as she dipped the ladle into the stew and carefully put it to her lips. It needed a touch more pepper, she decided, and maybe just a pinch of plain flour to thicken it. It had to be just right, for her two married boys and their wives had come round for their usual Tuesday evening meal.

Lizzie always felt happy when the family gathered together, and tonight Geoff's wife Mary had filled her cup to overflowing by quietly and calmly announcing that she was pregnant. It meant so much to Lizzie. The war had taken her three sons away from her but now they were all home again, and in good shape. She had despaired of ever becoming a grandmother but now, the good Lord willing, she would soon have her dearest wish granted.

Sounds of merriment drifted out from the parlour and then she heard her husband's loud voice. ' 'Ow much longer are we gonna wait, Liz? There's a lot of 'ungry mouths ter feed 'ere, yer know.'

Lizzie ignored Eric's light-hearted impatience and continued humming to herself. They would have to wait a little longer, she thought. She prided herself on her beef stews and was not about to lose her good reputation by rushing an underdone stew in to her hungry tribe.

Geoff suddenly appeared in the doorway and winked knowingly at his mother. 'Good news, Ma, ain't it?' he grinned.

Lizzie smiled happily at her eldest son. 'You better take care of 'er now, boy,' she commanded. 'I don't want nuffink 'appenin' ter that baby.'

Geoff grinned. 'I'll do the winders now, Ma, but she'll still 'ave ter fetch the coal and chop the logs,' he told her.

Lizzie ignored him in feigned disgust. Geoff was thirty-seven years old, the eldest and most outgoing of her three lads. He was stocky like his father, with a thick mop of dark hair and blue eyes. His chin was square and his thin lips constantly on the move, betraying his wicked sense of humour. He had served in the navy as a stoker during the war, and had now settled back into his civilian job as a lighterman.

Geoff ambled back into the parlour to join the rest of the family. His father Eric sat near the fire talking quietly to Mary and Steve's wife Connie, while Steve and Eddie sat together discussing Millwall's chances that coming Saturday. Geoff sighed contentedly as he slumped down in the one remaining chair. The family had been very lucky, he realised. They had mercifully all survived the war and were back working in the docks. Steve was in the Royal Docks and Eddie, the youngest, had just found himself a regular gang that worked the Tooley Street wharves. Like his older brother, Steve had felt compelled to volunteer at the outbreak of war, and he had been at Dunkirk as well as with the Eighth Army in the Middle East. Like Geoff he was stocky, though fair of complexion like his father. Eddie was the odd one out, it seemed to Geoff. He was quiet and thoughtful, with a love of football, and in particular Millwall, following the team religiously. He was the only one of the three still single and he appeared not to be in any hurry to get married. He was dark, with wide-spaced, large brown eyes which tended to look sad at times. He had gone into the army later than his two older brothers and had served in the Royal Tank Corps from D-Day to the Rhine crossings.

Lizzie came into the room carrying a large dish which she set down in the centre of the table and the family gathered round. She ladled the steaming stew on to big dinner plates, and as was the custom at the Cassidys' everyone waited for the matriarch of the family to take her place before they started eating. The huge pile of thick bread slices quickly diminished as the meal got under way and when Eric took the last slice to wipe his plate clean Lizzie briefly raised her eyes to the ceiling.

'Mind yer don't make an 'ole in that plate,' she said.

Eric leaned back from the table and rubbed his stomach with relish. 'That's what I call a good meal,' he declared, looking round the table at the grinning faces.

'That'll do fer two,' Mary said, smiling at Lizzie.

'Yer gotta keep yer strength up when yer carryin',' Eric said, reaching for his tobacco pouch. 'I always maintain that if yer fill yer belly yer stave orf trouble. Now you take me.'

'Look, Eric, they don't want ter listen to all that

again,' Lizzie said with another quick glance at the ceiling. 'Now why don't yer go an' make us all a nice pot o' tea while I clear the plates away?'

Eric grinned widely and gave Mary a saucy wink as he got up from his chair. 'She don't leave me alone, gel. Nags me narrer, she does.'

Lizzie ignored his joking and started to pull the emptied plates towards her, but Connie got up quickly. 'You stay there, Mum, me an' Mary can wash up,' she told her.

Geoff idly watched as Steve rolled a cigarette and then he took the proffered tobacco pouch. 'The river's very quiet,' he remarked.

Steve nodded. 'We've not bin doin' much since Christmas.'

Eddie turned to him. 'Our gang's bin busy lately,' he added.

Geoff's mouth twitched. 'Well, they'd 'ave ter be, wouldn't they?' he answered.

' 'Ow's that?'

'Well, when yer carryin' someone, it's bloody 'ard.'

Eddie leaned back from the table, weaving his fingers together over his middle. 'Let me tell you two that I'm very well thought of by my gang,' he announced. 'We're considered ter be the fastest gang in Tooley Street. Wait till the bonus loads start arrivin'. The rest o' the gangs won't live wiv us.'

'I ain't said nuffink, so don't get on ter me,' Steve said with mock indignation.

The banter went on for some time, with Eric Cassidy joining in as he poured the tea, then suddenly Lizzie brought her hand down sharply on the table. 'Oi, you lot! Stop arguin'. This is s'posed ter be a family get-tergevver.'

Geoff blew out a cloud of tobacco smoke and chuckled. 'It's all right, Ma. We're just sortin' our flash little bruvver out.'

When the table had been cleared Lizzie sat in her favourite armchair with her family around her and she held court. 'Queenie Bromley's boy's bin in trouble again,' she told them. ' 'Er Charlie got caught nickin' at the market, by all accounts. 'E'll end up in Borstal if 'e's not careful.'

'I noticed there's curtains up at number three. 'Ave yer seen the newcomers yet?' Mary asked.

Lizzie shook her head. 'Elsie Carmichael told me she'd met 'er though. Nice young woman, accordin' to 'er. Apparently the woman's got 'er farvver livin' wiv 'er, an' a sister wiv two kids.'

'That Elsie's a right scatty mare,' Eric cut in. 'She caught me goin' ter work the ovver mornin'. I was tellin' yer, wasn't I, gel?' Lizzie nodded. 'She asked me if I could open 'er front-room winder. It 'ad got wedged apparently. Anyway, I couldn't budge it, then I noticed it'd bin nailed shut. It was that dopey ole man of 'ers. She told me the next day. 'E was fed up wiv 'er leavin' it open an' 'e stuck these bloody great six-inch nails frew it.'

' 'E seems a strange bloke at number six,' Connie said. 'I've seen 'im strollin' up an' down the Row once or twice wiv 'is 'ands be'ind 'is back. Is 'e all right?'

'That's Wally Stebbin's,' Lizzie replied. ' 'E's a nice quiet chap. Sad really. 'E lives wiv 'is ole mum an' 'e works in the office at the box factory in Weston Street, so Mrs Stebbin's told me. 'E acts a bit strange, but it's 'is nerves. Wally's farvver used ter knock 'im black an' blue, by all accounts.'

'Is Wally's farvver dead, Mum?' Connie asked.

'Yeah, 'e is now, but 'e run orf wiv anuvver woman when Wally was a youngster,' Lizzie told her.

'She's a right kill-'em-an'-eat-'em, that woman in the first 'ouse, ain't she?' Mary remarked with a grin.

Lizzie laughed. 'Queenie Bromley, yeah. The one

whose boy Charlie I was tellin' yer about. She was the first one ter move in the Row when it was done up last year. I don't 'ave a lot ter do wiv 'er, but I s'pect she's all front. That sort usually are. Funny fing, but I used ter notice 'er goin' out all dressed up every Sunday afternoon, before it got too cold. On 'er own she was. Always on 'er own.'

'P'raps she was goin' ter church,' Eric volunteered.

'What, Sunday afternoon?' Lizzie countered quickly.

'She might 'ave bin goin' ter see 'er fancy feller,' Connie remarked.

Lizzie puckered her lips. 'I dunno, but I often used ter wonder.'

'Yer should 'ave asked 'er where she was off to,' Geoff suggested with a wry smile.

'She'd 'ave told me ter mind me own business,' Lizzie said with a chuckle.

'If she starts goin' out again I'll ask 'er ole man where she's orf to when I see 'im up the boozer,' Eric said, winking at his sons.

'Yer'll do no such fing,' Lizzie told him sharply. 'I don't wanna get the name o' bein' a busybody.'

'They seem a pleasant enough couple next door, though,' Mary said.

'Yeah, Bridie Molloy's a nice woman,' Lizzie told her. 'She's very quiet. 'Er ole man's a decent bloke too. 'E likes a drink though. 'E's a gas-fitter. They moved in same week as we did, last September. As I say, Queenie was the first ter move in. Last July it was, an' the Carmichaels followed 'er a couple o' weeks later, so she told me. As they finished doin' each place up they moved people in. They 'ad a lot o' trouble wiv number three. Somefink ter do wiv the pipes, by all accounts. That's why they've only just let it.'

Eric reached down by his feet and retrieved his tobacco pouch, a humorous look on his face. ' 'Course yer know that these 'ouses are s'posed ter be 'aunted,' he said suddenly.

The younger women stared at him with surprise and the young men grinned at each other, but Lizzie looked hard at her husband. 'Yer shouldn't be frightenin' the gels,' she said sharply, 'not in Mary's condition.'

Mary laughed. 'It's all right, Mum. Go on, tell us about it, Pops.'

Eric undid his pouch and took out a paper with some strands of tobacco. 'Well, yer see, this 'ere Row was s'posed ter be the place where all the ole pedlars congregated,' he began. 'They used ter rest 'ere when this area was grass an' trees. Now I've lived round 'ere all me life an' these 'ouses went up in 1880, an' that was before I was born, but us kids grew up wiv the stories about this place.'

'I've lived round 'ere all me life too, an' I ain't 'eard about the places bein' 'aunted,' Lizzie cut in.

Eric ignored his wife's comment and proceeded to roll his cigarette. 'Well, they chucked the pedlars orf this spot ter build these 'ouses an' one o' the ole geezers was s'posed to 'ave put a curse on the place,' he went on. 'Our parents scared the life out of us kids wiv the stories. If we wouldn't go ter sleep they used ter threaten us wiv Gypsy Joe.'

'Gypsy Joe?' Mary echoed.

' 'E was one o' the pedlars,' Eric continued. 'The one who put the curse on the place. People used ter be scared of 'im. If Gypsy Joe knocked at their door they 'ad ter buy somefing orf 'im or 'e'd put a curse on 'em. Mind yer though, some women told 'im ter piss orf – sorry gels – told 'im ter get goin' an' not ter come back, but there was ovvers who were really scared of 'im an' they bought from 'im, afford it or not. I did 'ear once that one woman's 'usband chased Gypsy Joe away from the street

43

an' a few weeks later they found 'im dead in a doorway. 'E'd bin stabbed, so it was said.'

Lizzie was getting concerned for Mary. 'Yer frightenin' the gels, Eric,' she said pointedly. 'Why don't yer shut up.'

Both Mary and Connie were intrigued by the story, however, and they urged their father-in-law to continue. 'Was it Gypsy Joe who did it?' Mary asked.

Eric shrugged his shoulders. 'No one ever found out, but they said it was 'im what done it. I tell yer though, not many of us kids ventured round 'ere when we was small. The place was gaslit at the time an' on winter nights it looked really ghostly. That's 'ow this Row got its name, because o' the pedlars that used ter frequent it. As a matter o' fact I remember my ole grandmuvver tellin' me an' me bruvvers the story. She told us that the evil curse Gypsy Joe called down would last as long as the places lasted, an' that one day lightnin' would come from the sky an' these 'ouses would crumble to dust.'

'Well, they did, sort of,' Geoff cut in. 'These 'ouses were gutted durin' the Blitz, so I s'pose that was the lightnin' from the sky. They stood empty after that until they were done up last year. I remember seein' the state o' the Row after that land mine fell on Cooper Street. I was 'ome on leave at the time.'

'I don't believe in that load o' twaddle about curses an' bad luck,' Lizzie said with conviction. 'Yer make yer own luck, an' what's ter be will be. The Lord Almighty don't need no promptin' from the likes o' Gypsy John.'

'Gypsy Joe, Mum,' Steve corrected her.

'Gypsy Joe then. Anyway, that's enough, Farvver, now go an' put the kettle back on.'

Laura Prior was sitting back in an armchair beside the

brightly burning fire, darning one of Terry's socks. Opposite her, Albert sat reading the evening paper. The wireless was turned down low and a lilting melody was quietly drifting through the room. Laura felt a little less worried this evening. The coalman had delivered and she had chopped up a large box which she had found in the back yard. Lucy had got up for work that morning looking bright and breezy, which was unlike her, and the boys had gone to bed without much fuss. Her father was feeling better and this evening he seemed quite cheerful.

Albert put down the paper and proceeded to scratch vigorously behind his ear. 'They say there's gonna be a break in the weavver soon,' he announced suddenly.

'I wouldn't bank on it,' Laura said. 'I fink we're still in fer some snow.'

'I might start keepin' rabbits again,' he told her.

'That'll be nice,' Laura replied, knowing that her father would no doubt change his mind by the morning.

'Yeah, I bin finkin',' Albert went on. 'I used to 'ave some good rabbits when we lived in Leroy Street.'

'I know yer did,' Laura said.

'Soon as I feel well enough I'm gonna clear out that yard an' build a few 'utches,' he continued. 'Nuffink like a nice rabbit pie. Rabbit stew's nice too. Yer muvver made us some nice rabbit stews. Mind yer, yer gotta know what yer doin' when yer keep rabbits. Yer gotta look after 'em. Yer gotta know 'ow ter keep 'em clean an' make sure they don't get ill. If one rabbit goes down wiv somefing then yer can be sure that the rest are gonna go down wiv it too. That's the way wiv rabbits.'

Laura was beginning to get a little tired of hearing about rabbits, but she knew there was no way to tell her father without hurting his feelings. 'This room 'keeps warm,' she remarked in an effort to change the subject.

'Not as warm as Leroy Street,' Albert replied. 'That was a lovely warm 'ouse there. I liked Leroy Street. Nice people lived there.'

'I expect there's nice people livin' 'ere, Dad,' Laura said quietly. 'Trouble is, we ain't 'ad much of a chance ter meet the neighbours yet.'

'D'yer remember that night when we got bombed out?' Albert said.

' 'Ow could I forget it?' Laura replied. 'I remember that shelter actually liftin' wiv the blast. Then when we saw the state o' that little turnin' I couldn't believe it. It was terrible.'

'No one was killed in the street that night, an' when yer look at the damage what was done yer gotta say it was nuffink short of a miracle,' Albert declared.

'Not much in the paper, Dad?' Laura asked, hoping to draw her father away from memories which always left him feeling depressed.

'I remember that next mornin' when we 'ad ter get our bits an' pieces tergevver,' Albert continued as though he hadn't heard her. 'We lost a lot o' stuff. That lovely wardrobe an' dressin' table. Made of satin walnut they was. Yer couldn't buy the likes o' that now. Losin' that furniture really upset me. Shame about that old 'ouse in Leroy Street. Terrible place, those Buildin's.'

Laura put down her darning and stretched in her chair. 'Well, I fink it's time fer a nice cuppa, Dad,' she said, realising that it was the only way to stop her father going on with his reminiscences.

The scullery felt cold and Laura shivered as she turned the gas on under the kettle. Suddenly there was a loud knocking and she hurried to the front door. Elsie Carmichael was standing there looking very distressed.

46

'I'm really sorry ter trouble yer, luv, but I don't know what ter do,' she said tearfully.

'Whatever's wrong?' Laura asked quickly.

'It's my Len. 'E's in agony. 'Is shoes 'ave burnt away an' 'is feet are in a terrible state.'

Chapter Five

Len Carmichael had worked at the local brewery as a maintenance man for more than twenty years, and during his first year there he had married Elsie. Their marriage had been blessed with two daughters: Patience, who was nineteen, and Priscilla, who was nearing eighteen. Both daughters had been living at home when the Carmichaels applied to the council for rehousing; Patience was engaged to a local lad, and Priscilla was pregnant. When the family were offered the house in Pedlar's Row Len and Elsie were delighted, and Elsie had got it all worked out. Patience could go ahead and get married, and she and her husband could live with the Carmichaels. After all, there were three bedrooms. As for Priscilla, well, she could get married quickly and live with them too, if she could persuade the father of her unborn child to do the right thing by her.

However, things had not quite worked out the way Elsie had planned and Len realised that there could be serious repercussions. Patience had married a draughtsman who felt that there were many more opportunities in Australia for skilled men, so he and Patience applied for assisted passage. Priscilla too had had decisions to make. Her young man agreed to make an honest woman of her, on one condition: that they found their own place. Events moved at a very rapid pace, and by the time the move to Pedlar's Row took place both Patience and Priscilla were already waiting to move away from the family nest.

As Len began his two-to-ten shift at the brewery on Tuesday he was a very worried man. It was not all sweetness and light as far as things went with their next-door neighbours and he felt that it wasn't beyond that loud-mouthed Queenie Bromley to report him and Elsie to the council. They rented a three-bedroomed house and as far as the authorities were aware they had two single daughters living with them. The real facts were that Patience and her husband were now in transit to Australia, while Priscilla and her husband were living in Peckham.

Len was engaged in rerouting a complicated pipe-run in a disused part of the brewery and the maintenance foreman had told him to pump a caustic de-scaler through a blocked section of the piping to clear it. Under normal circumstances the process would have been quite a straightforward operation, but that day Len was preoccupied with Queenie Bromley and the borough council. He forgot that he had already removed one pipe connection and as he set the pump working the dangerous liquid began to leak out and form a large puddle on the factory floor.

It was late in the evening before Len discovered his error, and by that time he had tramped back and forth through the chemical puddle and his shoes were beginning to rot. At first there was just a slight itching between his toes, and he noticed that the leather sole on one shoe had come unstitched. By the time he was gathering up his tools at the end of the shift, however, he was in agony. The itching had become unbearable and there was a burning sensation on the soles of his feet.

Len cycled home from work as quickly as he could and Elsie gasped as her unfortunate husband collapsed in a chair and kicked off all that was left of his shoes and socks. Large blisters and bright red patches covered his feet.

'Oh my good Gawd! Whatever is it?' Elsie cried.

'Bloody industrial bleach! It's burnin' me feet orf!' Len groaned.

'Bleach? What yer bin doin' wiv bleach?' Elsie asked, staring down at him.

'Don't stand there gawkin', yer silly cow!' he shouted. 'Go an' get us a bowl o' water.'

Elsie hurried into the scullery and by the time she had filled the bowl Len was on his feet and dancing like a dervish. 'Me toes are burnin' orf!' he moaned.

Immersing his feet in the cold water did not seem to help and Elsie began to panic. 'Stay there, I'll go an' phone fer an ambulance,' she told him, fighting to stay calm.

'I ain't goin' nowhere,' Len groaned as he stared down at his painful feet.

Elsie grabbed her coat from the back of the parlour door and as she ran out of the house she suddenly realised that she had never been in a phone box. For a few moments she hesitated, then in sheer desperation she knocked at the house next door.

On Saturday morning women hurried to and from the Tower Bridge Road market and enterprising children scrounged empty boxes to chop up for firewood. The pennies that the youngsters earned selling the sticks of wood were spent on hot sugary doughnuts oozing with raspberry jam, and there were usually enough coppers left over for the Saturday morning cinema. Men studied the morning papers and took their bets to the local street bookie, and at midday as the docks and wharves closed for the weekend the pubs began to fill up. The Sultan public house in Weston Street was doing a roaring trade, and the manager, Jack Murray, was in earnest conversation with a well-dressed individual, who occasionally nodded to the customers.

'They've bin makin' fings difficult lately, an' Muvver Jordan's told the bookie she's fed up wiv 'im divin' in an' out of 'er place all the time,' Jack told him.

The smartly dressed man studied his whisky for a few seconds before replying, and when he spoke his voice was gruff. 'We can't pay 'em off while fings are the way they are. There's a new guv'nor at Tower Bridge nick an' 'e's out ter make a name fer 'imself.'

Jack Murray stroked his unshaven chin. 'What about settin' up anuvver snatch? Won't they go fer that?'

Archie Westlake dusted an imaginary piece of fluff from his camel-hair overcoat and then thoughtfully adjusted the white silk scarf that was showing beneath. 'It won't work this time,' he said. 'They'll just grab the poor bleeder, bail 'im to appear, an' then they'll be back the next day. Word 'as it that this new inspector is after takin' us right off the streets. I expect 'e's after the Commissioner's job.'

Jack Murray filled Archie's empty glass and leaned forward on the saloon bar counter towards his boss. 'What about changin' the pitch?' he suggested.

The local villain nodded his head slowly. 'It might be the fing ter do,' he replied thoughtfully. 'If we can find the right spot, an' be a bit shrewd, they won't cotton on fer a few weeks, an' by that time the pressure might be off. We might even be able ter bung 'em a few shekels ter keep 'em 'appy like we used to.'

The publican grinned slyly. 'I fink I've got the right spot,' he said in a whisper.

'Yeah?'

'Yeah. Pedlar's Row.'

'Pedlar's Row? That's where Queenie Bromley lives. Do we know anybody there apart from 'er?' Archie asked.

Jack Murray nodded. 'The young sort who cleans 'ere lives in Pedlar's Row. She might be willin' ter let us use 'er place. Apparently she's at 'ome durin' the day. She looks after 'er farvver. 'E's 'ad a stroke, by all accounts.'

'Yer look after that then, Jack,' the villain said, gulping down the remainder of his drink. 'I've got some business ter take care of.'

Elsie Carmichael stood at her front door on the bright cold Saturday morning talking to Annie Stebbings. 'I tell yer, luv, I was terrified,' she said, pushing her thick spectacles back up on to the bridge of her nose. 'My poor Len was in agony. I thought 'is toes were gonna drop orf.'

'Good Gawd,' was all Annie could say.

'I run out ter phone fer an ambulance but I suddenly realised I didn't know 'ow they worked,' Elsie went on. 'I've never 'ad cause ter use a phone box. I didn't 'ave any coppers on me anyway.'

'Good Gawd,' Annie said.

'Well, I tell yer, luv, I was at me wits' end, I expected ter come back an' find 'im walkin' about on stumps, no lie.'

'Good Gawd.'

'Anyway, I suddenly thought about the Prior girl who's just moved in next door. She seemed a sensible young woman an' I wondered if she could 'elp. She come in wiv me an' when she see Len's feet she was shocked. They was all blistered an' red. Like a couple o' boiled lobsters they was.'

'Good Gawd.'

'Well, anyway, she asked 'im what it was 'e'd stood in, an' when 'e tells 'er, the girl asks me if I've got any vinegar in the 'ouse.'

'Vinegar?'

'Yeah, vinegar.'

'Good Gawd.'

'As it 'appened I did 'ave some. My Len won't eat 'is fish an' chips wivout soakin' 'em in vinegar. So I gave 'er the bottle out the cupboard an' she poured the 'ole lot in the bowl that Len 'ad 'is feet in.'

'Good Gawd.'

'Yer never seen such a difference. One minute Len's in agony an' the next minute the burnin' 'ad stopped altergevver.'

'Good Gawd.'

'It was the vinegar, yer see. It's what yer call a counteraction or somefing. Anyway it done the trick.'

Annie Stebbings felt obliged to say something. 'Good job she knew what ter do. 'Ow's Len's feet now?' she asked.

'Well, 'e went ter the 'ospital an' they put some ointment on 'em. 'E's gotta stay orf of 'em as much as possible.'

'Well, I 'ope they get better soon,' Annie said.

Elsie tucked her hands into her apron and hunched her shoulders against the cold. ' 'Ow's Wally?' she asked. 'I ain't seen 'im about fer a few days.'

Annie pulled a face. ' 'E's bin very quiet lately,' she replied. 'I do wish 'e'd find 'imself a nice gel. It'd be the makin' of 'im. I fink that job's gettin' 'im down too. They seem ter put on 'im at that factory.'

' 'E works in the office, don't 'e?'

'Yeah. 'E does the books.'

' 'E must be pretty bright.'

'Oh yeah, my Wally's clever enough, but 'e's jus' so quiet.'

' 'Ow old is 'e, Annie?'

' 'E's jus' turned forty.'

'Ain't your Wally never 'ad a gelfriend?'

'Well, there was one once. It didn't last long though.

She was in the Salvation Army an' she got Wally ter join.'

'Didn't 'e like it?' Elsie asked.

Annie shook her head vigorously. 'Nah. They wanted 'im ter go roun' the pubs wiv that paper they sell.'

'The *War Cry*, yer mean?'

'That's the one. Anyway my Wally couldn't do it. 'E don't like goin' in pubs,' Annie told her.

'Yeah, but 'e didn't 'ave to 'ave a drink, did 'e?'

'Nah, but Wally can't stand the places.'

'So it all finished?'

'Yeah. I was sorry ter see 'im leave. 'E looked very nice in the uniform too, once 'e got 'is cap sorted out.'

'Oh?'

'It was too big, yer see,' Annie explained. 'It come right down over 'is ears an' the kids used ter shy-'ike 'im. They was little bleeders where we used ter live. Never left 'im alone. I fink that was what turned Wally. Shame though, 'cos she was a nice gel.'

'Well, never mind, luv, I s'pose it's all fer the best,' Elsie said.

Annie picked up her shopping bag. 'Well, I'd better be orf,' she sighed. 'Wally'll be wantin' 'is grub. 'E likes 'is food, does Wally.'

Charlie Bromley was a very knowledgeable eleven-year-old and he had formed an immediate friendship with Terry Grant at the Webb Street School. Now that Terry had moved into Pedlar's Row Charlie was delighted.

'I'm really glad yer livin' 'ere, Tel,' the young delinquent said. 'We can do lots o' fings now.'

'Like what?' Terry asked.

'Well, we can't go nickin' apples at the market any more, 'cos the coppers told my mum I'll go ter Borstal if they catch me there again, but we could bunk in the Trocette.'

'Cor yeah!' Terry enthused.

'I got this bit o' tin, yer see,' Charlie went on. 'Yer can get in easy wiv this.'

Terry stared at the thin piece of metal that Charlie had taken from his trouser pocket, and then his face became serious. ' 'Ere, what's Borstal?' he asked.

Charlie's expression changed to one of horror. 'It's the worstest place in the 'ole world. It's worse than Devil's Island,' he said with conviction. 'If yer get caught nickin' or doin' bad fings they take yer ter the court an' the ole git there sends yer ter Borstal. It's 'undreds o' miles away an' yer can't see yer muvver or farvver. They give yer the cat-o'-nine-tails an' sometimes they lock yer up in the cellar all night long wiv the rats.'

'Cor! I don't never wanna go there,' Terry said with a shudder.

'That's why we can't go nickin' in the market,' Charlie told him.

'S'posin' they catch us bunkin' in the Trocette?' Terry said.

'That's different,' Charlie explained. 'There's only this ole bloke who stands on the door an' 'e's got tanner-each-way feet. 'E can't run fer toffee. We could easy get away from 'im.'

'Yeah, but s'posin' we did get caught? Would we get sent ter Borstal fer bunkin' in the pictures?' Terry asked, wide-eyed.

'Nah. All they do is clip yer round the ear an' chuck yer out,' Charlie told him. 'A clip round the ear's nuffink. Better than the cat-o'-nine-tails. That really 'urts.'

Terry was convinced. 'Okay then. Let's bunk in the Trocette.'

As they walked along Weston Street Charlie fished into his coat pocket and took out a small tin box. 'I got itchy powder in 'ere,' he announced.

Terry looked at the scorched sides of the tin. 'Why's it black?' he asked.

'That's 'cos it's bin over the fire.'

'Why's it bin over the fire?'

'Ter roast the grass'oppers.'

'Grass'oppers?'

'Yeah. When yer put grass'oppers in the tin an' roast 'em they make a noise.'

'That's cruel.'

'No it ain't. Not as cruel as what Alan Parish does. 'E puts goldfish frew the mangle.'

They hurried along Tower Bridge Road, past the stalls and busy shops, and Charlie set a fast pace with his hands pushed deep down into his trouser pockets. He was determined to avoid Borstal at any costs, and his face had taken on an angelic expression.

When they reached the Trocette the two young lads ambled up to the fire exit and Charlie looked left and right before applying the strip of metal to the formidable-looking door. In no time at all the two friends were sitting very quietly in the 'one-and-nines'. Soon the main feature started and Charlie groaned aloud. 'Cor, what a swizz! I've seen this picture before.'

Chapter Six

On Monday morning Laura was a few minutes late getting to her job at the Sultan. Her father had fallen as he was getting out of bed and shaken himself up. By the time she had settled him into the armchair, made him a strong cup of tea and reassured herself that he would be all right, it was five minutes after nine o'clock. Laura prided herself on keeping good time, and as she hurried along Weston Street she thought about Jack Murray. He might have been put out a bit by her coolness towards him, and if he had decided to get rid of her then her lateness would be an ideal excuse.

Laura told herself to stay calm as she hurried up to the pub door. She was being silly. She was only ten minutes late and could make that time up, provided the manager didn't keep her chatting.

'Mornin', luv,' Jack said, looking over from behind the counter. 'It's a cold'un terday.'

'Mornin', Jack. Sorry I'm late,' she replied.

'That's all right, not ter worry,' he said, smiling.

Laura hung up her coat and set to work. She began as usual by emptying and washing the ashtrays, then she swept and mopped the public bar, and it was some time later, as she was setting to work polishing the tables, that the publican came over to her.

'I've bin finkin'. Ow would yer like to earn a few extra bob a week?' he asked, stroking his stubbled face.

'Doin' what?'

'Nuffink much. I got a bookmaker pal who needs a pitch.'

'At my front door?'

' 'S'right, luv.'

Laura's mind was racing. It would be unthinkable, the way her father was. He felt the cold and she couldn't allow the front door to be kept open in all weathers. Besides, he was a worrier. He would fret over getting in trouble with the police, and then there was the council to consider. People had got notice to quit through allowing bookies to take betting slips in their doorways. 'I'm sorry, but my dad's too ill. I've gotta be careful the way fings are,' she replied.

Jack Murray's face dropped and he shrugged his shoulders. 'Never mind, I understand the position,' he said. 'What about yer neighbours though? One o' them might like to earn a few extra bob. There's no risk attached. There'll be two lookouts, one at each end o' the Row. If they see the coppers they'll give the signal an' the bookie goes inside an' shuts the door till they've gone. It's only a couple of hours mornin' an' evenin', an' it pays well.'

Laura thought that it would do no harm at least to ask her neighbours for him. 'All right, I'll talk to 'em,' she replied.

His expression brightened. 'Good gel. Do yer best.'

As she set about the polishing Laura felt a little relieved at his reaction, but she wondered how she was going to approach the neighbours in the Row. The only person she had got to know so far was Elsie Carmichael, though she had chatted briefly to Queenie Bromley and nodded to some of the other neighbours as they passed by.

Laura just finished the polishing by opening time, and hurried back home anxious to see how her father was feeling and eager to get to the market before the best of the vegetables were sold. As she walked into the Row she saw Queenie. She was busy cleaning her windows and she turned as Laura passed her.

'I 'eard yer sorted that silly git's feet out,' she said sardonically.

Laura nodded. 'Did Elsie tell yer?' she asked.

Queenie snorted. 'That silly mare wouldn't tell me anyfing. We don't get on, me an' 'er. It was Annie Stebbin's who told me.'

'Annie Stebbin's?'

' 'Er at the end 'ouse,' Queenie went on. 'That's 'er boy Wally. Yer might 'ave seen 'im walkin' up an' down 'ere. Always got 'is 'ands be'ind 'is back. Looks like Percival the Preacher. I've told my boys ter keep away from 'im. There's somefing strange about that fella.'

'It might just be nerves,' Laura offered.

'Yeah, an' it might not be,' Queenie replied. 'If I was you I'd do the same as me. Tell yer boys ter stay clear of 'im.'

Laura took a deep breath, wondering whether she should put Jack Murray's proposal to the aggressive woman. She might be the sort of person who could handle it, and she would no doubt be grateful for the extra money. In any case there would be no harm in mentioning it, she decided.

' 'Ow's yer farvver?' Queenie enquired before she could say anything.

'Well, as a matter o' fact 'e fell gettin' out o' bed this mornin'. It shook 'im up,' Laura told her.

'They're a bloody worry when they're gettin' on a bit,' the large woman replied, brushing a hand down the front of her floral apron. 'I 'ad it fer years lookin' after my ole muvver. She's dead now though.'

Laura took another deep breath. 'I was asked ter let a

bookie stand at my front door, but I can't, not the way Dad is,' she said casually.

Queenie's large blue eyes narrowed suddenly. 'That'll be one o' Westlake's bookies,' she said venomously. 'I wouldn't give 'em 'ouse room. Archie Westlake poisons everyfing 'e touches. Anyway, 'ow come you got asked?'

Laura told her about working at the Sultan and how Jack Murray had approached her, feeling intimidated all the while by Queenie's eyes staring at her. 'As I said, I couldn't do it,' she concluded.

'Yer done right,' Queenie replied. 'I wouldn't give Archie Westlake a crust o' bread if 'e was starvin'. The man's an evil bastard.'

Laura made her excuses to leave the angry woman, shocked by the spite in her voice. Maybe it would be better to forget the whole thing, she decided. Jack Murray would have to do his own canvassing, like it or not.

Lucy Grant was deep in thought as she worked away at her machine in the biscuit factory. The constant clatter of tins and the pulsating throb of the machinery made it hard for her to concentrate fully, but as she went through the repetitive process of pulling and pushing on the levers in front of her she tried to form a clear picture in her mind of how Roy would look. It had been so long and she realised that he would have changed. He would not look anything like the fresh-faced young man who had said goodbye to her and the children that summer day on King's Cross Station. He would be older, thin and gaunt, and perhaps he would have a haunted look in his eyes that would frighten her.

Lucy instinctively touched her breast pocket where the letter from Roy was resting and she gulped hard. It had dropped through the letterbox just as she was leaving for work that morning and she had read it in the changing room. The factory hooter had sounded too soon for her to reread it and she was impatiently willing the lunchtime whistle to sound. The letter was postmarked Cape Town, and in it Roy said that he would be sailing soon and that his ship would dock at Liverpool on the third of February. In two short weeks he would be back home after an absence of over four and a half years. Would they be able to pick up the pieces after so long apart? Lucy wondered anxiously. How much damage had been done to his mind during the terrible years of slavery? Would his body be scarred? Perhaps he would be a physical wreck, not able to work. Numerous questions flashed through her troubled mind and she felt sick with doubt and dread as she glanced up at the clock for the hundredth time.

The sound of the factory whistle was music to Lucy's ears, and as she hurried away from her machine to the refuge of the canteen Val Bennett hailed her. The fat, motherly woman had taken Lucy under her wing from the beginning and had become a confidante. When the wagging tongues and derogatory remarks had hurt and upset Lucy, Val Bennett had been there to give her support and encouragement. Now, as Lucy turned to see the large woman approaching, she smiled and tapped her breast pocket.

'I got a letter from Roy this mornin',' she said, smiling.

Val beamed. 'When's 'e gettin' in?' she asked, puffing to catch her breath.

'On the third o' February,' Lucy told her as they hurried out of the large factory hall.

After lunch the two women sat talking together in the noisy canteen, and Lucy looked worried as she confided in her friend. 'It's bin so long,' she said. 'I won't know what ter say to 'im, Val.'

Val's wide face puckered up into a grin. 'Once yer

61

alone tergevver the years'll roll back. It'll be like 'e's never bin away. You'll see.'

'I'm just worried what 'e's gonna look like,' Lucy fretted. 'Roy was a good-lookin' fella. Gawd knows what those four an' 'alf years 'ave done to 'im.'

Val shrugged her shoulders. 'Years don't sit easy on any of us, gel. None of us get any nicer wiv keepin'. What yer gotta remember is, that no matter what's 'appened durin' the time yer fella's bin gone, yer gotta ferget it. Put it out o' yer mind an' make a fresh start.'

Lucy nodded slowly as she looked into her friend's large soft eyes. 'I've finished wiv Pat,' she said simply.

'Yer done right,' Val told her as she leaned forward over the table. 'Don't listen ter the chitchat, an' don't let the snide remarks get ter yer. 'Alf o' them ain't so bloody righteous anyway. Jus' tell yerself yer makin' a fresh start, an' don't feel too guilty about what's 'appened while yer fella was away. Just remember, a couple o' slices out of a cut loaf ain't gonna be missed, are they?'

Lucy smiled affectionately at the large woman. Val was a good friend. She had a large brood of her own and a diminutive husband who adored her. She had a saying to fit almost every occasion and she made a lot of sense. There was no point in dwelling on what had happened during the past few years. There was no undoing, and she would have to live with her indiscretions. Roy was going to need her and that was all that mattered now. They had been happy together, despite her mother's fears that she was too young and hadn't known Roy long enough. She was just nineteen and Roy twenty-one when they wed. She had become pregnant almost immediately and Reg was born just after her twentieth birthday. It had been hard, what with the shortage of money and Roy being thrown out of work when the cabinet-making trade went into decline, but they had coped.

Things would be better now. Roy would probably go back into the furniture business and they could find a decent place to live, maybe in one of the new towns that were being built.

'Penny fer yer thoughts.'

Lucy looked up quickly. 'Just daydreamin',' she said, smiling.

'Yer know it ain't gonna be easy,' Val remarked.

'Yeah, I know that,' Lucy replied. 'We were only kids when Roy went in the army. We're both older now, older an' more wise. We'll manage.'

'I'm sure yer will,' Val said with an encouraging smile.

Lucy was quiet for a while, absent-mindedly twisting the gold wedding ring around on her finger. Then she suddenly looked up. 'Yer know what, Val?' she said. 'I fink I'll go in fer anuvver baby, before I'm too old.'

' 'Ow old are yer?' Val asked.

'Thirty-three.'

'Yer just a spring chicken,' Val said grinning. 'Go in fer it soon as yer can. There's nuffink like a baby ter put a bloom in yer cheeks. Look at me. I've 'ad seven. I 'ad my Doreen when I was forty-one. I shouldn't wait that long though if I was you.'

The factory whistle sounded and the workforce tramped out of the canteen. Lucy settled herself at her machine, vowing to follow Val's good advice and do her best to make Roy happy. All that had happened was water under the bridge, she told herself. She could live with it. After all, other people had to live with their guilty secrets. Her sister had to live with hers and she had come to terms with it. Laura was strong, and she would be too.

Len Carmichael's feet had shown a marked improvement, so much so that he felt he could survive a trip to the Sultan. He was well known at the local pub, however, and he found himself greeted with a certain amount of leg-pulling.

' 'Ello, Len. Wassa matter wiv yer plates o' meat?' someone remarked.

'I see yer got yer dancin' shoes on,' another said.

Len looked down at his carpet slippers which were held on with strips of bandage threaded through holes cut into the sides. 'Accident at work,' he replied sheepishly.

'They're swollen, ain't they?' someone said. 'I thought that was Charlie Chaplin comin' frew the door.'

'Cor blimey! I thought me eyes was playin' tricks fer a minute,' another wag remarked as he stood staring at Len. 'Yer look just like Charlie Goldfish.'

'Charlie Goldfish? 'Oo's 'e?' Len asked.

June Morrison, the barmaid, leaned her chubby arms on the bar counter and looked at Len. 'Before yer get stuck listenin' ter Tubby, what yer gonna 'ave?' she asked.

'I'll 'ave a pint o' mild an' bitter, an' one fer yerself,' Len said, putting a ten-shilling note down on the counter.

'Bit brassy, ain't we?' Tubby said.

'Matter o' fact I'm on the panel an' I'm boracic lint,' Len replied. 'This is the rent money. I told the rent man I'd pay 'im double next week.'

The barmaid passed over the frothing beer and when he had taken a large gulp Len turned to Tubby. ' 'Ere, Tubby, who's this Charlie Goldfish?'

Tubby put his glass down and leaned his elbow on the counter. 'Charlie Goldfish was always in 'ere one time o' day,' he began. ' 'E's dead now though. Charlie loved a mild an' bitter. I never known 'im ter miss a day wivout 'avin' 'is mild an' bitter. One day 'e walked in 'ere just like you did. Charlie's feet were all bandaged up an' 'e 'ad a right miserable look on 'is face. I sez ter Charlie,

"Oi, Chas, wassa matter wiv yer kippers?" Well, Charlie gives me a right look, an' I tell yer, mate, if looks could kill then I'd be six feet under by now. "Industrial bleach," 'e sez. "Bleach?" I sez. " 'Ow that 'appen then, Chas?" "I bloody trod in this bleach at work," 'e sez. "Gettin' better an' all they was. Then all of a sudden two o' me bloody toes dropped orf." True. True as I'm sittin' 'ere,' Tubby declared, still leaning against the counter. 'Anyway, a couple o' weeks later I bumped inter Charlie Goldfish's ole woman. " 'Ow's Charlie?" I asked. " 'E's gorn," she said. "Gorn?" I said "Gorn where?" " 'E dropped dead last week," she said. Apparently they found out at the inquest that Charlie shouldn't 'ave bin drinkin'. What 'appened was, the beer 'e drunk started all the bleach up again an' it finally travelled up 'is leg an' touched 'is 'eart. Terrible fing, really.'

Len Carmichael put his half-empty glass down on the counter and stared at it in horror for a few seconds, then turned on his heel and made for the door.

'Oi, where yer goin'?' Tubby asked, hiding a grin.

'I jus' remembered I left the gas on,' Len mumbled as he hurried out.

'That wasn't very nice,' the barmaid chided Tubby. 'Yer scared the life out of 'im. Was that what Len trod in, bleach?'

Tubby nodded. 'Len's missus told my ole dutch. Anyway, 'e shouldn't be drinkin'.'

'Why not? Beer won't 'arm 'im,' June said contemptuously.

'I know that,' Tubby replied. ' 'E borrered the rent money though. Dodgy game that, usin' the rent money fer booze.'

Chapter Seven

Bridie Molloy lived in the next house along from the Priors. She was a friendly woman in her late forties, and with fair hair which she wore short and tidy. She was slightly built and thin-faced, with pale blue eyes. Being an amicable woman, Bridie was very concerned about her neighbours, and for that reason she was at pains to nag at her large, easy-going husband who tended to get the worse for drink occasionally. Bridie did not mind Joe having a drink – after all, he worked hard as a gas-fitter and he was never nasty when he was under the influence, more the reverse – but it worried her that on the odd occasion when he was drunk he quite often tended to stagger home singing at the top of his voice.

Being keen to keep up appearances, Bridie kept her windows sparkling, the front-door area swept and the doorstep scrubbed clean every week without fail. She liked to get on with the neighbours and be able to chat to them, and when the Priors moved into Pedlar's Row she made a mental note to get to know the family as soon as possible. There had been little chance so far, but after what had just transpired, Bridie wondered if she could ever face any of her neighbours again, let alone the new arrivals.

Joe had been the cause of it and Bridie nagged him unmercifully.

'Whatever possessed yer, Joe? I won't be able to 'old

me 'ead up in front of 'em,' she stormed.

'Now don't be so silly, Bridie,' he said quietly. 'There's no 'arm in it. Everybody likes a flutter. I like a bet an' sometimes you pick a couple o' dogs out on Saturday night.'

'I ain't talkin' about 'avin' a bet. I know there's no 'arm in that,' she went on. 'What I'm concerned about is you agreein' ter let our place be used as a bolt 'ole.'

Joe sighed as he leaned back in his chair. 'Now listen, luv. It won't be no 'ardship. Yer back 'ome at 'alf ten from yer office-cleanin', an' yer said yerself yer could do wiv anuvver little job to 'elp out. Lettin' the bookie stand in the doorway won't 'urt, an' the money'll come in 'andy. Yer won't 'ave ter bovver about gettin' anuvver cleanin' job in the evenin's now.'

'But what'll the neighbours fink?' Bridie fretted.

'Yer shouldn't worry so much about what the neighbours fink,' Joe told her. 'Anyway, they'll all be runnin' up wiv their bets, mark my words.'

Bridie wished she didn't worry so much, because Joe was right about the extra money. Their elder daughter Kathleen was planning on getting married later in the year and young Pauline was going steady. Weddings were expensive and Bridie was determined that her two girls would have the best.

'I bet Queenie Bromley's gonna 'ave somefing ter say about it,' she muttered, rubbing her chin anxiously.

'That bolshy cow 'as somefing ter say about everyfing,' Joe replied dismissively.

Bridie continued to worry, knowing that she could not expect her two daughters to take her side in the argument. Like their father they thought that she was inclined to trouble herself too much about what other people might think and had often said as much.

Joe Molloy could not understand why Bridie was so upset. He had been pleased when Jack Murray approached him. He had known the publican for some years and knew that Archie Westlake was running the local bookies. Archie was a big man in the area and it was probably quite an asset being in with someone like him. Archie looked after his own and Joe felt secretly proud to think that he had been asked to help out, as it were.

Bridie Molloy was still feeling worried and apprehensive as she knocked at number three. Her new next-door neighbours had been there for more than a week now and she felt that it was high time to introduce herself.

'I 'ope yer don't mind, luv, but I thought I'd better knock ter say 'ello,' she said quickly. 'I'm Bridie Molloy an' I live next door.'

Laura smiled. 'I'm Laura Prior. Would yer like ter come in fer a minute? It's better than standin' at the door.'

Bridie followed Laura into the warm parlour and saw the old man huddled in front of the fire.

'This is my dad,' Laura said. ' 'E's not too bright this mornin', are yer, luv?'

'I am sorry,' Bridie replied, nodding to Albert. 'The weavver don't 'elp neivver.'

Albert gave her a weak smile and returned his gaze to the flames.

Laura motioned to a chair. 'Make yerself comfortable,' she said. 'Would yer like a cuppa?'

Bridie shook her head as she sat down on an upright chair beside the table. 'No, it's all right, fanks. I'm just off shoppin' as a matter o' fact an' I thought it was about time I called in considerin' I only live next door. Trouble is, I do early-mornin' cleanin' an' I usually bring me shoppin' in wiv me. I don't go outside the door then, while it's so cold. Well, anyway, 'ow d'yer like it 'ere?'

'We're gettin' settled,' Laura answered with a smile. 'We came from Crystal Buildin's in Long Lane. We were put in there after we got bombed out o' Leroy Street.'

Bridie brushed her hand down the lapel of her coat. 'I used ter live the ovver end o' Long Lane,' she said. 'Queenie Bromley lived there as well. As a matter o' fact, the Bromleys an' the Carmichaels lived in Long Lane fer years. George Bromley's aunt Clara lived in Crystal Buildin's. So did Aggie Carmichael, Len's gran'muvver. Those buildin's 'ave bin up fer donkeys' years. I bet yer glad ter get away from there, ain't yer?'

Laura nodded emphatically. 'We were up on the fourth floor. Dad 'ad a job wiv the stairs. 'E's 'ad a stroke. Gettin' this place was a godsend.'

Bridie glanced at Albert who was still staring into the fire, then quickly turned back to Laura. ' 'Ave yer met any o' the other neighbours yet?' she asked.

'I've met Elsie next door,' Laura told her.

' 'Ave yer met the Cassidys?'

'Not yet.'

'They're a lovely family,' Bridie said. 'What about 'er at number one?'

'Queenie Bromley, yer mean? Yeah, I 'ad a brief chat wiv 'er,' Laura replied.

Bridie's expression had changed noticeably. 'So yer've met our Queenie Bromley. I 'ope she didn't bend yer ear too much.'

Laura smiled. 'Just a bit.'

'Well, don't you go lettin' 'er upset yer,' Bridie said quickly. 'Queenie's all right, I s'pose. 'Er bark's worse than 'er bite. She does try to act like she owns the place though.'

'Yeah, I did notice,' Laura said, smiling.

'Is there jus' you an' yer dad?' Bridie asked.

'No, my sister an' 'er two boys live 'ere. She's at work durin' the day,' Laura told her. ' 'Er 'usband's bin a prisoner o' war in the Far East. 'E's not 'ome yet. 'E's expected any time now.'

Bridie nodded. 'I bet she's all on pins.'

'Are yer sure I can't get yer a cup o' tea?' Laura asked her.

'No, I'm fine, fanks very much,' Bridie replied, a worried look suddenly appearing on her face. 'There's somefing I wanted ter let yer know while I'm 'ere, though, an' I 'ope it won't cause any problems. It's about the bookie.'

'Bookie?'

'Yeah. Yer see, my Joe's bin an' told the bookie 'e can stand at my front door ter take 'is bets, wivout talkin' ter me first. That's my Joe all over. I 'ope yer don't mind?'

Laura's face relaxed into a large grin. 'No of course I don't,' she told her. 'As a matter o' fact I was asked if the bookie could stand at my door, but I couldn't say yes, not the way Dad is. 'E feels the cold an' I couldn't 'ave the door left open.'

Bridie looked surprised. 'They asked you?'

Laura nodded. 'The guv'nor o' the Sultan asked me. I do the mornin' cleanin' there,' she explained.

'That's who asked my Joe,' Bridie replied. 'Are yer sure yer don't mind?'

Laura shook her head. 'Certainly not. Dad likes a bet now an' again, don't yer, Dad?'

Albert nodded without much enthusiasm. 'When I feel up to it,' he said in a tired voice.

Laura gave Bridie a reassuring look and waved away her concern. 'Don't give it anuvver thought.'

'Oh, I am pleased,' Bridie said. 'Yer know I bin worryin' meself sick over what the neighbours might fink. I know Queenie's gonna 'ave somefing ter say.'

'Why should it concern 'er?' Laura asked.

Bridie leaned forward over the table. ' 'Ave you 'eard the name Archie Westlake?'

Laura nodded. ' 'E owns the Sultan,' she replied. 'I've seen 'im in there a few times.'

'That's not all 'e owns,' Bridie told her. 'My Joe said that Archie Westlake owns a couple o' grocery shops round 'ere an' a drinkin' club over in Camberwell, as well as runnin' the local bookies. Durin' the war 'e made 'is money in the black market. 'E's a big villain round 'ere an' 'e's made a few enemies in 'is time. Queenie Bromley's one. It was common knowledge down Long Lane. Everybody knew she couldn't stand the man, but funny fing was, nobody ever found out why. Oh, there was a lot o' rumours flyin' about, but that's as far as it got. Somebody did say that Queenie an' 'im was fick as fieves at one time but somefing went wrong. All I know is, she's gonna 'ave somefing ter say when she finds out about the bookie.'

Laura smiled sympathetically. 'Well, I wouldn't take no notice, Bridie,' she said. 'It's none of 'er business anyway.'

Bridie stood up and adjusted the collar of her coat. 'Well, it's bin nice meetin' yer, Laura, an' you too, Mr Prior. I 'ope yer feel better soon,' she said, making for the door.

Albert nodded briefly and mumbled a goodbye, as Laura showed Bridie to the front door. 'Pop in any time, I'm in most o' the day,' she told her.

The evening meal over, Lucy stood beside the stone sink in the scullery, drying the crockery Laura passed over to her. There was a thoughtful expression on her pretty face and occasionally she glanced at her older sister as they chatted together.

'I shouldn't be in too much of a rush ter tell Roy yer lookin' fer anuvver place,' Laura was going on. 'Just give 'im time ter settle in 'ere first. It's understandable 'e's gonna feel strange. 'E's gonna need ter feel relaxed an' comfortable. Wait till the time's ripe. After all, there's no immediate rush.'

Lucy nodded. 'I won't rush 'im, Laura, but we do need a place of our own as soon as possible. Besides, I'm finkin' o' goin' in fer anuvver baby soon as I can.'

'I 'ope yer'll let Roy inter the secret,' Laura said with a sigh of resignation.

Lucy nodded. ' 'E'll be involved.'

For a while they fell silent, then Lucy glanced at her sister. 'Would it make any difference ter the council if I did find anuvver place?' she asked quickly.

Laura shrugged her shoulders. 'I dunno. Elsie an' Len next door are on their own. Besides, I could always take in a lodger,'

'Yer wouldn't, would yer?' Lucy said with concern. 'Yer'd 'ave enough ter do lookin' after Dad.'

Laura's face became serious. 'We both gotta realise that Dad's gettin' on, an' that stroke's really aged 'im,' she pointed out. 'What about the future? I can't be expected ter live 'ere all on me own. I don't s'pose the council would let me, anyway.'

Lucy sighed deeply. 'I do wish you'd find a nice fella, Laura. I worry over you at times.'

Laura shrugged again. 'I don't get much opportunity, do I?' she replied.

Her younger sister finished drying the last of the plates and gathered the pile up, placing them carefully on the bottom shelf of the old Welsh dresser, then she looked up from where she was crouching. 'Yer know, Laura, I sometimes fink yer don't wanna find a man,' she said quickly.

Laura's face had become set firm as she watched Lucy moving the clean crockery around. 'What makes yer fink that?' she asked coldly.

'Well, yer never did 'ave a real steady fella after Ralph Knight, did yer?' Lucy said. 'Oh, there were plenty o' fellas, but yer never seemed ter take any of 'em seriously. I often wonder if you were punishin' yerself by not

72

gettin' prop'ly involved wiv any o' those lads. After all, one or two were really nice.'

Laura bit back an angry reply, knowing that her sister was nearer the truth than she realised. When Ralph's wife was found gassed that terrible Sunday morning Laura had felt as though she herself had turned on the tap. She had been inconsolable, wishing that she was dead too and didn't have to face the awful guilt. There was no suicide note, and Ralph had been quick to stress again and again to her that he and his wife were living apart when his affair with Laura began. Laura remembered how she had tried many times to convince herself that she was in no way to blame for what had happened but she was the one who had taken Ralph's wife's place in his affections. She would never know the truth. Had Ralph been playing fast and loose with his wife's loyalty? Had he told her about his new love? Had the poor woman been hoping against hope that they would somehow mend their marriage? Whatever the situation had been, the inescapable fact was that she had finally decided that life was no longer worth living.

Laura averted her eyes from her sister's enquiring gaze as the memory of that time irresistibly filled her mind. Ralph had tried hard to continue with their relationship, they both had, but the death of his wife had weighed heavily on them both and they finally realised that they could no longer go on together. The break had been mutually agreed and Ralph had left London to start another life somewhere else. He had promised to let her know how he was getting on and she had received just two letters, a short one from Somerset; and a second letter just after the outbreak of war in which he said that he had volunteered for the army. That was the last she had ever heard of him. She had scoured the casualty lists and pored over newspaper photographs but had failed to find any trace of him.

'Laura?'

'I'm sorry,' Laura replied with a start, suddenly realising that Lucy was speaking to her.

'I was askin' if yer still thought of 'im,' Lucy said slowly.

Laura shook her head. 'Not in any big way,' she told her. 'I sometimes wonder what 'appened to 'im, but it was over long ago, before the war started.'

Lucy leaned against the dresser as she picked at her fingernails. 'But yer still carry the guilt around inside yer, Laura. Yer gotta let go of it, an' until yer do, until yer bury the ghost once an' fer all yer'll never build a lastin' relationship wiv any man.'

Lucy was right; there had been other men friends as she tried hard to pick up the pieces of her life, but the very thought of another serious relationship developing had caused her to panic. Only at home, within her very close family, had she felt safe, and she had begun to avoid and disregard altogether the attentions of young men. The onset of war had been an excuse for a while. Most of the young available men were either in the services or going in shortly. Her mother's death, Roy going into the army and her father's illness had all affected her dramatically, changing her thinking, moulding her into what she had become. She would never wed now. Her life was settled, comfortable, predictable, and lonely. So very lonely.

Lucy suddenly clapped her hands together. 'I know what. Let's go up the Sultan fer a drink,' she said, smiling widely. 'Let's drift in there like we're a couple o' tarts.'

'I don't know 'ow ter do the walk,' Laura replied, attempting to be cheerful. 'Anyway, Dad's not so good. I can't leave 'im.'

Lucy shrugged in resignation and sighed as she picked up Roy's letter from the dresser and stared at it for a while. 'S'posin' it was somebody else who wrote the letter for 'im?' she said suddenly. 'S'posin' 'e can't write? There could be somefing wrong wiv 'im.'

Laura took her younger sister by the shoulders and held her firmly.

'I'm tellin' yer, that's Roy's 'andwritin'.'

'Yer don't know fer certain,' Lucy replied, her eyes filling with tears.

'Look, are yer sure yer've got no samples o' Roy's 'andwritin' lyin' around anywhere?' Laura asked.

The younger woman shook her head. 'I've bin searchin' in all the drawers. There's nuffink.'

'I could be dyin' fer want of a cup o' tea in this 'ouse.'

The two young women turned to see Albert standing in the doorway.

'Sorry, Dad. We've bin talkin',' Lucy replied quickly.

'Yeah, I 'eard what yer said about that letter, an' about the 'andwritin'.'

'I searched 'igh an' low an' I can't find anyfing wiv Roy's 'andwritin' on,' Lucy said with a sigh.

Albert had a smirk fixed on his gaunt face. 'You two are married, ain't yer?' he asked Lucy sarcastically.

'Eh?'

'The marriage lines. What about the marriage lines?'

Lucy rummaged through the sideboard drawer for a few moments then gave a grunt of satisfaction. ' 'Ere it is.'

The two sisters pored over the marriage certificate, comparing Roy's signature with the handwriting in the letter.

'Look, it's the same, yer can see clearly,' Lucy said excitedly. 'Look at the way 'e's done that letter, an' look at the squiggly bit at the end.'

'I told yer, didn't I?' Laura said, smiling.

Albert shuffled back to his place beside the fire. Since his stroke he found it tiring being on his feet too much, and as time weighed heavily on him he had taken to reading almost every word in the newspapers, as well as listening to the wireless most of the day and during the evenings. He had not missed much of the current news and topics that were being discussed, and he had heard a lot of what was being said about compensation for the maltreated Far Eastern prisoners of war. A lot of terrible stories were beginning to emerge, and he worried for his young son-in-law, dreading what sort of state he would be in when he returned home.

The two young women were chatting away together when Laura suddenly looked over at her father. 'Are you all right, Dad?' she asked with concern.

Albert continued to stare fixedly into the fire, the poker held in his bony hand.

'Dad, d'yer 'ear me?' Laura said louder.

'Sorry, gel, I was jus' finkin',' Albert replied.

'Why don't yer read yer paper?' she suggested.

Albert shook his head slowly. 'There ain't much in it these days,' he lied.

Chapter Eight

On the last Saturday morning in January the bookie walked into Pedlar's Row and knocked at number four. ' 'Ello, gel. Everyfing all right then?' he asked.

Bridie looked at the large, broad-shouldered man with a mop of grey wavy hair, a black Crombie overcoat and black patent leather shoes and she smiled nervously. 'I'll leave the door open,' she said.

'Yeah, it would be advisable,' the bookie replied with a saucy grin. 'Just in case the boys in blue decide to 'ave a little stroll round 'ere. Anyway, my name's Conrad, but everyone calls me Con. I fink me muvver must 'ave fancied a Russian.'

'I'm Bridie, an' I 'ope yer don't get pounced on,' the nervous woman told him.

'I'm sure we'll be okay,' he said, still grinning broadly. 'If I do get the signal I'll just step in the passage and close the door. Yer won't know I'm there.'

Bridie found it a little unsettling for a time, with the front door open and snatches of conversation drifting inside, but her two daughters thought it was quite exciting. 'What d'yer get fer aidin' an' abettin' bookies, Mum?' Kathleen asked.

Pauline looked through the lace curtains and sighed. 'That bookie looks quite 'andsome, in a rugged sort o' way,' she remarked in a husky voice. ' 'E looks a bit like Clark Gable, 'cept 'e's got grey 'air.'

77

'Come away from the curtains,' Bridie admonished her. 'It's enough of a poppy-show wivout you joinin' in.'

Kathleen smiled affectionately at her mother. 'You ain't still mad at Farvver over this, are yer?' she asked.

Bridie shook her head. 'Nah, yer farvver was only finkin' o' me, I s'pose,' she replied. 'Like 'e said, the money'll come in 'andy.'

'Did mouth-an'-trousers say anyfing to yer, Mum?' Pauline asked.

Bridie shook her head.

'Yer did tell 'er, didn't yer?' Pauline pressed.

'I was goin' to, but I ain't seen anyfing of 'er lately,' Bridie replied.

'Wait till she finds out,' Kathleen said, glancing at her sister and pulling a finger across her throat.

Bridie did not fail to notice. 'It's no laughin' matter,' she said sharply. 'I don't like fallin' out wiv neighbours, but I tell yer straight. If she starts shoutin' at me I'll give 'er a good mouthful. The likes o' Queenie Bromley don't scare me.'

'I'd tell Farvver to 'ave a word wiv 'er if I were you, Mum,' Pauline suggested. 'Yer know Dad, 'e can charm the birds out o' the trees.'

'Not bloody vultures though,' Kathleen cut in.

'Oi, you watch yer tongue, me gel,' Bridie scolded her. 'I don't want my daughters talkin' like dockers.'

Pauline slumped down into an armchair. 'Seriously though, Mum, yer not frightened o' that tub o' lard, are yer?' she said.

Bridie afforded a smile. 'It's not a question o' bein' frightened o' the woman,' she replied. 'I just don't like arguments. There's nuffink worse than grown women shoutin' out at the top o' their voices at each ovver, wiv all the street knowin' their business.'

Kathleen stuck out her fists like a boxer posing. 'Jus' give 'er a bunch o' fives if she starts, Mum,' she laughed.

★ ★ ★

Queenie Bromley was well aware of what was going on in Pedlar's Row, and had been for the past week. Joe Molloy had been talking to Len Carmichael and Len had passed on the information to George Bromley. It was all done in an innocent and typically careless way in the public bar of the Sultan, but when George told his wife she raised the roof. 'I'd put 'im away if I could,' she stormed.

'Look, gel, yer shouldn't take it to 'eart so,' George said soothingly. 'Yer know 'ow it starts yer blood pressure orf. D'yer wanna end up in 'orspital again?'

'Take it to 'eart?' Queenie echoed. 'What am I s'posed ter do, give the whoreson me blessin'? After what 'e done?'

George became quiet. He knew from long experience how the name Archie Westlake inflamed her. Queenie would cross the street so as not to pass the villain. She would rant and rave at the very mention of him, and his name was seldom spoken in the Bromleys' house. George was sorry he had told his wife about the bookie, not thinking at the time that he would be one of Westlake's men.

Queenie had decided not to approach Mrs Molloy about the bookie using her front door as a pitch, for she realised that it wasn't her doing. It was that drunken husband of hers who had instigated it. Queenie also had a sneaking regard for the quiet Bridie, although she would have died sooner than admit it. What she did decide to do, however, was let Archie Westlake know through the bookie's runner that she hoped he would choke on his dinner and die in rotten agony for daring to put a bookie in the respectable Pedlar's Row.

As soon as the bookie took up his post outside number four and his two runners were in position, one at each end of the Row, Queenie stepped out of her house and

79

took a deep breath, preparing to verbalise the nearer runner into a state of extreme shock. When she caught sight of the familiar figure standing at the entrance to the Row, however, she was taken aback.

'What the bloody 'ell are you doin' workin' fer that ponce Westlake?' she said in a slightly deflated voice.

John Bannerman looked sheepishly at Queenie and attempted a smile. 'It's a question o' bread an' butter, luv,' he replied. 'I bin away.'

'In nick, yer mean?'

' 'S'right.'

'Are yer still wiv Marge an' the kids?'

'Yeah, there's four of 'em now.'

' 'Ow's Marge?'

'She's fine, luv. 'Ow you bin keepin'?'

'I wasn't complainin', till I 'eard about Westlake puttin' 'is dirty, stinkin' mark on my Row,' Queenie spat out.

John Bannerman shrugged his narrow shoulders. ' 'E employs me,' he said, nodding towards the bookie. 'I 'ave nuffink at all ter do wiv Westlake. Ter be honest I'd much sooner get a regular job, but yer know 'ow it is when yer got form. "Sorry, pal, but we can't take a chance." It's always the same.'

Queenie sighed deeply. 'Well, I can't say I'm 'appy seein' yer workin' fer Westlake, 'cos make no mistake about it, son, it's Westlake's money that pays yer wages, not 'is,' she said, nodding towards Bridie Molloy's front door.

The thin young runner looked down at his shoes and Queenie suddenly took him by the arm. 'Give my best ter Marge, an' give us a knock before yer leave,' she said quietly. 'I've got a few bits an' pieces for yer.'

Lucy Grant's two sons were enjoying Saturday morning. Reg at thirteen considered himself a little too old for the children's matinee show at the Trocette, and after he had strolled back from the Tower Bridge Road market he ambled along to the bookie to see what was going on. For a while he stood lolling against the factory wall opposite, watching the man. He noticed how quickly it was all done. People would walk up to the bookie and then pieces of paper were quickly handed over and money was thrown into a deep pocket inside the man's overcoat. Sometimes the bookie paid out money after first consulting a long, thin book, the pages of which he flipped over and marked with the stub of a pencil. Reg very soon decided that he was going to be a bookie when he grew up. It was exciting, dodging the police and having men looking out for you. After a while he sauntered over.

'Excuse me, mister, but 'ow d'yer be a bookie?' he asked.

The large man looked down at him with a broad smile on his face. 'Well, first of all yer gotta get yer certificate,' he replied.

'What for?'

'Yer gotta 'ave a certificate before yer can be a bookie.'

'Where d'yer get it from?'

'School.'

'School?'

' 'S'right. Yer gotta know yer sums.'

Reg looked a little downcast and the bookie grinned at him. 'Now listen ter me, son,' he said. 'Yer can't be a bookie unless yer very clever at sums. If yer work 'ard an' get good at sums yer can ask yer teacher fer a bookie's certificate when yer leave school ter go ter work.'

'Fanks, mister,' Reg replied, perking up.

'Yer welcome,' the bookie said, reaching into his

overcoat pocket for his notebook. 'Now off yer go, I'm gonna be busy.'

Reg decided that maybe he should stick to train driving and he ambled off to see what other exciting things there were to be done on Saturday morning.

Lizzie Cassidy was humming to herself as she pegged out the washing in the back yard but her mind was working overtime. It was Elsie Carmichael who had told her about the new arrivals to the Row and she had been full of praise for the way in which Laura Prior had tended Len's 'terrible injury', as she put it. Elsie had gone on to tell her more about the Priors, and Laura in particular, and it seemed to Lizzie that here might be an opportunity for her finally to get her son Eddie out from under her feet.

Lizzie realised that she would have to be careful. The last time she had attempted to play Cupid it all ended in disaster. For some time she had been worried over her son's apparent reluctance to leave the nest and had decided that something would have to be done to get him married off. Unfortunately Eddie had no such desire, but Lizzie persevered, and when she made the necessary introduction at a recent wedding that the family attended things seemed to be progressing nicely. One of the bridesmaids was a pretty young thing, so Lizzie steered her in the direction of her son, and the two young people began happily chatting together, until the girl's boy-friend arrived on the scene a few hours later. It was obvious to all and sundry that he had spent quite a bit of time in the boxing ring. He had a flattened face, one cauliflower ear and a nasty temper into the bargain. He took umbrage at the attention his girlfriend was paying the young stranger and decided to sort him out.

Eddie's two older brothers had spotted the danger and warned him of an impending altercation but the young man dismissed their fears. ' 'E might be a scrapper but 'e can't be all that good, just look at 'is face,' he remarked.

Geoff and Steve stood close at hand, and when the inevitable argument broke out they were ready. The irate boxer threw a punch which missed, and then as he threw another Eddie ducked under it and delivered a hard jab to his stomach which winded him. The Cassidy brothers felt that no assistance was needed, but as they turned away the bridesmaid suddenly rounded on Eddie and thumped him in the chest with her clenched hands for daring to injure her beau. Finally order was restored and the offended party quietly removed, and Lizzie vowed to be more careful the next time she attempted to act as matchmaker.

As she finished hanging out the washing Lizzie was wondering how to make an introduction which would not appear too contrived. She had nodded once or twice to Laura Prior but as yet she had not really found an opportunity to stop her for a chat. Lizzie was a resourceful woman, however, and before the next lot of washing was out of the boiler she had things all worked out.

Charlie Bromley and Terry Grant were becoming inseparable. Wherever one was to be seen it was certain that the other was near at hand. They stuck together like glue, and on Saturday morning as they were strolling along shoulder to shoulder Charlie suddenly suggested that they should go and watch the eels get slaughtered.

'We could 'ave pie an' mash afterwards,' he suggested.

' 'Ow much is pie an' mash?' Terry asked.

'A tanner. I got a tanner, 'ow much you got?' Charlie asked him.

Terry looked disappointed. 'I've only got fourpence,' he said.

'We only need tuppence more then,' Charlie said brightly. 'We can soon get tuppence.'

Terry had complete faith in Charlie Bromley and he grinned at him as they strolled off along Weston Street towards the busy Tower Bridge Road.

The market was crowded as usual on that Saturday morning, and as the two young lads dodged and weaved between the shoppers Charlie was already rehearsing his role. Outside the doughnut shop there was a fruit stall run by a fierce-looking woman with a bright red face and bristles sprouting from her chin. Maggie Palfrey's appearance concealed a heart of gold and her weights were never short. She always found time to listen to her customers' troubles, and it was her fruit stall that the two young lads made for.

' 'Ello, Mrs Palfrey. D'yer want us ter get yer tea?' Charlie asked politely.

' 'Ello, luvvies. No fanks, I've jus' got it,' she replied.

Charlie looked suitably disappointed and the two lads stood watching Maggie weighing up a scoopful of carrots. 'Anyfing yer want us ter do?' Charlie asked her.

Maggie shook her head as she slipped the carrots into a customer's shopping bag. 'You two should get orf 'ome out the cold,' she urged.

Terry was about to walk away but Charlie Bromley was more streetwise and those few words were just the cue he needed. 'We're not allowed ter go 'ome yet, Mrs Palfrey,' he told her in a quiet voice.

'Oh, an' why's that?' Maggie asked curiously as she weighed up two pounds of potatoes.

'The lady said we can't go 'ome till Mum's 'ad the baby,' Charlie explained.

Maggie and her customer exchanged shocked glances while Terry stood wide-eyed, too scared to look at Charlie's nonchalant face.

'When's the baby due?' Maggie asked.

'The lady said it should be 'ere by ternight,' Charlie replied, hunching his shoulders.

Maggie's customer, a large woman with ginger hair, tut-tutted. 'Yer mean ter say you an' yer bruvver 'ave bin chucked out by this woman?' she said in a loud voice.

'We can go 'ome ternight,' Charlie told her, wiping the sleeve of his coat across his nose.

'I fink it's disgustin',' the large woman ranted.

Maggie nodded and looked down at the budding actor. 'Yer mean ter tell me yer gotta walk the streets all day wiv no food in yer bellies?' she said, trying not to smile.

'No, she give us tuppence each ter get a doughnut,' Charlie told her cheerfully.

The large ginger-haired woman was becoming more angry by the second. 'I've a good mind ter fetch a copper ter this woman,' she said fiercely. 'The bloody nerve of 'er.'

Maggie Palfrey had enjoyed the act, but she felt that it was time to bring down the curtain. ' 'Ere we are, luvvies,' she said, handing over some copper coins and hiding a grin. 'There's fourpence each. Now yer can go an' get a nice pie an' mash.'

'Cor, fanks, Mrs Palfrey,' Charlie said, taking the coins.

'Yeah, fanks, Mrs Palfrey,' Terry echoed, his face beaming.

Maggie watched the two of them hurry away and then turned to her still-fuming customer. 'That saucy one is Charlie, Queenie Bromley's boy,' she informed her. 'If Queenie's 'avin' a baby then I'm the Duchess o' Kent.'

'Yer mean it was all lies?' the woman said with a look of shock.

'Lies, stories, call it what yer like, but it does 'elp ter brighten up the day, don't yer fink?' Maggie chuckled.

Jack Murray was collecting the glasses at closing time after the Saturday lunchtime session when Archie Westlake walked in and seated himself at the counter with a nod, running his hand through his thick greying hair.

'It went off well,' he announced. 'No problems at all. Con's 'appy wiv it.'

Jack nodded. 'I didn't expect any problems, did you?'

Archie leaned his elbow on the counter and looked down at his shoes for a few moments. 'Well, apart from one particular party, no I didn't, but yer never know about these fings,' he replied, glancing up at the publican with his dark eyes. 'Anyway it's bin a good mornin' accordin' ter Con.'

Jack busied himself washing the glasses and up-ending them on the shelf below the counter, then he paused to look up at his boss. 'I got word about Levy this mornin',' he said hesitantly.

Archie fixed him with a hard look. 'Oh?'

' 'E's comin' out next week, by all accounts,' Jack informed him.

For a few moments Archie's eyes seemed to smoulder, then he gave Murray a brief smile. 'I did know. I've bin keepin' tabs on Levy. Look, Jack, I want yer ter set up a meetin'.'

The publican nodded. 'No sweat. What's the details?'

Archie shook his head slowly. 'Just tell 'im I'll be contactin' 'im. I wanna give Levy time ter ponder.'

Jack Murray went back to washing the glasses. He had been involved in a number of ways with Archie Westlake over the years, as a minder, an associate, and also as a partner in crime, and he knew much of the man's affairs and dealings. The Levy connection was something that went beyond the confines of local villainy, and the normally calm publican began to feel a little uneasy.

Marcus Levy was a very talented man from a wealthy and respectable Jewish family who had made their fortune in the clothing and textile trade around the turn of the century. The youngest of four sons born to Alex and Ada Levy, the young Marcus had been doted on and given a first-class education. He had studied art and architecture in Paris, Rome and New York during the twenties, travelled the world on a regular and very tidy allowance, and become embroiled in more than one scandal concerning wealthy women, which had been kept out of the papers by the financial intervention of his long-suffering parents.

Marcus had many talents, but they were overshadowed by his weakness for women and gambling. He had narrowly missed being apprehended in France over the sale of a Gauguin forgery during the thirties and had managed to escape to England, where he lay low in London's East End. Marcus had friends in the area and he survived by using his artistic talents to produce forged passports for refugees and aliens. It was in Whitechapel that Archie Westlake was first introduced to the young Hebrew when he went to get a passport for a wanted confederate in crime who was fleeing the country. Archie was impressed by the artist and he saw the huge potential in cultivating a friendship.

Unfortunately, Marcus Levy had fallen madly in love with a society belle and he was already living way above his means again. He began to run up substantial gambling debts and in desperation he embezzled a large sum of money from an art foundation he had become involved with, landing himself in prison for five years in 1937. On his release he went into hiding, fearing the wrath of those to whom he still owed money, and it was then that Archie Westlake found him and was able to put his talents to good use once more. The war was on and there was a market for forged ration books and clothing and petrol coupons. Marcus was older now but not a lot wiser where the fair sex was concerned, and it was not long before he was convicted of misappropriating cheques, one of which belonged to a woman he was having an affair with who happened to be married to an East End villain. For that offence Levy was sent to prison for a further three years.

The misguided artist realised that prison would not be a safe haven and he feared that he would be sought out there and dealt with by one of the prisoners in the pay of the aggrieved party. He appealed to Archie Westlake for his intervention and managed to get a reprieve. Marcus knew that there would be a price to pay and that he had a distinct choice – either to pay off his debt to the Bermondsey villain by working for him when he got out of prison, or else to disappear. Archie Westlake was well aware of the man's dilemma now that his release date was drawing near, and it was for that specific reason that he had decided to let Marcus Levy ponder for a few days.

Chapter Nine

Laura was beginning to feel more at home in Pedlar's Row now that she was becoming acquainted with her neighbours. They seemed a friendly lot, with the exception of Queenie Bromley, who did not go out of her way to chat unless it was to say something uncharitable concerning the rest of the tenants in the little row of houses. Laura could not help feeling some pity for Queenie. She seemed a very unhappy woman who found it difficult to raise even the smallest smile. There was something in the woman's past that had caused her to be so unsociable, Laura felt, and the whispered asides she heard tended to confirm her suspicions. She had learned of the woman's mysterious trips on Sunday afternoons, when she was smartly dressed and always unaccompanied, and she had also heard that Queenie had once been close to the local villain. Laura knew how she detested Archie Westlake and she remembered the look in Queenie's eyes when she mentioned his name. What had changed her? And what had made her so bitter?

Laura raked out the white ashes from under the fire and added two small knobs of coal to the flames. The room felt cosy and peaceful, with the relaxing soft rhythm of a South American band playing on the wireless in the far corner. Her father was sitting facing her, his head buried in the evening paper, and Lucy was settled at the table sorting through a large pile of assorted buttons. The two boys had gone off to bed some time earlier and now the muffled noise upstairs had ceased.

Laura let her thoughts wander as she settled herself down in the armchair. It had been nice of Lizzie Cassidy to call, realising that there was no fit man in the household who could do the everyday tasks such as changing a tap washer or putting a picture up. Her offer to send her husband in to help out, or maybe her son, Eddie, set Laura at ease. She had got by so far with a hammer and nails, and she had managed to put a new line up in the back yard, but there would no doubt be a time when she found herself unable to do something herself and the offer of help would be welcome.

Lizzie seemed a nice, friendly woman, warm and devoted to her family. It must have been terrible having three sons away at war, and how happy she must be now that they were all home safe and well. She had said as much but did not make too much fuss about it. She was excited about becoming a grand-mother in the autumn and Laura felt happy for her. Lizzie had said that Eddie was the only son still at home and that he seemed in no hurry to get wed. Laura had not set eyes on the young man, but Lizzie had described him to her in detail and she felt that she would immediately know him should she spot him in the Row.

Albert had put down his paper and was yawning widely. 'I s'pose there ain't any chance of a man gettin' a cup o' tea in this gaff, is there?' he asked.

Laura smiled and started to rouse herself but Lucy got up quickly. 'All right, I'll put the kettle on,' she said. 'I've gotta see if my stockin's are dry.'

As soon as Lucy had gone outside Albert looked at

Laura. 'Well, it won't be long now. 'E'll be 'ome on Sunday,' he said.

Laura nodded. 'We'll all 'ave ter be a bit patient wiv 'im, Dad,' she remarked. 'After what 'e's bin frew.'

'Well, I won't upset the man,' Albert said quickly. 'I always got on well wiv 'im.'

'I know that, Dad, but 'e's gonna be different. It's gonna take 'im time ter get used ter the family again. I bet 'e can't even remember what the kids look like.'

'Yeah, it's bin a long time. I wonder if 'e's all right?' Albert said suddenly.

'What d'yer mean, all right?'

'What I say. 'E could be missin' a leg, or an arm, or somefing.'

' 'E'll be fine,' Laura said with conviction.

Albert picked up the paper again and proceeded to turn the pages. 'There was a bit in 'ere I was readin' just now,' he said, 'if I can find it. It was all about those prisoners on the Burma railway. Terrible it was.'

Just then Lucy came into the room. 'What was that you was sayin', Dad?' she asked.

'I was jus' tellin' Laura about the new ration list in 'ere,' he said. 'Gawd knows 'ow long the rationin's gonna go on for.'

Lucy went back out to check on the kettle and Laura leaned closer to her father. 'Yer better be careful what yer say in front o' Lucy,' she warned him quietly.

'I wasn't sayin' anyfing in front of 'er. She was out the room,' he replied testily.

Laura felt a wave of tiredness sweeping over her and she leaned back in her chair and closed her eyes. The music was sweet and soft, and she could hear the sound of the wind soughing in the chimney. Sleep overtook her and suddenly she saw Roy coming along the street towards them. He was on crutches and there was a bandage wrapped tightly around his head. His hair was grey and his back stooped. He was thin too, terribly thin, with a gaunt face and large staring eyes which seemed to be pleading for help. He opened his mouth to speak but nothing came out. Lucy was sobbing and she hid her face from him. Roy came nearer and nearer, and Laura could see his face more clearly now. He had a scar down the length of one cheek and his mouth hung open, revealing his broken yellow teeth. He reached her and pointed to Lucy who was crouching down on the paving stones. He put out his hand and Laura felt his strong grip on her shoulder. He was shaking her, pleading with her to make Lucy face him, but there was nothing she could say.

Laura opened her eyes and realised that Lucy was gently shaking her shoulder. ' 'Ere's yer tea. Yer've bin mumblin' in yer sleep, yer nearly knocked it out of me 'and,' she said.

At number one on Sunday night Charlie Bromley lay in bed and wondered if Soapy was all right. It was cold outside and he wasn't sure if Soapy liked the cold. Was it cold where Soapy came from? he wondered. Never mind, tomorrow he would take him some food. Terry Grant would help him. The two of them should be able to get Soapy back home. Perhaps it would be better if they just killed him, Charlie thought. They could do it quick with a hammer, or better still the chopper. It couldn't be very nice being cooped up in that dustbin with the lid tied down. He was probably starving by now too. All they had been able to get him was a crust of stale bread and a tiny piece of Spam. He hadn't seemed too keen on the Spam but perhaps he would eat it later.

Charlie glanced at his younger brother who was fast asleep in the other bed. Frank had said it would be wicked to kill Soapy, but what did he know, he was only nine. Charlie knew he mustn't let Fred and Billy find out about Soapy. They'd be sure to take him away. Fred thought he knew everything, just because he was fourteen and going to work this year. Billy wasn't so bad, only when he was with Fred. Anyway, tomorrow after school he would go with Terry and see Soapy, and if he didn't look happy they could decide what to do with him.

Wally Stebbings had had a hard day. The auditors were due soon and the books had to be balanced. There were also the two large orders to be dealt with and invoices to check through. Everyone had seemed very tense and edgy today, Wally thought as he put on his raincoat, adjusted the warm scarf around his neck and put on his trilby hat. Mondays were always strained days, but never mind, Monday night was bubble-and-squeak night. There were some good programmes on the wireless Monday nights too, and if he did not feel too weary after tea he could get on with some fretwork.

Wally left the box factory in Weston Street and walked the short distance to Pedlar's Row. As he turned into the paved area he spotted two young lads bending over a cardboard box outside number three. Natural curiosity got the better of him and he sidled up and peered over the boys' shoulders. 'My goodness,' he said.

Charlie and Terry looked up at him. 'That's Soapy,' Terry said quickly.

'Where did you get it?' Wally asked.

Charlie was always careful when asked where he got things from and he thought fast. Terry was learning fast too, and he stepped in first. 'It fell out o' the tray,' he said quickly.

'At the pie shop?' Wally asked.

'Yeah, it was wrigglin' over the floor an' the man just

93

left it there, so we picked it up in case it got trod on,' Charlie added.

Wally had often stood watching the pie man cut up the eels and he was at a loss to understand how an eel could manage to get out of the deep tray. Still, it was nice to see the two young lads trying to take care of it and he smiled down at them. 'So that's Soapy, is it?' he said.

'Yeah, we called it Soapy 'cos it feels jus' like when yer get 'old o' wet soap,' Charlie told him.

'Well, it looks half dead to me,' Wally said.

Terry looked up at him. 'We was gonna kill it ter put it out of its misery, but we don't want to,' he said with a sad look on his dirty face.

'Eels need to be kept wet,' Wally told them. 'If they get dry it affects them. That eel should be in water, river water.'

'We can't chuck it in the river ternight, it's too far,' Charlie said. 'My mum said I gotta go in fer me tea in a minute.'

'I can't eivver,' Terry cut in. 'Same fer me.'

Wally pulled at his chin with thumb and forefinger. 'I tell you what. I might be able to put Soapy in the river, if you want me to?'

'Cor, could yer, mister?'

'I think so. After tea of course.'

'Fanks, mister.'

'Yeah, fanks, mister.'

Wally picked up the cardboard box. 'I'll take it home and put it in a bucket of water. That should do until I put it in the river,' he told the two lads.

Annie Stebbings looked horrified when Wally showed her what was in the box. It would have been quite normal for a young lad to bring home such things, but not a grown man. 'What d'yer intend ter do wiv it?' she asked him irritably.

Wally took off his trilby and fiddled with it awkwardly. 'I'm going to drop it in the Thames,' he said.

Annie sighed deeply. 'Well, wash yer 'ands, yer tea's ready. Yer'll 'ave ter make it snappy too if yer gonna go down ter the river, or yer'll miss *Monday Night at Eight*.'

Elsie Carmichael was fuming when her husband got home on Monday evening. 'Did you see that mess outside our front door?' she raved.

Len shook his head. 'I didn't notice anyfing,' he replied.

Elsie stood glaring at him with her hands on her hips. 'You must walk about wiv yer eyes shut,' she shouted. 'Go out an' 'ave a look at what those Bromley kids 'ave done under our winder.'

Len Carmichael sighed as he went to the front door. Elsie was a gem, but she did tend to make a mountain out of a molehill, he thought.

When he returned Elsie was standing with her mouth puckered up in temper. 'Did yer see it?' she yelled. 'Did yer see that bloody mess?'

'It looks like 'orse shit,' Len replied.

'It is 'orse shit,' Elsie raved on. 'They done that on purpose. I 'eard those Bromley kids under me winder before yer come in, but I couldn't go out to 'em 'cos I 'ad me feet in a bowl o' water.'

'I don't s'pose they meant any 'arm,' Len replied, not wanting a confrontation with Queenie.

Elsie was adamant that something had to be done, however. 'You get next door an' tell 'er ter make those kids clean up the mess,' she shouted at him.

Len was about to take off his coat but Elsie stopped him. 'Go there now. It's no good leavin' it. I cleaned outside the door once terday an' I ain't 'avin' that mess stuck there all night, so there.'

Elsie's dutiful husband sighed in resignation and wondered how to avoid an open conflict as he knocked on Queenie's front door. 'I'm sorry ter trouble yer, luv, but I fink yer lads left some 'orse shit under our winder,' he said quietly as the virago appeared in the doorway.

Queenie gave him a dark look and tilted her head back towards the passageway. 'Oi, Fred, Billy. Get yerselves out 'ere,' she bawled.

The two lads came to the door looking worried and Queenie glared at her eldest son. 'What did I send you two out for earlier?' she asked him.

' 'Orse shit fer the tomato plants,' Fred replied, looking puzzled.

'Well, 'ow comes 'alf of it's outside Mr Carmichael's winder?'

'The bag 'ad an 'ole in it, Mum,' Billy answered quickly. 'Some fell out when we put it down fer a rest.'

'It's all right, we still 'ad plenty fer the plants,' Fred added.

'Well, that's all right then,' she told them, and turning to the bemused Len she said, 'It's okay, we've got enough, yer welcome to it,' and promptly closed the door in his face.

When Len reported back to Elsie she gave him a look of disgust. 'Well, didn't yer tell 'er ter get it cleared away?' she stormed.

'I never got a chance,' he said meekly, finally taking off his coat.

'Right, that does it,' she growled, pushing past him.

Len heard his wife mumbling to herself as she hurried into the scullery and as he collapsed into an easy chair and opened the evening paper he heard the front door open. In a few moments Elsie was back with a satisfied look on her face.

'I've just swept it all up from under our winder,' she told him.

'That's the spirit, luv. It don't take five minutes ter put it in the dustbin, does it,' Len said, smiling at her.

'Dustbin nuffink,' Elsie snorted. 'It's all under 'er winder now.'

Chapter Ten

The week seemed to drag on endlessly for the occupants of number three. Lucy became steadily more anxious each day and Laura tried hard to be a calming influence, without much success. The continuing cold weather meant that Albert remained house bound and he became increasingly edgy, shouting at the boys for little reason. The two lads tended to keep out of his way as much as possible; for Terry it wasn't too difficult, as every evening after school he went off with Charlie Bromley, but for Reg it was more of a problem. He was growing up fast and was now in his last year at school. Albert had started lecturing him about taking up a trade and he became angry when the lad shrugged his shoulders and showed little if any enthusiasm.

'What's 'e gonna do, go in a factory?' he moaned to Lucy. ' 'E should be finkin' about gettin' an apprenticeship somewhere. Yer nowhere wivout a trade these days.'

'I've talked to 'im, but 'e don't seem ter know what 'e wants ter do,' she replied. 'I can't take 'im by the 'and, Dad. Reg is gonna 'ave ter make 'is own mind up.'

'All that boy seems ter fink about is football. That ain't gonna do 'im any good, is it?' he went on.

Lucy had other worries on her mind but her silence angered Albert still further. 'Yer'll 'ave ter get Roy ter sort 'im out when 'e gets 'ome,' he told her in front of the young lad, 'ovverwise 'e's gonna end up in the bagwash factory or in some bloody ware'ouse luggin' 'is guts out.'

All the heated talks about his future tended to confuse Reg more and more and he avoided thinking about what he would do once he left school. The pictures painted by his ailing grandfather of slavery in such places as the bagwash factory frightened him, and he became very withdrawn.

Con the bookie had taken a liking to Reg, however, and he would let him take the dog bets from the punters during the evening session. Sometimes he sent him on errands for change or cigarettes, and occasionally when the runner waved his handkerchief as a signal that the local bobby had turned the corner Reg would slip into Bridie Molloy's house with Con until the coast was clear. It seemed exciting and daring being a bookie and Reg hero-worshipped the friendly character. Nothing was too much trouble for the young lad where Con was concerned and he was never more pleased than when the bookmaker asked him to do some favour or other.

Reg's younger brother Terry and his bosom pal Charlie Bromley were forming their own friendship with Wally Stebbings, and when Queenie found out that the two boys had actually been in his house she grilled Charlie.

' 'Ow comes yer go in that man's 'ouse? What d'yer do in there?' she asked.

'Well, we 'ad this live eel, yer see, Mum,' Charlie told her.

'A live eel? Where d'yer get a live eel from?'

Charlie looked down at his shoes, expecting to get a clip round the ear any second now. 'Well, this man was cuttin' their 'eads off an' choppin' 'em up in little pieces,' he started to explain. 'There was just this one left. It wasn't very big like the ovvers. It was more like a baby one, an' me an' Terry Grant took it out o' the tray when the man went in the shop fer a minute. We put it in a paper bag first of all, then it dropped out an' I wrapped it in me coat.'

Queenie was trying to keep a serious expression on her face but was finding it very difficult. 'What's this gotta do wiv that man Stebbin's?' she asked sternly.

'Well, me an' Terry 'id Soapy, that's what we named 'im, on the bomb site in this old dustbin, yer see, Mum. We took 'im some food on Sunday an' 'e looked like 'e was dyin' on Monday after school. Then Mr Stebbin's saw 'im. 'E said 'e'd put 'im in the river fer us.'

'But 'ow comes yer went in 'is 'ouse?' Queenie urged.

'Well, next day me an' Terry wondered if Mr Stebbin's did put Soapy in the river so we knocked on 'is door last night to ask 'im. Mr Stebbin's let us see all the fings 'e's made, an' 'e said we could go an' 'elp 'im if we wanted to.'

Queenie took the lad gently by the shoulders. 'Look at me, Charlie,' she said quietly. 'When you an' Terry were in Mr Stebbin's 'ouse did 'e touch yer? Did 'e touch yer in any rude places?'

Charlie looked wide-eyed at his mother. 'No, Mum. 'E give us milk an' a rock cake.'

'Are yer tellin' me the trufe, Charlie?'

'Cross me 'eart an' 'ope ter die, Mum.'

'Was Mr Stebbin's' mum there when you two were there?' Queenie asked.

Charlie shook his head.

'Well, I don't want yer ter go in that man's 'ouse ever again, now do I make meself clear, son?'

The young lad looked down at his feet. 'Why, Mum? Mr Stebbin's is gonna build us a fort. 'E promised.'

Queenie put her hand under her son's chin and lifted his face to meet her stern gaze. 'Listen, Charlie,' she began. 'Sometimes men take little boys inter their 'ouses an' they do nasty fings to 'em. Sometimes they 'urt the little boys. They're nasty, wicked men an' that's why I don't want you goin' in Mr Stebbin's 'ouse.'

'Mr Stebbin's ain't like them men,' Charlie said with conviction. ' 'E's pretty nice really. 'E give us milk, an' a rock cake.'

'I'm not sayin' 'e's one o' those nasty men, but I can't be sure, so I'm tellin' yer now not ter go in there any more. I'll be 'avin' a word wiv Terry's muvver too. Now I want yer ter promise me yer'll do as I say.'

'I promise,' Charlie mumbled, dropping his head glumly.

Queenie pulled him against her apron and ruffled his hair. 'By the way, what 'appened ter Soapy?' she asked.

' 'E died, so Mr Stebbin's put 'im in the dustbin,' Charlie said sadly.

' 'E most likely went into Annie's stew pot,' Queenie muttered to herself.

Marcus Levy eased his thin frame out of the carriage seat and stepped down on to the platform at Waterloo Station. He was in his early forties and round-shouldered, the ends of his receding black hair resting on the collar of his brown pinstripe suit. His large brown eyes stared warily out of a lean, pallid face which showed patches of stubble, and he carried a brown paper parcel that contained a change of underclothing and a shirt. In his pocket he had the princely sum of five shillings.

Marcus tried to take comfort from the fact that he had a place to stay and a few pounds hidden away, enough to tide him over until he sorted himself out. The problem was that he was still a wanted man in some quarters and went in fear of his life. Archie Westlake had made sure that the heat was off him while he was a guest of His Majesty, but now he was back in circulation and word would have preceded him. Could the Bermondsey villain protect him now? Well, he would have to lie low and see what transpired. Archie knew where to find him and he would no doubt be getting in touch before many days were out.

As he walked off the platform Marcus caught a brief glimpse of a large man wearing a white raincoat and black trilby hat who got up from a platform seat and fell into step behind him. The man wore his hat low over his forehead, shielding his face, but he had looked vaguely familiar. At the barrier Marcus handed over his ticket and hurried on across the large station concourse. He could hear the steady clip of the man's shoes and as he increased his pace so the steps behind him accelerated too. Marcus had no doubt now that he was being followed. The man had obviously bought a platform ticket and been sitting there waiting for Marcus's train to arrive, and he obviously knew who he was waiting for.

Marcus quickly turned left at a kiosk and hurried towards a mound of luggage on a four-wheeled bogie truck. He quickly darted behind the luggage, ducked down and pretended to tie up his shoelace. He knelt there for several minutes listening to his heart pounding in his chest as he tried to be inconspicuous, then he slowly straightened up and looked around. There was no sign of the man in the white raincoat, and the fugitive artist sighed with relief. He would not give up yet though, Marcus thought. Better to lie low for a while until his tail had done another circuit of the station.

For fifteen minutes Marcus sat on a toilet seat in a basement cubicle, waiting anxiously, holding his breath every time someone walked into the washroom. His pursuer was not one of Westlake's men or he would have approached him on the platform, Marcus felt sure. This man was out to get him, maybe stick a knife between his ribs at the first possible moment.

At last he stood up and pulled the chain. It was time to go, he decided. Carefully he opened the toilet door, reassuring himself that the washroom was empty. He stepped over to the hand basin, put down his parcel and turned on the tap. At that moment the man came strolling in. Marcus could only stare in horror as he sidled up to him, turned on the tap of the next basin and proceeded to wash his hands. There was no escape, no way out this time.

' 'Ello, Marcus. We bin 'avin' a little sit-down, 'ave we?' the man said, giving him a brief smile.

Levy gulped hard and shook his head, waiting with a racing heart for the man to reach into his pocket for a gun or a knife, but instead the stranger walked over to the roller towel and took his time drying his hands thoroughly. He finally turned and slipped his hand under his coat and Marcus stepped back, waiting for the inevitable to happen, but the man pulled out a folded piece of newspaper and opened it up casually.

'It's a good likeness, don't yer fink?' he said, smiling.

Marcus tried to control his shattered nerves as he stared at the photo of himself. It had been taken at the Whitechapel Art Gallery just before he was convicted and sent to prison. It showed a group of dinner-suited businessmen and local artists at a charity function which had been organised to raise money for promoting the arts in the East End.

'It's not a bad photo,' Marcus said, attempting a smile.

The big stranger pocketed the piece of paper and adjusted the collar of his raincoat. 'I wouldn't 'ave missed yer anyway,' he said. 'Not many people get off a train carryin' a brown paper parcel under their arm, do they? Yer stood out like a sore thumb.'

' 'Ave yer come from Archie Westlake?' Marcus asked, praying he had.

'Yeah, Danny Steadman's the name. I've got a message for yer, Levy,' the man told him gruffly. 'Westlake said 'e wants a meetin'.'

Marcus gulped in sheer relief. 'Sure. Any time,' he said quickly in a voice he could hardly recognise.

'Where yer stayin'?' the man asked, pulling out a small notepad from his raincoat pocket.

'Colman Buildin's, number twelve,' Marcus replied quickly. 'It's in Friar's Court, Whitechapel.'

The man jotted down the address and pocketed the notepad again. 'Right. We'll be in touch soon, so stay put there, okay?'

Marcus caught the warning in the stranger's hard voice and he stood transfixed as the man turned on his heel and walked casually from the washroom.

On Saturday morning, after she finished cleaning at the Sultan, Laura came back and went right through the house. The curtains and bedding were changed in all the bedrooms, a fresh lace curtain was hung in the parlour and the whole place was dusted and polished. Lucy had done the shopping and when everything else was finished the two sisters went to the front bedroom and got it ready. They put all of Laura's personal belongings in her large linen chest, and as she gathered up the few books lying on the bedside cabinet, Laura smiled to herself. She had never managed to finish that love story, she reflected.

'I do 'ope yer gonna be all right in that chair-bed,' Lucy said.

'It's nice an' comfortable, so don't worry,' Laura told her. 'Now let's get this room finished an' you can sleep in 'ere ternight ter get used to it.'

'I'm scared, Laura,' Lucy said suddenly, slumping down on the edge of the unmade bed.

'I s'pose it's natural, but you'll be all right,' Laura replied, touching her sister's arm as she sat down beside her.

'This time termorrer 'e'll be 'ere. It don't seem possible,

after all this time. 'E'll still love me, won't 'e, Laura?' Lucy asked, her dark eyes wide with misgiving.

'Of course 'e will. Roy won't 'ave changed, 'e'll still be the same fella,' Laura said, smiling affectionately. 'Now come on, I want yer to 'elp me unclip the chair-bed so I can air the cushions.'

The two sisters took hold of the linen trunk and manhandled it down from the bedroom and into a recess beside the coal cupboard under the stairs.

'That'll 'ave ter do fer the time bein',' Laura gasped. 'C'mon, let's try the chair-bed.'

The wide armchair had a backrest that let down and a folded spring under the bottom cushion. When opened it was a full-size bed and quite comfortable, but it had been kept shut since being salvaged from the bombed family house in Leroy street. Laura pulled it out from the corner of the parlour while Lucy moved the table nearer the heavy oak sideboard.

'It'll open right out now,' Lucy said.

Laura threw off the large cushion and took hold of the folded spring, watched closely by Albert who had got out of his chair.

'It won't budge,' she panted, her face red with exertion.

'Let me 'ave a go,' Lucy said, elbowing Laura out of the way.

'It's jammed,' Albert commented knowingly.

The two young women looked up at him in exasperation.

'We can see that, Dad,' Lucy said quickly.

'Yer need a bar or somefing ter lever it wiv,' Albert explained.

'It must 'ave bin the blast,' Laura sighed as she sat down on the spring. 'It's all warped.'

'What we gonna do now?' Lucy asked in an irritated voice.

'Don't worry, I'll sort it out later,' Laura replied. 'Let's get it back in the corner an' I can get the tea ready.'

Albert resumed his place in the armchair. 'I only wish I was all right,' he moaned. 'It needs a bit o' muscle ter shift it.'

'Well, don't fret, Dad, it'll get done,' Laura told him.

Albert picked up his tobacco pouch and pipe from the hearth. ' 'Ere, I know. Why don't yer slip along ter see that woman who called in the ovver day?' he said suddenly. 'She said 'er ole man'd give yer 'elp if yer needed it.'

Laura nodded. 'Good idea, Pops. I'll give 'er a knock after tea.'

Lizzie Cassidy was sitting beside the fire reading a romantic short story in the *Evening News*. Now and then she glanced over at the slumbering figure of her son Eddie. His hands were clasped on his middle and he was snoring lightly. He had come in soaked to the skin that evening, moaning about his favourite team Millwall going down by the odd goal.

'It was a lousy game, Ma, not werf gettin' wet for,' he had growled as he hurried up to his room to change. Now he had eaten his fill he was sleeping soundly and Lizzie felt it was a shame to wake him. She glanced up at the clock on the mantelshelf and saw that it was almost time. Eddie had said he wanted calling at seven thirty as he was due to meet a couple of mates in the Sultan later that evening.

The knock at the door made her jump and she threw the paper down on the floor as she eased herself out of the chair. Eddie had not stirred and she had to step over his feet to get to the door, mumbling to herself as she did so about him taking up all the room.

'What's up, luv?' Lizzie asked as she saw Laura's anxious-looking face.

'I'm so sorry ter trouble yer, Lizzie, but I need a bit o' muscle. It's a chair-bed that's got jammed,' she said, smiling with embarrassment. 'I don't s'pose yer 'usband's in, is 'e?'

'Nah, luv, 'e's gone dog racin', but the boy's in. I'll give 'im a call,' Lizzie told her with a friendly grin.

'Don't bovver 'im if it's awkward, there's no immediate rush,' Laura said quickly.

Lizzie waved away her concern. 'The lazy sod's dossin' but 'e's due ter be woken up now anyway. I'll send 'im in soon as I rouse 'im,' she said, smiling.

Ten minutes later Laura opened the door to see a tall, slim young man standing there. He smiled a greeting and she noticed that his eyes were still puffy from sleep and his dark wavy hair was slightly dishevelled.

'Eddie?'

'That's me.'

'I'm sorry, I wouldn't 'ave knocked at yer mum's if I'd known yer was asleep,' Laura said.

'It's okay, I was only nappin',' Eddie replied as he stepped into the passage.

Laura showed him into the parlour and pointed to the chair-bed in the corner. 'I've tried ter get it open but the fing won't budge,' she told him. 'It's bin shut fer ages.'

Albert looked up from his paper. 'It's bin like that since we got bombed out,' he added.

'This is me dad,' Laura said by way of introduction.

The young man nodded pleasantly and turned his attention to the chair-bed. 'I can see what's wrong. The metal frame's twisted,' he said, taking hold of two corners and up-ending the thing.

Laura watched while he prised and levered, then suddenly the folded spring dropped free. Eddie righted the chair-bed and opened the spring with a fierce tug, and as he did so he winced. A sharp piece of projecting wire had caught his index finger.

Laura's hand went up to her mouth as she started, and Eddie laughed at the look on her face. 'It's all right, it's only a scratch,' he said dismissively, sucking on the cut.

Laura took his arm. 'Come out in the scullery, I've got a bandage in the drawer,' she told him.

'It's okay, it's nuffink,' he replied.

'No, I insist,' she said, smiling. 'I wouldn't want yer finger ter get septic.'

Eddie followed her into the scullery and stood watching her while she rummaged through a small box that she took from the dresser drawer. She finally found what she was looking for and Eddie pulled a face as she took out a bottle of iodine and a small wad of cotton wool.

'Yer better sit down,' Laura said with a smile. 'This might sting.'

Eddie grinned. 'Ave yer got anyfing ter bite on?' he asked her.

Suddenly they were both laughing and Laura felt her face redden slightly. It was a long time since she had been in a young man's company, and a very handsome young man at that. She took a deep breath to control the sudden nervousness she felt and concentrated on the job that needed doing. She tipped up the bottle and watched as the small dark brown stain grew on the cotton wool pad. Eddie was watching the process and as she took his hand and pulled it toward her he winced. She glanced quickly into his eyes as she held the pad against the deep cut but they were sparkling with amusement.

'Yer know, when I was a kid I was terrified of iodine,' he said, smiling at her. 'My muvver was always usin' that on us kids.'

Laura nodded, taking the pad away from his finger and glancing at the results. 'Well, it's clean anyway,' she remarked. 'Now I'll just put a bandage on.'

'It's all right,' he said.

'No, we've gotta keep the dirt out,' she replied quickly.

Eddie sat quietly watching Laura binding up his finger and he noticed how gently she did it. He felt the warmth of her hands on his and he could hear her shallow breathing as she concentrated on making a neat job of it. When she had finished he wiggled the bandage at her.

'Is it too tight?' she asked with concern.

'No, it's really comfortable,' he replied. 'Yer've done a first-class job.'

Laura got up and gathered the bits and pieces together, putting them back in the cardboard box. 'Look, would yer like a cuppa? I was just goin' ter make one before yer came in,' she told him.

'If it's no trouble. Muvver woke me up an' kicked me out wivout one,' he laughed.

'I'm really sorry about that,' Laura said as she put the filled kettle over the flaring gas jet. 'Yer mum did say that if I needed a bit o' muscle I should knock.'

Eddie held his palms up to reassure her. 'It's all right, really. That's one fing yer can guarantee in our 'ouse. There's plenty o' muscle, if a shortage o' brains.'

Laura spooned the tea leaf into the pot from a brightly coloured caddy and stood leaning against the dresser. 'I 'ad ter get that chair-bed sorted out. It's gonna be my bed from ternight,' she told him.

'Yeah?'

'My sister an' 'er two children live 'ere wiv me an' Dad, an' now 'er 'usband's comin' 'ome from the Far East,' she explained. ' 'E's due 'ome termorrer evenin'. 'E was on the Burma railway.'

Eddie's face suddenly took on a serious look. 'I 'ope

everyfing works out all right. I expect yer wonderin' 'ow yer gonna find 'im.'

Laura nodded, averting her eyes as he looked at her intently. 'Yer mum told me you an' yer bruvvers were in the war,' she said.

'Yeah, me an' Steve were in the army, but our elder bruvver Geoff was in the Andrew,' Eddie replied.

'Andrew?'

'The navy. Geoff was a stoker.'

The kettle started puffing steam rings and Laura took two cups and saucers down from the dresser and placed them on the table. 'I understand yer work in the docks,' she said.

Eddie nodded. 'We all do. Farvver as well. It's 'ard at times but I'd sooner that than bein' stuck in a factory.'

The kettle was boiling fiercely and Laura prepared the tea. 'I 'ope I've not put yer be'ind,' she said, looking up quickly.

'There's no rush really,' Eddie told her. 'I'm jus' gonna see a few pals. As a matter o' fact I've enjoyed our little chat, an' the first aid,' he added, grinning.

'Well, if it needs anuvver bandage yer must call in,' Laura said with a smile, feeling immediately self-conscious.

'I'll certainly call in fer a check-up,' Eddie replied.

The two young people sat sipping their tea and Laura felt strangely nervous as the young man occasionally fixed her with his large dark eyes. Eddie was feeling comfortable and relaxed, intrigued by the pretty young woman who seemed to have taken on the responsibility of looking after her family.

'D'yer get the chance ter go out much?' he asked her.

'Not really,' she replied. 'There's so much ter do.'

Eddie finished his tea and stood up. 'Well, it's bin nice talkin' ter yer,' he said, smiling, 'an' fanks fer the bandage.'

Laura got up to show him out. 'Fank yer fer all yer 'elp.'

Albert was waiting when she came back. 'Oo's 'e?' he asked curiously.

'That's Eddie Cassidy,' Laura replied, feeling suddenly aglow.

Chapter Eleven

Sunday morning dawned bright and clear and Lucy Grant turned over in her unfamiliar new room, glancing sleepily at the bedside clock. It showed ten minutes past eight. She yawned and stretched leisurely under the covers, and then suddenly she sat bolt upright. Roy's ship would have docked and he was probably getting on the train about now, she thought with a jolt. He had said in the letter that he should arrive in London around teatime and expected to be home between five and six o'clock.

Lucy slid her feet over the edge of the bed and found her slippers. She stood up and put on her dressing gown, tying the band around her waist as she crossed the floor to look out of the steamed-up window. Down below the Row was empty, except for the buxom figure of Queenie Bromley who was sweeping a pile of what looked like leaves away from her window. Lucy watched with curiosity as she made a neat pile under the window of the house next door.

Lucy went out on to the landing and looked into the back bedroom. Her two boys were still sleeping soundly and she went down the stairs into the cold scullery, yawning widely as she picked up the box of Swan Vestas. The gas jet spluttered and popped into flame and Lucy scratched her head, yawning again as she stood leaning against the dresser with her arms folded. This was the day she had prayed and waited ages for, and feared would never come, and now it had arrived she could feel no great excitement. She had carried a suspicion for so long deep down inside her that Roy would never return home and she had tended to live her life accordingly. It was natural to feel the way she did, Lucy told herself. The four and a half years of waiting, dreading hearing the worst at any time, was enough for anyone to cope with. It was understandable to feel confused and a little numb. It would be different once he was home.

The kettle was spouting steam and still Lucy stood pondering. What if the two of them failed to pick up the pieces of their war-torn lives together? What if time and separation had altered them so much that they now saw each other as strangers? No, she must not think that way. The two boys needed their father and she needed her husband. She must try hard to bury all her guilty feelings and understand how Roy was feeling, help him to readjust. It was the only way to happiness for both of them.

The kettle boiled over and extinguished the gas flame, startling Lucy out of her troubled thoughts. Five minutes later she took a cup of tea into the parlour where her sister was stirring.

'Did yer sleep well?' she asked her.

Laura sat up in the bed and gave a big yawn. 'Yeah, it was nice an' comfortable,' she said as she took the cup of tea.

Albert noisily sipped the tea Lucy brought him and then pulled the bedclothes back over his head, knowing that it was better for him to keep out of the way on this of all mornings.

Lucy went in to wake up the two lads and sat with them on the edge of the bed as they roused themselves. 'Well, yer'll be seein' yer dad this evenin',' she told them with a smile.

Reg scratched his head and yawned. 'Mum, d'yer fink Dad'll take us ter football matches?' he asked.

Lucy nodded. 'Yer dad used ter go all the time,' she answered him.

'What about Charlie, Mum? Can 'e come in an' see Dad terday?' Terry asked sleepily.

'We'll 'ave ter wait till yer dad gets settled in,' she told him. 'Don't ferget 'e's come a long way an' 'e's certain ter be very tired.'

'Is where Dad's bin as far as Australia?' Terry asked.

'I expect so,' Lucy replied.

'Will Dad 'ave a long beard, Mum?'

'Well, I 'ope not. Why d'yer ask that?'

Terry sat up straight in bed and clasped his hands over his knees. 'Well, me an' Charlie bunked in the Trocette last Saturday an' we saw *The Count of Monte Cristo*,' he said with his eyes widening. 'This man was in a dungeon in this 'orrible castle an' 'e 'ad a long beard.'

Lucy hid a smile and attempted to look stern. 'What 'ave I told yer about bunkin' in the pictures?' she said quickly.

Laura came into the boys' bedroom and sat on their bed next to Lucy, her dressing gown wrapped tightly around her. 'You two should get up an' out early,' she remarked. 'It's a lovely bright day.'

Lucy nodded. 'Aunt Laura's right. Besides, there's a lot ter be done an' we don't want you two under our feet.' Then she turned to her sister. 'I didn't come down last night when that fella was 'ere in case yer thought I was bein' nosy,' she said quietly with a ghost of a smile playing on her pale face.

Laura ignored her evident curiosity. She stood up and stretched. 'Well, I better get dressed,' she said.

' 'E was 'ere fer quite a while,' Lucy went on, probing. 'I looked out o' the bedroom winder when 'e left. 'E looks very nice.'

'Yeah, 'e's a nice fella,' Laura replied.

Lucy smiled at her sister's reticence. 'Is 'e courtin'?'

' 'Ow the 'ell should I know?' Laura retorted.

'Well, yer could 'ave asked 'im,' Lucy replied quickly.

' 'E'd fink I was bein' nosy.'

'Well, so yer should be, where a fella's concerned.'

As Laura was leaving the bedroom she turned at the door to face Lucy, who had got up and was looking out of the window. 'If it'll satisfy yer curiosity, I don't fink 'e's courtin',' she said, smiling.

Lucy turned away from the window. 'I saw Queenie sweepin' outside 'er door earlier an' now there's Elsie at it,' she told her.

Laura chuckled. 'There's a trial o' strength goin' on wiv them two. It's bin carryin' on all week,' she replied.

'What's it over?' Lucy asked.

' 'Orse shit,' Laura whispered with her back to the boys.

At eleven o'clock Conrad the bookmaker walked into Pedlar's Row and stood by Bridie Molloy's front door as usual, and ten minutes later Archie Westlake joined him. The two stood talking together for some time. Archie was wearing a fawn raincoat over his smart grey suit, with the belt loosely buckled at the back. He had on a light brown fedora and smart black patent shoes, and around his neck he wore a white silk scarf. He was puffing on a large cigar and occasionally he removed it from his mouth and delicately tapped the rim of ash off with a snappy movement of his forefinger.

Reg Grant was as ever hovering in the background and suddenly Conrad called him over. 'Oi, Reggie boy. Can yer run up ter Bert's paper shop an' get us the *News o' the World*?' he asked him.

Reg hurried over, smiling, and the bookie turned to Archie. 'This is my little 'elper. 'E wants ter be a bookie when 'e grows up, don't yer, Reg?'

The young lad looked up shyly and nodded.

'Well, p'raps yer can do me a favour while yer at the shop,' Archie said, taking out a padded wallet from his back pocket. 'Tell Bert yer called fer Mr Westlake's King Edwards. Can yer remember that?'

'Yeah, I can remember, Mr Westlake,' Reg replied, smiling broadly.

Archie handed the lad a ten-shilling note. 'Yer can keep the change fer goin',' he said.

When Reg hurried off the villain turned to Con. 'Queenie Bromley's not bin givin' yer any grief, 'as she?' he asked.

Con shook his head. 'A few black looks, that's all.'

'That was my only reservation about 'avin' the pitch down 'ere,' Archie said. 'I didn't want 'er causin' trouble. By the way, I'll be seein' Levy this afternoon. I'm gonna spell it all out to 'im. I want 'im ter start as soon as possible.'

Con nodded. 'I've bin 'avin' a few discreet words wiv some o' the lads. We can get a good team tergevver wiv no sweat,' he replied. 'If we work it right we'll make a tidy fortune.'

Archie winked slyly at his confederate. 'We'll certainly do that,' he said quietly.

Albert Prior had decided that it was about time he got a breath of fresh air. After he had finished his breakfast he put on his overcoat and cap, picked up his stick and calmly announced that he was going to the paper shop.

'Are yer sure yer gonna be all right?' Laura asked him. 'Yer not bin out on yer own fer some time.'

'All the more reason I do go out then, I need a bit o' fresh air,' Albert replied sharply.

'Well, be careful, we don't want you back in 'ospital,' Laura said, equally sharp.

Albert let himself out, nodded pleasantly to Con and Archie, then set off at a slow pace.

Queenie was standing at her front door eyeing the mobile pile of manure, her face a dark mask, and she nodded curtly.

'Nice day,' Albert said amicably.

'It was,' Queenie replied sharply.

'What's wrong, luv, yer look a bit put out,' Albert remarked.

'It's that pile o' shit,' she replied, nodding down at the manure. 'I can't seem ter get the message 'ome ter the silly mare next door, but I will, mark my words.'

Albert had heard of the battle going on between the two neighbours and he decided not to take sides. 'Well, good luck, gel,' he said as he turned on his heel and walked slowly out of Pedlar's Row.

A few paces along Weston Street Albert bumped into his happily grinning grandson. Reg was hurrying along carrying a newspaper under his arm and a box of cigars in his hand.

'Look what this man gave me fer goin' on 'is errand, Grandad,' he said breathlessly, displaying a half-crown in his sweaty palm.

'What man?' Albert asked quickly.

'Mr Westlake,' Reg replied. ' 'E's a friend o' Con the bookie.'

Albert stood watching until his grandson turned into Pedlar's Row, then he walked on slowly, reminding himself to have a word with Lucy about the lad hanging round the bookie and his cronies.

The paper shop was only a hundred yards or so along Weston Street but by the time Albert returned to Pedlar's Row he was feeling tired. Queenie was still eyeing the neat pile of dried manure, which was now under Elsie Carmichael's window, and Albert gave her a knowing grin.

'Can yer tell yer daughter I'd like a word wiv 'er,' Queenie said.

'Which one?' Albert asked.

'Terry's muvver.'

'Lucy, yer mean?'

Queenie nodded. 'Kids are a bloody worry, one way an' anuvver.'

Albert went into the house to find Lucy on her hands and knees raking out the ashes. 'Queenie wants yer,' he said. 'I fink it's somefing ter do wiv the kids.'

'I 'ope our Terry ain't bin in any trouble,' Lucy replied. ' 'E's got really cheeky since 'e's bin 'angin' round wiv 'er Charlie.'

'Well, you should keep 'im away from 'im then,' Albert said, slumping down in his armchair.

Lucy went out to find Queenie still leaning on her broom, with a satisfied smirk on her red face.

' 'As my Terry bin up to any mischief?' she asked the older woman.

'Nah, it's just that your Terry an' my Charlie are gettin' too pally wiv that Stebbin's bloke at number six,' Queenie replied. 'The two of 'em 'ave bin goin' in 'is 'ouse an' I don't fink it's right. I don't trust that fella. 'E seems a bit strange ter me, an' I've told my boy ter keep out o' there. If I were yer I'd keep yer boy away too. Yer can't be too careful the way fings are.'

Lucy nodded. 'I'll 'ave a talk ter my Terry. Yer right, yer can't be too careful.'

'While yer at it I'd 'ave a word wiv yer ovver lad as well,' Queenie added. 'I see 'e's gettin' friendly wiv that bookie. I've seen the boy 'angin' round 'im. That sort lead the kids astray. They're a bad lot, an' I know from experience.'

Lucy saw the hard look that had appeared in Queenie's eyes and she suddenly felt troubled. 'Fanks fer lettin' me know. I'll talk ter the both of 'em,' she told her.

The Sultan public house was filling up at lunchtime and Len Carmichael sat waiting for George Bromley to arrive. Both men were regular customers and Len felt that here, in the sanity of the public bar, reason would prevail. George was a good sort, he thought. He wouldn't want the saga of the shifting manure to get out of control but he would have to be encouraged to stand on his own two feet for a change instead of jumping every time that loud-mouthed bitch of his opened her big gate. He certainly wouldn't put up with his own wife behaving like that, he told himself. Elsie knew how far to go and if she overstepped the mark he'd soon put her in her place.

'Wotcher, Len, 'ow's yer plates o' meat?' George asked as he sidled up to where Len was leaning on the counter.

'Good as gold, mate,' Len replied. 'I'm back at work this week.'

George got a round of drinks and then stood wondering how to broach the subject. Len was a decent enough bloke but he was dominated by that four-eyed old cow of his, he thought. The feud would have to come to an end soon or the two families would be a laughing stock in the Row.

'George, I don't want ter spoil yer drink, but there's somefing me an' you need ter sort out,' Len began.

'Don't I know it,' George winced.

' 'Ave yer spoke ter your missus?' Len asked.

George nodded grimly. 'What about you?'

Len's reply came as no surprise to his next-door neighbour. 'It's like talkin' ter that pianer,' he grumbled.

'Same 'ere.'

The two men sipped their pints silently for a few

minutes then Len suddenly brightened up. 'I know. Why don't me an' you take our brooms an' shovels out and clear it up tergevver?' he suggested.

George shook his head slowly. 'Queenie would kick up 'ell.'

Len's face dropped. 'Yeah, Elsie would too, come ter fink of it.'

The glasses were replenished and again the two lapsed into silence for a while. Suddenly George looked at his drinking partner. 'When I go back 'ome I'm gonna tell 'er straight,' he declared. 'Enough's enough.'

Len hiccupped. 'I'm gonna do the same. It's bloody stupid the way they're carryin' on.'

It was not very long before the next round was bought and the two men were getting more confident that they could resolve the rift.

'She better not go on at me, Len, 'cos I've just about 'ad enough,' George said firmly.

'Me too,' Len replied, taking up his drink with a stern look on his rapidly reddening face. 'I'm gonna tell 'er straight. If she wants ter fall out wiv 'er neighbours over a dollop of 'orse shit, I don't.'

At two o'clock precisely the inebriates left the Sultan and walked rather unsteadily along Weston Street. Len was thinking about what he was going to say to Elsie, and George was getting ready to give Queenie a piece of his mind. As they reached Pedlar's Row they suddenly stopped and glanced at each other with puzzled frowns. The pile of manure was nowhere to be seen.

Elsie was sitting reading the *News of the World* when her husband walked into the parlour and she looked up in the disdainful way she usually did when he came in from his Sunday drink.

'Where's the muck gone?' Len asked.

'We cleared it up,' Elsie replied, returning her eyes to the spicy article she was reading.

'We?'

'Yeah, me an 'er next door,' Elsie said mysteriously.

' 'Ow comes?' Len enquired, slumping down in the armchair facing her. Elsie put down the paper and tilted her head to look at him through glasses which had slipped down her nose. 'Well, it was funny 'ow it 'appened,' she began. 'I went next door ter the Priors ter borrer a pinch o' bakin' powder fer me rock cakes, yer see, an' the nice young woman was tellin' me that 'er 'usband's comin' 'ome ternight from the war. 'E's bin away fer over four years an' the poor little cow's like a cat on 'ot bricks. Jus' fink of it, four years. It must 'ave seemed a lifetime. Roy, 'is name is. Captured by the Japs, 'e was. 'E's bin on that there Burma railway, poor bleeder.'

Len was beginning to get very puzzled and he sat up straight in his chair. 'Look, Elsie luv. I might be a bit sozzled, but what the bloody 'ell does all this 'ave ter do wiv a pile of 'orse shit?'

'I'm comin' ter that if yer wait a minute,' she replied quickly. 'When I 'eard about 'er Roy I got ter finkin'. The poor bleeder's bin a prisoner o' war fer all that time, away from 'is wife an' those lovely kids, an' now at last 'e's gonna come marchin' down the street, inter Pedlar's Row, an' what's the first fing 'e's gonna see. A pile o' bloody 'orse shit. What a welcome 'ome fer the poor sod.'

'I got yer now,' Len said grinning. 'So yer decided ter bury the 'atchet an' clear the shit up?'

'We decided tergevver,' Elsie replied with a smug look on her face. 'I went an' knocked on Queenie's door. I told 'er I was gonna clear the 'orse shit up, not fer 'er, but fer the woman's 'usband. Well, ter give 'er 'er due, she didn't argue. She said she'd clear 'alf of it, not fer me, mind, but fer the woman's 'usband. So that's what we did.'

'Well, I'm glad yer did, 'cos me an' George was gettin' sick o' this bloody carryin'-on,' Len said with a note of authority in his voice. 'Now what about servin' me dinner up?'

'You can bloody well wait till I've finished the paper,' she growled.

Chapter Twelve

Archie Westlake walked leisurely along the Whitechapel Road and into Brady Street. The cold winter sun was already dropping down behind the railway arches as he turned into a narrow side street and entered Colman Buildings, a dingy, gaslit tenement block that backed on to the railway sidings. Archie climbed to the third floor and knocked at number twelve, looking around him with distaste as he waited. He could hear movements inside and then a nervy voice. 'Who is it?'

The Bermondsey villain smiled with satisfaction. 'It's me, Archie Westlake,' he replied.

There was a short pause and then the bolts were slid back. Marcus Levy looked scared as he stood aside and invited Archie in with a brief smile and a curt nod.

'Long time no see, Marcus. What's it feel like ter be back in circulation?' Archie asked, holding out his hand.

Marcus gave the villain a weak handshake. 'I'm getting used to it,' he answered, quickly sweeping a pile of old newspapers from a chair and motioning Archie to sit down.

Archie undid his topcoat and slumped down heavily, his eyes taking in the untidy room. The floral-papered walls were streaked with dampness in several places and the ceiling was stained yellow with smoke, its ancient coating of distemper peeling and flaking. The coverless old table standing in the middle of the small room was littered with dirty crockery and empty beer bottles, and there was a pile of books stacked against the wall. Apart from two chairs and a tattered armchair, the only other piece of furniture was a sideboard, a heavy object in carved oak, which looked out of place in the squalid surroundings. Marcus went over to it and took two glasses from the cupboard. 'You still take Scotch?' he asked.

Archie nodded and watched while his host filled the glasses from a bottle of Johnny Walker. He noticed that Levy's hands were unsteady and he could see that the man's face had the distinctive prison pallor. He was clean-shaven but the heavy jersey he wore was holed at the elbows and made him look slovenly. He avoided Archie's eyes as he handed over the drink and then seated himself in the other upright chair beside the fire.

'Well, we managed ter keep yer in one piece, Marcus,' Archie said, twirling his drink. 'It wasn't easy, mind. A certain party wanted you boxed up while yer was inside an' it wasn't easy gettin' 'im ter cancel the arrangement.'

Marcus Levy took a sip from his glass before replying. He knew full well that it had not been an act of charity, and he was aware that there would be a price to pay for his continuing wellbeing.

'I'm grateful. Very grateful,' he said, putting his glass down on the edge of the table and self-consciously fidgeting with his fingers.

' 'Ow did yer come by this dump?' Archie asked.

'A friend of mine used to let me use it when he was out of London. He's away at the moment, which was opportune,' Marcus replied.

' 'Ow yer fixed fer cash?' Archie asked him.

'I'm all right, for the present.'

The Bermondsey villain drained his drink and put the empty glass down on the table at his elbow. 'I fink we should get straight down ter business, Marcus,' he said quietly. 'I've got a job for yer. It's somefing I know yer capable of, but it's gotta be the very best.'

Levy continued to stare down at the drink held in his thin, tapering fingers. 'I take it to be of an artistic nature, this job?' he replied with a note of self-mockery.

Archie smiled to himself and reached into his coat pocket, taking out a thick wallet from which he removed two one-pound notes. 'Look at these,' he requested, passing them over. One was crumpled but the other was crisp and new.

Marcus Levy studied the two notes for a few seconds then his pale eyes came up to meet his visitor's intent stare. 'The crumpled one is a forgery,' he said.

'That's good, very good,' Archie replied, handing him his empty glass.

Levy went to the sideboard and proceeded to pour him another drink, feeling like a cornered animal that was about to be pounced on. 'It's a poor job of work,' he said quietly as he handed the villain his refilled glass.

Archie fixed the thin-faced Marcus with a hard stare. 'I want you ter show me 'ow it should be done,' he said, sipping his drink.

The fallen artist's eyes widened noticeably and he shook his head in agitation. 'I can't do it,' he replied. 'It's bin too long.'

Archie lowered his eyes and ran his forefinger slowly round the rim of his glass. 'I'm countin' on yer, Levy,' he said in a low voice.

'Look at me, Archie. Look at these,' Levy appealed to him, holding out his shaking hands. 'I couldn't manage that sort of work. I'm finished.'

'Yer will be, if yer don't come across,' Archie said, smiling evilly. 'Now listen. You owe me, pal. I want the plates ter print pound notes. They've gotta be good. In fact they've gotta be the best work you've ever done. Yer know me ter be a very reasonable man. I'll see yer very well rewarded fer yer efforts.'

Levy slumped in his chair and took another swig from his glass. 'I don't know. I've bin out o' circulation fer a long while,' he groaned.

Archie Westlake smiled patronisingly. 'You're the best, an' I've got confidence in yer ter produce the real item,' he said quietly. 'I've bin plannin' this caper fer a long time. I've put money an' effort inter this, an' a lot o' time. I've got the best quality paper and printin' materials all lined up an' ready ter roll. I want yer ter produce a masterpiece an' set me in motion, Marcus.'

'But yer don't understand just what it entails, Archie. I'll need time,' Marcus pleaded. 'I can't just start right away, it's not like sketching a portrait or making a piece of furniture.'

'I wouldn't want yer ter fink I was bein' inconsiderate,' Archie replied sarcastically, putting a sealed envelope down on the table. 'You know me better than that. There's two 'undred oncers in that packet. There'll be anuvver four 'undred due when yer've finished the plates, provided of course they're perfecto. Now if I were you I'd get out o' this bug-'utch fer a spell. Brighton's bracin' this time o' the year. A couple o' days should do it. Then get ter work. I expect to 'ave the plates in three weeks.'

'That's impossible,' Levy groaned. 'I'd need at least a month.'

'Three weeks, Marcus,' the villain said with emphasis.

'But you don't understand,' Levy pleaded desperately. 'There's a workplace to set up. I can't work here. I need special materials too, and they're not easy to come by.'

Archie looked hard at the worried man for a few seconds, then his face relaxed somewhat. 'Yer got it, one month,' he told him, passing his empty glass over once more.

Marcus Levy knew that he had no choice in the matter

and he ran his fingers nervously through his lank, thinning hair. The villain had invested in him and was claiming his dues. There was no way to escape. He could try to disappear, but he was on parole and had to report to the local police station every week. As soon as he failed to turn up on the appointed day the police would come looking for him, and if they didn't find him, Archie Westlake would. It meant being behind bars once more, or being fished out of the river. Either way the Bermondsey villain would get him. He had no choice but to comply.

Archie took his third drink and felt the warmth seeping through him. Levy was an artist and he could be expected to produce a work of art, the villain told himself. He was also a lecher who relied on a regular supply of money to finance his way of life. He would be no trouble, since it seemed to have become perfectly clear to him that failure to deliver was tantamount to signing his own death warrant.

Archie rose from the chair and buttoned up his coat, content for the time being, while Levy stood next to the sideboard watching him, like a small animal waiting for the killer to attack.

'Remember, Marcus,' Archie said as he left, 'yer've got one month, and I'll be sendin' a messenger regularly ter monitor yer progress, so take that couple o' days' break and then get ter work, savvy?'

The afternoon wore on and at number three there was an air of expectancy. Albert sat humming constantly and tunelessly and poking at the fire, while Lucy kept walking in and out of the parlour, glancing in the wall mirror at her hair and straightening her dress. Laura tried to read the newspapers but found herself going over the same article time and time again without taking it in. Reg was sitting on the bed in his bedroom, reading an old edition of the *Rover*, his mind alert for a knock on the front door.

'Is Terry not in yet?' Lucy asked her sister, knowing full well that he had gone out with Charlie Bromley and not yet returned.

'Why don't yer sit down an' I'll make a cup o' tea?' Laura volunteered.

'I've got tea runnin' out o' me ears,' Lucy replied. 'I wonder 'ow much longer 'e'll be?'

'It's only five o'clock,' Laura said kindly. 'Roy said about six but the train might be late. Why don't yer go an' stretch out on the bed fer a while, it'll do yer good.'

Lucy shook her head and sat down at the table, clasping her hands tightly. 'I do 'ope Terry's not gone too far,' she said anxiously. 'It gets dark early these nights.'

Laura sat down at the table facing her. 'I wonder if there is anyfing in what Queenie said about that Stebbin's bloke?' she ventured.

'I dunno, but I told Terry not ter go in there any more,' Lucy replied. 'Trouble is they don't seem ter take a blind bit o' notice what yer tell 'em.'

'Yer can't be too careful,' Albert joined in. 'Remember that bloke they caught messin' about wiv little kids when we first moved in the Buildin's? They nearly killed 'im before the police come. Yer'll 'ave ter make sure that lad knows what's what.'

'I can't do no more than tell 'im,' Lucy said sharply. 'I can't be be'ind 'im all the time.'

Laura rose quickly and took up the empty teapot. 'Well, I'm gonna make us anuvver pot o' tea,' she announced, trying to dispel the rising tension. 'Lucy, why don't yer 'elp us wash the cups up?'

At number six Wally Stebbings was sitting at a small table in his scullery, watched very closely by Terry

Grant and Charlie Bromley as he worked the fretsaw along the curved pencil line. On the far side of the table stood the framework of a desert fort, already displaying one square tower. Wally hummed contentedly as he slowly turned the thin plywood to complete the cut.

'There we are,' he said with a grin. 'That's the opening for the gates.'

'Is that gonna be stuck on there?' Charlie said, pointing to the front of the fort.

'That's right. Then we'll cut the ramparts,' Wally replied, brushing the sawdust from his trousers.

Terry looked at Charlie with a wide grin breaking out on his grubby face. 'We'll be able ter put our tin soldiers in there,' he said excitedly. 'They can be firin' over the wall.'

Charlie leaned on the table with his chin resting in his cupped hands. 'Will it 'ave a drawbridge, Mr Stebbin's?' he asked.

Wally laughed. 'No. Desert forts don't have drawbridges. They have big opening gates. There's no water in the desert, you see,' he explained. 'Drawbridges are for letting down over moats.'

'What's moats?' Charlie asked, looking enthralled.

'Well, moats are ditches of water that go around castles and forts,' Wally said, enjoying their enthusiasm. 'They were put there to stop opposing armies from getting in the castles.'

The boys both nodded and Terry looked innocently at Wally. 'You're really clever, Mr Stebbin's,' he said. 'Is it 'ard cuttin' that wood?'

'Well, it takes a bit of practice,' Wally replied, looking happy at the compliment paid him. 'I tell you what. I'll let you both do some cutting next time you come in. Now it's time to do some gluing.'

Annie Stebbings looked into the scullery. 'I fink it's

about time those lads went 'ome,' she said. 'It'll be dark soon.'

Wally took off his glasses and wiped the lenses on a large spotted handkerchief. 'Next time you call in, the gluing should be set,' he told the lads.

As soon as Charlie and Terry had left, Annie rounded on her son. 'You shouldn't encourage those two boys,' she said sharply. 'It's not right they should be 'ere all the time.'

Wally looked downcast as he started to gather up his tools. 'There's no harm in building a fort, is there, Ma?' he asked her. 'They're nice, polite lads and they just stand watching.'

'I know there's no 'arm in it,' Annie replied,'but people are inclined ter talk. You 'ave ter be so careful, especially when yer dealin' wiv ovver people's kids.'

'What are you saying, Ma?' Wally asked quickly. 'Do those people think I'm the sort of man who would harm children?'

Annie sighed deeply. 'Look, Wally, yer nearly forty-one an' yer still livin' at 'ome. It'd be different if yer were married. People tend ter fink it's not right fer somebody yer age ter form an attachment ter young lads, that's all I'm sayin'.'

Wally lapsed into a moody silence as he finished clearing away his tools, and later he put on his overcoat, gloves and trilby and took his usual Sunday evening stroll through the cold and empty back streets.

Euston Station was seething with service personnel. The Liverpool train had just arrived and there were scenes of joyous reunion along the whole platform. The fair-haired figure in uniform wearing the cap badge of the Sherwood Foresters walked slowly to the guard's van where suitcases and kitbags were being unloaded. The soldier was tallish and slim, with pale

130

blue eyes that stared out of an angular face. The familiar sight of Euston Station brought back sad and poignant memories to Roy Grant as he stood looking at the piles of kitbags. The last sight of his tearful wife and the young children as he waved to them from the departing train had been etched into his mind, sustaining him and comforting him through the long years of separation. He had thought about his homecoming and had decided to make the last few miles alone, forgoing a reunion at the station and meeting his family at long last in the privacy of their home. It felt important to him that it should be that way, even necessary, and as he pulled his kitbag from the pile Roy knew that he had made the right choice.

The short journey from the platform to the main concourse left the young soldier breathless and he slipped the kitbag from his shoulder and stood motionless above it, his heart pumping wildly. It was still early days and he had been warned that it would take time. Months of recovery supervised by doctors and nursing staff from Ceylon to Cape Town and during the various stages of his voyage home had strengthened him, building his skeletal frame into a lean figure, though still some pounds underweight, but the long years of suffering and starvation had taken their toll. He needed regular doses of vitamins, malaria tablets and salts, and as he bent down to take up his heavy kitbag he already felt exhausted.

' 'Ere, 'old on, pal. I'll give yer an 'and.'

Roy looked up to see a soldier standing next to him. He was huge, with a tanned face and the Eighth Army insignia on his uniform. 'Where yer makin' for?' he asked.

Roy grinned sheepishly. 'Tower Bridge Road,' he replied. 'I was gonna take the underground, but I fink I'll settle fer a cab. That bloody kitbag weighs a ton.'

'Far East?' the soldier asked as he lifted the kitbag and threw it over his shoulder.

Roy nodded. 'I was on the Burma railway.'

'I guessed as much,' the soldier replied. 'Look, I'm goin' ter Waterloo. Fancy sharin' a cab? I could drop yer off first.'

The taxi drove along Kingsway, around Aldwych and into Fleet Street, then wove its way through the empty streets of the City and over London Bridge.

'It's bin a long time, pal,' the soldier said, staring out of the window. 'There's nuffink ter touch it, is there?'

Roy nodded. The sight of the tall buildings illuminated by streetlamps and the familiar grey mist of winter hanging over the River Thames made him catch his breath. The noisy tram running alongside the cab, the evening revellers, muffled and wrapped against the cold as they hurried through the foggy streets, the laden red bus and the glowing traffic lights ahead were the realities of London, realities that for so long had been nothing but visions mustered by a fevered mind in the hellhole of the disease-ridden jungle. The half-strangled memories of his city had helped see him through, despite the beatings, the starvation and the sickness of the long trek in slavery from Singapore to Siam and the killing labour beyond. And now everything was so bright and vivid that he suddenly thought with a pang of anxiety that it was still only a dream, too beautiful to be real.

The taxi turned into Tooley Street, took a right into Tower Bridge Road and then swung into Weston Street. The soldier turned to Roy and held out his hand.

'Well, 'ere you are, pal. Good luck.'

Roy shook the soldier's hand warmly and placed two half-crowns on the seat beside him as he alighted from the cab. 'Good luck ter you, an' fanks,' he said as he hoisted the heavy kitbag on to his shoulder.

The night fog had thickened as Roy turned into

Pedlar's Row. He knew the place of old, and remembered the row of bomb-damaged houses, empty for so long but now his home. He laboured under the weight he was carrying, his feet echoing on the greasy paving stones, and at the door of number three he dropped the kitbag with a thud. As he reached up to the knocker, the door was yanked open.

'It's Roy!' Lucy screamed as she threw herself into his arms, moulding herself to him in the doorway. Roy felt the warmth of her shaking body and he buried his face in her hair, his lips against her slim neck. He closed his eyes and fought back the rising flood of emotion that he feared would overwhelm him as her body clung even tighter to him. There were no words he could find for the moment and he just held her in his arms. Albert was standing in the passageway with Laura and behind them were Reg and Terry, both looking wide-eyed at the scenes of joy. At last Lucy released her hold on her husband and excitedly pulled him in out of the cold night. In the dark passage she reached up and found his lips in a short, breathless kiss before Laura threw her arms around him and hugged him tight.

'Don't keep the boy out here,' Albert said as he turned to lead the way into the warm parlour.

Laura took hold of the kitbag and dragged it into the passage while the boys stood looking up at their father. Roy suddenly bent down and swept the two lads up in his arms, choking back tears of joy as he kissed their faces and held them close. Albert stood back, his face twitching, his rheumy eyes filling with tears, and then the young soldier straightened up and embraced the old man. Albert suddenly broke down and wept, his frail body shaking violently as Roy fondly patted his back.

Outside, the fog swirled and starlets of frost began to spangle the ground, but inside the little house a fire flared brightly as the family sat together. Albert occupied his usual place beside the hearth and Roy sat opposite him, Lucy perching on the edge of his chair with her arm around his shoulders. Laura had the upright chair beside the table and the two boys sat cross-legged on the hearthrug, their excited eyes glancing from face to face. Roy was plied with questions, and his answers were interrupted by still more questions until Albert finally took a hand.

'Why don't yer give the poor sod a chance ter catch 'is breath?' he urged them. 'Laura, go out an' put the kettle on.'

Lucy could feel her husband shaking still with excitement and the emotion released by his homecoming. He looked surprisingly well, she thought, though he was thin-faced and obviously underweight. She quickly brushed a tear from her eye and squeezed him fondly, and he looked up at her, smiling happily.

The two lads had been very patient but finally Reg could stand the suspense no longer.

'Dad, are yer gonna take me ter see Millwall?' he asked.

Chapter Thirteen

The hour was late and in the empty street outside, the fog lay like a blanket. Inside the little front bedroom a small fire was dying in the grate but it had served to warm up the freezing cold room. Lucy lay on her back beneath the mound of bedclothes and stared up at the ghostly shadows of the fire playing on the ceiling. Next to her Roy was breathing irregularly as he slept on his side, his back towards her. Lucy turned her head and watched until the rise and fall of the bedclothes reassured her. She had worn her nightdress, a low-cut, revealing satin gown in a pale lemon shade, bought for Roy's homecoming. She had gone to him, standing at the foot of the bed enveloped in his arms, and she had felt him trembling as he kissed her tenderly on her open mouth, his hands moving greedily down the length of her back. It had been so long she had forgotten how his loving felt, but his touch restored her memories as if releasing her from a spell. He was always gentle and considerate, though there had been times when her needs were greater than his and she had wanted him to ravish her, take her on to a higher plane of ecstasy in a wild, domineering display of his sexual prowess. Tonight she had wanted to hold him, love him gently and let the pain of the long parting melt away in a tender, unhurried union, but Roy had been anxious, too anxious.

Lucy turned to face him, reaching her arm out over

him and feeling the rising and falling of his chest. He stirred and she moved slowly closer, wide awake and hungry for him although the hour was late. The whole day had seemed unreal and the moment she had waited for so long had left her unfulfilled. Roy had held her, drawing out the passion and urgency of her craving with his soft, almost delicate caresses. She had moved with him round to the side of the bed and then, as she sensed that his passion was threatening to overwhelm him, she had tried to move away from his tight embrace, but he had forced her down on top of the covers, tugging up her nightdress and groaning with desire as he went into her. She had wrapped herself around him, thrusting out her hips to await the pleasure of his movement but he was immediately spent. She had held him tightly, pressing his head down on to her heaving bosom, but he had struggled, pulling himself away from her as if fighting for breath. The magical moment was lost and Lucy had let her body go limp.

The shadows on the ceiling had all but disappeared and Lucy turned on to her back once more. She had been too demanding, too impatient to make him love her, and all her good intentions had been forgotten in her desire for him. She would have to be patient and give him time. He had tried too hard too soon and she was to blame.

Roy mumbled in his sleep and as he turned she reached out for him. Suddenly he stiffened and pushed her away with an unintelligible jumble of words, then he sat bolt upright, soaked in sweat and trembling. Lucy slipped out of bed and grabbed a hand towel from the washstand.

'It's all right, darlin', yer've bin dreamin',' she whispered, dabbing at his chest.

Roy snatched the towel from her and buried his face in it, groaning as though in pain, then he suddenly fell back

136

on the pillow and was still. Lucy brought the bedclothes up round his chin and very gently dabbed at his wet face. After some time he settled down and became quieter and she buried her head in her pillow, suddenly feeling afraid and willing herself to sleep.

Laura rose early on Monday morning, and while she waited for the kettle to boil she cleared out the ashes from the grate, laid the fire and set the screwed-up paper alight. The small sticks of wood started to crackle and spark but the room still felt icily cold and Laura shivered, wrapping her dressing gown tightly around her as she went out into the scullery. The rear window that looked out on to the back yard was patterned with ice on the inside and she could feel the coldness of the stone floor beneath her fluffy slippers. The house was quiet and she decided not to wake the boys yet, not until the parlour had warmed up. She idly watched the kettle puffing steam rings as she sat at the small table and her thoughts went back to Saturday evening. Eddie had come into the house at her request, and he had unknowingly tilted her little world on its axis. She had not been able to get him out of her mind. It had both worried and excited her. He was a friendly character, with good looks and a nice personality. He had made an innocent joke about coming back for a check-up, but those few words had pierced the hard shell of her loneliness. She wanted him to call again, but at the same time she found herself reinforcing her defences. How could she let him know that she wasn't really available without hurting his feelings?

The kettle started to boil and Laura made a pot of tea. It was still only seven thirty; there was plenty of time yet before she needed to call the boys for school. She took the teapot and cups into the parlour and sat down beside the growing fire. She was being silly pretending that

Eddie had any designs on her, she told herself. He most likely had a string of girls eager to go out with him. Why should he be interested in someone like her, a frumpy stop-at-home who didn't know how to dress – that was what Lucy had told her once? Perhaps she was being too hard on herself, she thought. Eddie might be a shy sort of bloke who didn't feel at home with the smart girls-about-town. His mother had said he was quiet and didn't have a girlfriend.

Laura poured herself a cup of tea and sat sipping it thoughtfully. Suddenly she got up and went over to the wall mirror, staring at herself as she stretched her mouth open. Her teeth were white and even, and her face was still unlined. Her hair was a mess though. She half turned to look at the reflection of her shoulders and bust. She was round-shouldered, or was it just the way she was standing? She held her back straight as she walked over to the fireside, thinking that she should see Lucy about her hair. Her sister had said she would give her a cut and perm. After all, there was no need to let herself go just because she never went anywhere. A woman had to have pride in her appearance.

Albert suddenly walked into the parlour and sat down heavily in his chair. 'I didn't sleep very well,' he said as Laura got up again to pour him a cup of tea. 'I was finkin' about Roy. 'E looked very thin and weak, that's fer sure.'

'Well, it 'as bin over four years, Dad, an' look what 'e's bin frew,' Laura replied.

Albert nodded. 'I s'pose yer right,' he said, taking the cup of tea from her. 'I 'ope the two of 'em pick up the pieces. It won't be easy fer eivver of 'em.'

Laura folded up the chair-bed and then took her clothes out to the scullery to get dressed. She splashed cold water over her face, then combed out her long fair hair and pulled it tightly behind her ears with slides.

Lucy had said that she looked like a middle-aged school-matron and Laura realised as she studied herself in the mirror how right her sister was. She quickly removed the slides and took up her hairbrush, and within a few minutes she was able to gaze at the results and smile to herself. Her hair was shining from the vigorous brushing and she had fixed it into waves over her forehead with the aid of clips. The long strands hung down over her shoulders and she shook her head daringly. It was much better. She dressed quickly and when she went back into the parlour her father looked up at her.

'I fink I'll take a walk up the shop fer the paper,' he said, making no move to get up.

'You stay put,' she told him. 'It's a very cold mornin' an' there's frost about. I'll go an' get yer paper.'

Albert sat back in his chair and stuck out his feet towards the fire. 'What yer done ter yer 'air?' he asked.

Laura hid a grin. 'I did it different fer a change,' she told him.

'I liked it the way yer 'ad it before,' he replied.

When she had given the boys their tea Laura put on her warm coat and slipped out of the house. It had started to snow and the flakes were settling. She pulled her collar up around her ears and bent her head against the wind as she walked the short distance to the shop. It was as she was coming out with the paper that she almost collided with Eddie. He was wearing a reefer jacket with a red scarf knotted docker-fashion and a cap at a jaunty angle.

' 'Ello, Laura. What you doin' out on a mornin' like this?' he asked her with a smile.

Laura returned his smile as she brushed a strand of wet hair away from her face. 'Dad's paper,' she replied.

Eddie slipped into step beside her. 'I'm just goin' back 'ome. There's no work at the wharf this mornin',' he told her.

139

' 'Ow's yer finger?' she said.

Eddie chuckled and held it up. 'D'yer fink I need a new bandage?' he asked.

Laura shook her head. 'You'll survive,' she laughed.

'Is the chair-bed workin' okay?' he enquired.

'Fine.'

They turned into Pedlar's Row and Eddie held up his finger. 'I still might need ter take yer up on that first aid.'

Laura let herself into the house, taking the newspaper from under her coat and handing it to her father. 'It's snowin',' she announced, going to the mirror to check her lank wet hair.

'Lucy's bin down. She's taken a cup o' tea up ter Roy,' Albert said, opening his *Daily Mirror*.

'Well, she's picked the right time ter stay off work,' Laura remarked, wondering what Eddie must have thought of her dishevelled hair.

The two boys had started squabbling over breakfast and Terry was looking particularly angry.

'Big mouth.'

'Big 'ead.'

'It's not as big as yours.'

'Yes it is, your cap could 'old five pound o' spuds.'

'Shut up, big mouth.'

Laura came over to the table. 'Now what's the trouble wiv you two?' she asked.

'All I said was, " 'Ow's the fort comin' on?", an' 'e called me big mouth,' Reg told her, hiding a grin.

'What fort?' Laura asked.

'That one Mr Stebbin's is buildin' fer 'im an' Charlie Bromley,' Reg replied.

'Shut yer big mouth!' Terry shouted.

Laura looked hard at Terry. 'Yer not still goin' in Mr Stebbin's' 'ouse, are yer?' she asked.

Terry shook his head. 'No, Aunt Laura.'

'Yer know what yer mum said. She'll clout yer if you are.'

'Honest, Aunt Laura,' Terry replied. 'It's just Reg tryin' ter get me in trouble.'

'Right you two, eat yer porridge an' not anuvver word out o' yer, understood?'

The boys nodded and bent their heads over their breakfast, then Terry looked up at Laura. 'What's wrong wiv Mr Stebbin's?' he asked.

Laura sat down at the table. 'Well, I don't fink there's anyfing wrong wiv 'im, but 'e acts a little bit strange at times,' she replied.

'What d'yer mean, strange?' Reg asked.

'Well, Mr Stebbin's sometimes mumbles to 'imself an' it's not right fer small boys ter pester 'im,' Laura told him, wondering how she could best get the message over.

' 'E could be singin',' Terry suggested.

'Yer mean 'e could be mad an' kill people?' Reg asked her.

Laura smiled. 'No, of course not, but sometimes there are men who like ter be wiv little boys,' she began.

'Mr Stebbin's does,' Terry cut in.

'What I mean is, there are some men who like ter touch little boys, an' sometimes they 'urt 'em, or even worse,' Laura continued, feeling more and more out of her depth.

'Like Jack the Ripper?' Terry asked, wide-eyed.

'Some wicked men do 'urt little boys, but I'm not sayin' Mr Stebbin's is wicked or that 'e would do anyfing bad. Yer mum just wants yer ter be very careful,' Laura explained.

'Mr Stebbin's is really nice,' Terry said. ' 'E's makin' me an' Charlie a lovely fort. 'E'd never 'urt anybody. 'E wouldn't even 'urt Soapy, but Soapy died so Mr Stebbin's put 'im in the dustbin.'

141

Reg had been let into the secret of the pet eel and he pulled a face. 'P'raps Mr Stebbin's strangled Soapy an' then chopped 'im up inter little pieces,' he suggested.

'You're really stupid,' Terry scowled at his older brother. 'Mr Stebbin's wouldn't 'urt nuffing, not even you.'

'Who's Soapy?' Laura asked.

'It was an eel what me an' Charlie saved from gettin' cut ter pieces,' Terry told her.

'They nicked it out o' the tank at the pie shop, if yer ask me,' Reg said.

'No one's askin' yer, rat-face,' Terry growled.

'Shut yer trap, pigs' brains,' Reg countered.

Laura startled the two boys by banging her hand down sharply on the table. 'Now listen ter me,' she said with authority. 'Yer father's just come 'ome from the war, an' all yer can do is argue. What will 'e fink of yer? Now go an' get yerselves off ter school, an' look out fer each ovver, okay?'

When the boys finally set off, Laura stood watching from the front door. Reg had slipped his arm around his younger brother's shoulders and she smiled.

'D'yer reckon that boy's still goin' in Stebbin's place?' Albert asked her when she went back in.

'I reckon so,' she replied. 'I fink I'll 'ave a word wiv Annie Stebbin's this afternoon.'

Queenie Bromley had finished baking the last of the rock cakes and she set them out on the dresser to cool. She had made enough for her hungry tribe and a few extra for John Bannerman. He could do with some good food inside him, she thought. He looked thinner now than when he was a regular visitor to her house in Long Lane. John Bannerman was a genuine fellow, but a born loser. He had been in love with her younger sister, Mary, since the first day they met. How long ago it all seemed.

They had been little more than children and they seemed to be so happy together. If only he had been in a position to marry the girl it would all have turned out different. Queenie sighed sadly. Mary had been very keen on him too, but there was no future for the two of them while the boy was still the breadwinner for his family. Then that rat Archie Westlake had come on the scene and quickly turned her head. She had been silly to fall for a man like him but she was young and impressionable and it was understandable. Westlake could give her all that John couldn't. It had broken the young lad's heart when she gave him up for that evil git, Queenie recalled. He had drifted into trouble of one sort or another, then he seemed to settle down when he married Marge Blake after getting her pregnant. Now there were four mouths to feed. Yes, John Bannerman was a gaolbird, a born loser, and he was going nowhere while he involved himself with the likes of Archie Westlake, but then who was she to judge? People like John needed a helping hand now and then, Queenie told herself, and those rock cakes would probably help fill the bellies of his poor kids.

Chapter Fourteen

On Monday morning Marcus Levy went to see an old friend in the clothing trade and purchased a smart lounge suit off the peg. He also bought a few shirts, a dinner jacket and a pair of black patent shoes similiar to the ones worn by Westlake which he had admired so much. Marcus got a generous discount, and feeling well done by he decided to fork out on a new tie. His shopping was progressing nicely and he next went to see another old friend who sold him a pair of matching brown leather suitcases, again with a generous discount.

Marcus looked at himself in the window of Cornbloom's the pawnbroker and felt that he had some work to do on his appearance. He visited Manny Silverman who cut his hair and gave him the full treatment, a close shave and hot towels, finishing off with a spicy aftershave. For services rendered Marcus tipped Manny Silverman handsomely and set off to see Ira Stanley, complete with his purchases in the suitcases and smelling as fresh as the morning dew. Ira was an old and trusted friend who could be relied upon to keep a secret, and it was with Ira that he discussed his predicament over a meal of gefilte fish and fresh bagels. At three thirty Marcus boarded the train to Eastbourne wearing his new clothes, and he sat back in the carriage feeling happier and more confident than he had done for a long while. He had told Ira everything and explained his detailed plan of action, and his old friend had been very helpful, promising to be his contact, should events overtake him.

The weather was cold and bleak and Marcus tired of watching the scenery flash by the carriage window, so he decided to catch up with the news. He had bought the *Daily Telegraph*, feeling that it was the paper most in keeping with his new-found image. At the quiet and almost deserted seaside resort Marcus booked into the impressive-looking Spa Hotel facing the sea and immediately made a few very subtle enquiries. He was feeling lonely and in need of a woman's company that night, and he was quite prepared to pay for her services. Two crisp pound notes discreetly passed over to the head porter worked wonders and an introduction was made. That night Marcus Levy invited a voluptuous brunette back to his room and allowed himself to forget his troubles. Breakfast was a leisurely affair and the former artist spent the rest of the morning familiarising himself with the hotel and its environs.

Paying for sex was something that Marcus did very often, although not usually with women of the night. He preferred the sense of conquest, the seduction of vulnerable and gullible females who frequented prestigious hotels and were there for the taking, as far as Marcus Levy was concerned. The problem was that those supposedly gullible and vulnerable females very often turned out to be aspiring, calculating creatures who were out to take people like him for every penny and more, and they often did. Marcus was well aware of his past failings in the art of selection and he vowed to be more careful in future.

The second evening seemed to be going well and Marcus got into a casual conversation at the hotel bar with a middle-aged couple from Canada. After he had introduced himself as a portrait painter, interior designer and freelance art critic he found himself discussing

French nineteenth-century Impressionist painters with the couple. The man, who was getting steadily drunk, told him that he was an exporter and that he had his own collection of Manet, Renoir and Degas. The man's wife, a large honey-blonde with an expensive taste in clothes and jewellery, was showing some interest in Marcus and he decided there and then that the chance meeting might be of some advantage to him.

Having wormed his way into joining the couple for dinner at their table, Marcus totally charmed the lady, and he accepted her invitation to accompany her on the dance floor to the music of a quintet. He was discovering that she had an enormous capacity for drink. The champagne, wine and earlier cocktails had made her heady and carefree, but they had taken a heavier toll on her husband, however. Following a few more after-dinner drinks at the bar the exporter was helped to his room by the giggling pair of conspirators, who then retired to Marcus Levy's room for the night.

When the reckless artist finally left Eastbourne to start work on the counterfeit plates back in Whitechapel he had entirely changed his future plans. The chance meeting with the Canadian couple had opened up new horizons and he would have to discuss his daring new scheme with his old friend Ira Stanley.

At the first opportunity Laura went to see Annie Stebbings. She had nodded to the woman occasionally in the Row but she had not as yet spoken to her. Laura realised that it was going to be difficult to broach the subject, but it would have to be done; Lucy had been worried about her lad's involvement with Wally ever since Queenie voiced her concern. As Laura had taken on the responsibility of caring for Lucy's two boys while their mother was at work she felt it gave her the right to approach the woman tactfully.

'I'm sorry ter trouble yer, Mrs Stebbin's, but I'm Terry's aunt, Laura Prior. I look after the boy durin' the day,' she said by way of introduction. 'I'd like to 'ave a word if I may?'

Annie looked worried as she showed Laura into her tidy parlour and offered her a chair. She sat down facing her, guessing already the nature of the visit.

'I know that our Terry 'as bin spendin' some time wiv your son Wally an' we're a bit concerned,' Laura began.

'My Wally's not bin up to anyfing 'as 'e?' Annie asked quickly.

Laura shook her head. 'No, but fer a start we don't want our lad pesterin' yer, an' secondly we'd sooner see 'im mixin' wiv children of 'is own age,' she replied.

'Are yer worried that Wally might interfere wiv your Terry an' that ovver lad, Charlie?' Annie asked coldly. ' 'Cos if yer fink that, yer wrong. Wally's a nice man. 'E likes ter be friendly wiv everybody, an' jus' because 'e's not married an' livin' 'ere wiv me don't make 'im one o' those sort.'

Laura reached out her hand and touched Annie's arm in a show of sympathy. 'Look, Mrs Stebbin's,' she said quietly. 'I know it must be terrible for yer ter know that people might fink the worst o' your son, but you 'ave to understand our feelin's. It is unusual fer a man Wally's age ter befriend children to the degree 'e does.'

'What d'yer mean by that?' Annie asked quickly.

'Well by invitin' the kids in an' spendin' a lot o' time wiv 'em. That's what I mean,' Laura told her.

Annie stood up. 'I wanna show yer somefing,' she said, beckoning Laura to follow her.

She led the way out to the scullery and pointed to the table set against the wall. 'Look at that. That's what Wally spends 'is time doin' when the kids are 'ere,' she said. ' 'E's makin' it fer them.'

Laura looked at the intricate Foreign Legion fort on

the table and she felt ashamed for having doubted Wally's intentions. The plywood model was almost finished, with detailed ramparts, double swing gates and squared towers set at each corner. The centre tower was complete with a tiny wall ladder leading up to the turret and a flagpole. Wally had started painting the fort and Laura could see the bits and pieces of offcuts, tubes of glue and a couple of small clamps lying around on the table. There was a rough drawing too which Annie picked up to show her. 'Wally went ter the library ter copy that,' she told her. ' 'E got the idea when 'e went ter the pictures an' saw that film, *Beau Geste*.'

'It's lovely,' Laura said with feeling. 'It must 'ave taken 'im ages ter get this far.'

Annie nodded. 'When the boys come in Wally sets ter work on it. They stand around watchin' 'im an' sometimes 'e lets 'em 'elp 'im, like sandpaperin' an' gluin' pieces on. Most times I'm in the 'ouse, but if I'm out I don't 'ave any worries. My Wally wouldn't do any 'arm ter those boys, Laura.'

Laura turned to go, feeling quite embarrassed. 'I'm sorry if I've upset yer, Mrs Stebbin's, but . . . '

'My name's Annie.'

'Well, Annie, after what yer've shown me I don't mind our Terry comin' in provided you don't mind.'

Annie Stebbings smiled briefly. 'I'm well aware o' the fact that people do gossip about my Wally,' she said 'but they don't know anyfing about 'im. When 'e was a little lad 'is farvver used ter clout 'im a lot, or else ignore 'im altergevver. 'E never 'ad any time fer 'im, an' Wally tended ter stay close ter me. When 'e was eight years old 'is farvver left us. 'E's bin dead fer years now, but at that time Wally couldn't understand why 'e should run off. 'Ow d'yer tell an eight-year-old that 'is dad's got anuvver woman? Anyway, Wally never mixed much wiv the ovver kids an' they tended ter take the rise out of 'im. It was 'cos 'e was so quiet an' shy. When 'e grew up 'e found it 'ard ter talk ter gels. 'E never 'ad a gelfriend until this Salvation Army gel came along. Wally liked 'er an' seemed ter get on well wiv 'er at first, but it wasn't ter be an' they parted. It's a long story, but Wally settled fer bein' a bachelor an' that's the way it is. 'E's got a decent job in the office at the box factory in Weston Street an' 'e likes the pictures. Ovver than that 'e stays in an' does fretwork an' models. Wally's a bit ole fashioned in 'is way, but yer've no need ter worry about 'is motives, of that I can assure yer.'

Laura left number six feeling much happier, if a little ashamed, and her thoughts turned to Reg. He was probably more at risk hanging round the bookie than his younger brother was with Wally Stebbings.

Lizzie Cassidy was preparing the weekly feast and the family were gathering. Geoff and Mary were the first to arrive and Lizzie did her usual fussing. 'I 'ope e's lookin' after yer, luv. I'm not gonna 'ave 'im puttin' on yer or 'e'll answer ter me,' she said firmly.

Geoff smiled. 'I don't want 'er pilin' on too much weight, Ma, so I'm keepin' 'er on the go,' he said with a straight face.

Lizzie's murderous look was enough to send him hurrying from the scullery to seek the sanity of the parlour. Steve arrived a few minutes after his older brother, and as he eased his stocky frame into a vacant armchair he was as usual very vociferous about the current bad form of Millwall. His father was equally damning, much to Eddie's disgust. He could see little wrong in his favourite team and he was quick to say so. 'All they want is one more experienced forward an' wiv a bit o' luck they could go up this year,' he asserted.

'They've got about as much chance o' gettin' promoted as you 'ave of gettin' married,' Geoff told him.

'I don't know so much about that,' Eddie replied with a sly smile.

Steve turned to Geoff. 'Now be fair. Who'd 'ave 'im?' he said, keeping his face serious. 'Just look at 'im. 'E's scruffy, lazy, an' 'e's got this fixation on Millwall. If 'e ever got married it would 'ave ter be in the closed season.'

Eddie took the ribbing with his usual good-natured aplomb. His brothers were always trying to wind him up and he knew that it irritated them more when he refused to rise to the bait. He was not above turning the tables on them occasionally, however. 'I reckon it is possible ter get married in the mornin' an' then 'ave time ter go an' see Millwall in the afternoon, if yer tell the vicar to 'urry it up,' he grinned.

'I s'pose all the guests would go along too,' Steve replied.

'Yeah, the vicar as well,' Geoff added. ' 'E could say a prayer before they started. That bloody team needs a miracle ter make 'em win.'

Out in the scullery Lizzie was chatting eagerly to her two daughters-in-law. 'This young woman 'ad some trouble wiv a chair-bed or somefing an' she asked if we could 'elp,' she was explaining. 'I'd already made meself known to 'er an' told 'er Eric or Eddie wouldn't mind 'elpin' wiv anyfing if she needed it. There's no man in the 'ouse yer see. Well, there's 'er farvver, but 'e's gettin' on a bit an' 'e's 'ad a stroke. Mind you, 'er sister's livin' there as well an' 'er 'usband's just come 'ome from a Jap prison camp. But this was before 'e got back. Anyway, Eric was at the dogs so Eddie went over. 'E was there fer ages, an' when 'e come back 'e was whistlin' to 'imself all 'appy like. 'E looked like the cat that swallered a canary. I reckon there could be somefing on the cards there. Don't dare let on I said anyfing though,' she warned them.

★ ★ ★

Each morning Con the bookie took up his place outside number four and each evening he was back for the dog bets and to pay out winnings from the day's horse-racing. The snow had almost cleared by now but the weather remained cold, so Bridie Molloy took the occasional cup of tea out to him, and Joe chatted briefly whenever he got the chance. One evening when the two were exchanging pleasantries Wally Stebbings came by with his head held low. He seemed to be mumbling to himself.

'Is 'e all there?' Con asked, grinning.

' 'E's a strange bloke,' Joe replied. 'We don't 'ave much ter do wiv 'em. There's just 'im an' 'is ole muvver.'

'I was watchin' 'im the ovver night,' Con said. ' 'E was standin' by 'is door talkin' to a couple o' the kids. 'E's a bit simple, ain't 'e?'

'I dunno about that, 'e works in an office, but 'e's certainly strange,' Joe answered.

Len Carmichael walked up and handed Con a betting slip, and seeing Joe standing at his front door he nodded.

'We've just bin talkin' about ole Wally,' Joe said.

'Bloody strange bloke, that one,' Len replied.

' 'E's bin chattin' ter the kids, so Con told me,' Joe informed him.

' 'E was in the Salvation Army once, accordin' ter my Elsie,' Len said, folding his arms. 'She said they chucked 'im out 'cos 'e wouldn't go collectin' in the pubs. 'Avin' it orf wiv one o' the Salvation Army gels, 'e was.'

'Well, I didn't like the way 'e was chattin' up those kids,' Con cut in. 'We'll 'ave ter keep our eye on 'im. There's only one way ter deal wiv people like that.'

'Too bloody true,' Joe added.

Lucy had managed to get three days off work to be with Roy, and when she returned to the factory her good friend Val Bennett was eager to hear all the news.

' 'Ow did it go?' she asked.

Lucy's face told her that all was not well. 'Roy keeps 'avin' these nightmares,' she said, toying with her teaspoon.

'Well, that's ter be expected, I s'pose, but yer gotta be patient. It'll pass,' Val told her. 'But what about the love bit? Can 'e still do it?'

Lucy shrugged her shoulders. 'It's all right, I s'pose, but it's all over too quick.'

'Yer gotta take into account 'e's not done it fer ages, 'e's bound ter be stale,' Val said encouragingly.

'Well, 'e never ever made a meal of it in the past, but I don't like rushin' it,' Lucy replied.

Val Bennett leaned forward over the table. 'When me an' my ole man first started doin' it 'e was on an' off like a robin,' she said, smiling broadly, 'but it got better as time went on. Yer get complacent about it all after a time though. Now I tell 'im to 'elp 'imself but don't ferget ter pull me nightdress down after 'e's finished.'

Lucy smiled briefly. 'Roy's very quiet too a lot o' the time an' I keep on sayin' ter meself that it's because of what 'e's bin frew, but it gets me all screwed up inside. It's like we've 'ad a row, which we've not.'

' 'E'll be better once 'e gets back ter work,' Val told her.

'Maybe yer right,' Lucy replied. ' 'E's goin' ter see about gettin' 'is ole job back terday.'

'What's 'e do fer a livin'?' Val asked.

' 'E's a cabinet-maker.'

'Well, there's plenty o' work in that trade, I should fink,' Val said.

'I don't want Roy ter rush back ter work but it might 'elp 'im get over those nightmares,' Lucy said hopefully. ' 'E wakes up in a terrible sweat, an' 'e keeps on about the bangin'. I've tried talkin' to 'im about it but 'e just

152

clams up tight. Gawd knows what did go on in those camps.'

The factory whistle sounded and as the women hurried out of the large canteen Val took Lucy's arm. 'Be patient, luv,' she urged her. 'It'll all work out. Yer just wanna remember, the grass is no greener on the ovver side.'

Chapter Fifteen

Chief Inspector Ben Walsh sat down heavily at his desk in Dockhead Police Station and thumbed quickly through the sheaf of papers lying in front of him. It would all have to wait, he decided. There was another development that needed all his attention, and from the information he had gathered it was serious. Walsh picked up the internal phone and held it under his chin while he flicked through the folder he had taken from the desk drawer. 'Eh, is Ashley in yet?' he asked. 'Right, well tell him I want to see him as soon as he arrives.'

Ten minutes later Detective Sergeant Gordon Ashley knocked on the door and walked in. 'You wanted to see me, guv?' he asked.

Ben Walsh waved him towards a chair beside his desk without looking up from the papers he was studying. Ashley sat down and reached into his coat pocket for his notebook. He was a big man, well over six feet tall and broad-shouldered. His thick dark hair was combed back from his forehead and his eyes were a pale blue beneath heavy eyebrows. He had been stationed at Dockhead for over fifteen years and felt that there wasn't much going on in the area that he didn't get to know about, one way or another. Gordon Ashley had the reputation of being a hard man who was not afraid to bend the rules when it suited him. He had been overlooked for promotion on more than one occasion because of his tendency to cut corners, but he was respected by his colleagues and detested by the criminal fraternity.

Ben Walsh, however, was a stickler for the rules. He did things by the book, and his reputation for getting results had preceded him to Dockhead. In the five years he had been in charge there two well-known villains from the neighbourhood had been put behind bars and a black-market ring which had been flourishing in Bermondsey since the early days of the war had been stamped out. Chief Inspector Walsh was a tenacious character, short and stocky, with a large mop of ginger hair and grey eyes. His ruddy, flat face had a humorous look about it and tended to make him appear easy-going and charitable, a mistake that many people had made during his long career as a policeman.

After a minute or two the inspector swivelled in his chair to face his subordinate and tossed the folder down in front of him. 'There's definitely something big going on in this manor, Gordon, and I just can't put my finger on it,' he said.

Ashley opened the folder and glanced at the top sheet of paper. 'Well, guv, what I've managed to pick up would bear that out, but it's still very sketchy.'

'What exactly have you got?' Walsh asked, leaning back in his chair and clasping his hands together on his lap.

Sergeant Ashley flipped over the top leaf of his notebook. 'Well, it would appear that Archie Westlake's branching out. It seems he's got himself involved in some way with a new printing works in Long Lane. Carlton Press it's called. Westlake's been seen there frequently and he often drinks with the firm's boss in the Leather Bottle at lunchtime. Also, there's something I've got from my snout which could possibly tie in with that. Apparently there's been talk of, quote, "working the tracks". There's something else too.'

'Oh, an' what's that?'

Ashley leaned forward in his chair. 'My snout feels that they're waiting for somebody.'

'Couldn't he be more specific?'

Ashley shook his head. 'He's not one of their cadre, so it's only snatches of conversation he's picking up here and there.'

'What's it all mean?' Walsh asked.

Ashley shrugged his shoulders. 'I don't know yet, but there seems to be a lot of excitement on the manor,' he replied. 'Another thing. Conrad Noble's changed his pitch. He's at Pedlar's Row now. Westlake's often there with him and the two are thick as thieves, if you'll pardon the pun.'

'Spare me that,' Walsh said grimacing. 'I think we'd better go easy on the bookie for the time being. We don't want to let them know we're watching. Let's allow them to settle in there and see how your snout does.'

'Do you think Archie Westlake's going to start printing ration books or petrol coupons?' Ashley asked, pocketing his notebook.

The inspector leaned forward over his desk. 'Not if the bookies are involved,' he replied. 'Can you imagine them pushing ration books at the racetracks? I'm more inclined to think it's counterfeit money they're after printing. Anyway, let's see what we've got. Westlake's suddenly involved with a new printing company, which could possibly be his own firm running under a cover. Then there's this talk of working the racetracks. We know that our friend runs the local bookies, and his little team would be ideal outlets if the assumption about counterfeit money is right. They know the tracks and the layout there. Just think what they could do at Epsom, Ascot, Newmarket, to name a few. Then they could cast their net wider. Counterfeit money could be pushed around like confetti all over the place.'

Ashley stroked his chin thoughtfully. 'You mean they'd back the field?' he suggested.

'Why not?' Walsh said quickly. 'It's been tried before. I remember when dud money was pushed at Catford dog-track some years ago. Trouble was the notes looked like toy money and the bookies spotted it straight away. If Westlake printed good stuff, and I'm sure he would, then the track bookies wouldn't spot it. They'd be too busy taking money. Our friend's cronies could spread themselves around the track and back every horse in each race. They could net a fortune for Westlake, provided they didn't get too greedy.'

'So we go to source, like concentrating on the printing works?' Ashley asked, looking dubious.

Walsh puffed out his cheeks. 'We'll need a lot more from your snout,' he said. 'We won't be able to get a search warrant to raid a legit company without something positive to go on, and besides, there's no guarantee that the money will be printed there. If the Carlton Press does belong to Westlake he could merely use their facilities, such as ink and paper, and a small press. He could set a small press up anywhere.'

Sergeant Ashley leaned forward and consulted the open folder for a few seconds then he looked up at the inspector. 'What about the printing plates, guv, any ideas?'

'I haven't forgotten what that snout of yours said about waiting for someone,' Walsh said thoughtfully. 'It might be their engraver, or it could be someone who's cutting the plates now, or maybe even someone capable of doing the job who's due for release from prison very shortly. I know it's a bloody long shot but we can't afford to sit on this one, Gordon. We've got to follow up every lead. I'll tell you what I intend to do. I'm going to take a chance and send a preliminary report to the Yard, with a request for a rundown on recent releases and pending releases of prisoners convicted under Section Fourteen. It might open a can of worms, but we need to set the ball rolling if we want to stay on top of this one.'

Ashley nodded. 'I'll be leaning on my snout. He may come up with something in the next few days.'

'Don't lean too hard, Sergeant,' Walsh warned. 'We need him and we can't afford to balls this one up. Just remember, as soon as Scotland Yard get my report they're involved, whether we like it or not, and the penpushers like things done by the book.'

When Ashley left, Inspector Walsh picked up the phone. 'I'll be out the office for the next couple of hours,' he said. 'If I need to be contacted urgently I'll be at the Leather Bottle in Long Lane. I hear they do a good lunch there.'

Laura had been busying herself at the Sultan for more than an hour on Saturday morning when Archie Westlake arrived. He was accompanied by a large man wearing a white mackintosh. The two ignored her and sat down at the counter talking quietly with Jack Murray. Occasionally Westlake looked in her direction, and after a time he walked over to where she was polishing.

'I understand you live in Pedlar's Row,' he said amicably.

Laura nodded. 'We've not long moved in there,' she replied, still polishing the table surface.

' 'Ow d'yer get on wiv the neighbours?' he asked.

'They seem a nice crowd,' Laura told him, wondering where his questions were leading.

'They're not worried about the bookmaker standin' in the Row, are they?' he asked, smiling to reveal even white teeth.

Laura shook her head. 'Not as far as I know,' she said cautiously.

'Not even our Queenie Bromley?' he pressed.

'I wouldn't know,' Laura replied. 'I've not 'ad much ter do wiv 'er.'

'That's not your young lad that chats ter the bookie, is it?' Westlake asked.

'That's Reg, my sister's elder boy,' Laura told him.

' 'E's a sensible young lad. I understand 'e wants ter be a bookmaker when 'e leaves school,' Archie said, smiling.

'I don't think 'e knows what 'e wants ter do, after all 'e's only thirteen,' Laura replied.

' 'E'll go a long way that boy, mark my words,' the villain said, brushing an imaginary piece of fluff from his coat lapel.

Laura was beginning to feel uncomfortable under his gaze and she was relieved when he went back to the counter. He was certainly a handsome man, with dark wavy hair greying at the temples, a square chin and thick neck, but he was big and seemed to impose himself. His clothes were obviously expensive and there was an arrogant air in the way he carried himself. Laura found him insidiously menacing and she began to wonder about his connection with Queenie. She had made no bones about her detestation of the man, and Westlake had been eager to find out about the woman's attitude to the bookmaker. Something must have happened between the two of them. Maybe they had been lovers once, Laura thought, suddenly realising that she had been absent-mindedly polishing one spot on the table for ages. It was none of her business anyway. She had enough to worry about caring for her own family.

The two visitors had gone into the back room with the pub landlord and Westlake was doing the talking. 'Danny, I want yer ter go over Whitechapel this afternoon. Levy won't be expectin' anybody ter call until next week,' he said. 'I wanna keep the pressure on 'im. Levy's like a slippery eel, an' if there was any way 'e could wriggle out o' this arrangement 'e would. As it 'appens I've got 'im by the balls, fer the time bein'. 'E's short o' cash. 'E wouldn't be dossin' down in that bloody fleapit if 'e was flush, but nevertheless we can't get complacent, there's too much at stake.'

The big man in the white mackintosh nodded. 'Don't worry, I'll put the evil eye on 'im,' he replied. ' 'E'll remember me right enough. I thought 'e was gonna crap 'imself when I got to 'im on the station.'

The other two laughed aloud and then Jack Murray clasped his hands together on the table. 'I can't 'elp finkin' about Ben Walsh showin' up at the Bottle,' he remarked. 'All right, I know 'e gets round the manor quite a lot, but why that particular pub?'

Westlake smiled. 'I told yer not ter worry about it, Jack,' he replied. 'There was nuffink going on fer 'im ter latch on to. Just a crowd o' businessmen 'avin' a comfortable lunch tergevver. Besides, 'e was the ovver side o' the bar. 'E couldn't 'ave over'eard anyfing.'

Jack Murray was not altogether satisfied. 'I just got a feelin' about 'im bein' there. I can't 'elp wonderin' about us not gettin' a visit from the tecs eivver. Con's bin in Pedlar's Row fer a couple o' weeks now an' the local cozzer's bound to 'ave spotted the runners.'

'Yer gettin' nervous in yer old age, Jack,' Westlake chided him. 'It's not like yer.'

Jack smiled. 'P'raps I am, but this business we're settin' up ain't yer run-o'-the-mill stuff. We can't afford ter take chances. It only wants someone ter get a bit pissy an' start talkin', an' we could all be lookin' at a ten stretch.'

'Nobody's gonna open their mouth, Jack,' Archie said, trying to reassure him. 'There's only a few of us in the know an' I'm sure none of us would be stupid enough ter spread it around.'

'What about Con's runners?' Murray asked.

'They're completely in the dark,' Archie told him. 'Besides, they can be trusted ter keep mum if they do over'ear anyfing. Con picked 'em 'imself. Dickie Jones is family, 'e's married ter Con's sister, an' as fer John Bannerman, 'e's just out o' nick. They've both got good pedigree, so stop worryin', fer Gawd's sake.'

Murray smiled briefly. 'Yeah, all right, but we can't be too careful wiv what's at stake. We only want a grass on the manor an' we could be in dead trouble,' he went on.

Archie rubbed his chin and looked hard at the publican. 'Well then, we'll just 'ave ter be very careful we don't start gettin' loose-lipped,' he replied.

The large man in the white mackintosh had been idly staring through the open door at Laura polishing the tables, and he turned suddenly to Westlake. 'That's a nice-lookin' sort. Did yer make any 'eadway wiv 'er, Archie?' he asked.

'I was just passin' the time o' day,' Archie replied dismissively.

'That's a definite no,' Jack cut in. 'I've already chatted 'er up. She's 'ousebound.'

' 'Ousebound?'

'Yeah, she ain't married or nuffink, but she looks after 'er farvver. 'E's gettin' over a stroke, so she told me.'

'What a waste,' Archie said, grinning. 'Anyway, I'd keep tryin' if I were you, Jack, yer may catch 'er on a good day.'

That Saturday morning was dry and bright; the last of the snow had disappeared and Pedlar's Row seemed to be a hive of activity. Charlie and Terry were sitting at Queenie's front door thumbing through packs of cigarette cards, while Reg stood beside Con feeling very grown-up as he collected the occasional betting slip and money from punters. Annie Stebbings was sweeping her doorstep and Lizzie Cassidy was out talking to Bridie Molloy. Queenie was busy cleaning her windows and Albert Prior occasionally went to stand at his front door to survey the scene. Inside the Prior house Laura was unpacking the shopping when Lucy walked into the scullery, looking worried.

'Roy's just gone out fer a pint,' she said, leaning in the doorway.

'It'll make a change fer 'im,' Laura replied. ' 'E's not bin out much since 'e got 'ome.'

'That's not my fault,' Lucy answered sharply. 'The weavver 'asn't bin all that good, an' besides, Roy didn't seem ter wanna move from the 'ouse.'

'Look, Lucy, yer gotta remember, Roy's bin used to a different climate, 'e's bound ter feel the cold fer a while,' Laura reminded her.

'I 'ope 'e don't 'ave too much ter drink,' Lucy said, sighing.

'Didn't yer wanna go wiv 'im?' Laura asked.

Lucy shook her head and pulled a face. 'The pubs are full o' fellas talkin' about bettin' an' football on Saturdays. I'd only be in the way.'

'Are you an' Roy 'avin' problems?' Laura asked her quietly.

Lucy shrugged her shoulders. 'I dunno what it is,' she said, looking down at her feet. 'It just don't seem like I thought it'd be.'

'Well, yer didn't expect it ter be all wine an' roses, did yer?' Laura said, closing the dresser door and straightening up. 'Yer knew it was gonna take time.'

Lucy sighed deeply. 'Yeah, I knew that, but we can't seem ter talk, an' Roy's bin 'avin these terrible dreams. 'E's bin wakin' up in a pool o' sweat nearly every night since 'e's bin 'ome an' I can't get ter the bottom of it. It's like 'e's puttin' the shutters down on me. What more can I do except try gettin' 'im ter talk about it? P'raps I should ignore it an' pretend it's not 'appenin'? I dunno what ter do, Laura.'

'Maybe it's too painful ter talk about,' Laura replied. 'I'd just see 'ow fings go when 'e gets back ter work, if I were you. Once 'e's settled back in 'is job wiv ovver men around 'im 'e might be better.'

Lucy did not look too convinced. 'I dunno, I'm sure,' she sighed. 'Reg asked 'im if 'e'd take 'im down Millwall this afternoon but Roy said 'e couldn't manage it this week. When I asked 'im on the quiet why not, 'e told me 'e couldn't face bein' in a crowd. Roy's sick, Laura. 'E's really sick.'

' 'Ave yer suggested 'e goes an' sees Doctor Chandler?' Laura asked. 'P'raps 'e could prescribe somefing ter settle 'is nerves.'

'There's a drawer full o' medicine, vitamin tablets, sleepin' pills an' Gawd knows what, in our bedroom. Roy's takin' all sorts o' tablets, but they don't seem ter be doin' 'im any good,' Lucy told her, shaking her head sadly.

'Yeah, but is 'e takin' 'em regularly?' Laura asked her.

' 'E seems ter be,' she replied. 'I dunno, I'm worried sick.'

The conversation was interrupted as Albert walked into the scullery. 'Reg is out wiv that bookie again, Lucy,' he told her. 'I've just seen 'im from the winder. Yer'll 'ave ter keep 'im away, or that kid's gonna end up in trouble, mark my words.'

'What d'yer want me ter do, keep 'im indoors all day long?' Lucy shouted. 'Anyway, 'e's not doin' any 'arm jus' standin' there.'

Albert walked back into the parlour without replying and Lucy followed him out and ran up the stairs to her bedroom. Laura heard the door slam shut and she sat down heavily in a chair and sighed. It was all supposed to be so good once Roy got back home, she thought. Instead, after just one week there was Lucy sulking in her room, Roy at the pub on his own and Albert sitting mumbling to himself. Reg was going the right way to becoming a hardened criminal, if the lad's grandfather was to be believed, and goodness knows what young Terry was getting up to in the company of Pedlar's Row's little terror Charlie Bromley. They were most probably robbing the local pawnbroker this very minute.

Laura sat for a while in the quiet scullery and looked around, trying to find something to do, anything that would occupy her mind. The dresser had been tidied earlier, and she cast her eye along the line of blue willow-pattern plates standing upright on the top shelf, and below them the matching teacups hanging from cupboard hooks. She had taken the china down and washed it only the previous day and it was all shiny clean. There was a pile of ironed bedclothes on the chair and a clean piece of net curtaining up at the back-door window. The stone floor had been scrubbed, as well as the iron gas stove, and she had tidied the food cupboard up that morning. She had been thinking about putting a coat of blue distemper on the stone walls, or maybe a shade of pink, but they were so often wet with condensation. There was nothing that needed doing for the moment and it was too early to start getting the evening meal ready. A resentment started to well up inside her. Her whole life seemed to be centred around the next meal, cleaning, washing and ironing, and trying to keep dependable and cheerful in an atmosphere that was slowly becoming unbearable. Her own individual feelings and desires seemed to be stifled under the burden of the family responsibilities she had taken on.

Suddenly Laura stood up and grabbed her coat. She

had to get out of the house for a while, if only to walk down to the market, mingle with the shoppers and try to get rid of the depression that was suddenly weighing down heavily upon her.

'Will yer be all right fer a while if I go down the market, Dad?' she asked.

'I thought yer done the shoppin',' Albert said, looking up at her with a miserable expression on his gaunt face.

'Yeah, but there's a few extra bits an' pieces we need,' Laura told him. 'I won't be long.'

She set off in the crisp midday air and walked along past the box factory, following the bend of Weston Street that led out into the centre of the milling Tower Bridge Road market. She felt better for the brisk walk and listening to the cries of the stall owners, the rattle of passing trams and the rumble of voices. A piquant aroma of boiling oranges drifted down from the jam factory and blended with the strong odour of fresh fish, the flowery scent of ripe fruit and the sweet smell of sugared doughnuts straight out of the hot fat. She tarried at Cheap Jack's stall, looking over the thousands of items the stall owner had tipped on to the ever-diminishing pile. Next to him Sammy Israel was working away at his fish stall with a razor-sharp knife, removing fins and tails from plaice and skate. Further along the line of traders steam rose up in the cold air from a flue-pipe poking out above the gaily painted stall of the sarsaparilla man.

'Warm yer bellies 'ere an' take a bottle 'ome wiv yer!' he cried out continuously. 'Good fer the nerves, purifies the blood.'

Opposite the stall there was a clothes shop where hard-pressed women took their children and self-consciously passed over Provident clothing cheques as though it were a crime to buy clothes in such a way. A few shops along from the children's shop there was a ladies' outfitters, and it was there that Laura had seen the dress. It was a black crepe creation which had been pinned tightly to the model, of mid-calf length, ruffled round the hips, and with a V neckline that plunged daringly. The shoulders were puffed out, and on each side of the bodice a triangle of sequins reached down to a point at the slender waist.

The dress had been in the window for some weeks now and Laura stopped to glance at it every time she went to the market. Today she had time to tarry and for a few minutes she stood looking in the shop at the various fashions, her eyes constantly coming back to it. She had dreamed of walking into a ballroom, a restaurant or a theatre wearing that very gown and of all heads turning to admire her. She would wear her blonde hair loose and softly curled so that it danced on her shoulders, and of course she would put on sheer black stockings and high-heeled black patent shoes with black velvet bows. The dress was her size, and Laura felt as though it had been made just for her. It was not priced, but then the best of the dresses in that particular shop never were.

Laura reluctantly walked away from the clothiers and along to the shoe shop. The pair of black patent shoes with the velvet bows were still in the window, high up on the shelf and almost hidden, but she had spotted them and matched them the first day she saw the dress. There was no use standing there wishing though, she told herself, and she turned away with a sigh.

The last of the doughnuts were being pulled from the deep, hot fat in the cake shop, and outside at her stall Maggie Palfrey was standing with one hand on her hip, sipping a mug of steaming tea.

'Wotcher, luv. Still shoppin'?' she asked pleasantly.

Laura smiled. 'Just winder-shoppin',' she replied.

'Lucy's fella's 'ome then,' Maggie said. 'I was talkin' ter yer sister this mornin'.'

'Yeah, 'e looks well, considerin',' Laura remarked.

'The ole fella's not too good, I 'ear.'

' 'E'll be better when the weavver breaks. 'E can't get out much since the stroke,' Laura told her.

A customer had arrived at Maggie's stall and Laura nodded a goodbye. There was time to take one more look at that dress, she thought, turning and retracing her steps to the shop.

'It's lovely, ain't it?'

Laura turned round suddenly to see Lizzie Cassidy standing beside her.

'I look at that every time I pass,' Laura said, smiling.

'That would 'ave fitted me, about twenty years ago. Never mind, I couldn't 'ave afforded it anyway,' Lizzie chuckled, picking up her two bulging shopping bags again.

'Are yer goin' 'ome?' Laura asked her.

'Yeah, I've gotta 'urry up an' get meself sorted out. We're all goin' out ternight,' she replied.

'I'm on me way back 'ome, let me take one o' those for yer,' Laura offered.

The two women turned into Weston Street chatting away together, each carrying a heavy shopping bag. 'We all go up the Queens Arms in Abbey Street now an' then on a Saturday night. It makes a change,' Lizzie was saying. 'The boys an' their wives come as well, an' my Eric usually does a song on the mike. There's a nice pianer player an' anuvver bloke plays the accordion.'

'It must be nice, wiv all the family as well,' Laura replied, wondering if Eddie went too.

'Yeah, I enjoy it, an' so does my Eric. It's nice ter keep the family close. You should try an' get up there,' Lizzie said. 'Bring yer farvver, it'd do 'im good. They sing all the ole songs.'

'I'll 'ave a word wiv 'im,' Laura replied.

They turned into Pedlar's Row and Lizzie took her

167

bag from Laura. 'Fanks, luv,' she said, smiling gratefully. 'Don't ferget to 'ave a word wiv yer dad. I'm sure my Eddie'll be glad if yer go. 'E gets fed up wiv talkin' to all the ole fogies.'

Laura had a sudden surge of high spirits, and as she went into the house her depression had disappeared.

Chapter Sixteen

Terry and his best friend Charlie had decided to have a council of war, and because of the seriousness of the problem they left Pedlar's Row for their secret hideout.

'My muvver said she'd give me a clout round the ear if I went in Mr Stebbin's 'ouse any more,' Charlie said as they ambled along Cooper Street.

'I thought yer told me a clout round the ear was nuffink,' Terry replied.

'Yeah, not from that man at the Trocette, but my mum's different,' Charlie said. 'She can clout really 'ard.'

'Well, my mum said it was all right ter go in there, but she said I wasn't ter let 'im touch me or anyfing,' Terry told him, kicking a large pebble along the road.

'Mums are stupid, ain't they?' Charlie remarked. 'Fancy sayin' fings like that. Mr Stebbin's wouldn't 'urt anybody. Anybody'd fink 'e was Captain Blood or somefing.'

'Who's Captain Blood?' Terry asked.

' 'E was a monster who used ter get kids an' strangle 'em an' cut 'em up inter little pieces,' Charlie informed him. ' 'E used ter cut ladies up as well, but mostly boys.'

'Cor! Was it true or just in the pictures?' Terry asked, wide-eyed.

' 'E was real,' Charlie replied. 'Captain Blood killed fousands o' kids but they never caught 'im an' then when 'e got old 'e went ter live in the country.'

The two lads continued on along the quiet turning, passing the leather factory and tannery. Cooper Street was a favourite haunt of the local youngsters. All the houses there had been destroyed by a land mine during the Blitz and the ruins had been boarded up with corrugated sheeting and abandoned, while various public bodies argued over what should be done about the place. One year after the cessation of hostilities the housing land in Cooper Street was still a derelict ruin, and parts of the metal fencing had disappeared, making the site easy to get into and a favourite haunt of youngsters who built their camps in the shells of the houses and on the weed-covered land.

At a certain spot where the corrugated sheeting was missing the two lads entered the wasteland and made their way into the ruins of a house. The stairway was still intact although the banisters had gone, and it was there under the stairs that Charlie and Terry had established their hideaway, to which they adjourned whenever there was something serious to be discussed.

'Why don't we knock an' ask Mr Stebbin's if 'e's finished our fort?' Terry suggested. 'That wouldn't be like going in.'

'My mum would still clout me,' Charlie said, looking totally miserable as he leaned back on an apple box and rested his head against the wall. 'Besides, Mr Stebbin's would tell us ter come in. Then when I said I couldn't 'e'd ask why.'

'I know. I could go an' ask if the fort's ready an' I could say you was ill,' Terry offered.

'Yeah. You could tell 'im I've got scarlet fever, then 'e'd know I couldn't come wiv yer,' Charlie said, cheering up a little, ' 'cos people die wiv scarlet fever, but you

170

could tell 'im the doctor said I wasn't gonna die, I was jus' very ill.'

'Let's go back an' see Mr Stebbin's now,' Terry suggested.

'Let's see if our secret treasure map's still 'ere before we go,' Charlie replied, reaching into the darkness at the back of their den.

Terry watched while his friend slid a small stone slab to one side and reached down into the hole, bringing out a folded sheet of paper.

'No one could ever find it 'ere,' Charlie said, grinning.

Terry found himself thinking once more about the story of Captain Blood that Charlie had told him, and as he sat beneath the stairs of the ruin with the light fading fast he felt the hairs on the back of his neck beginning to stand up. 'Put the map back an' let's go 'ome,' he said, trying to sound casual. 'It'll be dark soon.'

The two young boys walked quickly along Cooper Street, and as they turned into the rear of Pedlar's Row beside Wally Stebbings' house Charlie turned to Terry. 'Don't ferget ter tell 'im I've got scarlet fever,' he whispered as he hurried off to his street door.

Terry waited until his best friend had disappeared inside, then he reached for the doorknocker of number six.

Across the River Thames, in a cellar beneath the Whitechapel Road, Marcus Levy had started work on the copper plates. He had set himself up in the room beneath the restaurant owned by his old friend Ira Stanley and had purchased all the supplies he needed, including gelatine and a carboy of acid. He had brought his scribing and cutting tools, and fitted up a desk lamp on the old workbench that Ira had cleared for him. The artist was comfortably settled by his own standards and he felt that the site was ideal. Above him customers were coming and going until the early hours and he could have his own meals sent down. It was much better than working in his dingy flat at the Buildings, and there was less chance of being found out by someone calling on him unexpectedly.

Marcus was making steady progress performing what he felt was his most difficult and exacting task yet. There could be no margin for error. The finished article must be a work of art if he was to be paid in full, and, more to the point, if he was to remain in the land of the living. He had no illusions about Archie Westlake's capabilities. He knew that the man was a monster. He was totally unfeeling, indeed callous to a biblical degree. Westlake was calling the tune, and he had already made it clear that there was no alternative. The job of work had to be done.

The artist straightened up from the bench and took off his green eyeshade. Staring at the etching lines and constantly consulting the intricate design of the pound note through the large magnifying glass had made his eyes tired and his head ache. He poured himself a large whisky and took a draught. In just over two weeks' time he had to have the plates ready and he considered how to finalise his own plans. It would be the last bit of work he would ever do for the Bermondsey villain, and if the powers that be looked favourably on him then he would be well out of it; a continent away, in fact, he thought, smiling to himself.

It had been a very opportune meeting in East-bourne. Magdalena Thorpe had been more than accommodating and she had made him a proposition he found impossible to refuse. She and her husband were going back to Canada after a very successful business trip and they were to begin refurbishing their new mansion just outside Toronto. Marcus recalled with pleasure the evening he had spent with the couple, and the night in his room with the insatiable woman. She had told him of her plans for the mansion, in which he played a large part. The huge dining room was to be redesigned in the mode of the Sistine Chapel in Rome, with wall frescos and ceiling paintings, and she also wanted him to do portraits of both her and Claude, which would hang in a place of prominence. The cost of his trip to Canada, accommodation and leisure-time expenses were to be taken care of by Claude, who was only too glad to keep his wife happy while he went off to wine, dine and bed his latest young conquest.

As Marcus sipped his whisky he thought about his problem. He had a criminal record and would not be welcomed in the dominion as Marcus Levy. He needed a new name on a new passport, and the chance to get to Canada without the attentions of Archie Westlake and his East End friends. In just over two weeks he must be ready to leave with the new identity of Hiram Stanley, interior design artist, fictitious brother to Ira Stanley, and with credible letters of introduction on his person from the Thorpes of Toronto, Canada. Magdalena was taking care of their side of things. His main concern was producing a fake passport that would pass muster, something which would test his old skills once more. Last of all, and of crucial importance, he needed to shake his pursuers. The only other way he would achieve freedom from the villains was by ending up deceased, and it was to avoid that outcome at all costs that Marcus Levy schemed.

In Pedlar's Row Laura and Lucy were washing up in the scullery after the evening meal, while Roy was slumped in a chair, warding off sleep. Albert sat facing him reading the *Evening News*, occasionally glancing at the two boys, who were trying to tune the wireless in to foreign stations.

'Yer gotta do it steady,' Reg told his younger brother.

'I know what I'm doin',' Terry replied. 'Look, that's 'Ilversum, I can 'ear talkin'.'

Reg puffed loudly. 'That's not 'Ilversum, that's Rome, yer got the switch on long wave.'

'Where's 'Ilversum?' Terry asked.

'I dunno,' Reg replied. 'I fink it's in Africa. Where's 'Ilversum, Grandad?'

Albert glanced over at them. 'Miles away,' he mumbled.

'It's a Dutch station,' Roy told him, his eyes closed.

'Cor! They're talkin' double Dutch on 'ere,' Terry said, chuckling.

The oscillation increased as the lads moved the pointer further along the illuminated dial, and Albert put down his paper with a loud puff.

'Yer'll wear that battery out between the two of yer. Why don't yer leave it alone,' he moaned.

'Come away,' Roy said, his eyes still closed.

Albert gave his son-in-law a disdainful look and picked up his paper once more, while the two lads, tired of twiddling with the wireless, walked out into the scullery.

'Is yer farvver asleep?' Lucy asked them.

'Nearly,' Reg replied.

'What about Grandad?' Laura asked.

' 'E's awake,' Terry answered. ' 'E jus' told us off fer touchin' the wireless.'

'Look, why don't yer go upstairs an' get yer comics down, then the two of yer can sit quiet an' read. Anyway, it'll be time fer bed soon,' Lucy said, glancing quickly at Laura and raising her eyes to the ceiling.

Reg considered himself a bit too big to be packed off

to bed at such an unreasonable time and he skulked out of the scullery. Terry remained in the doorway, leaning against the jamb.

'When Mr Stebbin's finishes the fort can I 'ave Charlie in?' he asked. 'It's 'alf Charlie's.'

'Wait till it's ready an' then we'll see,' Laura told him.

' 'Ave yer seen Mr Stebbin's lately?' Lucy asked him.

'I went there terday, but Mr Stebbin's was out,' Terry replied. ' 'Is mum said the paint wasn't dry yet.'

'Yer don't want ter keep pesterin' the man,' Lucy said sharply. 'Besides, yer shouldn't go in there too much.'

'But you an' Aunt Laura said it was all right if I was careful,' Terry fretted.

'Yeah, but not too often. Now go up an' get yer comics or yer'll 'ave ter go ter bed early.'

Terry turned away and Laura smiled resignedly at Lucy as they heard the slow, protesting footsteps on the stairs. 'Dad does get on to those boys, an' they're no trouble really,' she remarked.

' 'E's gettin' really miserable lately,' Lucy replied, taking the last of the plates from her.

'When we've finished 'ere I'm gonna see if 'e wants ter go up the pub ternight,' Laura said.

'Are you gonna take 'im?' Lucy asked, surprised.

'Well, I wouldn't expect 'im ter go on 'is own,' Laura replied quickly. 'I just thought it might buck 'im up a bit. After all, 'e don't get out much.'

'I'd come wiv yer but I can't leave the boys,' Lucy said. 'Roy could go though, if 'e wants to.'

When Laura suggested a drink at the pub Albert felt pleased, but in keeping with his current mood he stroked his chin thoughtfully before he answered. 'I dunno. I need a shave,' he said finally.

'Well, that won't take yer five minutes,' Laura said.

'What about you, Roy? D'yer fancy a drink?'

'Not really, Laura,' he replied. 'I've got a bit of a fick 'ead from dinnertime. Yer could see if Lucy wants ter go, though.'

While Albert got to work on his two-day growth of beard Laura and Lucy retired to the upstairs bedroom to get ready.

'Yer can't go out wiv no lipstick on, Laura,' her sister chided her. 'Yer could do wiv a bit o' powder too. It'll take the paleness off. No, not those shoes, they're too low. Put those navy ones on, they'll go nice wiv yer dress, an' yer can borrer my navy coat. It'll look a treat.'

Laura was brushing out her long blonde locks, holding a hairslide in her teeth, when she caught sight of Lucy staring at her in the mirror. 'What's wrong?' she asked quickly.

Lucy shook her head slowly. 'D'yer know, if I didn't keep my eye on yer we'd go out lookin' like ole muvver Riley an' 'er daughter Kitty,' she said, smiling affectionately. 'It's Saturday night. Leave those slides out, fer Gawd's sake. Come 'ere, I'll fix yer 'air. Don't argue, gimme the brush.'

At ten minutes to eight they left the house. Albert looked spruce in his clean shirt and silk scarf, wearing his best blue serge suit, and his daughters walked on either side of him, each taking an arm. Lucy looked very pretty in her powder-blue two-piece suit and high-heeled shoes. She had used the curling tongs on her dark hair and it was shaped around her ears and neck. She carried a small clutch bag and wore a silk floral scarf knotted loosely around her throat. Laura was wearing the edge-to-edge coat in French navy that Lucy had lent her and a dusty pink dress, with its collar raised over the bandless neck of the coat. Her blonde hair was loosely curled and resting lightly on her shoulders. Lucy had taken pains to

176

apply subtle touches of make-up to good effect and Laura was pleased with the result.

Laura had already told Albert what Lizzie Cassidy had said about the Queens Arms and he was looking forward to a good old musical evening. Lucy had felt from the beginning that Laura was hoping to see Eddie there but she refrained from mentioning it. She was secretly worried about Roy and his attitude towards her. He had hardly spoken since he came back from his lunchtime drink and he seemed preoccupied.

Laura was feeling nervous. She had not gone into a pub to drink for quite some time, not since Victory night, she recalled. She tried not to think about Eddie. He might have decided not to go after all. She should have popped along and told Lizzie she intended taking her father out for a drink, but they had all been so long in getting ready. She blushed a little to remember how Eddie had flirted gently with her and how it had excited her, and privately she hoped he would be there.

Roy Grant leaned back in his armchair and brought his hands up to his neck, gently massaging the muscles beneath the base of his skull with his fingertips. The hangover he had inflicted on himself by drinking too much in the pub that lunchtime had started to ease and the pressure of his fingers felt good. He had needed to get out of the house, away from the noise of the kids, Albert's changing moods and Lucy's constant worried glances at him. It felt as though she was expecting him to die suddenly, or explode into some sort of frenzy. The only saving grace was Laura's attitude towards him. She did at least try to treat him as a normal person, someone who had come back home after long years away and needed some time to feel comfortable with everyone again. It had been a frightening experience for them all, he had to admit. The children were growing up and suddenly they were faced with their father coming back to them after almost five years, a father whom they could not even remember. It had been hard for Lucy too. She had waited so long and needed his love.

Roy changed his position in the chair and cupped his chin in his hand as he stared into the fire. It had been sad to see the change in Albert. He remembered his father-in-law as a strapping man and now he was just a shell of his former self, angry and resentful at his incapacity, snapping at the children. It was strange, he thought, but only Laura seemed not to have changed much. Lucy had told him how Laura had held them all together in times of crisis, and he remembered how she had been a cornerstone for her father after he lost his wife that first year of the war. That was the way Laura was, and he knew that he owed her a great deal.

As he sat alone in the parlour, the two boys asleep upstairs, Roy thought about Lucy. He had not been able to love her fully, but maybe when he got back to work it would be different. He would have a job to occupy his mind instead of just sitting round with too much time to think. These last few days had been very hard without the personal attention he had grown accustomed to from the medics. Now he had recovered, so they had told him, recovered enough to go home and make a new life for himself and his family, but the nightmares had returned and he was reliving them almost nightly.

He remembered the horror as though it were only yesterday. He was still weak from beriberi but had been sent out to work, and in the stifling heat he had dropped on to the length of track, ignoring the screams of the brutal guard who prodded him viciously and relentlessly with the butt of his rifle. He remembered rising slowly and grabbing his tormenter by the front of his uniform in utter despair, then being beaten mercilessly and dragged away into the bush. He recalled the feeling of knowing that it was the end, waiting for them to perform some sadistic torture that would rip out the last gasps of his life, but instead they slung him into the tiny tin hut. All day he squatted in the stifling heat without food or water, unable to sit upright, deafened by the guards beating on the hut periodically with their rifle butts. At sunset he was dragged from his tiny prison and left there in the dust for his comrades to carry him back to the makeshift sleeping quarters and clean him up. Three days he suffered the torture, and on the third night his guards left him in the hut.

In the quietness of the cosy room Roy jerked nervously and shivered. He remembered how he had not expected to survive the war and had hoped that Lucy would find a new man to take care of her and bring the children up in a loving home. The end of the war had come abruptly, however. The guards suddenly became sullen and uninterested in their prisoners, and it was not long before the teams arrived: army doctors and nurses, medicines and food, lorries to transport the survivors to airstrips and Dakota aircraft which ferried the pitiful-looking survivors of the Burma railway to specially prepared centres for recovery. He had been one of the lucky ones, and during the long months in India and Ceylon he thought of nothing else but his family. He recalled how they sat in groups and talked about going home, about their families and what they would find when they returned. The subject of infidelity did not get discussed but he knew that, like him, many of the survivors thought a great deal about how they would react and cope if they discovered that their wives had been unfaithful.

The fire was burning low and Roy added another few pieces of coal. They would all be in soon and no doubt feeling cold. He went out to the scullery and lit the gas under the kettle, leaning against the dresser and staring abstractedly into the roaring flame. He had not asked Lucy if she had been faithful, realising that she would certainly feel insulted and angry at the question, but she had not reassured him that she had been. Perhaps she felt that she did not need to. Maybe it was the way it should be. The past was over and irretrievable, and the future was still to come. It was only now that really mattered.

Chapter Seventeen

The Queens Arms had filled early on Saturday evening and when Albert Prior entered the public bar on the arm of his daughters he looked around quickly. 'Bloody 'ell, it's packed in 'ere. I can't stand all night,' he moaned.

He was soon reassured as Lizzie Cassidy hurried over. 'I'm really glad yer made it,' she said smiling broadly, casting a quick glance at Laura. 'Bring yer dad over 'ere, 'e can sit wiv us.'

Lizzie and her family had commandeered the far corner and they had spread themselves round two tables on the soft, upholstered seats. Albert sat down gratefully and Laura looked around at the family. There was no sign of Eddie and her heart sank.

Lucy had opened her bag to get out her purse but Lizzie put her hand on her arm. 'Sit yerself down, luv. Eddie's at the counter. What'll it be?'

Albert asked for a pint of bitter while Lucy and Laura both chose a light ale. Having dispatched Eric to the bar with the new orders, Lizzie fussed about making room for the two girls, and when they were both seated she took a deep breath. 'Right, now this is Albert who lives at number three, an' these are 'is two daughters, Lucy an' Laura,' she began, then she started pointing around the table. 'That ugly one is my Geoff, 'e's the eldest, an' the pretty one next to 'im is 'is wife, Mary. That's Steve an' 'is wife Connie, an' the ole sod comin' over wiv the drinks is Eric my 'usband. Yer've met Eddie already,' she concluded, smiling happily.

The piano player had taken his seat and began tinkling on the keys.

'Do eivver o' you gels sing?' Lizzie asked.

Laura and Lucy shook their heads vigorously.

'Anybody can get up an' sing 'ere, yer know,' Lizzie informed them.

'I used ter do a song at one time,' Albert said, sipping his beer.

Both his daughters looked horrified. 'I don't fink they'd go a lot on your sort o' songs, Dad,' Laura remarked.

'Let 'im 'ave a go if 'e wants to,' Lizzie said, chuckling.

Eddie came over with two light ales and placed them on the table in front of the two sisters, and as he caught Laura's eye he winked saucily. 'That one's fer services rendered,' he said.

Laura felt her face start to go red and she smiled shyly as Lizzie said quickly, 'Oi, Eddie, be'ave yerself, yer'll embarrass the gel.'

Eddie sat down next to Laura and grinned. 'No, seriously, Laura came ter my rescue,' he said. 'She bandaged my finger up the ovver evenin' when I scraped it on a piece o' metal.'

Geoff turned to Steve. 'Pity it wasn't 'is tongue,' he grumbled.

'Take no notice,' Lizzie said, leaning towards the two young women. 'They're like this all the time.'

The piano player struck up with 'Some of these Days' and a large middle-aged woman stepped up on to a raised area in the far corner of the bar and sang lustily into a microphone which she held close to her lips. The customers tapped their feet and nodded their heads in time to the piano and some joined in with the words. Loud applause greeted the end of the song and there was a short pause in the revelries while the piano player picked up his refilled glass of ale and took a large swig.

Albert had a happy look on his face as he turned to Eric Cassidy. 'I ain't bin out fer ages,' he said. 'It makes a nice change, 'specially 'earin' some o' those ole songs.'

Lucy had struck up a conversation with Steve's wife Connie while Laura sat quietly listening to Lizzie and Mary discussing the film *State Fair* that was currently running at the Old Kent Road picture house.

'Is this yer first time 'ere?' Eddie asked suddenly.

Laura nodded. 'It seems a lively pub,' she replied, feeling nervous with Eddie so close to her.

'Just wait till Geoff gets up,' he grinned. ' 'E usually empties the place.'

Laura smiled, noticing how Eddie's lips moved expressively and how his eyes seemed to twinkle humorously. 'Do you ever get up an' sing?' she asked.

Eddie shook his head. 'I did once, but they weren't very impressed,' he replied, smiling.

Eric's loud voice cut across their conversation as he started to tell Albert about the latest development on the Tooley Street quayside. 'Nearly every time the *Bolsover* berths at Mark Brown's Wharf there's anovver poor sod 'idin' in the 'old,' he was saying. 'It's the Batavier Line ship from Poland. It must be terrible out there fer the poor bleeders ter take a chance like they do. They're 'alf starved an' terrified when our stevedores find 'em stuck be'ind the cargoes. What we do is tell 'em ter stay put until we're sure there's nobody clockin' us, then we get 'em on the crane wiv the load, an' up they go.'

'I 'eard that if they get discovered they're put in irons until the ship sails, then they're shot an' chucked overboard on the way 'ome,' Steve cut in.

'I shouldn't be at all surprised,' Eric replied.

Mary was curious as usual. 'What 'appens to 'em when yer land 'em on the quayside?' she asked.

'Well, first of all they're given a meal an' a drink, then the police are called. They take 'em ter the immigration people,' Eric explained. 'Mostly they're allowed ter stay but some get sent back. They could be Russian spies, yer see.'

'What a depressin' subject ter get on to on a Saturday night out,' Lizzie declared loudly. 'Why don't yer fink o' somefing 'appier ter talk about?'

'Tell 'em about ole Bonky Masefield, Dad,' Geoff prompted.

Eric's face lit up and he was about to begin his saga when the compere picked up the microphone.

'Now for your pleasure, ladies an' gentlemen, we've got a renderin' from Eric Cassidy.'

Lizzie turned to Laura as a roar of encouragement went up. ' 'E does this song every time we come up 'ere an' they still stand fer it,' she grinned.

Eric took the microphone in one hand and slipped the thumb of his other hand underneath his coat lapel in a typical costermonger pose. The piano struck up and Eric began his Cockney ditty.

'No more up an' down the Covent Garden Market,
'Umpin' all the sacks o' spuds abaht.
No more corduroys an' 'obnail boots,
When I takes me missus aht.
I gave up all me coster pals,
An' I frowed away the end o' my cigar.
An' when I'm out a-strollin',
The gels, they all declare,
" 'Ere comes the man who don't know who 'e are." '

Eric got his usual enthusiastic round of applause and he walked back to the family beaming happily.

Eddie smiled at Laura and then his face became serious. 'Muvver said she told yer about this pub but I never thought yer'd make it ternight. I'm really glad yer did,' he said quietly.

'I'm glad too,' Laura replied, her blue eyes matching his gaze. 'It's bin so long since I've 'ad a night out.'

'Maybe you should do it more often,' he said, still looking at her.

Laura merely pursed her lips and nodded and Eddie leaned towards her and gently touched her forearm. 'I'd like ter take yer out one evenin',' he said softly.

'That'd be nice,' Laura replied, feeling suddenly brave.

Eddie caught sight of Geoff and Steve looking over and he drew his hand away from her self-consciously. 'I tell yer what,' he said. ' 'Ave yer ever bin dog-racin'?'

Laura shook her head.

'I fink yer'd like it,' he went on. 'We could go ter New Cross an' then go fer a meal after. Maybe we could round it off wiv a drink.'

Laura felt a strange sensation thrilling through her. It had been so long since she had spent time in a man's company, albeit with his family, and it was nice. Eddie was a handsome young man with a reckless smile that made her legs feel weak. It was easy to talk to him and he was so attentive. His dark eyes seemed to look right into her mind and his manner was pleasingly gentle, though there was a confidence about him that made her feel safe and secure. She had never experienced those feelings before, not even with Ralph, and she wanted the night to go on forever.

Geoff bought a round of drinks and the two families continued to chat together genially. A smoke haze hung in the air and the buzz of conversation and occasional raucous laughter got louder as the night wore on.

Albert slipped his hand into his waistcoat pocket and took out a pound note which he passed over to Eric, despite the profuse objections. 'I'm gettin' this drink,' he declared.

It was Geoff's turn to sing a song and Lizzie turned to Laura as her son confidently strode up to the piano. ' 'E does this one well,' she said, 'but it makes me wanna cry every time 'e sings it.'

As the pianist swept his fingers over the keys in the introductory few bars, Geoff winked over at his mother.

> 'One bright an' shinin' light,
> That taught me wrong from right,
> I found in my mother's eyes.'

Lizzie looked sad as her eldest son sang the words loudly and clearly.

> 'Just like a wanderin' sparrow
> One lonely soul,
> I'll walk the straight an' narrow,
> To reach my goal.
> God's gift sent from above,
> A real unselfish love,
> I found in my mother's eyes.'

Lizzie blew hard into her handkerchief as the applause rang out. 'I'll bloody well murder that boy,' she growled. ' 'E knows 'ow it affects me.'

Laura felt strangely moved as she watched Geoff walking back to the table, being patted on the back and congratulated by his friends. It was plain to see that the Cassidys were a close, loving family. If one of them was cut then they all bled, as the saying went. The banter and leg-pulling were just rough ways of showing each other that they cared, there was no animosity. It was fun to be with them, and Laura smiled as Eddie patted his mother's hand.

The night seemed to have flown, Laura thought, as the 'last orders' bell sounded. Lucy was laughing constantly with Connie and Mary, and Albert was getting steadily intoxicated. Suddenly Eric caught the eye of the compere, who came over to him. A few whispered words were exchanged and then Eric got up and helped Albert out of his seat. The Prior girls looked at each other in dismay as the compere led Albert on to the raised dais.

'Ladies an' gentlemen, Albert's gonna sing a little ditty entitled "The Bobby's Song".'

To shouts of encouragement Albert grabbed the microphone and took a deep breath.

'I'm a bobby an' I know my beat,
You can tumble by my saucy looks.
I go moochin' roun' the 'ouses,
Dustin' the little boys' best blue trousers.
Last night I was on my beat,
An' I saw two chaps, what'o.
'Avin' a rare ole chim-chase there,
Because they did not know.
I was there a-watchin' 'em,
I was there a-watchin' 'em.
While they was arguin' I got my staff.
I jobbed 'em in the tiddly an' I made 'em laugh.
Oh good gracious, it was a pantomime.
Eye-ty idly-idly, Eye-ty idly-idly,
I's a-watchin' all the time.'

Loud applause greeted the end of the song and Albert returned to his seat with the help of Eric Cassidy, a wide grin on his flushed face.

The bar bell was finally rung for the last time and Eddie surreptitiously put his hand over Laura's. 'Is that a date then, New Cross, Tuesday night?' he asked.

Laura met his eyes and nodded. 'I'd love to,' she said.

The two families walked home together along the quiet Tower Bridge Road. The night had got chilly but Laura was glowing inside as she held on to her father with Lucy on his other side. Eddie was walking next to her, chatting cheerfully, while the two elder Cassidy brothers took their mother's arms and Eric followed in their wake between Connie and Mary.

Eddie turned up the collar of his suit coat and slipped his hands into his trouser pockets. 'Well, we missed out on Farvver's saga about Bonky Masefield,' he said, 'but yer'll most likely 'ear it before long, that's if yer come up the Queens Arms again,' he added quickly.

Laura smiled. 'I'm lookin' forward ter the story,' she replied, smiling. 'Is it naughty?'

Eddie shrugged his shoulders. 'I'll let yer decide fer yerself,' he said, a smile playing around the corners of his mouth.

The party turned into Weston Street and by the time they reached Pedlar's Row Albert was starting to sag, although he was still chattering on about the way his song had been received. At the door of number three, Laura turned to give Eddie a smile, and he winked back.

'I'll call fer yer about seven, if that's okay,' he said. 'We'll catch the first race then.'

'I'll be ready,' Laura replied. 'Good night, Eddie, it's bin really nice.'

Chief Inspector Ben Walsh had gone into his office early on Saturday morning, and when his assistant looked in just after nine o'clock he threw a sheet of paper across the desk. 'Take a dekko at that report from the Yard,' he said.

Ashley studied the communication for a few seconds and then shook his head slowly. 'Well, that doesn't help us any,' he replied, looking downcast.

The inspector smiled briefly. 'Okay, so there were no releases of offenders convicted of forgery or counterfeiting during the past six months and there are none pending,' he said, 'but let's not get too disappointed. Sit down for a minute, Gordon, and let's shuffle this business around a bit. As a matter of fact I came in the office early this morning to catch up with the paperwork, as it's been piling up since I got this bee in my bonnet about Archie Westlake. Amongst it all there was the usual stuff from the Probation Office, including the update list of parolees coming back on the manor. As you know, it has the prisoners' details on it, addresses and occupations etcetera. Well, I've been through the update list and the back lists as well, and I can't find any likely candidate. None of those listed have got the expertise to cut printing plates. So to all intents and purposes we've drawn a blank.'

Ashley pulled a face. 'What do we do then, guv, leave it all on file?'

Chief Inspector Walsh leaned back in his chair and stroked his chin thoughtfully for a few moments, then he looked up at the sergeant, his eyes narrowing. 'I've still got this gut feeling that we're on the right track, Gordon, so how do we progress?' he asked him.

'Well, it'd take us a month of Sundays to get probation reports from all twenty-three divisions, then there's the time we'd need to sift through them all,' Ashley replied, 'and that's assuming that our man is coming out of prison. Westlake could be waiting for someone to arrive from another part of the country, and it could be someone who's clean anyway.'

Walsh nodded. 'You're right, of course, but I feel we should try one other area while we're still rolling. I'm thinking about the East End. Whitechapel and Stepney, to be precise.'

Ashley looked uncertainly at the inspector. 'I don't follow you,' he said.

Walsh smiled kindly. 'I've not forgotten the old adage, east London, south London, never the twain shall meet, but there's always exceptions to the rule,' he said with a raise of the eyebrows. 'Let me refresh your memory. Remember when we broke up that black-market set-up and grabbed those piles of ration books and petrol coupons?'

Ashley's face relaxed into a smile. 'Yeah, I remember. The Yard report said that the printing could well have been done in the East End. The forensic tests showed that our haul matched perfectly with exhibits they were holding from a police raid on a printing firm in Stepney.'

Walsh grinned. 'You got it. Now I don't know the details of the raid, or who they nicked, but I do remember from the report that it took place in nineteen forty-one or forty-two, and I'm sure it was Leman Street Police Station that was involved. As it happens I know the guv'nor there. I can get the reports from their files as well as their probation lists without much trouble. Okay, I know it's still a long shot. If the person who made the plates was nicked he would have got a lengthy sentence and he won't be getting out yet awhile, but he might have gone down at any time on some lesser charge. It's all in the lap of the gods, but at least we'll be doing something, instead of sitting on our backsides until it's too late.'

Sergeant Ashley nodded enthusiastically. 'I've always felt that Archie Westlake was the big one behind that black-market business, but we didn't have anywhere near enough evidence to charge him,' he said.

'I've a feeling Archie Westlake might be getting just a little too cocksure,' Walsh remarked. 'He might just overstep himself this time. Let's hope we can nail him to the dock.'

Chapter Eighteen

Early on Monday morning Roy Grant left the house and walked to the Trocette picture palace, where he caught a number 42 bus to Aldgate and then took the number 8 to Bethnal Green in London's East End. It was there, the centre of the furniture trade, that Roy had learnt his craft as a young apprentice. He was a skilled cabinet-maker and French polisher, and he was going back to his old firm, Dennis Bromfield & Sons.

As he stepped down from the bus and walked the short distance along the Bethnal Green Road Roy was feeling queasy with anticipation. He was keen to get back to work once more and meet his new workmates, and a few of the old crowd, if any of them were still employed there. He knew that starting work as soon as possible was the only way he would be able to get back to normality, and the only answer to his problems. Unless he sorted himself out he was surely going to lose Lucy. She had turned to him for love and he had failed her. His efforts to show her how much he still loved her and had missed her had been pathetic, he knew only too well. She had been very patient and understanding, but it could not go on for much longer. If only he could bury those terrible memories which rose up again and again like a monster to overwhelm him.

Roy glanced at his wristwatch and saw that it was twenty minutes to eight. He slowed his pace, not wanting to seem over-keen to the rest of the workforce. Lucy would be thinking about him this morning, he imagined. She had kissed him goodbye as he was leaving and he had held her close, but she would be thinking about the night before. He had turned to her in bed when she snuggled close and he had initiated the first gestures of lovemaking. His kisses had aroused her and she seemed frantic for him to love her fully. He had tried so hard to relax and forget all the bad memories of his captivity, but they had rushed into his mind just as they always did. He had broken out in a cold sweat and then the drumming in his head had started. Why? What was it inside him that provoked those cruel attacks at such intimate moments?

Roy walked through the gates of Dennis Bromfield & Sons and entered the workshop. Men were gathering around the time clock and he stood back, taking in the scene and familiarising himself with the factory once more. He could smell casein glue, stain, varnish and sawdust, and he glanced along the alleyways at the milling machines, the saw benches and veneer presses, and saw the large routers and the stack of drying timbers and plyboards. It was like coming home again, he felt, emotion welling up within him, squeezing at his throat and gripping his stomach like a vice.

On Monday evening when Wally Stebbings walked into the Row he saw the two young lads sitting in the doorway of number three but they appeared not to have noticed him. He walked past them, glancing over casually to see if they would say hello, but they seemed to be preoccupied.

Charlie had seen Wally before he turned into the paved area. 'I'm s'posed ter be ill, Tel,' he whispered.

Terry looked down at his feet. 'Pretend we ain't seen 'im,' he whispered back. 'When I go an' see 'im I'll tell 'im yer can't come out 'cos yer still not prop'ly better.'

Charlie held his head low until Wally had passed, then he smiled at Terry. 'I've bin sortin' out all my soldiers. I got ten Scotch 'Ighlanders,' he told him.

'They're no good fer a fort,' Terry replied. 'They're layin'-down soldiers. Yer gotta 'ave standin'-up soldiers fer a fort.'

' 'Ow many 'ave you got?' Charlie asked.

'I've got six, an' a few wiv no 'eads on,' Terry answered.

'Yer can stick matchsticks in 'em ter keep their 'eads on,' Charlie informed him.

'Yeah, if yer got the 'eads, but I ain't,' Terry said sadly.

Charlie was quiet for a few moments, then suddenly his face brightened. 'I got a good idea,' he said. 'We could play cards wiv those kids in the Buildin's, but instead o' playin' fer cigarette cards we could play fer soldiers.'

Terry grinned broadly. 'We'll win fousands o' soldiers,' he replied, having been let into the secret of Charlie's specially prepared deck of cards.

Queenie Bromley came to the door. 'Yer tea's ready, Charlie,' she called out, 'an' yer better say good night ter Terry. Yer can't come out any more ternight.'

Charlie mumbled under his breath as he stood up. 'Don't ferget ter see about the fort, Tel,' he reminded his friend. 'We'll play them kids at cards after school termorrer.'

A few minutes later Terry walked along to the last house in the Row and knocked on the door. ' 'Ello, Mr Stebbin's. I've come ter see if the fort's ready yet,' he said hesitantly.

Wally smiled at him and stepped back. 'C'mon in,' he replied. 'I've just had a look at it and the paint's dry. I put the last touches to it last night.'

Terry followed Wally into the scullery and his eyes

nearly popped at what he saw. The fort was indeed ready. It had been painted in a sand-coloured shade with thin lines to represent the stone blocks of the walls and tower. The wall ladder had been painted black and Wally had fixed a small paper flag on the flagpole and painted it in stripes of blue, white and red to make a Tricolour.

'You can take it with you if you like,' Wally said, smiling.

'Cor! It's the best fort I've ever seen,' Terry gasped. 'Charlie an' me will never let anybody touch it 'cept us.'

' 'Ow is Charlie?' Wally asked.

' 'E's not very well so 'e can't come ter see yer,' Terry said quickly. ' 'Is mum said 'e mustn't go out yet, only ter my door.'

'Oh, I see,' Wally replied. 'Well, there you are. If you take hold of it I'll go in front and open the door.'

Terry carried the fort home and proudly set it down on the table in the parlour. 'That's just like a real Foreign Legion fort, Aunt Laura,' he said, his eyes shining. 'Mr Stebbin's copied it from pictures in books.'

Laura gazed down at the model with her arms akimbo. 'It's really nice,' she enthused. 'Look at this, Dad.'

Albert stood up and studied it for a few moments. 'It's a clever bit o' work,' he said, nodding. 'Yer better take it up ter yer room in case it gets damaged.'

'Wait till Dad sees it,' Terry said as he gingerly took hold of the fort and carried it out of the room.

Laura turned to her father. 'Nobody's gonna convince me that there's any 'arm in Wally Stebbin's when 'e can make somefing as nice as that fer two little lads,' she said with passion.

Albert nodded. 'Trouble is, gel, people tend ter see what they want ter see. I've noticed the bloke walkin' past 'ere wiv 'is 'ands be'ind 'is back, mumblin' to 'imself on occasions. It's a bloody shame.'

'It's just nerves,' Laura answered. 'I've noticed 'im too, an' ovver days 'e seems quite normal.' She shook her head sadly. 'Well, I'm gonna make a point o' talkin' to 'im next time I see 'im, if only ter fank 'im fer makin' the fort,' she said firmly. 'Now get yer bits an' pieces off the table, I'll 'ave Roy an' Lucy in soon fer their tea.'

Queenie Bromley was standing in the scullery frying a large saucepan of chips, and George was cutting up a loaf of bread, his shirtsleeves rolled up over his elbows and his thinning grey hair tousled from sleeping in the armchair.

'There's a ship docked in Wilson's Wharf terday. I should get a call-on in the mornin',' he said, in an effort to pacify Queenie.

'About bloody time. Yer done bugger all fer the past two weeks,' she moaned.

George turned his large brown eyes dolefully in her direction. 'It's a food ship an' they like a quick turn-round,' he went on. 'I expect it'll be a bonus job.'

'Yer'll 'ave ter get yerself goin' if it's a bonus job,' she replied sharply, 'or they'll leave yer standin' on the cobbles.'

George felt peeved as he began spreading margarine on the thick slices of bread. 'I can still do me share,' he retorted. 'Trouble is, the young blokes back from the army get picked first every time. Us older ones 'ave ter wait most o' the time until there's extra men wanted.'

'Can't yer do anyfing about it?' Queenie asked, turning the chips over with a big spoon.

'Not really. It's the way the system works,' he answered. 'Mind yer, there'll be work all this week fer everybody. The *Bolsover*'s docked at Mark Brown's Wharf as well.'

Queenie suddenly regretted her cutting remarks as she looked at her ageing husband. He had been a good provider over the years, and it was only lately that he had started to slacken. The hard life on the quayside, working in all weathers, had taken its toll, and he was looking older than his years. She pulled another pan towards her and started breaking eggs into the hot fat. 'Are yer goin' out ternight?' she asked him casually.

George shook his head. 'I can't, luv, I'm skint,' he replied.

'The tallyman ain't bin round this week, yer can borrer ten bob from the tin, if yer like,' she told him, easing back as the eggs spat in the pan.

George's eyes brightened. 'Fanks, luv. I'll be able ter put it back on Friday.'

The boys were hovering round. 'Is tea nearly ready, Mum?' Fred asked.

Queenie turned to see her fair-haired son standing in the doorway with his hands in his trouser pockets. 'I'm waitin' on the chips. Go in an' sit down,' she told him.

Billy was never far away from his older brother. 'Don't ferget ter turn my egg over, Mum,' he called out over Fred's shoulder.

'Yer tell me that every time, now go in an' sit down,' she ordered.

Charlie came out to the scullery and stood for a few moments watching his mother as she splashed fat over the sizzling eggs. 'Terry Prior's gonna get our fort if it's ready,' he said suddenly.

'Oh yeah?' Queenie replied.

'I could 'ave gone wiv 'im, if yer'd let me,' the young lad moaned.

'Yer know what I told yer, so don't keep on about it,' she snapped. 'It's not right fer young boys ter go in men's 'ouses, 'specially Wally Stebbin's' 'ouse.'

'Terry can go in there, 'cos 'is mum said 'e could,' Charlie persisted.

'I don't care what Terry's mum said. If she don't care

about 'im, that's 'er lookout,' Queenie shouted. 'Now that's enough. Get in there an' sit down at the table, I'm bringin' yer tea in.'

George had been careful not to get involved and he gave his sons a warning glance as he put the plate of sliced bread down in the centre of the table. 'Now be'ave yerselves round the table,' he said quietly, then he spotted the vacant place. 'Fred, go up an' tell Frankie 'is tea's ready.'

Fred left the table and shouted up to his younger brother. There was no answer so he ran up the stairs quickly, and in a few moments came back into the room. 'Dad, Frankie's not there,' he said.

George looked around at his sons. 'Where's 'e gone?'

Charlie looked up. ' 'E came in wiv me from school an' then 'is mate knocked fer 'im,' he replied.

George puffed loudly. 'I'll tan 'is arse fer 'im. 'E knows what time tea is,' he growled.

Queenie came in with the plates of food. 'Where's Frankie?' she asked.

'The little sod's not come in yet,' George told her.

'Well, you lot eat yer tea, I'll go an' look fer 'im,' she said, reaching for her coat behind the parlour door.

'I'll go,' George volunteered, but Queenie flapped her hand at him to sit down.

'You keep yer eye on them, I'll 'ave my tea later,' she said quickly.

' 'E went round the Buildin's wiv Stanley Felstead,' Fred said, reaching for a slice of bread.

Queenie left the Row and walked quickly along Weston Street. A winter's gloom was settling in as she turned into Farrow Street and entered Brady Buildings, a dingy tenement block that was long overdue to be pulled down. Queenie knew Mrs Felstead quite well and Frankie often went to her house after school to play with Stanley. She was puffing loudly as she reached the fourth floor and knocked on the door.

'Is my Frankie 'ere, Bet?' she enquired.

'No, luv. 'E left 'ere about five o'clock,' Mrs Felstead told her.

Queenie felt a sudden knotting in her stomach and she hurried down the stairs, vowing to give Frankie a good hiding when she did find him.

Weston Street was full of homeward-bound factory workers as Queenie hurried back to Pedlar's Row, willing her youngest boy to be there when she arrived. John Bannerman, the bookie's runner, was standing on the corner. ' 'Ave yer seen my Frankie come by?' she asked him breathlessly.

John shook his head. 'I shouldn't worry, 'e'll be in soon, yer know what kids are,' he replied, trying to be helpful.

Queenie hurried into her house. 'Is 'e in?'

George was looking worried as he shook his head. 'You sit down an' 'ave yer tea. I'll go an' find the little bleeder,' he said.

' 'Ow can I eat me tea while Frankie's gone missin'?' she replied.

George squeezed her arm gently. 'Sit down, luv, an' get yer breath. Fred, get yer muvver a cup o' tea. I'm goin' ter look fer 'im.'

Queenie sat sipping her tea, the knot in her stomach tightening in pain as she thought of all the mishaps that could befall a small lad. He might have been taken away by someone, or maybe he had fallen in the Thames, she brooded. Perhaps he had been playing on the bomb sites and had an accident. He might be lying dead somewhere this very minute, she told herself, tears forming in her anxious eyes.

It had seemed like an eternity, but the clock told Queenie that her husband had only been gone for an hour when she heard his footsteps in the Row. George walked in, looking very worried. 'I can't find 'im anywhere,' he said, standing in the middle of the room.

'I'm goin' ter the police,' Queenie announced, getting up quickly.

'I've already called in at Tower Bridge nick,' he told her.

Darkness had settled down over the Bermondsey back streets as George renewed his hunt for his youngest son. He scoured the immediate area again, picking his way over the rubble-strewn bomb site in Cooper Street, calling out his son's name. As he retraced his steps he bumped into Len Carmichael coming home from his shift at the brewery.

'Young Frankie's gorn missin', Len,' he said as he caught his breath. ' 'E didn't come 'ome fer 'is tea. Gawd knows what's 'appened to 'im.'

Len patted his neighbour's back encouragingly. 'I'll just pop in ter let Elsie know then I'll 'elp yer look,' he told him.

The two men walked back to Pedlar's Row and George waited while Len went into his house. In two minutes he came out carrying a large torch. 'We might need this,' he said. 'Now where d'yer wanna try next?'

Elsie Carmichael had never liked her next-door neighbour and she avoided Queenie as much as possible, but as she sat sipping her tea she imagined what she must be going through. Suddenly she put down her teacup and stood up, briefly patting at her hair as she studied her reflection in the mantelshelf mirror before slipping on her coat.

'My Len told me about your boy, Queenie, an' I jus' wanna say, if there's anyfing I can do . . . ' she said hesitantly.

Normally Queenie would have given her short shrift but she was near to tears and feeling sick to her stomach. She was convinced that something terrible had happened to Frankie and any company was welcome. 'Come in, gel, I've just made a pot o' tea,' she said.

Hours earlier Frankie Bromley had left the Buildings and walked out into Weston Street where he saw the Chandler brothers coming towards him. Like Frankie, Jimmy Chandler was a nine-year-old, and always bragging about the tricks he and his older brother Peter got up to.

'We're goin' down Shad Thames,' Jimmy announced. 'We're gonna get nuts an' coconuts out o' the barges.'

Frankie was impressed. Being the youngest in his family and forbidden to do anything dangerous or exciting, he often felt left out. It would be good to go home with nuts and coconut pieces and tell his older brothers that he had been on the barges. Tea would be ages yet, he thought. There was plenty of time to go to Shad Thames. 'Can I come?' he asked.

Peter Chandler thought for a moment. 'If yer good at climbin',' he said.

'Frankie's a good climber,' Jimmy said in support.

'All right then,' Peter replied. 'Yer gotta watch fer the rats though. We chuck bricks at 'em ter scare 'em away, then we climb down the rope.'

Frankie did not quite understand what it all meant but it sounded very exciting and he nodded his head enthusiastically.

It took the three boys only fifteen minutes to reach the quiet riverside lane lying in the shadow of Tower Bridge. Frankie could smell the spices and hear the lap of the turning tide as they clambered down the slippery stone steps beside Butler's Wharf. To their right was an empty barge moored against the pilings and Jimmy pointed. 'That's the one,' he said.

The river was beginning to rise and the muddy water was already lapping around the keel of the barge. That night when it was afloat it would be taken out to midstream by a tug, ready for its return trip to Tilbury, but the three lads were in blithe ignorance of the lightermen's plans as they began their dangerous manoeuvre, edging along the thick, greasy piling that protected the brickwork of the wharf. They eased themselves along slowly, Frankie beginning to feel very frightened but desperate not to show it, and in a short time they were directly over the barge and about five feet above the narrow decking which skirted the cargo area. Frankie's eyes widened as he saw the coconut-strewn planking at the base of the hold. Peter leapt down and steadied himself on the walkway and his younger brother Jimmy followed him. Frankie looked down at the two brothers and hesitated. If he missed the decking he would fall between the barge and the wharf into the rapidly rising tide. He took a deep breath and jumped, landing perilously near to the edge, but Peter grabbed his coat and steadied him.

'Right then, let's get the rope,' Peter said, hurrying around the walkway. Jimmy and Frankie helped him to uncoil the length of hawser and fix the eyelet over the mooring cleat. Peter kicked the jumble of rope into the hold. 'It's easy ter slide down, but can yer climb up it?' he asked, looking at Frankie.

The young lad nodded, although he was feeling more than a little frightened.

Peter led the way down and Jimmy followed. Frankie eased his body over the decking and grasped the rope. Using his feet to slow his descent he found it was easy, and at the bottom he stood grinning at the brothers.

'Right, let's get the big pieces o' coconut,' Peter said, taking a folded sack from under his jersey. 'Leave all the tiddly bits. It's a good job there's no rats in this barge.'

The three lads set about collecting the coconut pieces and soon the sack was full. Peter dragged it to the bottom of the rope and then climbed up with ease. Once at the top he pulled out a ball of twine from his trouser pocket and holding on to one end let it drop into the hold. 'Tie it tight,' he called out.

Jimmy tied the end of the string on to the sack and his older brother hauled it out of the hold.

'C'mon, Frankie, let's go,' Jimmy said, taking hold of the rope.

Frankie watched his friend climb it confidently. It looked a very long way up and he chewed his lip nervously. As Jimmy pulled himself on to the decking Frankie heard a shout and saw the two brothers disappear from sight. There were hurried footsteps and more shouting, then it suddenly became quiet. Frankie stood in the shadows of the hold for some time, listening to the lapping water and feeling the movement of the barge. It remained quiet and he finally decided to make the ascent. He grabbed at the rope and started to climb up. He found it difficult and painful, and before he had gone halfway up his arms shook and his strength left him. He felt his grip slipping and he slid down the rope and landed in a heap. For a time he sat steeling himself for a second attempt, and then taking a deep breath he tried again. He got less than halfway this time before he slid down to the bottom once more, his hands rope-burnt. Frankie looked up at the evening sky and rubbed the tears from his eyes. It would be dark soon and he would have to stay here all night, he realised. He felt hungry and thirsty and very frightened, not least at what his mother would do to him when he eventually got home, if he ever did.

The tug skipper swung hard on the wheel and let the craft drift on the running tide until it bumped gently against the empty barge. A lighterman leapt across from the tug and caught the hawser thrown by his colleague.

Once he had secured it to the barge he prepared to jump back aboard the tug when he suddenly spotted the length of rope trailing down into the hold.

'Oi, Geoff, somebody's bin down 'ere,' he called out.

Geoff Cassidy joined him on the barge and the two peered down into the darkness of the hold.

The tug skipper was becoming impatient. 'C'mon, lads, the tide's runnin' fast,' he called out.

Geoff cupped his hands. 'Throw us a torch,' he bellowed.

Frankie blinked and covered his eyes as the sharp beam picked him out, and he moved out of the shadows. Geoff shinned down the rope and took him by the shoulders. 'Yer muvver's gonna 'ave a few words wiv you, me lad,' he said, softening his voice as he saw the boy's tear-streaked face. 'Where d'yer live?'

'Pedlar's Row,' Frankie said, trying to look brave.

'Well, I'll go ter the foot of our stairs,' Geoff said, grinning and scratching the back of his head. 'Are you Queenie Bromley's boy?'

Frankie nodded. 'I couldn't climb up the rope,' he said quietly.

In no time at all the young lad was hoisted out of the hold and put into the cabin of the tug. 'I'll whistle fer the river police,' the skipper said, eyeing Frankie coldly.

Geoff sidled up to the skipper. 'Let it go, Bert,' he said conspiratorially 'Wasn't you ever 'is age?'

The skipper looked hard at Geoff, then his face broke into a smile.

'What d'yer want me ter do wiv 'im, throw 'im overboard?'

'Drop us at Cherry Garden Steps. I can take 'im 'ome by tram,' Geoff replied.

Chapter Nineteen

Laura tried to stay calm as she sat in front of the dressing-table mirror in the front bedroom. It had been a mad rush all day. First Lucy had been late home from work, and the simple dinner of sausages, peas and mash seemed to take ages to prepare. It was after six o'clock when Roy got in and by the time the meal was over and the table cleared it was almost time for Eddie to call. Laura had put a match to the copper earlier that day and there had been plenty of hot water for her strip-down wash before the meal, but she was interrupted constantly. The boys were in and out, and Albert seemed to be forever calling for her with some request, though Lucy had helped by doing the washing-up. Now as Laura tried to catch her breath she felt nervous. Her hair was a mess and Lucy wasn't making things any easier by sitting on the edge of the bed and going on about work and Roy's apparent unwillingness to talk about how he was settling in at his job.

'I might just as well not be 'ere,' she groaned. 'Last night was the same. All I got out of 'im was, "It's all right. I'll soon settle in." What sort of an answer is that? I was worried about 'im all day an' then 'e just ignores me. At least 'e could tell me about what 'e's doin' an' 'ow 'e's gettin' on wiv the ovver fellas. I dunno, I'm sure I don't.'

Laura tried to hide her irritation as she brushed out

her hair vigorously, but when she finally slipped on her mustard-coloured coat and glanced in the mirror to adjust her silk scarf Lucy looked at her critically and said, 'Yer not goin' out in them brown shoes, are yer? Yer black ones look much better.'

Laura gritted her teeth as she delved into the bottom of the large wardrobe she shared with Lucy and fished out the black shoes.

'I dunno though. Those brown ones do look better, come ter fink of it. They are dark.'

Laura sighed deeply. 'Are yer sure? Are yer quite sure?' she said sarcastically.

Lucy nodded, ignoring her older sister's exasperation. 'If yer go out lookin' anyfing but yer best it tends ter knock yer confidence. That's what I feel anyway,' she went on. 'You've got a good figure an' yer can carry clothes well, but yer gotta get more colour-conscious.'

Laura smiled at Lucy despite herself. Eddie would be knocking at any minute and she did want to look her best. Besides, it wouldn't be very good if she was having a blazing row with her younger sister when he called.

Lucy got up from the bed and delved into the dressing-table drawer. ' 'Ere, sis, let's give yer a squirt o' this,' she said, taking the top off a tiny bottle of perfume. 'It's the real stuff.'

Laura held out her arm and when Lucy had applied a tiny spray she rubbed her wrists together and dabbed them against her ears. 'It smells really nice,' she said.

Lucy smiled slyly. 'That should send yer young man wild.'

Laura tried to look shocked but Lucy was not fooled and she suddenly reached out and pulled her older sister to her. 'I really 'ope it goes well,' she said warmly. 'I'm so pleased fer yer.'

A loud knock startled Laura and she smiled affectionately at Lucy before hurrying down the stairs.

Eddie was wearing a navy blue overcoat with the collar turned up, over a grey suit. His shoes were highly polished, his blue shirt looked immaculate and he had put on a plain silver tie. His dark wavy hair was well groomed and combed back, covering the tips of his ears.

'Yer look very nice,' he said, smiling at Laura.

'Yer look very smart yerself,' she replied as she stepped out of her house.

As they turned into Weston Street Eddie held out his arm and Laura took it, feeling slightly uncomfortable at first but soon relaxing. He had a way of making her feel at ease and his chat warmed her to him.

'If we walk ter the Bricklayer's Arms we can get any tram,' he told her.

The winter night was cold, with a threat of fog. Streetlamps glowed brightly, and as they walked along, Laura could smell the distinctive aroma of new leather. She gave Eddie a shy glance and noticed that she came just above his shoulder in her high-heeled shoes. He looked broad-shouldered in his overcoat and he held himself very erect.

'D'yer go ter the dogs often?' she asked.

'Just now an' then,' he replied, smiling. 'Mainly when I get a good tip. A pal o' mine races dogs. There's one of 'is runnin' at New Cross ternight.'

They soon reached the Bricklayer's Arms junction and a tram came along almost immediately. Laura noticed how strong his arm was as he helped her aboard, and when they were seated on the lower deck he turned and smiled at her, revealing his white teeth. 'D'yer spend all day at 'ome wiv yer farvver?' he asked.

'No, I've got a cleanin' job at the Sultan,' she told him. 'It's just two hours a mornin' but it 'elps out. My sister Lucy works full time, an' I look after 'er two children till she gets 'ome.'

'It must be 'ard,' Eddie replied.

The conductor was standing beside them, holding out his hand and looking bored, and Eddie quickly fished down into his overcoat pocket. 'Sorry, pal, I didn't know we 'ad ter pay,' he said, smiling. 'Two threes, please.'

The joke was lost on the conductor as he flicked two tickets from a clip and slipped them into the ticket punch before handing them over.

Eddie turned to Laura and saw the humorous expression on her face. 'I wanted ter be a tram conductor when I was a kid,' he said, smiling back at her. 'It was the ticket punch that got me, but then I s'pose most young lads 'ave the same idea.'

' 'Ow did yer come ter work in the docks?' Laura asked.

'It's a family job,' Eddie replied. 'It's tradition, passed down from farvver ter son. Our Geoff was the first in out of us three, bein' the eldest, but 'e wanted ter be a lighterman, so Farvver got 'im apprenticed to a good lighterage company. Steve works the quays same as me though.'

Laura felt warm and safe sitting next to Eddie and as the tram rocked and swayed she could feel his arm pressing against hers. She had often daydreamed about being alone with a man since taking on her current responsibilities of managing the family home and looking after her sister's children and her semi-invalid father, but she had dismissed the thoughts by telling herself that it was never likely to happen anyway. She had almost resigned herself to spending her future years alone, despite the times when things piled in on her and she yearned to fall into a man's arms and let him take away her lonely feelings and ease her burden. Now she was alone with a handsome young man who made her feel good, who had stirred the deep emotions she had determinedly buried for so long.

The New Cross Dog Stadium was brilliantly lit up, and

as the two young people climbed the steps to the rim of the arena Laura caught her breath. A large crowd was milling around inside the stadium, and hurrying back and forth to the betting windows and the bookmakers' stands to place their bets as the dogs for the first race were paraded. It was all so new to Laura and she felt the excitement mounting inside her as Eddie pointed down to the track. 'That one's the favourite, the one wiv the black an' white stripes,' he told her. 'It's five ter four. The one in blue is the outsider.' He glanced quickly up at the tote. 'It's one 'undred to eight.'

Laura watched with fascination as the dogs were pushed into the traps and as the bell sounded she saw the mechanical hare start to move, slowly at first but quickly gaining speed until it seemed to be flying. The crowd roared as the traps flew open and the greyhounds dashed out. At the second bend the favourite was knocked out of its stride by the outsider and the dog in the blue marking slipped inside and ran close to the rail. The crowd roared even louder as the favourite made up the distance lost and narrowed the gap. Laura followed the dogs excitedly, willing the favourite on, and as they rushed past the post it was too close to call. After a few seconds the result was called out on a loudspeaker over their heads. The favourite had won.

Eddie smiled broadly as he caught Laura's expression. 'I see yer wanted the favourite ter win,' he said.

Laura nodded. 'The ovver dog cheated,' she replied quickly.

Eddie chuckled loudly. 'There's a café over there,' he said, pointing towards the tote. 'Let's get a warm drink. I'm waitin' fer the fourth race.'

They stood at the back of the stadium, looking down on the scene, as they sipped steaming Bovril from thick mugs, and when their eyes occasionally met they smiled happily at each other. Eddie noticed how Laura kept looking up at the illuminated tote, watching the constantly changing numbers, and he touched her arm. 'Can you understand all that?' he asked.

'It's all so confusin',' she replied, looking bemused.

Eddie began to explain the combinations of possible results and how the betting was going. 'So yer see, yer bet on the first an' second, an' yer can get some idea of which way the bettin's goin'. Look, I tell yer what. You pick a combination an' I'll put a bet on fer yer. If yer win it's yours.'

Laura shook her head but Eddie was determined. 'C'mon, pick a combination,' he urged.

'Okay then. One an' two,' she answered.

Eddie laughed aloud. 'All right, but I 'ave ter tell yer, it's a bookie's delight.'

'What's that mean?' Laura asked.

'Well, I'd say yer got about as much chance o' winnin' as I 'ave o' skippin' over the moon,' he joked.

As soon as they had finished their drinks Eddie took Laura's arm and led her down to the tote window. The dogs were being paraded as they walked back to a vantage point and Eddie handed her a ticket. ' 'Old on ter that, 'cos if yer do win yer gonna need it,' he told her.

Once more the hare started up and suddenly a roar erupted as the greyhounds leapt from the traps. Laura was starting to jump up and down in her excitement as the number one dog went out in front. On each of the bends it increased its lead and she screamed out her encouragement. Eddie tugged on her arm and shouted in her ear. 'Look at the two dog, it's catchin' up.'

At the final bend the number two dog passed number three and four and almost overtook the number one dog as they crossed the line. Laura suddenly turned to Eddie and threw her arms around him ecstatically. 'It won! It won!' she screamed.

Eddie slipped his arms around her automatically and

suddenly the expression on Laura's face changed from excitement to embarrassment and she looked into his eyes for a brief moment. He took his arms from her waist and gripped her shoulders gently but firmly, and gazed at her, willing her to raise her eyes once more. Laura glanced up and the look that passed between them was full of passion and fire. Suddenly she moved away, frightened by her own impulses, secretly wishing that he would kiss her on the mouth. Eddie let his arms fall to his sides, moved by the strange promise in her pale blue eyes.

The numbers were flashing again on the totaliser board and suddenly Eddie gasped. 'Yer've won two pounds!' he said excitedly.

Laura stepped back a pace and looked up at the illuminated display. 'I can't believe it,' she said breathlessly.

Eddie took her arm and steered her towards the pay-out window. 'C'mon, let's get yer winnin's.'

The evening seemed to be full of magic as Laura sat facing Eddie in a small restaurant in the Old Kent Road. They had a window seat and as they sipped their coffee they glanced out at the passing crowds and traffic through the net curtains. They had eaten a grill of egg, bacon and tomatoes, and Laura was still feeling excited at her unexpected win. Eddie had not been so fortunate. His selection had come in a poor last, but he had managed to break even by backing a nine-to-four winner in the last race.

'It's bin a lovely evenin',' Laura said, looking across at him.

The young man smiled. 'I've really enjoyed it,' he replied, 'but the best bit was when I saw your dogs come in first an' second. Talk about beginner's luck.'

Laura looked down at the chintz tablecloth for a few moments, then her eyes came up to meet his. 'Yer know,

I feel a beginner in more ways than one,' she said softly.

'What d'yer mean, Laura?' he asked.

'Well, it's bin so long since I've gone out on a date an' I felt I was gonna spoil it for yer,' she replied.

Eddie's handsome face relaxed and he smiled at her. 'Look, in the first place I wouldn't 'ave asked yer out if I felt I was gonna be bored or fed up wiv yer company. I wanted to ask yer out that first night when I called in your place. I've really enjoyed ternight, an' I'd like us ter go on seein' each ovver, if yer'd like to.'

Laura stared into his eyes, seeing his sincerity and honesty, and she nodded. 'I would, Eddie, very much so, but yer need to understand the way fings are, what wiv the responsibilities I 'ave ter me family an' the way it's affected me as a person,' she told him. 'It's changed me. I'm not a carefree, 'appy-go-lucky person inside any more. I'm thirty-four years old, tied ter the family through circumstances and not able ter get a regular job that'd allow me ter buy nice clothes an' get me 'air done occasionally. I didn't feel that I could accept a young man's offer of a night out because it wouldn't be fair, to 'im I mean. Wiv you it was different. Yer knew a bit about the way things were an' yer still asked me out. Besides, yer very 'andsome an' a gel would 'ave ter be mad not ter jump at the chance.'

Eddie shook his head slowly as though disbelieving her, but he could not hide the smile playing on his lips. He was surprised and flattered by what she had said, and however she saw herself, to him she was a very attractive young woman with a charming personality. 'Listen, Laura,' he began. 'I must admit ter datin' quite a few gels since I got out o' the army, but none of 'em 'ave rung any bells wiv me, if that's the right way o' puttin' it. I 'ave ter say that they were generally pretty but empty-'eaded an' I 'ad no ulterior motive fer datin' 'em anyway. I mean I wasn't lookin' fer a wife or a steady relationship, just a good time, an' I don't mean that in a bad way. Wiv you though, I saw somefing else. I saw a carin' young woman who was very pretty wiv a lovely smile an' a nice personality. You've struck a chord wiv me, Laura, I 'ave ter say it, but I also understand the way fings are. Let's get ter know each ovver better. Let's spend some time tergevver an' enjoy it. We don't need a commitment. What d'yer say?'

Laura had not taken her eyes from Eddie's face while he was speaking and she sensed a maturity and understanding beyond his years. He seemed to be responding to the way she felt by reassuring her in his own way. 'I'll go along wiv that,' she replied, smiling gently.

It was late when Laura and Eddie walked back into Weston Street. They had left the restaurant and caught a bus to Tower Bridge Road, then strolled along to the George public house. It had been quiet and almost empty and they had sat in a secluded corner, chatting cheerfully, until the landlord called time. Laura had let Eddie take her hand in his as they crossed into Weston Street and walked slowly along the deserted pavement. Near Pedlar's Row they stopped in the shadows of the box factory and suddenly she was in his arms, her mouth feeling the pleasure of his gentle, lingering kiss. It had happened so suddenly, so naturally, and she closed her eyes, wanting it to last forever.

'Can I see yer soon?' he whispered huskily as their lips parted.

'I'm sure yer will,' Laura answered him, smiling happily.

They walked the short distance to her front door and Eddie brushed her lips as they parted. 'I'll knock termorrer evenin' an' we can arrange somefing, if yer like?' he said.

'I'd like,' Laura replied as she let herself into her house.

★ ★ ★

Marcus Levy had decided that he would have to be very careful. His old friend Ira was taking a big risk by letting him use the basement room under his restaurant. If the police discovered the workshop Ira would certainly be implicated. More worrying to Marcus was the possibility of his being tailed by one of Westlake's men and his workshop being discovered. It would be so easy for someone to follow him right into the restaurant and then sit down for a meal to allay suspicion. Westlake's man could be any one of the nightly diners, and there was no way of telling whether or not it had already happened. Ira had been taken into Marcus' confidence and he had suggested that they should not act like friends while in the restaurant; then if any questions were asked it was just a business arrangement with a total stranger who was doing some freelance artwork for a magazine and had paid a month's rent in advance for the use of the basement workshop. The plates were coming on nicely anyway and Marcus had made the decision to work only in the evenings now. Should he be followed and seen going into Ira's restaurant it would appear quite normal, provided the place was open for business at the time.

Marcus refilled his glass from the half-empty bottle of Johnny Walker and took a draught as he stood beside the sideboard in his dingy flat. His passport was ready and he had received a letter from Magdalena saying how much she missed him, and that she would be sending on his letters of introduction soon. That side of things was progressing well, but there were other problems to consider, Marcus reflected. He was determined to finish the plates well before the allotted time, in line with his future plans, and he had decided on a devious scheme to thwart any nasty idea that Westlake might come up with.

A loud rat-tat on the door startled Marcus and he

looked quickly around the room before going to answer the knock.

Danny Steadman looked menacing as he walked into the room, ignoring Marcus' invitation to sit. 'What's the progress?' he asked quickly.

The artist went to the sideboard and picked up a clean glass. 'Care for a drink?' he said, trying to look relaxed.

Steadman shook his head. 'I'd like ter see the plates,' he said in reply.

Marcus smiled disarmingly. 'I don't keep them here, it'd be asking for trouble. I could get a call from the police or the probation officer at any time,' he told him.

'Where are they?' the big man asked suspiciously.

'They're at my workshop,' Marcus replied.

Steadman motioned to the door. 'Okay, let's go.'

Marcus realised that it was useless to argue and he picked up his coat from the back of a chair. He led the way down the dusty wooden stairs and out into the early-evening air. They crossed into Brady Street and out on to the broad Whitechapel Road. Steadman did not speak until they were almost at Ira Stanley's restaurant. 'By the way, there's a change o' plan,' he said casually. 'We need the plates by the end o' next week.'

'I don't know,' Marcus replied, looking shocked. 'It's intricate work. I can't rush it.'

'I'm afraid yer got no option,' Steadman said coldly. 'Next Friday.'

They entered the restaurant and Ira purposely ignored his friend when he saw Steadman with him. There were only a few customers there and the two men walked through to the kitchen and down a steep flight of stairs which led to the workshop.

Steadman looked around curiously. 'Where are they?' he asked.

Marcus reached down and took a bundle from a shelf under the workbench, laying it carefully on the wooden surface. The villain watched quizzically while Marcus unwrapped the bundle and he stared down for a few moments at the copper plates. 'So this is what it's all about,' he remarked. 'They don't look much.'

'Well, they're nowhere near ready yet,' Marcus told him. 'You can see the roughness of the cuts. Just run your finger along the surface. You can feel how rough they are.'

Steadman looked out of his depth as the artist explained the complicated process in detail, making it all sound as technical as possible. He nodded stiffly and turned away from the bench. 'Well, like I say, the boss wants 'em on Friday next. So yer better get workin',' he warned as he made for the stairs.

Marcus showed him out and then went back to speak with his old friend. 'I'm sorry, Ira. That was Westlake's right-hand man,' he told him. 'He's a very nasty piece of work. I had to bring him here, I had no choice.'

Ira took off his thick-framed glasses and polished them on a handkerchief, his eyes squinting beneath bushy eyebrows. He was a short, stocky man in his fifties, with a mop of grey hair and an angular face. He nodded as he went on with his pastry-making. 'I hope you know what you're doing, Marcus,' he said.

The artist smiled confidently. 'They've brought the date forward, which is nothing more than I expected,' he replied. 'It just means a slight alteration to my plans. It doesn't change things for you though, Ira. As soon as I'm finished I'll clean up and get rid of all the equipment. No one would know I'd ever been here.'

'I hope you're right,' Ira remarked. Being a close friend of the artist certainly made life interesting, if not positively dangerous at times.

Chapter Twenty

The families in Pedlar's Row were only six in number, and since they were living in a somewhat isolated little nook of Bermondsey it might have been expected that they would strive to band together, like all good neighbours, as much as they were able. Queenie Bromley, however, did not help to further anybody's good intentions by her attitude to all and sundry in the Row, and Annie Stebbings was compromised by her son's seemingly strange behaviour and was inclined to be suspicious and protective whenever she talked to anyone. Bridie Molloy tried to be friendly toward her neighbours, but she still felt a little ashamed for allowing her house to be used at the local bookmaker's convenience, and she tended not to tarry too long in casual conversation in case the subject came up. As for her daughters, they were young and in love, and they couldn't care less what their neighbours thought anyway. The Carmichaels were very often embroiled in their own petty squabbles, and it was only when Elsie had exhausted her venom on her long-suffering husband that she was able to take an interest in what was going on around her.

The Cassidys were a large family and Lizzie was a match for most, but her main concern was for her matriarchal duties and social dallying tended to get neglected. As for the Priors, Laura was new to Pedlar's Row and still becoming acquainted with the neighbours, while Lucy was out at work all day and found little time or inclination to stand at the front door chatting. All in all, there seemed little chance for a community spirit to flourish, but unforeseen circumstances caused the families to draw closer together regardless.

Queenie Bromley was almost out of her mind when Geoff Cassidy brought a sorry-looking Frankie home from his adventures on the river, and the normally hard-faced woman almost wept on the lighterman's shoulder with relief and gratitude. She also made a point of speaking to Lizzie Cassidy about her eldest son's good deed and said that, in her opinion, if anyone else but a neighbour had found her Frankie hiding in the barge they would most certainly have handed him over to the police.

Concern for her sister's boy had first led Laura to approach Annie Stebbings, but she was now on first-name terms with Wally's protective mother, and she had also made an ally of Elsie Carmichael, who had had good reason to be grateful for her next-door neighbour's help when Len burnt his feet with bleach. Elsie herself had won a truce at least when she offered her support to the volatile Queenie Bromley in her hour of need.

As far as the men were concerned, the Sultan public house was the main haven of sanity, a place of refuge when things got tough indoors, and the neighbours of Pedlar's Row drank together there in friendship. Albert Prior had found out about the men's meeting-place and when he felt up to it he managed the short distance for a pint, knowing that there was usually someone on hand to see him home. The only exception was Wally Stebbings. His eccentric behaviour and the fact that he was teetotal did not endear him to the rest of the men. They treated him with suspicion and tended to shun him in the street.

Wally Stebbings had been thirty-three when the war broke out. He was working as a clerk in a City shipping office at the time, and when he went for his army medical he found out that he was colour-blind. He also discovered that he had a perforated eardrum and flat feet. He went back to the office feeling rather relieved that he would not be called up to fight in the war, but he felt he should do his bit for the country and he volunteered for the City of London fire-watching team. Always a loner, Wally buried himself in his hobbies: fretwork, model-making and reading historical novels. After the war finished he decided, in a rare moment of resolve, that it was about time he changed jobs, and he found a similar position nearer to his home.

Apart from his one brief relationship with a young lady Salvationist, Wally had never had any women friends, and as he grew older he became more and more old fashioned in his attitudes. He tended to dress beyond his years, and being constantly under the influence of his doting mother, who was always concerned for his health, he heeded her advice and always wore a scarf around his neck, woollen gloves, and a trilby to keep his head dry.

Wally liked to listen to the wireless, and he was in the habit of going for quiet walks whenever possible. On Sunday evenings he would stroll as far as Tower Hill, spending some time in the Tower gardens, feeding the pigeons and watching the rivercraft passing to and fro, and sometimes during the week, if there was nothing of interest on the wireless, he would go as far as the Old Kent Road and back.

On Tuesday evening Wally went out for a walk, and just as he started to retrace his steps back home he heard children's singing voices coming from a mission hall. Sweet strains of 'Jerusalem' carried out on the night air and he stopped to listen. Curiosity got the better of him when he noticed that the front door of the mission was ajar, and he peeped in. The group of young girls and boys at choir practice seemed to be enjoying the hymn and they sang it with gusto, egged on by the choirmaster, who waved his arms about vigorously. Wally stood peering in through the door after the hymn had finished, hoping that there would be another delightful rendering after the choirmaster had finished instructing the children.

Joe Molloy had stopped off at the World Turned Upside Down on his way home from his shift at the Old Kent Road gasworks, and after having one drink he had met an old acquaintance, who bought him another. The drink was returned and when Joe Molloy finally left the pub he walked home briskly, until he saw the familiar figure of Wally Stebbings peering into the mission hall. Sounds of children's laughter carried out and Joe got suspicious. What was Stebbings doing there? he wondered.

Wally finally realised that the singing lesson was over and he walked away, wanting to be home in time for the Tuesday drama hour on the Home Service. Unknown to him he was being followed at some distance by Joe Molloy, who felt angry and disgusted at him for spending all his spare time hanging round children, either talking to them or spying on them. What was wrong with the man? he wondered. He was a danger to little children and one day he could quite well do one of them some harm. A man like him should be locked up, Joe raged.

At the Bricklayer's Arms Wally took out his pocket-watch and consulted it. There was time yet before the programme started, he thought, deciding to take the longest way home via Cooper Street. Joe Molloy kept his distance as he followed Wally along Great Dover Street and the roundabout route into Cooper Street. It was dark now and the turning looked sombre with the rising moon shining down on to the factories and bomb site and the deserted cobbled road.

Wally Stebbings had been emotionally stirred by the

children's rendering of his favourite hymn. As he neared the rear entrance to Pedlar's Row he was humming the tune, and thinking that he was alone in the dark turning, he imitated the choirmaster by throwing his arms about.

Joe Molloy was now totally convinced that Wally Stebbings was a raving bloody lunatic, and he would definitely have something to say when he met the lads for a drink.

On Wednesday morning Chief Inspector Ben Walsh sat studying the report sent to him from Leman Street Police Station in the East End. It made very interesting reading and Walsh was pleased with himself when he finally closed the folder and rang for his subordinate.

'I think we've come up trumps, Gordon,' he said, smiling.

Sergeant Ashley pored over the file while Walsh sat back in his chair and filled his pipe from a leather pouch.

'They didn't bag Mr Big,' Ashley remarked, looking puzzled.

Ben Walsh puffed a cloud of tobacco smoke towards the ceiling before answering. 'No, the two convicted were done for handling forged ration books and petrol coupons. You can see what it says in the report. The owner of the printing works went missing. Now take a look at the latest probation report and where I've ringed.'

Ashley read out the details. 'Marcus Levy. Twelve, Colman Buildings, Friar's Court, Whitechapel. Freelance artist and interior designer. Convicted of embezzlement at Bow Crown Court, January nineteen forty-two. Sentenced to five years. Released on parole January nineteen forty-six. Could this be the man they're waiting for, guv?'

Walsh threw another folder across his desk. 'Read that. It's Levy's file,' he said, smiling slyly.

Ashley's face broke into a grin as he studied it and he whistled excitedly. 'Levy was suspected of forging ration books and petrol coupons but nothing proved,' he said. 'That was his second conviction for embezzlement. Well known in the Whitechapel area. Comes from a wealthy background. Mixes with high society.'

'I'm convinced that Levy is our man. I can feel it,' Walsh said conclusively. 'He was suspected of producing those forged coupons, and the Yard report said that they were expertly done. I'd bet that Levy's working on those counterfeit plates right now. Point is, where do we go from here?'

Ashley stroked his chin for a few moments. 'We could ask Leman Street to put a tail on him for a few days. Or we could get them to pay him a visit. Just a social chat, of course.'

'I prefer the first option,' Walsh replied. 'We've got to be careful, or Levy might realise we're on to him and bolt. Besides, a tail might lead us to something.'

Ashley looked pleased as he passed the file back. 'It looks good, guv. We could be getting on top of this,' he said enthusiastically.

Ben Walsh puffed away at his pipe. 'I was going to go to the Leather Bottle again for my lunch today, but I think I'll give it a miss. If my hunch *is* right and they're getting ready to print, I don't want them thinking we've sussed anything.'

Lucy had expected Roy to feel much better once he got back to work, being in an environment he was used to and doing the job he was skilled at, but she had not realised how much it would take out of him. He came home the first day looking pleased but very tired, and within minutes of finishing his tea he was fast asleep in the armchair. The same thing happened the next day. He looked exhausted and snapped at the boys for the least little thing, and Lucy had to rouse him when it was time to go to bed. That night he woke her up when he suddenly sat upright in the early hours and screamed out. He was sweating profusely and she could see that he was in some distress. By the time he settled back to sleep it was time to get up, and at breakfast Lucy was determined he should seek help.

'We just can't go on like this, Roy,' she said firmly. 'Yer not gettin' proper sleep an' nor am I. Why don't yer go an' see the doctor? P'raps 'e can give yer somefing ter make yer sleep.'

Roy looked ashen-faced as he sat sipping his morning tea, and he nodded. 'I'll go ternight,' he replied.

Lucy kissed him goodbye as he left for work, and noticed that it seemed almost too much trouble for him to return her kiss. He was verging on a breakdown, she felt sure. His mental state was beginning to affect her too. She was missing his love, and she was helpless to do anything about it. Roy had never been over-passionate, but at least they had always enjoyed regular lovemaking. Now, however, it was nonexistent.

Laura had overheard the conversation as she came into the room and she was quick to approach her sister once Roy had left for work. 'D'yer fink sleepin' pills are the answer?' she asked.

'What else is there?' Lucy retorted angrily.

'What about you goin' wiv Roy ter see the doctor. Maybe 'e can put yer in touch wiv somebody who can 'elp 'im,' Laura suggested.

'Like who?'

'Like a psychiatrist or somebody.'

Lucy sighed deeply as she sat down with Laura at the breakfast table. 'I dunno. I'm at my wits' end. Roy won't listen ter me anyway. 'E finks it'll all go away once 'e settles back ter work. I can't see it, meself. In fact last night was the worst yet. 'E woke up terrified an' 'e was

223

covered in sweat an' shakin' like a leaf. I can't stand much more of it,' she groaned.

Laura got up and poured a cup of tea to take to her father. 'I'd certainly go wiv Roy ter see the doctor,' she told her. 'Tell 'im what yer just told me. Doctor Chandler's a decent sort, 'e'll give yer good advice. 'E was very good when Dad 'ad the stroke.'

Lucy merely nodded, and by the time Laura returned to the parlour she was standing in front of the mirror putting the finishing touches to her make-up. 'I fink I will go wiv Roy ternight,' she said as she gathered up her handbag.

The house was quiet and while Laura sat sipping her tea before leaving for the Sultan, she thought about Eddie. It had been a lovely evening and he was so easy to talk to. His good-night kiss was just wonderful, she recalled. She must make sure not to let things get out of hand though. He was a very attractive man and it would be easy to lose her head over him. She would have to ensure that he was still serious about her, and make him aware that she needed time. Eddie would understand, she felt sure.

Queenie had been up early that morning, and as George got ready to go off to work she had some words of advice for him. 'Now don't ferget ter come straight 'ome ternight fer yer tea. I ain't keepin' it in that oven like I did last night. Besides, you was a bloody job ter rouse this mornin',' she told him. 'It won't be any good you workin' yerself silly one day an' losin' the next 'cos you overdone it, now will it?'

George nodded obediently. 'I'll be straight 'ome, gel,' he promised. 'Last night it was different. We 'ad our union dues ter pay at the Ship an' yer can't run in an' out, 'specially when yer've 'ad a good day. They'd all fink I was right under the cosh.'

'Well, you are, ain't yer?' Queenie replied with a stab at humour.

George ignored the joke as he laced up his boots. If the rest of the week went off as well as the first two days Queenie was going to be pleasantly surprised when he put his pay packet on the table, he thought. There was another ship waiting to berth and that was a bonus cargo as well.

'By the way, if the weavver's not too bad I'll be goin' on Sunday,' she informed him.

George nodded as he got to his feet. It was starting all over again, he thought. Queenie was always miserable for a couple of days after a visit, and he had not been able to persuade her that it did not serve any purpose to continue going, other than keeping her powerful feelings simmering. It was not as though she needed any reminding of what had happened. Loving memories and bad memories each had a rightful place in everyone's mind, but Queenie seemed in danger of not being able to separate the two, and it was slowly killing her.

John Bannerman slipped into the Sultan at eleven o'clock as usual for his morning constitutional before taking up his position at the entrance to Pedlar's Row at noon. He usually met Dickie Jones at the pub and the two would spend the hour chatting away together, more often than not about Dickie's unhappy marriage and his fear that Con Noble might find out about the new woman in his life.

'I tell yer, John boy, if it ever got ter Con's ear, 'e'd slice me up good an' proper,' Dickie moaned. 'Con might give the impression o' bein' easy-goin' but I know different. 'E's a bloody animal.'

John sipped his beer thoughtfully. He was under no illusions about the bookie's capabilities and he wondered how he himself would fare if Con or Archie Westlake ever discovered that he was having regular meetings with Detective Sergeant Ashley. His only comfort was that neither the bookie nor the Bermondsey villain had found salvation in Christianity. The only time either went into a church was for a wedding, a christening or a funeral, and knowing that made John feel reasonably safe when he met with the detective in the shadow of the altar in St James' Church.

'Yer'll just 'ave ter be careful then, Dickie,' he told his friend. 'Keep away from this manor whatever yer do. Somebody's bound ter see the two o' yer tergevver an' put a word in Con's ear.'

'Don't I know it,' Dickie groaned. 'Con was only tellin' me yesterday about what Jack Murray was sayin'.'

'Oh, an' what was that?' John asked casually.

Dickie looked over to make sure the publican was out of earshot. ' 'E told Archie Westlake that there could be a grass on the manor,' he said softly. 'Archie told Con an' Con told me.'

John Bannerman felt a lance of fear strike at his stomach but he hid his feelings by smiling. 'The trouble is, Dickie, fings 'ave got a funny way o' gettin' around,' he remarked. 'Just like I was sayin'. Every time the story's told one more gets to 'ear it. Still, yer got no need ter worry on my part. If I was a grass you'd be in 'alf a dozen different bags by now, or sittin' up in a concrete bucket at the bottom o' the Thames.'

Dickie shivered. 'Leave orf, John, yer puttin' the fear up me.'

'Seriously though, yer don't fink there is a grass on the manor, do yer, Dickie?' John asked.

'Nah, course not,' Dickie replied. 'Con reckons Archie don't fink so, an' nor does 'e. It was all over the guv'nor at Dock'ead nick goin' in the Bottle fer 'is lunch. Apparently Archie was 'avin' a meet in there wiv some pals at the time an' they saw the cozzer. It was just a coincidence. There was nuffink dodgy goin' on anyway.'

John smiled and took another swig from his glass. It had been a stroke of bad luck that got him involved with Ashley in the beginning. He had been caught red-handed by the vigilant detective while trying to sell some stolen fountain pens, and although the articles were cheap and insignificant Ashley had made capital out of it by reminding him that he was still out on probation and a further conviction, however trivial the offence, would put him back behind bars once more. John had been finding it difficult to provide for his wife and four children and knew that with his record it was unlikely he would ever get a decent job. Sergeant Ashley had laboured the point and given him an offer he could not very well refuse, and thus John Bannerman became the detective's informant.

When he'd bumped into Dickie Jones quite by accident in a Rotherhithe pub a few weeks later, John had learnt that there might be an opening for him as a bookie's runner. Dickie had been a fellow prisoner in Pentonville and the two had become friendly during the time they spent there. During their chat in the pub Dickie Jones mentioned that the big villain Archie Westlake ran the bookies, and that he would talk to him personally, 'being good pals', as he put it.

John Bannerman's first instinct was to decline the offer, for Archie Westlake was no stranger to him, but he was in a very awkward situation. Sergeant Ashley was getting impatient for some information to work on, yet the reluctant informant was loath to be the cause of anyone ending up in prison. With Archie Westlake it would be an entirely different kettle of fish, he thought. Apart from his own hatred of Westlake, the man had laughed at the law for years and had spent the whole war making a fortune in the black market by charging housewives exorbitant prices for food and little luxuries.

He had also gathered around him a callous and brutal team of minders, and had crushed any competition that might have been a threat. It was how he had come to control the street bookies and now he considered himself untouchable.

When he was successful in getting the job with Con Noble, John bought himself some time. Sergeant Ashley was no fool and he realised that his snout would have to establish himself within the organisation before he was fully trusted. Here was a chance to get enough information finally to nail the Bermondsey villain once and for all.

John Bannerman had had a bit of luck bumping into Dickie Jones in the first place and now, being a confidant, he had gathered some very useful information from his unsuspecting friend. As they sat chatting together that morning John Bannerman was about to learn something which would be of vital importance to Ben Walsh and his detective sergeant.

Chapter Twenty-One

On Wednesday evening Eddie called to see Laura, and she felt a little embarrassed having to talk to him at the door.

'I'd invite yer in but me dad's sittin' in the parlour an' Lucy's ironin' in the scullery,' she said with a sheepish smile.

Eddie reached out and squeezed her hand. 'It's all right, I understand,' he replied, smiling. 'I was finkin' yer might like ter come ter the pictures termorrer. There's a good film at the Trocadera.'

'I'd like to,' Laura said quietly.

'Did yer really enjoy last night?' he whispered.

'It was lovely,' she answered. 'I don't remember ever 'avin' such a nice time.'

'Same 'ere,' Eddie said, looking along the Row quickly.

Laura was aware that the bookie was standing next door and she beckoned Eddie into the passageway. 'I don't wanna go but I've got a load o' work ter do if I'm comin' out termorrer,' she said, trying to keep her voice down.

Eddie smiled and clasped her hand gently but firmly. 'Could I 'ave a kiss before I go?' he asked.

Laura raised her hands and clasped his arms as he came close. He bent his head and found her lips in a soft, lingering kiss which left her breathless.

'I've not 'ad yer out o' me mind all day,' he whispered.

'It was the same fer me,' Laura replied, feeling her face getting hot.

'Until termorrer then,' he said, not moving.

'Until termorrer.'

'Can yer be ready by seven?'

'Yes.'

'Will yer miss me?'

'Terribly.'

'Really?'

'Really.'

'Laura, there's a bloody draught comin' under that door,' Albert called out.

Eddie winced. 'All right, I'll see yer at seven,' he said, stealing a quick kiss as he turned to leave.

The Sultan was quite busy for a weeknight and Len Carmichael was waiting at the counter.

'Two pints o' bitter, two pints o' mild an' bitter an' one fer yerself, June luv,' he said cheerfully.

The barmaid smiled cheekily as she pulled down on the beer pump. 'If yer fink a drink's gonna get yer anywhere wiv me yer dead right,' she quipped.

Len chuckled as he gathered the pints. 'I couldn't afford yer, June. Besides, my Elsie'd 'ave me guts fer garters.'

At the table George Bromley and Eric Cassidy were listening to the angry Joe Molloy. 'I tell yer fer nuffink, if that bloke ain't stopped we're gonna be sorry, all of us,' he growled.

Eric Cassidy sipped the froth from the top of his drink. 'Yer might be right about the bloke not 'avin' all 'is marbles but that doesn't mean 'e'd 'arm kids,' he replied. 'Them sort are evil bastards, but it strikes me that Wally Stebbin's is just an 'armless nerve-case who wouldn't 'arm a fly.'

'Well, if you'd 'ave seen 'im last night yer'd change yer tune,' Joe told him. 'I've got two daughters meself an' I wouldn't 'ave wanted a bloke like 'im 'angin' round my gels.'

George Bromley nodded in agreement. 'We've stopped our Charlie goin' in the bloke's 'ouse,' he added. 'Me an' Queenie don't trust 'im.'

Len had made himself comfortable at the table once more and he nodded at George's remark. 'My Elsie was tellin' me that Wally Stebbin's was in the Sally Army at one time,' he said.

Eric Cassidy thought the conversation was getting ridiculous. 'What's wrong wiv bein' in the Sally Army?' he asked sharply. 'Those people do a grand job. Look at the work they did durin' the war.'

'I'm not sayin' anyfing about them,' Len answered quickly. 'What I was gonna say was, Stebbin's packed it in 'cos 'e wouldn't go in a pub. All those Sally Army people go in pubs fer collections. That's all I'm sayin'.'

Joe Molloy leaned forward over the table. 'Yer've only gotta look at the facts,' he went on. 'We've all seen 'ow 'e walks up an' down the Row, mumblin' to 'imself. Then there's the way 'e dresses. 'E looks like Sharkey the bomb-thrower. 'E chats to all the kids 'e sees, an' on top o' that 'e's a Peepin' Tom. I can vouch fer that. Ter crown it all 'e goes orf 'is 'ead every now an' then. I saw 'im performin' last night in Cooper Street.'

Eric shook his head sadly. 'Look, Joe, I know yer got the best intentions in sayin' what yer do, but yer gotta be careful. There's nuffink wrong in talkin' ter children. We all do it some time or anuvver. As fer 'im bein' out of 'is tree, well that's nerves. We've all seen it. The war an' the Blitz in particular pushed fousands o' people over the edge. 'E could be one o' those poor bastards.'

'Yeah, an' 'e could be a nonsense-case too,' Joe persisted.

George Bromley turned to Eric. ' 'Ere, what was that docker's name who was accused of interferin' wiv those little gels?' he asked.

Eric stroked his chin for a moment or two. 'Bassey. Ted Bassey.' He turned to Joe Molloy. 'Now there's a case in question,' he said. 'Ted Bassey was always chattin' ter the little kids, especially gels. Anyway one day somebody was s'posed ter see 'im touch one an' they called the police. Poor ole Ted was took down the nick an' it was only the kid's muvver who saved 'is bacon. She was standin' by 'er front door an' saw it all. Ted was just pattin the kid's 'ead like we all do at times but because 'e was always 'angin' round kids somebody got the wrong end o' the stick. The kid's muvver went down the nick when she 'eard what 'ad 'appened an' they released 'im. What most people didn't know was that Ted Bassey 'ad lost 'is own daughter when she was only four years old. 'E jus' loved kids. After that the poor sod couldn't live down the gossip that was flyin' around, an' one day 'e jus' walked on to the ship we were workin' an' dived 'eadlong inter the 'old. Killed stone dead, 'e was.'

'Well, that might be so, but Wally Stebbin's ain't married an' 'e ain't lost a daughter,' Joe replied. 'I just don't trust the bloke an' I'm gonna keep me eye on 'im. I'd advise yer ter do the same, George. After all, you've got young lads.'

The large church garden had a winter look about it, with the tall, bare plane trees moving gently in a cold wind. The wide flagstone path was strewn with dry brown leaves, and on both sides winter flowers had opened up to add a delicate colour to the dark, hard earth. A lone squirrel sat up on its hind legs and turned a kernel round in its paws before scampering up the nearest tree as footsteps approached.

The young man walked quickly, looking around him

nervously as he neared the flight of curved stone steps that led up to the massive, iron-studded door of St James' Church. With a last furtive look round he climbed the steps quickly and entered the elegant Georgian building. Inside he was immediately aware of the stale, damp smell, and with an accustomed eye he glanced around. The rows of pews were empty, and in the silence he noticed how the pale light shone through the large stained-glass window above the altar.

John Bannerman went and sat in a middle pew, looking around at the stone wall plaques and the tall columns that supported the railed balcony. He was early and it suited him. If he kept Ashley waiting he was sure of a hard time, even in the sanctity of a church. Ashley was an atheist, he felt sure. The man seemed to have no reverence at all.

For ten minutes the young man sat quietly, thinking about the situation he found himself in, wondering how it was all going to end. Would he ever be able to shake off the yoke and walk proud and tall, or would he be compelled to carry the burden for the rest of his life, forever glancing over his shoulder? Maybe they would let him alone once they had squeezed enough information from him. The alternative was too depressing to dwell on. It would mean that one day he would be offered up to the wolves when his usefulness was expended.

John heard the footsteps echoing on the marble stones and he did not turn around as he heard the creaking of a pew behind him. He kept his head low as if in meditation until Ashley spoke.

'Well, my son, what have you got for me?' the sergeant said in a low voice.

John raised his head and gave Ashley a half-glance. 'It's gettin' very dicey,' he whispered. 'They're worried in case somebody's bin talkin'.'

'You've not been silly, have you?' Ashley asked quickly. 'I don't want you blowing your cover, not at this stage.'

'No, it's jus' talk, but I can't push it. There's definitely somefing in the wind,' John assured him.

'Well, what's new?' Ashley asked.

John looked down at his clasped hands. 'I 'eard terday that they've moved a printin' press.'

'When? Where to?'

'I dunno where they took it to, but it was loaded yesterday afternoon,' John replied. 'The bloke I was talkin' to said they got 'im to 'elp 'em load it on to a lorry. It was already dismantled, so 'e said.'

Ashley felt pleased at what he had just heard. It was all coming together, he thought. If things worked out right it could mean an important crowd of villains in the bag, and certainly an overdue promotion for him. They would not be able to ignore him then. He looked with a grudging respect at the thin young man sitting in front of him. 'You've done well, son,' he said, reaching out and touching John's shoulder. 'Now, I want you to keep your ears and eyes open. Any little bit of information is going to help us. I need to know where that press went to. Okay then, you go out first. I'll wait a few minutes longer.'

John Bannerman left the church and walked home to Rotherhithe with a feeling of unease. Dickie Jones had told him much, believing that he was to be trusted, but he might recall those casual conversations and put two and two together if and when the bubble burst. The only answer was to get right away from the area, John realised. Maybe he could get a new start in a new town. He had to consider Margie and the kids.

Ben Walsh had lost no time getting things moving, and after a long talk on the telephone with the chief inspector at Leman Street Police Station, the two detectives agreed to combine their efforts. A rota of plain-clothes officers would be assigned to watch and report on the movements of one Marcus Levy. The detectives would operate a shift system, changing every four hours from dawn until midnight for one week, and then they would review the situation.

Walsh felt pleased with what had been accomplished, and when Ashley reported back that evening the inspector felt that they had earned a drink.

'It's looking very promising,' Walsh said, sipping his gin and tonic as they sat in the saloon bar of the Grapes. 'If we get a result from the Leman Street boys and your snout can find out where that printing press went to, we can pick our time to pounce. I won't be satisfied with the chicken shit, Gordon. I want the rooster this time,' he growled.

'You still think it's money they're going to print?' Ashley asked.

Walsh nodded emphatically. 'I'm sure of it. I'm just curious to know where Westlake would set up a press,' he said, stroking his chin. 'It wouldn't be at the back of one of his shops, I feel sure. I don't think it would be at his club in Camberwell either. In the past the bugger's always got away unscathed by not directly involving himself. I think that he'll use a secure location, probably premises hired under an alias, but there's no way any small fry are going to take a chance of doing a ten stretch without a fair share of the proceeds. Make no mistake about it, this is the big one. If we nab anyone at all we've got to make sure it's the one who's pulling the strings.'

Sergeant Ashley studied his drink for a few seconds, then looked up at the inspector. 'Where did we go wrong before, guv?' he asked quietly.

Ben Walsh ran his finger thoughtfully round the rim of his glass. 'I don't think we can win either way,' he replied with a sardonic smile. 'Take you, now. Fifteen years you've been in the force and you're still a sergeant. And why? I'll tell you why, because you tend to cut corners, play it your own way. Am I right, would you say?'

'I wouldn't argue with that assumption,' Ashley replied cynically. 'My record stands up with any other officer's as far as getting results goes, but unfortunately the powers that be look at the small print when they do the assessment. They see the complaints, the criticisms and the comments of the judiciary on trial reports about my methods and they're swayed. That's my honest opinion.'

Walsh nodded slowly. 'Well then, take my case as a comparison. I've been in the plain-clothes division for ten years. I'm looking for promotion later this year, and I'm confident I'll get it,' he said quietly. 'You see, I've always played it strictly by the book. I've had my share of glory and I've got a good record. As far as the judiciary goes I'm lily-white, clean as the driven snow. Now with someone like Westlake, you cut corners and step out of line and his brief will crucify you. The result is, the villain walks free. In my case I played it right, did all the paperwork and waited until I'd covered my backside as required, then I went in. What happened? We netted the small fry and Westlake laughed at us. We both know he was the brains behind the black-market set-up that we stamped on, but we couldn't nab him. That's what I mean by saying we can't win either way.'

Ashley looked downcast. 'Unless we catch Archie Westlake with the counterfeit plates in his possession we can't nail him,' he said.

Walsh laughed. 'I wouldn't be at all surprised if he still walked free,' he replied. 'Westlake could say he was merely going to exhibit the plates in some bloody museum he was setting up, or he was going to decorate his lounge with them. No, we've got to catch him printing money and all the paths have got to lead to his door, not some tuppenny-ha'penny hireling.'

'It's not going to be a pushover, that's for sure,' Ashley remarked.

Ben Walsh leaned forward in his chair. 'I want Archie Westlake. That villain's been a bane on my life for quite a few years now and I want him out of circulation for a long time. I need a result that bad I'd be prepared to change the habit of my working lifetime.'

Ashley looked closely at his superior officer. 'What are you saying, guv?' he asked.

'I'd be prepared to do a deal to nail Westlake, but of course a lot depends on what the Leman Street boys come up with. Let's just leave it at that for the time being,' he replied quietly.

Chapter Twenty-Two

Archie Westlake walked into Pedlar's Row on Thursday morning and stood talking to Con for some time. He wore a dark suit, a camel-hair overcoat, and his usual black patent leather shoes. He stood tall and wide, with a confident air about him. Bermondsey was his territory and he felt supreme, surrounded by his own team of workers, minders and people who jumped to oblige when he wanted something done. He liked to consider himself first and foremost a successful businessman, and with certain justification. Both his large grocery shops were doing exceptionally well, mainly due to his flourishing wholesale provision business. His drinking club in Camberwell was thriving too. It was a place where local businessmen gathered for an after-hours tipple, and small-time villains congregated to scheme and later celebrate. Archie himself was often seen there, but only as a customer, usually with a young woman on his arm. The club was efficiently run by Larry Petersen, an ex-boxer who commanded respect in the Camberwell district and had his own team of young heavyweights to stamp out any trouble before it got serious. Archie Westlake allowed his manager to run the club in his own way, realising that Petersen's success in the boxing ring ensured a regular clientele of fight fans. Moreover, at a moment's notice Archie would use the club minders when he needed some muscle.

The Bermondsey villain stood listening to Con with his hands thrust down into his overcoat pockets.

'Feelin's are beginnin' ter rise, an' they seem ter feel the bloke's becomin' a risk ter the kids,' the bookie was saying.

'Who's they?' Archie asked.

'The men who live 'ere,' Con replied. 'Joe Molloy was tellin' me 'e spotted the geezer spyin' on some kids in a church 'all the ovver night, would yer believe, an' 'e said the women 'ere are runnin' scared. They've warned the kids not to 'ave anyfing ter do wiv 'im. As it 'appens one o' the punters told me this mornin' that there was a geezer seen lurkin' round by Brady Buildin's the ovver night. 'E reckoned that this nonsense-case was watchin' the little gels playin' in the square an' offered one of 'em sweets ter go fer a walk wiv 'im. Luckily one o' the men spotted 'im in time an' chased 'im off. The description matched this Stebbin's bloke. Mind yer, I've not said anyfing ter Joe Molloy yet about that incident but I'm goin' to, first chance.'

Archie shook his head. 'I wouldn't, Con,' he said quietly. 'It might be best ter keep it ter yerself fer the time bein'. We don't want the men ter get riled up an' start takin' the law inter their own 'ands. Next fing yer know the cozzers are gonna be swarmin' round 'ere an' give the place a bad name. Better if yer leave it ter me. I can sort this out. Where's the geezer work, any idea?'

'I can soon find out,' Con replied.

Archie pulled his coat collar up against the chill wind and took out a cigar from inside his overcoat. 'I've got the press sorted out an' Danny's bin ter see our little friend,' he said with a wry smile. 'If all goes well we'll be in business very shortly.'

Con pulled a box of Swan Vestas out of his coat pocket as he saw Archie fumbling for a light. 'What d'yer fink about Levy? Is 'e ter be trusted?' he asked darkly.

Archie lit his cigar and puffed on it until it was burning evenly. 'I've bin givin' it a lot o' thought,' he replied. 'That's the weak link in the chain. I've gotta nurse 'im fer the present, but when the time's ripe I'll decide what needs ter be done. One fing's fer certain. Levy ain't gonna be in any position ter pull us all down.'

Con nodded and caught the callous look in Archie's eyes. He had known the villain for a number of years, from when they had first teamed up with a violent gang of young men before the war. They had made their mark in Bermondsey and Archie soon became one of the ringleaders. He had never looked back, and it hadn't been very long before he was running the mobs, Con recalled. Despite being involved with most of the criminal activity in the area over the years he had never been convicted of any offence, which afforded him great respect in the eyes of his associates, and the police had been frustrated on more than one occasion when it looked certain that they had finally got him. The Bermondsey villain would leave nothing to chance, and would do whatever was necessary to prolong his reign.

Marcus Levy had been working into the early hours for the past few nights and on Thursday morning it was almost midday before he roused himself. He washed in cold water and had a meagre breakfast of dry toast and coffee before taking a leisurely stroll along Whitechapel Road to the paper shop. Being an artist by profession Marcus was always very observant. He took in scenes, absorbed the colours of sunsets and shades of light in the sky. He watched people, their mannerisms and their expressions, and he drew inspiration from his observations. He listened too, feeling motivated by sounds, the throb of engines, the rattle of trams and the high-pitched whine of the trolley buses. He loved the pulse of the East End and felt comfortable there.

On Thursday morning, however, his trained eye and ear told him that all was not well. It was just an idle observation at first. The tall man in the grey overcoat with the turned-up collar seemed to be looking intently through Hymie Goldblatt's shop window, and nobody ever did that. People either glanced in in passing or they went directly into his shop. Hymie was a tailor of repute, and nowhere else in the East End could a person get a better suit made. People came from far and wide to get measured up at Hymie Goldblatt's, but his shop window was a disgrace. Everyone knew it, including Hymie himself, but he was unrepentant. 'So I'm a tailor,' he had once said to a visiting window-dresser. 'I make suits with my material. Why for should I pay to have you put it all in the window? The piece in there now is an offcut. It wouldn't make a pair of trousers for a midget. I got a sign over the shop, what else do I need?'

Marcus had heard the story several times and he glanced once more at the man in the grey overcoat before he crossed the busy thoroughfare and turned left. When he reached the delicatessen he stopped as he invariably did to take note of all the different food on display in the window. Out of the corner of his eye he noticed the man in the grey overcoat again. He had crossed the road too and this time he seemed to be looking around him as though he was lost. Marcus walked on to the paper shop to buy the *Daily Mirror*, his ear attuned to the regular footsteps behind him. When he came out of the shop he carried on in the same direction until he arrived at Whitehall Court, a narrow byway filled with jewellery shops. The artist instinctively knew that he was being followed. He turned into the court and quickly slipped into a tiny shop to his left. He immediately nodded a greeting to the assistant and then bent down to retie his shoelace.

'Do you make rings to order?' he asked casually,

glancing through the window.

'Yes, sir,' the assistant replied, looking down at him with a smile.

The man in the grey overcoat passed by the window at that instant and Marcus stood up quickly. 'Good for you,' he said, and darted out leaving the young man standing open-mouthed.

When Marcus Levy finally turned into Friar's Court and walked into the Buildings he knew that he was still being followed. He made a pot of coffee and while he sipped the steaming hot black brew his mind was racing. Westlake would have no need to put a tail on him, he thought. The villain would ensure that his investment was left in peace to finish the plates. That left the police. But why should they be interested in him now that he had finished his sentence, unless they suspected something? Marcus poured himself another coffee and as he sat drinking it he was feeling very worried. He could quite easily lead the police to his workshop if he was not careful. That would be the end of everything.

At seven o'clock Marcus left his flat and walked briskly to Ira's restaurant. He knew that whoever had been assigned to follow him would have been relieved by now. Someone else would be dogging his footsteps and would have the cover of darkness.

Marcus reached the restaurant and strolled into the warm interior. Normally he would have walked straight through the passageway and down to the workshop, but on this occasion he sat at a table and waited for Ira to come to him. He looked around at the few occupied tables and was relieved to see Ira approaching him with a smile.

'They're all regulars,' Ira said quietly as he sat down. 'You look worried, Marcus. Is everything all right?'

The artist shrugged his shoulders. 'Can we talk?' he asked.

Ira led the way into his small office behind the kitchen. 'What is it?' he asked quickly.

'I think the police are following me,' Marcus replied. 'In fact I'm positive.'

'What will you do?' Ira asked anxiously.

Marcus sat down heavily in a chair beside the desk and clasped his hands together. 'I expect to be finished by tonight,' he replied. 'I've got everything else sorted out. The trouble is I can't stay here too long if there is a tail on me. I'd better get to work right away.'

Ira nodded. 'I shouldn't think they'd come into the restaurant, more likely wait in the shadows until you go out,' he said reassuringly.

Marcus stood up. 'What will you do if the policeman does comes in?' he asked nervously.

'How would I know?' Ira replied. 'I shouldn't worry though. I don't get many strangers in here until the pubs turn out, but if someone comes in asking for you I'll say you've paid your bill and left by the back door.'

'Supposing he wants to look around?' Marcus asked.

'I'll just ask for his search warrant. I know my rights,' Ira replied, grinning widely.

Marcus sighed deeply and bit thoughtfully on his lip. 'Can I use your phone, Ira?'

'Help yourself.'

Marcus reached out for Ira's hand. 'Things may go crazy in the next few days, old friend,' he said quietly. 'Just in case I don't get another chance, I want you to know I'll be forever in your debt. One day we'll meet again, I know it.'

The two embraced warmly and there were tears in Ira's eyes as he stood back. 'I owe you much. My family owe you much,' he said quietly. 'How can I ever forget that without your help my mother and father would probably be lying buried in some huge, nameless pit in one of the concentration camps? I know they thank you as I do. Now they can at least live out their few remaining years in peace and safety.'

Archie Westlake walked into the saloon bar of the Sultan with a stern look on his broad face. 'Jack, get somebody ter relieve yer. We gotta talk,' he growled.

The publican called June from the public bar to take over, then he ushered Archie into the small back room and closed the door after him.

Archie slipped out of his thick overcoat and threw it over the back of a chair. 'I've phoned fer Danny Steadman and Con Noble,' he said. 'They'll be 'ere soon. I fink we'd better 'ave a drink.'

Jack Murray reached down into a low cupboard and took out a bottle of Scotch whisky and some glasses. He did not ask Archie what was going on. Instead, he carefully filled two glasses in silence and handed one to the villain. There was trouble brewing, he could sense it. He had expected as much since Levy's release. The artist was bad news.

Archie had a stern look about him as he sipped the Scotch. ' 'Ow much longer are they gonna be?' he grumbled aloud.

Five minutes later Con Noble walked in, closely followed by Danny Steadman. Both men had a look of expectation on their faces as they sat down and picked up their filled glasses.

Archie Westlake lost no time in beginning. 'We've got a problem,' he said simply.

'What's the trouble, Archie?' Danny asked.

'Levy's finished the plates,' he replied. 'Problem is the dozy bastard's got 'imself a permanent shadow.'

'The cozzers?' Con asked.

Archie nodded darkly. 'Don't ask me the reason. I just don't know,' he growled. 'Levy phoned me an hour ago. 'E said I was ter go personally to Ira Stanley's restaurant in Whitechapel Road termorrer evenin' at seven o' clock wiv a female companion, those were 'is words. I'm to 'ave the money parcelled up an' take a seat nearest the door. It'll be marked reserved, an' I'm ter wait fer instructions.'

'What game's Levy playin' at?' Danny asked angrily. 'That's the place 'e's got the workshop, as I told yer.'

Archie's face was hard with rage as he sipped his drink in silence, and his companions sat waiting for him to say something.

'I'll crucify that little Yid if 'e's pullin' a fast one,' Archie thundered suddenly.

'I say we should go visit 'im ternight,' Danny suggested. 'I fink 'e's tryin' ter bluff us wiv the story about bein' tailed.'

Archie shook his head. 'I don't fink so. I reckon 'e's runnin' scared,' he answered. ' 'E certainly sounded it on the phone. If we go over ternight an' crash in on 'im, we've implicated ourselves by just bein' there.'

Con Noble put down his empty glass and looked around at the company. 'All right then. Let's say we do as 'e instructs us ter do,' he said. 'We get the plates an' when we try 'em out they're duff. We're six 'undred smackers down the drain. No, we've gotta bring Levy back 'ere, an' if the plates are rubbish then we do what we 'ave ter do.'

'If 'e is bein' tailed then we've got a problem,' Jack Murray pointed out. 'I fink we should do as 'e sez.'

Archie took the bottle of Scotch and proceeded to refill all the glasses. 'As much as I don't like bein' told what ter do, I'm gonna foller the instructions ter the letter,' he announced. 'I'll tell yer this though. If Levy puts one foot wrong I'll personally cut 'is froat.'

The night was dark, with a pale moon peeping fitfully from heavy cloud, as the two young people walked home arm in arm. Laura was quiet, thinking about the film, and about the attention Eddie had paid her as they sat in the back row of the half-empty cinema, the soft kisses he had stolen in the darkness. She was falling in love and it frightened her.

Eddie turned his head briefly to smile at her without saying anything as they walked along the wide pavement beneath a row of huge plane trees. He felt the warmth of her hand resting gently on his arm, and Laura could feel the closeness of his athletic body as they made their way unhurriedly to Pedlar's Row.

They had settled down in the darkened cinema feeling comfortable and warm, and very soon Eddie had reached out and clasped her hand. She felt safe and secure, enjoying the gentle caressing of his fingers, and later, when the Hawaiian moon cast silvery light on the sheltering palms and the heroine melted to the sounds of the strumming guitars on the large screen, their lips met in a secret kiss. It was soft, warm and delicious, and she felt a deep thrill inside her. His arm was around her shoulders and she leaned close to him, aware of the smell of aftershave and his slow, even breathing. She closed her eyes and imagined him loving her fully, and she snuggled closer, willing him to kiss her once more.

Now, as they walked home in silence, Laura knew that she wanted him, wanted to be with him for ever, and the intensity of her feelings frightened her. They lived so near to each other, just a few houses apart, but the strictures of circumstance could so easily tear them asunder. She must control her feelings, she told herself, let their relationship grow steadily and not let her emotions rule her head.

Eddie broke the silence, as if knowing what she was thinking. 'It's good that we live so near to each ovver, but it could be difficult at times,' he said.

'I know what yer mean,' Laura answered him.

246

'You are my gel now, ain't yer?' Eddie asked, his dark eyes full of anxiety as he looked at her.

'Yes, I am, as long as yer want me ter be,' she replied, smiling warmly at him.

Eddie squeezed her hand firmly in both his. 'I really like yer a lot, Laura,' he said softly. 'I feel really good when I'm wiv yer.'

'That's 'ow I feel,' she replied. 'I never felt as good as I do now, Eddie. I want us ter be tergevver always, but yer gotta remember the position I'm in.'

'I understand,' he told her, and with a sudden burst of enthusiasm he said, 'look, 'ow d'yer like ter come to a social evenin' on Saturday night? It's the dockers' club dance. I've bin before on occasions, but it's just bin a boozy evenin'. This time I want you ter come wiv me. I wanna show yer off ter me pals.'

Laura laughed aloud. 'Yeah, I'd like ter come. Can yer dance?'

Eddie shook his head firmly. 'No, I've got two left feet.' With a sudden afterthought he said, 'But if you like dancin' I'd manage a waltz, or maybe a quickstep.'

'I'll teach yer ter dance,' she laughed. 'I used ter be pretty good, if I say so myself.'

'Yer on,' he said quickly. 'Where shall we practise, in the Row?'

They laughed gaily and then Eddie's face suddenly became serious. 'I need ter know, Laura. 'Ave I got a rival anywhere?'

She shook her head and gave him a sweet smile. 'There's nobody else, an' there's not bin fer a long while now. There was someone once, but that's bin over fer years. One day I'll tell yer about 'im, if yer want me to, but not now.'

They had reached Weston Street and as they turned into the quiet side road he slipped his arm around her slim waist. 'I've really enjoyed ternight,' he told her. 'I can't wait till Saturday. Wait till the lads see yer comin' in the club on me arm. I'm gonna feel really proud.'

They stopped in the shadow of the box factory and moved into the darkness of the recessed entrance. Immediately they were in each other's arms and their lips met in a passionate kiss. Laura felt his body pressed against her and she melted to him, allowing his hands to stroke her back as they cuddled close. Her whole life had suddenly changed. There was a man now, a man she was growing to love and who was loving her. He seemed so gentle, yet he was so strong and protective. He had come into her life not a moment too soon, rekindling the physical desire and affection she had always secretly yearned to feel for someone, but feared had gone forever.

They tarried for some time in the darkness and seclusion, their arms around each other, their lips meeting in exciting kisses, and Laura felt her body trembling. Never in her whole life, not even with Ralph, had she ever experienced such exciting sensations of love. She wanted Eddie, needed him badly, and her head began to spin. Suddenly she was kissing him in a way she had never kissed, her mouth open, her lips forcing his open too, her tongue moving sensuously in wild abandon, tempting him, daring him to greater expressions of love, then quickly she broke free and gasped for air, resting her head on his shoulder. 'I'm fallin' in love,' she whispered.

'I already 'ave,' he replied, his cheek pressed against hers, his arms enveloping her tightly.

'I must go in now,' she whispered. 'I don't want to but I must.'

They walked out of the shadows and along into Pedlar's Row. The night had grown misty and it was beginning to swirl.

'I'll call fer yer Saturday,' Eddie said, smiling lovingly at her.

Laura squeezed his hand and watched him walk the few yards to his own front door. 'Good night, Eddie,' she said in a soft voice.

He lifted his hand in a wave. 'Good night, Laura,' he replied.

Chapter Twenty-Three

Wally Stebbings closed the ledger on Friday evening and stroked his eyebrows with the tips of his fingers. The accounts had not made sense and he had started to panic as he struggled with the figures. There had been a large deficit and as he searched the columns for some solution he had suddenly spotted the omission. The Barrington account had not been rendered. Why had he not entered it? he wondered. It was not like him to be so lax. Maybe he had been preoccupied with something or other at the time. Whatever the cause he would have to put it right before he packed up for the evening. He could not go home with that worry on his mind.

It had taken him the best part of an hour to get the accounts straight and when he finally finished he was feeling exhausted. It was silly to worry so, he knew, but being efficient and spot-on with the figures had become very important lately. The firm was changing. New managers were in control and new contracts were coming in all the time. The management team were younger, of a different calibre than the older, more fatherly figures he had grown used to dealing with. The younger team had recently dismissed two female clerks for laziness and had made it very clear that they would not tolerate slothfulness or incompetence.

Wally put the heavy ledger back on to the shelf and stretched before reaching for his coat and hat. He must be getting old, he thought. Normally he would have finished the monthly balances by early afternoon and it was now almost five thirty. His mother would be concerned at his lateness, though she would guess he had had some extra work to do. He remembered telling her that he might be a little late that evening. Never mind, it was all sorted out now and there was a good night's entertainment on the wireless. His regular copy of *Hobbies* should have arrived too and he was looking forward to reading through it in search of new fretwork projects to get started on.

As he adjusted his scarf and slipped on his trilby Gladys Ward came into the office. 'You're late this evening, Wally,' she said. 'You must like your job.'

Wally smiled sheepishly. 'I've been very busy,' he replied.

Gladys gave him a long look through her pink-rimmed spectacles. He was so timid, she thought. The poor man needed a good woman to sort him out, not that she could fancy him. Humphrey Bogart or Spencer Tracy were her kind of men. They were masterful and romantic, not like poor Wally. He would go all jellified if a woman made a pass at him. Perhaps she should have a word with Molly French. She was looking for a man and had been for as long as she had known her. Molly would be the right woman for Wally Stebbings. She was desperate and not too fussy, as long as he was able.

'Going out tonight?' she asked.

Wally shook his head. 'No, I'm going to be busy tonight,' he replied.

'Well, don't be late in the morning, Wally. The manager wants us to be here sharp for the staff meeting,' she reminded him.

Wally needed no reminder of the meeting. It had been on his mind all day, and as he walked down the stone stairs to the street he began to worry. It might mean that the management were going to reorganise their set-up, he thought. It could mean that there would be some cutting of staff, particularly the older members. He would have to make sure those ledgers were kept up to date. He could not afford to make any more mistakes like the one today.

The cold hit Wally as he left the factory and he pulled up his coat collar as he turned towards Pedlar's Row. The fog was settling down and the night air was chill but he did not mind. It was nice to just sit beside the fire and read his *Hobbies* monthly on a night such as this.

' 'Ello, mister. You're Stebbin's, ain't yer?'

Two heavily built young men had fallen into step with him and Wally looked nervously from one to the other. 'Yes, I'm Mr Stebbings,' he replied. 'What do you . . . What . . . '

The men had each taken an arm and they began propelling Wally along Weston Street. 'We need ter talk,' the man on his right said gruffly. 'It won't take long.'

Wally started to protest. 'But I live here. I've got to . . .'

'It's all right. I said it won't take long,' the young man told him forcefully. 'Just keep quiet or it'll get a bit unpleasant.'

As Wally was hurried along past the entrance to Pedlar's Row, he felt a cold fear gripping at his insides. This sort of thing only happened in films, not in Bermondsey. He was being abducted and there was nothing he could do. The two men looked like prize fighters, young and powerfully built. He glanced from one to the other and saw only a dead look on their faces. Where were they taking him? What was going to happen to him?

The men swung left at the next narrow turning, with the thoroughly frightened Wally Stebbings wedged between them and unable to resist. At the end of the road they turned left into Cooper Street.

'We wanna show yer somefing,' the vocal one said.

Wally now feared for his life as they dragged him through a gap in the corrugated fencing on to the bomb site. There was no one about, no one who could help him, and Wally began to plead. 'Look, I'm just going home from work. You must have mistaken me for somebody else,' he whined. 'What have I done?'

Suddenly a fist landed square in Wally's face and he staggered back and fell on to the rubble. For a time he could only see bright lights in front of his eyes and when his vision cleared a little he saw one of the men standing above him with his legs apart.

'Get up, Stebbin's.'

'Let me go, please let me go,' Wally pleaded, bringing his hand up to his face and feeling the wetness under his nose and on his lips.

'I said get up.'

'Please don't hurt me. What have I done? I don't even know you,' Wally cried out in panic.

The man who until now had been silent pushed his colleague to one side and stood over Wally. 'We don't like nonsense-cases round 'ere, an' yer better believe it,' he said menacingly. 'We like our kids ter be able ter play in the streets in safety, wivout the likes o' you dirty ole bastards interferin' wiv 'em. Now do you understand what it's all about?'

Wally felt a wave of revulsion. How could anyone suspect him of interfering with children? The little boys in Pedlar's Row would be able to testify that he had no such ideas. 'I've never touched any child,' he said imploringly. 'Anyone would tell you that.'

The violent one came forward. He slowly and deliberately undid his coat and took out a short length of hosepipe that had been tucked in his belt. 'Unfortunately fer you, it's time fer yer comeuppance,' he said quietly and menacingly. 'Now are you gonna get on yer feet an' take it like a man, or are yer gonna sit there an' get kicked from 'ere ter breakfast time? It's up ter you.'

Charlie Bromley and his best friend Terry Grant had long faces as they walked slowly home from Brady Buildings in Farrow Street.

'They're just scared,' Charlie grumbled. 'Fancy them sayin' we're cheaters.'

Terry laughed aloud. 'Anybody would fink those cards o' yours was cheatin' cards.'

Charlie's dirty face broke into a wide grin. 'It don't matter about them kids not playin' cards wiv us, I've told me mum I want soldiers fer me birfday, standin'-up soldiers.'

'I've told my mum too,' Terry replied. 'Trouble is my birfday's years away. I gotta wait right till November.'

'That's not fair,' Charlie said sympathetically.

The two ambled along, their coat collars pulled up against the cold, their socks round their ankles, and Charlie scheming as usual.

'I reckon those Buildin's kids would buy our treasure map fer six stand-up soldiers,' he said thoughtfully.

'We could give 'em our bag o' marbles if they give us anuvver six,' Terry added.

'What time's yer tea?'

'Six o'clock.'

'Mine's quarter ter six, but it's never ready when I go in,' Charlie grumbled. 'I know, let's go an' get our map an' the marbles. We can see if they wanna do a swap.'

The two young lads clambered quickly over the rubble of the Cooper Street bomb site to their secret hideaway.

'I fink nobody in the world could find our secret 'ideout,' Charlie said as he ducked under the stairway.

Terry crawled in after him and helped him slide the

small stone slab from over the hole. 'We could 'ide anyfing 'ere,' he remarked.

Charlie fished out the piece of folded paper and the bag of marbles. 'One day when I'm really rich I'm gonna come 'ere an' stash a lot o' real treasure,' he said.

'I wonder if this place will always be 'ere?' Terry said, looking up at the timbers above their heads.

'I should fink so,' Charlie replied. 'It's bin 'ere fer years an' years. My dad said the Germans dropped a fousand-pounder on this bomb site.'

'Cor, that must be a very big bomb,' Terry remarked.

Suddenly the lads heard a disturbance outside and then faint muffled voices. Charlie peered out from the hideaway and saw Wally Stebbings being dragged on to the bomb site. 'It's Mr Stebbin's,' he whispered.

The two youngsters watched wide-eyed as Wally was manhandled on to more level ground, and then they saw the first punch.

'Cor! Those men are beatin' poor Mr Stebbin's up!' Terry gasped.

'Let's get a copper,' Charlie hissed.

Unseen, the two lads crept out of the bomb site and ran as fast as their legs could carry them back towards Pedlar's Row.

' 'Ere, what's the rush?' Joe Molloy shouted as Charlie crashed into him at the entrance to the Row.

'There's two men murderin' Mr Stebbin's,' Charlie gasped.

'Where?' Joe asked, looking sceptical.

'On the bomb site up there,' Terry panted, pointing along Cooper Street.

'Go an' get yer farvver, Charlie, quick,' Joe shouted as he rushed away.

George Bromley hurried out of the house, still putting his coat on and bumped into Eddie Cassidy, who was walking into the Row. 'Trouble on the bomb site,' he shouted, hoping Eddie would follow him as he broke into a trot.

Wally looked up at his tormentor as the man stood over him and repeatedly slapped the hosepipe against the palm of his hand. 'Please. I've done nothing. I wouldn't dream of hurting young children,' he begged.

'C'mon. On yer feet,' the villain goaded.

'Please let me go,' Wally cried.

The young man moved a step nearer. 'Right, I've told yer fer the last time,' he growled. 'Now I'm gonna kick six buckets o' shit outta yer.'

'I don't fink so,' a voice said from behind him.

The young tough looked round in surprise and saw the large figure of Joe Molloy standing at the edge of the bomb site, his legs planted firmly apart and his thumbs hitched into his wide belt.

'This doesn't concern you, pal, so scram,' the tough said calmly.

'Oh yes it does,' Joe replied, equally calmly. 'I've got a stake in what 'appens ter that fella.'

The quiet one of the two young villains walked towards Joe. 'Look, pal,' he said slowly, 'this geezer 'as bin interferin' wiv young kids. We're gonna make sure 'e don't do it again, so why don't yer go 'ome an' put yer feet up, okay?'

Joe smiled disdainfully. 'I may be a bit older than you, pal,' he said, emphasising the last word, 'but I can still 'andle meself. So piss orf while yer in front, okay?'

The young thug wielding the hosepipe came and stood next to his colleague. 'D'yer fancy endin' up in Guy's, then, Pop?' he grated.

Just then George Bromley stepped on to the bomb site and walked over to stand next to Joe. 'I've bin listenin' outside,' he said quietly. 'I've come in 'ere to balance it up a bit.'

The mouthy tough laughed. 'You two ole fellas wouldn't stand a cat in 'ell's chance against me an' Nobby. Why don't yer piss orf an' let us get on wiv our business.'

Wally had risen to his feet shakily and was brushing his trilby on his cuff. His face was bloody and already swollen from the one heavy punch he had taken.

'You stay where you are, mister. You ain't goin' nowhere,' the other thug ordered him.

'C'mon, Wally, walk over to us,' Joe called out. 'They won't touch yer anymore.'

Wally hesitated and the villain wielding the hosepipe took a step nearer to Joe and George. 'If yer don't piss orf right now we'll turn you two over, understood?'

Suddenly Eddie Cassidy appeared. He sauntered across in front of the two toughs, looking them up and down with a mocking sneer on his face, and took Wally by the arm. 'C'mon, ole mate. Yer okay now,' he said quietly.

Charlie and Terry were peeping into the bomb site, their eyes wide with excitement.

'Cor! This is like a cowboy picture,' Charlie gasped.

'Yeah!' was all Terry could say.

Wally started to move but the villain with the pipe turned towards them. 'D'you want some too?' he growled at Eddie.

'If yer come at me wiv that, pal,' Eddie said quietly, 'I'll take it off yer an' beat yer poxy brains out wiv it.'

Joe and George walked over to join Eddie. 'What brains?' Joe said, smiling derisively.

'All right, all right, what's goin' on 'ere then?' a voice said from the edge of the derelict site.

Everyone turned to see the portly figure of PC Carmody brandishing his truncheon. 'Is this a private fight or can anyone join in?' he asked.

Joe Molloy was first to speak. 'It's all right, Constable.

Me an' me pals are jus' leavin'. C'mon, Wally, say goodbye ter yer friends.'

PC Carmody looked suspiciously at everyone, and particularly at the young toughs. 'Yer ain't from round 'ere, are yer,' he said. 'I know most o' the young bucks from these parts. An' what's that yer got in yer 'and if it ain't yer plonker.'

The thug dropped the hosepipe at his feet. 'I just picked it up 'ere,' he replied in a subdued voice.

'Right then, you lot, let's see yer off the premises,' the policeman said, stern-faced, 'unless anybody wants ter press charges?'

The young toughs left quickly, giving Wally blinding looks as they went. Joe Molloy and Eddie supported the terrified man as they picked their way over the waste-ground and made their way back to Pedlar's Row. Behind them came Charlie and Terry, walking beside George Bromley.

'Did you two find the copper?' George asked them.

'Yeah, Dad. 'E wouldn't come at first, but we told 'im you'd go down the nick about 'im if 'e didn't,' Charlie replied, grinning.

'Well, at least they know me down there, don't they?' George replied, ruffling Charlie's fair hair.

The Sultan was packed, as was usual on a Friday evening, and when George called in for his nightly beverage he had a few questions for Joe Molloy. 'You was the one who reckoned Wally Stebbin's should get a good seein'-to,' he remarked. 'Why the sudden change of 'eart?'

Joe shrugged his broad shoulders and took a large gulp of his pint before answering. 'Well, it was my Bridie really,' he replied. 'Yer see, George, I was tellin' 'er all about what we was sayin' the ovver night concernin' Wally, an' she told me a few fings.'

'Like what?'

'Well, fer starters, Wally Stebbin's spent a lot o' time makin' a model fort fer your lad an' young Terry Grant. I didn't know. On top o' that she told me about what Wally's ole lady showed 'er. D'yer know Wally got a commendation durin' the war. Apparently 'e rescued a crowd of office gels who were trapped in a burnin' office block. 'E done it all on 'is own, in fact. The ole buildin' was in danger o' collapsin', but Wally still went in. It's true 'cos Bridie saw the newspaper cuttin'. Wally's ole lady's got it framed an' she showed my missus last night when they were talkin' about Wally. So yer see, when your lad bumped inter me in the Row an' told us what was goin' on I 'ad ter do somefing. Wally's 'armless, I'm sure. I fink I was wrong ter suspect ovverwise an' I 'old me 'ands up. I don't fink a bloke like 'im could 'arm little kids. Trouble is, yer gotta be so careful. They caught a nonsense-case yesterday, so I 'eard. 'E was caught offerin' sweets ter some young gels. Apparently it's the same bloke who was seen round Brady Buildin's.'

George put a ten-shilling note down on the counter. 'This one's on me, pal. By the way, did yer expect trouble ternight?'

'Yeah, as a matter o' fact I did,' Joe replied.

'We was lucky,' George said. 'What wiv that 'osepipe the geezer was carryin'.'

'Well, I wasn't exactly unarmed,' Joe told him. 'As I run round ter the bomb site I picked up an empty beer bottle. I 'ad it tucked down me belt.'

'Bloody 'ooligan,' George growled.

Chapter Twenty-Four

Archie Westlake sat back against the deep cushioned rear seat and gazed out of the shiny black Wolseley saloon as it crossed Tower Bridge. Beside him was June, the Sultan's barmaid, feeling a little uncomfortable at being asked to accompany the Bermondsey villain into the East End. Archie had merely said that he was on a business trip and needed a partner to help relax the atmosphere, and that a meal was involved. June was puzzled by it all but felt obliged to accept the invitation. Working for the people she did often involved strange requests and she was used to it. Anyway it was good to get away from the pub for a couple of hours on pay, and with a meal thrown in as well.

Danny Steadman was driving, preoccupied with his own private thoughts as he steered the car into Leman Street. He glanced down at the instrument-panel clock and noticed that it was twenty minutes to seven. They would be at their destination in a few minutes and would find out just what was going on. He felt that Marcus Levy was trying to pull a fast one and had invented the story about being followed. The police had better things to do than spend their time tailing an ex-con with no known associates and who was living in a dingy flat, he reckoned. They had no way of knowing that Levy was involved in anything illegal, unless someone had talked. That was impossible. Only he, Jack Murray and Con

Noble were in on the money scheme, apart from Archie himself. Even Ernie Jackson, the foreman printer at Carlton's, had not as yet been told of the project, and he would be a safe bet anyway.

The car pulled up outside Ira Stanley's Kosher Restaurant and Archie stepped out on to the pavement, helping June from the car.

'Now look, luv. Whatever 'appens, don't worry,' he told her. 'It won't concern you. Just stay pretty an' keep a smile on yer face, okay?'

June nodded and stood waiting while Archie had a quick word with Danny. She was wearing a silver fox-fur coat and black high-heeled shoes and she had added an extra touch of make-up to her puffy face, feeling that she should try to look her best while being escorted by the very smartly dressed villain.

Archie watched his driver pull away to park in the next street, then he took June's arm, glancing up at the restaurant frontage. He noticed that full net curtains covered the large window and it was impossible to see who was inside. He pushed open the door and steered June into the warm interior, removed his camel-hair overcoat and hung it on a clothes-stand, then helped June off with her coat and moved the chair out for her at the reserved table before sitting himself down. There were only two other tables occupied, one by a couple of elderly men who appeared to be discussing business, and the other by a young couple who only had eyes for each other.

June glanced at Archie and sat waiting expectantly as the elderly waiter came over and put two menus down on the table.

'We're waitin' fer somebody, we'll eat later,' Archie said quickly. 'Can we get a drink 'ere?'

'I'm sorry, sir, but we're unlicensed,' the waiter told him. 'Can I get you tea or coffee?'

'Two coffees,' Archie replied, not waiting for June to decide what she wanted.

As the waiter was walking away, Marcus Levy entered the restaurant and sat down at the table, looking a little breathless. He was wearing a thin grey overcoat that had seen better days and a grubby white shirt with a thin strip of a tie. He smiled a greeting at Archie and nodded to June, who was beginning to feel that she should have declined the offer of a free meal. The restaurant was not the sort of place she would have picked herself, and Archie's business colleague looked more like a down-and-out.

'There's a plain-clothes tec standing across the street,' Marcus said quietly. 'I wasn't joking on the phone yesterday.'

'Why should they be tailin' you?' Archie asked, his eyes full of suspicion.

'I just don't know, but it's creepy,' Levy replied. 'I've been trying to think why. There's no chance of a leak at your end, is there?'

Archie shook his head dismissively. 'It's tight as a drum. You've not bin openin' yer trap to anyone, 'ave yer?' he asked.

Marcus leaned forward on the table, his long thin fingers clasped nervously. 'Give me some credit, Archie,' he replied quickly. 'I know the score.'

'Right then, 'ow are we gonna play it?' the villain asked, his dark eyes glaring at the frail-looking artist.

Levy looked around quickly before replying. 'Right. You'd better order the meal now, just in case my tail decides to come in. I can't be seen sitting here anyway.'

'What if 'e walks in this minute?' Archie growled.

'I'll be trying to sell you this cigarette case,' Marcus said, taking a slim silver case from his inside pocket and laying it down on the table.

'So what now?' Archie demanded.

'Have you got the money with you?' Levy asked.

Archie tapped the front of his coat. 'It's 'ere,' he replied coldly.

The waiter came over carrying a tray with a coffee pot, a jug of cream, sugar and two cups.

'Leave it, we'll see to it,' Archie said bluntly as the waiter started to unload the tray. He redirected his glare at Marcus. 'I wanna see the plates first.'

The artist sighed and lowered his head slightly. 'You've got to play it my way or it won't work,' he said, impatience creeping into his voice.

'All right, I'm waitin',' Archie growled.

Levy glanced quickly towards the door and then spoke in little more than a whisper. 'I'll take the money now, then I'll give you the package. After that I'll leave and walk straight back to the flat while you eat your meal. It's now ten minutes past seven. I want you to leave here at eight fifteen. Get in the car and drive to where I live. It should only take you a couple of minutes. Stop in Brady Street, well short of Friar's Court, and wait until I come out at eight twenty exactly. Now this is important. I'll be wearing a disguise, it's the only way to shake off whoever's watching my flat. I'll be walking on sticks and I'll be bent over. I'll look like an old man. Let me walk through the Brady Street arch before you pull away and approach me. This is for your benefit, remember. If you stop to pick me up too soon the tec might smell a rat and jot down the number. Is that clear?'

Archie was seething inside. He was not used to being told what to do by anyone, but he realised he had little choice on this occasion. He was not going to submit readily without an argument, however. 'You give me the necessary an' then I'll give you the money when yer get in the car,' he said quietly. 'Ovverwise yer could give me a load o' rubbish an' disappear wiv the cash. I can't take that chance.'

'I'm sorry, but you must do it my way,' Marcus replied firmly. 'You've just got to trust me. I'll be helping you set up the operation anyway, and once you're satisfied with the workmanship we'll part good friends. Doing it your way means that I might never get the chance to spend that money. I think you know what I mean.'

'No, I don't,' Archie replied, struggling to keep his voice down. 'If that's what's worryin' yer, what benefit would it be ter yer if I gave yer the money now? Yer still 'ave ter be involved in settin' everyfing up, unless yer was finkin' o' runnin' off somewhere?'

Marcus looked intently at the villain. 'When you give me the money I'm going to leave it behind the counter,' he said in a measured tone. 'The manager here has got instructions to hold on to it until a messenger calls for it. If the amount is right then he'll bank it and send the receipt to me, care of a certain address. In the meantime I'll be helping you set everything up. There'll be no problems on that score. I have to tell you now that the messenger has also got a sealed letter addressed to Scotland Yard. If I don't personally collect that letter from him by next Tuesday evening then he'll post it. Now I don't think I need explain the contents of it to you. What I do have to tell you is, once everything is set up and we part company, I'm going to move away from London. We won't be meeting again, that's for sure.'

Archie slumped back in his chair, his face dark with anger. Levy had really thought it all out very thoroughly, he had to concede. One thing was for certain. He would track Levy down one day, wherever he went.

June had been sipping her coffee in silence throughout the whole discussion and she could feel the tension around the table. She saw the thinly disguised fear and anxiety in the scruffy individual's face, and the murderous look in her escort's eyes. She wanted to have the promised meal and get back behind the bar of the

Sultan as soon as possible. The atmosphere here was frightening.

Marcus Levy was sitting in silence, nervously waiting for the Bermondsey villain's decision, and it wasn't long in coming.

'All right, 'ere's the money,' Archie said sharply, taking a package from inside his coat. 'It's all there.'

Marcus picked it up quickly and as he left the table the door opened and two couples came in laughing together. The diversion was opportune for Marcus as he handed the package over to Ira with a quick wink and took a carpetbag in return. He sat back down at the table and placed it at Archie's feet. 'I should order a quick meal now,' he said with a ghost of a smile. 'Remember I'll be walking through the arch at eight twenty. So until then.'

As Marcus Levy left the restaurant Archie raised his hand to attract the waiter, then he turned to his companion. 'In business we can't always pick an' choose who we deal wiv, unfortunately,' he said with a cold smile on his face. 'As far as you're concerned, June, this meetin' never took place, okay? Right, now let's eat.'

Danny Steadman sat behind the wheel of the car and lit another Gold Flake. He was in his early fifties, a hard, callous man who had been associated with Archie West-lake since the early days when they ran with the same team of tearaways. Like the Bermondsey villain Danny had made his money by involving himself in shady wheeling and dealing. His intimidating manner had first made him an ideal minder and collector for Westlake, but he had gathered together his own small team of ruthless villains and Archie had come to see him as a potential threat to his dominance in the area. Danny Steadman was now an associate and business partner, and Archie Westlake remained wary.

The winter night was cold and misty and as Steadman

wound down the side window to chuck out his cigarette he heard footsteps. Archie came into view carrying a bag and holding on to June's arm.

'Righto, Danny, let's get goin' ter Levy's place,' he said quickly as he and June climbed into the car.

Danny drove into the Whitechapel Road and swung into Brady Street, pulling up where Archie indicated. 'What's goin' on?' he asked, and getting no answer from Archie who was staring out of the side window he said, 'Do I get ter know what's goin' on?'

'We're waitin' fer the Yid, Danny. 'E's gonna be playin' at dressin' up,' Archie replied gruffly. Suddenly he stiffened. 'There 'e is, look, the ole boy,' he said quickly. 'That's Levy. Let 'im get frew the arch before we set off.'

Danny Steadman shook his head slowly as though he was imagining it all. 'Oo the bloody 'ell does 'e fink 'e is, Sherlock 'Olmes?' he growled.

Archie tapped Danny on the shoulder. 'Right, off yer go, an' take it steady. Let 'im get right frew.'

As the bent figure emerged at the other side of the long, dark arch, the car pulled up and Archie opened the door. 'Get in, Levy.'

The figure walked on, taking no notice and Archie leapt from the car, reaching out and grabbing the man's arm roughly.

'Mein Gott. Vas is dis?' the old man shouted, his eyes wide with fear as he stared at the Bermondsey villain.

Archie released the man's arm and muttered his apologies. As he turned away towards the car, he suddenly felt the weight of the old man's walking stick across his shoulders. 'You svine! I show you vat you get!'

Archie jumped into the car and slumped back against the upholstery as Danny put his foot down on the accelerator. ' 'E's tricked us, Danny,' he groaned. 'I'll cut the bastard inter little pieces when I do find 'im.'

Wally Stebbings emerged from the casualty department of Guy's Hospital feeling very shaky. He had a
plaster spread across his broken nose, and the area
round his eyes was already beginning to turn black.
The casualty sister had seemed sceptical when he told
her that he had tripped and fallen against a tree. She
was an old hand at dealing with assault victims and
knew the difference between a tree and a clenched fist.
She was also aware that there was probably a very
good reason why such patients preferred not to tell the
truth and press charges. She fixed his nose, handed
him the doctor's prescription and pointed him in the
general direction of the pharmacy. He looked a sad
figure, she felt, but there was no time to stand
wondering. Other cases were waiting.

Wally walked out of the hospital feeling very grateful
to the men who had come to his aid. At least they didn't
think he was a child molester, and they were his neighbours. Who could have been responsible for the attack?
he puzzled. He had not done anything to warrant
suspicion. His mother had warned him about having
those young lads in the house, but Charlie's father had
been one of the men who came to his assistance. It must
be something else, something he had done inadvertently
to arouse suspicion. In future he would talk to no one,
not even the two lads. What would they think in the
office? he wondered. Would they believe his explanation? The casualty sister certainly didn't, he felt sure.
Never mind, he would have to try and forget what had
happened. There was a good programme on the wireless, and he still had the *Hobbies* magazine to look
forward to.

On Saturday lunchtime Ben Walsh looked thoughtful as
he beckoned his sergeant into a chair. 'I've just had a

phone call from Leman Street, Gordon,' he said. 'Marcus Levy's gone missing.'

'Gone missing?' Ashley echoed with a puzzled frown.

'Adam Burrows just gave me the details,' Ben Walsh went on. 'Apparently Levy's been tagged constantly and the only place he visited was a restaurant in Whitechapel Road, apart from a daily stroll to buy newspapers. He made two evening visits to the restaurant, and the second time, which was last night, he only stayed for about fifteen minutes. He went straight back home, presumably to bed. The relieving officer was a bit concerned when Levy failed to appear this morning to get his papers. He went up to the flat and discovered that there was someone else living there, a Mr Ruben Solomon. He told the officer that Levy had been staying there and that he'd left to go on a holiday.'

'He must have given the officer the slip somehow,' Ashley remarked. 'What was he doing, dossing on the job?'

'Levy might have left after midnight,' Walsh replied. 'He could have caught a night train somewhere.'

'We should have had a twenty-four-hour watch on the man,' Ashley said irritably.

'They couldn't do it,' Walsh told him. 'They're working flat out at Leman Street. There's two unsolved murders and God knows what else. I had to almost plead with Burrows as it was.'

'You say that Levy visited a restaurant twice. Would there be any tie-up there?' Ashley asked.

Walsh shrugged his shoulders. 'The man went there to eat, what else?'

'It's a pity we didn't turn the flat over,' the sergeant remarked.

'Like I said before, Gordon, it's all a question of playing it by the book. We had no solid reason to get a search warrant. It was only gut feelings, and that's not reason enough, sad to say.'

'We could get Leman Street to slip in the restaurant for a few discreet enquiries,' Ashley suggested.

Walsh nodded. 'I suppose it wouldn't do any harm. I'll get on to Adam Burrows first thing on Monday morning.'

Ashley got up and stretched. 'I'm off home now, guv, if that's all.'

As Sergeant Ashley was going out, the phone rang, and just as he was closing the door behind him, Ben Walsh shouted his name. He came back into the office and waited until his superior officer put the phone down.

'Yes, guv?'

'That was Leman Street. Marcus Levy threw himself into the Thames late last night,' Walsh said quietly. 'He left a suicide note.'

Chapter Twenty-Five

On Friday evening Marcus Levy left Westlake in the restaurant and breathed a huge sigh of relief. His ploy had worked. The Bermondsey villain had been left with little room to manoeuvre. He couldn't take the chance of being seen together with him in the street and he had been forced to comply with the arrangement. Ira Stanley would do his part and look after the money, once he had made sure that it was all there.

The artist turned into Brady Street feeling quite elated. The plain-clothes officer would no doubt be close behind him, but it did not matter now. Everything was under control. He had to make the necessary last-minute arrangements with Ruben Solomon and then get into his disguise. Ruben had been quite excited when asked to make a comeback, even if there was to be no audience to speak of. Ruben had trod the boards for years in minor roles but he would never know how important his coming role would be. It could even be seen as a starring part, Marcus thought, smiling to himself as he walked into the Buildings.

The ageing Ruben pocketed the five-pound note and picked up his walking sticks. 'I think I'll go and sit with Golda Cohen until it's time for the curtain to go up,' he said. 'Tonight will be the performance of my life. Tonight I shall join the immortals, Sir Henry Irving, the Barrymores.'

'Just be careful, old friend,' Marcus warned him. 'Don't do anything silly. The man's an animal.'

Ruben clasped hands with Marcus. 'Good luck, my friend. May fortune chance to smile on you.'

Once Ruben had left, Marcus stripped out of his grubby suit. It took him quite a while to perfect his disguise, his eyes constantly on the clock. At ten minutes to eight he walked out of the flat carrying a shopping bag containing his coat, trousers and shoes. He walked with a slight movement of the hips, anxious that he did not wobble in his high-heeled shoes, and when he finally reached the Whitechapel Road he hailed a taxi. The driver did not give him a second glance when instructed to go to the Cherry Tree pub in Wapping, and when Marcus gave him a large tip as he alighted, the driver managed a saucy wink.

In the darkness and solitude of Wapping Steps the artist took out his suit from the bag and folded it neatly before putting it down above the high-water mark at the top of the slimy stone steps. On top of the folded suit he placed his shoes and inside the left shoe he tucked a sealed envelope. His task completed, Marcus retraced his steps and walked out on to the Wapping Highway. Fifteen minutes later he arrived at Ira's house in Bow and let himself in with a key. Everything was there: his clothes, suitcases, a few books and some mementoes he would take with him to the new world. He had better hurry, he thought. Ira's messenger would arrive soon with the money.

The night was clearing and a full moon came out from behind a cloud as the taxi pulled into the forecourt of Euston Station. The well-dressed man alighted, pulled his cashmere overcoat over his shoulders and adjusted his fedora. 'There you are, my man, keep the change,' he said in a cultured voice.

As the taxi sped away, Marcus Levy took a last look at

the city outline, and turning on his heel Hiram Stanley, artist and interior designer, possessor of introductory letters from the influential Thorpes of Toronto, flicked the ash from his cigarette holder and ordered a porter to take his fine leather suitcases to the Liverpool train.

Lucy Grant had a long chat with her good friend Val Bennett on Saturday morning after they had both finished work for the week. Lucy had always found Val to be very sympathetic and understanding, and she needed desperately to talk to someone. She could not bring herself to discuss her problems with Laura, partly because her sister was unmarried and also because she was too close for Lucy to feel comfortable talking about such things with her. Val was more approachable and perhaps she could offer good advice, Lucy thought.

Val Bennett shook her head sadly as they sat together in the little café that the factory women frequented. 'I fink there's a danger wiv takin' sleepin' pills, luv,' she said quietly. 'If it 'elps 'im in the short term it'll be fine, but 'e can't afford ter rely on 'em.'

'That's what I'm worried about, ' Lucy replied. 'We might as well be bruvver an' sister the way fings are goin'. We just don't make love anymore. As soon as 'is 'ead touches the piller 'e's asleep. I know it's stopped those terrible nightmares 'e was 'avin', but I'm gettin' ter be a nervous wreck. I need 'im, Val. I need some lovin'.'

'Ain't yer sat down an' 'ad a chat to 'im about it?' Val asked.

' 'E just won't talk about it,' Lucy replied, toying with her teaspoon. 'When we went ter the doctor's tergevver I expected 'im ter be referred ter someone who could sort fings out. You know the sort o' places I'm talkin' about. There's that special clinic at Guy's.'

'Yeah, I've 'eard about it,' Val replied. 'Maybe yer should've suggested that ter the doctor.'

'Well, I did, sort of,' Lucy answered.

'What d'yer mean, sort of?' Val asked.

'Roy didn't want ter be seen as a nervous wreck. 'E just said 'e couldn't sleep an' 'e needed some medication,' Lucy replied. 'I only started ter suggest that 'e see a specialist an' even then 'e shut me up quick, an' when we got 'ome 'e really told me off. We've gotta go back ter see the doctor next week an' Roy's already told me that 'e's gonna get anuvver supply.'

'Well, yer gotta try an' get 'im ter talk, Lucy, or yer'll be a suitable case fer treatment yerself,' Val said with a sympathetic smile.

Lucy pushed the teacup back and reached into her handbag for a cigarette. 'It's impossible. I even tried ter frighten 'im by sayin' that if 'e didn't talk about 'is problems our marriage'd break up. 'E just told me I was bein' melodramatic. 'E said that I should be more patient wiv 'im. What does 'e expect of me, Val? I've already waited fer more than four years fer 'im ter come 'ome, an' now it's just terrible.'

Val reached out and squeezed a tearful Lucy's hand. 'Look, I dunno what yer wantin' me ter say, but I'm not gonna encourage yer ter take a lover, if that's it. First yer gotta try an' get Roy ter take yer out at weekends. Go to a lively pub fer a few drinks. That might relax 'im enough ter be more responsive in bed, but if 'e won't go, then yer gotta get out yerself. Go out wiv a friend, or even Laura. P'raps Roy might pull 'imself tergevver then, 'specially if 'e finks yer up fer grabs. If all that don't work then yer 'ave ter decide fer yerself what yer gonna do about it. There's plenty o' fellas who can oblige, an' I mean the sort who don't want any commitments. If yer do decide to 'ave a bit o' fun, remember yer gotta be ready fer Roy when 'e does come round, 'cos I'm sure 'e will.'

Lucy smiled affectionately at her friend. 'Yer always

seem ter know what I wanna 'ear, Val,' she told her gratefully. 'I do love Roy, truly I do, an' I dearly want our marriage ter be as it was, but I can't stand 'is indifference terwards me.'

'Well, if yer finally do decide to 'ave a bit on the side, just make sure there's no deep involvement,' Val warned. 'Treat it as a stop gap, not some wild romantic affair.'

Lucy drew hard on her cork-tip cigarette. 'Tell me somefing, Val. 'Ave you ever 'ad an affair?'

The big woman chuckled loudly. 'Six weeks after I first met my ole man 'e 'ad me in bed,' she replied. 'I got pregnant straight away, so it was a quick weddin', I've got seven kids now, so where the bloody 'ell d'yer fink I could 'ave found the time ter go gallivantin'? Mind yer, there was the odd time when I was tempted. We 'ad a lovely milkman who used ter call on us. 'E always stopped fer a chat an' a cuppa when 'e came round fer the money. Trouble was though, I was always up ter me armpits in shitty napkins an' Farley's rusks. I did like 'im though. I bet I could've made 'is eyes sparkle.'

Lucy laughed aloud, beginning to feel much better for the chat with her old friend. 'Well, I'd better be off 'ome,' she said. 'Fanks fer everyfing, Val. I really appreciate it.'

Val stood up and buttoned her coat up over her ample proportions. 'Just remember what I said, luv. All yer gotta do is be careful, an' if yer can't be careful, remember the date.'

On Saturday lunchtime, in a room above the Sultan which was normally used for union meetings, Archie Westlake sat at the head of the table with a large cigar in his hand and a glass of Scotch whisky at his elbow. The three men sitting with him looked serious as he went over the events of the previous evening, and when he finished talking and reached for his glass, Jack Murray was the first to speak.

'Until we get the plates set up on the machine we won't know if Levy's done the business,' he remarked.

Archie glanced at his wristwatch. 'Ernie Jackson'll be 'ere soon,' he replied. ' 'E can 'ave a look at 'em, 'e should be able ter tell us.'

Danny Steadman drained his glass and pulled a face. 'If that little Yid 'as done us down we'll find 'im, no matter where 'e tries to 'ide. We've all got a stake in this,' he growled.

Con Noble had managed to get a stand-in to take his place in Pedlar's Row while he attended the meeting, and he was concerned by what Archie had said. 'When d'yer plan to 'ave the press goin' then, Archie?' he asked.

The Bermondsey villain smiled mysteriously. 'We're startin' ternight.'

'Ternight?' Danny said incredulously. 'The printin' machine's not even set up yet. It'll take us at least a couple o' days.'

'We're doin' the print-run at Carlton's,' Archie said quietly for effect.

The puzzled looks around the table only served to encourage his cryptic reserve. 'Ernie Jackson'll be 'ere any minute. Let's wait fer 'im,' he said, reaching for the bottle of Scotch.

Jack Murray poured himself a drink next, looking away from Archie Westlake's thoughtful gaze. He was feeling uneasy and finding it difficult to relax.

'Yer look a bit worried, Jack. Is everyfing all right?' Archie asked him suddenly.

The publican nodded quickly. 'Yeah, I'm fine,' he replied, taking a large gulp from his glass.

'There's no problems wiv the pub, is there?' Archie pressed.

Jack struggled to control his sudden attack of nerves. 'No, I've 'ad a run-in wiv Alma,' he answered. 'She's comin' on 'eavy again. It's nuffink I can't sort out.'

'Wives are a bloody nuisance. My ole woman told me the ovver night she'd like a place in the country,' Danny said, grinning widely. 'Can yer imagine me prunin' roses an' growin' spuds? I'd be a ravin' lunatic inside two weeks.'

The general laughter was cut short when Ernie Jackson walked in. He was middle-aged, tall and lean, with a bald head and a bulbous nose which he had acquired through heavy drinking. He wore thick-lensed spectacles in dark frames and as he nodded to the gathering and sat down, he immediately glanced lovingly at the half-empty bottle of Scotch.

' 'Elp yerself, Ern,' Archie said genially. 'Then I want yer ter take a look at somefing an' give us yer expert opinion.'

Carlton's foreman printer poured himself a stiff draught, swallowed it in one gulp, and then looked around at the amused smiles of the assembly.

Archie reached down by his feet and lifted up a carpetbag, which he placed on the table. 'Pass it over to 'im, Jack,' he said.

Ernie handled the contents of the bag as though they were delicate pieces of china, peering closely at them and moving them around in his long fingers. 'They seem very good, excellent in fact,' he announced. 'Of course we'll have to see how the colour-match looks. That's the secret, you see.'

The relieved faces slowly assumed puzzled frowns as Ernie pointed out the intricacies of colour printing. 'These plates overprint,' he told them. 'Each one has to complement the other, so to speak.'

'All right, Ernie. You can start this evenin' then,' Archie said.

Con Noble, Murray and Steadman looked at each other and then stared at Archie Westlake's grinning face.

'What was the point o' dismantlin' a machine an' takin' it down ter the yard if we're not gonna use it?' Danny asked.

'Ben Walsh, that's why,' Archie replied, his face becoming serious. 'All right, I know I dismissed yer fears about 'im showin' up at the pub, but wiv someone like Walsh we've gotta be one step in front all the time. We may 'ave a grass on the manor. I don't know, but it seems strange that the cozzer suddenly shows up when we're all there. I gotta tell yer now that the press we took out o' Carlton's wouldn't do the job. It's a duff bit o' machinery, an' as far as the print workers knew, it was bein' sold as scrap. That's what Larry Petersen's muscle boys were told when they shifted it, an' apart from them, only us in this room knew the destination. Nevertheless, I ain't takin' chances wiv Ben Walsh. If 'e's 'ad a sniff o' what we plan ter do, 'e'll be spendin' 'is time tryin' ter find out where the press went to. Ernie's gonna do the print-run termorrer, all bein' well, so let's 'ave a drink on it.'

Both Con Noble and Jack Murray hid their displeasure at being kept in the dark, but Danny glared at Archie. 'Yer've obviously put Ernie in the picture, why weren't we told?' he asked him.

Archie leaned forward over the table. 'I've put a lot o' time, as well as our capital, inter gettin' this venture off the ground, Danny,' he said coldly. 'It was my idea in the first place, an' I was given the okay, remember? Now I don't see why I should 'ave ter justify the way I play it. Don't lose sight o' the fact that we stay in business only as long as we play our cards close to our chests. If any of us show our 'and or get a bit loose-tongued, then the likes o' Ben Walsh'll stamp on us.'

Before Danny could say anything, Con Noble cut in. 'Look, we all know the score, so let's take that drink, shall we?' he said quickly, seeking to diffuse the tension.

Jack Murray waved away the proffered bottle. 'I've gotta see 'ow fings are goin' downstairs, lads,' he said, getting up from the table.

Archie watched as Murray left the room, then he turned to Danny. 'What's all this about 'im an' Alma?' he asked.

'It's about uppin' the maintenance fer 'er an' the kids,' Danny replied. 'The scum-bag she was shacked up wiv pulled out an' left 'er penniless.'

'Does Alma know about Jack's barmaid movin' in wiv 'im?' Archie asked.

'Yeah, she knows, but she's not concerned. 'Er an' Jack were finished long ago,' Danny said, sipping his drink.

'That geezer Alma was livin' wiv, does Jack know 'im?' Archie enquired.

'I dunno, Jack don't say too much about it,' Danny replied with a shrug of his broad shoulders.

'Well, I don't want 'im back on the bottle, not wiv what we've got lined up,' Archie said firmly.

Danny smiled cynically and glanced at Ernie Jackson, who was refilling his glass. ' 'E can put it away,' he remarked.

Archie took the point. 'Ernie always works better when 'e's pissed. Besides, 'e knows the score. Wiv 'is past record they'd chuck the key away next time they feel 'is collar.'

Con looked around the table. 'I'd better be gettin' back ter the pitch if we're finished,' he said.

Archie nodded then turned to Ernie Jackson. 'Right, let's get the goods in the car then I'll run yer over ter the factory. Yer can't be seen 'umpin' that lot frew the streets.'

There was a gentle tap on the door then June looked into the room. 'Sorry ter disturb yer, but I thought yer should see this,' she said, passing over the midday edition of the *Star*.

Archie frowned as he looked at the item the barmaid indicated.

WAPPING TRAGEDY

River Police scour the Thames after a suicide note was found beside a bundle of clothes on Wapping Steps. Victim believed to be Marcus Levy, a well-known figure in London's East End. Levy was recently released from prison after serving a five-year sentence for embezzlement. Police are withholding the contents of the suicide note for the time being. A police spokesman confirmed that the bundle of clothes was discovered before midnight and stated that the body could have been carried downriver on the high tide.

Archie turned to the barmaid. 'Is Jack in the bar, luv?'

' 'E's slipped out fer a while,' she replied.

The villain passed the paper across the table. 'If that bastard's gone in the river then I'm the Duke o' Kent,' he growled.

'What d'yer make o' that suicide note?' Danny asked.

'I reckon Levy's coverin' 'is tracks, that's all,' Archie replied.

'I 'ope yer right,' Danny scowled. 'That mongrel could crucify the lot of us.'

Chapter Twenty-Six

On Saturday morning Laura went to the market early as usual, and as she left Maggie Palfrey's vegetable stall she glanced at the black crepe garment in the shop window. It seemed to be waiting for her to buy it, she thought wistfully. How wonderful it would be to go to the social in that dress, looking really glamorous, with her hair done specially and wearing those black patent high-heels she had picked out earlier.

The shopping bags were heavy, and by the time Laura reached Pedlar's Row her arms and shoulders were aching. Albert had a pot of tea ready and insisted on pouring her a cupful of his own strong brew.

'Yer wanna get Lucy ter give yer some 'elp wiv the shoppin', gel,' he said, shakily, handing her the cup and saucer.

'She works nearly every Saturday,' Laura replied. 'I can't expect 'er ter dash down the market as soon as she gets in, Dad.'

'Look at the time, it's nearly one o'clock. She should be in by now,' Albert remarked, sitting down heavily in his armchair.

'She's most likely doin' some of 'er own shoppin',' Laura replied, kicking off her shoes and massaging her ankles. ' 'As Roy gone out?'

Albert nodded. ' 'E's shot orf up the pub. 'E ain't 'ardly said two bloody words this mornin'.'

Laura sighed. Things were not looking too good between Roy and Lucy, she thought. His getting back to work had not seemed to make any difference and he was still inclined to be short-fused with his two lads.

'Is Eddie takin' yer out again ternight?' Albert asked, cutting across her thoughts.

'Yeah, we're goin' ter the dockers' club social,' Laura told him. 'Yer don't mind, do yer?'

Her father shook his head and picked up the poker to stab at the live coals. 'I reckon that Eddie's a decent bloke. They're a nice family, the Cassidys. I was talkin' ter Lizzie Cassidy the ovver mornin' when I went fer the paper. She was askin' me 'ow I was gettin' on down 'ere.'

'What d'yer tell 'er?' Laura asked.

'I told 'er it was a bloody sight better than the Buildin's,' Albert replied. 'Mind yer, I can't make that Queenie Bromley out. I nod to 'er whenever I see 'er but she ain't one fer chattin'. She seems ter change like the bloody weavver, one minute she's all right an' then the next minute yer can't get a kiss-yer-arse out of 'er.'

Laura was still sipping her tea when she heard the front door go and Lucy came in.

'Where's Roy, up the pub?' she asked.

Albert nodded and Lucy pulled a face as she sat down heavily in a chair. 'I've just bin talkin' to Elsie Carmichael,' she said. 'Wally Stebbin's got beaten up last night.'

Laura's hand came up to her mouth involuntarily. 'Oh no! Who did it?'

'Accordin' to Elsie, a couple o' fellas grabbed 'im as 'e come out o' work last night an' dragged 'im round ter the bomb site in Cooper Street,' Lucy told her. 'Elsie said they would 'ave killed 'im if it wasn't fer our Terry an' Charlie Bromley. Apparently they was playin' on the bomb site when the two fellas dragged Wally on there an' they run off an' told Joe Molloy. 'Im an' Charlie's dad an' Eddie run round just in time, by all accounts. Wally's got a broken nose an' 'e was badly shook up.'

'Why ever should they wanna pick on Wally Stebbin's?' Laura asked. 'What 'arm could 'e 'ave done anybody?'

Lucy shook her head. 'I dunno, but somebody must 'ave 'ad it in fer 'im.'

'It was a good job those two lads saw it,' Laura remarked.

'That little sod o' mine didn't say a word last night when 'e came in. I wonder why?' Lucy puzzled, shaking her head.

'Probably 'cos yer told 'im 'e wasn't ter go on that bomb site,' Laura said.

'Come ter fink of it, 'e did look a bit flushed when 'e came in,' Lucy replied. 'Where's 'e gone now?'

'Charlie called fer 'im early this mornin'. They've not bin back since,' Laura told her. 'I gave Terry a tanner fer pie an' mash, so 'e won't be back until 'e's 'ungry again.'

'Fancy pickin' on someone like Wally Stebbin's. I wonder who could 'ave done it,' Lucy said thoughtfully.

At that moment Reg walked into the parlour. 'Got the midday paper, Grandad?' he asked, flopping down in a chair.

Albert nodded. 'What d'yer want it for?' he asked.

'I wanna study the form,' Reg replied casually.

Laura and Lucy exchanged quick glances and Albert glared at the young lad. 'Yer wanna study form, at your age? Yer'll be stickin' a tanner each way on next,' he said sarcastically.

'I could do. I got money. Con gave me a sprarzy fer gettin' 'im some fags,' Reg replied with a saucy grin.

'It seems ter me yer goin' the right way ter land up in trouble, my lad,' Albert said quickly.

Reg ignored the remark and slipped out of the chair to get the *Star*, but Lucy stopped him. 'Oh no yer don't. I don't want yer gettin' involved in bettin' at your age,' she said sharply, 'an' I want yer ter keep away from the bookie, understand?'

'I'm not doin' any 'arm,' Reg protested. 'Con's a good bloke. 'E lets me 'elp 'im take the bets an' do 'is errands. Con reckons Mr Westlake might give me a job when I leave school.'

'Doin' what?' Lucy asked quickly.

'Workin' in the ware'ouse,' Reg replied.

'Well, yer can get that notion right out of yer 'ead,' Lucy shouted. 'I'm not 'avin' a son o' mine workin' fer Westlake.'

Reg pulled a face. 'Why?' he asked.

'Never you mind why.'

'I bet I'd get good wages.'

'I don't care about the wages.'

'I don't wanna work fer peanuts,' Reg complained.

Laura stopped herself smiling. 'Yer wanna try an' get a trade, Reg,' she said sternly. 'Workin' in a ware'ouse might seem a good idea now but yer gotta fink o' later.'

'I might be a bookie when I get older,' Reg said casually.

Lucy shook her head in dismay. 'I can see you endin' up in Borstal the way you're goin' on. If a boy o' your age gets caught 'elpin' a bookie that's just where they'll send yer.'

'The cozzers 'ave gotta catch yer first,' he said, grinning.

Lucy was about to lose her temper but Laura cut in quickly. ' 'Ave yer seen Terry?' she asked him.

'I saw 'im at the pie shop wiv Charlie,' Reg answered. 'They said they was goin' off ter play cards wiv the kids in the Buildin's.'

Lucy raised her eyes to the ceiling but Laura couldn't help smiling. Albert looked very stern, however, poking away at the fire and mumbling to himself about sparing the rod.

The attack on Wally Stebbings seemed to be the sole talking point amongst the folk in Pedlar's Row, and when Queenie saw the victim pass her door with both eyes blackened and a strip of plaster covering his nose, even she felt sad at what had happened to him. 'I must admit I don't go a lot on the bloke, but 'e don't deserve that sort o' treatment,' she remarked to her husband.

'Who could'a put 'em up to it?' George asked her.

'Well, yer ain't gotta look very far, 'ave yer?' she replied. 'Yer told me yerself all yer drinkin' pals were goin' on about 'im up the pub, an' yer said Joe Molloy 'ad bin chattin' ter the bookie about 'im. Put two an' two tergevver.'

'Yer mean . . .'

'Yer know who I mean,' Queenie snapped. 'That's the sort o' fing 'e would do, just ter prove what a big man 'e is. 'E's got no feelin' fer anybody whatsoever. One o' these days somebody's gonna swing fer 'im, you mark my words.'

'Long as it ain't you, gel,' George joked.

Next door Elsie Carmichael was sitting in her tidy parlour talking to Annie Stebbings. 'I felt really sick when I saw poor Wally's face this mornin',' she said sadly. 'It must 'ave bin a terrible shock when 'e came 'ome last night.'

Annie was still feeling upset and she shook her head slowly. 'I thought I was gonna pass out when I saw 'im come in,' she told her. 'Eddie Cassidy an' Joe Molloy was 'oldin' on to 'is arms an' 'e seemed ter be in a daze. Eddie told me what 'ad 'appened. Anyway, I made Wally a strong cup o' tea an' 'e said 'e felt better after that. 'E wanted ter go ter bed, but I made 'im go up Guy's. I could see 'is nose was in a right state. I wanted ter go up the 'ospital wiv 'im but 'e wouldn't 'ear of it.'

Elsie sighed sadly. 'Poor sod. Who could'a done it?' she asked.

'Somebody was put up to it,' Annie said. 'I got my suspicions. Wally said that the bookie always gives 'im nasty looks every time 'e sees 'im.'

'I don't know why Bridie Molloy lets 'im stand outside 'er front door, really I don't,' Elsie replied. 'I wouldn't allow it. I was tellin' my Len only the ovver day, it ain't right. We 'ave all sorts walkin' in an' out the Row ter put their bets on. The bleedin' place ain't our own, the way fings are.'

A couple of doors along, Bridie was talking to her two daughters. 'I know it's terrible ter say it, but yer farvver's gotta take some o' the blame fer Wally gettin' beaten up,' she said firmly. ' 'E's bin goin' on about 'im recently, an' I 'eard 'im talkin' ter the bookie about 'im the ovver evenin'. I gave 'im a right mouthful when 'e came in that night. 'E was really surprised when 'e found out what Mrs Stebbin's told me about 'er Wally bein' in the paper, an' about that lovely model fort 'e made fer the two lads. Yer just can't tell wiv people. All right, I know Wally looks a bit peculiar, what wiv 'im mumblin' the way 'e does, but it's most prob'ly nerves. It's down ter the war, I shouldn't be at all surprised.'

Bridie's daughters were unusually subdued and they both knew that their mother was right. 'Do yer really fink the bookie was be'ind it?' Kathleen asked.

'I reckon 'e instigated it,' Bridie replied. 'Yer farvver was sayin' that Archie Westlake runs the bookies, an' 'e's got a right name in this area. 'E's an out-an'-out villain. I'm certain 'e got some blokes ter do it.'

'If that's the way yer feel, Mum, why don't yer get Farvver ter tell the bookie 'e can't stand outside our front door anymore?' Pauline suggested.

Bridie nodded. 'I was already finkin' o' that. I never

liked the arrangement in the first place. It was yer farvver's doin'.'

'Well, at least Dad stopped Wally gettin' badly 'urt,' Kathleen cut in. 'I fink 'e was really brave ter face them blokes.'

'Yeah, so do I,' Pauline added.

Bridie smiled proudly. 'That's yer farvver all over. 'E'd stand up ter King Kong.'

'Well then, get Dad ter stand up ter the bookie, Mum,' Kathleen said. 'Let's get the 'orrible git out of Pedlar's Row.'

For once Bridie did not protest at her daughter's rough language. 'Yeah, I fink we will,' she said firmly.

On Saturday evening Laura and Eddie walked through Abbey Street on their way to the Catholic church hall in Dockhead. Laura was wearing a floral dress, a hand-me-down from Lucy, under her fawn winter coat, and a chiffon scarf tied loosely around her slim neck. She had bought a pair of stockings from the market that morning and Lucy had tonged her hair and lent her a suitable pair of grey high-heeled shoes. She felt reasonably smart for a night out, and when Eddie squeezed her arm supportively as they made their way over to a group of his friends at the bar, Laura felt that she was going to enjoy the evening.

Eddie was wearing a dark pin-striped double-breasted suit, black shoes and an immaculately laundered white shirt with a silver tie. His dark hair was well groomed and he walked upright with a slight sway of the shoulders. His face broke into a wide grin as one of the young women took his arm and looked at Laura. 'If yer get fed up wiv this fella, luv, just send 'im my way, will yer?' she joked.

Eddie winked at Laura reassuringly. 'What'll it be?' he asked.

Laura settled for a light ale and Eddie decided on a pint of bitter, declining the offer of a drink from one of the group.

'They're a decent enough crowd but those women can be a bit overpowerin' at times,' he told her as he carried their drinks over to a vacant table. 'Besides, I want yer all ter meself this evenin'.'

The band was getting ready to play and Laura looked around the hall. Groups were standing round chatting together, and most of the women seemed to know everyone else. They constantly waved and darted here and there to have a conversation with another group, while the men stood holding pints of beer and laughing loudly amongst themselves. Eddie seemed relaxed and happy as he sipped his pint and he never stopped glancing at Laura, making her feel flattered by the attention he was paying her.

'They're all dock workers, an' this is a regular gatherin',' Eddie said presently. 'Yer see, it's always bin a close-knit community on the river. We tend ter clan tergevver. I s'pose it's 'cos o' the job we do. Most o' the people 'ere are Catholics, incidentally. Our family are too, although I 'ave ter say we're not regular churchgoers. The last time I went ter church it was a weddin', an' I ended up gettin' involved in a punch-up at the reception. No fault o' mine though, I'd like yer ter know.'

Laura wanted to ask him about the previous evening's incident with Wally Stebbings, but instead she waited, hoping he would tell her without prompting just what had happened. He appeared to have forgotten, however, or had decided it wasn't the thing to talk about on a night out. He would no doubt mention it later, she felt.

The band struck up loudly and one young couple immediately went out on to the dance floor. Everyone stood watching as the pair expertly tripped round, elegantly executing the dance movements, the girl with a dreamy look on her face as she floated round the floor in her long, swirling dress and the young man stepping smartly as he led her, a proud grin on his face.

'They start the dancin' every time there's a social,' Eddie said quietly. 'They're very good, as yer can see, but not so long ago that fella was lyin' in Guy's wiv a broken back. A load fell out of a crane sling an' flattened 'im.'

'I expect a lot of accidents 'appen in the docks,' Laura replied.

Eddie nodded. 'It's not the easiest of jobs, but I wouldn't change it fer anyfing,' he said firmly.

The dance ended and the couple got a warm round of applause.

'Now the dancin' starts in earnest,' Eddie said, chuckling.

Couples took the floor for a foxtrot and Laura glanced hopefully at Eddie, but he merely smiled and shook his head. One of his friends walked over to the table and looked down at Laura.

'Would yer care to, luv?' he asked. 'This fella won't mind, will yer, Eddie?'

Laura got a reassuring grin from her escort and she went out on to the floor. Eddie watched as she was whisked around. She seemed to be enjoying it. She was a good dancer, he could tell, and as he watched her he felt deeply moved. She was such a beautiful woman; her figure was slim and shapely, and she had a certain manner about her. Her blonde hair was shining under the bright spotlights and her hips swayed in a way that discomposed him. He desired her madly, needed to hold her and passionately love her, and he began to wonder. She had made it clear from the start that she was duty-bound to look after her family and that had to be her priority, but it was obvious she had had men friends before. She had hinted as much, and one day, she had said, she would tell him about her past life.

The dance ended and Laura walked back to their table, smiling. 'It's your turn next,' she joked. 'I'm not lettin' you get away wivout a dance.'

Eddie returned her smile. 'Yer dance very well,' he remarked.

'I used ter go a lot, at one time,' Laura replied.

The young man caught a certain nostalgic look in her eyes and it secretly troubled him, but there was no time to sit pondering. The band struck up a waltz number and Laura glanced at him expectantly.

Eddie smiled at her and got to his feet. 'All right, if yer wanna take a chance,' he told her.

They clasped each other closely as they stepped on to the dance floor and Eddie felt the delicious softness of her warm body and smelled the sweet fragrance of her hair. She leant her head against his shoulder and her hips were pressed to his as she discreetly initiated their progress round the floor. He looked down at her and she smiled at him in a way that made his heart jump. He had never felt this way about any woman but now, now he was smitten.

As they left the floor Eddie caught sight of his brothers and their wives coming into the hall. Following on were Lizzie and Eric Cassidy, arm in arm and looking very well groomed. Lizzie had had her raven hair permed and she was wearing a pink dress. Eric was looking spruce in his grey suit, and the two were smiling genially as they came over to the table.

As the evening wore on Laura became very relaxed, and she was starting to feel a little light-headed. She had danced with both Geoff and Steve, and Eddie had managed to try a foxtrot. The conversation had been witty and light-hearted and the drinks were still flowing. The men were standing near the bar chatting together and occasionally Eddie looked in Laura's direction and gave her a smile and a reassuring wink or two. At the table Mary was talking with Connie about her forthcoming happy event and Lizzie took the opportunity of speaking quietly to Laura.

'I'm really glad you an' our Eddie 'ave got tergevver,' she said, smiling warmly. ' 'E's a nice lad but 'e needs a good woman ter keep 'im in line. I fink yer make a good match.'

'I'm very fond of 'im,' Laura replied.

' 'E's very fond o' you too, I can tell,' Lizzie said knowingly. 'Just don't let 'im 'ave it all 'is own way though, the little cowson's bin gettin' away wiv murder wi' me lately.'

Laura laughed aloud and just then Eddie came over. 'It'll be the last dance soon,' he said. 'Shall we get a bit of air?'

Laura took his hand as they stepped out into the quiet paved area and walked slowly along the path skirting the lofty church building. Eddie was silent until they reached an arched door and then he swung her round suddenly and was embracing her, pulling her to him as they stepped into the shadows. 'I love you,' he whispered, his lips brushing her neck.

Laura felt a delicious shiver of pleasure run through her and she closed her eyes as he found her open mouth. She could feel his hands caressing her back and the tightness of his body against hers arousing her, and she responded with a sensuous movement of her hips against him. The drinks they had both had made them feel daring and Laura did not try to stop Eddie as he moved his hand on to her firm breast, her breathing growing more rapid as he gently felt her. She wanted him to explore her body and feel the desire she had for him right now, and Eddie struggled to master his wild passion, pulling back gently as he took her by the shoulders and gazed into her smouldering eyes. 'Yer know I love yer,' he said in a whisper. 'Yer know I want yer badly.'

'I want yer too,' she sighed.

'I couldn't take my eyes off yer when yer were dancin',' he told her. 'Yer looked gorgeous.'

Laura smiled and reached up with her hands to clasp him round the neck and pull his head down to her. Her initiating kiss told him everything and he clutched her in a tight, almost crushing embrace as they kissed long and sensuously. The night was cold and damp but Laura felt only the hot flush of desire in that secret moment among the shadows. She wanted it to last forever and she was beginning to lose control, but something inside her urged her to draw back. It would be so easy to let him take her at that very moment, and she gasped for breath as he eased his pressure on her and raised his head to look adoringly into her eyes. Laura knew that he had felt the same as her and was fighting to restrain himself. 'Let's go back, darlin',' she whispered. 'I don't want to, but we'd better.'

The last waltz was playing inside the hall and everyone seemed to be on the floor. Laura closed her eyes and thought how lovely the night had been. She felt safe and secure in Eddie's arms and knew that whatever happened in the future, whatever fate had in store for her, she would never forget this evening.

Chapter Twenty-Seven

All through Saturday night, Carlton's printing works was destined to be a hive of industry. Archie Westlake and his friends had given Ernie Jackson time to set up the plates in the print roller, and when they called later the foreman printer told them he was ready to begin printing. The villains waited with bated breath while the paper was fed into the press, and when they saw the early results they were delighted. Marcus Levy had not let them down, but Archie sounded a warning.

'I've known Levy fer a long time,' he said. 'I fully expected 'im ter do a first-class job on those plates. Wiv 'im it would be a matter o' pride, but I'm worried about 'is disappearance an' that suicide note.'

'Yer don't fink the Yid done a deal wiv the cozzers, do yer?' Danny asked.

Archie looked troubled. 'I dunno. I wouldn't put it past 'im, but I'm sure 'e ain't floatin' in the river,' he said thoughtfully. 'Though I can understand the logic be'ind it. If Levy wanted ter take on a new identity 'e'd 'ave ter get rid o' the old one, it stands ter reason. 'E'd like us ter fink 'e topped 'imself, but 'e knows very well that even if we don't believe 'e chucked 'imself in the river we can be sure 'e ain't 'angin' round 'ereabouts ter turn witness on us. After all, 'e couldn't very well drop us all in the cart wivout droppin' 'imself as well. What worries me is that suicide note.'

'Levy could 'ave told the police everyfing that way,' Con Noble remarked.

Archie nodded, leaning against the workbench and folding his arms. 'If the cozzers pull us all in fer questionin' Levy's got time ter disappear. 'E could be out the country before we 'ad time ter do anyfing about it,' he said with a frown. 'Some'ow I don't fink Levy 'as shopped us though. Fer my money I fink Ben Walsh is 'angin' on ter that note ter get us all worried.'

'Well, if that's the case 'e's certainly doin' a good job,' Danny replied.

'Let's assume that is the case,' Archie went on. 'Walsh wants us ter get panicky an' make a slip-up somewhere along the line. Point is, 'ow much does 'e know already? If 'e knows of our tie-up wiv Carlton's 'e'll also more likely than not know that we moved a printin' press recently. 'E'd assume we wouldn't chance printin' the money in a legit printin' firm. That's why I covered our arses. What we 'ave ter do now is get the job done soon as possible then remove all traces of a print-run by Monday mornin' when the workers come in. Ernie knows the score, right, Ernie?'

The print foreman nodded. 'I can be all through by the morning,' he said confidently.

'The set-up's pretty good,' Archie said quietly. 'We're at the back o' the factory an' nobody on the outside would suspect there's anyfing goin' on 'ere durin' the night, but should the night-beat cozzer get suspicious, Ernie'll tell 'im that 'e's come in ter service a machine ready fer Monday mornin'. It wouldn't be the first time it's 'appened.'

'That's right,' Ernie cut in. 'I had a word with the night-beat copper some time ago when I was coming in to do an emergency service. They'd probably take no notice now if they did hear the machine going.'

'All right, it sounds good, but yer've bin doin' a lot

293

o'supposin',' Jack Murray cut in. 'Let's suppose Ben Walsh 'as primed up the night-beat cozzer, an' if 'e gets the word there's somefing goin' on 'ere ternight an' they raid the firm, what then?'

Archie turned to Ernie. 'Tell 'im, Ern,' he said.

'I'm doing a service on a duff machine, remember? It wouldn't take a few seconds to destroy the plates with that acid there,' he said, pointing to the carboy on the bench. 'The same applies to the print-run. The lot could be destroyed with ink inside a few seconds. It'd take the police longer than that to break through the bolted door. All right, they'd find the place in a poxy mess, but I'd tell them it's a machine gone bandy, and they'd have a job disproving that.'

'Okay, let's leave Ernie ter get on wiv it,' Archie said. 'Give us a ring when yer've finished the run an' it's ready fer cuttin', Ern.'

The print foreman nodded, then turned and took a quick swig from a bottle of whisky before he put on his tin-rimmed spectacles.

'Don't get too pissed,' Archie said as he beckoned his friends to follow him.

On Sunday morning Elsie Carmichael was humming to herself as she swept the pavement outside her front door. Along the Row Lizzie Cassidy was chatting to Annie Stebbings, while Bridie Molloy was busy cleaning her parlour window. Wally Stebbings walked into Pedlar's Row with the Sunday newspapers tucked under his arm, holding his head low, embarrassed by the condition of his face. His eyes were blackened and his lips puffed up and there was a plaster covering his swollen nose. He nodded sheepishly to Elsie and then to Lizzie as he passed by. The women were all saddened and angry at Wally's misfortune and Bridie was all the more determined that the bookie would have to go.

Queenie stepped out of her front door and without a glance at the women she walked out of the Row. She was looking very smart in her black coat and matching hat and she wore a pair of low-heeled, buckled shoes. She was carrying a black bag in one hand and a canvas shopping bag in the other.

'I see Queenie's started goin' out again,' Elsie commented to Bridie.

Lizzie looked at Annie Stebbings. 'It's strange ter see 'er all dressed up,' she remarked. 'I wonder where she goes?'

'She always used ter go out in the afternoons,' Annie replied. 'She wouldn't be goin' ter church, not Queenie. Besides, she 'ad a shoppin' bag wiv 'er.'

Elsie had walked up to them. 'I reckon she's got a bloke, don't you?' she said, grinning.

'I dunno. It's very mysterious,' Lizzie remarked.

'Well, she's certainly done up in 'er best bits,' Elsie went on. 'When yer see 'er round 'ere she looks a right scruff, wiv 'er 'air in curlers an' that scraggy old apron she wears. Mind you, she's got 'er work cut out, what wiv those boys of 'ers an' 'er George. 'E never seems ter be in work fer more than a few days at a time. I fink 'e's a bit of a lazy git, don't you?'

Lizzie and Annie did not want to get into a lengthy dialogue with their neighbour and they both gave a noncommittal shrug of the shoulders. Elsie was not finished, however. 'The police was in there the ovver night,' she told them. 'It was somefing ter do wiv 'er boys Fred an' Billy. Apparently they'd bin over Billin'sgate an' they was caught comin' over London Bridge wiv a bloody great skate stuck down Billy's jumper. Queenie didn't tell me 'cos yer know me an' 'er don't get on very well. It was 'er ole man what told my Len. As it 'appened this copper spotted the fish-tail stickin' out o' Billy's jumper, an' when 'e stopped 'em they told 'im they found it on the cobbles an' it must 'ave fell off a barrer. Just then a market porter come runnin' up. The two little sods 'ad nicked the fish from off 'is barrer while 'e was pushin' it up the 'ill. George told my Len that Billy's clothes stunk to 'igh 'eaven. I tell yer, those boys are gonna end up in prison before long.'

Annie and Lizzie both made their excuses to get away from their loquacious neighbour, and Elsie went back to her cleaning convinced that Queenie was going to meet her fancy man.

On Monday morning Wally Stebbings woke up and looked into the hand mirror on his washstand. The area round his eyes looked greenish-black but his lips were less swollen. What would they think? he wondered. How could he tell them all in the office that he had been assaulted? He would have to stick to the story that he had fallen against a tree. At least everyone at Clyde's knew he didn't touch alcohol, so they couldn't assume he had been drunk at the time.

Wally ate his breakfast of porridge oats and drank his weak tea, still worrying, and when he finally slipped on his coat, hat and scarf he was feeling very apprehensive. Gladys Ward would no doubt have a lot of questions to ask and Molly French would make him embarrassed by her reaction. She always seemed to be smiling at him and making excuses to come into his office for one thing or another. Molly was a very kind person and he liked her, but he always felt uneasy in her presence. She was much like his mother in the way she tended to fuss over him.

Wally walked slowly along the Row and out into Weston Street. He always left himself enough time to get into work early. The management had said at the last meeting that good timekeeping was very important and they were going to clamp down on persistent latecomers. Well, they had little to worry about as far as he was concerned, he thought to himself. He had never been late during his time there, apart from the one morning when he had had a bad stomach upset. Even then he had managed to struggle into work by nine thirty.

As he entered the building and climbed the stairs to the first-floor offices, Wally felt shaky. The attack had taken more out of him than he had realised.

Gladys Ward put a hand up to her mouth when she saw him, as if in genuine shock. 'Oh my good God! Whatever have you done!' she cried, playing her part well.

'I'm afraid I slipped and hit my head on a tree,' Wally said flatly.

Gladys felt the revulsion rising up within her but she maintained her guise of concern. She had heard all about the attack on Wally from her friend Betty Johnson whom she had met at the market on Saturday. Betty had heard it from Elsie Carmichael when they had bumped into each other earlier that morning. Elsie had been eager to give Betty her view of things and made the mistake of mentioning that Wally had been suspected of interfering with children, and that was why somebody had decided to warn him off in a very violent way. She had been quick to say that she felt Wally Stebbings was completely innocent and incapable of such evil doings, however, but Betty had already closed her ears to Elsie's view. The two women worked together at Clyde's box factory on the assembly bench and she considered Elsie to be a complete scatterbrain. Betty had had her own view of Wally Stebbings for some time, and she was quick to pass on her version of what had happened.

Gladys Ward had nodded her head in staunch

agreement as Betty Johnson told her all about it near the fish stall, and by Monday morning her path was decided. It was her duty to bring the events of Friday night to the attention of the management. After all, none of the women were safe with a sex maniac on the payroll. Now, as she stood facing the battered creature, Gladys felt she had done her colleagues a service in exposing his dirty secret. The man was obviously guilty. Why would he lie to her about the attack unless he had something to hide?

'It was a strange thing to happen, wasn't it?' she remarked. 'I could understand it if you had had a drop too much to drink, but you don't touch the stuff, do you?'

Wally shook his head. 'I must have tripped over something,' he said timidly.

'Well, I hope you feel better soon,' she said, wanting to get away from the monster as quickly as possible.

Wally set about the new monthly trial balance as soon as he got seated. Work was the best therapy, he told himself.

'Er, Mr Stebbings? Mr Lancing wants to see you right away,' the chief clerk told him.

Wally got up and closed the ledger, fussing with his tie and pulling on his coat as he left his office. What would Mr Lancing want with him so early on Monday morning? he asked himself. Normally the office manager did not appear until nearly lunchtime, and even then it was unusual for him to send for him.

'Close the door behind you, Mr Stebbings,' Lancing said, raising his head briefly from a sheaf of papers.

Wally stood upright, feeling very uncomfortable and apprehensive as he waited.

'Take a seat,' the manager said sharply. 'I'll be with you in a moment or two.'

The book-keeper nervously looked around the office,

realising that during his time at Clyde's he had only ever been in this room on one other occasion, and that was when he was summoned and told that he was being put in charge of all the accounts and was to receive a salary increase of two and sixpence per week. That was when old Mr Brian was in charge. This new manager seemed very distant. There was no familiarity where he was concerned. Old Mr Brian knew every one of the staff by their Christian names, but Mr Lancing would be hard pressed to recite even the surnames of his staff, Wally shouldn't be surprised.

The manager looked up. 'I see you've had an accident,' he said coldly. 'Do you mind telling me what happened?'

'I'm afraid I bumped into a tree on my way home from work on Friday evening,' Wally answered.

'Um. Very unfortunate,' the manager remarked, lowering his head again.

Wally waited patiently while papers were shuffled, the inkstand was adjusted and the blotting pad was squared off. Finally when the manager was finished, he looked at Wally with a sickly smile on his pallid face. 'I'm sorry, but I have some bad news,' he said, coughing nervously. 'I have to trim the staff, not my decision, you understand. It came from the directors. Under the circumstances I have to tell you that your services will no longer be required and you will be given a month's notice from today.'

'But – but – why me? Surely you've never had reason to fault my work?' Wally replied in a shocked voice. 'I've always given of my best.'

'We are not faulting your work, Mr Stebbings,' the manager said in a flat tone. 'It's a question of who we could best spare. Your job will be taken over by another member of staff.'

'If it's a question of doing two jobs I could . . . '

'Can you type?' Lancing cut in sarcastically.

'No, but . . . '

'I'm afraid the directors' decision is final,' Lancing said quickly. 'We won't expect you to work out the month. You can leave immediately. If you come back this evening I'll make sure your month's salary is ready for you. Good day, Mr Stebbings.'

Wally rose from his chair, feeling shocked and nauseated. There was only one possible reason for his sudden dismissal. Word had got around about the assault and he wasn't being allowed the benefit of the doubt. He had been branded as a child-molester. Angry tears welled up in his eyes as he left the office, forgetting to close the door after him. He had to get out into the fresh air or he would faint.

The Monday morning market was quiet as usual after the weekend rush and as Wally walked slowly along the row of stalls his head was reeling. Why should they suspect him? he asked himself again and again. What had he done to make them all so convinced that he would harm a child? It was the only reason he had been dismissed from Clyde's. None of the typists could perform his duties. It was just a pathetic excuse to get rid of him as quickly as possible. The month's salary in lieu of notice told him that. Clyde's would normally want their pound of flesh, they always had. They must have badly wanted him out of the way immediately.

Wally Stebbings stood at the edge of the pavement, waiting to cross the busy Tower Bridge Road, with his mind in turmoil. Where could he get another job now without the stigma following him? A tram rumbled past, and another, and Wally was still standing beside the kerb contemplating his future. Finally he made his way almost blindly across to the other side of the road and walked on, hardly knowing where he was going until he suddenly breathed in the tangy smell of hops. He was walking past the bottling store of the Courage brewery and ahead was the tall, majestic edifice of Tower Bridge. He glanced way up above the rising struts which supported the main bridge and he saw the walkway, now closed for repair. Many a person had ended their life by jumping from that high parapet into the swift-flowing waters of the River Thames.

The wharves were bustling, with tall cranes dipping and swinging and cargoes being hauled from the holds of trampers and freighters. Dockers were shouting and cursing as they manhandled the bales, crates and bundles down below Wally. He stood watching the eddying muddy water, and as he stared down it suddenly seemed very inviting. How easy it would be to lean over, just enough to lose his balance, and topple down, down into oblivion. Who would mourn his passing? His mother, yes, but she would surely know that he was at peace, and that nothing more could hurt him now. There was no one else who would feel sad. The neighbours would shake their heads and get on with their lives. Mr Lancing would lose no sleep over him, that was for sure.

'Not finkin' o' jumpin', are yer, mate?' a voice said in his ear.

Wally turned quickly to see a very tall policeman standing beside him, and he shook his head. 'I'm just looking,' he said meekly.

'We get a lot o' people contemplatin' jumpin',' the policeman went on. 'Many 'ave, an' fer some it was a quick way ter go. But let me tell you, fer every one who goes in, ten more turn round an' walk away. I've seen it. Yer get ter sense it in my job. Twenty years I've bin on this bridge. I stopped a bloke goin' over the top once, an' yer know what 'e told me? 'E said 'e wanted to end it all 'cos 'is missus was playin' about wiv anuvver man. We 'ad a long chat an' 'e ended up so angry that I'm sure 'e went 'ome an' gave 'er a good 'idin'. I 'ope 'e didn't clout

301

'er too 'ard though,' the policeman chuckled.

Wally smiled briefly. 'I'm not married,' he said quietly.

The tall policeman rocked back on his heels. 'Anuvver time there was a bloke who climbed up that girder right ter the top,' he went on. 'I called fer 'im ter come down but 'e said 'e was gonna chuck 'imself in an' no one was gonna stop 'im. We got the fire brigade an' they went up on one o' their extension ladders until they were only feet away from 'im. The man screamed out that if they got anuvver inch nearer 'e'd jump. I was standin' right below. It looked 'opeless, until a couple o' blokes came out from the brewery. They started shoutin' at 'im, givin' 'im a load o' verbal. Well, the bloke on the girder got really angry, an' it didn't exactly mollify 'im when these blokes from the brewery told 'im they was goin' 'ome fer their dinner an' could 'e jump now, so they wouldn't miss anyfing. D'yer know what the man did? 'E called fer the ladder ter come nearer an' 'e jumped in the cage, screamin' out ter the brewery workers ter wait till 'e got down 'cos 'e was gonna smash their 'eads in.'

Wally stood listening, his eyes never once leaving the policeman as the story unfolded. 'Did he get to them?' he asked.

'Nah. They disappeared before the cage reached the ground, but they obviously saved 'is life,' the officer said, smiling broadly. 'It takes a lot o' work an' it's often dangerous too when yer tryin' ter prevent a suicide. I got six kids. I don't wanna 'ave ter jump in that water after some silly bleeder who's decided to end it all. Well, I've said me piece, so why don't yer go on 'ome an' stop me worryin', not that I expected you ter jump in, yer understand.'

Wally smiled at the policeman and turned for home. He walked slowly, trying to compose himself. It couldn't be as bad as it seemed. At least the neighbours trusted him, and he could hold his head high. Surely with his experience he could find a job somewhere. He had his own pursuits too. There was his fretwork, and the wireless to listen to.

The tall policeman watched Wally's progress from the bridge, noticing his sudden quickening of pace, and he smiled to himself. 'That was a near one or I'm a bloody Dutchman,' he said aloud.

Chapter Twenty-Eight

When Con Noble walked into Pedlar's Row on Monday lunchtime Bridie Molloy was waiting for him. As he approached she stood at the door with a very determined look on her face. 'I 'ave ter tell yer, I don't want yer usin' my front door fer yer pitch any more,' she said firmly.

Con looked shocked. 'Why, luv? What's the trouble?' he asked her.

'It's just that I don't want yer 'ere any more,' she told him, looking him square in the eye.

'I ain't upset yer in any way, 'ave I?' he enquired. 'If I 'ave I'd like ter know about it.'

Bridie was getting a little impatient. 'Look, I don't 'ave ter tell yer anyfing, now will yer find somewhere else ter go,' she insisted.

'All right, if that's the way yer feel,' Con said, shrugging his shoulders. 'Yer can give me a few days though, can't yer? I'll 'ave ter find anuvver pitch an' I'll need ter let me regulars know.'

'I'm sorry but yer'll 'ave ter be away by termorrer. That's the way it's gotta be,' Bridie said, turning on her heel and going into the house.

Con stood stroking his chin in consternation. He could not recall having upset the woman in any way. It must be to do with the Friday night business, he realised. Strange though. He would have thought the people round here would be only too glad to get a nonsense-case warned off. Maybe the woman felt that it had been too violent, but it was the only way to deal with that sort of problem. Westlake wouldn't be pleased. There was not much time to get another pitch by tomorrow. Perhaps he should have a chat with the woman next door to Queenie, Con decided. She seemed a decent sort. It wouldn't take a minute to talk to her, even if it was not the ideal spot to stand.

When Elsie opened her front door she was holding a stiff-bristled brush and her hands were smothered in black lead. 'Yes?' she said, looking at the bookie in irritation.

'I was wonderin', luv. Would yer mind if I used yer front door fer me pitch?' he asked, smiling pleasantly. 'The lady at number four can't 'ave me there anymore.'

Elsie looked up at him through her thick-lensed spectacles. 'I should fink not,' she said sharply. 'As fer me, I wouldn't tolerate yer at any price. I fink it's a terrible fing that poor Mr Stebbin's gettin' beaten up the way 'e did.'

'That was nuffink ter do wiv me, luv,' Con said quickly. 'I'm a bookmaker not a strong-arm man.'

'Well, maybe not, but that bloody guv'nor o' yours is, an' don't try ter tell me 'e wasn't be'ind it, 'cos I know different,' Elsie retorted sharply. 'Everybody round 'ere knows it too, so I wouldn't try knockin' at any ovver door. Yer'll get the same answer as I'm givin' yer now.'

'I fink yer got it all wrong,' Con replied, glaring at her. 'I don't know who put that bit o' scandal about, but I can assure yer Mr Westlake wasn't involved in the attack on your neighbour.'

'Don't give me that load o' tosh,' Elsie said, her voice rising. 'Yer've turned this nice little place into a bloody public convenience wiv yer bettin'. I tell yer this much. If yer don't piss orf an' leave us alone we'll all do somefing about it, mark my words.'

As soon as Con Noble walked away from Elsie's front door Queenie appeared and gave her neighbour a big smile. 'I 'eard what yer said. Good fer you, gel,' she told her, loud enough for the bookie to hear. 'I never thought yer 'ad it in yer. That's the way ter deal wiv those sort. That's the only language they know.'

Elsie threw her shoulders back. Getting praise from Queenie was something indeed. 'People like that don't frighten me,' she said proudly. 'I soon told 'im where ter get orf. Anyway, I've got the kettle on, luv. Fancy a cuppa?' she asked.

Queenie was not in the habit of going into her neighbours' homes for cups of tea, but she considered this to be a special occasion. After all, Elsie Carmichael might be a scatterbrained mare, but the woman certainly had guts to tell the bookie a few home truths. She had also shown her true colours by coming over to the Bromleys when young Frankie went missing. Queenie should try to be a little more pleasant towards her. 'All right, luv, but I can't stop, I've got a meat pie in the oven,' she replied.

On Monday afternoon Archie Westlake sat in his office at the warehouse in Bermondsey Street, puffing on a large cigar. Outside in the yard a lorry was unloading a consignment of dried fruit and another laden lorry was parked beyond the gates waiting to drive in. Business was booming and Archie's two shops were doing very nicely. He was thinking of extending that side of his operations by opening another shop at Dockhead. He would soon need a larger warehouse too, he realised. It was getting more and more difficult finding the space to store all the provisions.

The lorry driver walked into the office, puffing from his exertions. 'That's twenty cases then,' he said, looking expectantly at the roll of money Archie had taken out of the desk drawer.

'Right then, fifteen shillin's a case, that's fifteen quid,' the villain said quickly, passing over the money.

The driver's face dropped. He had expected the usual price of seventeen and six for the cases of sultanas and he had lost fifty shillings on the deal. He could barter, but then Archie bought anything and everything, which was very convenient at times. It wouldn't do to haggle with the man over fifty shillings. 'Righto, guv. See yer then,' he said, snatching up the money and hurrying from the office.

Archie sat back deep in thought while he waited for Reg Grant to call, having promised to have a word with the lad after school that afternoon. The weekend had gone off better than even he had expected. Ernie Jackson had printed twenty thousand one-pound notes and they had been packed into a suitcase and hidden in a place of safety. The plates too were deposited at the secure location known only to Archie and his three associates, Danny Steadman, Con Noble and Jack Murray. The four men had agreed not to tell Ernie Jackson where the counterfeit money was stashed, although he was an equal partner in the deal. Ernie had not been at all curious in any case, but then he was in a very comfortable position. The print foreman knew that he was the one with the know-how and the villains relied on his expertise.

Archie puffed on his cigar and blew a cloud of smoke towards the ceiling. They would all have to be patient. In early April the flat racing season started and it was then that the plan could be put into action. The first operation would take place well away from London, possibly at Newmarket or one of the northern racecourses, then later they would switch the operation south for big paydays at Ascot and Epsom. If all went well there was a bigger prize to aim at with the new contacts he had made, but for the time being Archie Westlake preferred to keep that to himself.

It was just after four o'clock when Reg Grant walked into the yard and presented himself at the office. Archie beckoned him into a chair and smiled benevolently at the nervous young lad. 'My pal Con tells me yer'd like ter work 'ere on Saturdays, is that right?' he asked.

Reg nodded. 'Yes, Mr Westlake.'

'Well, yer'll 'ave ter work 'ard. We don't like slackers 'ere,' he said, knocking the ash off his cigar. 'My foreman will show yer what yer gotta do an' if yer a smart lad there'll be a good future 'ere for yer. Yer'll be able ter learn the business an' when yer leave school we might be able ter give yer a full-time job. It all depends on 'ow yer shape up of course, okay?'

Reg nodded enthusiastically. 'I can work 'ard, Mr Westlake.'

'Right then. We'll pay yer ten shillin's ter start wiv, an' then after a couple o' months we'll see if yer've earned an increase,' Archie told him. 'Yer'll be expected ter get 'ere fer nine in the mornin' an' yer finish at five. Can yer start this Saturday?'

'Yes, Mr Westlake. I'll be 'ere fer nine sharp,' Reg replied, looking very pleased.

'Right yer are, off yer go now. I'll see yer Saturday,' the villain said, amused at the young lad's enthusiasm.

Roy Grant stepped off the bus at the Trocette cinema earlier than usual and walked along the Tower Bridge Road in a troubled frame of mind. The throbbing of his bandaged hand had eased somewhat and he was eager to get home and put his feet up. Since he had started taking the sleeping pills on a regular basis his limited energy seemed to have deserted him and he felt exhausted most of the time. Last night was the first

308

time he had tried to do without the pills but he had tossed and turned all night. Lucy's sleep had been disturbed and she had been irritable this morning. He had gone to work feeling jaded, and it was tiredness which had been the cause of his accident. He had run a chisel into the palm of his hand that afternoon and the cut had needed six stitches. The manager was quick to spot his condition and suggested that he go to his doctor and get a medical certificate for the rest of the week.

As Roy crossed the main thoroughfare and turned into Weston Street he was feeling breathless and his head ached. He knew he would have to break his dependence on the sleeping pills, regardless of the recurring night-mares. He could not go on like this for much longer. He was slowly losing Lucy, and the two lads as well. They were understandably reluctant to speak to him, and he could sense the invisible barrier between him and his family growing every day.

When Roy let himself into the house he tried to make light of his injury but Laura fussed over him, helping him off with his coat and making him comfortable in the armchair, and Albert looked closely at him. ' 'Ow many stitches did they put in?' he asked.

'It was only a small cut but it wouldn't stop bleedin',' Roy replied. 'They put a couple o' stitches in it an' told me ter go straight 'ome an' take the rest o' the week off.'

Laura hurried into the scullery to make a pot of tea, and by the time Lucy arrived home from work Roy was feeling a little better.

'I'm glad yer got the rest o' the week off, yer don't look well at all,' she told him when he explained what had happened.

Laura had started to fold the clean washing and she glanced over at him with concern. 'Are yer still takin' those sleepin' pills, Roy?' she asked.

'I left 'em off yesterday,' he answered. 'I was awake all night though.'

'Tiredness, that's 'ow yer got that,' Albert said in his usual forthright manner.

Roy smiled to accommodate him. 'Yeah, I got careless. It was silly really.'

Reg had been sitting near his father, listening to the conversation and looking anxious, and when Lucy went into the scullery he followed her out. 'Mum, I've got a Saturday job workin' fer Mr Westlake in 'is ware'ouse. I'll get ten bob, an' if I do well 'e's gonna see about a rise,' he said excitedly.

Lucy turned and glared at him. 'I told yer I wasn't gonna let yer work fer that man,' she said sharply. 'Don't you ever listen ter what I say?'

'But it's not like workin' fer a bookie, Mum. I'll be workin' 'ard fer the money,' he told her. 'I done it to 'elp out. I can give yer seven an' six a week now.'

Lucy's heart melted as she saw the look in her son's eyes and she sighed deeply as she slipped her arm round his shoulders. 'Look, Reg, I know yer mean well, but men like Archie Westlake are a bad influence,' she tried to explain. 'Yer gotta realise that the man's a villain. 'E makes 'is money by robbin' an' bettin' an' 'e runs this neighbour'ood by puttin' the fear o' God inter people. Mr Stebbin's got beaten up by some o' Westlake's thugs. That's the sort o' man 'e is.'

'I know Mr Stebbin's got beat up but Mr Westlake wouldn't 'ave done it,' Reg replied. 'Why should 'e?'

Lucy knew that she had to make a decision. Her son seemed determined to go to work for Westlake and by refusing him she would only add to her already mounting problems. Maybe it would be a good idea to go and see Westlake herself, she thought suddenly. She could spell out her requirements for Reg then. Earning money doing a Saturday job was not the issue. Many young lads earned money doing paper rounds and helping milkmen, and others worked in the market running errands and stocking up the stalls. In her son's case he would be working for a known villain and he could quite possibly become influenced by the man's attitude and lifestyle. That was how more than a few impressionable young men got into a life of crime, she felt sure.

' 'Ave yer said anyfing ter yer dad about this?' she asked him.

Reg shook his head. 'I was waitin' ter see you,' he replied.

'I'll let yer start on one condition,' Lucy said firmly. 'I wanna 'ave a word wiv Mr Westlake first. Where's 'is yard?'

'It's in Bermondsey Street next door to a pub on the left-'and side,' Reg told her. 'I'll show yer if yer like.'

'No, you stay 'ere an' sit wiv yer farvver, but don't say anyfing to 'im till I get back,' Lucy said as she put on her coat. 'I won't be long.'

It was only a ten-minute walk to the warehouse but Lucy hurried there, hoping not to miss Westlake, and by the time she arrived she was breathing heavily. Men were unloading a lorry as she walked into the yard and they gave her lecherous looks as she tried the office door.

Danny Steadman was checking the goods and he walked over. 'Who d'yer want, luv?' he asked.

'I'm lookin' fer Mr Westlake,' Lucy replied.

' 'E left about ten minutes ago,' Danny told her, and seeing the look of disappointment on her face he said, 'yer could try the pub next door. 'E often goes in there fer a pint when 'e leaves 'ere.'

Lucy thanked him and hurried out of the yard. She was always loath to walk unaccompanied into a pub, but she steeled herself with a deep breath and pushed open the saloon-bar door. There were two men standing at the counter talking quietly, and in the far corner three men sat around a table enjoying a joke. One had his back to her and when he looked round she saw that it was the Bermondsey villain.

'Mr Westlake, can I 'ave a word wiv yer?' she said, feeling uncomfortable at the stares she was getting.

Archie got up and came over to her, a puzzled look on his face. 'Don't I know yer from somewhere?' he asked.

'I live in Pedlar's Row,' Lucy replied. 'I'm Reg Grant's mum.'

Archie smiled. 'Well, well. I didn't know Reg 'ad a mum as pretty as you. What can I do fer yer?'

'Well, ter be honest, I'm a bit concerned about Reg comin' ter work fer yer,' Lucy told him.

Archie steered her away from the door towards a seat some distance from the other men. 'Before yer tell me why yer so concerned, can I get yer a drink?' he said.

'Well, I . . . '

'What'll it be?' Archie said quickly.

'I'll 'ave a stout, if yer don't mind,' Lucy answered.

The villain went to the bar and exchanged a few quiet words with the barman, who smiled broadly and looked in the young woman's direction. Lucy averted her eyes, feeling out of place, but by the time Archie came back with the drinks she had got herself prepared to spell out a few things.

'Before yer say anyfing, did yer know about this mornin'?' Archie asked.

'What about this mornin'?' Lucy said, looking puzzled.

'My bookie got 'is marchin' orders this mornin',' the villain replied. 'It seems we're no longer welcome in Pedlar's Row.'

Lucy looked closely at the man facing her. She had heard much about him and knew that his name was a household word in Bermondsey. He was an imposing man, heavily built with wide shoulders and a strong face. His dark greying hair was well groomed, he was dressed immaculately and she noticed his thick hands and manicured nails as he toyed with his glass of whisky, but he had a certain menacing look in his dark eyes.

'I'm sorry about that,' she replied, 'but my concern is fer my son.'

Archie smiled disarmingly. 'Your Reg is a smart lad. 'E's likeable an' very willin'. That's why I wanna give 'im the job,' he said, sipping his drink. ' 'E'll work in the yard from nine till five every Saturday, an' I'll pay 'im ten shillin's. If 'e shows promise I'll up the wages after a couple o' months. It'll be a good start fer the lad, an' 'e can learn the business.'

Lucy took a deep breath. 'Look, I know all that. Reg told me about the conditions,' she replied. 'It's just that I'm concerned about 'im workin' fer you.'

'Oh? So it's my reputation that's worryin' yer?' he said, smiling mischievously.

'Well, you must admit you're not exactly a run-o'-the-mill employer, are yer?' she replied forthrightly.

'I 'ave ter say I like yer style,' Archie remarked, still smiling. 'I can see you're an intelligent woman too. It's right yer should 'ave concern fer yer lad's wellbein'. When I was twelve years old my ole man came back ter live wiv me muvver again an' I was kicked out on ter the street every Sunday wiv a slice o' bread an' marge while 'e took 'is usual Sunday exercise at me muvver's expense. After 'e 'ad 'is way wiv 'er 'e'd knock 'er about a bit. When I was Reg's age I took a club 'ammer an' opened 'is 'ead wiv it after I caught 'im punchin' 'er senseless. I got off because o' the ole man's reputation fer violence and the fact that I was protectin' me muvver. What I'm tryin' ter say is, Reg won't come ter no 'arm workin' fer me. All right I know I've got a bit of a reputation, if yer get my meanin', but it don't extend ter beatin' kids up.'

Lucy laughed and then dropped her eyes under Archie's gaze. 'I wasn't worried on that score,' she replied quickly. 'I jus' want 'im ter get a decent trade when 'e leaves school.'

Archie shrugged his shoulders. 'That's all right, but a tradesman can only earn the goin' rate. There's no end ter what a bright lad like your boy can earn, once 'e learns the business. He could branch out on 'is own, open up a shop wiv all the knowledge 'e'll pick up.'

'It sounds good, but I don't want 'im goin' wrong, Mr Westlake, if yer know what I mean,' Lucy said earnestly.

'Call me Archie,' he said quickly. 'All my friends do.'

'Yer do understand, don't yer?' she persisted.

'Yeah, I understand,' he replied. 'I'll personally keep my eye on that lad an' I promise yer 'e'll be fine.'

Lucy raised a brief smile. 'Okay, I'll let 'im start this Saturday,' she told him, aware that the villain was studying her closely.

'Can I get yer a refill?' he asked.

Lucy shook her head. 'I must get back 'ome. They'll be 'oldin' the tea up until I get in,' she replied.

Archie downed the last of his drink. 'Look, if we're gonna both keep our eye on yer lad I fink we should get ter know each ovver a little better,' he said. 'So why don't yer come ter my club one night? There's a cabaret an' dancin' on Saturday nights. Do yer like dancin'?'

Lucy smiled. 'I'm a married woman,' she replied.

'Well, I'm not after yer body, if that's what yer finkin',' Archie laughed. 'Like I say, it'll be fer the lad's benefit. What about it?'

'We'll see,' Lucy said, getting up.

Archie stood and held open the door for her. 'Look, fink about what I just said. Yer can find me in the yard most evenin's, or in 'ere. In any case the yard manager

314

can always contact me by phone if need be.'

Lucy gave him a smile and as she stepped out into the street the villain touched her arm momentarily. 'I 'ave ter say you're a very attractive woman,' he remarked, giving her a saucy wink.

Lucy walked home quickly, unable to get Westlake out of her head. Although he had a bad reputation he was a very attractive man, and he seemed to know just how to treat a lady. He had made her feel good with his flattery, and the way things were just now, the opportunity of a night out with him seemed very exciting. After all, it wasn't as if she was going to be disloyal to Roy. He wasn't interested in going out anyway. Like Westlake had said, it was in her son's best interest that they keep in touch, she thought, but she knew that she was only trying to justify herself. If she did agree to go out to Archie's club it would only be because she wanted to see him again.

Chapter Twenty-Nine

On Monday evening Wally Stebbings left his house and walked the short distance to Clyde's box factory feeling as though he was in a dream. He found it hard to take in all that had happened to him in the last few days. On Friday evening he had closed his books and left the factory as he had always done, looking forward to a quiet and relaxing weekend, then suddenly his whole world had been tipped upside down in a few short minutes. People now looked at him in a new way. His neighbours had not said much to him but he could see by the looks on their faces that they felt sorry for him. His mother had taken it hard when he arrived home that morning and told her about his dismissal. She had wanted to go to the firm and confront the manager herself, and he had responded by shouting at her and telling her that he was a mature man not a child any more, and that it would only make him a laughing stock.

Wally climbed the flight of stone steps to the first floor and almost collided with Molly French who was hurrying out from the main office. For a moment she stood staring at him and then a mournful look appeared on her face.

'I'm very sorry to hear that you're leaving, Wally,' she said, tilting her head sideways for effect. 'I think it's a damn disgrace. What are they thinking of?'

Wally smiled sadly at the willowy lady and he could

see the genuine concern in her pale blue eyes. Her thin lips were pinched up too as though she was fighting to control her emotions, and he touched her arm in a spontaneous show of gratitude. She was the only member of staff who had ever shown him friendship. All the others had always kept their distance to a degree, and had tended to poke fun at him and his way of life. Molly was having to put up with the same sort of thing too, he thought. Life had not been too kind to her but she always seemed to find time for a few words and a warm smile. 'I suppose it's all round the office by now,' he said, looking down at his feet in embarrassment. 'Friday evening, I mean.'

Molly had flushed under his touch. He had never touched her before and she had often dreamed about such a thing. 'There's a lot of talk going on in there,' she replied, nodding toward the office, 'but I don't pay any attention to that scandalous nonsense.'

'Well, that's nice of you to say so,' Wally said, looking into her eyes. 'I suppose you could say I was a victim of circumstance, and people tend to believe the worst about us, don't they?'

Molly nodded. How intelligent and knowledgeable Wally was, she thought. Such a distinguished, upright man, and so noble in the face of those terrible accusations levelled at him. He was kind and considerate and would never hurt a living soul. At this moment he needed a friend and she must let him see that she would be that friend, no matter what anyone thought or said. 'I just want you to know that I'm going to miss you very much, Wally,' she said, daringly reaching out and touching his hand. 'I hope we don't lose touch now you're leaving Clyde's.'

Wally felt a lump rising in his throat. What a nice person Molly was. He had never really appreciated her friendship in the past. 'Thank you, Molly,' he replied quietly and with feeling. 'Perhaps we could meet for a quiet chat some time soon?'

'I would like that very much,' she answered, her face colouring again. 'Look in before you leave and I'll give you my address. You might care to drop me a line once you've got yourself settled in another job.'

Wally nodded quickly, trying to cover his own embarrassment. 'I certainly will,' he replied.

Gladys Ward suddenly emerged from the office and gave the two a hard look as she flounced by, and Molly responded by pulling a face.

'Well, until we meet again, goodbye and thank you for your support and friendship,' Wally said in a serious voice.

Molly French walked into her office and sat down carefully in her chair. Her heart was pounding and her throat felt dry as she tried to compose herself. She had never experienced these sort of feelings ever, and they were delicious.

John Bannerman left his home in Rotherhithe on Monday evening feeling very apprehensive. That day he had spent his regular hour at the Sultan with Dickie Jones, and his fellow runner had been unusually talkative, though he often became very loose-tongued after a few drinks anyway. Dickie prided himself on his inside knowledge of what was going on and was keen to impress his trusted friend. What would he do if he knew that his drinking partner was a police informer?

John dug his hands deeper into his shabby overcoat and rounded his thin shoulders against the cold evening air as he walked to the tram stop. His thinning hair blew in the wind and his small face looked pinched as he joined the few waiting passengers. He was due to meet with Ashley after the evening session and he also wanted to talk to Queenie Bromley. God knows what her reaction would be when he told her what he had learned that day from Dickie Jones, but she had a right to know, he thought, whatever her response.

The number 68 tram ground to a halt and John climbed aboard. He heard the loud laughter and banter of the homeward-bound rivermen and factory workers and wished that he too could go home at that time in the evening with the toil and cares of the day forgotten. In his case all he had to look forward to was the monotonous hanging around on a draughty street corner for a couple of hours, watching out for the police and making small talk with the punters, and all the time worrying about his involvement in the goings-on and the deadly implications should someone suspect him of being a grass. Westlake would have no hesitation in getting rid of him. The man was totally ruthless, and he had access to hard-men who would be paid exceptionally well to carry out his orders without question or pangs of conscience. How had he allowed himself to become embroiled in such a perilous game? How was he going to extricate himself and start a new life away from all the worries and dangers facing him? There was no chance, not while Detective Sergeant Ashley found him useful. There was no way out. Once he was no longer any help to the man he would become expendable. A discreet word could be put about and before he knew it the villains would come looking for him. It was the usual way grasses went, once their usefulness was at an end. He had been such a fool allowing Ashley to manipulate him in the first place. He should have bluffed it out and let the worst happen. All right, it would have meant another spell inside, but when he had finished his time he would have been a free man, not tortured by the dire situation he was in now.

The tram lurched round the sharp bend at Dockhead and John Bannerman felt inside his coat pocket for his cigarette tin. With the regular information with which he had been supplying Ashley it wouldn't be long before the police pounced on Westlake and company. They might not be successful in convicting the villains – they never had been in the past, after all – and this time Westlake could be sure that someone had talked. Dickie Jones would no doubt have his suspicions, considering the amount of information he had passed on.

The worried bookie's runner rolled himself a cigarette, suddenly aware that his hands were shaking. He was not looking forward to seeing Queenie later that evening but he knew he had to tell her what he had learned from Dickie Jones. The woman had been good to him and his family and the cakes and pies she baked were a godsend. Queenie had a heart of gold behind that sometimes frightening exterior and he loved her like a mother. Perhaps he should spare her the information. It would only add to the burden she already carried.

The tram turned into Tower Bridge Road and by the time it shuddered to a halt at the Trocette cinema John Bannerman had smoked his cigarette and was rolling another in his nervousness. It was no good trying to conceal the truth from Queenie, he finally decided. She had to know.

Laura Prior hummed happily to herself as she peeled the potatoes over the scullery sink on Monday evening. It was hard for her to believe what a meaningless existence she had been stuck in until recently. There was a man in her life now whom she had come to love dearly in a few short weeks, and it was incredible how he had managed to lighten her burden. Her father's mood swings no longer upset her in the way they used to, and the obvious problems between Lucy and Roy did not weigh down on her quite so heavily as she might have expected. Everything now seemed surmountable, and Laura felt almost guilty at the happiness she enjoyed. She would be popping into the Cassidys' home to spend a couple of hours with Eddie later this evening, and while they chatted with Lizzie and Eric they would secretly hold hands under the tablecloth and steal brief glances full of silent desire.

Albert was sitting beside the fire in the parlour, reading the evening paper, and Roy was lounging quietly in the armchair facing him, his eyes staring into the glowing coals. The two boys had gone up to their bedroom, and for a short while Laura had time to reflect. Her romance with Eddie had come at a crucial time in her life and now she was thinking of things she had never imagined before. She wanted him desperately and felt that he wanted her just as much. The chemistry that existed between them was electric, each aware of the other's need. It was excitingly apparent every time they got near to each other, and it was inevitable that they would become lovers very soon. They were finding it hard to keep their hands off each other and it took an ever-increasing amount of restraint.

Lucy had just come in and Laura heard her hurry up the stairs. Soon she came back down and walked out into the scullery with a deep sigh.

'Well, I've seen Archie Westlake,' she said, leaning against the small table. ' 'E's told me there's nuffink ter worry about where Reg is concerned. I told 'im though that I wasn't too keen on Reg workin' fer 'im.'

'Oh, an' what did 'e say ter that?' Laura asked, glancing up from the sink.

' 'E was quite nice really,' Lucy replied. ' 'E didn't take offence or anyfing. In fact 'e was tellin' me about when 'e was a lad.'

'I s'pose there's no 'arm in Reg workin' in the ware'ouse, provided yer keep yer eye on fings,' Laura remarked. 'The trouble is, lads of Reg's age tend ter be impressed by those sort o' people.'

Lucy nodded. 'As a matter o' fact Archie Westlake wanted me ter go to 'is club in Camberwell one night,' she said, toying with a frayed edge of the stiff tablecloth.

Laura frowned as she looked at her younger sister. 'Yer not finkin' o' goin', are yer?' she asked sharply.

'Of course not,' Lucy replied quickly. 'I wouldn't dream of it.'

Laura could see the unhappiness reflected in Lucy's eyes and her heart went out to her. 'Look, I know that it's really difficult wiv Roy at the moment but I'm sure you'll get it all sorted out in the end,' she said sympathetically. 'Yer knew it wasn't goin' ter be easy.'

Lucy snorted dismissively. 'I'm fed up o' tryin', ter tell yer the trufe,' she replied. 'It seems ter be gettin' worse. I can't talk to 'im an' the boys seem scared to ask 'im anyfing. Reg wanted 'is dad ter take 'im ter see Millwall play last Saturday, but 'e was frightened to ask. That's not right, is it? It's the same wiv young Terry. 'E never seems ter spend five minutes in the 'ouse more than 'e 'as to, an' yer know 'ow 'e used ter sit fer hours in the corner wiv a book.'

'I don't fink Roy's got anyfing ter do wiv that,' Laura answered. 'Terry's got in wiv young Charlie an' the two of 'em are very close. 'E's just growin' up fast an' 'e prob'ly wants ter get out more.'

'I dunno, I'm sure,' Lucy sighed.

Laura scooped the potatoes into a large pot and put them over the gas. 'Tea's gonna be late ternight, an' I wanted ter clear away early too. I'm goin' in ter see Eddie later,' she said.

Lucy smiled widely and drew a sharp retort from Laura. 'What you grinnin' for?'

'Just thoughts,' she replied, pulling on the loose tablecloth thread.

'Oh, an' what thoughts?' Laura quizzed her.

'I was just finkin' 'ow different you are lately,' Lucy replied. 'Could it be love, by any chance?'

Laura coloured slightly and needlessly lifted the pot lid to peek at the potatoes. 'Don't be silly,' she countered.

'Well, yer could 'ave fooled me,' Lucy persisted.

Laura saw that there was no use hiding the fact any longer and she turned to face her sister. 'We are very close,' she said, meeting Lucy's amused gaze. 'Eddie's a special fella an' I'm pretty sure 'e feels the same way about me, at least I 'ope so.'

Lucy could feel the emotion in her sister's words and she smiled affectionately. 'I'm very glad for yer, fer both of yer,' she answered. 'I've bin worried over yer lately, an' Dad 'as too. It's not right yer should 'ave the worry of us lot. It started to age yer, I could see it slowly 'appenin'.'

'Well, fank you very much,' Laura said sarcastically. 'That's a great boost to a woman's morale, I must say.'

Lucy slipped her arm around her sister's waist as they stood together in the small scullery. 'I didn't mean it like that,' she replied. 'Yer still a good-looker an' yer figure's as trim as it ever was. It's just that yer seemed ter be gettin' like all the married women round 'ere. All yer talked about was the rationin', the weavver, an' 'as the coalman bin yet this week? Yer never talked about clothes, or what was on at the pictures, an' yer never spent much time wiv yer 'air or yer nails like yer used to, at least up until yer met Eddie.'

'Ter be honest, there isn't much time fer anyfing when yer lookin' after a family, Lucy, but it's all gonna change from now on,' Laura said positively.

'I'm glad to 'ear it,' Lucy replied. 'Yer know, when yer dress up an' do yer 'air yer look stunnin'. I can understand Eddie fallin' fer yer.'

Laura smiled. 'By the way, I must tell yer. I've seen

this beautiful dress in Marley's winder. It's black crepe wiv a plungin' neckline an' it's got panels o' sequins on the bodice. I keep lookin' at it every time I go past the shop.'

' 'Ow much is it?' Lucy asked.

'I dunno, it's not priced, but then the best dresses never are.'

The potatoes started to boil over and Lucy reached forward to turn the gas down. 'I'll lay the table if yer like,' she offered.

Laura nodded. 'I'll just check the meat pie, it should be ready by now,' she answered, feeling closer to her sister than she had for a long time.

Darkness had settled over Bermondsey and the wind had got up, stirring the barren plane trees and sending a trail of loose earth across the paved church path as John Bannerman climbed the wide steps and entered St James' Church. There was a choir practice taking place in the body of the church and John sat just inside the door, feeling the draught around his feet. He had managed to see Queenie before he left Pedlar's Row and he had been shaken by her response to the information he gave her. He had been prepared for her to rant and rave but she did not. Instead, she seemed numbed by what he had told her, and he had sensed that she was near to tears. It was so unlike the woman he had come to know as hard and vengeful, and he was glad when he finally got out of the house.

The door creaked open and Gordon Ashley stepped inside the church, wearing a reefer jacket with the collar pulled up around his ears and a red scarf tied loosely at his throat. He looked like the average dockworker, an impression he wanted to give to any curious bystander.

'Wotcher. It's a nasty night,' he said, sitting down in a pew a couple of feet away.

John nodded, waiting for some prompting from the detective.

'Well, what tasty bit of info have you got for me?' Ashley asked in an insinuating way that made the runner want to go for his throat.

He took a deep breath to allay his disgust and looked down at the hymn book on the pew rack. 'It's counterfeit money fer sure,' he whispered. 'There's a large amount already bin printed.'

Ashley cursed under his breath, suddenly remembering where he was and wincing. 'You've let me down, John, I was expecting you to come up trumps on where they took that printing press,' he said in a low, slow voice that had a definite threat in it.

John glanced sideways at the sergeant. 'It wouldn't 'ave made any difference,' he whispered earnestly. 'The printin' was done at Carlton's.'

'Are you sure?' Ashley grated.

'That's the word,' John replied. 'It was done over the weekend.'

'So moving that printing press was a ruse, then,' Ashley said, clenching his fists tightly in anger. 'I hope this wasn't a devious move on your part. You do understand what I'm saying, Bannerman?'

John nodded his head vigorously. 'Look, I'm just a runner, an' like I said, I'm not in the know of anyfing that goes on,' he explained. 'All my information comes from a pal who's got an inside contact, that's 'ow dicey it all is. I'm a trusted friend, an' that's all.'

'What's the play?' Ashley asked.

'Well, it seems that they're gonna wait fer the flat season ter start an' then they'll flood the courses,' John told him. 'My contact is gonna be one o' the punters, if 'e's ter be believed.'

'So they're going to back some winners,' Ashley said archly. 'I expected that was the plan.'

'Well, it wouldn't want much workin' out, would it?' John replied with a rare show of spirit. 'It's just toy money wiv a guaranteed return. They'll just back every 'orse in every race. It only wants a few outsiders ter come in an' they'll make a fortune.'

'They stand to make a fortune anyway,' Ashley growled, 'if they're not stopped. Anyway, what's the first track they'll visit?'

'I dunno,' John replied. 'I should fink it'll be one o' the northern courses.'

'Oh, and what makes you think that?' Ashley asked quickly.

'It's what my contact reckons.'

'Well, keep your ears to the ground, and don't let me down this time,' Ashley warned him.

'I'll do me best.'

'I want more than that. I want a result, understand?'

'I can't do the impossible. Besides, I ain't in a position to ask those sort o' questions,' John replied in anger.

Gordon Ashley leaned across and with a quick glance towards the performing choir he grabbed the young man's arm in a tight grip. 'Don't get cheeky, Bannerman, or you might find yourself on the run, and I don't mean from me only,' he hissed.

'I said I'll do me best,' the runner replied, feeling the power of the detective's grip.

'Tell me, what's the news on Jack Murray's love life?' Ashley whispered letting go of the frightened young man and leaning back.

'Well, as far as I understand, Murray's bein' pressurised by 'is ex-wife fer more money,' John told him. 'There's a whisper that 'e's bin playin' about wiv the books, but it's all rumour at the moment. I don't fink there's any foundation in it, or Westlake would 'ave sorted 'im out by now.'

Ashley glanced quickly at his informant. 'What about Murray's ex?'

John Bannerman shrugged his shoulders. 'Not a lot. Apparently 'er fancy man moved out an' there's someone else moved in, accordin' ter what the barmaid at the Sultan told my contact,' he whispered out of the corner of his mouth. 'Murray never talks about 'is ex-wife, publicly that is, an' 'e's in the bar most o' the time.'

Ashley breathed heavily. 'Right, that's all for now. We'll meet same time next week, unless there's something important you want to tell me. In that case the procedure's the same, okay?'

John Bannerman walked out of the church with mixed emotions. It might have been worse, he thought, but then how much worse could it get? He had been told in no uncertain terms what was in store for him if he did not continue to deliver what was expected. He glanced up at the figure of Christ nailed to a cross at the church gates and sighed deeply. He himself was being crucified for his sins, and his family along with him.

A tram was pulling away as he reached the stop and with a few fast strides and a giant leap he scrambled aboard.

'Tired o' livin'?' the conductor remarked sarcastically.

Sergeant Ashley left the church garden deep in thought. Alma's main fear was that someone would find out about their relationship and bring down a load of trouble on their heads. He would have to be extra careful from now on.

Chapter Thirty

The pleasure launch from Greenwich Pier chugged along on the high tide and sailed under the centre span of Tower Bridge. As the boat entered the Pool of London the few passengers seated on the upper deck could see the hustle and bustle on the quayside as cargoes were unloaded from two freighters docked on the south bank. On the north side of the Pool the white stone walls of the imposing Tower of London stood out in the early spring sunshine. The day was pleasantly mild, with a light river breeze carrying the sour tang of mud as it ruffled a few loose strands of the young woman's hair. Beside her the man sat quietly watching the activity on the wharves, his bandaged hand resting in his lap, and he turned and smiled briefly as his companion tucked the dark wisps of her hair into the white linen headscarf she was wearing.

'Are yer cold?' he asked.

Lucy shook her head and took in a deep breath of river air. 'It's a long time since we did this,' she said, glancing at him.

Roy merely nodded and turned to look at the quay-side, and Lucy tightened her lips in exasperation. She had wanted him to remind her that it was on one of these short trips to Westminster Pier that he proposed to her, though she would never have needed reminding. She was a romantic at heart and would always remember that rainy day when they sat on the lower deck, their arms around each other, and she heard Roy whisper the words which set her heart pounding. How different it all was now. He had been very reluctant to leave the armchair, and seemed indifferent when she told him she had decided to take time off work so that they could spend the day together.

Lucy pulled the collar of her fawn-coloured coat up around her ears as the breeze rose, and sighed deeply as she recalled the few words Roy had mumbled as he lay in bed, his body bathed in sweat and his hands clenched tightly on his chest. He had seemed to be pleading with someone, and then he was suddenly wide awake, his eyes staring at the ceiling. She had tried to comfort him but he had turned away from her, sitting on the edge of the bed with his head in his hands and shaking violently. She had pleaded with him to tell her what it was that was tormenting him, what was so terrible that he couldn't even tell his own wife. She had sat with him in the early-morning light, her arm around his shoulders, coaxing him to let her share his burden, but it was no use. Roy seemed determined to shut her out, and she realised that unless he opened up to her, unless she could find some way to reach him, then their marriage would break apart.

The launch passed under London Bridge and moved on upriver, past the old Southwark Cathedral and St Paul's and on towards Blackfriars Bridge.

'It's a nice view from 'ere,' Lucy remarked, searching for conversation.

'Yeah, it is,' Roy replied. 'See 'ow the sun lights up that spire.'

Lucy slipped her arm through his and let her hand rest lightly on his own. 'Are yer feelin' better fer comin' out?' she asked.

He nodded and gave her a wan smile. 'I'm sorry about last night,' he said quickly. 'It's leavin' those pills off.'

'Are yer goin' ter start takin' 'em again?' she asked.

'I fink I'll 'ave to,' Roy said with a sigh. 'I can't seem ter get by wivout 'em.'

'Look, we've got the whole day to ourselves, let's just enjoy it,' Lucy said, nestling closer to him.

Roy did not reply immediately, instead staring ahead at the approaching bridge. He was silent until the launch neared Westminster Pier. Suddenly he said, 'Let's take a walk in St James's Park.'

They left the pierside and climbed the steps on to the Embankment, glancing up at lofty Big Ben and the Houses of Parliament before hurrying across to Parliament Square. Lucy held Roy's arm and noticed how rigid he felt. In the past he would have given her a little sign by squeezing his arm to his side or patting her hand with his free one, but it was different now. He walked straight-backed and stiff, not talking unless prompted and with his jaw set in a determined line.

Inside the park they made for the pond and walked around the perimeter, looking at the ducks that were swimming near the bank and watching an old man throwing pieces of stale bread into the water. They remained silent as they left the pond and walked further into the park, sitting down on an empty seat under a small tree whose buds were bursting into leaf.

'Me an' Laura used ter bring the kids over 'ere while you were away,' Lucy said after a while. 'Dad came wiv us sometimes. 'E was always frightened the kids would fall in the water.'

Roy eased back on the seat and stretched out his legs. 'It must 'ave bin 'ard fer yer, not knowin' if I'd ever come back,' he replied.

'It was terrible, 'specially before I got word you were a prisoner o' war,' Lucy told him. 'I couldn't 'ave managed wivout Laura. She was a tower o' strength, always there fer me, fer all of us, an' I owe 'er a lot.'

Roy nodded. 'She seems ter be set on this Eddie,' he replied. 'I'm glad fer 'er. I just 'ope it works out.'

Lucy could see that he was starting to relax a little and she began to feel encouraged. 'I bet yer was really surprised ter see 'ow big the boys 'ad got,' she remarked.

'I was,' Roy replied. 'It feels sad to 'ave missed those years seein' 'em both growin' up. Don't ferget they were babies when I left.'

'Tell me, Roy, was there a time when yer really felt yer'd never see us again?' Lucy asked quietly.

Roy looked down at his clasped hands for a few moments. 'Most o' the time we were starvin' an' forced ter work long hours in a terrible climate. Everyone was constantly goin' down wiv malaria, beriberi an' jungle ulcers, as well as dysentery an' sheer physical exhaustion, but most of us kept ourselves goin' by finkin' of 'ome an' the people we loved. It was a way o' survivin', but one mornin' one o' the men collapsed wiv cholera an' it swept through the camp in no time at all. That was one time when I felt I'd never get back 'ome.'

Lucy reached out and touched his hand, urging him to carry on, but Roy stirred awkwardly on the bench with a strange pained look in his eyes, and she knew that a veil had closed over his memories.

'Well, I prayed for yer every night, an' I made the boys say their prayers too,' Lucy told him. 'They never missed sayin' their prayers.'

Roy slumped back on the bench and studied his hands for a few moments. 'Tell me,' he said after a while, 'wasn't yer ever tempted ter go out wiv somebody while I was away? After all, yer didn't know if I'd survive.'

Lucy felt a sudden tightening in her stomach. It was the question she had been dreading, and she knew that she could never tell him the truth. 'I s'pose there were gels who 'ad plenty o' time on their 'ands and were tempted,' she replied as casually as possible. 'Don't ferget the boys were only babies an' I was workin' full time. I 'ad no time ter go drinkin' or dancin', an' that's where the temptation was.'

'Plenty o' women couldn't wait,' Roy said searchingly. 'I bet there were a lot who jumped inter bed wiv anuvver bloke as soon as their ole man was out the door.'

'P'raps there were,' Lucy replied quickly, 'but we shouldn't judge. They were bad times fer all of us. We should just be fankful that we 'ave each ovver, some weren't so lucky. All I want is fer us ter get back ter normal.'

'Don't yer fink I want that too?' Roy said, raising his voice in anger. 'I know I'm not any good in bed at the moment, yer made that clear, right enough, but it won't always be like it is now. I just need time.'

' 'Ow much more time d'yer need?' Lucy retorted. 'Six months, a year? If yer'd only confide in me, tell me what it is that causes those bad turns, I might be able to 'elp. One fing's fer sure, yer can't go on takin' those sleepin' tablets every night. They're knockin' the life out of yer.'

'What's there ter tell?' Roy shouted. 'They're just bad dreams. I'm back on the railway an' I'm relivin' the nightmare. It's not surprisin', is it?'

Lucy bit back angry tears, realising that the day was spoiled. 'Somefing 'appened ter yer that yer won't face up to,' she replied, her voice full of emotion. 'It's somefing yer pushin' ter the back of yer mind an' until yer bring it out inter the open yer not gonna be any different.'

'What are yer, a psychiatrist now?' Roy said sarcastically.

'No, I'm just talkin' common sense, an' you know I'm right,' Lucy told him, taking a handkerchief from her handbag and dabbing at her eyes.

Roy lapsed into an angry silence and when Lucy had

composed herself he stood up. 'I fink we'd better get back 'ome,' he said. 'It's started ter cloud over.'

Lucy felt a wave of depression closing in around her. For one brief moment it had looked as though she was finally breaking through Roy's defences, but she was forced to concede that nothing had changed. She realised with a sinking feeling that nothing would, unless he faced up to the fact that their marriage was teetering on the brink of disaster.

The two walked from the park in silence and caught a tram back to Bermondsey. Roy stared impassively out of the window for most of the journey, while Lucy sat beside him with her thoughts racing. How could he be so insensitive to her feelings? Didn't he understand how much she needed him to love her, to hold her close, to tell her how much he loved her? Well, he would be made to understand, she vowed, however painful it might be. She had tried hard to save their marriage but she had not succeeded. He was too sure of her, that was it. Well, perhaps if he was shocked into realising that she wasn't prepared to wait indefinitely then he might pull himself together. It was the only answer.

At Dockhead Police Station Ben Walsh swivelled round in his chair, his face dark with anger. 'Ashley, they're taking the piss and I'm not going to stand for it, do I make myself clear?' he barked.

The sergeant gripped his fist in the palm of his hand. 'I put the fear of Christ into that snout of mine,' he answered. 'There's no way he gave me false info. I think we can take it as read that Westlake pulled a fast one. We go looking for a site while they print money at the last place we expect them to.'

Walsh sat back and shook his head slowly. 'Either I'm getting too old for this job or the villains are getting more and more sophisticated,' he growled. 'One thing's for sure, Ashley. I'm going to nail that bastard if it's the last thing I do.'

'Well, the flat season starts in a couple of weeks and they'll be pushing that money,' Ashley said. 'With a bit of luck we might have the location.'

'If it's luck we need you can forget it,' Ben Walsh replied. 'We get a lead on a possible engraver and then he goes and tops himself, and you've got a snout who leads us up the garden path. In the meantime Westlake prints counterfeit money and sits back laughing at us. If we have to depend on luck I may consider putting in for my retirement.'

Ashley leaned forward on the desk. 'I got one bit of info that could be a change of fortune,' he said quietly. 'It seems that Jack Murray is cooking the books. Westlake doesn't know as yet. I think it's all about Murray putting his own booze in the pub, you know the sort of thing, sticking his own spirits on the optics and pushing dodgy cigarettes. There are some shrewd customers use the Sultan and I suspect they've noticed things. That's where the rumours usually start and it won't take long for word to get to Westlake.'

'Then the fat will be in the fire,' Walsh remarked.

'Exactly,' Ashley replied. 'If the big four fall out then we might get the break we're looking for.'

'There's a good pal of mine on the management at Wenlock's,' Walsh said, smiling slyly. 'I might just give him the tip that one of his pubs would benefit from a visit by the area manager. That should alert Westlake.'

'A sprat to catch a mackerel, eh?' Ashley laughed.

'Too right. Now let's see what else we can do to get the ball rolling,' Ben Walsh said, picking up a folder. 'I want a blitz on the bookies. Get yourself a team and hit 'em tomorrow lunchtime.'

'That's a bit short notice,' Ashley said quickly. 'We've

got a squad on that pilfering thing in Tooley Street and there's . . . '

'Sod Tooley Street,' Walsh cut in sharply. 'This is about thousands of pounds of counterfeit money, not a bloody hock of bacon stuck up some docker's jersey. Take a wagon, and when you round them up put one of our men in with them. Mind who you put in though. I want someone who looks the part. We'll keep them hanging around in the charge room as long as possible. Anything we can pick up will help.'

Ashley left the office in a hurry. If the round-up of the bookies was going to be successful there was much to do.

On Tuesday evening George Bromley sat sipping his beer with a long face, despite having several reasons to be happy. He had had a good spell at the Tooley Street wharves and there was a chance that it would continue into the next week or so. Fred and Billy had been placed on probation, and young Charlie had quietened down no end since he had teamed up with the lad from number three. Even Frankie had been on his best behaviour of late, apart from the little episode when he kicked a tennis ball through Ginger Morgan's front-room window and nearly caused a fight between George and the hare-brained tram driver. If it hadn't been for that idiot John Bannerman calling in and priming Queenie up, everything in the garden would be lovely, George thought.

He drained his glass and sat contemplating the line of froth around the rim. He had hoped that Queenie would not go back to her weekly ritual but he had known in his heart that she would. He could manage to live with that, but now the bookie's runner had really put the cat amongst the pigeons. He should have kept the knowledge to himself instead of running to Queenie with it.

' 'Ello, mate, fancy a pint, or are yer gonna sit lookin'

at that empty glass all night?' Len Carmichael asked with a grin.

' 'Ello, cock, I didn't see yer come in,' George replied. 'I was jus' finkin'.'

'I shouldn't. It could be dangerous,' Len laughed, picking up George's empty glass and going to the counter.

'Wassa matter wiv that mate o' yours?' Tubby Jeffreys asked as he turned and leaned his elbows on the counter. ' 'E looks like 'e's jus' done 'is last shillin'.'

'It's Queenie, I shouldn't be at all surprised,' Len answered. 'She leads 'im a dog's life at times.'

June leaned over the counter. 'What'll it be, two pints o' the same, Len?' she asked with her usual smile.

Len nodded and turned to Tubby. 'I wouldn't put up wiv what 'e puts up wiv,' he announced. 'My ole dutch don't give me any grief since I straightened 'er out.'

Tubby caught June's eye and winked quickly. ' 'Ow did yer straighten 'er out then?' he asked.

'Well, she started on about me goin' out fer a pint, so I done no more an' give 'er what for,' Len replied, laying down a half-crown on the counter.

'What for?'

'Yeah, what for.'

'Yer mean yer belted 'er?'

'Nah, I just give 'er what for.'

'What for?'

'Yeah, that's what I said.'

'That's what I thought yer said.'

June gave Tubby Jeffreys a blinding look. 'Can you two continue this conversation somewhere else?' she said wearily.

'What for?' Tubby laughed.

Len Carmichael felt he was wasting his time trying to talk sense to Tubby and he picked up the filled glasses.

George Bromley sipped his beer and then reached into

his coat pocket for his tobacco tin. 'I 'eard Wally Stebbin's got the push,' he said.

Len nodded. 'Yeah, my Elsie told me. Bloody shame. I dunno if it's anyfing ter do wiv that ovver turn-out, I expect it is.' He lifted his glass. 'I understand Joe Molloy's ole woman moved the bookie on then,' he remarked.

' 'E tried ter stand outside your door, didn't 'e?' George said.

'Yeah, but I wouldn't tolerate it,' Len replied, wiping the froth from his lips with the back of his hand. 'I told Elsie what ter say. If 'e gives yer any ole cheek call me out, I sez to 'er. I was on late shift at the time, yer see. Nah, I wouldn't stand fer it. The bloody Row was gettin' like a Cantonese brothel, what wiv all the comin's an' goin's.'

'It was nice an' quiet terday, accordin' ter Queenie,' George remarked.

The two glasses were soon emptied and George got up. 'Same again?' he asked.

Len considered for a moment or two. Elsie had given him strict instructions not to stay too long and she was going through one of her more vitriolic patches. 'All right then, one more fer the road,' he said, hoping it might give him the courage of his convictions. Elsie might well benefit from a good 'what for'.

Chapter Thirty-One

Laura turned over on the chair-bed and stretched, her eyes going up to the mantelshelf clock. It was ten minutes past seven and she could hear movement coming from upstairs. It sounded like Lucy was awake and would be down soon. The room felt cold and Laura pulled her feet back up under the covers as she stared up at the grimy ceiling. She heard footsteps passing the parlour window and she smiled to herself as she realised that Eddie would be going off to work about now. She sat up quickly, pulled her quilted dressing-gown from the back of a chair and wrapped it around her as she made her way out into the scullery to boil the kettle. She always enjoyed the quietness at this time of day, but it would have been nice to spend another few minutes under the blankets.

Lucy walked into the scullery looking miserable and mumbled a good morning. Her eyes were puffy and her face looked very pale.

'Roy was awake again last night,' she sighed. 'I 'ad a job gettin' back ter sleep.'

Laura took hold of her sister's arm. 'Go in the parlour an' sit down. I'll bring in a cuppa soon as it's ready,' she said kindly.

Lucy walked out of the scullery with her shoulders hunched and Laura shook her head sadly. Things were not improving between her sister and Roy and she could see trouble ahead. Lucy had never been one to sit about the house during the evenings. She and Roy had always gone dancing or to the pictures when they first got together, and even after the children were born they had still been able to manage the occasional night out. Yesterday was the first time they had gone out together since Roy came home, and that appeared to have ended disastrously. Lucy had come in looking downcast and Roy had not had much to say for himself.

Laura nibbled at a stale biscuit and thought about the previous night, as she waited for the kettle to boil. She had enjoyed the evening at number five and they had all made a fuss of her. The whole family were gathered there, as was the custom on Tuesday evenings, and Eddie had taken a lot of ribbing. It was obvious to her how close the Cassidys were and Eddie seemed to enjoy his position as baby of the family. Most of the time he had winked surreptitiously at her before opening up some topic of discussion and then sat back calmly while his brothers did their best to wind him up. There was no malice or bad feeling, but the conversation did sometimes become heated. Lizzie had constantly interrupted with the warning that she was not going to tolerate brothers arguing but Eric merely laughed and egged his sons on. The evening ended on a light note with Eric being drowned out when he attempted to tell the tale of Bonky Masefield, and Laura wondered if he would ever manage it. She had left around ten o'clock, and Eddie saw her to her front door and kissed her good night. Laura had wanted him to hold her in his arms for a while, but Joe Molloy had walked into Pedlar's Row at that moment in a state of intoxication and the moment had gone.

The kettle came to the boil and Laura filled the enamel teapot. The boys would need to be roused soon and Albert would be waiting for his morning tea. Lucy would want to get ready in the scullery for work and she would need hot water. Laura refilled the kettle and put it over the gas before pouring the tea. There were a few minutes left for a quiet chat with Lucy before the house came alive.

At number two, Elsie Carmichael sat drinking her morning tea, hoping that her doctor was going to allow her one more week before he signed her off the panel. After what Clyde's had done to Wally Stebbings she felt no guilt whatsoever in scrounging another week on the sick list. At least they couldn't sack her while she was on the panel, although the manager would no doubt give her notice at the first opportunity because of her erratic timekeeping. It wasn't much of a job anyway, she told herself. She could earn more at the tin-bashers, or at Crosse and Blackwell's. The rag-sorters were always advertising, though it was said the women there brought home fleas. Maybe she could get a start at Collins in Tower Bridge Road. One of her friends had got a job there recently and she was earning good bonuses packing toy soldiers and small plastic model kits.

Elsie looked around the room. The lower half of the walls were wood-panelling and it was all looking really grimy. Len had promised to scrub it clean while he was on late shift and she would have to make sure he didn't forget. It would be a good idea to leave him a note, she decided. He would get up while she was at the doctor's and it was a stone certainty he would sit around for at least an hour before he roused himself. If she went to the market straight from the doctor's and then went to enquire about the job at Collins it would give him enough time to get on with the cleaning. He might even be finished by the time she got back home.

At Dockhead Police Station everyone was getting

primed up for the blitz on the street bookies. The black maria was standing ready and a variety of disguises were being issued. Ben Walsh was supervising the last-minute preparations and he was determined that his briefing would leave no one in any doubt as to the importance of the operation. This wasn't to be just another run-of-the-mill street betting clean-up. This operation had a twofold dimension and if it was successful it would no doubt enhance his promotion prospects enormously.

Sergeant Ashley was feeling uneasy as he made his own last-minute preparations. Alma had told him that Jack Murray had not given up hope that they might get back together again, though for her it was out of the question. He had been a violent husband and had had a string of affairs over the years. He had always been wildly jealous, and if he suspected that there was a new man in her life he would have no hesitation in causing trouble. Ashley realised only too well that he, a police officer, could not afford to have anything of that sort happen. In fact it would be totally disastrous for him if it became known that he was consorting with a known villain's ex-wife.

Ben Walsh was ready to start his briefing and he called a heftily built policeman to one side. 'Right, Baker, all being well we'll be picking you up in Long Lane just by the church at ten past twelve or thereabouts,' he said. 'As soon as the back doors of the wagon open, try to make a run for it, understood? Hopefully by that time we'll have a few customers in the wagon. It'll look good if you attempt to get away. Give the arresting officers a bit of verbal for effect. You know the score. We're counting on you conning a bit of information, and watch your step. Good luck, Baker.'

Len Carmichael sat sipping his tea and wondering if he should take a stroll down to the papershop for the midday *Star*. There were a couple of afternoon dog-meetings and he might be lucky to pick a win double. Maybe he should just put his feet up for an hour or two. The late shift was proving to be very tiring and there was that dismantling job to finish when he went back. Elsie had said she was going to see the doctor and then go on to the market, so she wouldn't be home just yet, he thought, running his fingers through his thinning fair hair. It might be a good idea to have a quick tidy up though, just to keep the woman happy.

Len settled his lean frame comfortably in the armchair by the fire and rested his hands in his lap. The wireless was on and soft strains of theatre organ music lulled him into a torpor. He drifted between sleep and waking for some time, and when he finally roused himself he noticed that the clock said eleven thirty and realised that Elsie would be home soon. It was then, while he was tidying the parlour table, that he saw the note.

'Bloody Ada!' he exclaimed aloud. 'She'll 'ave my guts fer garters!'

Cursing to himself, Len slipped on his overcoat and cap and hurried out of the house. The oil shop in Weston Street was the nearest, he figured. The man there would know the best stuff to use on greasy woodwork.

'Well now, the best fing fer paintwork is Manger's Sugar Soap, but yer gotta be careful if yer got cuts on yer 'ands,' the shopkeeper told him. 'It stings like billy-o. On the ovver 'and, yer can try turpentine wiv a drop o' machine oil. That's pretty good. Mind yer, I don't use any o' that meself. I always use Polson's Paint Preparation. That's the best yer can get. It's a bit dearer, mind.'

Len scratched his head. 'I'm only doin' a spot o' tartin' up, I ain't renovatin' Buckin'ham Palace,' he said sarcastically.

'Well then, I'd use turpentine an' oil,' the oil-shop man said, stroking his chin.

'All right then, that'll do,' Len replied, feeling a little confused.

The man went away and came back rubbing his bald head. 'I'm out o' turpentine till termorrer,' he announced.

'All right then, give us some o' that Mangy sugar soap,' Len said wearily.

'Manger's, yer mean,' the shopkeeper corrected him.

'Yeah, that,' Len sighed, glancing anxiously at the wall clock.

Finally Len walked out clutching a packet of Manger's Sugar Soap with the shopkeeper's words ringing in his ears. 'Don't ferget ter read the instructions before yer start.'

As he neared Pedlar's Row Len glanced at the instructions on the back of the packet and he automatically slowed down. The printing was very small and he stopped still on the corner of the Row while he studied the words. He took no notice of the two overalled workmen who were approaching him and he was amazed when they suddenly grabbed him roughly by the arms. 'Right, yer nicked fer street bettin',' one said sharply.

Len was still speechless when he found himself being bundled unceremoniously into the back of a black maria.

'I fink it's a bloody disgrace. Downright criminal,' a voice said above him.

Len picked himself up off the floor of the van and sat down heavily on a low bench beside a well-dressed individual. 'What's this all about?' he asked incredulously.

'They're 'avin' a blitz, by the look of it,' the bookie replied.

Len was still holding on to his packet of sugar soap as the van lurched round a corner and squealed to a halt. The doors opened and another man was bundled into the dark interior.

'Pity they ain't got nuffink better ter do,' the bookie opposite Len growled.

Spiv Martin picked himself up off the floor and squeezed on to the bench. 'I've a good mind ter sue 'em fer impersonatin' a postman. Yeah, that's right. I got done by a copper disguised as a postman,' he grumbled.

Benny Copland nudged Len. ' 'Ere, they could 'ave done wiv that,' he grinned, pointing to the packet in Len's hands. 'They're 'avin' a right clean-up terday.'

Len Carmichael stuffed the packet into his overcoat pocket. 'I don't know what the bloody 'ell they nicked me for,' he groaned, unaware that he had been mistaken for a runner.

Spiv Martin straightened his tie and brushed a hand over his sleeked-back dark hair. 'They dropped a clanger wiv Con Noble,' he chuckled. ' 'E's moved ter Brady Buildin's terday.'

'Are you all bookies?' Len asked.

The man next to him nodded. 'Why, yer wanna place a bet?' he quipped.

Suddenly the van drew to a sharp halt and the doors were flung open once more. 'Gawd 'elp us, if it ain't Morry Baines,' Spiv exclaimed, helping the ageing bookie into the van.

'The bastards caught me dead ter rights,' Morry fumed. 'This bloke walked up 'oldin' ole Muvver Price's arm an' nabbed me just as I took 'er bet. Wait till I see that cow.'

'That silly ole mare wouldn't know any better,' Spiv remarked.

Len had realised by now that he had been mistakenly arrested and he settled back on the bench with a grin on his thin face. Wait till Elsie finds out, he thought. She'll never believe me.

Spiv Martin banged on the side of the van as it pulled

up again sharply. 'Oi, be careful! Yer got passengers aboard,' he shouted.

Morry Baines nudged Len in the ribs. 'I don't know yer,' he said sharply. 'Yer ain't one o' the regulars. I'm the local bookmakers' association secretary, so I should know yer.'

'Well, I'm on the late shift this week,' Len began, ' 'an . . . '

'Late shift? What bloody late shift?' Morry cut in.

'At the brewery,' Len told him.

'We ain't got anybody in there yet, 'ave we?' Morry asked, looking around at the rest.

The doors suddenly opened and there was a commotion. Two policemen were grappling with a well-built man who was cursing them loudly. Finally he was roughly bundled into the van and the doors slammed shut. Len helped him to his feet and made room for him on the bench.

'I don't know 'im eivver,' Morry remarked, glancing suspiciously at Spiv Martin.

Spiv made a quick motion across his throat and Morry nodded and then turned to another of the bookies. 'Bloody outsiders,' he growled. 'Bermondsey's gettin' full of outsiders. We'll 'ave ter call a meetin' soon as possible. It'll be nigh on impossible to earn an honest crust before long, the way fings are goin'.'

PC Baker sat hunched on the bench, feeling that he was going to have a disappointing day. 'Where did they nab you?' he asked, turning to Len.

'Pedlar's Row,' Len replied. 'I'd just bin ter the oilshop in Weston Street, which is just as well. They've got nuffink on me.'

PC Baker made a mental note. Bookies often passed over bets and stakes during the day in case they were nabbed. The oilshop would certainly be marked down for a visit. 'Bin on that patch long, then?' he asked.

'Last year. The council won't be very 'appy when they find out about me changed circumstances though,' Len remarked.

'Oh, an' why's that then?' PC Baker enquired.

'Well, yer see, when the council give me the okay they thought I 'ad me two daughters wiv me. They'd both pissed orf by the time we got the nod.'

The black maria drove into the police compound and pulled up sharply, sending Spiv Martin and Morry Baines into a heap on the floor.

'I dunno about us, I fink they should nick that stupid git fer dangerous drivin',' Spiv growled.

The men were all hustled into a large room and one by one they were led in front of a sergeant and told to empty their pockets. Len stood next to PC Baker. 'I'm not partin' wiv this,' he whispered, tapping the bulge in his pocket. 'This is me evidence.'

The undercover policeman shook his head slowly. Either Bermondsey Borough Council were aiding and abetting street bookmakers or the man next to him was a raving lunatic. 'It wasn't a bad day fer you, gettin' ter the oil shop in time,' he remarked.

'Yer can say that again,' Len said, smiling. 'I'd be right up the Swanee ovverwise.'

'There's bin a lot o' rumours flyin' around lately,' Baker whispered to him as they stood waiting in line. 'I dunno what ter make of it all.'

Len wasn't sure either. 'No, neivver do I,' he replied.

'What's the latest your end?' Baker asked.

'Well, there's bin a lot o' rumours about poor ole Wally Stebbin's, but there's no trufe in it, none whatsoever,' Len told him, shaking his head. 'I never believed what they was sayin' about 'im, nor did my Elsie, come ter that.'

'Right, turn out yer pockets,' the duty sergeant ordered.

Len reached into his coat pocket. 'I paid fer that an' yer can check up at Spratt's oil shop,' he said, banging down the packet of sugar soap on the counter.

The sergeant looked wide-eyed at it for a moment or two, then he shook his head slowly. 'Turn out the rest o' yer pockets,' he ordered.

Len searched through his overcoat and brought out a slip of paper which he laid down sheepishly on the counter. The sergeant picked it up and his face suddenly contorted as he read the message: 'Len, Clean that bloody woodwork down or you'll be getting bread and jam for your tea. Your loving wife, Elsie.'

'Yer can keep it if yer like,' Len said quietly.

One hour later Ben Walsh glanced through the glass-panelled door into the room and gave the order for the bookies to be charged and bailed to appear at Tower Bridge Magistrates Court the following morning. It had not been a success. Con Noble had somehow eluded the net, and Spiv Martin had nothing on his person anyway. PC Baker seemed to be getting the silent treatment, and all that had come to light, apart from a few betting slips, was a packet of Manger's Sugar Soap and one loving note.

Chapter Thirty-Two

There was a shock waiting for Laura when she walked into the Sultan on Wednesday morning. The public bar counter and tables were littered with dirty glasses and the whole place was a mess. Normally Jack Murray and Sonia, the saloon barmaid, cleared the tables and counter and washed the glasses after closing time, but last night nothing had been done. Jack Murray had only just woken up in time to let Laura in, and he was still suffering an outsize hangover.

When Laura saw him emerge from the back room she could tell immediately the state he was in and she decided it would be better to start work without comment.

Jack Murray walked around the bar and sat down heavily in a chair. His face was ashen beneath his black stubble and his hands were shaking as he lit a cigarette.

'I'm sorry fer the mess,' he said flatly. 'Sonia walked out on me last night. Yer might as well know, it'll be public knowledge five minutes after openin' time.'

'I'm very sorry,' Laura replied, filling a large tray with glasses.

'Yer don't fancy a barmaid's job, do yer?' Murray asked.

Laura shook her head. 'I'm sorry, but yer know my position,' she answered.

The publican drew on his cigarette and coughed

loudly. 'Sonia always cooked me a breakfast,' he said. 'I s'pose I'd better get used ter doin' it meself now.'

Laura put the tray down on the table and walked behind the bar into the little back room. 'I'll cook yer somefing,' she said, searching for the frying pan. 'I'll be able ter clear up an' wash the glasses, but there'll be no dustin' done terday.'

Jack Murray sat watching while Laura turned the bacon and broke two eggs into the hot fat. 'It 'ad ter come, I s'pose,' he told her, taking two slices from a cut loaf and spreading them with a thick coating of margarine. 'We seem to 'ave bin at each ovvers' froats fer the past two weeks.'

Laura did not want to hear the details but Jack Murray seemed intent on describing everything to her. 'Sonia knew she was always gonna be second best to Alma. She knew that from the start but she reckoned fings'd change.'

'Is Alma yer wife?' Laura asked out of politeness.

'Ex-wife,' Jack corrected her. 'We got divorced two years ago, but I'd 'ave 'er back termorrer.'

Laura scooped up the eggs and placed them on a plate beside the thin rashers of bacon. 'There you are,' she said. 'I'll make some tea while yer eat that then I'll 'ave ter get on.'

Laura was hard pressed to finish cleaning the two bars before opening time, and when she slipped on her coat at eleven o'clock Jack Murray appeared from the back room again. He had shaved and put on a clean white shirt, but his face still showed the signs of a heavy night's drinking.

'Put that in yer pocket,' he said, handing Laura a pound note. 'You earned it.'

Laura thanked him and set off home. She had heard stories about the Sultan's manager from her father, who frequented the place. He had said it was common knowledge that Sonia was living with Murray but they always seemed to be getting at each other's throats. Albert had also told her that there were after-hours sessions for a privileged few in the saloon bar every weekend and there were some strange faces to be seen there lately. Everyone knew that Westlake owned the pub but he was occupied at his drinking club every weekend and most evenings. The question the customers were asking was, did Westlake know about the late drinking sessions, and if not, how would he react when he found out?

Laura went straight to the market, knowing that Roy was at home to keep an eye on Albert, and she decided to put the morning's business out of her mind. It was no concern of hers anyway, except that it had meant extra work, but at least she had been paid a bonus for her troubles.

When she had been to the fruit and veg stall Laura walked slowly by the clothes-shop window. The black crepe dress was still there and it seemed to look more beautiful than ever. Laura vowed that one day when she had summoned up enough courage she would go in the shop and price the dress. Not this morning though, she decided.

On Wednesday morning Wally Stebbings got up early and put a fresh blade into his razor before shaving. He took down his clean white shirt that was hanging from a clothesline in the scullery and he sorted out his smartest tie. He had to look his best today, he knew. Molly French had put a note through his letterbox on her way home from work the previous evening, telling him that Messrs. Cox and Sons, a provision merchant's in Tooley Street, were looking for an experienced book-keeper clerk and he would do well to pop along, saying that Miss French had sent him.

Wally had been surprised when he read the note, but he had no time to dwell on the whys or wherefores. Molly must obviously know someone in the company, he reasoned. He had to concentrate on getting himself into the right frame of mind. Going for an interview was not the easiest of things to do. One little slip or one wrong answer could lose him the job and he knew that presentation counted for a lot. His mother had been very inquisitive about the note. 'Who is this mysterious Miss French?' she had wanted to know.

Wally adjusted the knot of his tie and decided to leave his scarf at home. After all, the weather had turned comparatively mild and the scarf tended to hide his nice clean shirt. Wally's only concern was his leather boots. They had developed a squeak and it troubled him, though his mother had laughed it off, saying that boots only squeaked if they hadn't been fully paid for. Wally wasn't worried on that score. Everything he had was purchased cash down. His mother had taught him early on that once the tallyman got his talons into people they could never get free.

Wally put on his dark overcoat and brushed a few specks of dust from the lapels before putting on his trilby. 'There we are,' he said aloud.

'Don't ferget yer scarf, Wally,' his mother called out.

The hopeful candidate walked steadfastly out of Pedlar's Row and turned right into Weston Street. He must keep calm, he told himself. A brisk pace would do it. He kept his face to the front, not wishing to look over at Clyde's, but Molly French was waiting.

'Coo-ee,' she called out from the office window. 'Good luck, Wally.'

He turned and looked up to see Molly waving a handkerchief and smiling broadly. With a stab at being debonair Wally waved his hand in a regal gesture and marched on at an even faster pace.

351

Elsie Carmichael had been successful at the surgery. The doctor had agreed with her that her back would not stand up to the rigours of work just yet and he gave her another week on the panel. Elsie was in a good mood as she strolled along the market, until she bumped into Betty Johnson. She was the one who had carried the news of Wally's attack into work on Monday morning, and it was a certainty that she had made much of the reason for the assault, Elsie told herself. It was silly of her to have mentioned anything to the woman, but it was too late now. She might have known that Betty would immediately go running to that horrible Gladys Ward with the news.

'Hello, Elsie, you're looking better,' Betty remarked.

Elsie bit back on a sharp reply and smiled instead. 'I'm feelin' a bit better but the doctor won't sign me off just yet,' she answered.

'It was a shame about Wally Stebbings,' Betty went on. 'I could have cried when I heard he got the sack.'

Elsie had a strong urge to swing her laden shopping bag in the woman's gob but she smiled sympathetically instead. 'Yeah, it was a shock. Such a nice man,' she said. 'Funny fing though, 'e fell in the shit but come up smellin' o' roses.'

'Oh?'

'Yeah, 'e got a job over the City, so 'is muvver told me. Double the pay an' a bonus every month,' Elsie lied.

'Well I never.'

Elsie looked hard at the woman, suddenly getting an idea. ' 'Ow's Gladys feelin' now?' she asked with feigned innocence.

'She's fit and well, why do you ask?' Betty queried.

'Oh, it's just that I saw 'er at the doctor's the ovver evenin'. She didn't see me though. P'raps I shouldn't 'ave mentioned it,' Elsie said, making a good job of looking worried and compromised.

'Strange,' Betty remarked, pinching her chin. 'She never mentioned anything to me.'

'Well, she couldn't, could she?' Elsie said mysteriously.

'Why ever not?' Betty asked.

'I shouldn't say any more,' Elsie told her, looking even more worried.

'Look, Elsie, you know me,' Betty whispered. 'I'm discretion itself. You can feel safe confiding in me.'

'Promise yer won't let this go any furvver, Betty, 'cos if yer do I'll know where it come from,' Elsie warned her. 'Apart from me, an' Gladys 'erself, no one else knows about it.'

'You can trust me implicitly,' Betty said, holding a hand over her heart for effect.

Elsie put down her shopping bag and moved closer. 'When I was waitin' ter go in the doctor's surgery I saw Gladys come out,' she began in a hushed voice. 'She didn't see me, like I said, an' she was lookin' all agitated. You know, like when yer got an' itchy back an' can't reach it. She looked really perculiar, if yer ask me. Anyway, I got a prescription fer me painkillers an' I took it ter the chemist near the Trocette, the one that's always open late. Gladys must 'ave left 'er prescription ter be done, 'cos the bloke in the chemist got mixed up an' thought I was 'er. "Mrs Ward?" 'e said. "No, I'm Mrs Carmichael," I told 'im. Well, 'e got all flustered and snatched the bottle back quick, but not before I'd got a look at it.'

'Whatever was it?' Betty asked, her eyes open wide.

'Lockwood's Lotion,' Elsie whispered.

'Lockwood's Lotion? Whatever's that for?' Betty asked.

'It's fer relievin' the itchin', in certain places, yer know what I mean,' Elsie said, nodding collusively as she picked up her shopping basket.

'Yer don't mean,' Betty started in a shocked voice, 'yer don't mean she's got— .'

'Seems like it,' Elsie cut in quickly as she turned for home. 'Most likely caught 'em at work.'

Fred Bromley and his younger brother Billy had vowed that they would be on their best behaviour from now on, after their last brush with the law, and after the few words their father had had with them both. 'Yer muvver's got enough ter worry about, what wiv one fing an' anuvver,' he growled. 'Any more turn-outs like the last one an' she could well end up in 'ospital. Yer know she ain't bin at all well lately.'

Fred, being the eldest, felt that he should set a good example and he called a brothers' meeting. 'There's gonna be no more nickin' an' no more smashin' winders, right?'

Billy, Charlie and Frankie all nodded dutifully, but Frankie had a question. 'What about if a kid gets stroppy? Can't we even punch 'im one?'

'Yer gotta come an' see me first,' Fred said.

'Cor! It's gonna be really borin',' Billy groaned.

'We don't want Mum ter go in 'ospital again, do we?' Fred reminded them.

'Me an' Terry Grant don't get in trouble,' Charlie cut in.

'None of us must get in any more trouble, so if yer get any ideas yer gotta see me first, all right?'

'Why you?' Billy asked.

' 'Cos I'm the eldest, that's why,' Fred told them sternly. 'Now I want yer ter promise.'

'We promise,' the boys said in unison.

Fred felt that he had done his duty, but he was put in a difficult position the following evening when Billy approached him.

'What we gonna do about all that old iron we found the ovver day?' his young brother asked.

Fred scratched his head thoughtfully. 'I dunno. Best ter leave it where it is fer the time bein',' he replied.

Billy looked disappointed. 'But we said we was gonna sell it ter Percy the totter. There's enough ter fill ole Percy's cart. 'E'd give us more than two quid fer all that lot, I bet.'

'It's werf more than two quid,' Fred told him. 'More like a fiver.'

Billy's eyes lit up. 'We could give Mum four quid an' still 'ave ten bob each, an' it ain't like doin' nickin'. Finders is keepers,' he said, smiling.

Fred sat down on their front doorstep to ponder. Billy was right. They had come across the pieces of machinery one evening when he and Billy had climbed over a wall into the overgrown gardens behind the bomb-damaged Scout hall in Long Lane. The main building itself was in ruins but the lads discovered that the brick-built outhouse was still in one piece, its double doors secured with a padlock. They had peered through the barred windows and spotted the pieces of machinery, then, with a little ingenuity, they had prised off the padlock with a heavy iron bar and gone inside to have a closer look. They decided that the machinery must have been dumped there by the Scouts and left to rust.

'If the Scouts was still usin' the place it would be nickin',' Fred reasoned. 'But they ain't, are they?'

'Nah. We might as well take it before somebody else does,' Billy replied.

'Right then. We'll go an' see Percy the totter termorrer,' Fred told him.

'What about the 'orse an' cart?' Billy asked.

'We could climb over the wall again an' take the bar off the back gates,' Fred replied. 'There's no padlock ter worry about an' Percy could drive right up ter the shed.'

'D'yer fink 'e'll take the stuff?' Billy asked him.

'Course 'e will. Percy takes anyfing. Remember that ole wringer we dragged off the bomb site an' sold to 'im fer a shillin'?'

Queenie's loud voice summoned the lads in for their tea and further planning was deferred while they ate in silence. George Bromley eyed the two with suspicion, however. They were too quiet this evening and it could only mean that something was afoot.

On Wednesday evening Annie Stebbings answered a knock on her door to find a strange woman standing there, looking rather nervous.

'I'm so sorry to trouble you, but I felt I had to call,' the visitor said anxiously. 'I'm Molly French and I wondered if Wally got the job.'

Annie eyed the willowy woman with caution. 'As a matter o' fact, 'e did,' she replied. 'P'raps yer'd like ter come in fer a minute.'

Molly followed Annie into the neat and tidy parlour and saw Wally sitting beside the fire reading the *Evening Standard*. He got up quickly, looking embarrassed.

'Thanks for telling me about the job, Molly,' he said, quickly adjusting a cushion on the armchair facing his and motioning his guest to sit down.

Molly settled herself and clasped her handbag on her lap with both hands. 'I'm so glad,' she said smiling. 'I found out through Mr Tweed on Monday evening that they wanted a book-keeper. Did he interview you for the job?'

Wally nodded. 'Yes, he was very nice. I start on Monday.'

Molly pressed her hand against her flat chest. 'I'm so pleased for you. I'm sure you'll get on very well there. Cox and Sons are a very old-established firm. Old

Mr Cox used to belong to my church and Mr Tweed is a regular there too.'

'Oh, an' what church is that then?' Annie asked coldly as she stood with her arms folded in the middle of the small room.

'It's the Methodist mission in Dockhead,' Molly replied, looking up at her. 'I was at Bible classes on Monday evening and we said a prayer for Wally. That was when Mr Tweed told me about the vacancy.'

'That was very nice of you,' Wally said, glancing up quickly at his mother. 'It seems your prayers were answered.'

Annie sniffed loudly. She had visions of her son walking around with a Bible tucked under one arm and Molly French on the other and it worried her. Wally seemed happy to see the woman though, and she had at least found him a job. Perhaps she was being a little premature in judging her.

'Would you like a cup o' tea?' she asked her.

'That would be very nice,' Molly replied. 'I can't stop too long though, I've got the Brownies tonight.'

Annie left the parlour with a quick, exasperated glance at the ceiling while Wally settled himself back in his chair. 'The church must take up a lot of your spare time,' he remarked.

'Yes, it does, really,' Molly replied. 'There's Bible classes on Monday and the Brownies on Wednesday evenings, then there's the women's group on Friday evenings. I go to Sunday school as well as the evening service. I mark the star cards, you see.'

'Star cards?' Wally queried.

'Yes, the children have to attend Sunday school before they can belong to the junior club, which is held on Tuesdays and Thursdays, six till nine. If the children get enough stars on their cards during the year they get presented with a nice Bible,' Molly explained.

Annie had been listening, and as she came in and put the cup of tea down on the table beside Molly she gave Wally a quick warning glance. 'D'yer go ter the club as well?' she asked.

'Goodness me, no,' Molly replied with a smile. 'I need a little time to myself. There are the usual chores to do, and rehearsals every Thursday evening.'

'Rehearsals?' Wally said, frowning.

'I belong to the South London Operatic Society,' Molly told him proudly. 'We perform for charity.'

Annie stifled a vexed sigh as she saw the look of mutual admiration exchanged between her son and Molly. If this woman gets her claws into him, she thought, not only will he be walking around like Preacher Proctor, he'll be singing baritone at the operatic concerts as well.

Molly finished her tea and made to leave, but Wally seemed keen to delay her departure. 'Won't you stop for tea?' he asked. 'I'm sure Mum has enough to go round.'

Annie gave Wally a blinding look and nodded. 'I'm sure we can manage,' she said flatly.

'Thanks all the same, but I must go now,' Molly replied. 'Brownies starts at seven and I've got to get ready. Perhaps you'd like to come to the Sunday evening service?'

Wally nodded enthusiastically. 'Yes, that would be nice,' he said, getting up quickly. 'I'll see you out.'

Annie had some harsh words for her son when he returned to the parlour. 'I 'ope yer ain't fergot the last turn-out,' she reminded him. 'That woman sounds like the ovver one yer got involved wiv. Goin' ter church is all right, but if yer not careful she'll 'ave yer goin' ter Sunday school to 'elp 'er wiv the bloody star cards next, or yer'll be up on the stage singin' bleedin' opera. Yer gotta remember yer place in life. Opera indeed.'

Wally had been feeling elated at the prospect of

starting his new job, but now he suddenly felt flat. Molly was a nice, refined lady and she had been a tower of strength to him these last few days. He intended to build on his new-found friendship with Molly, and his mother would have to put up with it, like it or not.

Chapter Thirty-Three

The first weekend of April started bright and sunny, and early on Saturday morning Reg Grant hurried past the market stalls on his way to start work at Archie Westlake's provision warehouse in Bermondsey Street. His younger brother Terry had rushed his breakfast and was waiting impatiently for Charlie Bromley to knock, while upstairs in the front bedroom Roy was sleeping late. In the small downstairs bedroom Albert turned over and winced at the pain around his middle.

'First bloody nice sunny day we get this year an' I'm stuck in 'ere,' he groaned to Laura as she straightened his bedclothes.

'Well, yer just gotta put up wiv it,' she told him firmly. 'The doctor said yer need a lot o' rest wiv shingles.'

Albert pulled a face and allowed his daughter to adjust his pillows. 'I'll be all right ter get up later,' he insisted. 'A nice cup o' tea'll put me straight.'

'Yer stayin' there terday, an' I want no arguments,' Laura replied, looking at her father sternly. 'I don't want you goin' down wiv anyfing else, I've got enough on my plate as it is.'

A few minutes later Laura brought Albert in a mug of hot tea and he sighed as he took it from her. He had heard the few words exchanged between his girls earlier that morning and he had been thinking about them both. Lucy had been in a vile temper and had gone to the market in a huff. Laura was bearing the brunt of it all as usual, he thought. Another girl would not put up with it.

'Are yer feelin' better now?' Laura asked as Albert rested the mug on his lap.

'Yeah, luv, them tablets 'ave started to ease the pain but I feel so weak.'

'Yer will do,' Laura told him. 'Just take it easy an' I'll bring yer the papers in soon as I get a chance ter pop out.'

'Is Roy up yet?' he asked.

Laura shook her head. 'Lucy said 'e woke up feelin' rough this mornin'. She left 'im in bed.'

Albert sighed deeply. 'I dunno what's gonna become o' them two. I 'eard you an' Lucy at it this mornin'.'

'Lucy's bin gettin' on at Roy ter take 'er out ternight an' she warned 'im that if 'e didn't she'd go out wiv one o' the gels from work,' Laura explained. 'I was tryin' ter tell 'er that she was askin' fer trouble, that's all.'

'Yeah, I can see that comin',' Albert remarked. 'She can't start layin' the law down yet awhile. After all, Roy ain't bin 'ome all that long. It's bound ter take 'im time. Trouble is Lucy can't stop in, she never could. She likes a good time does that one.'

'Don't we all,' Laura replied with a brief smile.

'It was no good 'er shoutin' at you though,' Albert said, frowning. 'It ain't your fault.'

'I didn't take any notice, Dad,' Laura replied. 'Lucy's very worried about Roy. I fink she's just tryin' ter shake 'im out of 'imself.'

'Anuvver fing. If I was 'er I wouldn't let young Reg go ter work fer Westlake, not at any price,' he asserted. ' 'E could turn that boy wrong.'

Laura walked round the bed and adjusted the net curtaining. 'Why don't yer get back ter sleep fer a bit?' she suggested. 'Yer didn't 'ave a very good night, I 'eard yer coughin' on an' off.'

Albert shook his head. 'I'll wait till I see the papers,' he replied. 'I wanna put a bet on if yer can do it for me. The bookie stands in Brady Buildin's now.'

Laura went back to the parlour and sat down heavily in the armchair, feeling irritated. Eddie had asked her to go out to the pub with his family that evening, and with Lucy pressing Roy to take her out and Albert in bed ill it looked as though she would have to say no. She couldn't leave her father unless he brightened up during the day, even though Lucy had suggested that Reg could keep his eye on him. It wouldn't be fair, Laura thought. The old man could take a turn for the worse or he might have a fit of coughing. Reg could not be expected to cope; after all, he was only a lad. Lucy seemed quite insensitive at times. What if their father decided to get out of bed and slipped over? She would never forgive herself if anything happened to him and she wasn't around.

After a short rest Laura tackled the job of clearing the grate and laying the fire. As soon as Lucy got back she would go for the papers and see if Eddie was in from work. He was usually home just after twelve, she thought, scooping up the ashes on a small shovel and placing them on a sheet of newspaper. Perhaps Roy would decide to stay in regardless of what Lucy threatened, but then she couldn't rely on him to watch out for her father. Roy was prone to drop off to sleep at any time while he was on those sleeping tablets and he wouldn't hear a call for help. No, she would have to tell Eddie exactly how things stood, he would understand.

Lucy came back into the house, carrying a laden shopping bag. 'The market was packed,' she sighed as she slumped down into a chair. 'Ain't Roy up yet?'

Laura shook her head as she poured out the tea. 'Will yer take 'im up a cup?' she asked.

Lucy got up, puffing. 'I'd better, or 'e'll sleep all day,' she moaned.

Laura filled an extra cup. 'Are yer still goin' out ternight if Roy doesn't want to?' she asked.

'Bloody right,' Lucy said angrily. 'I've 'ad enough sittin' in. I don't mind if it's pictures or the pub. I'd even settle fer a walk, but I'm not sittin' in ternight, that's fer sure.'

Laura passed her cup over. 'P'raps Roy might agree ter go ter the Queens Arms,' she suggested. 'It's a lively pub. We 'ad a good night there wiv the Cassidys.'

Lucy snorted. 'I asked 'im last night about goin' there but 'e said it was too noisy. The only pub 'e feels 'appy in is that flea-bitten 'ole in Cooper Street.'

'The Anchor?'

'Yeah, the Anchor. It's full of old men smokin' pipes an' the guv'nor looks like 'e could do wiv a bath,' Lucy said in distaste. 'Roy took me in there the ovver week an' I couldn't get out fast enough. If 'e finks I'm spendin' Saturday night in that pub 'e can fink again.'

Laura could see that it was useless talking to her and she reached behind the door for her coat. 'Keep yer eye on Dad, I'm goin' fer the papers,' she said tersely.

Outside in the Row Queenie was wiping her windows over, and nearby Elsie stood talking to Annie Stebbings. Queenie's youngest son Frankie was leaning against the high factory wall that faced the row of houses, idly watching a group of older boys from Brady Buildings playing cards with Charlie and Terry. In Weston Street people were going to and fro, and Percy the totter came by, standing on the back of his cart with his battered trilby pulled down on his head, his horse trotting at a lively pace. Overhead the calm blue sky was streaked with patches of fleecy cloud which drifted fitfully across the warm sun, and a light breeze carried the sweet smell of oranges through the mean back streets as the early Spanish Sevilles were pulped and boiled in the huge cauldrons at the jam factory.

Laura glanced in Queenie's direction as she passed by, but the large woman did not notice her. Elsie was in earnest conversation but she managed a brief smile as she was talking. At the paper shop in Weston Street Laura bought the midday edition of the *Star* and a half-ounce packet of Old Holborn for her father, and as the day was fine she decided to continue on to the market. It would be nice to see the dress once more, she thought, before it disappeared from the shop window for ever.

Len Carmichael had been hard pressed to persuade Elsie that he really had been snatched from the street corner by the police, and she was still not fully convinced of his sincerity as she chatted with Annie Stebbings that sunny morning.

'They're all the bloody same,' Elsie went on. 'Yer give 'em somefing sensible ter do an' they fink of all the excuses in the world ter get out of it. I tell yer, Annie, if 'e don't set ter work on that woodwork before long I'm gonna play merry 'ell wiv 'im. I've bin askin' 'im fer Gawd knows 'ow long ter do it.'

Annie nodded sympathetically. 'When my ole man was around 'e wouldn't do sod all,' she told her. 'I 'ad ter do everyfing meself. I still do. Mind yer though, my Wally's a good boy. 'E'd do fings but 'e's so slow. I'd sooner get on wiv it meself.'

'Is 'e all right now, after that turn-out, I mean?' Elsie enquired.

'Yeah, 'e seems all right,' Annie replied. ' 'E's got anuvver job anyway, that'll settle 'is mind.'

'I am pleased,' Elsie said, smiling. 'Where's 'e workin' now then?'

'It's a firm in Tooley Street. They're takin' 'im on as a manager, by all accounts,' Annie told her. 'My Wally's got a good 'ead on 'is shoulders an' 'e's not afraid of 'ard work. 'E worked 'ard at Clyde's. Trouble was, they never appreciated 'im, an' when they sacked 'im the way they did I sez ter meself, that boy's better out of it.'

Elsie pushed her spectacles up on to the bridge of her nose and nodded. 'Yer right, 'e's too good fer the likes o' them.'

Annie slipped her hands through the armholes of her flowered apron. 'I am worried though,' she said in a quiet voice. 'I fink Wally's got 'imself involved wiv a woman. She works in the office at Clyde's an' she come round ter see Wally in the week. I thought I'd mention it ter yer, 'cos I know you work there. I wondered if yer might know 'er.'

'What's 'er name?' Elsie asked.

'Molly French,' Annie replied.

'I work in the factory but I do know 'er,' Elsie told her. 'She seems a bit stuck-up ter me, though I ain't 'ad much ter do wiv 'er. The office staff don't come on the factory floor much.'

'She seems a strange woman, if you ask me,' Annie went on. 'She's wrapped up in the church, by all accounts, an' she belongs ter some opera society or somefing. She certainly seems to 'ave impressed my Wally. She's even got 'im ter go ter church termorrer. I don't like the sound of it, especially after the last turn-out I told yer about.'

'I shouldn't worry too much,' Elsie tried to reassure her. 'Wally's old enough ter take care of 'imself an' I don't fink 'e'll be too taken in after what's 'appened to 'im lately. After all, 'e's not a child.'

'That's the trouble,' Annie said, sighing. 'In some respects 'e is. I s'pose it's partly my fault. I've tended ter shelter 'im too much, but yer 'ave to understand there was just me an' 'im. I've 'ad no man be'ind me fer years now.'

Elsie was eager to get back indoors to make sure that Len had started on the cleaning. 'Well, I just 'ope everyfing works out fer the both of yer, Annie,' she said, making to move, 'an' I shouldn't worry too much about that woman. She might be the makin' of 'im.'

Annie Stebbings sighed deeply as she turned back to her house. It was all right for people like Elsie Carmichael to talk. She didn't know what it was like. Anyway, Molly French had better watch out. If she became too possessive towards Wally she would soon be told where to get off.

Lucy picked up the betting slip and the half-crown from the parlour table, having offered to take it to the bookie on her way back to the market. As she walked out into the sunshine she was feeling very angry. Roy's words were still ringing in her ears. 'I don't feel like goin' out ternight, an' if yer can't see yer way ter sittin' in then it's up ter yer. I can't force yer ter stop in, an' yer not draggin' me out, so please yerself.'

Lucy was shocked by the venom in Roy's voice and she had bitten on an angry reply. He wasn't himself, but he never would get back to normal with the attitude he was taking. Well, maybe he needed to be taught a lesson.

As she hurried along Weston Street Lucy was making her mind up about her plans for the evening, and when she stepped into Brady Buildings clutching the betting slip and spotted Archie Westlake standing with the bookie her heart leapt.

'I 'ope you're not takin' ter gamblin',' Archie said, grinning.

Lucy gave him a big smile. 'It's fer me dad. 'Ow's Reg doin'?'

Archie shrugged his shoulders. 'I've not bin in the yard this mornin' but yer've no need ter worry. 'E'll be looked after. More important, who's takin' care o' you?' he asked her.

Lucy handed the bet to Con Noble and felt Archie's hand on her arm as he guided her to one side.

'Look, why don't yer take up my offer an' come ter the club ternight?' he said quietly. 'Yer'll enjoy yerself.'

'I don't fink I'll be able ter coax my 'usband out ternight,' Lucy said, with a sly grin creasing her lips.

'Well, yer can always come on yer own,' Archie told her. 'I'm there from early evenin' an' I'll chaperon yer.'

Lucy raised her eyes momentarily as if questioning him. 'As a matter o' fact, I was gonna pop round the yard this afternoon ter see 'ow Reg was gettin' on an' ter tell yer I'd like ter take up yer offer,' she replied, hoping she did not sound too forward.

'Well, that settles it then,' the villain said, smiling widely. 'I shouldn't go round the yard now though, yer'll only embarrass the lad. Let 'im get on wiv it. Yer've no need ter worry, 'e'll be fine.'

Lucy looked up into Archie's dark, smouldering eyes and felt a tingling sensation course along the length of her back. He had a look of authority about him and he was charming, but she knew that behind that polite, attentive manner there lurked a dangerous animal. She saw it in his eyes, she had seen it the first time she had spoken to him, and it excited her.

'No, I won't go round there,' she replied.

Archie took hold of her arm again in a firm grip. 'I'll pick you up at seven thirty,' he told her, 'outside the Buildin's, if that's all right? Will you 'ave eaten?'

'Yes,' Lucy replied.

'Okay, then we'll go straight ter the club. The cabaret starts at nine an' there's dancin' till the early hours. Yer can leave when yer ready an' I'll lay a cab on for yer, now I can't be no fairer, can I?'

Lucy walked on to the market feeling strangely

excited. She had never met anyone before who had had such an effect on her. It was his eyes, she knew. It was as though they had undressed her and caressed her and she had to admit to herself that she welcomed it, though her better sense told her she was playing with fire. At that particular moment though she did not care, and she walked along in the sunshine feeling elated.

At number five Pedlar's Row Lizzie Cassidy was hanging out a line of washing in the back yard when Laura knocked, and she answered the door with a bundle of clean shirts thrown over her shoulder. 'Come in, luv,' she said, smiling. 'Go in the parlour, I won't be long.'

Laura followed Lizzie out into the back yard, however. 'I wanted ter see Eddie,' she said. 'I can't make it ternight.'

Lizzie's face became concerned. 'Is there anyfing wrong?' she asked quickly.

Laura picked up the box of pegs and held them for her while she explained. The older woman stretched out the last of the shirts and secured it at the end of the clothesline, then she sat down on a rickety chair and brushed the back of her hand across her forehead. 'I'll tell Eddie when 'e comes in,' she replied. ' 'E told me 'e was goin' straight ter Millwall from work. There's a big match there terday, by all accounts. Yer know 'ow Eddie is wiv football. That boy won't miss a match.'

Laura smiled wanly. 'We were lookin' forward ter goin' round the Queens ternight,' she said, sighing, 'but I just can't leave me dad while 'e's ill, especially after that stroke.'

Lizzie reached up and took Laura's hand in hers. 'I'm sure Eddie'll understand,' she said softly. 'We're a close family, as I'm sure yer've come ter realise, an' we all know only too well that there's always sacrifices ter make when yer've got a lovin' regard fer yer family. I can understand it ain't easy for yer, but yer won't regret the love yer give 'em, 'cos that love comes back tenfold. It's like someone said once, yer cast yer bread upon the water an' yer sow yer seeds.'

Laura put her other hand on Lizzie's shoulder and smiled. 'Me an' Eddie are gettin' very close, Lizzie. I want ter be wiv 'im all the time. I love 'im an' I want 'im ter feel the same way about me.'

Lizzie squeezed the young woman's hand tightly. 'I'm sure 'e does, luv,' she replied. 'I've seen the change in the lad, we all 'ave. I fink yer make a lovely couple, an' if 'e starts showin' off when I give 'im yer message I'll come down on 'im like a ton o' 'ot bricks. I wouldn't worry too much, 'e'll most likely call round ter see yer later.'

'Tell 'im 'e mustn't stay in on my account,' Laura said quickly. 'I wouldn't want ter spoil the evenin' for 'im.'

Lizzie got up from the chair and pulled at her apron strings. ' 'Ave yer got time fer a cuppa? I need one meself.'

The two women sat in the parlour for a short time, sipping their tea and chatting amiably, then suddenly there was a sharp knock on the door. Lizzie got up quickly to answer it and Laura heard her sister's anxious voice. 'Can yer tell Laura ter come quickly? Dad's 'ad a bad turn!'

Chapter Thirty-Four

The evening had turned chilly and Laura had lit a fire. It burned low in the hearth and she sat deep in thought, her eyes fixed on the smouldering coals. The wireless was switched on and the soft orchestral music was having the effect of making the young woman feel melancholy as she sat alone in the small room. The doctor had seemed pessimistic that afternoon as he leaned over the table and wrote out a prescription. 'You have to realise that your father is getting on in years,' he had said. 'He could possibly have another stroke. Anyway, I'll give you these tablets to help with the pain, but I think the cause of his blacking out was through trying to get out of bed too quickly. He must stay there for the next few days at least, then we'll see how things are.'

Laura stretched out her legs and let her head rest against the hard cushion. It was just like her father to be obstinate. It seemed to be a family trait. That evening Lucy had spent some time getting ready to go out while Roy sat in moody silence, occasionally picking up the paper and glancing quickly through the pages. Neither of them had been willing to give way, and after Lucy finally left the house with a gruff goodbye, Roy suddenly decided that he would go to the Anchor for a couple of pints.

Laura had all but given up trying to get Roy to open up a little, but that evening he had been slightly more forthcoming before he went out to the pub. 'I don't mind Lucy goin' out wivout me, Laura,' he had said. 'I know she likes 'er Saturday night, an' I trust 'er, but I wish she'd try an' understand my feelin's. I just can't face crowds, not yet anyway. I dunno, p'raps I'll get over it soon, I 'ope ter God I do. The trouble is, I keep gettin' this buzzin' noise in me ears an' I feel like I'm gonna pass out. I've told Lucy, but she finks I can beat it if I just go out more. It's not as simple as that.'

Laura had sighed deeply as she looked at the slim young man in the doorway preparing to leave. She did not share Roy's confidence that Lucy would be on her best behaviour. In fact she did not feel too sure that her sister was going out with a workmate that evening. It seemed wrong to think the way she did, but she knew Lucy as well as anyone.

'Does the buzzin' 'appen while yer at work?' she had asked Roy.

He shook his head and seemed a little embarrassed at the question. 'There's a lot o' machine noise in the factory, but I s'pose I'm used ter that now.'

Laura tried to make sense of it all as she sat alone in the parlour. Roy might well be lying about the buzzing in his head, using it as an excuse not to go out in the evening, but he was prepared to go alone to the grotty pub in Cooper Street. Maybe he just wanted to sit in silence, alone with his personal horrors. That she could understand. It had been that way with her when she fought her own demons, blaming herself for what had happened. In her case she had survived by using her family as a crutch, seeking salvation through their needs and becoming their matriarch. Roy would have to find his own way of coming to terms with all that had happened to him, and one day he would have to open up completely, however painful and traumatic it might be.

Laura got up and went into her father's bedroom. He

was sleeping soundly and for a time she stood over his bed, watching his chest slowly rising and falling, then she went up the steep stairs to the boys' room. Reg was sitting on the bed, propped up against a pillow, reading a book, and Terry was lying out on the floor, his chin resting on his hands as he scanned a *Beano* comic. They both looked up as she came in.

' 'Ow's Grandad?' Reg asked her.

' 'E's sleepin' quietly. 'E should be feelin' better in the mornin',' Laura replied.

'It was good terday, Aunt Laura,' Reg told her. 'I 'ad ter stack a load o' boxes an' then I done some packin'. The foreman's a nice bloke. I kept gettin' cups o' tea.'

Laura sat down on the edge of the bed and ruffled Reg's hair. 'So yer a workin' man now. Keep up the good work an' yer might even get a rise soon,' she said, smiling.

Terry got up from the floor and sat down beside Laura on the bed. 'Aunt Laura, what's doolally tap mean?'

'Where did yer 'ear that?' she asked, laughing aloud.

'Charlie said 'e 'eard 'is dad say that to 'is mum when they was arguin' the ovver night.'

'Well, it's a way of sayin' that someone's goin' mad,' Laura told him.

'Charlie reckons 'is mum's goin' funny,' Terry said in a serious voice. ' 'E said she's started goin' out every Sunday an' 'is dad won't tell any of 'em where she goes. When she comes 'ome all of 'em 'ave ter be quiet an' no one must ask where she's bin.'

Laura slipped her arm around the young lad's shoulders. 'Maybe there's a simple answer,' she replied quietly. 'P'raps Charlie's mum goes ter see someone who's ill an' it upsets 'er afterwards. Maybe she's too upset ter talk about it.'

'Well, it's a long way away where she goes,' Terry told

her. 'Fred an' Billy follered 'er one Sunday an' they saw 'er get on a bus.'

'P'raps she goes ter somewhere like Bedlam,' Reg cut in.

'Where's that?' Terry asked.

'It's a lunatic asylum,' Reg answered.

Laura got up and straightened her blouse, feeling that the conversation was getting a little too serious. 'Right, you two, it's gettin' late. Come downstairs an' I'll do yer supper. I promised yer mum I'd make sure yer didn't stay up too late. An' don't make too much noise, I don't want yer ter wake yer grandad up.'

When the boys had been settled for the night Laura made herself a cup of tea, banked up the fire and sat back in the armchair to listen to the wireless. The Cassidys would be at the pub by now, she thought. Eddie would be winding up his brothers as usual and the women would be chatting away together. There might even be some good-looking girls there and Eddie might be eyeing them up. Was he thinking of her that very minute? she wondered anxiously. Why hadn't he called in before he left for the pub?

Her thoughts were beginning to upset her and she decided to wash her hair. She got up, filled the kettle and put it over the gas flame, and as she came back into the parlour there was a knock at the door. She glanced at the time. It was nearing nine o'clock, and she felt a little apprehensive as she went out into the dark passage.

Eddie was standing there, the collar of his reefer jacket pulled up around his ears, and there was a wide grin on his handsome face. 'I wondered if yer needed some company,' he said.

Laura felt she wanted to leap into his arms at that moment. She stood back with a small sigh of relief and beckoned him in. 'I thought yer was at the pub,' she said, smiling at him.

Eddie walked into the parlour and slipped out of his heavy jacket. 'Well, as a matter o' fact I was goin',' he said, 'but then I realised it wouldn't be the same wivout you, so I cried off. I thought I'd better let yer get fings sorted out before I called.'

Laura looked into his dark eyes and suddenly she was in his arms, her head pressed against his chest. He held her close, realising that she was feeling emotional, and gently stroked her back as they stood together in the middle of the room. She looked up at him and he saw that her eyes were filled with tears.

'I was missin' yer,' she whispered.

Eddie leant his head down and his lips found hers in a soft, lingering kiss. He could feel her hands moving up his neck, her fingers straying into his thick dark hair, and he slipped his arm round her waist and pulled her tightly to him. 'I love yer, Laura Prior,' he whispered.

'I love yer too, Eddie Cassidy,' she replied in a low voice.

The sound of Albert coughing made Laura start and she quickly let go and hurried into the back bedroom. She was back in a few moments with a look of relief on her flushed face. 'It's all right, 'e's still sleepin',' she said, feeling slightly uneasy as Eddie's eyes appraised her. 'I was just goin' ter wash me 'air.'

Eddie sat down and looked up at her with a smile. 'Go on then, I'll be all right. I can read the paper.'

'I was only gonna do me 'air ter kill time. I don't need ter now,' she said, moving towards him.

Eddie reached out and pulled her down on his lap, hugging her to him as he rested his hand on her thigh. He could feel the strands of her fair hair on his cheek and the pressure of her firm breast against his chest and he kissed her hard on her open mouth. 'I do love yer, Laura,' he whispered.

'I was feelin' all miserable a few minutes ago an' now I

feel wonderful,' she said, wrapping her arms round his neck. 'D'yer know somefing, I want us ter make love, Eddie, but it's awkward right now. The boys are upstairs an' there's me dad in the back room, an' Roy's gonna be comin' in soon.'

Eddie smiled and gently stroked her back. 'I wanna make love too, darlin',' he whispered into her ear. 'D'yer know what, I fink we should try an' get a weekend away somewhere, if yer can manage it.'

Laura laid her head on his shoulder, her hand stroking his hair. 'Soon, darlin',' she sighed.

The sound of a key being inserted in the front door made Laura get up quickly and a few seconds later Roy walked into the parlour, his face flushed with drink. He stood for a moment, looking from one to the other, then he mumbled his apologies and went out into the scullery.

Laura and Eddie exchanged sheepish smiles as she went out to the small back room to see how Roy was. She found him leaning over the stone sink, his head bowed and his shoulders hunched.

'What is it, Roy?' she asked him, her hand gripping his arm gently.

He turned to face her and she could see the pain and anguish in his frightened eyes. 'I couldn't stay in the pub. I 'ad ter come 'ome. I'm losin' 'er, Laura,' he croaked, tears beginning to fall down his pale cheeks.

Laura reached out and took him in her arms, holding him like a baby and patting his back as she tried to comfort him. 'It's all right,' she whispered, 'it's gonna be all right.'

Eddie had come out into the scullery and she signalled to him with her eyes. No words were needed, and he gave her a reassuring wink and a nod before going back into the parlour. He slipped on his coat and sighed ruefully as he quietly let himself out of the house.

★ ★ ★

Lucy stepped into the warm car and adjusted her tight black dress around her knees as Archie put his foot down on the accelerator. She had taken considerable care in getting ready that evening and she was feeling confident. She had spent some time with the curling tongs, and her short dark hair was set around her ears and curled softly on to her forehead. She was wearing her pearl-drop earrings and a matching brooch pinned to the lapel of her grey pinstripe three-quarter coat. Her make-up had been carefully applied and she wore a bold red lipstick which accentuated her full lips, and on her extra journey to the market that morning she had bought a pair of fully fashioned black stockings which she felt complemented her black patent high-heeled shoes. A small black clutch bag sat on her lap, and she had a silver chiffon scarf draped round her slim neck.

Archie smiled approvingly as he swung the car into the Old Kent Road and accelerated along the wide thoroughfare. 'Yer look very pretty,' he said, giving her a quick glance.

Lucy turned her head towards him and gave him a friendly smile, noticing how smart he looked too. His white shirt was immaculately ironed and he wore a dark brown tie with his expensively tailored brown herringbone suit. The lapels were hand-stitched and the shoulders neatly padded, and it was set off with a top-pocket handkerchief that matched his tie. Lucy could smell his aftershave and she noticed how smooth his wide jawline looked. She was impressed, and she nestled back against the leather upholstery as they turned into Albany Road and picked up speed.

The evening was beginning to turn dark as Archie pulled the car into the kerb at the busy Camberwell Green, and Lucy saw the bustle of people milling around outside the nearby Camberwell Variety Palace. Archie stepped from the car and came round to the front, opening the nearside door and taking her arm as she eased herself out from the seat.

'Well, this is it,' he said, waving his hand towards the brightly lit frontage of his club.

Lucy looked up at the impressive blue neon sign which said 'Larry's Club' above the wide-open doors. A heavily built man in a dark suit stood at the entrance with his hands behind his back, a serious expression on his ring-scarred face as he eyed the customers going inside. Archie took Lucy's arm and escorted her into the plush interior. She found herself in a wide foyer and ahead she could see through to the softly lit main room set out with round tables covered with white linen tablecloths. Archie exchanged a few brief words with the doorman and then he smiled at Lucy as he led her into the hall. A small area had been cleared for dancing and at the far end of the room there was a raised dais. People were gathering at the long bar to one side of the hall and taking drinks over to the tables.

Lucy felt a glow of pride as Archie slipped his arm around her waist and steered her over to the bar, nodding to people and acknowledging the greetings coming his way. She could feel their eyes staring at her and she imagined what might be going through their minds. They would probably assume that she was his new mistress and some of the young women assembled at the bar were no doubt envious of her. Well, she would play the part, she decided, just for devilment.

'What's it gonna be, then?' Archie enquired.

'A gin an' tonic, please,' she said, fluttering her eyes at him under the inquisitive stares of two well-dressed young women who stood nearby.

'We'll 'ave this drink then I'll show yer upstairs,' Archie said, taking out a wallet from inside his coat.

Lucy watched him, wondering if he was going to pay for the drinks, but he took out a couple of cards and handed them to the two curious women. 'There we are. Enjoy the evenin', an' if yer fancy the job yer can see the manager later.'

The women gave him sweet smiles and Archie handed Lucy her drink and held his up to her. 'Well, 'ere's to a lastin' friendship,' he said.

Lucy caught a hint of mockery in his voice that belied his friendly smile, but she was feeling excited by his attention and she could see other women glancing at her as she sipped her drink.

'Those two are lookin' fer barmaids' jobs,' Archie whispered to her. 'My manager's very careful who 'e employs. This club's got a very good reputation an' 'e's keen ter keep it that way.'

'D'yer spend much time 'ere?' Lucy asked him.

'Quite a bit, especially at weekends,' he replied. 'Let me take yer drink an' I'll show yer upstairs.'

Lucy followed him out into the foyer and through a side door that led up a long flight of red-carpeted stairs. At the top there was a square landing with panelled doors leading off. Archie opened the first door to her left. 'That's where the business is done,' he said, smiling.

Lucy glanced in at the long polished table and plush decor, and then when the villain opened the next door she gasped with surprise. It was a bedroom, beautifully decorated, with draperies set out over the head of the huge bed. The curtains looked very expensive too and everything seemed to match perfectly.

'Impressed?' he asked.

Lucy nodded enthusiastically. It was like stepping on to a film set and she half expected romantic music to start playing. 'It's lovely, really lovely,' she said, turning towards him.

Archie smiled as he pulled the door closed. 'That's special,' he told her, looking very mysterious.

There were so many questions rushing into Lucy's

head, but she dared not ask them. She could only imagine that this room was where he brought his women friends, and he had seen fit to show it to her.

'This is the kitchen, and this is the bathroom,' Archie went on, standing back to let her see inside the rooms.

The bathroom contained a large corner-bath and a separate shower cubicle. Everything was in emerald green, and Lucy noticed the row of toiletries standing on a long glass shelf under the huge mirror.

'It takes my breath away,' she said reverently. 'I've never seen anyfing like it.'

Archie's face was suddenly serious. 'I lived up 'ere wiv my wife at first, but we split up years ago. It was all very calm and sensible, an' then when the divorce went frew I 'ad the place gutted and redesigned. This is the result. I can see yer like it.'

'Like it? It's unbelievable,' Lucy gasped.

Archie took her arm and stared down into her eyes. 'I'd like ter get ter know yer better,' he said in a low voice. 'It's a long time since I've met anyone like you.'

Lucy felt her heart pound and she found it hard to answer. 'What, wiv all those lovely women downstairs? I bet yer 'ave ter fight 'em all off,' she managed with a smile.

'You're different,' he said, his eyes boring into hers. 'Fer a start, yer wasn't intimidated first time yer come ter see me. I liked that. I like the way yer look too, an' I'd like yer ter come out wiv me one night soon. I could show yer a good time.'

'I'll 'ave ter fink about it,' she said, backing away slightly, fearing that he would suddenly sweep her up in his arms, but he closed the doors to the rooms and turned towards the stairs.

'I wanna introduce yer to a few people,' he said. 'I've got a bit o' business ter take care of while I'm 'ere, but it shouldn't take long. Yer can watch the show.'

Downstairs in the hall, cigarette smoke hung in the air, and up on the dais, a pianist was tinkling on the keys while another musician sat tuning his guitar. Archie led Lucy over to a large table and slipped his arm around her waist as he smiled at the group sitting there. 'This is Lucy, a good friend o' mine,' he told them. 'I want yer ter make 'er welcome while I'm busy, okay?'

A large middle-aged woman, heavily made-up and wearing an off-the-shoulder dress and gaudy earrings, motioned Lucy to sit down beside her. 'I'm Sadie Steadman, luv,' she said. 'Make yerself at 'ome, none of us bite.'

Lucy sat down and smiled at the woman, aware that she was being appraised by the rest of the group.

'This is Bel Noble an' those two lovebirds are Dickie and Sara Jones,' Sadie went on.

Lucy smiled at the large blonde woman and guessed that she was nearing fifty and the colour of her hair probably came from a bottle. She glanced over at the younger couple and got a brief nod from Dickie but his wife Sara merely stared at her.

Archie had left Lucy alone with the group and she felt uneasy as she strove to join in the conversation. It did not take her long to realise that she had little in common with the women round the table. They seemed a crude lot, ill mannered and loud mouthed. Dickie too was talking in a loud voice and his wife seemed to be bored with the whole evening. It soon became apparent to Lucy that the business Archie was attending to was of a more serious nature than he had led her to believe. The two older women at the table kept glancing over to where the villain stood with his cronies, and occasionally they exchanged worried glances. Lucy recognised one of the men with Archie as Con Noble the bookie and she gathered that the other man must be Sadie Steadman's husband.

Once or twice a waiter came over with a tray of drinks and Lucy began to relax a little more. The show started and after the comic had finished his act, both Bel and Sadie got up to dance with well-dressed men. When Dickie Jones got up and sauntered over to the bar, his wife Sara turned to Lucy and gave her a cold smile. 'Are yer enjoyin' yerself?' she asked.

Lucy smiled back. 'It's really nice 'ere,' she remarked.

'Yeah, it is,' Sara replied, displaying little enthusiasm.

'Don't you like ter dance?' Lucy enquired, trying to make conversation.

Sara shook her head. 'Ter be honest I'd sooner go ter the pictures, but 'e likes it 'ere,' she replied, nodding her head in her husband's direction.

Lucy lapsed into silence and turned her head towards the dais as the guitarist began crooning into a microphone, but Sara seemed uninterested in the performance.

'Are yer Westlake's girl?' she suddenly asked, taking Lucy by surprise.

'No,' Lucy answered quickly. 'I 'ardly know 'im.'

Sara gave her a cynical smile. 'My advice ter you is, be careful,' she said, glancing briefly towards the bar. 'I don't go a lot on Archie Westlake's crowd. They're not my sort. I only wish my ole man would see sense an' break away from 'em instead o' runnin' round after 'em like a bloody lapdog.'

Bel and Sadie were coming back to the table and Lucy glanced over at the bar. Archie and the two men were still in a huddle and their conversation looked very intense.

'I wouldn't like ter be in Murray's shoes,' Bel whispered to Sadie.

Lucy heard the comment and she glanced quickly at the two women.

Sadie was nodding towards the bar. 'It looks like we'll

be takin' ourselves 'ome ternight,' she replied.

Lucy saw that the two men standing with Archie were putting on their coats. The villain said something to the pair and then came over to the table. 'Look, luv, I've gotta leave. It's urgent business,' he said, resting his hand on Lucy's shoulder. 'I'll be in touch. Enjoy the rest o' the show an' when yer ready ter go tell the doorman to order a cab for yer. There's the fare.'

Lucy clutched the pound note and watched in surprise as Archie walked quickly out of the hall. She looked around at the women and Sara Jones gave her a secret look, as though reinforcing the warning she had uttered just a few minutes ago.

At eleven o'clock Lucy climbed into a taxi and slumped back in the seat with mixed feelings as it drew away from the club. The evening had been an education, if nothing else. She knew full well that she could be playing with fire if she allowed herself to become emotionally involved with Archie Westlake, but the man excited her. He seemed to exude an animal magnetism, and she knew from the feeling in the pit of her stomach that she had to see him again, and soon.

Chapter Thirty-Five

Jack Murray slid the bolts over after the last of the Saturday lunchtime customers had left and with a shaking hand poured himself a large measure of Scotch. On Thursday he had had a surprise visit from the brewery's area manager who wanted to see the condition of the cellar and the stock, especially the spirit supply. Normally there was a phone call to arrange a suitable time for a visit, but on this occasion there had been none. It was obvious that Wenlock's had become suspicious over something or other and were checking up. Archie had not shown any great surprise on Friday morning when he was told of the visit, and Murray had found that odd. It was as though it had been planned with the connivance of the villain, who was expecting to catch him dead to rights.

It was just as well he kept his private supply of spirits up in the flat above the pub, Jack Murray thought. It was fortunate too that he had not yet replaced the empty bottles on the optics with his own supply when the area manager called. The man had not seemed too happy when he scanned the books, though. The recorded takings were down again and there had been a few awkward questions to answer. It didn't matter now, he had had enough. It was time to get out before the first of the race meetings. He had never agreed with Archie's plan to spread the counterfeit money around the tracks.

He had been outvoted when he suggested they should market the money abroad. That way they would be done with it, and there would be no comebacks. It was all right for Archie. He had no police record and he would keep his own hands clean, as usual.

Murray took the morning's takings from the till and slipped them into an envelope, along with a bundle of notes he had removed from the hiding-place in the cellar, then he took a sealed envelope from the side-board drawer and slipped it into his coat pocket. There was little time to waste if he was going to succeed in his plan. He must see Alma immediately. He had to make her see sense. They could patch up their differences, he felt sure. He had money now, and he would receive a tidy sum once he finally handed over the suitcase of notes. There was much to be done this evening, while Archie and the rest of them were at the club. By tomorrow he would be long gone.

Jack Murray poured himself another Scotch and sat alone at the bar, waiting for the expected phone call from Ernie Jackson. The printer had agreed with him that Archie Westlake's plan to spread the money around the race-tracks was too risky. Printing the money was not a problem, but disposing of it was another matter. When the plates were in his possession Ernie could do more print-runs and there would be a regular sum split two ways. Ernie Jackson was no fool, despite his liking for the booze. He had understood the potential in the alternative scheme put to him.

The phone bell startled Murray and he leaned across the bar quickly and picked up the receiver. He listened for a few moments and then a smile creased his bloated features. 'Okay then. I'll meet yer there. Nine sharp.'

He put the receiver down and hurried out to the back room, where he reached under the small table and pulled out a canvas bag, checking the contents before he zipped it up. Then he quickly let himself out of the pub. He had to see Alma first, and then drop the pub keys off to June the barmaid so that she could open up that evening. There was no going back now, he realised.

Archie Westlake's face was set hard as he drove along the Old Kent Road. Next to him Con Noble sat staring ahead, dreading the coming confrontation with Jack Murray. Con had always stayed well clear of any violent score-settling with Archie's enemies but tonight he had no choice. Murray had been stupid to think he could filch that amount of money from the pub without being found out, and if Archie was right about the man's intentions to turn them all over, then Murray was living on borrowed time.

The car reached the Bricklayer's Arms and swung right into Tower Bridge Road. 'We'll look in the Sultan first, just in case 'e's turned up,' Archie growled.

Danny Steadman reached under his coat and took out his Mauser pistol from a shoulder holster, checking again that it was ready to use before slipping it back. He had never liked Jack Murray and had often signalled to Archie his distrust of the man. Now he had been proved right, and putting a bullet into the double-crossing whoreson's head would not give him any sleepless nights.

The Bermondsey villain had been looking forward to a pleasant evening with the pretty young woman from Pedlar's Row. He had felt that Lucy was out for some excitement and she had been impressed by what she saw at the club. With a few double gins inside her she would have been an easy conquest, he felt sure. There were more important matters to take care of now though. It was fortunate one of his men had mentioned not seeing Murray at the Sultan when he called in there for a drink before going on to the club. It was very unusual for the publican not to be there on Saturday evening and it had set alarm bells ringing in Archie's mind. That information, coming on top of the brewery report about the books and suspected double-dealing with the spirits, had been enough to alert the villain. He had noticed how Jack Murray had become a changed man over the last few months, obsessed with winning back that ex-wife of his, despite the fact that she had now taken a new lover. The woman was bad news, and it was common knowledge that she hated the sight of Murray, which was understandable considering the way he had ill-treated her over the years. All right, that was his business, Archie conceded, but robbing his own was something else. Loyalty was everything, especially at this particular time.

Archie turned the car into Weston Street and pulled up sharply outside the Sultan. 'I'll wait 'ere, Con. Slip in an' take a dekko,' he ordered.

Con Noble was soon back. 'The barmaid's doin' 'er nut,' he said as he got into the Wolseley. 'Murray left 'er the keys this afternoon an' told 'er to open up this evenin'. Murray's bird ain't turned up eivver. June's 'ad ter get a replacement fer the saloon bar.'

'Where do we start lookin'?' Steadman asked.

'We go ter the ware'ouse first,' Archie said, jamming the car into gear. 'We can't leave the stuff there any more. Not now.'

Steadman swore under his breath as Archie swung the car out into the deserted Tower Bridge Road. If his hunch was right and Jack Murray was intending to run off with the counterfeit money and plates, then there was no time to lose. He knew that Westlake and Noble both shared his fears, although they had earlier voiced their doubts that Murray would go that far. The man was a loser anyway, Steadman thought as he patted the bulge at his shoulder.

Archie drove into Bermondsey Street and parked the Wolseley some way short of the warehouse gates. 'We don't wanna advertise,' he said quickly as he switched off the engine and stepped out on to the pavement.

The three men walked swiftly along the quiet turning and when they reached the warehouse Archie tested the padlock on the wicket gate. 'Let's check round the back first,' he said in a low voice.

They walked on a few yards and turned into a dark alley. At the end they ducked into a narrow gap between two high walls and clambered over piles of rubbish and old tin cans until they reached the back wall of the warehouse.

'This is a bit too 'igh fer Murray ter climb up,' Con remarked.

Archie nodded and led the way back into Bermondsey Street. 'Unlock the wicket gate, Danny,' he said. 'I'll go an' bring the car up.'

Jack Murray hurried along Bermondsey Street, feeling very upset at not seeing Alma. He had gone to her flat in Walworth but she had not answered his repeated knocking on her front door. The woman opposite had come out, looking concerned at the noise, and told him that Alma had gone away the previous day carrying a suitcase and had said she would not be back for two weeks. Murray did not believe the woman and for nearly an hour he had hung about in the street below, hoping to catch sight of his ex-wife, but to no avail. Finally he had had to leave, and now he tried hard to stop thinking about it as he walked past the warehouse and slipped into the alley with his heart pounding.

He crouched down in the darkness and opened his canvas bag, taking out a coiled rope ladder. At the second attempt the grappling hooks bit on the top of the brickwork and Murray clambered up, puffing loudly as he reached the top. He pulled up the ladder and held it under his arm as he dropped down on to a stack of wooden cases. Looking furtively from left to right, he crossed the yard and fished into his coat pocket as he bent down beside the office door. He had considered himself an expert lock-picker in his younger days and he was gratified to find that he had not lost any of his skills. It took him only a few seconds to pick the mortise lock and as he entered the office his spirits began to rise. He realised that he could always get Ernie Jackson to contact Alma for him. Once she read his letter and found out that he was a man of means she would be only too glad to come to him.

Murray bent down and took out a torch from his bag, for it was too dangerous to turn the light on. He took out the crowbar he had packed, and moving the chair away from the office wall he set to work in torchlight. Once the plasterboard was pierced it did not take him long to tear out a full panel, and as he reached down into the recess he grunted with satisfaction. He lifted out the suitcase and a small weighty bundle which he quickly put into the canvas bag with the torch and crowbar. He glanced at his wristwatch and saw that it was twenty past nine. Ernie would be getting anxious by now, he thought. Just then he heard a noise by the front gate and he bent low as he hurried out across the yard, carrying the suitcase and bag. As he was about to climb back on to the stack of cases by the back wall he heard footsteps crunching over rubble in the back alley and he cursed under his breath. It could be a tramp looking for a suitable sleeping place, he thought, or a curious policeman on patrol. Soon it became quiet again, and a few moments later he heard what sounded like the padlock being undone on the wicket gate. He hurried on tiptoe to one side of the yard and ducked down behind the parked lorry, his heart missing a beat as he heard Danny

Steadman's voice. They were on to him.

Murray held his breath as the big man crossed the yard and tried the office door. He heard Steadman curse loudly and call out to Con Noble, who was waiting beside the wicket gate. 'The bastard's bin 'ere!'

Con Noble made to enter the yard but Steadman held up his hand. 'Stay by the gate, I'll go an' switch the lights on,' he called out.

Murray knew that he had to make a move now, before the yard lights gave him away. He quietly took the crowbar from the bag and eased round the lorry, edging silently towards the wicket gate. With a quick movement he stood up straight, and as the bookie turned in surprise Murray smashed the crowbar down heavily on top of his head. Con Noble collapsed in a heap and Murray grabbed up his two bags and slipped out into the narrow street. A car was coming towards him, the headlights picking him out. He heard Westlake scream out at him and he dashed across the cobbles, jumping for his life as the car tried to mow him down.

Murray ran as fast as he could towards the Leather Bottle pub. He could see the car quickly reversing into a narrow lane and Steadman was shouting something. There was no time to lose and in the brief moment before the car turned fully towards him he slipped into the pub. Ernie Jackson was sitting by the door and his face became alarmed as he saw Murray gasping for breath. Customers stared curiously as the fugitive grasped Ernie by the arm and propelled him into the passageway which led to the toilets.

'Quick, take this!' Murray gasped as he quickly unzipped the canvas bag and took out the bundle containing the counterfeit plates.

Ernie stood, looking confused, but Murray grabbed his arm again and shook him into action. 'C'mon, they'll be in 'ere in a few seconds!' he shouted.

The two men hurried along the passageway and slipped out through a back door into a yard filled with empty kegs and beer crates. 'Where's that lead to?' Murray gasped, still trying to regain his breath.

'The church garden,' Ernie replied, looking over his shoulder in fear.

Murray threw the canvas bag into a corner and then helped the printer up on to a stack of beer crates, following him up on to the wall. He let the suitcase fall into the flowerbed below and together they dropped down into the dark safety of the secluded garden.

'Right now, you get on 'ome an' 'ide those plates somewhere safe. Yer'll be okay. Nobody knows you're involved in this,' Murray whispered. 'I'll contact yer soon as I'm settled somewhere.'

Ernie held out his hand. 'They'll be safe with me. Good luck, Jack. Take care,' he said quietly.

The men parted company at the garden gates which led into Tower Bridge Road and Murray crossed the main road and turned into Abbey Street. He intended to get to London Bridge Station but realised that taking the wide roads would be asking for trouble. He had to keep to the back alleys and lanes that were unsuitable for vehicles. He set off quickly with his overcoat collar pulled up around his ears, gripping the suitcase tightly. He hurried through back streets and narrow alleyways, and eventually found himself in a small turning off the brightly lit Bricklayer's Arms. He stopped for a moment to catch his breath, putting the suitcase down by his feet and rubbing his numb hand. If he could negotiate the busy junction without being spotted by Westlake and Steadman he could weave his way to the station via the back alleys.

As he started off again Murray wondered about Con Noble. He had been forced to hit him hard to make sure that the man was incapacitated, and he felt some regret.

Noble was the best of the bunch, but there had been no time for niceties. The hunted man gritted his teeth as he quickly crossed the thoroughfare and slipped into the shadows once more. So far so good, he thought. Once he was in Cooper Street he would feel better. The turning was quiet, with a large bomb site he could use for cover should he need it, and at the end of the road there was a narrow alley that led out at the foot of London Bridge Station.

Danny Steadman jumped back into the car, mouthing a curse, as Archie reversed into a narrow alley. 'The bastard's staved Con's 'ead in!' he shouted.

For a moment Archie sat looking at Steadman's blood-covered hands. 'Con's dead?' he said in a shocked voice as he jammed the car into gear and then roared back up Bermondsey Street.

'Where's that bastard gone?' Steadman growled.

Archie screeched the car to a halt outside the pub. 'Quick, check in there,' he shouted. ' 'E can't be far.'

Steadman ran into the pub and when he came back out again he waved quickly to the villain as he jumped into the car. 'Turn left at the end,' he shouted over the revving engine. 'Murray must've gone out over the back wall. An ole feller said 'e saw a bloke run in carryin' a couple o' bags.'

'Don't worry, we'll get the whoreson,' Archie snarled as he pulled hard on the steering wheel.

As the car travelled quickly along the quiet Tower Bridge Road the two men tried to control their seething anger as they scrutinised the few passers-by.

'It's no good goin' up an' down 'ere,' Archie said, easing back on the accelerator pedal. 'Murray's dived inter the back streets. Where would 'e be makin' for?'

'If 'e's not already 'oled up somewhere 'e'll be wantin' ter get out o' the area as soon as possible, that's fer sure,'

391

Danny replied. 'I'd take a bet 'e's makin' fer the railway station.'

Archie lapsed into silence as he turned the car round and drove past the Trocette cinema, swinging quickly into Weston Street. 'I reckon 'e'll go via Cooper Street, if that's 'is game,' he said. At the end of the road he pulled up. 'I'll cruise up ter London Bridge Station an' make me way back. You go inter Cooper Street, an' be careful. Wait there for me, an', Danny, if yer catch 'im, just 'old 'im till I get there, understood?'

Steadman nodded as he got out of the car and he stood waiting until Archie drove away. The night was moonless and the white glow from a gaslight at the entrance to Cooper Street lit up the empty cobbled road. Steadman moved carefully into the turning, his hand tucked inside his coat resting on the automatic pistol. He moved in the shadows, his rubber-soled shoes making no sound. Suddenly he saw a figure hurrying along the deserted street towards him. It was Jack Murray. Steadman ducked into a factory doorway, took out the Mauser and cocked it, his breathing coming faster as Murray drew near.

The fugitive stopped dead in his tracks, a look of terror on his wide, scarred face as he saw the broad-shouldered man step out of the shadows in front of him.

'Yer shouldn't 'ave done it, Jack,' Steadman said calmly as he pointed the pistol at him. 'There's no doin' yer own, you should know that.'

Murray dropped the suitcase and looked left and right in desperation.

'Don't try it, or I'll drop yer,' Steadman snarled. 'Just turn around slowly an' go down on yer knees.'

'Look, Danny, there's plenty fer both of us. I've got a buyer ready. 'E'll take the lot,' Murray said in a pleading voice. 'I warned yer all it was too chancy the ovver way. Westlake ain't takin' the risks, we are, don't yer understand? My way's best.'

'Yer killed Con,' Steadman said quietly. 'Now do as yer told. Turn round an' go on yer knees.'

Murray suddenly leapt forward and felt a thud in his shoulder as the gun went off. He grappled with Steadman, sinking his teeth into his ear as he fought for his life. Steadman screamed in pain and struggled to point the gun at Murray but the heavier man was too powerful. Steadman's wrist was twisted outwards and a knee came up into his groin. He doubled in agony, still trying to point the muzzle of the revolver towards his foe. The men fell in a heap, Steadman's head hitting the kerb with a sickening thud. A bright light flashed in front of his eyes with a deafening report and Danny Steadman went limp.

Murray staggered to his feet, feeling the warm trickle of blood travelling down his arm and over the back of his hand. He stared down at the still-smoking revolver clasped in Steadman's lifeless hand and saw the neat hole in the dead man's temple. He bent down painfully and picked up the suitcase, and with a last look at the dead body crumpled at his feet he staggered off towards the bomb site, aware that Westlake would not be far away. As he reached the safety of the derelict land, his arm hanging loosely at his side, he heard a car engine and saw the sweep of the headlights on the cobbles.

At ten o'clock on Saturday evening the elderly doctor answered the knock on his front door and caught a fainting man in his arms. 'Quick, Magda! Help me!' he shouted. 'This man's bleeding to death!'

Chapter Thirty-Six

Doctor Tressel leaned over the unconscious figure, his hands shaking as he worked doggedly to stem the bleeding. After a while he gave a grunt of satisfaction and slowly straightened up. 'He was very lucky, it missed the bone,' he said, dropping a blood-sodden swab into a kidney dish. 'A half-inch to the right and he'd have had a splintered shoulder.'

Magda Tressel fondly patted her husband's arm. 'A very good job, my dear,' she said, smiling.

'He'll need good care for a few days, but he can't stop here. It's too risky,' the doctor said, looking under his eyebrows at his wife.

'I know, dearest,' Magda replied. 'I'll phone Angela. Her husband can bring the car for him.'

Doctor Tressel removed his surgical apron and washed his hands over the stained sink. He was a tall, thin man with a pronounced stoop. His wispy grey hair was rapidly receding but his pale blue eyes, half hidden behind thick-lensed spectacles, still sparkled with a quick intelligence. Doctor Robert Tressel considered himself to be retired, but in reality he had been thrown out of the medical profession through improper conduct. A liking for gin had been his downfall, but the doctor had seen the error of his ways and signed the pledge. He eked out a living by performing abortions and catering to the criminal fraternity. They are all God's creatures, he had once told his adoring wife, and who was he to discriminate. Tressel chose to omit from such philosophical pronouncements the fact that he was paid very well by his patients, who for obvious reasons could not go to a hospital with gunshot or knife wounds, but his wife understood his benevolence very well.

Tressel never asked questions, nor did he name a fee. His clients would come to him out of need and in desperation and he always got paid, eventually. In the present emergency, when he and his wife had dragged the heavy man into the makeshift surgery and were undressing him, they had seen the bulky package as they slipped off his coat and had taken a peek. The man would be able to pay for services rendered, Tressel realised as he made an initial examination of the contents. 'About five hundred pounds I'd say at a glance,' he remarked.

'Well, we won't worry about that just yet, dear,' Magda replied.

'I wonder what's in the suitcase?' Tressel said as he reached for another cotton swab.

'More money, like as not,' Magda answered. 'He seemed reluctant to part with it.'

The venerable doctor smiled as he bent over the patient. 'Ours is not to reason why, dearie,' he said in his colonial voice. 'Pass me the suture, will you.'

Just after midnight a car pulled up in a narrow lane behind the row of Edwardian houses and a very groggy patient was helped out down the back garden and through a gate into the vehicle, his shoulder heavily bandaged and his arm secured in a sling. The Tressels watched the car move off, then they hurried back into the house to examine the contents of the suitcase.

'Pass me the small screwdriver, will you,' Tressel said as he bent over the lock. 'Ah, there we are.'

Magda watched as her husband slowly raised the lid of

the suitcase, and her eyes suddenly popped. 'Good Lord!' she exclaimed.

'Well I never,' Tressel remarked. 'Brand new. I'd say there was fifteen to twenty thousand pounds here, old dear.'

Magda picked up a bundle of notes and slipped one from the band. She studied it for a while, gently testing the quality of the paper, and then she gazed at the bundle as she turned it in her hand. 'Good Lord!' she cried again.

Tressel examined the note and compared it with the rest of the bundle. 'Well I never,' he repeated. 'Virtually the real thing.'

'This is big stuff,' Magda said, feeling suddenly excited.

'We must be very careful, dearie,' Tressel told her. 'We've got involved in big business.'

Before the Tressels went to bed that night they went down into their cellar and hid the suitcase beneath a pile of old rugs and carpets. It was past one o'clock when they finally slipped between the sheets and turned out the bedside lamp. Suddenly Magda sat up straight in bed. 'You don't think the money in the package is counterfeit too, do you, dear?' she asked.

Chief Inspector Ben Walsh finished his coffee and filled his cup once more from the steaming pot. He had received a phone call from the station just as he was about to turn in and he had lost a complete night's sleep. He and Sergeant Ashley had gone to the scenes of the two killings, and from there to the police morgue, before going back to look for clues. Now, as he sat in his office, Walsh was wide awake. The adrenaline was flowing and sleep was the last thing on his mind. It was quite possible that his decision to speak to the brewery manager about the Sultan pub was somehow linked to the killings, and he remembered thinking at the time that the move might open a can of worms. It could well have done just that, and he would have a clearer picture once Archie Westlake was brought in. Ashley had been gone for over an hour and he should be back soon, he thought.

Walsh picked up his phone. 'Send DC Wakely in,' he said, reaching for his coffee cup.

An expectant-looking young detective knocked on the door and walked in. 'Yes, sir?'

'Wakely, I want you to go to the Leather Bottle pub in Bermondsey Street and see what you can get from the guv'nor there,' the inspector said quickly. 'Then go on to the Sultan in Weston Street. Find out if the manager, Jack Murray, was there last night.'

The young detective looked instinctively at his watch and Ben Walsh banged his cup down on the desk. 'I know it's only nine o'clock but knock 'em up, man. We're dealing with a couple of murders, not noise complaints.'

The detective hurried out and Walsh leaned back in his chair and studied the ceiling thoughtfully. The last month had been a frustrating time, with all the rumours and speculation, but it now seemed that things were beginning to fit into place. There had obviously been a major crisis amongst the villains, and it was a stroke of luck that the night bobby had been on his toes during his patrol along Bermondsey Street last night. If he had failed to notice that the padlock was missing from the wicket gate then things could have turned out quite differently. As it was, Westlake had some explaining to do.

The phone rang and Walsh picked it up quickly. 'Take him to the interview room,' he said. 'I'll be along shortly.'

Archie Westlake sat slumped in the back of the police

car as it sped towards Dockhead Police Station. He had looked out of the bedroom window of his house in Bermondsey Square to see the police car pull up, and had stubbed out his third cigar of the morning before going down to answer the door. He had been expecting the call since dawn and by now he was feeling confident that he had not forgotten anything and that his story would hold up. If it didn't, then that was Ben Walsh's problem; the police had nothing concrete against him anyway. He had his own problems to worry about. He had lost good, loyal friends in Con Noble and Danny Steadman, and that whoreson Murray would have to answer. It was vital that he find Murray before the police did. If they got to him first they might well recover the counterfeit money and coax him into making a full statement. Murray would know that he was finished. He might well decide to plead self-defence and do a deal to beat the hangman. Ben Walsh would be keen to trade, Archie felt sure. It would be a feather in his cap if he could boast that he was the man who finally nailed Westlake. Well, the game wasn't over yet, Archie told himself.

The police car pulled up outside Dockhead Police Station and Westlake found himself being led along a maze of corridors. He was shown into a small room that was bare except for a steel table and two chairs and he sat down with a weary sigh, gazing up distractedly at the high barred window. He could still see Danny Steadman's lifeless eyes staring up at the heavens, his head resting in a pool of blood from the black hole in his temple. Archie recalled how he had followed the trail of blood spots on to the bomb site in his search for Jack Murray, only to find that it suddenly disappeared. Murray must have staunched the flow somehow. Archie had hurried back to Bermondsey Street but there was already a police car outside the warehouse. He had driven on past the gates and gone home to Bermondsey Square, hardly able to comprehend all that had happened in the past hour or so.

A ray of sunlight shone down on the table, lighting up the specks of dust in the air, and the muffled rumble of a passing tram drifted into the room. Footsteps sounded outside and the door opened.

'I'm sorry to have dragged you here on such a lovely morning, but it's urgent business,' Ben Walsh said as he entered the room.

Archie looked up at the inspector with a puzzled frown. 'I couldn't get anyfing out o' that sergeant o' yours. 'E does talk, I presume?'

Ben Walsh sat down facing Westlake and clasped his hands on the table-top. He had decided to play things the villain's way. He would not let the man goad him into anger; instead he would demoralise him with his calm confidence. It was only a matter of time now before he had him. 'I'm afraid I've got some bad news,' he said quietly. 'Last night one of my police officers happened to spot that the padlock on the gate of your warehouse was missing, and when he opened the wicket gate he found a body lying just inside the door. It was Con Noble, and his skull had been smashed in with a blunt object.'

'I don't believe it,' Archie gasped. 'Con Noble? Yer must be mistaken.'

'There's no mistake,' Walsh replied. 'I've seen the body myself. It was Noble right enough. That's not all. About the same time last night there was another murder, in Cooper Street. It was Danny Steadman and he'd been shot in the head.'

Archie stared up at the inspector with his mouth hanging open, then he brought his hand up over his eyes and slowly squeezed his temples. 'I can't believe it,' he muttered. 'Who would 'ave done it? It don't make sense. What was Noble doin' in my ware'ouse on Saturday night, an' what was Danny Steadman doin' in Cooper Street? It just don't make sense.'

'That's why we've asked you to come here,' Walsh said pointedly. 'We thought that you might be able to throw some light on the mystery.'

Archie shook his head slowly as though trying to take it in, and prayed that he was playing his part well. 'Last night I went to a club in Camberwell,' he began. 'Larry's Club in Camberwell Green. I 'ad a young lady wiv me an' we got there at about eight o'clock. I'd arranged ter meet Con Noble an' Danny Steadman there wiv their wives. We chatted fer an hour or so an' then I left.'

'Alone?'

'Yeah, Steadman an' Noble were still at the bar when I went.'

'What about the young lady?'

'I gave 'er the cab fare before I left.'

'That seems a little strange,' Walsh remarked. 'You take a young lady to a club then ditch her an hour later. What did she have to say about it?'

'As a matter o' fact I was sufferin' wiv me stomach. I've got an ulcer, yer see,' Archie replied, tapping his middle with his open hand. 'It started ter give me gyp, so I told the young lady I 'ad some business ter take care of. It was just an excuse.'

'She couldn't have been too happy though,' Walsh persisted, staring into Westlake's eyes.

'She was fine,' Archie replied. 'I'd already introduced 'er ter the men's wives an' she seemed ter be enjoyin' 'erself.'

'Can you give me the young lady's name?' the inspector asked.

'Look, she's a married woman,' the villain said quickly. 'There's nuffink goin' on between us, but 'er ole man might fink ovverwise if 'e gets to 'ear about where she was on Saturday night.'

'We'll be discreet, but you've got to remember we're dealing with two murders here,' Walsh replied tersely. 'It's routine, I'm sure you understand.'

Archie nodded. ' 'Er name's Lucy Grant an' she lives at number three, Pedlar's Row, off Weston Street.'

Walsh jotted the address into his notebook. 'I know that Danny Steadman was your yard foreman, but what about Con Noble?' he enquired. 'He's known to us as a street bookmaker. Where did he fit in?'

'Con was a good friend.'

'One you trusted?'

'Implicitly.'

'Then what was he doing breaking into your yard on Saturday night?' Walsh asked suddenly.

'Ow d'yer know 'e was breakin' in?' Archie countered. ' 'E might 'ave bin walkin' past an' surprised somebody who shouldn't 'ave bin in there.'

'Oh, I see. He just happened to be passing,' Walsh said with cold sarcasm. 'You left Noble at the club in Camberwell at nine o'clock and at nine forty-five your good friend is found in Bermondsey with his head caved in. You dropped Noble and Steadman off in Bermondsey last night, didn't you? Why?'

'I've already told yer, I left 'em drinkin' at the bar,' Archie said calmly.

The door of the interview room opened and Sergeant Ashley looked in. 'Wakely's back,' he said.

'If you'll excuse me for a few minutes,' Walsh said, getting up quickly.

Archie lit a cigar and puffed a cloud of smoke towards the high window. Where would Murray be holing up? he wondered. He couldn't have got far, not with the amount of blood he left behind. There was one possibility, but he would have to be very careful. Walsh might decide to put a tail on him.

The inspector came back into the room and sat down.

'Right now, where were we?'

Archie shrugged his shoulders. 'I've bin tryin' ter puzzle out what Con Noble was doin' at the ware'ouse,' he said, a look of dejection on his face.

'Last night I went to your warehouse and noticed that the office door was unlocked. Inside the office I found that a chunk of wall had been knocked out,' Walsh told him. 'Now you'd agree with me that either Noble, or the person he surprised, was responsible for the damage to that wall, wouldn't you? Unless you've got any other explanation?'

Westlake shook his head slowly and Walsh leaned back in his chair.

'Do you keep any money at the yard, in a wall safe, for instance?' the inspector asked, staring intently at the villain.

'No, I don't 'ave a wall safe. I only keep a few pounds in the office, in a cash box in the desk drawer, and there's never more than a fiver in it,' Archie replied calmly.

'What was the intruder looking for, Archie?' Walsh asked suddenly. 'It wouldn't be counterfeit money by any chance, would it?'

'Yer jokin',' the villain replied, looking shocked. 'Me? Bent money? Jesus Christ, what next?'

Walsh smiled wryly. 'All right, let's turn to Danny Steadman,' he went on. 'When he was found he had a Mauser automatic gripped in his hand. The gun had recently been fired and we've established that two bullets were missing from the magazine. There were powder burns on Steadman's temple around the wound, and I'm certain that when the autopsy report comes through we'll see that the bullet that killed him came from his own gun.'

'Yer mean 'e killed 'imself?' Archie said incredulously.

'I don't think so,' Walsh answered, 'unless he tried

to gnaw his own ear off in the process. It was almost bitten through and there was heavy bruising on the back of his gun hand. No, whoever killed Steadman turned the man's gun on him during a violent struggle, after being hit by the first bullet. There was a trail of blood leading away from the murder scene. It led on to a bomb site and we found a few spots at the far end. The killer left through a gap in the back fencing. We know that he was carrying something too. It was most probably a suitcase. Where the blood trail ended we found four marks in the dust. They could well have been made by the metal studs that are usually fixed on the bottom of a suitcase. We also found another stud imprint by the back fencing. It follows that the killer ran on to the bomb site, put the case down while he staunched the bleeding, then carried on to the back fencing, putting the suitcase down again while he prised open the corrugated sheeting. The effort caused the bleeding to start again. Now the question is, what was in the suitcase? It was something heavy. We could tell by the depth of the stud imprints.'

Archie sat up straight in his chair. 'Look, I don't wanna sound rude, but why waste time tellin' me all this?' he asked. 'Wouldn't yer be better off lookin' fer whoever killed Danny? It shouldn't be too difficult, after all, the bastard's most probably bleedin' ter death.'

'Oh, we'll get him, sure enough,' Walsh replied calmly. 'In the meantime I'd like you to listen to my theory. There's a falling-out of villains, and one villain decides to abscond with the loot, in this case a suitcase of bent money and possibly the printing plates. He goes to the secret cache and removes everything, only to be surprised by the other villains, who have been alerted to his double-dealings and have found that he's gone missing. Now their main concern is to move the suitcase before he can get his hands on it. They're too late though

403

and in his escape the villain kills one of his partners in crime and then hurries off. The remaining villains pursue him and finally he's cornered in Cooper Street. He's not finished, however, and he makes his escape after a violent struggle, during which he gets a bullet in the gut, or in the chest, maybe. Certainly not in his leg, because the footmarks didn't indicate that he was limping.' Walsh paused for a moment and stared at Westlake. 'Now I have to ask myself the question, which one of the villains stole the loot? Certainly not you, Archie. You're not bleeding all over my interview room. That leaves Jack Murray. You know and I know that he was fiddling the books. Like you I got that information from the brewery. Like you I also know that Murray wasn't at the pub last night, which was unusual, considering Saturday night is the busiest night of the week. Murray hasn't been seen since he closed up yesterday lunchtime, except by June Morrison, the barmaid who he gave the keys to. One last observation. Jack Murray had form. He was done for grievous bodily harm on two occasions. He was also involved in a fracas at a race-track some years ago when he was badly scarred with a razor. Murray is a violent man and quite capable of looking after himself. It had to be a very strong man who could tackle and overpower Danny Steadman, not to mention Con Noble, wouldn't you say?'

Archie had sat expressionless all through Ben Walsh's speculations, and when the detective finished he smiled cynically. 'It all sounds very nice, an' full marks fer perspicacity,' he replied, 'but yer wrong. Danny Steadman was my yard manager, Con Noble was a personal friend and Jack Murray manages me pub. As fer the allegations that Murray was fiddlin' the books, most managers take their perks an' the brewery are well aware o' the fact. I knew it an' I overlooked it, like most pub owners do, providin' it stayed at an acceptable level.

Murray's so-called fiddlin' was peanuts, an' I 'ave ter tell yer that the breweries don't always get their sums right. Wenlock's sacked two o' their area managers last year fer incompetence. Yer got nuffink on me, Ben, so why don't we call it a day an' let me get back 'ome. I can feel my ulcer playin' up again.'

'You're free to go,' Walsh said, showing no emotion as he got up slowly. 'When we find Murray I believe we'll recover the suitcase too. We'll talk again then.'

Archie Westlake walked out of the police station deep in thought, troubled by Walsh's calm manner. There was a visit to make, but first he had to be sure that he wasn't followed. If he gave anything away now the game might well be up.

Chapter Thirty-Seven

Laura was up early on Sunday morning. When she had gathered her thoughts she looked in the back bedroom to see that her father was sleeping soundly and she pulled her dressing gown tightly around her as she went out into the scullery to make the morning tea. She must call in to see Eddie after what happened last night, she thought. It was nice the way he had discreetly left, seeing that she was trying to comfort her brother-in-law, and he would probably be wondering how Roy was. It was so sad, Laura thought, sighing. Lucy had come in at eleven thirty, looking very pleased with herself, and had taken the news about Roy's upset very calmly. She could be so irritating at times. Unless the two of them made a big effort very shortly their marriage was doomed.

Laura took the kettle from the gas stove and filled the large china teapot. Already the sun's rays were filtering into the scullery and the young woman afforded herself a secret smile. She had been very bold in telling Eddie how much she needed him and he had responded in a way that made her tingle all over. The thought of a weekend of love with him was delicious. The feel of his hands on her body and his passionate kisses melted her completely. She could hardly wait to be alone with him, without the fear of interruption.

Albert was looking chirpy this morning, Laura thought as she dressed quickly; he had even managed a smile when she took him his tea. She quickly folded up the chair-bed and cleared the ashes from the grate. There were no sounds coming from upstairs and she decided to slip out for the morning papers.

The sun on her face was nice and it seemed that the worst of the weather was past. The old ash tree on the bend of Weston Street was breaking into leaf and the sky above was blue, tinged with wisps of lazy cloud. It was a morning to enjoy, Laura felt as she entered the corner shop.

'Did you 'ear about the murder last night?' Peggy Taylor asked, her eyes bulging.

Laura shook her head, suddenly wondering whether she was still dreaming.

'There was a bloke found shot just round the corner in Cooper Street,' Peggy went on. 'The police 'ave bin flyin' around everywhere. I 'eard 'e was shot in the 'ead, but you 'ear so many different stories. I dunno what next. Just fancy, a murder on our doorstep. It don't bear finkin' about.'

'Who was it, do they know?' Laura asked.

Peggy shook her head. 'Nobody seems ter know, but it'll be in the papers termorrer fer sure. Ole Mr Dawkins told me about it this mornin'. 'E saw the ambulance takin' the body away. 'E said that the police cordoned off Cooper Street. They wouldn't let anybody near the turnin'.'

Laura walked back home, trying to take the news in, and as she reached the entrance to Pedlar's Row she saw Elsie Carmichael standing by her front door, talking to Annie Stebbings.

'Did yer 'ear about the murder?' Elsie asked.

'The woman in the paper shop just told me,' Laura replied.

'My Len reckons there was anuvver one last night,' Elsie told her. 'In Bermondsey Street, by all accounts.

Someone told 'im as 'e was comin' 'ome from work this mornin'. I reckon there's a bloody maniac walkin' the streets. Gawd 'elp us all.'

Annie Stebbings put her hand up to her face. 'We'll be frightened ter go out next,' she remarked.

Laura let herself into the house where she found Lucy sitting beside the empty grate, sipping a cup of tea. 'I've just 'eard there was a shootin' last night,' she said, putting the papers down on the table. 'A man was found dead in Cooper Street, an' Elsie next door just said 'er Len told 'er there was anuvver murder in Bermondsey Street.'

Lucy brought her hand up to her mouth, suddenly realising that the murders might be connected with the urgent deliberations that had gone on at the club. 'They don't know who it was, do they?' she asked.

Laura shook her head. 'It's sure ter be in the papers termorrer.'

Lucy stared down into the grate. Archie had his warehouse in Bermondsey Street, she thought. It could be him, or he could have done the shooting. Con Noble would be doing the paying-out at the Buildings later that morning. She would have to make an excuse to slip out and see him.

Word had spread like a rushing wind that Sunday morning, and in the small back streets folk stood around at their doorsteps, talking in hushed voices and nodding their heads knowingly. Villainy in the area had grown like a throbbing abscess and it had suddenly burst wide open on the streets. It had been inevitable and expected, but it was hard for everyone to comprehend that it had finally happened, and in such a brutal way.

Lucy left the house around noon and walked quickly to Brady Buildings, hoping to find Archie there with the bookie, but when she turned into the forecourt she saw a strange man standing in the block entrance, paying out some money to an elderly woman. Nearby she saw the familiar figure of Dickie Jones sitting on a low wall and she walked over to him. He nodded on recognising her. 'I take it yer've 'eard the news,' he said quietly.

'I only 'eard there's bin a shootin' an' somefing about anuvver murder,' she replied, looking at him apprehensively.

'Con Noble an' Danny Steadman were both killed last night,' Dickie told her in a solemn voice. 'Bel an' Sadie are both out o' their minds. My Sara ain't stopped cryin' all night. Con was 'er favourite. 'E was found at the ware'ouse wiv 'is 'ead smashed in. It was terrible, really bloody terrible.'

Lucy stared at him in horror. 'Oh no,' she sighed. 'What about Archie? Is 'e all right?' she asked anxiously.

'Yeah, 'e's okay. I 'eard the police took 'im down the station though,' Dickie told her. 'They'll be grillin' 'im about Jack Murray.'

'Jack Murray?'

'Yeah, the guv'nor o' the Sultan. 'E's the missin' link,' the runner said, stifling a yawn. 'I thought there was somefing up when they all dived out o' the club a bit sharpish.'

Lucy nodded and Dickie stood up, adjusting the lapels of his coat. He looked pale and drawn, and his eyes were heavy-lidded through lack of sleep. He glanced at her closely. 'Are you Archie's girl?' he asked.

'No, just a friend,' she said quickly. 'I was really worried when I 'eard about what 'appened last night.'

Dickie shook his head sadly. 'Archie should be back 'ome soon, I should fink. They've got no reason to 'old 'im.'

'Do yer know where 'e lives?' Lucy asked him.

'Bermondsey Square. Number six. But don't tell 'im I gave yer the address, will yer?'

'Don't worry, I won't,' she said, smiling.

'I'd be careful if I were you,' Dickie warned her. ' 'E's bound ter be screwed up over what 'appened. Con was a good pal of 'is, an' so was Danny. It's a bloody shame.'

Lucy nodded. 'It's terrible. It seems so senseless.'

'You don't know the 'alf of it,' Dickie muttered. 'There's a lot more. It might all come out one day, but it's best yer don't know anyfing. It's safer that way.'

Lucy walked back to Pedlar's Row shocked and at the same time relieved, full of conflicting emotions. She remembered how she had lain in bed beside Roy, listening to his shallow breathing and feeling guilty about her secret fantasies. Her marriage was in crisis and all she could think about was Archie Westlake. He had aroused her in such a way that she could hardly wait to see him again. He was a big man, powerful and respected by everyone at the club. They had looked at her with admiration and envy and it had excited her. She had felt intoxicated by it and wanted more.

Now, as she walked into the Row, Lucy knew that she must stop before she became ensnared. It was madness to consider starting a relationship with another man, and especially with a man like Archie Westlake. It would only end in tragedy, she felt sure. She had to think straight. She had a husband and children who needed her. They must be her only consideration from now on.

There was a strange atmosphere at the Sultan that Sunday lunchtime. June Morrison looked unusually serious as she stood behind the counter, and the piano was not being played. Men stood around, chatting quietly, and in one corner two young men sat together, talking in low voices, their eyes darting about the bar to make sure they were not being overheard.

'I'm better off out the way,' Dickie said, sipping his pint. 'Bel's got all Con's family wiv 'er. My Sara's gone round there too.'

John Bannerman nodded. 'I still can't believe it's 'appened. 'E was a nice bloke, Con.'

'I wouldn't like ter be in Jack Murray's shoes when Archie catches up wiv 'im,' Dickie remarked.

'Are yer positive it was Murray who killed 'em?' John asked. 'It's only spec.'

'It was Murray, yer can bet yer last shillin',' Dickie assured him. ' 'E's not 'ere, is 'e?'

'Nah, but that don't mean 'e's definitely the one who done it,' John replied.

Dickie put down his glass and leaned forward over the table. 'My Sara told me that Con an' Archie were worried about the bent money. It was kept in the ware'ouse,' he whispered. 'Con used ter tell my Sara everyfing. Archie thought Murray might try an' nick it. They knew that 'e was fiddlin' the pub books. Con told Bel on Saturday night that Murray 'ad done a runner an' they 'ad some urgent business ter take care of. They went ter the ware'ouse ter move the money, just ter be on the safe side, yer can bet yer life. Trouble was they caught Murray in the act. Who else would know where the money was 'idden?'

'Yeah, but they might 'ave surprised somebody else, somebody who was breakin' in the ware'ouse purely ter nick the stock,' John suggested.

Dickie shook his head dismissively and looked warily from left to right to make sure no one was paying them any attention. 'Nah. Archie called on Bel Noble just before midnight an' told 'er about Con,' he whispered. ' 'E told 'er it was Murray who done it. Archie said Murray 'ad nicked the money an' shot Danny Steadman as well. What I'm sayin' is fer your ears only though. Fer Gawd's sake don't breave a word to anyone, or they'll know where it's come from.'

John nodded. 'I didn't 'ear a fing,' he replied, picking up his drink. 'It's a shame they didn't find out about

Murray before they stashed the money though. What d'yer reckon's gonna 'appen now?'

'Well, yer can be sure that Murray's gonna be found. Danny Steadman put a bullet in 'im before 'e got killed,' Dickie whispered. 'Archie told Bel there was a trail o' blood leadin' on ter the bomb site. 'E must be 'idin' somewhere local.'

'Murray would 'ave ter get patched up an' 'e couldn't very well go to an 'ospital,' John remarked.

'Wherever 'e is Archie's gonna find 'im, that's fer sure,' Dickie said draining his glass.

'One more?' John asked.

'Nah, I better get orf 'ome,' Dickie replied. 'Sara's gonna need me when she comes in.'

John Bannerman thought long and hard as he sat alone in the Sultan. He was due to meet with Sergeant Ashley the following day and he was wondering how much the police already knew. He would have to be very careful now that the lid had come off. One false move and he would be in dire trouble.

Laura took Eddie's hand as they stepped out into Weston Street. The afternoon was mild, with a light breeze ruffling her long fair hair. They walked leisurely along the quiet turning and into Tower Bridge Road and Eddie looked at her occasionally, his eyes appraising her, his hand gently squeezing hers. They were quiet for a while as they passed the shuttered shops, both thinking about the violence that had suddenly erupted so close to the Row. Laura recalled seeing the murdered men sitting together one morning in the Sultan, and the horror on young Reg's face when Lucy brought back the news of Con Noble. The lad had become fond of the bookie and could not understand why he should have been killed so violently. Lucy had decided that it would be better if Reg did not go to work at the warehouse again, and Laura had had to agree with her. The boy had taken the decision without any fuss or tantrums. It was as if he expected it.

Eddie took Laura's arm as they crossed the road and continued on towards Tower Bridge. People were out that fine afternoon, some lingering on the bridge approach, looking down at the quiet quayside and up at the giant cranes that were standing idle. They heard children's laughter and saw the tall, bored-looking policeman who stood with his hands behind his back, gazing downriver. A tug hooted as it passed under the centre span of the bridge and Eddie pointed downstream. 'It's takin' that freighter out,' he told her. 'Yer can see it's slipped anchor.'

Laura leaned closer to him as they stood looking down into the murky water. 'Where exactly do you work?' she asked.

Eddie pointed out the quay. 'There, just where that freighter's easin' out from,' he said.

'Where's it goin' to?' she asked.

'It's a Danish ship. We call it the butter ship. It's goin' back ter Copenhagen.'

'Movin' on the tide,' Laura said, smiling.

'You're learnin',' he laughed.

They stood close, watching the movement of the water.

'See that eddy?' he said, pointing.

'I'm lookin' at 'im,' she joked.

The young man smiled at her and slipped his arm around her shoulders. 'Down there, that swirlin' patch o' water. If yer went in just there yer'd be sucked down. I've known dockers, strong swimmers, fall in the water an' fight fer their lives against those currents,' he said, serious-faced.

'It's very dirty,' Laura remarked as she stared down.

'It might be dirty, an' it's certainly treacherous, but it's

413

beautiful all the same,' Eddie replied.

Laura saw the distant look in his dark eyes and suddenly wanted him to hold her tight. She slipped her arm through his and leaned her head on his broad shoulder. 'Yer won't get fed up wiv me, will yer, Eddie?' she asked quietly. 'I couldn't bear it if yer did.'

'Not fer months yet,' he said, smiling impishly.

'Not never. Promise.'

'I promise,' he whispered.

They set off again, walking slowly over the centre span of the bridge and feeling the rocking movement beneath their feet. The thick white stone walls of the Tower of London were away to their left, and upriver they could see the long, gently curving arch of London Bridge, high-flowing water washing its granite piers.

'It's all so peaceful,' Laura sighed.

Eddie nodded. 'Termorrer the cranes'll be movin' an' there'll be a flood o' people crossin' that bridge,' he replied. 'There'll be ships waitin' ter dock an' ovvers sailin' out on the tide. Terday though is fer you an' me. Let's go down ter the gardens.'

They walked along to Tower Hill and strolled through the gates to the riverside gardens. Children sat on the Crimean cannons and pigeons strutted about the cobbled walkway. The Tower of London looked imposing and impregnable, guarded by a proud yeoman in his traditional uniform and large padded hat. Eddie led Laura to a vacant seat and for a while they sat idly watching the activity going on around them.

'Is Roy okay?' Eddie asked suddenly.

Laura shrugged her shoulders. 'I couldn't leave 'im last night, Eddie,' she replied. ' 'E looked so sad an' upset.'

'I know,' he answered. 'It's a shame.'

'If only 'e'd tell Lucy what it was that's troublin' 'im. I'm sure it'd make all the difference.'

'P'raps 'e just can't face it,' Eddie remarked. ' 'E must 'ave really suffered on that railway.'

'What was it like fer you, Eddie?' she asked. 'You was a soldier in the war. Yer must 'ave seen some terrible fings, 'ad some terrible experiences.'

He sighed, his eyes following a gliding seagull high above the river. 'I was different. I 'ad no wife an' children ter come back to, so I didn't really care what 'appened. I tried ter get through a day at a time. I was scared ter death most o' the time, but I soon come ter realise that we all were. Anyway it's over now. Let's 'ope it never 'appens again.'

'Yeah, the 'ole world's lickin' its wounds an' families everywhere are tryin' ter pick up the pieces,' Laura said quietly. 'I only 'ope Roy an' Lucy can get back ter bein' like they once were.'

Eddie slipped his arm round Laura's shoulders. 'They will. C'mon, let's walk back 'ome over London Bridge,' he said cheerfully.

Chapter Thirty-Eight

Jack Murray woke to find himself propped up in bed and he looked around the room in confusion. There was a dull ache in his shoulder and a heavy pounding behind his eyes. He shook his head in an attempt to clear the fuzziness and slowly the events of Saturday night came flooding back. He sank back against the pillow with a sick feeling in his stomach. He remembered knocking on Doctor Tressel's front door and stepping into the passageway, then he must have passed out. It looked like he was safe for the moment anyway. At least he was being taken care of. The bedroom was clean and tidy, and a bright sun was shining through clean lace curtains.

Murray closed his eyes against the pounding in his head and after a while he heard footsteps outside his room. The door opened and a middle-aged woman came in, carrying a tray.

'I was just about to waken you, Mr Murray. It's nearly twelve,' she said, smiling at him.

Murray studied her as she put the tray down on the bed beside him. The woman reminded him of a nursing sister. She had a stern look about her yet her manner seemed kind. 'Am I still at Doctor Tressel's?' he asked.

'No, you're in Peckham. This is the Brindley household,' she replied with a smile. 'My husband collected you last night. Don't you remember?'

'I've got a vague idea,' he said, blinking again.

'It was the anaesthetic. You'll feel better after you've drunk your tea and eaten something,' she told him. 'My name's Angela Brindley and I'm Magda's sister. Magda is Doctor Tressel's wife. There's no need to worry, you'll be quite safe here. Now drink your tea before it gets cold.'

Jack Murray winced as he reached for the cup. 'Will the doctor be comin' ter see me?' he asked the woman.

'Yes, he's due this afternoon,' she replied. 'He'll be taking a look at that shoulder. I can see by the dressing that it's not been bleeding. I was a trained nurse, so I do know a little about such things.'

Murray sipped his tea, fighting off another attack of nausea. He tried to remember about the suitcase. Yes, he recalled the doctor's wife taking it from him at the door. Had Ernie Jackson managed to get away from the church gardens without being spotted? he wondered. What a mess he had got himself into. They would all be looking for him now, the police as well as Westlake's men. Killing Steadman was unfortunate, but it had had to be done. Con Noble would be all right though, apart from a headache.

When he finished his breakfast of cornflakes and toast, Jack Murray leaned his aching head against the pillows and closed his eyes. He would have to write a long letter to Alma before he left London. She had to know that he was willing to try again. They could make it work together now that he had money. Once he traded in the printed notes he would have enough cash to be able to go anywhere. Maybe he and Alma could go to Canada or Australia. They were both countries with plenty of scope for someone with the means. He would at least be safe from Westlake's vengeance.

Jack Murray opened his eyes to see Angela bending over him. 'The doctor's here to see you,' she said quietly.

Doctor Tressel walked into the room and stared down at the recumbent figure. 'How's the shoulder?' he asked.

'It's pretty sore,' Murray answered.

'It's bound to be. Angela, will you pull the table over, please,' he said.

Angela set down a small table beside the bed and stood ready while the doctor unclipped his bag and removed a pair of sharp scissors which he slipped under the dressing.

'Yes, that's very nice,' he said, looking closely at the wound. 'It all looks quite clean, but you must rest for a few days more. Angela, will you put a clean dressing on, please. I'll be back in a few minutes.'

Murray sat forward in the bed while Angela padded and bandaged his shoulder.

'There we are, now take these,' she ordered, handing him two tiny pink tablets and a tumbler of water.

Murray did as he was told and waited while the woman shook up his pillows.

'You'll feel better very soon, those tablets are pretty strong,' she said, smoothing the bedcover.

Murray leaned back with a thankful sigh. He would have to rest as much as possible to recover his strength if he was to have any chance of making it out of London. Westlake would be putting his men to work and someone might think to pay Tressel a visit.

The doctor walked back into the room and sat on the edge of the bed. 'You were very lucky,' he told him. 'The bullet passed through the fleshy part of the shoulder and out the back. The wound is messy but you'll survive. By the way, I've hidden your suitcase, Mr Murray. It's Jack Murray, I believe. I took the liberty of looking through your coat and I found your driving licence.'

'Did you look in the suitcase, by any chance?' Jack asked him.

Tressel took off his spectacles and proceeded to polish them with a large linen handkerchief. 'No, Mr Murray, the case was locked, but perhaps you might enlighten me on the contents. After all, I am the keeper, until you're fit and well again.'

'It's just as well yer don't know what's inside, but can yer bring it ter me?' Murray asked.

'I'll bring it tomorrow,' Tressel replied.

'Tell me, what d'yer know about my, er, accident?' Murray asked.

'As a matter of fact, there was something on the eleven o'clock news broadcast this morning,' the doctor replied. 'Apparently there were two killings in Bermondsey last night and the police suspect that they were linked.'

'Two murders?' Murray cut in quickly, looking shocked.

'Yes. A police spokesman said that they were making enquiries and an arrest was likely soon. I hope that doesn't worry you too much, Mr Murray.'

The fugitive looked hard at the elderly doctor and managed a cynical smile. 'Why should it?' he queried.

'My own information service tells me that one of the victims was clubbed to death and the other was shot dead, but not before shooting his killer,' Tressel went on. 'To be honest, Mr Murray, I do not concern myself with such matters. We are living in increasingly dangerous times and my avowed task in life is to heal, not to destroy. The fact that you came to me in particular for medical assistance assures me that you know of my reputation and trust me. Secrecy and discretion are my passwords, so rest easy. I expect to be amply rewarded for my endeavours, however, and I'm content that the gratuity I receive will be linked to the grateful patient's ability to pay, of course.'

'I'm very grateful, an' yer'll be paid well,' Murray replied.

Tressel replaced his glasses. 'I never doubted your indebtedness, nor your creditable nature, Mr Murray. I'll leave you now to get some sleep. Mrs Brindley will look after your needs. I'll call in tomorrow, with the suitcase.'

On Sunday afternoon the tenants of Pedlar's Row were standing at their front doors, discussing the terrible events of Saturday night. Elsie Carmichael nudged Annie Stebbings as Queenie Bromley emerged from her house and walked swiftly into Weston Street without a glance at them. 'There she goes again, all dressed up in 'er best bits,' Elsie remarked.

Annie nodded. 'She's a strange woman, that one.'

Elsie took off her glasses and wiped her eyes on the corner of her apron. 'I expect we'll find out termorrer who it was got murdered,' she remarked. 'It's bound ter be in all the papers.'

'I 'eard it was the bookie who used ter stand in the Row,' Annie said.

'My Len said it was the guv'nor o' the Sultan,' Elsie replied. 'Len said 'e ain't bin seen since 'e closed the pub on Saturday afternoon. Mind yer, there's so many rumours circulatin'.'

Annie nodded. ' 'Ere, what d'yer fink? My Wally's bin ter church terday wiv that woman I was tellin' yer about.'

'Molly French?'

'Yeah. She called round this mornin'.'

'Did she?'

'Brought me a bunch o' flowers, would yer believe.'

'No, did she?'

'I 'ope she ain't finkin' she can butter me up,' Annie said quickly.

'Molly French don't seem to be that sort o' woman ter me,' Elsie replied. 'Mind yer, there's no 'arm in 'er, not as far as I can see. She spent a number o' years lookin' after 'er elderly muvver, so I 'eard. Bloody ole witch *she* was, by all accounts. I 'eard she wouldn't 'ave anybody in the 'ouse.'

Annie brought her hand up and pinched her chin. 'Molly might be a decent sort, but I worry about Wally, 'e's so trustin', yer see. It's 'ow 'e's gonna cope wiv fings when I'm gorn that worries me. 'E wouldn't put a scarf on if it wasn't fer me naggin' at 'im. 'E can't cook a proper meal fer 'imself. 'E can cook an egg an' fry a bit o' bacon, but it takes 'im so long.'

'Well, yer can't always be be'ind 'im, Annie,' Elsie told her. ' 'E's gotta learn ter fend fer 'imself. Anyway 'e's a bit too old fer yer ter go naggin' at 'im about wearin' a scarf. What about when 'e gets around ter the you-know-what. Yer can't be there then. Let 'im alone. Gawd a'mighty, gel, yer Wally ain't a kid. The man's forty years old, so yer told me.'

'I expect yer right,' Annie said, looking even more worried.

Elsie suddenly laughed aloud. 'At least yer won't 'ave ter worry about Wally puttin' Molly French in the club. She must be knockin' on fifty, yer know.'

'Yeah, but I worry about the difference in their ages,' Annie said. 'Wally only looks a boy compared to 'er.'

Elsie thought that Wally looked at least fifty, but she refrained from saying so. Annie was a good friend and she doted on her son. Once Molly French really got her hooks into him though, Annie was going to have something to worry about, she thought.

Albert Prior sat up in bed, reading the *News of the World*. He was feeling better that evening and well enough to give his opinion when Laura told him of the killings. 'It's a gangland war, mark my words,' he said, nodding slowly. 'It won't be the last of it neivver. It strikes me it's gettin' like Chicago in the twenties round 'ere. That Westlake's be'ind it, yer can bet yer life. Lucy's gonna 'ave ter keep young Reg away from that lot. I'll tell 'er straight too. I warned 'er at the beginnin' about lettin' the lad get in wiv that bookie. I was right, wasn't I?'

'Yeah, you was right, Dad,' Laura replied, smiling indulgently. 'Now ferget it an' read yer paper. I've got work ter do.'

Laura went into the scullery and joined Lucy, who had started washing up the teacups and plates. 'I couldn't ask yer in front o' Roy, did yer enjoy last night?' she enquired.

'Yeah, it was nice,' Lucy said offhandedly.

'Where did yer go?'

'A club.'

'A club? What club?'

'It was just a club in Camberwell,' Lucy replied quickly.

'Sorry I asked,' Laura retorted.

Lucy shook the suds off her hands and turned to face her sister with a sigh. 'I didn't mean ter be snappy, but it was this club Archie Westlake owns an' they were all there last night,' she told her.

'Who d'yer mean, they?' Laura asked, looking puzzled.

Lucy sat down heavily in a chair and looked up at her. 'When I said I was goin' out ter get some air this mornin' I went round ter Brady Buildin's ter see Archie Westlake. I was wiv 'im last night at the club.'

'Yer mean Westlake took yer ter the club?' Laura asked in a shocked voice.

'Yeah. There was no 'arm in it. I was worried about Reg workin' fer Archie an' I wanted to 'ave a chat wiv 'im about it,' Lucy told her.

'So yer went ter the club just ter talk about Reg,'

Laura said sharply. 'C'mon, Lucy, credit me wiv a bit of intelligence. Yer went wiv 'im 'cos yer wanted a night out, not fer Reg's sake. Surely yer know it's playin' wiv fire gettin' in Westlake's company? Yer know what 'e is. If Roy finds out yer was wiv Westlake last night 'e'll go mad.'

'P'raps I should tell Roy. It might 'elp 'im pull 'imself tergevver,' Lucy replied.

Laura leaned against the dresser and folded her arms. 'Did yer see Westlake this mornin'?' she asked.

Lucy shook her head. 'I was talkin' ter one o' the bookie's runners. It was 'im who told me about the murders,' she said quietly. 'They was all tergevver at the club last night. They all left early, Westlake as well. 'E gave me the cab fare 'ome.'

Laura stared at her sister for a few moments, trying to take it all in. 'D'yer know who it was done the killin's?' she asked. 'Was it Archie Westlake?'

'No, it was Jack Murray,' Lucy replied. 'At least that's what the runner seemed ter be 'intin'. Apparently the police took Archie in fer questionin' this mornin'.'

'I s'pose yer realise that the police could pay you a visit if 'e told 'em 'e was wiv you last night,' Laura pointed out. 'Roy's bound ter find out then.'

'I've bin finkin' about that,' Lucy said, looking worried. 'Maybe I should go ter the police station an' give a statement.'

'I wouldn't,' Laura advised her. 'Wait an' see what 'appens. If the police do come round I'll go ter the door an' tell 'em yer ill, an' that yer'll call in at the police station as soon as possible. If Roy asks anyfing I'll say that they're just checkin' on all the 'ouses ter see if anyone knows anyfing or saw anyfing. I'll make some excuse up, don't worry.'

Lucy gave her sister a warm smile. 'Fanks, Laura. You

always seem ter know the right fing ter do. You're always there fer me, fer all of us, in fact. I'm sorry I was grumpy just now, it's just that everyfing seems ter be goin' wrong.'

Laura smiled briefly. 'I fink yer better tell Dad where yer went last night, just in case the police do come knockin',' she said quietly.

Lucy bit on her lip. ' 'E'll go off alarmin', yer know 'ow 'e is,' she replied.

'I'll tell 'im if yer like,' Laura offered. 'I can 'andle 'im.'

Lucy nodded a reply and sighed deeply, her expression reflecting her worried mind.

Laura moved towards the chair and slipped her arm around Lucy's shoulders. 'I fink it's all gonna work out all right, believe me,' she said encouragingly. She sat down on the edge of the table, facing her sister. 'I know I went on about this last night, but when Roy come back from the pub 'e was really upset. 'E came straight out 'ere, an' when I came ter see if 'e was all right 'e just broke down. 'E's so worried that 'e might lose yer, Lucy. I put me arms round 'im an' tried ter comfort 'im as best I could. It really upset me ter see 'im like that.'

Lucy shook her head slowly. 'I'm gonna try ter get ter the bottom o' this,' she said firmly. 'Some'ow I've gotta get 'im ter tell me everyfing. Somefing terrible must 'ave 'appened to 'im while 'e was a prisoner, somefing so terrible 'e won't even tell me. I could 'elp 'im if only I knew what it was, Laura.'

'Yer not gonna see Westlake again, are yer?' Laura asked suddenly.

'No, I've bin selfish,' Lucy replied, looking down at her clasped hands. 'I realise I've done wrong, an' I swear I'm gonna change. From now on I'll be 'ere fer Roy an' the kids, no matter what.'

'Fings are gonna work out, Lucy. I'm sure they will,'

Laura told her, smiling affectionately. 'Roy loves yer very much, an' 'e knows 'e's gotta pull 'imself tergevver soon.'

Lucy got up quickly. 'Roy's bin dozin' in that chair long enough,' she said suddenly. 'I'm gonna wake 'im up an' ask 'im if 'e wants ter take me out ter that pub of 'is fer a drink ternight. I'll even put up wiv sittin' in that dozy 'ole if it'll do any good.'

Archie Westlake drove along the Old Kent Road, wondering about the phone call he had received that afternoon from Sonia Osbourne. She had sounded angry and said that she wanted to meet him urgently. She would not elaborate over the phone but he felt that it must have something to do with her split with Jack Murray. The villain knew that Sonia was a very volatile woman and her relationship with Murray had been a stormy one. Nevertheless the split-up had surprised the Sultan's customers and rumour had it that Murray's ex-wife was involved somehow. Archie had thought about this and decided to lose no time in meeting her. It was quite possible that she would be able to give him some indication of Jack Murray's whereabouts, and it was vital that the villain found him before the police did.

Archie pulled up outside a terraced house in Clapham Road and knocked on the door. Sonia looked red-eyed and unsteady on her feet as she let him in, showing him into her comfortably furnished front room. He sat, watching her closely, as she went straight to the drinks cabinet and filled two glasses from a whisky decanter.

'Was it Jack who did the killin's?' she asked, passing him a drink with a shaking hand. 'I 'eard about it on the wireless.'

Archie nodded. 'I understand you two 'ave split up,' he said.

'I never want ter see 'im again,' she hissed, putting the glass to her lips.

'Where is 'e, Sonia?' Archie asked quickly.

'I dunno. Don't you know?' she slurred.

Archie studied his drink for a few moments. He would have to play it carefully. Sonia might still be protective of the man, despite what she had just said. 'Jack got a bullet in 'im last night,' he said quietly. ' 'E's 'idin' out somewhere, an' I need ter find 'im. I thought you might be able to 'elp me.'

Sonia got up to refill her glass. 'I dunno where the whoreson is, an' what's more I don't care,' she told him. 'As it 'appens I've got some information fer yer. I didn't wanna talk over the phone.'

'What is it, gel?' he asked.

Sonia stared moodily at her drink, swirling it round with a sad look in her watery eyes. 'Me an' Jack could never be 'appy while that bitch Alma was standin' between us,' she went on. 'Jack's obsessed by 'er. I told 'im 'e 'ad ter ferget 'er, but 'e couldn't, or wouldn't. Now 'e's left me, an' 'e's took all the money I 'ad saved as well, every penny.'

'What is it yer wanted ter tell me, Sonia?' Archie said irritably.

'Alma's got a new man in 'er life,' she slurred.

'What's that gotta do wiv me?' Archie grated.

Sonia took another large gulp from her glass. 'When the bitch got shot of 'er last feller Jack seemed ter change. 'E was expectin' ter get 'is feet under 'er table again. Then when 'e found out about Alma's new bloke 'e went back on the booze. One night we 'ad a terrible row an' Jack told me straight that it was 'er not me 'e wanted.'

Archie was getting increasingly annoyed by Sonia's wanderings. 'Look, why 'ave yer got me round 'ere?' he growled. 'If yer got anyfing ter tell me then out wiv it, fer Chrissake.'

426

'Alma's new bloke's a copper,' she replied.

'A copper?'

'Yeah, 'e's a tec from Dock'ead nick.'

'D'yer know 'is name?' Archie said quickly.

'Ashley. Gordon Ashley.'

'Does Murray know?'

Sonia gave him a crooked smile. 'Jack 'ad Alma watched. I only found out when we 'ad the bust-up.'

'Are yer sure about this?' Archie asked.

'Sure? Course I'm sure,' Sonia shouted. 'Jack 'ad photos taken. I've seen 'em. 'E kept 'em in a drawer. I nicked a couple after we 'ad our last slangin' match. Don't ask me why. I dunno, p'raps it was ter chuck 'em in Jack's face at some time. Anyway, it's all over between us now, so it doesn't matter.'

'Can I see 'em?' Archie asked.

Sonia walked unsteadily over to the sideboard and took out an envelope. 'Yer can keep 'em, an' good riddance,' she slurred.

Archie studied the two snaps. There was no mistaking. It was Ashley, sure enough, with his arm around Alma's waist, and they appeared to be walking through a park.

Archie left the house feeling that his journey had been very fruitful. There was now room for manoeuvre, he thought. One thing was certain. Sergeant Ashley was going to be very worried that his liaison with a wanted villain's ex-wife could become public knowledge. Ben Walsh wouldn't be too happy either.

Chapter Thirty-Nine

When John Bannerman walked into the church gardens on Monday afternoon he was a very frightened young man. All hell had broken out over the weekend and he felt that it wouldn't be long before he was thrown to the lions. His only hope was that the animals would all be caged by then. Danny Steadman was dead and Con Noble too. Murray was on the run from the mob, and from the police, but Westlake was still very much in control. He still had his hirelings who would carry out his bidding ruthlessly.

John slipped into the quietness of the church and smelled the familiar mustiness as he sat down with a nervous glance around him. The place was empty, save for one old lady who sat near the altar, her head bowed in prayer. The sun's rays shone through the stained-glass window high up in front of him and the young man shivered. Only that morning Marge had pleaded with him to give up his job as a bookie's runner and try to find some decent work, even if it meant making a fresh start in one of the new towns that were being developed. He had tried to put her mind at rest by promising to call in at the labour exchange for information on his way home, but first there was Ashley to contend with.

John sat, waiting quietly, for more than ten minutes before the detective sergeant slipped into the pew behind him, and when he turned to glance at him he could see that the man was unshaven and weary-looking.

'Right, now don't waste any o' my time, Bannerman, I'm under the cosh,' Ashley growled. 'What's new?'

'Word's out that Jack Murray fell out wiv the mob an' 'e went fer the money,' John said in a low voice. 'Westlake was on to 'im an' they caught 'im red-'anded at the ware'ouse in Bermondsey Street late on Saturday night. It was Murray who killed Con Noble an' Danny Steadman.'

'Murray ran off with the counterfeit money?' Ashley queried.

'Yeah, it was kept at the yard,' John answered. 'The printin' was definitely done at Carlton's.'

'What about Murray? Where's he hiding out?'

'There's no news. Westlake's lookin' fer 'im.'

'Well, he would be.'

'Word is Murray's got a bullet in 'im.'

'We know that,' Ashley growled irritably. 'We also know that he couldn't have got very far. He's holed up in this area.'

John felt that he was fast becoming excess to requirements. The police seemed to know more than he did. 'Look, I've told yer all I know,' he said, turning to face the policeman. 'Give us a break. It's gettin' too dangerous fer me ter go on askin' questions. Sooner or later they're gonna be on ter me.'

'I'm sorry, but I need your help until we've got Westlake under lock and key,' Ashley reminded the frightened young man. 'Help us nail him and we won't trouble you any more. One other thing. I understand your bookie changed his pitch. Where to?'

'Brady Buildin's,' John replied. 'The people in Pedlar's Row didn't want 'im there any more.'

'Oh, and why was that?'

'Well, they blamed Con fer what 'appened ter Wally Stebbin's. Wally's an 'armless bloke but somebody put it

429

about that 'e was interferin' wiv kids,' John explained. 'Wally got bashed up an' everybody felt that the bookie was be'ind it, so they told 'im ter piss orf.'

'Are you sure there's nothing else you've forgotten to tell me?' Ashley asked.

'I've told yer everyfing I know,' John pleaded. 'Surely that's enough ter go on.'

'We'll see,' the sergeant replied, suddenly lowering his head as the old lady got up from the front pew and walked towards them.

John Bannerman emerged into the spring sunshine feeling desperate. He decided to go straight to the labour exchange without any more delay. The way things were moving, the sooner he got away from London the better, he told himself.

Lucy walked home from work on Monday evening, feeling that she had at least made a fresh start with Roy. They had gone to the Anchor the previous evening and she had suffered the drab surroundings and the depressing atmosphere of the place for his sake. They had sat quietly chatting, occasionally lapsing into periods of uncomfortable silence, and Lucy could understand why Roy chose the Anchor. It was never very full and people there tended to sit alone, staring thoughtfully into their glasses of beer and smoking their pipes. It was an old man's pub, the sort of place where a person could drop dead without being discovered until the following week, she thought, smiling to herself.

A car pulled up beside her as she turned into Weston Street and Archie leaned through the side window. 'Well, if it ain't Lucy. Jump in, luv,' he said, smiling widely.

'I'm almost 'ome,' she replied, suddenly feeling nervous.

'Get in fer a moment. I wanna talk ter yer,' the villain persisted.

Lucy reluctantly stepped into the car and Archie immediately pulled away from the kerb.

'Where we goin'?' she asked anxiously.

'It's all right, I just wanna talk. Yer don't want yer neighbours or yer ole man ter see yer wiv me,' he replied as he swung the car into a side turning.

'Dickie Jones told me about Con an' Danny Steadman,' she told him. 'Was Steadman the big man you was talkin' to at the club?'

Archie's face became serious as he nodded. 'Danny was a good pal, so was Con. That's what I wanted ter talk ter yer about,' he said.

Lucy was getting increasingly nervous as the car sped on. 'I've gotta get 'ome, they'll be worried where I've got to,' she said.

Archie turned the car into a quiet side street off the Tower Bridge Road and pulled up. Lucy could see that he had picked the right spot for secrecy. All the houses in the narrow street had been completely destroyed by the bombing, and corrugated sheeting extended along the length of the turning on both sides.

'Did the police pay yer a visit?' Archie asked suddenly.

'No,' Lucy replied. 'D'yer fink they will?'

'I dunno, they might wanna check up on my story,' Archie said. 'I told 'em the truth about leavin' yer there at the club. I explained that I 'ad some business ter take care of. The only fing was, I told 'em I left before Con an' Danny. So if yer do get a visit, just stick ter that, okay?'

Lucy nodded, beginning to feel that she was being drawn into a very dangerous situation. 'I can only tell 'em what I know,' she said quietly.

Archie smiled. 'I was really sorry I 'ad ter leave before

we got ter know each ovver a little better. I was lookin' forward ter that.'

Lucy turned to face him. 'I'm afraid I've gotta tell yer that I'm not lettin' my lad work at the ware'ouse any more, considerin' what's 'appened,' she said.

'I'm sorry about that, but I understand,' the villain replied. 'It shouldn't stop us gettin' closer though,' he added, his hand coming over and closing on her forearm.

Lucy felt a shiver pass through her and she pulled away from his grasp. 'Look, I'm a married woman an' I shouldn't even be 'ere wiv yer now,' she said sharply. 'I can't afford ter take the risk.'

'So it's only the risk o' gettin' found out, is it?' Archie said, smiling slyly. 'We don't 'ave ter take any risks. I could pick yer up somewhere an' we could go ter my club, or up West. Who's ter know?'

'I will,' Lucy told him firmly. 'I'm not gonna start cheatin' on my 'usband, especially after what 'e's bin frew. Roy was a Japanese prisoner o' war.'

'It wouldn't be the first time yer've cheated on 'im though, would it?' Archie said sneeringly.

'What d'yer mean by that?' she asked quickly.

'I 'appen ter know yer've bin out an' about while that bloke o' yours was away,' Archie revealed. 'Yer gotta remember I know a lot o' people, an' people tend ter talk about such fings.'

'Well, whatever I did is no concern of yours,' Lucy said with spirit. 'Now if yer'll take me 'ome I'll be grateful.'

' 'Ow grateful?' Archie said, leaning over and sliding his hand along her thigh.

Lucy pushed his hand away. 'Take me 'ome or I'll get out now,' she told him, her face flushed.

'What about a kiss, just one little kiss? Surely that's not askin' too much,' he said, sliding his hand along the back of her seat.

Lucy reached for the door handle but suddenly she found herself being pulled towards him. His strong arms went around her and she could smell onions on his breath as his lips closed on hers. She tensed her whole body and pressed her lips hard together, giving him no excuse to think she would succumb to him. Her hands were pinned to her sides and she felt as though all the breath was being forced from her body as his arms tightened around her. Suddenly his teeth closed over her bottom lip and she gave a cry of pain. He broke away and grinned at her, his breath coming fast.

'That wasn't too bad, was it?' he asked.

Lucy glared at him for a moment, then brought her hand up sharply and slapped his face. Archie blinked in surprise and then hit her hard with his open hand, knocking her sideways and banging her head against the car door. 'Don't ever do that again,' he snarled.

Lucy bit back angry tears as she threw open the door. 'I won't 'ave to,' she said, sneering at him. 'That's the last time I'll allow meself in yer company, yer bastard.'

She walked quickly out of the turning with her heart pounding, her face still stinging from the heavy blow. Westlake was a dog, she fumed, angry at herself for not seeing through him before. Things could have been very different if this had happened at the club. She touched her cheek, realising that she would have to be extra careful about what she said when she got home. Laura was very sharp-eyed and she would notice immediately that something had happened. Roy would be home by now too and he would be worried over her lateness.

Ten minutes later Lucy turned into Weston Street, and as she reached Pedlar's Row she saw a tall young man knocking at the front door of number three. Her heart missed a beat. It was the police, she felt sure. She turned quickly without being spotted and carried on along Weston Street with the passers-by returning from work. Last night she had felt that at last she was finally beginning to make a little progress with Roy. They had even cuddled in bed until Roy dropped off to sleep, but now everything would be undone if he found out about her going to the club with Westlake. Perhaps he wasn't home yet. Laura would get rid of the policeman, but if Roy was in it was going to be difficult for her.

Lucy reached the end of the long turning and then slowly retraced her steps. All seemed quiet when she reached the Row again, and taking a deep breath she let herself into the house.

Roy greeted her with a smile. 'Yer late, Lucy. We were beginnin' ter get worried,' he said.

Lucy kissed his cheek and slipped off her coat. 'I went on ter Tower Bridge Road an' called in at the chemist fer some aspirin. I fink I've got a touch o' neuralgia,' she said casually.

Laura was busy laying the table for tea and she sensed at once that something was wrong. 'Yer face does look a bit red,' she remarked quietly.

'I'll go an' take a couple of aspirin right away,' Lucy replied.

Albert was sitting in his regular armchair beside the hearth and he looked up. 'Aspirins ain't no good fer neuralgia,' he said firmly. 'Yer wanna use a bread poultice, or soak a piece o' brown paper in vinegar. That should do the trick.'

'Don't be silly, Dad, she'll look like a pickled onion,' Laura said, laughing aloud.

''You might laugh,' Albert went on. 'It was the same wiv me. All those pills an' rubbish the doctor give me. None of it beats a bottle o' Guinness.'

'Yer still shouldn't be up,' Laura scolded him, then followed Lucy out into the scullery.

'I saw the man at the door. Was it the police?' Lucy asked anxiously.

'No, 'e was from the borough council,' Laura replied. ' 'E was askin' if we'd noticed any dampness. 'E was tellin' me they're gonna do a survey next week.'

Lucy breathed a huge sigh of relief. Maybe the police wouldn't bother to call after all, she thought hopefully.

Laura handed her the morning paper. ' 'Ave yer seen this?' she asked, pointing to an article on the first page.

'No, I didn't get the chance this mornin',' Lucy replied as she sat down wearily in a chair and glanced at it.

'There's a big bit in there about the murders an' it says the police want ter know the whereabouts o' Jack Murray to eliminate 'im from their enquiries,' Laura told her. 'I like the way they put it.' She looked at her sister quizzically. 'You 'aven't took yer tablets, 'ave yer?' she said.

Lucy looked up quickly, catching the intonation. 'I'll take 'em in a minute,' she answered.

'Why were yer late?' Laura persisted.

'I told yer, I 'ad ter go ter the chemist.'

'There's no tablets in the 'ouse an' I've got a bit of an 'eadache, can yer give me a couple o' yours?' Laura asked craftily.

Lucy put the paper down and sighed as she saw her sister's amused expression. 'All right, I never went ter the chemist,' she admitted. 'As a matter o' fact I got stopped by Westlake.' Seeing the look of concern on Laura's face, she quickly added, 'It was okay, 'e just wanted ter know if the police 'ad called round. It was just as well I did bump into 'im, 'cos I told 'im I was stoppin' Reg workin' at the ware'ouse.'

'What did 'e say ter that?' Laura asked.

' 'E was all right really,' Lucy said. 'I told 'im me reasons an' 'e just shrugged 'is shoulders. What else could 'e expect after what's 'appened?'

'Good fer you,' Laura said, smiling. 'Now what about you givin' me some 'elp servin' up the tea?'

435

* * *

On Monday night there was usually a gathering of the clans at the Sultan public house, and on this particular Monday there was an added incentive for the regulars to meet. There was much to discuss and where better than at the hub of things, as Joe Molloy put it.

'It all started 'ere, if we're ter believe the papers,' he said in a low voice.

Len Carmichael nodded. 'I'm surprised the police 'aven't closed the place down,' he remarked to the group as they sat around a corner table in the public bar.

'Jack Murray was only the manager. Westlake owns the pub an' 'e'll soon stick anuvver manager in,' George Bromley said.

'I bet there's a few plain-clothes dicks in the saloon bar watchin' points,' Eric Cassidy cut in. 'Still, it's nuffink ter do wiv us.'

Len sat back and savoured his pint. It was unusual for all the group to manage to get out for a drink together, he thought. He was on early turn at the brewery and Joe was on an early shift too. Eric didn't always come out on Monday nights, but rumour was rife and none of them wanted to miss anything.

'We 'ad a bloke call round earlier from the council,' Joe said. 'Somefing ter do wiv dampness.'

'Yeah, 'e called on us too,' Len replied. 'My Elsie asked 'im what it was all about an' 'e said they was gonna do an inspection or somefing. Elsie reckons it's somefing ter do wiv the sewers. We was really worried when the bloke said 'e was from the council. Elsie was scared in case they'd found out about only me an' 'er livin' there. When we applied fer the place we 'ad two daughters livin' at 'ome.'

'I wouldn't worry about that,' Eric told him. 'Look at Annie Stebbin's. There's only 'er an' Wally livin' there.'

'Yeah, but it was a different situation wiv 'er,' Len

replied. 'The council 'ad ter re'ouse 'er an' Wally when they pulled those ole buildin's down they used ter live in.'

'I dunno if it is dampness they're worried about, but I ain't seen any,' Eric said. 'There's a bad smell comes up sometimes though. It could be the sewers, I s'pose.'

'Nah, that's Annie Stebbin's cookin' mutton stew,' George laughed.

Eric sipped his pint and leaned back in his chair. 'If it is the sewers they'll 'ave a big job on,' he remarked.

'It could be the foundations slippin',' George told the gathering. 'After all, the 'ouses took a right canin' durin' the war.'

Eric put his glass down and leaned forward over the table. 'That reminds me. Did I ever tell yer about Bonky Masefield?' he asked.

The blank stares encouraged him to go on. 'Bonky used ter live in Pedlar's Row before the places got blasted. Now 'e swore blind that there was a curse on the 'ouses.'

'We've all 'eard about the gypsy curse,' George cut in.

'Yeah, but yer don't know about ole Bonky,' Eric said. 'Bonky used ter work in the docks, yer see, an' 'e was convinced that Romany curses were different to any ovver curse.'

' 'Ow come?' Len asked.

'Well, ter start wiv, Romany curses work in cycles, yer see,' Eric began to explain. 'We've all 'eard about the stories of years gorn by an' 'ow people who lived in Pedlar's Row 'ad nuffink but bad luck. Then there was the ole tale about the curse stayin' until the places crumbled. Now some people thought that when the Row got blasted that was what the ole gypsy meant.'

'What's all this got ter do wiv Bonky?' George asked.

'Well, Bonky Masefield was supposed to 'ave gypsy blood in 'im,' Eric told them. 'One bitter cold mornin' we was all sittin' on the quay waitin' fer the bacon ship ter dock, an' suddenly Bonky gets all agitated. He stood up an' started walkin' back an' forwards an' 'e kept mumblin' to 'imself. I thought 'e was goin' orf 'is 'ead, ter tell yer the truth. Anyway, one o' the blokes said that 'e noticed 'ow Bonky 'ad chucked 'is paper down as though 'e'd seen somefing in there that upset 'im. So this bloke picks up the paper ter take a gander an' 'e spots this bit about numbers.'

'Numbers?' Len echoed.

'Yeah, numbers,' Eric repeated. 'Apparently if yer get different numbers put tergevver it can mean different fings.'

'Yer lost me,' Len remarked.

Eric went on regardless. 'This bloke reckoned that Bonky must 'ave got a bit upset by what 'e'd read. Now Bonky gets up on this bloody great crate an' starts rantin' off about the gypsy's curse. 'E was goin' on about all the signs and symbols bein' in the right place an' that it only 'appened every so many years. So what I'm sayin',' he concluded, 'is p'raps the numbers 'ave come up again, considerin' what 'appened last week.'

'Yeah, but that's nuffink ter do wiv Pedlar's Row,' Len replied.

'Well, the bookie who got murdered used ter stand in the Row,' Eric reminded him. 'Then there was that turn-out wiv Wally Stebbin's.'

'I don't believe such tosh,' George cut in sharply.

'Well, I'm only tellin' yer Bonky Masefield's idea about the numbers,' Eric said.

'What 'appened ter Bonky? Did 'e 'ave a lot o' bad luck?' Joe Molloy enquired.

'Funny you should ask,' Eric went on. ' 'Cos the next day Bonky was standin' on the quay along wiv the rest of us an' the weavver was atrocious at the time. Freezin' cold it was. Anyway, a set o' bacon swung round on the

438

end o' the crane an' knocked Bonky in the drink. Now at that time o' year, wiv the weavver bein' what it was yer'd expect the worst. There was a tide runnin' too. All the same Bonky surfaced an' started driftin' downstream. Finally 'e managed ter catch 'old of a stanchion. A tug fished 'im out an' 'e was back ter work next day large as life. So much fer bad luck.'

'Is 'e still about?' Len asked.

'I saw 'im only last week,' Eric replied. ' 'E must be pushin' ninety if 'e's a day.'

Chapter Forty

Archie Westlake sat reading the *Evening Standard* in the saloon bar of the Railway Arms, near Waterloo Station. The pub was a regular haunt of travellers, mainly businessmen who passed the time there while waiting for their trains. It was an ideal meeting place, Archie thought. It was far enough away from Bermondsey for him to spend an evening there without being recognised, and equally so for Gordon Ashley, who could not afford to be seen having a private meeting with a member of the criminal fraternity.

Archie glanced up at the large wall clock over the bar and saw that it was now after eight o'clock. Ashley had said over the phone that he would get there by seven forty-five, and the villain was counting on him showing up. After getting an assurance from the policeman that no one would be listening on the line, Archie had made it clear that the meeting was urgent and in Ashley's best interest.

Archie went to the counter and ordered another whisky. He could not afford to wait around indefinitely, there was other business to take care of that night. Just then Ashley walked into the bar.

'I was beginnin' ter fink yer wasn't gonna turn up,' Archie said irritably. 'What yer 'avin' ter drink?'

'Is that Scotch you're drinking?' Ashley asked. 'If it is I'll have the same.'

The two men took their glasses to a far corner table and sat down.

'I take it there's no tail bin put on me, or you wouldn't be 'ere,' Archie said. 'Unless yer've given 'em the night off.'

'We're too short of manpower to put a team on to watching you, Westlake,' the sergeant told him tersely. 'Now what is it you wanted to see me about?'

'Let's not be so formal,' Archie said, smiling. 'Call me Archie.'

Ashley eyed the villain with contempt and then picked up his glass and took a swig. 'All right, let's get talking. I've been up since five this morning and I'm hoping I might get home some time tonight.'

The villain leaned forward in his chair. 'I thought we might be able ter do each ovver a favour,' he said quietly.

'Like what?'

'A trade maybe?'

'What sort of a trade?'

'I get to Jack Murray first an' you get peace o' mind.'

'I've already got peace of mind,' Ashley said, his eyes hardening.

'Well, let me tell yer that yer peace o' mind would very soon be shattered if this ever got in the newspapers,' Archie replied, taking an envelope from his coat pocket and placing it on the table in front of the policeman.

Ashley opened it and as he looked at the photo his eyes narrowed. 'Where did this come from?' he asked sharply.

'It doesn't matter,' Archie told him. 'The point is, can we do business?'

'I take it you've got the negative,' Ashley said.

Archie shook his head. 'Unfortunately Murray's got the negative an' the rest o' the photos as well. There were quite a few snaps of you an' Alma tergevver. I've got anuvver one in a safe place though, in case yer finkin' o' tearin' that one up.'

Ashley stared hard at the villain for a few moments. 'You know I can't do that sort of trade. Getting Murray is top priority. The guv'nor's leading the enquiry from the front. There's no way I can step in front of Ben Walsh.'

'Well, I'm sorry about that,' Archie said, putting the photo back into his coat pocket. 'I really thought we could 'ave done business.'

'P'raps we still can,' Ashley said quietly.

'Tell me more,' Archie replied, clasping his hands together in his lap.

'I suppose you know that there's an active grass on your manor,' the detective said, downing the rest of his drink. 'Now we could have a trade there.'

'What's in a name? Yer could tell me I'm the grass, fer that matter,' Archie said, smiling. 'Like you lads, I'd need proof.'

'How's this for starters. You did the printing in the Carlton factory and the money was hidden behind the wall in your office,' Ashley told him. 'You have to ask yourself the question, how could we possibly know you were printing money unless we got a whisper from the grass? It would be a different matter if the money was being pushed around, but it's not been moved yet.'

'I fink we can do a trade,' Archie replied. 'Not that what yer said 'as any truth in it, o' course. The only worry you've got is that Jack Murray's 'oldin' the rest o' the snaps. I can't do nuffink about that until I get to 'im.'

'If we find Murray's been taken care of before we get to him we'll come looking for you personally, so bear that in mind,' Ashley warned the villain.

'Once I've finished my business wiv Jack Murray I'll be only too glad to 'and 'im over ter yer,' Archie said with feeling. 'I'll let the 'angman take care of 'im. After all, 'e does get paid for it.'

Ashley pushed back his empty glass. 'I've got to get off home,' he said. 'Bring the other photo into the station tomorrow afternoon and we'll talk. Ben Walsh won't be there, he's going up to headquarters for a briefing.'

Archie ordered another drink before leaving the pub. He had used a taxi to get to Waterloo, hoping to shake off anyone who might be following him. Now, as he hailed another cab and settled himself back in the seat, he felt reasonably confident that he was not being tailed, and that it would not be long before he discovered the whereabouts of Jack Murray.

Queenie Bromley caught a number 68 tram to Rotherhithe and sat staring out of the window with a sad expression in her eyes. The information that John Bannerman had given her had shocked her terribly and left her feeling that she was partially responsible for the tragedy. She could have helped more, been more understanding, she realised with regret. Instead she had allowed things to happen, things she could have helped prevent if she had only given her sister more of her time. It was too late now though. All she could do was to make sure that Mary's grave was well tended and not allowed to deteriorate like so many others had over the years. It had become a ritual, going to the cemetery, when the weather allowed, to place fresh flowers over the grave and spend some time weeding, washing the headstone and generally tidying up. She liked to speak to her sister, tell her all the news, how George was and how big the boys were getting. Queenie was sure that Mary could hear her, and that wherever she was she would know that she had been loved very much, even though her last year on earth had been full of misery and loneliness.

The tram swung round the bend at the Rotherhithe

Tunnel and rattled on towards the Surrey Docks. Queenie could see the tall cranes at rest and the high iron sheds of the huge timber wharves. The people who lived alongside the docks by the bend in the river were known as Downtowners, and everyone was aware of the reputation the small community had for its friendliness and comradeship. They were hardy folk, many of them earning a living at the docks and wharves as well as the factories in the area. The spur of land was serviced by a main road that followed the line of the river and passed over two narrow strips of water, one on the west side and one on the east, which linked the various timber wharves and allowed access to the Russian and Scandinavian ships. When the road bridges were raised for ships to pass under, the dock area became isolated, and this unusual situation set the Downtowners apart from the rest of the Rotherhithe folk. They considered themselves to be island people and proud of it.

It was to this part of Rotherhithe that Queenie came on her quest for the truth about her young sister Mary, and as she stepped down from the tram and walked into Redriff Road she dreaded what she might discover tonight about her sister's final days.

Doctor Tressel finished his evening meal and leaned back in his chair with a satisfied sigh. His wife reached for the blue china teapot and poured the tea into matching cups. 'How long do you think Mr Murray will have to stay at Angela's?' she enquired.

Robert Tressel stroked his chin thoughtfully. 'I want him away in a couple of days,' he replied. 'It's too risky to delay things.'

'Will he be fit to travel?'

'He's a bull of a man and I'm sure he'll survive,' he said, smiling. 'What we have to consider is that someone may come looking for him very shortly.'

'The police, you mean?' Magda asked, looking worried.

'I don't think so,' he told her. 'There's no reason for the police to come calling. No, I'm afraid any visitors we might have concerning Mr Murray will be from the criminal ilk. There was more in the papers today, did you see it?'

'Yes, I did, dear, and it frightened me, to be honest. Fancy us giving succour to a murderer,' Magda said in a hushed voice.

Tressel shrugged his shoulders dismissively. 'During the First World War when I was a young army doctor I had to tend the wounded, regardless of whose side they were on,' he said. 'When Mr Murray fell into our passageway he was bleeding to death. I couldn't very well ask him for his credentials.'

'Of course not, dear,' Magda replied. 'I'll be much happier though when the man's out of Angela's house.'

The Tressels finished their tea and retired to the comfortable lounge to listen to the wireless. Magda sat working on a piece of embroidery and Robert's eyes drooped as the soft music lulled him into reverie. The knock on the door startled them and Magda got up from her chair and went to the window.

'It's a man,' she whispered, gently easing the curtains back into place.

'Right, dear. Stay calm,' Tressel said in his military voice. 'You know the drill.'

The knock was repeated and Magda went out into the passage, taking a deep breath before she opened the front door.

'Is the doctor in?' the visitor asked.

'Yes, but he's very tired. He doesn't see anyone these days,' Magda replied, trying to steady her voice.

'I fink 'e'll see me,' the man told her. 'Tell 'im it's Archie Westlake.'

'You'd better come in then,' Magda said.

Archie followed the woman into the lounge and looked around. 'It's a nice room,' he remarked.

'Yes. I'll just see if my husband's awake,' she said, motioning him into an armchair.

Archie sat down and watched Magda closely as she left the room. This would be Murray's obvious destination to seek help, he thought. It was very near Cooper Street, and with a bullet in him and bleeding heavily he would not have been able to get very far. Doctor Tressel was well known to the criminal fraternity of old. He had treated quite a few fugitives from the law over the years and he could be trusted to be discreet, provided he was properly rewarded for his services.

Magda came back into the room and without saying a word she opened the door wide and went out again. Suddenly she was back, pushing a wheelchair. The occupant sat slumped, his mouth hanging open and his eyes half closed. He had a tartan rug covering his legs and he wore a woolly hat which was pulled down over his forehead. Archie stood up and stared at the sagging figure, trying to hide his disgust as the man's tongue started to protrude out of the corner of his gaping mouth.

'My husband feels the cold terribly since his stroke,' Magda said quietly, and turning to her husband, 'this is Mr Westlake, dear,' she shouted. 'He's come to see you. Say hello to him.'

Tressel slurred and gulped, a trickle of saliva dropping on to the rug, and Archie stepped back a pace as though frightened of catching some terrible disease. 'I'm sorry, there's been some mistake,' he said hurriedly.

'Won't you stay for a cup of tea and a slice of my caraway cake?' Magda asked, smiling pleasantly at the villain. 'I'm sure you'd like it. Robert likes my caraway cake, don't you, dear,' she said, raising her voice.

The elderly doctor nodded slowly, his mouth opening still wider.

'No, I won't trouble yer,' Archie said, making for the door.

'Perhaps you might like to come back some other time?' Magda pressed him. 'My husband is feeling rather tired this evening, I'm afraid.'

Archie hurried out of the house, cursing under his breath. He had wasted his valuable time, and he was only too aware that with every hour that passed Murray was more likely to be making his escape from Bermondsey.

Wally Stebbings walked purposefully along Weston Street with Molly French holding on to his arm. Wally had only ever once before experienced having a young lady holding on to his arm, and he was feeling proud and quite daring as they turned into Pedlar's Row.

'I do hope your mother will agree,' Molly said anxiously.

'Well, I don't see any reason at all why she should object,' Wally replied. 'After all, it's not as though we were teenagers. We're both mature people with adult views and an understanding of life. We've both taken our knocks and we both bear the scars. Mother likes you and I'm sure she'll have no objections.'

'You do make it all sound so romantic,' Molly said. 'You have a way with words. You could have been a poet, or maybe an actor. Yes, an actor. I can see you now in *Othello* or *Henry V* at the Old Vic.'

Wally stood outside number six, imagining what it would be like to receive the rapturous applause of a cultured audience. He was brought down to reality when the door suddenly opened and Annie stood there holding a couple of empty milk bottles.

'Yer scared the bleedin' life out o' me,' she moaned.

447

'Well, are yer comin' in or not?'

Wally walked into the parlour, followed by Molly, Annie bringing up the rear with her face set hard.

'I was just orf ter bed. I s'pose yer know what time it is?' she said crossly.

'It's only eleven o'clock, Mother,' Wally informed her.

'I thought yer'd be in before this. Yer never usually stay out late on weeknights,' Annie said, folding her arms. 'Yer can't afford ter be late fer work, 'specially now yer've got a new job.'

'I know, but Molly and I want to tell you the good news,' Wally said, smiling happily.

'Yer'll 'ave ter wait till I finish puttin' me curlers in,' Annie told him.

Wally sat down next to Molly and smiled at her. Annie's eyes shot up to the ceiling as she hurried out of the room. That woman was turning his brain, she felt sure. Wally would not normally stay out after ten thirty on weeknights. She looked a sight in that hat of hers. It was more like a bird's nest. And those shoes too. Fancy wearing high heels at her age. Wally would have to see the light before it was too late. He'd gone out tonight without his scarf and gloves too. 'I dunno,' Annie said aloud.

Wally gave Molly's hand a gentle squeeze just as Annie came back into the room, and he received a reproving look.

'I've got something to say, Mother,' he began.

Annie did not like Wally calling her anything other than Mum. He was getting too many airs and graces since that woman had come on the scene, she felt. 'Well, what is it?' she asked.

'As you know, Molly and I have been walking out together, and we have decided to give ourselves three months to see if we still like it. If so, we're going to get married next year. So I suppose you could say that we are unofficially engaged,' Wally announced.

' 'Ang on a minute,' Annie said, frowning. 'If yer like what?'

'If we like each other's company, of course,' Wally replied. 'We can get officially engaged in the autumn and marry early next year.'

Annie sat down heavily on a chair. 'I don't believe it,' she groaned. 'After all the years of lookin' after yer an' carin' for yer, now yer wanna run off an' get married.'

'We are not planning to run off, Mrs Stebbings,' Molly cut in. 'Wally's being open about our feelings. We do like each other and it's every person's right to get married if they wish to do so.'

'Oh, an' what about my feelin's?' Annie said sharply. 'Don't they count fer anyfing?'

'Of course they do, and we've already agreed that when we do get married you can come to live with us,' Molly told her. 'We'd be delighted, wouldn't we, Wally?'

'Of course,' he replied. 'We wouldn't want it any other way.'

'Mind you though, Wally will be the man of the house,' Molly asserted. 'I'd like my man to be strong and dominant, though not in a nasty way, more like making decisions and being firm and forthright, you know. A woman appreciates a strong man about the place, don't you agree, Mrs Stebbings?'

Annie was looking boggle-eyed at Molly French, staring in shocked silence, unable to believe what she was hearing. The woman was a raving lunatic, she realised. The two of them had only just started walking out together and she was already leading him along the fast track to a mental asylum.

'Well, what have you got to say, Mother?' Wally asked.

'I've bin sittin' 'ere listenin' ter the biggest load o' tosh I've ever 'eard,' she growled. 'Strong, dominant, firm, forthright. Yer talkin' about my son, lady, or Clark bloody Gable? I'm orf ter bed, an' as fer you, Wally, next time yer go out don't ferget ter wear yer scarf an' gloves, an' don't ferget ter get in at a reasonable time. An' anuvver fing. Don't bloody well keep callin' me Muvver.'

Chapter Forty-One

Ben Walsh was busy gathering his briefing papers together on Tuesday morning prior to his visit to Scotland Yard when Sergeant Ashley walked into the office. 'I've got a car coming soon, Gordon, so let's go through what we've got,' the inspector said quickly.

Ashley sat down and flipped through his notepad. 'Murray never checked in to Guy's or St Olave's Hospital, guv, so we can assume he must have got some emergency treatment privately,' he began.

'Well, he certainly needed some medical treatment, judging by the amount of blood he lost,' Walsh replied.

Ashley nodded and consulted his notepad again. 'The team checking on the local people came up with conflicting reports,' he went on. 'Apparently no one saw the killing in Cooper Street, which is not surprising considering there are only factories and the bomb site in the turning. Some tenants in Brady Buildings which backs on to the street reported hearing gunshots, however. Some said there was one shot, others said there were two, and one tenant said he heard three shots, but one sounded different.'

'Different?'

'Yes, like a car backfiring,' Ashley replied. 'All we got from the manager at the Leather Bottle pub in Bermondsey Street was that a stranger came in around nine thirty on Saturday night looking a bit dishevelled and carrying a suitcase and a grip bag. The manager thought he was a pedlar, but he was busy serving at the time and when he looked round the man had gone. He found a grip bag later in the back yard. We've got it here now. There was just a torch, a jemmy and a couple of screwdrivers inside it.'

'So Murray could have entered the pub with the intention of going over the back wall into the church gardens, to put space between himself and whoever it was who was after him,' Walsh suggested.

'The manager of the pub said he heard a screeching of brakes and the sound of revving outside,' Ashley continued. 'He said he thought it might have been a car chasing somebody, because just then a hefty-looking man ran into the public bar and said he was looking for someone carrying a suitcase. The manager told our officer he thought the man was a tec but he wasn't able to help him much.'

Ben Walsh stroked his chin thoughtfully. 'The question is, did Murray use the pub as a bolt hole, or had he arranged to meet someone in the bar, maybe to pass something over? Certainly not the money. Murray still had the case when he was shot, we've established that.'

'It could have been the printing plates,' Ashley suggested.

'Good point,' Walsh replied, nodding. 'He could have been carrying the plates in the grip bag. That would account for it being discarded. Now, who would he have passed them over to?'

'It could have been the person who did the original printing, someone who works at Carlton's, maybe,' the sergeant offered.

Walsh rubbed his chin pensively for a few moments. 'I think I'll call in to the firm again tomorrow,' he said slowly. 'My first impression was that the owner is in the clear. He certainly looked dumbfounded when I told him there was a possibility that counterfeit money had been printed at his works. When I put it to him that one of his workers could have been doing some unofficial overtime he said it would have been impossible without his print foreman knowing about it.'

'What about the foreman, guv?' Ashley asked.

'Reliable, good references, very efficient by all accounts,' Walsh replied. 'Anyway, I'll make a point of seeing him tomorrow.'

Ashley turned a few pages of his notepad. 'My snout's certain that the money was printed at the Carlton factory,' he said. 'As a matter of fact he confirmed it when I spoke to him yesterday.'

Walsh closed his eyes for a moment as he stroked his forehead with the tips of his fingers. 'The search of Cooper Street didn't throw up a spent bullet,' he said after a while. 'Now we know that the gun found on Steadman's body had two bullets missing from the magazine, and we know that one was lodged in his head. I think we can safely say that the second bullet was lodged in Jack Murray when he made his getaway. Unless we recover the bullet we can't be certain that it came from Steadman's gun though. So let's ask ourselves the question, where does Westlake fit into all this? It could well have been his car the pub manager heard that night. If so, then he was involved in some way in the killing. As a matter of fact, I've been thinking about this young woman who Westlake said was with him at the club on Saturday night. He wasn't using her as an alibi so I didn't see any reason to interview her, but I've had second thoughts. Westlake told us he left early, before Steadman and Noble, but he might have waited outside for them, or they might all have left together. The young woman may be able to help us clear that one up. Have you got her name and address?'

Ashley nodded. 'I'll get on to it,' he replied.

'One last thing,' Walsh said quickly as he gathered up his papers. 'Who do we know of locally who might have looked after Murray?'

'I've checked that out,' Ashley replied, glancing at his notepad once more as he got up from his chair. 'There were two possibles.'

'Were?'

'Yes. A Mrs Audrey Fuller, a retired nursing sister who carried out private abortions, and a Doctor Robert Tressel, who was struck off the medical register some years ago for malpractice. Audrey Fuller died last year but Tressel still lives locally. We're checking him out today.'

'Good man. Give me an update tomorrow,' Walsh said as he strode out of his office.

Sergeant Ashley went back to his desk, feeling decidedly uneasy. Westlake was due to pay a visit that afternoon and the villain knew full well that he was in a strong bargaining position. It could get very tricky.

Laura went to the Sultan that morning at her usual time and found a new manager in the pub. He was a tall, thin young man who introduced himself in a high-pitched voice as Arthur Bingley, temporary manager. He looked nervous and seemed to fuss about behind the bar, all the while humming tunelessly to himself. Laura set about her cleaning duties, becoming increasingly irritated by his needless interest in what she was doing.

'How did you get on with the last manager?' Bingley asked her as she was putting her coat on to leave.

'I didn't 'ave a lot ter do wiv 'im, ter be honest. 'E just left me ter get on wiv it,' Laura said pointedly.

'Well, I intend to make a few changes in here, the place needs a good sorting out,' he told her in a businesslike manner.

'I wish yer luck,' Laura replied, a note of sarcasm in her voice.

The temporary manager smiled briefly and came out from behind the bar. 'Yes, it's very important I begin in the way I intend to carry on, so I'll just check the cleaning before you go,' he announced.

Laura gave him a hard look as he walked between the tables, his eyes appearing to dart everywhere. 'Yes, that seems fine,' he said. 'Thank you, Mrs, eh . . . '

'Laura Prior, an' I'm not married,' she answered.

'I'll see you tomorrow then, Miss Prior,' the young man said, smiling.

Laura walked home, thinking that she would have to start looking for an alternative part-time job if Arthur Bingley remained at the Sultan, though she had a hunch that this new manager was not going to reign very long there.

Albert was sitting in his favourite armchair when Laura walked in, and he gave her a self-satisfied smile. 'I've made some tea. Sit yerself down an' I'll pour yer a cup,' he told her.

'Yer lookin' cheerful this mornin', Dad,' Laura said, taking off her coat. 'It must be the Guinness.'

'As a matter o' fact, I do feel better,' he replied. 'I went fer the papers this mornin'. I fink the walk done me good. I wanna pick a few winners. The flat racin' started terday.'

Laura reached for the teapot but Albert waved her into a chair. 'Yer take it easy, I said I'll pour the tea,' he said chirpily.

Laura sat down and kicked off her shoes. 'There's a new manager in the Sultan,' she told him. ' 'E looks a bit young ter be a manager, prob'ly a trainee.'

Albert pulled a face. 'I expect Westlake's asked the brewery ter stick somebody in until 'e finds a permanent manager,' he said. 'I wouldn't mind that job if I was a bit younger.'

Laura laughed aloud as she massaged her feet. 'I can just imagine yer be'ind the bar. Free drinks fer all yer pals. The pub would go bust in a few weeks,' she said, grinning.

Albert handed her a cup of tea. ' 'Ere, 'ave yer 'ad much ter do wiv that Annie Stebbin's?' he asked suddenly.

'I've spoken to 'er a few times. She seems a decent sort,' Laura replied. 'Why d'yer ask?'

'Oh, nuffink. I was 'avin' a chat wiv 'er when I come back from gettin' the papers,' Albert said casually. 'I asked 'ow 'er Wally was gettin' on after that trouble 'e 'ad. I told 'er I've bin queer wiv the shingles an' she said she thought she 'adn't seen me about. She seems a nice woman. As a matter o' fact she was tellin' me that 'er Wally's got a young lady friend. Well, she's not so young, accordin' to Annie. She's older than 'e is. Annie don't go a lot on 'er. She finks she's a bit of a madam. Still, that's Wally's affair. Anyway, we 'ad a nice chat.'

'So yer've found yourself a lady friend, then?' Laura said, smiling.

'Nah, she's just a friendly sort, that's all,' Albert replied dismissively. 'The poor cow's bin on 'er own fer years, apart from Wally, o' course. I s'pose she likes to 'ave a chat wiv a man now an' then.'

'Especially if 'e's a dapper character like you, Dad,' Laura said, grinning.

'She could do a lot worse,' Albert replied quickly. 'I might be gettin' on a bit in years but there's many a good tune played on an old fiddle, me gel.'

Later that morning Bridie Molloy knocked at the door. 'I was just wonderin' if the council's bin ter see yer,' she said when Laura showed her into the parlour.

'Yeah, they called yesterday,' Laura told her. 'They're

gonna do a survey. It's somefing ter do wiv the foundations or the sewers, so the man was tellin' us.'

Albert motioned Bridie into a chair. 'Would yer like a cuppa, luv?' he asked.

'Yeah, that'll be nice,' she said. ' 'Ow yer feelin', Albert? Laura told me you wasn't very well.'

'I'm a lot better, fanks,' Albert replied. 'I bin out fer the papers an' all this mornin'.'

'Yeah, an' 'e got talkin' to Annie Stebbin's no less,' Laura cut in with a quick wink at Bridie.

'She seems a nice woman. She's very lonely, if you ask me,' Bridie replied, returning Laura's wink. 'I fink she needs company, a nice man's company.'

Albert eyed the two women and decided not to take the bait. 'While yer 'avin' a chat I'm gonna sit in the scullery an' pick out a few winners,' he told them.

'I see yer've got yerself a nice young man,' Bridie said when they were alone. 'Is it serious?'

Laura smiled and nodded. ' 'E's lovely.'

'The Cassidys are a nice family,' Bridie remarked. 'I've known 'em fer years. We used ter live in the same buildin's as them. I remember when Lizzie Cassidy's boys all went off in the services durin' the war. Lizzie an' Eric were 'eartbroken. I've seen those boys grow up from bein' little tots. Always very close, they were.'

' 'Ave you 'eard that Wally Stebbin's is courtin'?' Laura asked.

'Yeah, Annie told me 'erself,' Bridie replied. 'I can see trouble brewin' there. Annie can't stand the woman. Mind yer, she does dote on 'er Wally. She treats 'im like a little kid. This woman might be the makin' of 'im.'

Outside in the scullery Albert was busy looking down the race entries, one ear cocked to hear what was being said in the parlour. It was understandable that Annie should dote on her son, he thought. He was all she had. What Annie needed was a man friend of her own, after

457

all she was still very presentable and not at all a bad-looker. Perhaps he might entice her out to the pub one night. Once she got a Guinness or two down her she'd be a different woman. He would have to play it careful though. It wouldn't do to give the woman the impression that he was looking for a permanent relationship, God forbid. Annie might be willing to settle for a bit of fun. It was worth a try.

Jack Murray eased himself on to the edge of the bed and gingerly stood up. The loss of blood had made him feel very weak, and as he slowly and awkwardly got into his clothes he realised that he would not be able to travel very far just yet. It was important that he get out of the area as soon as possible though. Tressel had been to see him that morning and had told him about his visitor. From the doctor's description Murray knew that it must have been Archie Westlake. The villain would have his hirelings out, scouring the Bermondsey area and further afield, and it was going to be very risky changing his place of security.

Murray glanced down at the suitcase that Tressel had brought and he frowned anxiously. He was going to look conspicuous if he carried the case through the streets, and the weight of it would slow him down in his condition. He would have to contact Ernie Jackson. He would be able to help him move as soon as it got dark.

Suddenly there was a tap on the bedroom door and Angela Brindley came into the room. 'You shouldn't be out of bed,' she said quickly, surprise showing on her face. 'That wound is not healed yet. You could quite easily start it bleeding again.'

Jack Murray sat down on the edge of the bed and smiled painfully at the woman. 'I've gotta get movin' ternight,' he told her. 'It'll be better fer you too.'

'Does Doctor Tressel know you're planning to leave this evening?' she asked.

Murray pointed to the sealed envelope lying on the bedside table. 'I've left some money in there fer the doctor,' he replied. 'I was gonna leave you somefing too.'

'There's no need for that, Mr Murray,' Angela said quickly. 'The doctor pays us for our services. You should let him know that you intend leaving though. He'll be able to give you something to ease the pain at least. Shall I phone and tell him?'

Murray shook his head. 'I'd prefer it if yer didn't,' he said. 'I'd be obliged if yer'd let me use yer phone though.'

'It's in the hall. Can you manage the stairs?' Angela asked.

Murray nodded, and when she left the bedroom he stood up again and gently touched his stiff shoulder. Then he leaned down and felt the weight of the suitcase with his good arm. He would be able to manage it to the taxi, he decided.

Archie Westlake walked into Dockhead Police Station that afternoon and asked to see Detective Sergeant Ashley. He was immediately shown into a small room by a bored-looking station sergeant, who gave him a curious glance as he left. A few minutes later Ashley came into the room and sat down, facing the villain across the metal table.

'Have you got the necessary?' the detective asked him.

Archie took out an envelope from his pocket and laid it down on the table, his large hand covering it. 'What about you?' he asked.

Ashley reached out and took the villain's wrist in a strong grip, sliding the envelope from beneath his hand. 'I'll need to see this first,' he said.

Archie watched the detective's face darken as he took out the photograph. 'You told me there were two,' he growled. 'Don't play games with me, Westlake.'

Archie reached inside his coat and took out another photo. 'Who's the grass?' he asked.

Ashley stared at the villain for a few moments. 'I'll need the negatives,' he said.

Archie puffed in exasperation. 'I've already told yer that Jack Murray's got the negatives,' he replied. 'If yer let me get to 'im first I could get 'em for yer.'

Ashley shook his head. 'We've got one or two leads on Murray, but I can't say anything more than that. Ben Walsh is leading the investigation and I've already told you I can't go above him.'

'Well, yer'd better pray I do get to 'im before you lot,' Archie said in a serious voice. ' 'E's most likely carryin' the photos wiv 'im, an' you're gonna look a bit silly when the desk sergeant makes 'im turn 'is pockets out.'

'Let me worry about that,' Ashley replied.

'So who's the grass?' Archie replied.

'It's one of your runners, John Bannerman to be specific,' Ashley told him.

Archie's face clouded with anger and he clenched his large hands into tight fists. 'I'll neuter the little bastard,' he muttered.

'So long as you don't remove him permanently,' Ashley warned. 'If we get his wife round here screaming I'll come looking for you.'

Archie stood up. 'Don't worry. I won't remove 'im, as yer put it, an' I can assure yer that the little rat won't be makin' any complaints against me.'

Sergeant Ashley looked into the steely eyes of the villain and saw slaughter, stark and undisguised. John Bannerman's days were numbered, that was a certainty, he thought. It was a pity it had to be this way, but it was a case of self-preservation. There would be a missing person report to deal with in the near future, sure enough, but the chance of finding Bannerman, dead or alive, would be remote. He would most probably end up at the bottom of the Thames with his feet set in concrete.

Archie paused at the door. 'Are yer sure there's nuffink yer can tell me about Murray's suspected whereabouts?' he asked.

Ashley turned in his chair. 'All I can say is, we followed up a lead this lunchtime,' he replied. 'A Doctor Tressel. He was suspected of harbouring Murray. We took a search warrant but we drew a blank. The place was searched from top to bottom, so you can take that one off your list.'

Archie grinned slyly. 'I 'eard that ole goat was confined to a wheelchair an' was on 'is way out,' he remarked.

'Don't you believe it,' Ashley answered. 'Tressel followed us all over the house. He's as sprightly as you and me.'

Archie's mind was working quickly as he walked out of the police station into the spring sunshine. The venerable Doctor Tressel was going to have some explaining to do.

Chapter Forty-Two

Laura hummed to herself as she straightened the clean white tablecloth and set the places for tea. Tonight she and Eddie were going to see *Gone With the Wind* at the Trocadera and she was feeling happy. The winter gloom that had lingered about the house seemed to be lifting at last. Her father was looking much better these last couple of days, she thought, and he was very cheerful since his chat with Annie Stebbings this morning. Lucy and Roy seemed to be making an attempt to patch up their differences too, and there was a spring feeling in the air.

The rat-tat startled her and she glanced quickly at her father before going to the front door. A tall young man held out his warrant card and put one foot on the doorstep.

'Dockhead Police,' he said. 'Does a Mrs Grant live here?'

Laura nodded, glancing quickly along the Row. 'She's not 'ome from work yet,' she replied.

'We need her to answer a few questions,' the detective said, slipping his hand into his trouser pocket.

'We thought yer might call,' Laura told him. 'Look, 'er 'usband's due 'ome at any minute an' it could be awkward for 'er. Couldn't she come down the station?'

The policeman nodded. 'Ask her to call after eight thirty. Tell her to ask for DC Thomas,' he replied.

'Who was that at the door?' Albert enquired with a frown as Laura walked back into the parlour.

'It was the police. They wanna talk ter Lucy about Saturday night,' she told him with a worried look on her face.

'I knew it. I just knew it,' Albert groaned. 'If I've warned that gel once I've warned 'er a fousand times about the way she carries on. She'll be the death o' me.'

'Come on, Dad, it ain't as bad as all that,' Laura said quickly, trying to console him. 'Lucy wasn't doin' any 'arm. She only went ter that club ter see Westlake about young Reg. It's nuffink ter worry about, so don't get yerself in a state.'

'You can believe that if yer like,' Albert snorted. 'I know she's me daughter but she can be a bloody shameless cow when she likes. She should fink o' that feller of 'ers an' them two boys instead o' gallivantin' all over the place wiv the likes o' that there Archie Westlake. The man's an out-an'-out villain.'

Laura took her father's arm and guided him down into his chair. 'Now look, Dad, Roy's gonna walk in any minute now, an' if 'e sees yer in that state 'e's gonna start wonderin' what's wrong,' she told him firmly. 'Just calm down. I'll get Lucy ter one side as soon as she comes in. Roy won't need ter know anyfing.'

Upstairs in the back bedroom Reg and Terry sat on the bed. Terry was very frightened. They had heard the knock on the door and had crept out on to the landing to hear the policeman announce himself.

'I'll go ter Borstal fer this,' Terry murmured, biting his nails.

'Course yer won't,' Reg said in an attempt to reassure him. 'They'll just tell Mum ter keep yer in fer a few days, that's all.'

'No they won't,' Terry groaned. 'Charlie's bin warned before, an' the coppers told 'is mum that the next time

463

it's Borstal. I was wiv 'im, so they're bound ter send me there too.'

'Well, yer shouldn't bunk in the pictures,' Reg said reprovingly.

'We wasn't doin' any 'arm,' Terry told him. 'Me an' Charlie was jus' sittin' nice an' quiet an' this bloke come up an' asked us fer our tickets. They always chucked us out before, but this bloke was a new one an' 'e wouldn't let us go. 'E took us ter the manager an' 'e took our names an' addresses.'

'Didn't yer tell 'em yer was somebody else?' Reg asked.

'Yeah, we did, but the bloke knew Charlie an' where 'e lived, an' 'e told the manager we was lyin', so we 'ad ter tell the trufe,' Terry explained.

Reg felt sorry for his young brother and he put his arm around his shoulders. 'Don't worry, I'll sort it out,' he said in a grown-up fashion.

'What can you do?' Terry asked him.

'I got money from that Saturday job I done,' Reg replied. 'I can go up the Trocette an' pay fer yer seats. That way they can't nick yer, not if yer offer ter pay.'

'Is that right?' the young lad asked.

'Yeah, so jus' leave it ter me.'

'Cor, that's smashin', Reg. Can I go an' tell Charlie?'

'If yer like.'

'Cor, fanks.'

Lucy came into the house a few minutes before Roy and she was immediately hustled into the scullery by Laura. While the two girls talked, Albert sat in the parlour, staring into the empty grate. It was different when there was a fire, he thought. Problems seemed to be easier to work out when the fire was burning brightly, but empty grates only made him feel more and more depressed. He stared down at the black-leaded ironwork. Lucy had brought it on her own head and she would have to face the consequences, he decided. He had enough to think about.

Roy walked in and slumped down into the armchair facing Albert. 'The buses were slow ternight,' he remarked as Lucy came into the parlour and leaned over to kiss him. 'The bridge went up as well. A quarter of an hour we were stuck there.'

The two lads hurried down the stairs to greet their father and Laura waved towards the table. 'Sit down there, you two,' she said with a look of authority. 'I'm gettin' the tea up right now.'

Tuesday night was mutton stew, at number three, but today as the family gathered round the table a strange silence prevailed. Laura was dreaming about her night out and the prospect of sitting in the back row of the Trocadera with Eddie's arm around her, while Lucy was worrying about the visit to the police station. Albert thought about how he would approach Annie Stebbings for a quiet drink, and the two boys sat eating their stew with their heads bowed resolutely over their plates. They feared an inquisition at any minute and dreaded what their mother would have to say when she got back from the police station. Roy sat at the head of the table, alone with his own problems, and when he occasionally glanced at Lucy she did not seem to notice him. He had stopped taking the sleeping tablets for a few nights now and last night the nightmare had returned. He had managed to ease himself out of bed to dry his sweat-drenched body without disturbing Lucy, and it was almost dawn when he settled back to sleep.

'I've got ter call round ter see Val Bennett ternight,' Lucy said suddenly. 'She's off work an' the forelady asked me if I'd collect 'er sick note, me livin' local.'

The two boys gave each other a furtive look and Roy

465

glanced up from his meal. 'Where does she live?' he asked casually.

'Brady Buildin's.'

'Want me ter take a walk round there wiv yer?' he asked. 'It's a bit creepy in those Buildin's when it's dark.'

'No, it's all right, I don't mind goin' round there on me own,' Lucy replied quickly.

'It's no trouble,' Roy told her.

'I said it's all right,' Lucy replied sharply. 'I'm not a kid.'

Roy gave her a hurt look and got up from the table. 'Seen the evenin' paper, Albert?' he asked with a deep sigh.

Laura waited until Terry had wiped his plate clean with a hunk of bread and then she got up. 'Come on, Reg. You can 'elp me wash up ternight. I've gotta be out in less than an hour,' she said, smiling fondly at the lad.

Out in the scullery she filled the enamel bowl with hot water and added a large knob of soda. She began washing the plates and cutlery, stacking them on the wooden draining board, occasionally casting a quick glance at the small alarm clock standing on the dresser. Reg picked up the tea towel and carefully started drying a plate.

'Aunt Laura, I 'eard the policeman knock. Will we be in trouble?' he asked anxiously.

Laura turned to face him, smiling reassuringly. 'It's nuffink ter do wiv you, luv,' she told him. 'The police are knockin' at all the doors about what 'appened at the weekend, an' we don't want yer dad 'avin' ter deal wiv 'em in case 'e gets upset. That's why yer mum's goin' ter the cop shop to answer the questions wivout Dad knowin'.'

Reg did not look convinced. 'Why would Dad get upset?' he queried.

Laura took the plate and tea towel away from the lad

and laid her hand on his shoulder. 'Yer gotta try to understand that yer dad suffered very badly in the war,' she said quietly. ' 'E was a prisoner fer a long time an' it might bring back bad memories 'avin' to answer questions. Can yer understand?'

Reg nodded slowly. 'I fink so.'

Laura began drying the plates. 'What 'appened ter yer dad was terrible an' 'e's tryin' ter ferget it all. You an' Terry can 'elp by givin' 'im all yer love, even when yer dad gets short-tempered wiv yer. Fings'll get better very soon, fer all of us.'

'Does Mum an' Dad still love each ovver?' Reg asked.

'Of course they do,' Laura replied quickly, giving him a warm smile.

'They argue a lot though,' he said, running his finger along the edge of the draining board.

'Mums an' dads often do, but it doesn't mean they don't love each ovver,' Laura said softly. 'You an' Terry argue quite a lot, but yer still love each ovver, don't yer?'

Reg nodded slowly and then looked directly into Laura's eyes. 'Will you an' Eddie get married?' he asked.

'I 'ope we will, one day,' Laura replied with a fond smile.

'Will yer go away ter live, miles away, I mean?'

'No fear. We'll live close by so we can come an' see yer every day,' Laura replied, hugging the lad tightly to her. 'Now you an' Terry be'ave yerselves while I'm out, an' tell Terry not ter let on ter yer dad where Mum's really gone.'

Reg walked to the door and then turned back for a moment. 'I'm glad yer not gonna move far away, Aunt Laura,' he said with a grin.

Archie Westlake drove to Camberwell Green in a hurry. There was one urgent matter to take care of before he paid another call on the theatrical Doctor Tressel, and it had to be arranged in a very professional manner. Ashley could think what he liked, but without any evidence to link him to Bannerman's disappearance he would be powerless to do anything about it. Besides, Ashley could not very well pull him in for questioning without implicating himself.

Archie walked into Larry's Club and slumped down at the counter while he waited for the doorman to fetch the club's manager. A young man was busy stocking the shelves and he gave the villain a nod of recognition before making himself scarce. Experience, and the recent events in Bermondsey, had taught the barman that the less he overheard the better. The cellar needed to be sorted out anyway, he told himself.

Larry Petersen walked into the large room and shook the villain's hand. 'I guessed it must be serious when yer said yer couldn't talk over the phone,' he remarked, sitting down on a bar stool. 'It's terrible about Con an' Danny. Both prime lads.'

Archie nodded. 'I got a job fer the boys,' he said, moving his face closer to the ex-boxer's. 'It's a job o' grass-cuttin'.'

Larry smiled, showing his newly acquired gold teeth. 'Tidyin' up the manor a bit.'

'I need Jack Murray fer that,' the villain muttered, making a fist.

'Yer need a close cut, I take it,' Larry said, fetching out a packet of Gold Flake from his coat pocket.

'I can't afford a botch-up, Larry,' the villain told him. 'This job needs doin' properly. I want the grass dumped, permanently.'

'It's no problem,' Larry said as he struck a Swan Vesta and put it to his cigarette. 'We'll feed the pigs a good supper.'

Archie took a piece of paper and a pencil from his

inside pocket and scribbled down an address. 'The contact'll meet yer there, at twelve noon,' he explained, passing over the slip of paper. ' 'E'll tell yer 'is name, Dickie Jones. 'E'll take yer ter the spot an' point out the grass, who'll come along about twelve twenty. Now as soon as yer've clocked 'im, drop Jones off and grab the grass. I want it done clean. That way no bloody upright citizen's gonna take the car number or try any heroics.'

' 'As this grass got a moniker?' Larry asked with a dark smile.

'Yeah, John Bannerman,' Archie replied, taking out a package from his coat pocket and dropping it down on the bar counter. 'It's the usual arrangement. The balance on completion.'

Larry picked up the money. 'Leave it ter me. It'll be a sweet job, no worry.'

Archie nodded. 'I want anuvver favour, Larry,' he said, getting up from the stool. 'I've got a lead on Murray. I'm makin' a move on 'im ternight an' I'll need two of yer best lads.'

Doctor Tressel spooned a liberal amount of sugar into his coffee mug and stirred the milky brew thoughtfully. The papers had been full of the murders for the last two days, and from the reports he had read it seemed that the police were confident Jack Murray was responsible, though they had not said so explicitly. 'Wanted for questioning in connection with the crimes' was the wording they used. Well, as far as the doctor was concerned, the sooner Murray left the Brindleys the better.

Magda looked up from the novel she was reading and gazed at her husband for a moment or two. 'You look worried, dear,' she remarked. 'Is it Mr Murray?'

Tressel nodded. 'Why do we do it, Magda?' he asked

her. 'Why do we involve ourselves so much in other people's troubles?'

'You're a doctor, dear, and a very good one, despite those bumbling fools in the Association,' she answered. 'You could no more have turned Mr Murray away from the door than you could the Pope himself. Don't judge yourself so harshly. Why don't you take a nice nap? I'll wake you when the concert comes on.'

Tressel smiled and sipped his coffee. 'I think I will, dearie,' he replied. 'I do feel rather tired.'

Magda continued with her novel, occasionally glancing up at her recumbent husband and over at the large ornate clock on the mantelshelf. At ten minutes to seven the doorbell rang and she jumped up with a start, quickly rousing the doctor. 'Come on, dear, into the other room, fast as you can,' she urged him.

A few moments later Archie Westlake followed Magda into the cosy lounge. He looked around as she motioned him into an easy chair beside the low fire.

'I'll see if the doctor's awake,' she told him, trying not to let him see that she was frightened.

The villain tensed his jaw in impatience and gripped the arms of the chair tightly. The woman seemed to be taking a long time.

Magda came back into the room with a rueful smile. 'I'm very sorry but the doctor's sleeping soundly,' she said.

Archie suddenly leapt from his chair and grabbed the startled woman by the arm. 'Let's stop the play-actin',' he growled. 'There was enough o' that the last time I called. Now show me ter the doctor or I'll really get rough.'

Magda's face went white as he bundled her out of the room into the wide hall. 'You've no right to barge in here threatening me,' she said bravely.

'Where's the ole man?' Archie growled, tightening his grip on her arm.

The door facing them opened suddenly and Doctor Tressel emerged. He raised his hands in a gesture of resignation. 'Don't you dare harm my wife,' he told the villain.

Westlake swiftly reached into his coat pocket and took out a flick knife. The menacing blade shot out from its socket as he raised it to Magda's throat. 'If you co-operate she'll come ter no 'arm,' he said in a low voice. 'Now, where can I find Jack Murray?'

'Jack Murray?' Tressel echoed.

Westlake pressed the knife a little harder against the terrified woman's throat. 'Don't mess me about, Tressel. You know who I'm talkin' about.'

'I treated a man for a gunshot wound on Saturday night, but he's gone,' the doctor replied, holding his palms up in front of him.

'Where is 'e?' the villain shouted.

'I'll tell you where he is. Please put that knife down,' Tressel implored him.

'No! Don't tell him!' Magda cried out courageously.

Tressel's shoulders sagged. 'He won't hurt your sister or her husband, dear. It's Murray he wants.'

Westlake pushed Magda back into the lounge and shoved her down on a chair. 'Yer've got more guts than brains,' he snarled at her. 'Now what's the address?'

A few minutes later the villain left the house holding on to Magda's arm. She was roughly bundled into the back of his car and found herself tightly wedged between two hefty-looking young men. She felt a sudden unreal elation, despite the traumatic experience of the past few minutes. It was like something out of a Hollywood gangster film, with her the heroine in dire circumstances, waiting for her hero to come racing after her.

Her strange excitement soon turned to cold fear as

Archie half turned and glared at her. 'We better not be on a fool's errand,' he growled.

There was no hero to rescue her, she realised, only her ageing husband, who was left on his own in the house, no doubt beside himself, praying for her.

Lucy arrived home feeling very relieved. She had not been able to tell the police much, but they seemed to have believed her account of the events on Saturday evening at the club. She now had to brazen it out with Roy. She had been gone for much longer than she had anticipated and he would no doubt fire questions at her.

As soon as she entered the house Lucy knew that something was wrong. Her father had a worried look on his face and there was no sign of her husband. Her two sons were sitting quietly in one corner, eyeing her anxiously.

'Where's Roy?' she asked.

' 'E's gone out lookin' fer yer,' Albert replied.

'Lookin' fer me? Why?' Lucy asked.

Albert looked into her anxious eyes. 'Val Bennett called round just after yer left,' he told her. 'She brought the dress material she promised yer.'

'Oh no,' Lucy groaned as she slumped down into a chair.

'I'm sorry, luv. Roy answered 'er knock,' Albert said dejectedly. 'Laura 'ad gone out an' I was dozin' in the chair at the time.'

'What did Roy say?' Lucy asked him.

' 'E jus' said 'e'd like ter know what was goin' on an' then 'e put 'is coat on an' went out. 'E said 'e was gonna look fer yer.'

'Was it all right at the police station, Mum?' Terry asked, looking worried.

'Yeah, it's nuffink ter worry about, luv,' Lucy told him with a quick smile. 'You two 'ad better get ter bed before yer farvver gets back. I don't fink 'e'll be in a very good mood.'

Doctor Tressel had been pacing the room ceaselessly for the past hour. Suddenly he heard a key being inserted into the front-door lock. He hurried down the stairs into the hall to see a very relieved Magda closing the door behind her. He held out his arms and embraced her, fighting to keep control of his emotions. 'What happened?' he cried. 'Did he harm you?'

Magda patted his bony shoulders comfortingly. 'No, dear. It all ended very civilised,' she said, smiling.

'But . . . but . . . '

Magda put two fingers against his mouth and took his arm, leading him into the lounge. 'When we arrived at Angela's house Mr Murray was just getting into a taxi,' she told him. 'I was bundled out of the car on to the pavement and they drove off after him. I was quite all right really, just a little frightened.'

Doctor Tressel put his arm round Magda's shoulders. 'I've been thinking, dear,' he said as he regained his breath. 'Remember that little cottage in the Fens you fell in love with? Well, I've decided it's about time we took another look at it.'

'But you don't like the Fens,' she said, looking into his pale blue eyes.

'I think I could quite easily change my mind,' he replied.

Chapter Forty-Three

Laura and Eddie walked home through the quiet streets late on Tuesday night after watching the long film epic *Gone With the Wind*, the passionate love scenes between Rhett Butler and Scarlett O'Hara still lingering in their minds. The night was becoming chilly and Laura wore her coat collar up around her ears. She felt Eddie's warmth as she snuggled close to him, her arm in his, and she sighed as he instinctively squeezed her arm against his side and smiled in that special way of his. They had sat in the back row, his arm around her, occasionally stealing secret kisses as the romantic saga unfurled on the screen in front of them.

It was nearing midnight when they reached Pedlar's Row, and Laura moved her arm to let his hand find hers. 'They'll all be in bed, would yer like a cuppa, or a coffee?' she asked him.

Eddie smiled in answer and slipped his arm round her waist as she put the key in the front door. 'Frankly, my dear, I don't give a damn,' he said in a deep voice, echoing Clark Gable's immortal words to Vivien Leigh.

Laura giggled as she led the way into the dark passage and turned to him. Suddenly their arms were around each other and their lips met hungrily in a passionate kiss. Eddie stroked his fingers gently along her slim neck and Laura moulded herself to him, her breathing coming faster as she felt the urgency of his passion. 'I need yer, darlin',' she groaned. 'I need yer so much.'

'I need yer too,' Eddie gasped, finding it difficult to control his hands. Her body felt delicious and her long fair hair tantalised him as he smelled her sensual fragrance.

Laura moved away from him in the darkness and took his hand, pulling him into the shadowy parlour. The fire was still burning low and the room felt warm and cosy. They stood together in the dim light from the fire and kissed passionately, Laura quivering in his arms and moving her hips in a provocative way, exciting him, driving him wild with desire. Eddie gasped as his hands glided down her body, reaching the tops of her thighs, his mouth open against hers. Suddenly Laura brought her hands up to his shoulders and urged him back momentarily while she fumbled with the buttons of her coat.

'God, you look lovely!' Eddie whispered hoarsely.

Laura slipped out of her coat and let it fall on to the chair beside her. Slowly and deliberately she reached up and undid the top button of her white blouse, pulling the garment out from inside her skirt. Eddie reached for her, slipping his hands inside and caressing her small, firm breasts. He could feel her hands on his body and quickly he undid his coat and threw it off. They came together once more, their kisses deep and full of fiery hunger. The waiting game had been exhausted. Now it was time for the real game of love and Laura was ready. She reached for the zip of her skirt while Eddie quickly pulled off his tie and opened his shirt.

He pulled Laura down on to the hearth rug, his body hovering over her and raised up on his tensed arms as she bared her thighs. In the dim light of the dying embers they made love, their bodies melting into one as their mounting passion threatened to explode. It was urgent and brief, fulfilling their long-smouldering desire in a sudden frenzy of delirious ecstasy, and at the very moment when their ardour burned white-hot they kissed wildly.

'I love yer, darlin', an' yer all mine now,' Laura whispered.

'I love yer too, Laura, an' yer mine ferever,' he said, gently stroking her hair as they lay together in the darkness.

On Tuesday evening Jack Murray said his goodbyes to the Brindleys and walked down the few stone steps of the house to the waiting taxi. Ernie Jackson stepped from the cab and took the suitcase from the white-faced fugitive. 'Come on, Jack, I've got you,' he said.

Murray allowed the printer to take his arm and as they stepped into the taxi headlights flashed in the turning. They heard the revving engine and saw a woman being roughly bundled out on to the pavement.

'Quick! Get movin'!' Murray screamed at the startled driver.

The taxi roared out of the turning, followed closely by the car.

'There's a fiver in it if yer lose 'em!' Murray shouted to the driver.

'Yer'd better lose 'em, or we're all in the shite,' Jackson shouted.

The taxi driver looked frightened as he bent over the steering wheel. He had picked up some strange characters in his time but this was something else, he realised. This looked like a gangland feud and it was just his luck to get himself involved. Well, he had been a cab driver for more years than he cared to remember and there wasn't much he didn't know about the streets and byways of south London. He had been hired to pick up the second passenger in Peckham and then go to a house in Deptford, which had been a straightforward request until now. He had to shake the car behind them, and quickly if he wasn't going to end up in dire trouble.

'Hold on!' he shouted as he suddenly steered towards the kerb, braked hard and then swung the steering wheel full over.

Murray and Ernie Jackson stared wide-eyed at the bus coming straight at them, expecting to be hit head-on, but somehow the taxi missed the vehicle by inches as it skidded round and did a complete turn and they saw the infuriated bus driver shaking his fist after them. The pursuing car carried on, unable to turn in such a tight circle, and the taxi driver grunted loudly with satisfaction. 'These cabs can turn on a sixpence,' he remarked.

Murray puffed heavily and looked at Ernie Jackson, whose face was chalk-white with fear. 'We can lose 'em now,' he said, glancing through the back window.

The driver swung left and then right, throwing his anxious passengers against each other. Murray felt pain shooting through his shoulder and Ernie gripped the seat-rest tightly, praying that they had got away cleanly.

'Gawd knows where we are,' Murray growled.

The taxi driver felt much better now that he was off the main New Cross Road. These back streets were mean and ill lit and they led down to Deptford circuitously via a network of railway arches.

In the other car Archie Westlake cursed his luck. His two passengers sat motionless, beginning to feel that they were not going to earn their money after all.

'The bastards must 'ave turned off down 'ere somewhere,' Archie growled. 'They wasn't that much in front.'

The two thugs constantly glanced at each other as the villain drove through a maze of back streets. It was obvious to them that they had lost the taxi but Archie would not give up until finally he found himself coming back out on the main New Cross Road. He was tempted to go back to the house in Peckham but he realised that Murray would certainly not have left a forwarding address. He cursed under his breath as he turned the car round. 'I'll drop yer off at the club,' he said sullenly. 'I need a drink anyway.'

The night sky was clear and filled with stars as Lucy stepped quietly out of bed and opened the blinds. A crescent moon hung high in the heavens, and she noticed how the roof slates seemed to glow silver-grey in the stillness. She heard Roy move in bed and she turned briefly to see him raise himself against the headrail in the darkness. He was wide awake and watching her, she knew, and as she turned back to the window Lucy realised that it had to be now or never. No longer could she stand his silence, his unpredictable behaviour and his looks of mistrust and anger. Everything must be brought out into the open, and it was time to do it now.

Roy sat up in bed, his stomach knotting as he looked at his wife. She seemed more beautiful than ever. Her slim figure was perfectly silhouetted by the spectral light of the moon and her dark hair cascaded round her shoulders and rested on her flimsy nightdress. She reminded him of a wild gypsy girl, a creature of passion and fire, too much for him to handle and too volatile to contain.

He leaned his head back against the cold iron. 'Couldn't yer sleep?' he asked her quietly.

'So yer can talk, then?' she replied with venom.

'I'm sorry, but what was I ter fink?' he countered. 'Yer told me a lie. Yer could 'ave bin anywhere.'

'Yeah, I was wiv my fancy man,' she said, curling her mouth disdainfully.

'Don't joke about it,' Roy said quickly.

Lucy suddenly turned away from the window and came over to the bed. 'Yer came in ternight wiv not a word ter say fer yerself,' she began. 'No questions, no third degree, only that bloody pained silence. Gawd 'elp us, Roy, we'll never get our marriage tergevver unless we can start talkin' to each ovver again.'

'Do yer want our marriage ter go on?' Roy asked, his pale blue eyes burning into hers.

'Of course I do,' she almost shouted. 'But I want a real, lovin' marriage, not a sham. I want love, I need yer love.'

Roy dropped his head. 'I love yer dearly, Lucy,' he said in a whisper. 'I want ter please yer, believe me I do.'

She suddenly reached out and took his hands in hers and he could see the outline of her full breasts beneath the nightdress. He felt a burning need to give her all the love and attention she longed for, and it cut him to his very soul. He had become impotent, useless as a man, and yet he had so much love for her locked up inside him.

'I want you ter listen ter what I've got ter say, Roy,' she told him quietly. 'Let me finish first, and then yer can decide what yer wanna do. Ter begin wiv, I went ter the police station this evenin'. Yer see, I was wiv Archie Westlake on Saturday night, not wiv me gelfriends. 'E invited me to 'is club when I went to 'is ware'ouse ter see 'im about young Reg workin' there on Saturdays. I know what the bloke was expectin', but it was the last fing on my mind. Okay, so I 'ad a few drinks at the club an' I met a few of 'is friends, but 'e left early, an' yer can guess why. I got a cab 'ome an' that was that. Nuffink 'appened, so there's no need fer you ter worry. Anyway, I've stopped Reg workin' at the ware'ouse after what's bin goin' on round 'ere. Yesterday, though, Archie stopped me as I was comin' 'ome from work. 'E tried ter get fresh, an' said 'e wanted me an' 'im ter get tergevver, but I told 'im straight that I was 'appily married an' wanted nuffink ter do wiv 'im. Now that's the gospel trufe, I swear on our two boys' lives. The reason I've told yer everyfing is ter clear the air. It's very important ter me, ter both of us, if we're ter make a go of our marriage,' Lucy said, gazing intently into his eyes.

Roy's face had become dark with anger at the Bermondsey villain as he listened in stunned silence, and he was about to interrupt when Lucy raised her hand. 'I know that yer feel unable ter satisfy me, Roy,' she said quietly, 'an' I know what it's doin' ter yer, but I'm also as sure as anyone could be that it's not a physical problem. It's all in yer mind. Those sweats, an' the times yer wake up shoutin' out, that ain't got nuffink ter do wiv any sickness in yer body, an' you've gotta recognise that. P'raps deep down inside yer know it, but until yer face it an' draw whatever's troublin' yer out in the open then there's no chance o' beatin' it, no chance fer us ter make love tergevver the way we once did. Can't yer understand that?'

For a few moments Roy sat staring into Lucy's eyes, then suddenly his head dropped and he sobbed. 'I can't,' he groaned. 'It's too terrible.'

'Yes you can,' Lucy urged him, her hands squeezing his very tightly. 'Try, darlin', fer Gawd's sake try.'

Roy gulped hard, crushing the bedclothes up in his fists as he fought with himself, his body tensing and starting to sweat. Lucy grabbed him and took him in her arms, pressing his head against her breasts. 'Tell me, darlin'. Tell me, please. Let it all out. Jus' try an' unburden yerself, fer me, fer us an' our sons.'

The crisp lace curtains fluttered in the gentle breeze coming in through the open window, and outside the moon shone down from a starry sky as Roy finally bared his soul.

'It was the last year of our captivity,' he began. 'We were up country an' we were gettin' word through the local villagers that the war was goin' bad fer the Japs. We were all scared that as soon as the railway was completed we were gonna be killed. I was very weak wiv the after effects o' beriberi an' jungle ulcers, an' one day I collapsed on the railway track. A Jap guard grabbed me an' tried ter pull me ter me feet, an' I lunged out. I was delirious. I didn't realise what I was doin'. Anyway, the Japs gathered around me an' beat me senseless wiv the butts o' their rifles, an' then I was thrown into a small tin shed. There was no room ter stand up straight an' it was stiflin'. Every now an' then the guards would beat on the tin sheetin'. The noise was unbearable an' I screamed out fer 'em ter stop. They only laughed an' carried on. I was kept there fer three days an' nights, accordin' to our camp officer. Yer can imagine the state I was in. I was lyin' in me own filth, unable ter stand up or stretch out. Then on the third night one o' the lads crept out from the compound an' opened the shed.'

Lucy held him close, biting hard on her bottom lip in an effort to check her emotions. Silent tears fell down her cheeks as she stroked his hair, urging him to go on.

'The soldier knew it was forbidden ter release a prisoner from that shed, but 'e came fer me anyway. I'll never ferget 'im. 'E was a young country lad about me own age. Anyway, the lads cleaned me up the best they could, an' next mornin' there was a parade in front o' the camp commandant. The Nips dragged me out in front of everybody an' told me to identify who it was who'd released me. I couldn't 'ave given the lad away, Lucy, not even if they'd killed me. They almost did that mornin'. I was beaten senseless an' when I came round I was in the sick bay. It wasn't until later that I found out about what 'appened ter the young lad. 'E stepped out o' the line ter save me an' they smashed 'im down an' beat him mercilessly. Finally . . . ' Roy paused for a moment and closed his eyes, gritting his teeth in an effort to go on. 'Finally they dragged 'im down ter the river's edge, and there, while I was lyin' bleedin' in the dirt, they be'eaded 'im. I can still see that young lad's face. I see 'im everywhere, in crowded pubs, on the street an' every night in me sleep I see 'im taken away ter be killed, over an' over again. If only I 'adn't provoked that guard the lad would still be alive. I caused 'is death. It was me that killed 'im.'

Lucy cried aloud as she hugged her distraught husband. 'There, there. It wasn't your fault,' she sobbed. 'Yer can't blame yerself.'

Roy sagged in her arms, crying against her as she gently kneaded his neck, and after a while she very slowly eased him down under the covers.

As the dawn light filtered into the small bedroom and spots of rain spattered the open window, Lucy and Roy lay fast asleep, wrapped in each other's arms.

Throughout that long night Dickie Jones lay twisting in his bed, unable to sleep, his mind tortured. Sara lay beside him, sleeping like a baby, and as it grew light the young man turned on to his back and stared up at the cracked ceiling, fighting with his conscience. She was right. She was always right, and it was a pity he had not taken any notice of her when she advised him not to get mixed up with the mob. Sara had told him what it would entail, and she knew only too well. Her brother Con had got himself tangled up with Archie Westlake and she understood just how easy it was to get involved and how difficult it became to get out. The mob demanded absolute loyalty. If a person defaulted in any way or posed a threat, then they were quickly dealt with. If a rival group dared attempt to move into the area, then the forces were marshalled. The mob demanded total commitment and at their head Archie Westlake had reigned supreme for a long time. Although things were changing now – the gang had lost two of its leaders and others were emerging from the shadows to take over – they would never change for him and Sara while he was a hireling, but what was he to do?

The young man stared fixedly at the ceiling, his mind racing. He was to be the Judas. His finger would point out the victim and then he would make his exit, leaving John Bannerman to his fate. Sara was right. How would he be able to sleep peacefully in his bed at night? How would he be able to look at himself in the mirror every morning without cringing? She had spelled it out to him in simple fashion. 'Warn Bannerman,' she had said. 'Nobody would be any the wiser.' But then Sara did not have to face the fury of the mob.

What was he to do? Could he front it out? Sara felt he could, but she was still distraught over her brother's killing. She had never liked Con being involved with the villains and when he met his brutal death it had broken her heart. She was still in a state of shock and not thinking clearly, or she would have understood that he had to go along with the gang's wishes.

As the rain started to beat down outside, Dickie Jones got out of bed and went to the scullery to make himself a cup of tea. John Bannerman had brought it on himself, he thought. He had betrayed a confidence and had put people at risk. He knew the rules and he knew full well that the mob would show a grass no mercy. John Bannerman had grassed and he would now have to pay the price.

Sara Jones suddenly walked into the scullery and sat down with a sigh in the chair facing her worried-looking husband. Her eyes were still heavy with sleep but there was a determined expression on her pale face. 'Now listen ter me,' she began.

Chapter Forty-Four

John Bannerman stubbed out his third cigarette and slumped back in the chair as he looked dejectedly around the empty room. It seemed so quiet without Marge and the kids, he thought. The high chair was gone, and the metal trunk that contained the children's toys was missing from the corner. There were no napkins hanging over the gas stove and the dresser was bare of crockery. The room was just how it had been when they first moved into the furnished flat. There was a table and four chairs, a tatty-looking settee and two easy chairs with well-worn cushions, and a wall cupboard with a door that would not stay shut. It was hanging open now and the young man could see the fresh newspaper that his wife had spread out on the shelves only last week.

Marge had been overjoyed when he found the flat in Rotherhithe. She had been heavily pregnant at the time, he recalled, and her mother had not wanted her to leave the family home until after the birth of the baby. Marge had been adamant, however. The rows were increasing and she was getting tired of the friction between her mother and her husband. She had made their new place comfortable and welcoming, as much as she was able, and here in this grotty two-roomed flat she had given birth to three more of his children. They had been happy, but money was always scarce, and he had been in and out of work until recently. Getting the job with the bookie had seemed a godsend at the time, as he had already fallen foul of Sergeant Ashley and the detective was pressing him for results. Things had soon turned bad, though, and now he found himself in the worst situation he had ever been faced with.

He had always tried to keep his dealings with the detective away from his wife but she had suspected right from the start that something dangerous was going on. It was hard to keep his appointments secret from her and finally he had been compelled to tell her all. Marge had taken it well, considering, but she constantly pressed him to try and find an honest job away from London, away from the mob, before he got in over his head. Now his worst fears had been realised. For some reason Ashley had decided to feed him to the lions, despite his numerous assurances to the contrary, and John knew only too well that his life was not worth a brass farthing.

Early that morning Dickie Jones had called, looking very disturbed, and had spelled it all out. He had made it plain that if it was left to him he would not have lifted a finger to prevent a grass getting his just deserts, but it had been his wife Sara who finally talked him into calling, and then only because of Marge and the kids. Dickie had a right to be angry, John thought. After all, his trust had been betrayed and he had been used, and it would be disastrous for him if Westlake ever found out whose tongue had been wagging in the first place.

John Bannerman lit another cigarette as he sat in the empty room, feeling sick to his stomach. There had been much to do in very little time. He had managed to get a friend to transport Marge and the kids home to her mother in Stepney for the time being, along with the bits and pieces from the flat, and he could not put out of his mind how sad and anxious he had felt as he watched the van leave the little Rotherhithe back street. Marge had pleaded with him to come with her and the children, but he had told her firmly that as long as Westlake was after him it would put them in too much danger. His only hope was to get well away from London, and as soon as he had settled in a job and found a place to live he would send for them.

The young man stood up and went to the window, checking the time with the church clock opposite. Normally he would set off at noon and catch the tram to Tower Bridge Road. This morning, however, John Bannerman had other plans. There was someone he wanted to see before he left the riverside borough, and as the church clock mournfully struck the hour of eleven he put on his coat and left the flat.

Val Bennett shook her head sadly when Lucy finished speaking. 'I don't fink we'll ever know the 'alf of it,' she said quietly. 'What must 'e 'ave bin goin' frew? Terrible, it's just terrible.'

Lucy sighed heavily as she sat in the works canteen alongside her old friend. 'I can understand a lot o' fings now,' she replied. 'Roy blames 'imself fer everyfing. I only 'ope we can start ter get closer now, Val. I do love 'im so.'

The large woman smiled fondly at her. 'I know yer do, pet. Be patient fer a little longer an' yer'll see the difference in 'im, mark my words.'

'I 'ope so, Val,' Lucy replied. 'Roy looked really strange when 'e left fer work this mornin'. I've never seen 'im like that before, even since 'e's come back from the war. It was as though 'e was preoccupied wiv somefing. There was a sort o' starey look in 'is eye. Me sister Laura noticed it too. She asked me if there was anyfing wrong. When I told 'er what Roy 'ad revealed ter me last night she was really upset.'

'Well, like I say, don't rush fings,' Val advised. 'Remember to undo the string carefully, don't just tear the wrappin's off. That's what my ole man always sez.'

Dickie Jones sat passively between the two large young men, his half-hearted efforts to strike up a conversation coming to nothing as the car pulled away from his house and drove to Weston Street. The men seemed to be priming themselves for the job in hand and they looked decidedly mean and moody. The driver looked very serious too and said nothing as he swung the car into the Tower Bridge Road and slowed down behind a tram.

The day was overcast and gloomy, with a threat of rain, and Dickie tried to remain calm as he looked out at the busy market stalls. On the surface everything looked quite normal, but he knew only too well that for one man it might well have been the last day he would ever see, had it not been for Sara. She was right. There had been enough killings already without another young woman being widowed. Sara had become convinced that Archie Westlake was finished, and that it was only a matter of time before the due processes of the law caught up with him. For too long he had ruled the neighbourhood with a mailed fist, his reign enforced by a trusted cadre of old associates in crime and a motley back-up crew of ruthless young men who considered themselves beyond the law. Now the Bermondsey villain had overstretched himself. Greed and power had begun to affect his thinking.

'Right, 'ere we are,' the driver said, pulling up short of Brady Buildings.

The young man sitting kerbside lowered his window slightly and glanced along the turning. 'As soon as yer spot 'im, give us the nod, an' keep yer 'ead ter the front,' he growled at Dickie. 'We don't want the geezer sussin' anyfing.'

Dickie could see a stretch of the pavement behind him in the driver's mirror and he made a play of watching carefully for the other runner. Occasionally he turned round to glance through the back window, and all the time he was aware of the tension building up around him. Westlake's men were getting impatient and the driver constantly drummed his fingers on the steering wheel as he slouched in the front seat.

'Where the bloody 'ell's 'e got to?' one of the men asked.

' 'E's always 'ere by twenty past twelve,' Dickie told him. 'Con was always 'ere on the 'alf-hour.'

'Yer don't fink 'e's sussed somefing, do yer?' the driver asked.

'There's no way 'e could 'ave done,' the man on Dickie's left replied. 'Apart from Archie an' us 'ere, no one was in on the business.'

Just then the bookie replacing Con Noble arrived and walked into the Buildings.

'It's turned the 'alf-hour,' Dickie remarked.

'If Bannerman don't show up, Archie's gonna be livid,' the driver grumbled.

Dickie shifted uncomfortably. 'I wonder if 'e's sick?' he said, attempting to look as impatient as the rest of them.

'We'll give 'im anuvver ten minutes then we'll go lookin' for 'im,' the man next to him replied.

At twelve forty-five the young villain glanced at his silent partner and then at Dickie. 'Right then, you know where Bannerman lives, we're goin' there,' he announced. 'Slip out an' tell yer bookie 'e'll 'ave ter do wivout runners terday, an' be quick.'

Dickie Jones stepped out of the car and hurried into the Buildings, praying that John Bannerman had not been stupid enough to remain in the flat. These men meant business and they were paid on results.

Ernie Jackson stared down at his whisky as he sat in the small bar of the Jolly Compasses. The little pub was sited in an alley just off the Tower Bridge Road and it was mainly frequented by market traders and local businessmen. Ernie was still shaking after the grilling from Chief Inspector Ben Walsh that morning, and now, surrounded by the lunchtime noise and smoke of the bar, he cursed the moment of madness which had got him involved with Archie Westlake's counterfeit scheme. He had a well-paid job with security and he was allowed to manage the print shop with little or no interference from his boss, and now he stood to lose that and his liberty as well if he was found out. It must have been the whisky that had befuddled his brain and stopped him thinking straight when the Bermondsey villain first approached him. Archie had done his homework and used his position of financial backer to obtain the information he needed from Mr Leadbeater, the firm's owner, and he would have found it the easiest thing in the world to pull the wool over that old fool's eyes.

Ernie downed his whisky and ordered another. He felt more at ease here than at his previous local. This place was definitely a much safer bet now than the Leather Bottle in Bermondsey Street, which seemed to be attracting half the Bermondsey CID of late. Ben Walsh in particular appeared to find the Leather Bottle a fascinating pub, and he had said as much that morning in Leadbeater's office. The inspector had gone on about the persistent rumour circulating in the underworld that counterfeit money had been printed at Carlton's, and he had asked questions about the printing press that had recently been taken out of the firm. Simon Leadbeater had been at pains to explain that when he bought the business there were one or two old machines that he had replaced and the originals had recently been sold for scrap.

Ben Walsh had harped on about the possibility of illegal goings-on behind the owner's back and Leadbeater had

had to concede that it was indeed possible, though extremely unlikely. It was a small firm and the workers would be aware of anything untoward, unless the illegal printing was carried out at night. In that case, Ernie thought, he was right there in the frame. He was the foreman printer and he sometimes serviced and set up machines at night. Leadbeater had been very quick to rubbish the likelihood of his foreman being anything less than one hundred per cent loyal and true. He was also quick to point out that as far as he was aware Mr Jackson was a devout Christian and a sidesman at the local church. Ben Walsh had seemed to be satisfied, but he was a senior police officer and no doubt adept at not giving anything away. The detective could be finalising his case against him right this very minute, Ernie fretted.

Ernie Jackson's lunch hour was almost over and as he walked swiftly back to Bermondsey Street he was filled with trepidation. The events of last night had almost given him a heart attack, he felt sure, and now he had been instructed by Jack Murray to set up a meeting with Archie Westlake within the next twenty-four hours. How he would go about it was his affair, but Murray had strongly hinted in a roundabout way that if anyone double-crossed him now it would be a very unwise move and would incur terrible retribution. Ernie's mind was racing as he entered the print works and he was still not clear just how a meeting could be arranged between the two sworn enemies.

Laura was going around with her head in the clouds all day after her wonderful romantic evening with Eddie, and she longed to see him again. She had gone to the Sultan that morning, feeling as though she was floating on air, and even the tiresome young manager could not dampen her spirits with his pettiness and pomposity. Later, when she was shopping at the market, she took time to look once again at the black creation that was still hanging in the clothes-shop window. It looked more beautiful than ever, and as she gazed at it, daydreaming, Lizzie Cassidy tapped her on the shoulder with a fond smile on her homely face. 'It's almost too good ter wear,' she remarked. 'I reckon that dress'll be there fer ever.'

Laura nodded with a self-conscious grin. 'I wish I 'ad the nerve ter price it,' she said.

'Go on, why don't yer?' Lizzie coaxed.

'I daren't,' Laura said, laughing. 'I might end up pawnin' the family heirlooms, well, the crockery, at any rate.'

The two women walked home to Pedlar's Row, chatting about the weather, the prices at the market and the continuing food rationing, and Lizzie mentioned the fact that Eddie was late for work that morning but had got up in a cheerful mood. 'Normally 'e's in a terrible mood when 'e's late fer the call-on,' she told Laura, 'but this mornin' 'e was singin' away to 'imself as 'e dashed about. I dunno what yer doin' to 'im, but don't stop, luv, whatever it is. I can't stand it when that boy o' mine's in a temper.'

Laura smiled to herself and hoped she wasn't blushing as the two of them entered Pedlar's Row. Last night had been lovely, she thought, but how much nicer it would be when she and Eddie managed to get away for their romantic weekend.

Archie Westlake leant forward over his office desk, his face bloated by the considerable amount of whisky he had drunk that lunchtime, his hands clenched into angry fists. 'I ask yer ter do a simple job an' yer go an' balls it up,' he snarled. 'Am I s'posed ter do everyfing meself?'

'It wasn't our fault, guv, the bloke never showed,' the young man facing him said quietly. 'We went ter where 'e lives but the 'ole family 'ad scarpered.'

Archie banged his fist down on the desktop. 'Couldn't nobody tell yer where they was?' he shouted. 'I take it they never vanished in a cloud o' smoke.'

'We spoke ter the greengrocer opposite an' 'e said that the woman an' kids went off in a van early this mornin',' the young man replied. 'Bannerman wasn't wiv 'em though.'

Archie waved the men from the office and sat back in his chair, raising his large hand to his forehead in frustration. It all seemed to be falling apart, he thought with a heavy sigh. Jack Murray was still hiding out somewhere, and with each hour that passed, the chance of recovering the money and plates was growing less likely. Even the relatively simple task of removing a grass from the manor had been thwarted. It was pure bad luck that Bannerman had decided to pick that particular day to skip the neighbourhood.

The office door opened and one of the yard men looked in. 'There's a young lad outside, guv,' he said quickly. ' 'E's got a letter for yer. 'E won't give it ter me.'

Archie puffed loudly. 'All right, send 'im in,' he growled.

That evening Laura sat chatting to Lucy while she waited for Eddie to call. They had planned to take an evening stroll and Laura was eager to feel his arms around her once more and experience again his passionate kisses that sent her weak at the knees. Her life was so good at the moment and as she listened to her younger sister she felt keenly sorry for her.

'I was 'opin' it would 'ave made some difference, but it don't seem to 'ave done,' Lucy was going on. 'Roy looked really angry when 'e went out. I do 'ope 'e don't 'ave a skinful ternight. 'E knows 'ow it affects 'im next mornin'.'

'I don't fink fer a minute it's you 'e's angry wiv,' Laura replied. 'I fink it's what yer told 'im about Archie Westlake that's troublin' 'im. I noticed 'ow 'is face changed when Dad was goin' on about the villains this evenin'. If looks could kill, Westlake would be dead by now.'

Lucy shrugged her shoulders and rubbed away at her fingernails with a small file. 'I 'ope Dad's gonna be all right ternight at the Sultan,' she said after a while. ' 'E's so unsteady when 'e's 'ad a drink.'

' 'E'll be okay. Joe Molloy said 'e'd see 'im 'ome ter the door,' Laura replied. 'Just make sure 'e gets inter bed properly. I don't fink I'll be too late, in any case.'

'Don't rush back,' Lucy told her as the doorknocker sounded.

Eddie and Laura walked briskly out of Pedlar's Row in the gathering dusk, his arm around her waist, the two of them smiling lovingly into each other's eyes. Lucy sighed as she peered through the parlour curtains, feeling a little envious at their uncomplicated and passionate love affair. How she hoped it would all come right for her and Roy very soon.

As the night settled in and storm clouds blacked out the moon, Bill Jordan got up and put on his reefer jacket. Sleep would be a better proposition, he thought wearily to himself, but he had to be fair to Susie. She had been cooped up in the house all day and she loved her evening out, no matter what the weather was like. 'Are yer ready, Susie?' he asked.

Susie came running and Bill fondly tickled her under the chin as he slipped on her lead and left his house in Weston Street. Susie pulled enthusiastically on the heavy-duty leash. She was a big mongrel, favouring an Alsatian but with a placid disposition, and only when he slipped the lead on the edge of the bomb site would she get excited.

Bill turned into Cooper Street and felt Susie straining against the leash. At the place where the corrugated fencing was buckled open he let her have her head and she bounded off into the darkness. Bill lit his pipe and waited. Susie was never more than a few minutes. As he stood in the blackness, feeling the warmth of the glowing pipe against his face, he suddenly heard her. It was not her usual bark, more like a throaty cough, and then she gave out a long, wolflike wail. Bill felt a shiver pass down his back and he hurried through the fencing on to the bomb site. Something was wrong, he knew. He called his dog's name and this time Susie answered with a full bark. He could see her now. She was standing further on, beside the ruined house, and she appeared to be snuffling warily at some kind of bundle. Bill reached her and suddenly a sensation of sheer horror paralysed his insides. There at his feet was the body of a man. He was lying on his stomach with his head turned to one side, his sightless eyes wide open. His throat had been cut from ear to ear, and the initials W.S. had been carved on his cheek.

Chapter Forty-Five

Laura and Eddie had spent a pleasant evening at Greenwich, and as they walked back into Pedlar's Row Laura felt deliriously happy. They had made many plans and the future looked exciting. Eddie had been very attentive and it felt good to have his arm around her as they strolled along the riverside and he smiled at her in that devilish way of his. He made her feel good and she knew that he was happy too.

When they walked into the parlour they found Lucy sitting alone and looking worried.

'Roy's not back yet an' Dad's still out as well,' she said with a sigh.

Laura slipped off her coat and hung it behind the room door. 'I don't s'pose they'll be back till the pubs turn out now,' she replied.

Eddie stood in the middle of the room, feeling a little self-conscious. 'D'yer want me ter slip up the Sultan an' see yer Dad 'ome?' he asked.

Laura shook her head. 'No fanks, Eddie, Joe Molloy said 'e'll bring 'im back,' she told him.

Lucy got up from her chair. 'Sit down, Eddie, I'll put the kettle on,' she said. 'It's boiled once. I bin waitin' fer Roy ter come in. 'E doesn't stay till the pub turns out as a rule.'

Laura gave Eddie a secret smile and followed her sister into the scullery. 'Don't get angry when Roy comes in, Lucy,' she said quietly. 'Yer makin' good progress, don't spoil it fer the two o' yer.'

Lucy nodded. 'Yeah, I know. I just 'ope Roy's not gonna start broodin' on what I told 'im. 'E must know I wouldn't 'ave said a word about it if there was somefing to 'ide.'

Sounds of singing came from outside the front door and Lucy pulled a face as she hurried into the passage. She heard some chuckling and Joe Molloy's deep voice bidding her father good night, and as she opened the door the old man staggered into the house, laughing his head off.

'Yer look like yer've 'ad a skinful,' Lucy remarked, propping him up as she led him into the parlour.

Eddie got up quickly and took Albert's other arm, guiding him down into his favourite chair. 'There yer go, Pop,' he said, smiling at Lucy.

'Yer a good lad, Eddie,' the old man slurred. 'I like yer, d'yer 'ear me?'

'Yeah, I 'ear yer,' Eddie replied, grinning.

'Our Laura's a good gel too. She deserves the best,' Albert went on as he tried to get his hand into his coat pocket. 'Where's me bloody pipe? I 'ad it when I went out.'

'There it is, yer just put it down on the fender,' Lucy told him crossly, glancing at Eddie and raising her eyes to the ceiling in exasperation. 'Now be careful, don't set yerself alight.'

Laura went down on her haunches and took the pipe from him. 'I'll fill it,' she said.

Albert smiled crookedly at Eddie. 'Yer got a good'un there, son,' he said, slowly raising his eyebrows in an effort to concentrate. 'She's a right little mum. Bin good to all of us, she 'as. I dunno what we'd 'ave done wivout 'er. Me wife died, yer see.'

Laura stood up and put her arm around her father's

shoulders as he broke down and wept. 'C'mon, Dad, yer better get ter bed,' she said kindly. 'Yer'll feel better in the mornin'.'

'I want me pipe,' Albert persisted.

'Now c'mon, Dad, it'll make yer cough ternight. Yer can 'ave it in the mornin',' Laura told him.

Albert allowed himself to be helped out of the room by Eddie and Laura. 'Bloody little squirt,' he growled. 'Who the bloody 'ell does 'e fink 'e is.'

'Who yer talkin' about, Dad?' Laura asked, grinning at Eddie.

'Why, that there publican,' Albert replied. ' 'E dunno 'is arse from 'is elbow. I dunno where they find 'em, I'm sure I don't.'

'C'mon, Pop, in yer go,' Eddie said, easing the old man's legs up on to the bed.

' 'E 'ad the cheek ter tell me an' Joe ter shut up,' Albert went on. 'Just 'cos me an' Joe was singin' "O'Reilly's Daughter". We told 'im ter piss orf. Joe said 'e was gonna slosh 'im but I told 'im ter be careful in case we got barred. It's nice an' 'andy, that Sultan.'

'Yeah, too 'andy at times,' Laura remarked. 'Now c'mon, Dad, settle yerself down.'

Ten minutes later there was a loud rat-tat on the door, and when Laura answered it she found Queenie Bromley standing there holding on to Roy.

' 'E fell against me door,' Queenie said. 'I couldn't get any sense out of 'im.'

Roy's face was chalk-white and he mumbled something as he was helped into the house. Lucy looked at Eddie appealingly. 'Can yer give us an 'and gettin' 'im upstairs?' she asked.

Eddie nodded quickly and slipped his hands under Roy's arms, straightening him up against the passage wall before taking him in a fireman's lift. Lucy followed them up the narrow stairs and signalled towards the bedroom.

Eddie gently eased Roy down on to the bed, turning him on to his back, and Lucy bent down and loosened his collar. 'I'd better get 'im undressed,' she sighed.

As Eddie started to remove Roy's clothes he noticed that his shoes and the turn-ups of his trousers were wet. He glanced quickly at Lucy and folded the trousers over a chair before she saw them. He helped make Roy comfortable and then went back down to the parlour.

'I'm sorry yer got lumbered,' Laura said, smiling appreciatively.

Eddie gave her a quick reassuring grin. 'It was no trouble,' he replied, looking towards the room door before showing her his hands. 'This came off Roy's shoes an' trouser turn-ups,' he said quietly. 'It's blood, by the look of it. It's still sticky.'

'Is Roy all right?' Laura asked anxiously.

'It didn't come from 'im,' Eddie told her. ' 'E must 'ave bin standin' in it.'

Laura's eyes widened. 'I won't say anyfing ter Lucy, she'll be worried enough as it is,' she murmured.

Eddie saw the concern on Laura's face and he reached out for her. She went to him and snuggled close, comforted by the feel of his strong arms around her as he held her tightly. 'Somefing bad's 'appened, Eddie,' she whispered. 'I can feel it.'

They moved apart quickly as Lucy came down the stairs, and both could see the worried look on her face.

'I fink 'e's bin drinkin' whisky. It smells like it on 'is breath,' she said. 'I've never known Roy ter touch whisky. Whatever it was certainly knocked 'im out anyway. 'E's sleepin' like a baby.'

Laura glanced briefly at Eddie. 'I'd better make that tea,' she told him.

'Fanks fer what yer did,' Lucy said, smiling at Eddie. 'I'd better knock at Queenie's an' fank 'er before she turns in fer the night.'

As soon as she left the house Laura hurried up the stairs and examined Roy's shoes and trousers. 'It's definitely blood,' she said to Eddie. 'I'll 'ave ter get it off as soon as Lucy goes ter bed. I don't want 'er ter see it.'

Wally Stebbings arrived home late that evening, feeling very pleased with himself. For years he had felt that he was walking in everyone else's shadow, and now he had finally stepped out into the light. His mother must never know what he had accomplished that evening, she would be horrified. In the fullness of time, however, she would come to see that her only son was well able to stand on his own two feet and make a life for himself.

Wally went into the parlour and saw his mother sitting beside an empty grate with her head resting against the back of the armchair and a piece of embroidery lying in her lap. She woke up suddenly and immediately glanced up at the ornate clock on the mantelshelf. 'You're late, I was gettin' worried,' she said irritably.

'It's only eleven o'clock, Mother,' Wally replied, taking off his overcoat and hanging it on the back of the door. 'Molly was playing me some of her operatic records. We didn't notice the time.'

Annie puffed loudly. 'I s'pose she realises yer've got ter go ter work termorrer.'

Wally sat down heavily in the armchair facing her. 'I've become very fond of Molly, and she's very fond of me,' he said quietly. 'I wish you could get to like her, Mum. She's a very feeling lady and she likes you a lot.'

Annie snorted. 'She's too bloody 'oity-toity fer my likin', an' she's got you right under 'er thumb already. Gawd knows what it'd be like if yer ever got married to 'er.'

'As a matter of fact, Molly would make a very nice

499

wife,' Wally said with passion. 'She's very considerate, she's good-hearted, and what's more, she's loyal. I've not forgotten how she stuck by me over that affair at Clyde's. You have to remember too that it was Molly who got me my present job. I don't know where I would have been without her.'

'Yer just too daft ter see it,' Annie went on. 'She's missed the boat as far as she's concerned, an' then you come along. It's 'er last chance an' she ain't gonna frow it up. She might be all sweetness an' light now, but just wait till she gets a ring on 'er finger. Yer'll be expected ter do everyfing for 'er. I know that sort only too well.'

Wally looked down at his clenched hands, trying to avoid making an angry retort. For years he had pandered to his mother's wishes, and he was beginning to see where it had led. She was old now and frightened of being left alone. Any woman he brought home would be given short shrift. If only he had asserted himself when he was younger, this situation could have been averted. Well, he had finally found a woman and he was not going to let his mother spoil it for him. Molly had been instrumental in helping him overcome his shyness and lack of confidence, and tonight he had proved himself.

'Yer'd better take yer cocoa up ter bed wiv yer or yer'll never get up in the mornin',' Annie said offhandedly as she got up to go to her own bedroom.

Jack Murray peered through the net curtains of his upstairs room at the dark cobbled street below. It was all quiet except for the night-patrol policeman who plodded slowly along the pavement, his thumbs tucked into his black leather belt. In Deptford nobody asked too many questions, and Murray felt that it was as safe as any area of London for a fugitive from justice. He had paid a month's rent in advance for the room and the elderly couple who lived in the house were more than happy with the arrangement. Here in riverside Deptford he could wait in reasonable safety until Ernie Jackson arranged the meeting with the money men. In a week or two his shoulder would be properly healed, and with a bit of luck he would be set up for the future and on his way to a new life. Once Ernie had contacted Alma and she had read his letter she would see that her future was with him. The detective she was seeing didn't mean anything to her, he felt sure. Alma would send him packing like the last man in her life.

Jack Murray went over to the dresser and poured himself a stiff whisky. He had been the dogsbody for Westlake for more years than he cared to remember and none of the mob had ever taken his opinions seriously. He was always seen as the hard man. 'You come with me, Jack, there might be trouble,' had been a favourite expression of Archie's. Well, now he had shown them all. The mob as a force to be reckoned with was finished. Its leaders were dead or had had it and the young villains stepping on to the scene were like a crew without a captain, he thought. The police would soon pick them off one by one, but they would never get him, not alive. He had done enough time to know what it was all about and he could not take another term of imprisonment.

Jack Murray carried his glass of whisky over to the window and peered out into the darkness once more. Suddenly he saw Ernie Jackson come into view beneath the light of the gaslamp. He was hurrying along with his coat collar turned up. Good old Ernie, Jack thought. He was the only one he could trust now and Ernie wouldn't let him down.

A few minutes later the foreman printer sat in front of the unlit gas fire, sipping his whisky. 'I managed to get the letter to Alma's sister,' he said. 'She promised to give it to Alma soon as she could.'

'Yer done well, Ernie,' Murray told him. ' 'Ere, let's top yer drink up.'

The printer held out his half-empty glass. 'I'll see about the phone call first thing tomorrow,' he said. 'It shouldn't be any trouble.'

'Are yer sure yer got the plates in a safe place?' Murray asked.

'They're as safe as in the Bank of England,' Ernie replied, laughing nervously.

The fugitive walked over to the dresser and took out an envelope from the drawer. 'I want yer ter take a look at these,' he said.

Ernie glanced at the photos and gave Murray a puzzled look. 'I can see it's Alma, but who's the bloke?' he asked.

'That's Detective Sergeant Gordon Ashley, currently stationed at Dock'ead nick,' Murray told him. 'I put one o' these snaps in the letter to Alma. Once she shows it ter the tec 'e'll be up an' runnin'.'

'Do you think she will show it to him?' Jackson asked.

'I fink she will,' Murray replied, smiling evilly. 'Alma soon tires of 'er fancy blokes. That'll be a nice way o' gettin' out from under, if yer get the drift.'

Ernie Jackson did not feel so optimistic but he nodded. 'I'm sure you're right,' he said tensely.

'I know I'm right. You'll see,' Murray replied.

The printer finished his drink and shivered involuntarily as he prepared to leave. It was all getting too dangerous, he thought. Doing a bit of counterfeiting was one thing, but being an accessory after the fact was something else.

'There's anuvver little favour I want yer ter do fer me, Ernie,' the villain said, pointing to the envelope. 'I want yer ter keep this in a safe place fer the time bein'. If anyfing 'appens ter me, yer know where ter send it.'

Ernie nodded, feeling himself slowly getting sucked

further and further into an inextricable situation. 'Sure thing,' he said anxiously as he buttoned up his coat.

In dark and gloomy Cooper Street Bill Jordan stood guard at the entrance to the bomb site. His dog Susie sat obediently beside him, enjoying her ears being ruffled. Bill had lived in Bermondsey all his life and never had he known such times. Talk of the recent killings was still on everyone's lips, and now there was another. This one was the most horrific of all, and he, or rather Susie, was the one who had discovered it. He had hurried over to the Anchor to make a phone call and the police had told him to remain at the scene until they could get there. 'We're gonna be in the papers termorrer, you an' me, ole gel,' he told Susie, shivering with a mixture of excitement and revulsion. Who could be so sadistic as to carve letters on a man's face? he asked himself. It was like the days of Jack the Ripper all over again.

Suddenly the quietness was shattered as police cars turned noisily into the street, and Bill stood talking reassuringly to Susie as he watched the first car skid to a halt. A large ginger-haired man got out and came towards him and Susie growled.

'Mr Jordan? I'm Inspector Walsh, Dockhead Police. Can you show me where the body is?'

Bill led the way, followed by the inspector and two other plain-clothes policemen. For a few moments Walsh stood looking down at the body, then he turned to his sergeant, a ghost of a smile touching his lips.

'So somebody finally sorted out Archie Westlake, then,' he said.

Chapter Forty-Six

When the milkman delivered to the leather factory in Cooper Street early on Thursday morning, he noticed police activity at the bomb site and saw that the area had been cordoned off. He was unable to get any information out of the two policemen guarding the fence, but when he delivered to the buildings where Bill Jordan lived he heard the full story. Bill also told the proprietor of the corner paper shop and within a very short time everyone in the area knew that there had been another killing.

People discussed the murder on their way to work and the Tower Bridge Road market was buzzing with the story. Strange faces appeared in the area and many questions were being asked.

'Yer gotta be careful wiv them reporters,' Maggie Palfrey told her customers. 'It don't do ter tell 'em anyfing. That Archie Westlake 'ad a lot o' people workin' fer 'im. One o' them reporters come ter me this mornin' an' asked me if I'd 'eard anyfing. I told 'im I didn't know what 'e was talkin' about an' 'e said there was a murder round 'ere last night. "Was there?" I sez to 'im. "Yeah, the local gang boss got bumped off," 'e sez. "Gawd 'elp us," I sez, just like that, an' 'e starts askin' questions about this Archie Westlake. "I don't know the bloke," I sez. "Yer'd better ask one o' the ovver stall-'olders." 'E went an' spoke ter Sammy Israel but I

504

don't fink 'e told 'im anyfing, not if I know Sammy.'

Early that morning Pedlar's Row was alive with rumour. Elsie Carmichael knocked on Queenie Bromley's front door and gave her the news.

'Archie Westlake got murdered last night, Queenie,' she said breathlessly. ' 'E 'ad 'is froat slit, by all accounts. They found 'im on the bomb site in Cooper Street.'

Queenie took the news in her usual way, showing little surprise, and making her customary acid comment. 'Well, 'e won't be bovverin' the likes of us again, that's fer sure,' she remarked.

Elsie was disappointed at the woman's response and she decided to try Annie Stebbings. Annie was more forthcoming and the two women stood talking eagerly together for some time.

'It's gettin' like old Chicago round 'ere lately,' Elsie went on. 'That's the third one in a week. Gawd knows what the place is comin' to.'

'Westlake got 'is just deserts, if yer ask me,' Annie replied. ' 'E was the one be'ind what they did ter my Wally. That boy's never got over it prop'ly. What wiv that, an' that woman 'e's got 'iked up wiv, it's enough ter put me in me grave.'

Bridie Molloy knocked at number three and told Albert the news, and he felt an urgent need to go and tell Annie Stebbings.

'Yeah, I've just 'eard,' she said. 'Elsie Carmichael told me.'

Albert cursed under his breath. 'I 'ope she didn't frighten yer, luv,' he said with concern. 'That woman does go on a bit.'

Annie nodded. 'I dunno why she come an' told me. As if I ain't got enough ter fink about.'

Albert saw his chance. 'Yer don't look very well, it must 'ave put the wind up yer,' he remarked casually.

'What you should 'ave is a nice Guinness. It steadies yer nerves, yer know. Why don't yer pop up the Sultan fer a bevvy? I'm goin' up there, I'd be pleased ter buy yer a drink.'

Annie smiled. 'I might just do that, Albert.'

'I'll give yer a knock about twelve,' he told her.

'No, yer better not,' Annie replied. 'Yer know 'ow people talk. I'll see yer up there.'

Albert went back into his house, feeling pleased with himself. He had been trying to think of some way to lure Annie out for a drink and now he had succeeded. He glanced at his reflection in the mantelshelf mirror and thought that it might be a good idea to wash his hair and have a shave. 'Where's she put that Lux Flakes?' he mumbled to himself.

Laura had left for her cleaning job at the Sultan unaware of the news, and when the manager told her about the killing her heart missed a beat.

'The milkman told me,' he went on. 'Someone walking their dog found him late last night. Terrible sight it was apparently. There was blood everywhere.'

Laura worked in a daze, constantly going over the events of the previous night in her mind. Lucy had told her how angry Roy had become when she confided in him about Archie Westlake, and he had gone out to the pub looking very strange. He had come in later with his shoes and trousers stained with blood and this morning he had gone off to work looking very pale and drawn. No, it was impossible that Roy could have had anything to do with the murder, Laura told herself. Roy was a gentle, easy-going man who had suffered terribly as a prisoner, and he was verging on the brink of a nervous breakdown. There was no way he could have been callous enough to slit the villain's throat, no matter how he felt about him.

As she walked home Laura was still deep in thought. Only she and Eddie knew about the blood on Roy's clothes. She had thought it better not to mention it to Lucy that morning, and by then all traces of the blood had been removed. She had washed Roy's trousers late last night and hung them in the back yard to dry, and this morning she had got up extra early to iron them. Lucy had been her usual miserable self when she got out of bed and had not even noticed the freshly ironed trousers hanging over the banisters outside her bedroom. Roy hadn't mentioned anything either before he left for work, and Laura felt that she should let the matter drop and cast the whole thing from her mind. The police would obviously be making calls, as they had over the other killings, and the less she remembered the better for Roy, for all of them.

Chief Inspector Ben Walsh had been hurriedly summoned from a retirement dinner for one of his old friends to go to the murder site, and he had only been able to snatch a few hours' sleep before the meeting with the Assistant Commissioner. He felt exhausted as he slumped down at his desk, and after his third cup of strong coffee he picked up the phone. 'Send Detective Sergeant Ashley in right away and bring us a fresh pot of coffee, Sergeant. Thanks.'

Ashley walked in, carrying a folder and looking heavy-eyed. His fatigue was obvious as he sat down facing his superior officer. 'How was the meeting?' he asked.

Walsh shook his head slowly. 'Sanders read me the riot act,' he growled. 'He said it was, quote, "unacceptable and disgraceful that the streets were given over to blood-letting by the villains", unquote. The gist of the meeting was that we apprehend the perpetrator at the earliest. At least we've got the manpower now. There's a murder squad coming in this morning from the Yard.

Our first priority is to find Jack Murray. Agreed?'

Ashley nodded and flipped open the folder. 'The path. lab report says that Westlake was killed instantly with a sharp, thin-bladed knife, which severed his right carotid artery as it was drawn across his throat from right to left.'

Inspector Walsh held out his hand for the report and leaned back in his chair, mumbling to himself as he studied the contents. After a while he threw the folder down on the desk and stood up. 'Right, Gordon, get down on your hands and knees,' he said suddenly. The sergeant looked surprised and Walsh pointed to the carpet. 'Come on, man, we haven't got all day.'

Ashley knelt down on all fours and Walsh stood to his left side.

'Now this is how I see it,' Walsh began. 'I'm pretty certain that Westlake was in that position when the knife was plunged in, so.'

Ashley lifted his head sharply as the inspector reached down under his chin and pressed a finger on the right-hand side of his neck, quickly drawing a line under his throat.

'That tells us that the killer was most probably left-handed,' Walsh continued. 'Now, we found Westlake lying a foot away from the wall of the derelict house. There was blood under him, and it had run down the slope and puddled a few inches behind his outstretched legs. We know that blood spurts from a severed artery, and there was no blood on the house wall, which is why I say that Westlake was in the position you're in when he was killed, but with his head facing downwards, as though he was looking for something. We can back that up by the marks on the small patch of sandy rubble. There were two deep indentations and toe marks, which looked like they were made by the victim kneeling. Unfortunately the attacker left no visible footprints because he was standing on the hard rubble to the left of the body. Now, when Westlake's throat was cut he fell forward, and his face was turned towards his attacker, who then sliced the initials on his cheek. After I sent you off home, Sergeant, I waited around until the body was taken away. Where it had been lying there was a small hole in the soil which was in fact a broken water pipe. Now, to the right of the pipe was a slab of concrete and I found scuff marks that had been hidden by the body. In other words, Westlake knelt down, removed the slab of concrete, and was just about to put his hand into the hole when he was killed. Are you with me?'

'It sounds right,' Ashley replied as he got to his feet. 'But what was Westlake looking for, and who was it who lured him on to the bomb site?'

The inspector sat down in his chair and stroked his chin thoughtfully. 'When Murray was being chased by the mob and dashed into the Leather Bottle pub, he was carrying a suitcase and a small grip bag,' he went on. 'Murray went out into the pub yard, over the back wall and made off. Now Westlake could have assumed he was still carrying the grip bag, which we believe contained the counterfeit plates that were presumably handed over to someone in the pub yard. Danny Steadman knew that Murray wasn't carrying the bag because he confronted him in Cooper Street, but Steadman's dead. So it's possible that Murray contacted Westlake to do a deal, luring him on to the bomb site with the story that he hid the plates there after he was wounded because they were too heavy to carry any further. It would follow that Westlake removed the heavy slab because he was aware that Murray was too weak from the bullet wound to do it himself. It was as he was fishing for the plates that Murray killed him. I know it's a lot of supposition,' Walsh concluded, 'and my theory doesn't explain away the carved initials, but we've got very little evidence to go on.'

Ashley nodded affirmatively. 'It sounds very plausible, if we're to assume that it was Murray who killed him,' he said.

'I'm building a case against Jack Murray on the basis that he's the last of the mob leaders,' Walsh replied. 'The others who are left we know to be small fry, without the brains or the inclination to don the mantle. We need to find Murray as soon as possible, or I'll be driven right up the bloody wall by the Assistant Commissioner. He wants results by yesterday.'

The conversation was interrupted by a tap on the door and the station sergeant put his head into the office. 'Got a minute, guv?' he asked.

'Come in, George,' Walsh replied.

'I've been going through all the stuff we have on the mob and there's one bit of info that I've just spotted which might be relevant,' the sergeant said, looking pleased with himself. 'A man who lives in Pedlar's Row was beaten up a few weeks ago by a couple of toughs who were in the pay of Westlake, according to the victim's neighbours. I found a copy of the beat bobby's report in the file.'

'There must be scores of people who've found themselves on the sharp end of Archie Westlake and company,' Walsh said quickly.

'Yeah, but this particular man's name was Wally Stebbings, guv. W.S.?'

'Good man,' Walsh replied. 'Get his address, we'll follow it up.'

Ashley suddenly recalled the meeting he had had with John Bannerman. The snout had said that a local man had been beaten up and that it was Westlake's doing. 'Do we bring him in, guv?' he asked.

'We've got to be seen to be moving on this one, Sergeant, or the newspapers as well as Sanders are going to crucify us,' the inspector grumbled. 'Bring the man in for questioning.'

★ ★ ★

Elsie Carmichael had finally decided that she would part company with Clyde's box factory, and she had managed to find herself some homework with a toy firm in Tower Bridge Road. It entailed painting faces on tiny soldiers which were made from a composite material and supplied in packets of ten to toy stalls in the market as Christmas stocking fillers. Once a week Elsie went to the firm and collected a dozen or so boxes of the soldiers, bringing them home on an old pram she had bought from the local totter, and for each box completed she earned the princely sum of two shillings and sixpence.

When Len first saw the work involved he became angry. 'There must be fousands in each box,' he said sharply. 'Yer've gotta paint a blob on fer the face, then when they're dry yer gotta put the eyes on. It's bloody slave labour.'

Elsie would have none of Len's negativity. 'Look, it's dead easy,' she told him. 'Yer put a dab of paint on 'ere an' line 'em up ter dry. I can do a box in two hours. Then when they're ready yer just dip the pen in the ink an' make the eyes. The firm gives yer the pink paint. I just 'ave ter get the ink.'

'That's very nice of 'em,' Len said sarcastically. 'Two hours ter paint the faces an' I reckon anuvver hour ter put the eyes on. That's three hours fer a box, an' at 'alf a crown a box I make it ten pence an hour. Bloody charmin'.'

Elsie was tempted to give her husband the sharp edge of her tongue, but she decided not to upset him because she had plans for him. If he were to put the eyes on the painted blobs then she could be getting on with the second box. It would mean him giving up the pub on a couple of his nights off, but it was for the benefit of them both in the long run, she told herself. Besides, working at home allowed her to have a break when she felt like it, and this morning Elsie needed to take time off and consort with her neighbours about the terrible events that were taking place locally.

As she stood talking to Bridie Molloy at the door of number four, a car pulled up at the Cooper Street end of the Row and three men got out. They were carrying clipboards and other items that Elsie could not see clearly.

'They're plain-clothes coppers,' she declared.

'I don't fink so,' Bridie remarked. 'They look like council men.'

Elsie and Bridie stood watching closely as the three men walked into the Row and started measuring the factory wall facing the row of houses. One of the men then came over to them. 'We'd like to inspect inside your homes if it's not too inconvenient,' he said.

Bridie looked at him suspiciously. 'What for?' she asked.

'I'm sorry, I should have said. We're from the works department of the Bermondsey Borough Council,' the man replied. 'We're doing a survey. We won't disrupt you at all. In fact the inspection won't take more than a few minutes.'

Bridie nodded reluctantly but Elsie was less co-operative. 'I dunno. I've got me soldiers all out on the table. I can't move 'em just yet awhile,' she said quickly.

The leader of the workmen gave Elsie a peculiar glance and decided not to enquire further about her soldiers. 'Maybe we could have a quick look in your house now,' he suggested to Bridie.

Elsie walked unenthusiastically back to her own house to get on with the face painting, thinking that Len might be right after all. She had spent at least two hours on one box of soldiers and it wasn't finished yet.

Albert Prior was feeling very chirpy that morning and was looking forward to his lunchtime drink with Annie Stebbings. He took a stroll to the paper shop at eleven o'clock to get the racing edition of the *Star* and when he came back he went straight out into the scullery where Laura was doing the washing. ' 'Ere, gel, there's a lot in the paper about that murder last night,' he told her. 'There's a big bit 'ere about the police not doin' their job prop'ly.'

Laura took the paper from him and sat down on the rickety chair while she read the article. In one column there was a photo of Jack Murray above a caption that said, 'Wanted for questioning'.

'It sez there that they're after Jack Murray fer the murder,' Albert remarked.

Laura felt sick with worry. Should she tell Lucy about discovering the blood on Roy's clothes, she agonised, or should she approach Roy in secret? Either way it could cause further problems in her sister's very precarious marriage. Perhaps it was best to let things rest. There could be a genuine reason for the bloodstains after all. Roy could have staggered on to the bomb site to relieve himself on his way home from the pub and inadvertently stepped into the blood. Yes, that was it. It had to be the answer, she told herself.

She put the paper down and sighed deeply. Albert was standing in front of her, looking very pleased with himself, and she realised that she had been ignoring him.

'I thought yer might notice me barnet,' he said, running a hand through his thinning grey hair that had suddenly become very fluffy.

'What yer bin doin' to it, Dad?' she asked him, hiding a smile.

'I give it a wash in Lux Flakes,' he replied. 'It certainly makes it stand up a bit. I 'ad a nice shave too.'

'I can see that by the bits o' fag paper stuck on yer face,' she said. 'Was it a new blade?'

'I'm goin' up the Sultan,' Albert announced with a large grin. 'I'm meetin' Annie Stebbin's there. I wanted ter look a bit decent. There's no sense in lettin' yerself go, is there?'

The loud knock on the front door startled them and when Laura hurried out to answer it she found Annie Stebbings on the step, looking very distressed. 'It's me poor Wally,' she said tearfully.

'Whatever's 'appened?' Laura asked, helping the frantic woman into the parlour.

'The police come fer Wally a few minutes ago,' Annie sobbed. 'I told em 'e was at work an' they wanted the address of 'is firm. They said 'e's wanted fer questionin' about that murder last night.'

Laura felt hot with fear and her heart was pounding as Albert took Annie by the hand and led her to a chair. 'Sit yerself down, gel. It won't be nuffink ter worry about,' he said kindly. 'It's only fer questionin'.'

Annie sat in the parlour of number three for some time, nervously twisting a handkerchief round her fingers as she tried vainly to halt her fits of crying. Albert finally managed to calm her down a little and coax her out to the Sultan for a quick drink, convincing the worried woman that a drop of rum and port was the finest thing for a nervous stomach.

Laura got on with the cleaning in an attempt to relieve her anxiety, and while she was washing down the dresser she discovered something that suddenly made her blood turn to ice. She had pulled the dresser slightly away from the wall and tilted it to flatten down a piece of floor covering when she heard something drop. She now pulled it far enough away from the wall to get her arm behind it and her fingers closed over something metallic. She drew out her hand to see that she was holding a long, thin knife. The blade felt very sharp and it was stained a dull red.

Chapter Forty-Seven

Wally Stebbings sat back in his chair and took off his glasses to rub his tired eyes. The figures seemed to be floating about on the invoices and he had already had to make a few adjustments to his calculations. It was unlike him, he thought. Usually the figures balanced correctly, and he could only put it down to his recent spell of late nights and his outings with Molly. His mother was probably right after all about the late hours affecting his job, though he dared not admit it to her. She was acting very coldly towards Molly and he knew that she was worried about his future. He would have to pull himself together before some mistakes showed up in the half-yearly figures.

The office junior hurried over to Wally's desk in the far corner of the spacious office and stood self-consciously in front of him. 'Mr Winston would like to see you in his office right away,' the lad said quickly.

Wally put his glasses back on and hurried along to the inner sanctum, observed curiously by the rest of the office staff.

'Come in, Mr Stebbings. Now what have you been up to?' the office manager said, peering over his gold-rimmed spectacles.

Wally looked in confusion at the rotund figure, whose belly seemed to be flowing out over the desktop. 'I beg your pardon, Mr Winston?' Wally replied.

'There's a policeman in reception and he would like to have a word with you right away,' Winston said in his nasal tone.

Wally shook his head nervously, feeling his face colouring up. 'I'm sure I don't know what the police would want with me,' he replied.

'You'd better find out then,' the manager told him abruptly.

Wally walked into the small reception area to see a young man sitting down on a low seat, reading a magazine. He got up quickly. 'Mr Stebbings?'

'Yes,' Wally replied, looking anxious.

'We're making enquiries about the murder in Cooper Street last night and we think you might be able to help us,' the detective said, smiling disarmingly.

Wally's face drained of colour and he made to sit down. 'I don't see as I can be of any help, but . . . '

'We'd prefer you to come down the station, Mr Stebbings, if you wouldn't mind?' the detective said quickly.

'Of course, but I'd better let the manager know,' Wally answered breathlessly.

Ten minutes later Wally Stebbings found himself sitting in a small room containing only two wooden chairs and a heavy oak table. The walls and ceiling were whitewashed and the door had a small glass panel through which he could see a constant parade of policemen. Wally glanced up at the high window and suddenly felt nauseous. What could the police want with him? he fretted. Surely they didn't suspect him of having anything to do with the murder?

The door opened and a stocky ginger-haired policeman came into the room. 'Mr Stebbings?'

Wally nodded. 'Yes, sir.'

The policeman introduced himself as Chief Inspector Walsh, then sat down and looked searchingly at the frightened man. 'I understand that a few weeks ago you were subjected to a beating by two young men, and this beating took place on the bomb site in Cooper Street, am I correct?'

'Yes, I was, but it was stopped by some of my neighbours before I was badly hurt,' Wally replied.

'Would you have been badly hurt if it wasn't for your neighbours, Mr Stebbings?' Walsh asked him.

'I feel that I might have been killed,' Wally said with conviction.

'You know who did this to you, I believe,' Walsh remarked.

'Everyone seems to think it was Archie Westlake who was behind it,' Wally replied.

'Everyone?'

'All my neighbours.'

'And what about you? Do you feel Westlake was responsible for your beating?'

Wally nodded. 'Yes, I do.'

'Can you tell me why Westlake would want to single you out for a beating?' Walsh asked.

Wally dropped his head and stared down at his sweating hands. 'I'm seen as something of a curiosity, I suppose,' Wally began. 'I'm single, I don't like pubs and I still live at home with my widowed mother. Recently there was an attempt to lure a little girl away from some buildings near where I live and I was suspected of being the person involved.'

'Were you?'

'Certainly not. I think that sort of thing is appalling. In fact I think it's evil,' Wally replied forcefully.

'Was there any other reason you could think of why you should be suspected of trying to lure this young girl away?' Walsh asked him.

'There are two young lads who live a few doors away from me and I was making them a model fort,' Wally explained. 'They used to come into my house to watch me building it. It's my hobby, you see.'

'Model-making, you mean?'

'Yes. I was never alone with the two boys. My mother was always there too.'

'I see.'

Wally felt the policeman's eyes boring into him, and he lowered his head once more. The sudden silence made him feel apprehensive and he swallowed hard. 'I'm afraid I can't help you any more, sir,' he said in a voice he could hardly recognise.

'I wonder why you didn't report the attack to the police, Mr Stebbings?' Walsh remarked. 'Were you too frightened, or were you intending to mete out your own justice?'

'I just wanted to forget it as quickly as possible,' Wally replied. 'I certainly didn't want to seek revenge.'

'Did you slit Archie Westlake's throat?' Walsh asked suddenly.

'No, of course I didn't,' Wally almost shouted. 'I couldn't kill anybody.'

'Can you give me an indication of where you were last night between the hours of nine p.m. and eleven thirty p.m.?' Walsh enquired.

Wally looked into the inspector's eyes. 'I was with a young lady,' he replied. 'She can vouch for me.'

'Is she your regular young lady?' Walsh asked.

'Yes, and we are intending to get married later this year,' Wally told him.

'Is there anyone else who could substantiate your movements last night?' the inspector asked.

Wally thought for a few moments, then shook his head. 'I went round to see Molly at about seven thirty and we played records for quite a while,' he replied. 'I left her house at ten minutes to eleven and the walk home took twenty minutes, give or take a minute.'

'You know why you've been asked to come in and see us, don't you, Mr Stebbings?' Walsh remarked.

'Because I was beaten up by Westlake's men and you thought I might have taken my revenge,' Wally said quickly.

'Yes, that's true,' the inspector replied, 'but there was another reason. Your initials are W.S. and those initials were carved on the dead man's face. So you see, Mr Stebbings, you're a suspect.'

Wally felt a wave of sickness rise up in his stomach and he swallowed hard. 'I wouldn't be so stupid as to advertise the fact that I'd killed him, if I had,' he answered firmly.

Walsh smiled briefly. 'It wouldn't be the first time that a killer left his personal visiting card on a body, thinking that we would not suspect such an obvious identification. It's an old ploy, believe me.'

'I think I want to be sick,' Wally said suddenly, his face chalkwhite.

'The toilet's across the passageway,' Walsh told him.

Later, after Wally had composed himself and made a statement, which he duly signed, the inspector stood up and sighed. 'You're free to leave, Mr Stebbings,' he said, 'but we might want to talk to you again in the near future, so if you've any plans to go anywhere, will you let us know?'

Wally put on his trilby, picked up his rolled umbrella and made for the door. 'I hope you catch the murderer quickly,' he said, turning. 'It's disgusting, the goings-on in this area lately.'

Inspector Walsh winced at Wally's remark, and when he left the interview room and saw Sergeant Ashley he shook his head slowly. 'If he killed Westlake then I'm the Duke of Clarence,' he growled. 'I suppose we'd better check his statement anyway.'

★ ★ ★

520

Molly French was ecstatically happy as her fingers flew over the typewriter keys. Normally she would have been feeling a little hard done by with all the work that was constantly piling up, but today was a special day for her. Molly recalled with a joyous feeling how last night she and Wally had consummated their love for each other, and she could still feel a tingle that constantly rippled up and down her spine. Wally had needed some prompting, and she herself had had to get over the embarrassment of him seeing her without most of her clothes, but true love had prevailed, regardless. They had turned off the light, nervously fumbling in the darkness to the emotional strains of *Aida*. Wally had been profuse with his apologies and she had had to suppress her giggles as he clumsily stroked her aching body, but then it suddenly happened. It was quick and urgent and she would have liked it to go on forever, but it mattered not. All her life she had waited for the right man and now she had found him.

'You're looking very chirpy today,' one of the typists remarked.

Molly wanted to tell her young colleague that she was in love, but instead she gave her a sly grin. The typist however took the first opportunity to pass a quiet remark.

'You don't reckon her Wally's given her one, do you?' she asked her close friend.

'You're joking,' the girl remarked. 'That feller of hers probably thinks it's for stirring his tea, I should imagine. People their age don't do it, anyway.'

Molly happily carried on with her work until lunchtime, then as she stepped out of Clyde's factory into the spring sunshine she saw Annie Stebbings hurrying towards her. Nothing was going to spoil today, not even Wally's miserable mother, Molly told herself. 'Hello,

Mrs Stebbings, you look worried, are you all right?' she asked pleasantly.

'I fink I've a right ter be worried,' Annie said quickly. 'The police came fer my Wally this mornin'.'

Molly had not bargained for news of that sort and her face dropped. 'Whatever for?' she asked.

'It's to 'elp wiv their enquiries about the Westlake murder, so they told me,' Annie replied. 'They wanted ter know where 'e worked. I s'pose they've gone there ter talk to 'im.'

Molly made her excuses and hurried off to Tooley Street. She arrived at Wally's workplace out of breath and feeling upset, and the receptionist only added to her anxiety by telling her that the police had taken him away and he had not come back as yet. There was only one thing to do now, she thought. She would have to go to the Dockhead Police Station.

As she hurried along Tooley Street Molly was getting more and more angry at the police for having the nerve to suspect her Wally, and by the time she arrived at the police station and ran up the entrance steps she was livid.

'What have you done with my Wally?' Molly shouted at the desk sergeant.

'I 'aven't touched yer Wally,' the sergeant replied, smiling at his jest.

'Don't you get saucy with me, young man,' Molly said angrily, looking up at him from her full five feet four inches. 'I want to speak to the officer in charge.'

Chief Inspector Walsh was finally summoned and he took Molly into the same room where he had interviewed Wally just a short time ago. 'How can I help you, Miss . . . er. . . '

'Miss French,' Molly replied quickly. 'I believe you're holding my future husband here, a Mr Stebbings, and I'd like to know what for.'

'We're not holding anybody at the moment, but we

did interview Mr Stebbings a short time ago,' Walsh told her. 'As a matter of fact he said he was with you last night. Is that correct?'

Molly sighed deeply as she took the proffered chair. 'Yes, Wally was with me,' she replied.

'And what time would that be?'

'We were together all evening, from seven until very late, around eleven, I would say.'

'You were in all evening?'

'Yes, we were.'

'Was anyone else with you?'

'Certainly not . . . I mean, no.'

Walsh stifled a smile. 'You'll understand we have to follow all leads,' he told her. 'If you don't know already you'll soon read it in the newspapers, but Archie Westlake, the murdered man, had initials carved on his cheek, presumably by his killer. The initials were W.S.'

'How awful,' Molly said, shivering. 'Why ever would they do a thing like that?'

'Weird and wonderful are the workings of the criminal mind,' Walsh sighed. ' "Though this be madness, yet there is method in't." '

'That's from *Hamlet*, isn't it?' Molly queried.

'Do you like Shakespeare?' Walsh asked by way of reply.

Molly nodded, feeling a little more relaxed now. This policeman was obviously cultured and he would not be likely to convict an innocent man. 'I enjoy literature, opera and art,' she told him, smiling. 'Wally is a music lover too, and I'm encouraging him to read more. Believe me, Officer, Wally Stebbings was with me last night, and he's incapable of harming a fly.'

The inspector nodded briefly. 'We have to follow all leads, Miss French. You do understand?'

Molly stood up and buttoned her long coat. 'I'm reminded of another quote from *Hamlet*,' she said,

smiling. ' "The lady doth protest too much, methinks."
I'm glad you didn't choose to quote that one.'

Inspector Walsh waited until Molly French had left the
room, then he sought out Detective Sergeant Ashley.
'Gordon. Assemble the team in my office, pronto,' he
growled. 'I want all the stops pulled out on this one.
We're going hunting for Murray.'

All day long Laura had agonised over her discovery of
the knife. She had placed it on top of the dresser,
puzzling over what had happened the previous night.
Roy had been helped into the house in a state of collapse
and Eddie had carried him to bed straight away. The
knife wasn't in Roy's belt or in his trouser pockets or
Eddie would have discovered it when he carried him up
the stairs and took off his clothes. If it was the murder
weapon then it must have been in his coat pocket, and
Roy had remembered to hide it before he went out to
work this morning. Alternatively, Lucy might have
found it in his coat when she hung it up in the bedroom
and then hid it herself after seeing the blood on Roy's
trousers. But then she had no way of knowing that Roy
had killed Westlake, Laura thought, unless he confessed
to her when he woke up this morning. Lucy could then
have hidden the knife before she left for work.

Laura pinched her bottom lip as she sat in the quiet
parlour listening to her father's even snoring. It still
seemed unreal to think that Roy might have gone out
and killed Westlake. Her brother-in-law was a gentle
man, kind and considerate, despite his strange behaviour
of late. His terrible experiences as a prisoner of war were
the cause of that, but had his personality changed
enough for him vengefully to murder a man who had
tried to seduce his wife? If Roy had done it, would he be
able to live with his terrible secret?

Albert woke with a start and shook himself, sitting up

straight in his chair and rubbing his face. The day had been spoiled by the police calling on Annie, he thought angrily. He had had it all planned, but instead of a quiet drink, a stroll and then maybe a little sit-down in Bermondsey Church gardens and a nice chat, he had been obliged to take her straight home from the pub. The woman had been like a cat on hot bricks in the Sultan. She had moaned nonstop about the police suspecting her Wally, and then all the way home she had chattered on about her son's lady friend, who they had met on the way back from the pub. Yes, he thought, Annie Stebbings was a difficult woman to make headway with, but he would persevere. There was another day tomorrow, he told himself.

Laura handed Albert his afternoon tea and he sipped it noisily. 'I wonder who it was killed ole Westlake?' he said, looking at his worried daughter. 'Mind yer, I say 'e got what 'e deserved. If yer live a violent life then yer die the same way as like as not.'

Laura could have done without her father raising the subject but she nodded in agreement. 'I don't fink there's many who'll cry over 'im, but 'e was murdered, Dad,' she replied.

'They're still lookin' fer Jack Murray, accordin' ter the papers,' Albert went on. 'There'll be more in the *Star* ternight. I fink I'll take a walk up the corner shop before tea. It'll stretch me legs anyway.'

Laura went into the scullery to check on the meat pie in the oven and she glanced up anxiously at the top of the dresser. If that knife was the murder weapon, why had Roy left it in the house? she wondered. He could quite easily have taken it to work with him and dropped it in the Thames, or disposed of it somewhere in the workshop. It wouldn't have been too difficult.

An hour later Lucy came home from work and hurried straight out to the scullery where Laura was straining the greens. 'Wasn't that terrible about Archie Westlake,' she said breathlessly. 'Everyone was talkin' about it at work. I still can't believe it.'

Laura looked at her sister quickly and she could tell that Lucy was genuinely shocked. It was quite obvious that she had not heard of the killing from Roy. 'There's a big bit about it in the *Star*,' she said, wiping the back of her hand across her hot forehead.

A few minutes later Roy came home and immediately ruffled Terry's hair and playfully sparred up to Reg before kissing Lucy on the cheek and then sitting down with a deep sigh. Laura watched him closely for his reaction as Lucy showed him the evening paper. 'Westlake was murdered last night,' she said, pointing to the front page.

Roy showed little emotion as he read the account, and then a derisive grin creased his face. 'It serves 'im right,' he remarked. 'The man was an out-an'-out villain. He got 'is comeuppance right enough. Good luck ter the bloke who killed 'im.'

Laura felt her stomach knot as she saw the look on Roy's face. His eyes had suddenly become cold and hard, and the chilling smile was lingering about his lips as he read on.

'It says 'ere that whoever killed 'im marked 'is face wiv the initials W.S. I wonder what that meant,' he said, glancing quickly at Lucy. 'I s'pose it could stand fer wife stealer.'

Chapter Forty-Eight

Eric Cassidy sat forward in his favourite armchair, his eyes wide and haunted as he addressed his family. 'You can laugh, but I tell yer straight, there's somefing 'angin' over this row of 'ouses. I said it before an' I'll say it again, that old gypsy's curse wasn't somefing people made up, it's true.'

Lizzie came into the crowded parlour, carrying a tray weighed down with a large teapot and cups and saucers. 'I wish yer wouldn't frighten those gels, Eric, what wiv Mary carryin' an' all,' she said, putting her load down on the table. 'It's all a load o' bloody eyewash anyway.'

Eric was not to be silenced. 'Look at those murders what's took place lately,' he said indignantly.

'That's nuffink ter do wiv Pedlar's Row,' Steve replied quickly, giving his brother Geoff a sideways glance.

'You can say that, but what about that there bookie who got done in?' Eric went on. ' 'E was usin' this Row fer 'is pitch, before Bridie Molloy give 'im the elbow. Then there's poor ole Wally Stebbin's. 'E got took fer questionin'. Those killin's 'ave touched this little place, an' who knows what's gonna 'appen next?'

'Fancy the police finkin' Wally 'ad anyfing ter do wiv the murder,' Mary remarked. 'You've only gotta look at the bloke.'

'Charlie Peace didn't look like a murderer, but 'e was a right evil git,' Eric replied.

Lizzie had gone out of the room to fetch the milk and sugar and a plate of rock cakes, and when she came back she sat down facing Eric and puffed. 'Yer ain't still on about that bloody curse, are yer?' she said irritably. 'Give it a rest, fer Gawd's sake.'

'I was talkin' about Charlie Peace,' Eric told her.

Lizzie raised her eyes to the ceiling and Mary and Connie looked at each other and smiled. 'It sez in the papers that the police are lookin' fer Jack Murray, but I don't fink 'e killed Archie Westlake,' Mary said, winking at Geoff.

'Who d'yer reckon done it, then?' Steve asked, acting as the foil.

'I reckon Len Carmichael topped 'im,' Mary went on. ' 'E found out that Elsie was carryin' on wiv the villain an' 'e went crazy.'

'Yer can't 'ave a sensible conversation wiv this lot,' Eric remarked to his sons as he got up and reached for a rock cake.

Mary got up to pour out the tea. 'Seriously though, Westlake made a lot of enemies round 'ere,' she said. 'The police won't be short o' suspects.'

Eddie had been sitting quietly, his mind focused on what Laura had told him earlier that evening when she met him in the Row on his way home from work. Finding the hidden knife had been a terrible shock to her. Together with the bloodstains on Roy's clothing, it had been enough to convince her that her brother-in-law had killed Westlake. As she had said, he had a motive, and he was emotionally insecure. Everything pointed to Roy being guilty, though Laura still found it difficult to accept. He was part of her family after all.

'You've not 'ad much ter say fer yerself, Eddie,' Mary remarked. 'Who d'you reckon killed Westlake?'

Eddie shrugged his shoulders dismissively and Geoff grinned. 'Take no notice of 'im, 'e's in love,' he said.

'Yes, an' she's a very nice young lady,' Lizzie said firmly.

'Are we gonna 'ave anuvver weddin' in the family soon?' Connie asked, smiling.

'It seems like it, by the look of 'im,' Steve laughed.

Eddie got up and stretched. 'I can't sit 'ere listenin' to all this nonsense, I'm takin' Laura ter the pictures,' he said, winking at Mary.

'There's a good picture on at the Astoria,' Steve remarked. 'It's a murder mystery.'

Eddie ignored the banter and went up to his room. He sat down on the edge of his bed and stared out of the window at the evening sky. That lunchtime he had fixed up a hotel reservation in Brighton and purchased the train tickets, and he hoped that Laura would still want to go after what had happened.

Early on Friday evening Alma Murray and Gordon Ashley sat together in a quiet Stepney pub, discussing the letter she had received from her sister that morning.

'I can't believe it,' Ashley growled. 'We've got everyone out hunting for Murray and he's trying to fix up a meet. He's just laughing at us.'

The smartly dressed woman leant forward on the table as she sipped her gin and tonic and looked at him with troubled eyes. 'I couldn't possibly meet him, Gordon, not after all that's happened,' she replied. 'It was the best thing I ever did, getting him out of my life. As if the money would make any difference. I've got too many bad memories.'

As Ashley gazed at Alma, at her short, neatly cut chestnut hair and her beautiful brown eyes, he grew angry to think of the cruelties that Murray had inflicted on her. Her full lips were parted over her even white teeth as she smiled dismissively, but although her make-up had been applied with considerable care the small scar over her left eye was clearly visible. Ashley remembered her telling him that Jack Murray had done it when he punched her in a drunken rage the night before she left him.

'What about that photo he put in the letter?' he asked. 'It doesn't worry you?'

'Why should it?' Alma replied. 'The question is, does it worry you?'

The detective sat back in his chair and sipped his whisky and soda. 'I've got to admit, it would be very awkward for both of us if our relationship was made public,' he told her. 'The papers would love it. I can just see it on the front pages. "Detective investigating Bermondsey murders involved with killer's wife." But there's no need for you to fret, Alma. I couldn't leave you, no matter what. Do you believe me?'

Alma reached across the table and rested her hand on his. 'I love you, Gordon,' she told him. 'You've made me really happy, happier than I've ever been in my whole life. I don't know what I'd do without you.'

Ashley looked around the quiet bar and sighed. 'I don't want us to always have to meet like this, in out-of-the-way places. I want us to be free to do what we want, go where we want, without the fear of someone spotting us together.'

'It won't always be like this, darling,' Alma said softly.

'It will be, as long as Jack Murray's on the loose,' he told her. 'I've got to get him, and soon. When he realises you're not going to him he might well post those photos on to the station. Once Murray's behind bars it wouldn't matter if our relationship came out into the open.'

'I can't help you, darling,' Alma replied. 'I don't know where he's hiding out and this letter doesn't give anything away. He could be anywhere.'

'You could help me,' Ashley said quietly as he squeezed her hand in his. 'You could do as he says and put the card up in the shop window.'

Alma looked shocked. 'Don't ask me to do that, Gordon. I couldn't bear to see him again, not ever.'

'But he's a murderer, Alma,' Ashley said with passion. 'He's killed three people, assuming that he was responsible for Westlake's murder.'

'They were gangland killings. It's not as though he's going around slaughtering ordinary people,' Alma replied, looking into her lover's eyes.

'Listen to me, darling,' Ashley said in a quiet voice as he leaned forward over the table. 'If you don't help me put him away you might live to regret it. No, listen. Supposing a member of the public got in Murray's way while he was trying to elude us. They could quite easily be maimed, or killed, even. Don't forget he's armed. Supposing a police officer recognised him and challenged him? Murray wouldn't hesitate to pull the trigger. If you make a meet with him we could catch him without a shot being fired, if it's well planned. All you have to do is make contact and leave the rest to me. You won't be in any danger, believe me.'

'You're asking too much, darling,' Alma pleaded with him. 'Please don't ask me to do it.'

Ashley sighed deeply and sat back in his chair. 'All right, forget it. It's only our happiness together that's hanging on this. If you really loved me you'd do it.'

Alma dropped her head, angry that Gordon would dare to question her feelings for him. Hadn't she proved her love over and over again? He was taking advantage of her, knowing that she could not refuse him anything. 'All right, I'll meet him,' she said, sighing.

Ashley's face brightened and he reached out his hand and squeezed her arm. 'I never doubted you, darling. You won't regret this, I promise.'

On Friday morning the council workmen were back in

Pedlar's Row and Elsie Carmichael sat painting little pink faces on the toy soldiers while she waited for the men to finish inspecting her house. One of them came into the parlour and went down on his hands and knees to have a look at the wainscoting, tapping it and prodding it with a knife. After a while he got up and stood by the table, gazing at her curiously.

'What yer doin', luv?' he asked.

'What's it look like I'm doin'?' Elsie answered sharply.

'Is it an 'obby, then?'

'No, it's not. It's outwork,' she said irritably. 'I get paid fer this, though I sometimes wonder why I ever decided ter do it.'

'It looks a fiddly bloody job if yer ask me,' the workman said. 'Yer must 'ave a lot o' patience.'

'I 'ave ter put eyes on these as well,' Elsie told him.

'Good Gawd.'

' 'Alf a dollar a box I get.'

'Good Gawd.'

'My ole man finks it's slave labour.'

'I fink 'e's right.'

'Still, what can yer do if yer need the money?'

'I couldn't do that,' the workman told her. ' 'Ere, 'ow d'yer put the eyes on 'em?'

'Wiv a pen an' ink.'

'Good Gawd.'

Elsie got up to stretch her back, mollified by the workman's interest in her artistry. 'Fancy a cuppa?' she asked.

'Well, I'm s'posed ter be inspectin' next door, but I fink I can spare a few minutes,' he said, smiling broadly at her.

When the workman left her house ten minutes later Elsie had learned quite a lot about the reasons for the council's inspection of Pedlar's Row, but for his part the workman was glad to get away. When he encountered

Elsie's next-door neighbour, he was confirmed in his opinion that there were some queer folk living in the Row.

'Yer'll 'ave ter wait there a minute,' Queenie told him when he announced himself.

He could hear a lot of urgent mumbling and then Queenie came back to the door, looking at him in a suspicious way. ' 'Ow do I know you are a workman?' she queried. 'Yer could be anybody.'

'Look, 'ere's me papers, luv. It distinctly sez Bermondsey Borough Council,' the man explained with a frown.

'All right, in yer come, but be as quick as yer can, I got fings ter do,' she told him.

The workman went about his inspection with Queenie following him around everywhere, and when he came back down the stairs with the large woman on his heels he turned and smiled bravely. 'Right' that's all, luv,' he said. 'No, wait a minute, I fergot the back yard.'

'Yer can't go out there,' Queenie said quickly.

'I've got to, gel, it's part o' the inspection, the back yards.'

'Yer'll 'ave ter wait 'ere a minute, then.'

The workman heard more mumbling and then Queenie returned. 'Right, quick as yer can, then,' she ordered.

He went out with the woman still behind him and looked around the tiny yard. 'I should check the toilet,' he said.

'No, yer can't, there's someone in there,' she replied quickly.

'Oh, all right then. I don't s'pose it matters that much,' the workman said, looking forward to getting out of the house.

Once he had left, Queenie hurried back out to the yard and opened the toilet door. 'It's all right, 'e's gone,' she told the anxious young man. 'We can't be too careful.'

John Bannerman came out of the dark closet, blinking, and sat down on an upturned beer crate. 'I gotta be goin' soon, Queenie luv,' he said. 'Marge an' the kids are gonna be worried sick.'

'I understand that, John, but yer gotta realise that yer could be picked up by the police as a suspect,' Queenie reminded him. 'That git Ashley left yer ter the mercy o' Westlake, an' yer was lucky 'e didn't get 'old o' yer. The cozzers might fink you 'ad somefing ter do wiv that evil sod's murder.'

'We don't know fer sure if Ashley told Westlake I was grassin' 'im up,' John replied.

'Be sensible, son,' Queenie said quickly. 'Yer told me Dickie Jones was plain enough about Archie Westlake bein' after yer. 'Ow would Westlake 'ave found out about yer unless Ashley told 'im? Only Ashley knew what yer was doin'. I reckon they done some sort o' trade. Some o' those cozzers are worse than the villains.'

'All right, Queenie, I'll give it a few more days,' the young man told her. 'Then I'll 'ave ter make a move. I wanna tell yer, though,'ow much I appreciate what yer done fer me. I'll never ferget it. I just 'ope I can repay yer kindness one day.'

'Listen, son,' she said quietly. 'I've known yer fer a long time, way back when you was a skinny streak o' piss wivout much idea about 'ow ter tie yer shoelaces. Yer've got a good 'eart, an' I ain't gonna stand by an' watch some evil bastards do yer. Just relax an' be patient. In a few days' time when it quietens down a bit yer can go ter Marge an' the kids. It's much too risky now though.'

John Bannerman got up and suddenly threw his arms around the buxom woman, kissing her on the forehead. 'Gawd bless yer, luv,' he said.

★ ★ ★

Eddie and Laura stepped down from the tram at the Bricklayer's Arms and walked along Tower Bridge Road to the Jolly Compasses pub. Eddie got the drinks and steered Laura to a corner table. The tiny public bar was quiet and there were only two other customers, an elderly couple who sat together at the far end of the room. Laura had not been able to concentrate on the film and Eddie had noticed how uneasy she was. They had decided to leave the pictures before the end and go for a drink, and as they settled down in the quiet pub Laura took his hand in hers under the table.

'Do yer fink I'm wrong in suspectin' Roy?' she asked anxiously.

'What else could yer fink?' Eddie replied. ' 'E comes in soaked in blood, an' the next mornin' yer find out that Westlake's bin murdered. Then yer find a bloodstained knife, or what seems ter be bloodstains.'

'It was the way 'e looked as well,' Laura told him. ' 'E didn't show much surprise when 'e saw the newspaper, an' 'e was smilin' to 'imself. I tell yer, Eddie, that look on Roy's face really scared me.'

The young man squeezed her hand comfortingly. 'Now, I want yer ter listen,' he said firmly. 'Yer can't change what's 'appened, an' yer not yer family's keeper. All yer can do is carry on as though yer don't know anyfing. It's no good you confrontin' Roy about it. 'E's not likely ter say, "Yeah, I did it." I know it's gonna be 'ard, an' yer worried fer 'im an' yer sister, naturally, but yer've got a life of yer own now, wiv me.'

Laura smiled. 'Yer right, Eddie. I feel so different when I'm wiv you. Yer really make me feel protected and safe. Yer won't never leave me, will yer?'

'Try an' make me,' he said, grinning broadly. 'In fact, I've got somefing ter tell yer. I'm gonna take us away fer a romantic weekend, if yer'll come.'

'Oh, Eddie,' Laura sighed. 'When?'

'Next weekend. I've booked us inter a hotel in Brighton, an' I've even got the train tickets,' he said, smiling.

'I do love you,' she whispered, suddenly leaning towards him and kissing his cheek.

'I love you too,' he answered.

They walked home hand in hand along the quiet thoroughfare, wrapped in their secret thoughts as they turned into Weston Street and strolled the short distance to Pedlar's Row. When they reached number three, Eddie slipped his arm around Laura. 'By the way, I've got a little present for yer,' he said with a big smile.

'Tell me, what is it?' she asked excitedly.

Eddie's face took on a mysterious look. 'I can't tell yer, yet,' he replied. 'I'll give it to yer before we go on our weekend trip.'

They kissed long and passionately, Laura relishing the comforting feel of Eddie's body against hers.

'You don't know 'ow much I need yer, Eddie,' she whispered into his ear.

'One 'ole weekend, just you an' me tergevver,' he whispered. 'I'll love yer madly, all night long.'

'Don't, Eddie, I'm gettin' all excited,' she said, nuzzling his chin.

They moved apart, still holding each other, and Eddie smiled. 'I fink yer'll like yer little present,' he remarked.

Laura looked at him lovingly. 'I'm so lucky,' she sighed.

Eddie backed away from her and raised his hand as if to wave. 'I'll call in termorrer evenin',' he said. 'Night, sweetie.'

'Good night, my lover,' she whispered as he walked away.

Chapter Forty-Nine

Alma breathed deeply in an effort to calm herself as she stood waiting outside the Lighterman's Arms in Down-town Rotherhithe. Overhead the Sunday evening sky was full of storm clouds, and a distant rumble of thunder echoed around the shuttered wharves as the first few spots of rain started to fall. Alma had followed the instructions given to her in Jack Murray's first letter by placing the coded message in Tom Draper's corner-shop window on Saturday morning. The advert, 'Pekinese puppies for sale. Phone Ber. 1227', was pinned up amongst the dozens of messages on the notice board, and as she left the little shop in Bermondsey Street she had been filled with misgivings. Gordon had been quick to reassure her that he would be at hand and there was nothing for her to worry about, providing she did not panic, but as she stood waiting in the darkening dock-land street Alma knew real fear.

The answer to her message had been swift, for late on Saturday evening a letter containing explicit instructions was quietly pushed under her front door. Alma had been alone in her flat when she discovered the letter and she hurried to the window, half expecting to see Jack Murray scurrying away in the darkness, but the street below was deserted save for a couple of young boys. She had discussed the contents of the letter with Gordon that morning and he had assured her that she would come to no harm and that Jack Murray would very soon be languishing in a police cell.

The Lighterman's Arms was a notorious public house that catered to the Scandinavian and Russian seamen who crewed the timber fleets which regularly tied up at the nearby Surrey Docks. Fights and skirmishes were a regular occurrence at the Downtown pub, where the local streetwalkers jealously guarded their pitch from outsiders. In the large, smoke-filled interior the visiting seamen sat gambling and drinking together, distinctive in their navy blue roll-neck jerseys and greasy peaked caps. The men eyed the street girls who hung around together at the bar counter and many an introduction was made over glasses of Russian vodka and schnapps. The painted women asked for shorts but drank tonic water on its own instead and pocketed half the difference in price with the collusion of the pub landlord, and when they left with their drunken customers they were invariably stone-cold sober.

In the smoky pub two hefty young men sat together, talking in low voices, ignoring the women but secretly alert, furtively glancing around the bar as they sought out the villain, whose face had been imprinted in their minds from lengthy study of a police photo. The two men felt reassured by the revolvers strapped under their armpits and hidden from view by the reefer jackets they were wearing. Their instructions had been explicit: observe and report; do not attempt to apprehend unless life is threatened.

Outside in the dark, dismal street Alma was already feeling conspicuous. One or two of the local street women had given her suspicious glances, although it was obvious from her appearance that she was not soliciting. She tried to comfort herself with the knowledge that two police officers were inside the pub and another was watching from the roof of the spice wharf opposite. The police car was well concealed and everything looked quite normal. Would Jack Murray be fooled though? she asked herself. He had told her many times that he could sense a police presence.

A taxi came into view, driving slowly towards her. Alma felt her heart race as it pulled up alongside her and the door opened.

'Quick! Get in!'

As the frightened woman stepped into the cab it quickly pulled away from the pub and accelerated along the grimy cobbled street. Alma stared into the pallid face of her ex-husband and was shocked by his appearance. He had aged noticeably and the heavy moustache he wore made him seem even more menacing than she remembered. He smiled cryptically as he studied her, his right hand raised to grasp the passenger strap.

'Yer lookin' very well,' he said at last.

'I'm keeping well,' Alma replied nervously. 'What about you?'

Murray turned to look out through the rear window, then his eyes met hers. 'I got a bullet in me shoulder but it's all right now,' he told her.

'Why, Jack? Why did you get yourself into this mess?' Alma asked. 'You were doing all right with the pub.'

Murray laughed aloud as he glanced nervously out of the cab window. 'It's a long story, but it wasn't meant ter turn out the way it did,' he growled. 'I could 'ave bin long gone.'

'But what possessed you? You knew they'd come looking for you,' Alma replied.

'I got in over me 'ead,' Murray told her. 'I owed a lot o' money an' the debts were pilin' up. I 'ad ter dive inter the pub money an' Westlake found out. There wasn't many options left open an' I 'ad ter make a decision. I wanted out from the mob anyway. They got too ambitious when they started printin' money, an' I was sure they'd come a tumble wiv their plan ter spread it round the race-tracks. I told Westlake that we should push it out o' the country, but 'e wouldn't listen. Doin' it their way would 'ave got us all banged up fer a long stretch, I was sure of it. There was too many people involved.'

'Did you kill Westlake?' Alma asked suddenly.

Murray merely smiled and Alma felt her stomach tighten as he twisted round to look out of the back window. If he suspected that they were being followed he would obviously think she had set him up. She had to stay calm and keep him talking.

'Where will you go, Jack?' she asked him.

'As soon as I've made the deal wiv the money, I'm leavin' the country,' he told her. 'I'm arrangin' passage on a cargo ship ter South America. I'll be safe there.'

Suddenly the cab driver slid the glass panel to one side. ' 'Ere we are, guv. Deptford 'Igh Street.'

'Turn left at the top an' go down Church Street,' Murray instructed him. He turned to Alma. 'Come wiv me, Alma,' he said quickly. 'Ditch that no-good copper an' come wiv me. I'll be set up good, an' yer'll 'ave a life o' luxury.'

'I've already left 'im,' Alma replied, looking down at her hands and trying to remain calm.

'Well then, there's nuffink ter stop yer, is there?' he said, suddenly squeezing her arm in a strong grip.

'Could we ever be happy together, Jack?' Alma asked him. 'Have you changed enough for me to take the chance? I couldn't live the way we were. I couldn't take any more beatings.'

Murray increased his grip. 'I've 'ad enough, Alma,' he said. 'I've changed, God strike me dead if I'm lyin'. I know I did yer wrong, but I'll never lift a finger against yer, not ever. We can start afresh. We was 'appy tergevver once.'

Alma looked away from his burning stare and he

turned forward suddenly to address the driver. 'Turn left 'ere an' pull up quick!'

'Where are we going?' she asked him.

Murray did not reply. He stepped quickly out of the cab and took her arm as she followed him out, then he leaned through the side window. 'We might 'ave bin follered, so turn first left and make yer way out ter the Broadway frew the back streets. Quick as yer can,' he instructed the driver, handing him a five-pound note. 'If yer stopped, don't tell 'em yer dropped us off 'ere, got it?'

The driver nodded, his eyes popping as he saw the money. He waved his thanks as he sped away, disappearing from sight into a narrow back street.

Alma saw that they were standing outside a pub and she glanced up at the name: the Cat and Fiddle. She caught the evil glint in Murray's eye as he took her arm and led her into the public bar.

'We can't be too careful,' he told her. 'I'm lodgin' nearby an' this is me local. People round 'ere don't ask questions an' I know the lan'lord o' this pub. We'll be safe 'ere.'

Alma stood just inside the door, waiting while Murray rubbed his fingers over the steamy pane and peered out into the darkness.

'It's all right,' he said, looking relieved. 'Let's take a seat over there an' I'll get the drinks.'

The few customers gave them only a brief glance as Murray led her into a far corner and pulled back a seat for her.

'D'yer still drink gin an' tonic?' he asked.

Alma nodded and quickly glanced around her. Murray was taking no chances, she realised. Their position at the far end of the bar gave him a good view of the door across the counter, and they would not be spotted immediately by anyone coming in from the street. There was a door to their left which led out to the toilets, and he would have made sure that he could quickly get out through the back of the pub in an emergency. If she guessed right, the rear exit would lead out to the pub yard and it would be easy for him to make a getaway through the back yards of the adjoining houses.

Murray returned with the drinks and he sighed loudly as he squeezed into a seat next to her. 'Tell me about Ashley,' he said abruptly. ' 'Ow come yer got tied up wiv a cozzer?'

'Don't let's talk about him, Jack. Let's talk about you,' Alma replied, trying to appear relaxed despite her anxiety.

Murray rubbed his tender shoulder as he eased down in his seat. 'I'll spare yer the gory details,' he said, smiling, 'but I 'ave ter tell yer I didn't wanna kill Con Noble. I only meant ter stun 'im. As fer Danny Steadman, it was me or 'im. Steadman was out fer my blood from the early days. 'E was jealous o' my close friendship wiv Westlake. What's more, I know fer a fact that 'e was after takin' over the mob. I tried ter warn Archie on more than one occasion but 'e wouldn't listen. Anyway, it's all water under the bridge now. Fings are gonna be different fer us two, I promise yer. Yer've give that cozzer the elbow an' you an' I can get back tergevver again. I'll be ready ter leave the country in ten days at the most. Yer can stay wiv me till the ship sails. Yer won't regret it.'

Gordon Ashley had spent the whole of Sunday planning his move on Jack Murray. He knew that he had to be very careful or Ben Walsh would be on his back. Fortunately the men he had picked to accompany him in capturing Murray were already armed. His story would be that a snout had informed him late that evening that the fugitive was loose on the streets and there had been no time to mobilise more than a few detectives. Walsh would no doubt have something to say about it, but if Murray was finally put out of circulation the inspector would be more than happy and he wouldn't make too much of a fuss about the flouting of rules and regulations.

Ashley felt the adrenaline flowing as he took the girl's arm and walked slowly along the dockland street. He was wearing a heavy reefer jacket over his seaman's jersey and his head was covered by a navy blue woollen hat that was pulled down around his ears. The girl smelled of cheap scent and her long, brightly painted fingernails gripped the sleeve of his coat like talons.

'Don't look over there,' he growled as a taxi pulled up outside the pub opposite. 'Keep looking at me.'

Donna Whitworth had been more than a little surprised when Ashley flashed his warrant card. The girls were usually left alone by the local constabulary, and she was annoyed when Ashley told her what he wanted her to do. She knew full well that she could lose her good name by aiding the police, but realising that she had little choice in the matter, she flickered her long eyelashes at the detective and gave him her cruellest smile.

Ashley glanced out of the corner of his eye and watched Alma stepping into the taxi, and as soon as the vehicle left the pub he burst into action. Donna watched wide-eyed as he broke away from her and ran across to the pub, diving inside. Seconds later she saw him come out with two other men and the three of them dashed across to the wharf opposite just as the gates sprang open. She watched as the men jumped into the police car and drove away at speed.

'What's that all about?' one of the girls called over to her.

'Gawd knows,' Donna replied with a shrug of her shoulders. 'I thought 'e was after me body at first.'

Ashley sat back against the seat cushion, breathing hard. 'Keep your distance, for God's sake,' he warned the driver. 'If Murray knows he's being followed he might well cut the woman's throat.'

The taxi was some way ahead and the police driver kept a safe stretch between them, driving on sidelights as the car rattled over the cobbled road which led out of the Downtown area. The taxi turned left at the main Rotherhithe thoroughfare and continued along towards Deptford. Suddenly it swung right and Ashley grunted. 'That's the High Street. Watch your distance, it's well lit-up.'

The driver nodded as he put the car into top gear. The detectives watched the taxi go through a green light at the end of the High Street and turn left, then a few hundred yards or so along the Broadway it swung left again into Church Street. The police car followed at a discreet distance and suddenly Ashley cursed loudly. The taxi had gone under the railway bridge straddling the dark turning and disappeared. The road ahead was deserted.

'They must have turned left there,' the driver said quickly, accelerating and swinging over hard on the steering wheel.

The warren of narrow back streets was quiet and gloomy, and the police driver puffed loudly as he wove the car in and out of the maze-like byways. Ashley felt his heart sink. There had been a choice to make, and in his concern for Alma it looked as though he had made the wrong one. If they had overtaken the taxi and grabbed Murray before he got over his surprise they would have been on their way back to the station by now.

As the police driver turned into another narrow back street Ashley spotted the tail lights of the taxi some way ahead as it drove out into a brightly lit street.

'Chase him!' he shouted.

The police car caught up quickly and forced the taxi into the kerb. ' 'Ere, what's goin' on?' the driver asked, looking very annoyed.

Ashley flashed his warrant card. 'Where did you drop your fare?' he demanded urgently.

'Just round the corner in Wilson Street,' the cabbie replied, jerking his thumb behind him.

'Come on,' Ashley growled to his colleagues. 'We've got some doorknocking to do.'

Alma bit on her lip in anguish as Jack Murray went to the bar to get some more drinks. He had been going on and on about how he was different now and would never treat her badly again, but she knew that nothing had changed as far as he was concerned. He was still the domineering, self-centred brute of a man who had never considered her feelings. He had decided without even asking her that she would be staying with him until the ship sailed. Why had she allowed Gordon to talk her into meeting him?

Murray came back with his usual swagger and sat down, glancing quickly towards the door. 'I don't want us ter be 'ere too long,' he said. 'When yer've finshed yer drink we'll go back ter my lodgin's. I'll feel safer an' we can talk more.'

Alma's mind was racing and she struggled to conceal the terror rising up inside her. Gordon would soon realise that they had slipped out of the taxi in the back streets and the pub would be the first place he would check. If he showed his face in the door Murray would spot him and he might well plunge a knife into her before darting off. She gulped her drink and looked at him with a forced smile. 'I think you're right,' she remarked. 'Your picture's plastered over all the papers. Someone might recognise you here.'

Murray drained his glass and started to button up his coat.

Alma picked up her handbag. 'I'll need to pay a visit,' she said casually.

'Don't be long,' Murray told her sharply.

Once she was in the lady's room Alma hurriedly searched through her handbag and found a pencil and a used envelope. Just as she finished scribbling a message, the door opened and an elderly woman came in.

'Will you please help me?' Alma said in a low voice. 'Wait five minutes and then give this to the landlord. Tell him to phone that number immediately and pass on the message. It's a matter of life and death.'

The woman eyed Alma suspiciously. 'Five minutes, yer say?'

Alma nodded. 'It's very urgent.'

The woman walked back into the bar and took her seat beside her friend. ' 'Ere, Bessie,' she said. 'See those two just leavin'? Well, that woman gave me this.'

Bessie screwed her eyes up at the printed message. 'What's it say, Clara?' she asked.

'I dunno. I ain't never bin one fer readin',' Clara replied.

'I reckon the silly cow's 'avin' yer on,' Bessie remarked.

'That's what I was finkin',' Clara said.

'Chuck it away, gel. It ain't nuffink ter do wiv us.'

Jack Murray poured himself a stiff drink. 'I'm sorry I've got no gin. Why don't yer try a whisky? It'll relax yer,' he said, smiling slyly.

'You know I can't stand whisky,' Alma replied, looking around the dingy room.

Murray took a large gulp and sat down in an easy chair facing her. 'D'yer remember the ole days?' he said. 'We couldn't keep our 'ands off each ovver.'

'That was a long time ago,' Alma replied.

'It could all be good again, if yer just let it 'appen,' he said in a low voice.

'I can't just turn it on, Jack. I'll need time,' she replied, feeling more and more anxious.

Suddenly he reached out and took her hands in his. 'I've bin missin' yer, Alma,' he said hoarsely. 'None o' those women meant anyfing ter me. It's you I want.'

She tried to pull away from his grasp but he stood up and dragged her out of the chair, his arms going around her and his open mouth pressing down on hers. Alma struggled fiercely but his greater strength left her gasping for breath. 'No, Jack, no!' she cried.

He reached down and tried to sweep her up in his arms but she kicked out quickly, her knee catching his sore shoulder. He let go of her with a grunt of pain and she backed away out of reach. Murray glared at her, his eyes narrowing.

'Don't fight me,' he snarled. 'Yer need it as much as I do.'

Alma quickly stepped behind the easy chair, her back to the window. 'Keep away, Jack. I'm warning you,' she said with spirit.

He bent down and pulled the chair away and as he straightened up his face was flushed. 'Come 'ere,' he growled, advancing slowly towards her.

She stepped backwards towards the window, reaching behind her for the heavy vase standing on the sill. Murray darted forward but she sidestepped him and ran back into the centre of the room.

'All right the game's over,' he said, grinning evilly.

As he came towards her Alma raised her hands and threw the vase with all her might, but he ducked quickly and it shattered through the windowpane. He pounced like a wild animal, grabbing her, squeezing her throat with his powerful hands. He was stopping her breathing and there was a pounding in her head. This is the end, she thought, as redness closed over her eyes.

Gordon Ashley stood by the police car, addressing his colleagues. 'We could spend all night doorknocking,' he said desperately.

'What else can we do?' the driver asked him.

'I'm sure that cab driver gave us the run-around,' one of the young detectives cut in. 'I reckon they got out the cab when it turned off of Church Street.'

'All right, we'll try there. Let's go,' Ashley said quickly, jumping back into his seat.

The police car drove into Comus Street and pulled up a few yards away from the Cat and Fiddle public house.

'I'll check the pub. You start doorknocking,' Ashley ordered.

At that moment the silence was shattered by the sound of breaking glass. 'Come on!' Ashley shouted as he broke into a run, throwing himself against the street door beneath the shattered window. Two wide-eyed, terrified faces stared out at him from a scullery as he dashed up the stairs, his revolver clutched in his hand.

The sound of splintering wood made Murray release his grip on Alma's throat and he let her fall as he pulled his gun from the sideboard drawer. He spun round as Ashley burst into the room. The first bullet caught the villain in the throat and he fell back against the easy chair. His eyes glazed as he tried to raise his revolver and the second bullet hit him between the eyes. Ashley's colleagues dashed into the room as he fired the second shot, their guns held at the ready.

Alma groaned as the detective bent over her. 'I never thought you'd get here,' she croaked.

'We'll need an ambulance, and you'd better sort those two out downstairs. I'll deal with this,' Ashley told his team.

He made Alma as comfortable as he could with a cushion behind her head, and then he hurriedly searched the room. Unable to find what he was looking for, he bent down and searched the body of Jack Murray, but to no avail.

Downstairs in the scullery, Dot Williams stood beside the gas stove, watching for the kettle to boil, her whole body shaking. 'Gawd Almighty! We could 'ave bin killed in our beds,' she said to the policemen gathered round her.

'Too bloody true,' her husband Toby replied.

Ashley walked into the room looking ashen-faced. 'We'll have to search the house. We're looking for a suitcase. Have you seen a suitcase, by any chance?' he asked.

Dot looked at her husband and he shook his head vigorously. 'Nah, can't 'elp yer, mate. 'E kept 'imself to 'imself. I ain't seen no suitcase,' he told the detective.

Later that night, as they sat alone, sipping their tea, Dot looked at Toby curiously. 'Why didn't yer tell 'em about the suitcase?' she asked him.

'It was up ter them ter find it, but they didn't,' he replied. 'Mind yer, I thought they'd spot it when they shone that torch in the coal cupboard. It was 'angin' up right over the cozzer's 'ead.'

'We can't keep all that dosh,' Dot said fearfully. 'We'd be done fer passin' bent money.'

Toby smiled slyly. 'I tell yer what we're gonna do,' he said. 'We'll skim off the top layer an' then we'll take it ter the police station. We'll tell 'em where we found it.'

'Won't they be suspicious?' Dot asked him.

'Nah, we'll just say 'e must 'ave 'id it in the coal cupboard when we was out,' he replied. 'After all, if the cozzers couldn't find it, 'ow the bloody 'ell was we expected to.'

'What'll we do wiv the money?' Dot asked.

'I'll pass a few notes at the dogs on Thursday,' Toby said, grinning. 'We'll dirty 'em up a bit wiv coal dust. The bookies won't know the difference.'

Chapter Fifty

Eddie smiled as he reached across the Sunday-morning breakfast table, gently stroking Laura's wrist with his fingertips. Their eyes met and she put her free hand over his. 'I'll never ferget this weekend,' she whispered.

The waiter was lingering nearby, eager to clear away and prepare the last of the tables in the room, trying to look unconcerned as he dusted an imaginary crumb from the adjoining table that was already set for lunch. Eddie gave him a quick glance and looked at Laura with an amused grin. 'We'd better get movin',' he said. 'I fink we're 'oldin' up the works.'

Laura took his arm as they walked out into the foyer. 'Eddie, could we take a last walk along the front before we leave?' she asked.

The young man smiled and nodded. 'You wait down 'ere while I get the cases an' settle the bill. We can leave 'em 'ere.'

Laura watched Eddie as he bounded up the wide flight of stairs and then she strolled over to the window seat and sat down with a contented sigh. Outside the sun was shining down brightly from a clear spring sky, making the white promenade dazzle, and glistening on the calm Channel water. The whole weekend had been like a wonderful dream, she thought. Early on Friday evening she had opened the front door to see Eddie standing there on the doorstep, holding a large, flat cardboard box, his face wreathed in a wide boyish grin. 'This is fer you,' he had said simply.

Laura smiled to herself as she recalled the excitement she had felt at that moment. She had hurried up into the front bedroom, undone the string impatiently and removed the lid to discover the black crepe dress, expertly folded between layers of tissue paper, the design of sequins about the bodice winking in the light as she reverently lifted it out of the box. She had been too overcome to speak. Instead she threw herself into the startled young man's arms in the doorway and wept unashamedly. She had never dreamed she would ever really possess the dress. It had remained for so long in the shop window, to be desired, coveted and fawned over, but never to be owned. Now it was hers, and when she slipped into it she found that it fitted her as if it had been made for her. Laura remembered the look on Eddie's face when she paraded herself for his approval. He had just smiled and nodded his head slowly, his eyes sparkling with pleasure.

Eddie was coming down the stairs of the hotel, carrying the two suitcases, and he winked at her as he placed them in a corner and walked over to the reception desk. Laura saw the young lady clerk exchange a few pleasantries with him and she suddenly felt a twinge of jealousy. It was stupid, she told herself. Eddie was a very handsome young man with a warm, friendly smile and charming ways, and she would have to expect young women to respond to him in a genial way. He was hers and hers alone. He had sworn his undying love in the quiet darkness of their hotel room as they lay together. They had made sweet, passionate love and Laura was feeling more alive than she had ever been before, still floating somewhere between fantasy and reality. His caressing hands had sent shivers down her spine and she had wanted his lovemaking to go on forever.

Now, as she waited for him, there was a dark cloud that had risen on her horizon. The weekend of love had been unbelievably wonderful, but they were going home, where the trouble was.

'Right then, let's take that stroll,' Eddie said cheerily.

Laura snuggled close to him as they walked down the stone steps of the hotel and crossed the wide thoroughfare to the promenade. 'I wish we could stay 'ere fer ever,' she sighed. 'It's bin the best weekend I've ever known.'

'I wish we could too,' Eddie replied with a deep sigh. 'We must try an' do it again, as soon as we can.'

Laura lapsed into silence as they strolled in the warm sunshine, her blonde hair rising in the fresh sea breeze.

Eddie gazed at her and sensed what she was thinking. 'Are yer worryin' about Roy?' he asked quietly.

She nodded. 'I just 'ope everyfing's all right back 'ome,' she sighed.

'I'm sure it is,' he answered. 'You told me Roy an' Lucy seemed ter be gettin' very close. Don't dwell on what's 'appened. Let it stay buried.'

'I wish I could,' Laura said. 'I'm just frightened that Roy might suddenly crack up. It must be a terrible secret fer 'im ter live wiv.'

Eddie squeezed her arm encouragingly. 'Look, the case is dead an' buried as far as the police are concerned,' he said firmly. 'It was in all the papers. They said it was a gangland vendetta an' they weren't lookin' fer anyone else. They're satisfied that Jack Murray killed Westlake, end o' story. Roy wouldn't be likely ter go to the police an' say, "I did it", now would 'e?'

'No, I s'pose you're right,' Laura replied. 'I just 'ope 'im an' Lucy don't let go of it all. It's bin so difficult fer the both of 'em, an' now it all seems ter be comin' tergevver. She really loves 'im, Eddie, an' Roy loves 'er too.'

The young man smiled jauntily. 'They'll be fine, just like us. Which reminds me.'

Laura gave him a questioning look. 'Yeah?'

'Oh, it's nuffink important,' he replied.

'What is it?' she asked.

'I just wanted to ask yer somefing, but it'll keep.'

'Ask me.'

'I dunno if I should.'

'Eddie?'

'Yeah.'

'What is it?'

'I jus' wanted ter know if yer fancied marryin' me.'

Laura stopped suddenly and turned to face him, her eyes wide with surprise. 'Is that an offer?' she laughed.

'If yer like,' he said, beaming, as she joyfully wrapped herself around him.

On Monday morning Ben Walsh sat back in his office chair and stroked his bristly chin as he looked down at the brown envelope lying on his desk. It had been addressed to him, marked Private and Confidential, and the contents had shocked him. There were niggling doubts in his mind about the Murray murder too, prompted by the police photos taken in the small upper room of the back-street house in Deptford. The body was sprawled against an armchair, arms spread out and head back, clearly showing the bullet wound in the throat. Obvious too was the revolver, still clenched in the dead man's right hand, not his left.

Ben Walsh heard footsteps in the corridor and he quickly put the envelope out of sight as Detective Sergeant Gordon Ashley walked in, his face pale and tired. He stood at the desk, hesitating for a moment.

'You wanted to see me, guv?' he said.

Walsh motioned to a chair. 'The Assistant Commissioner was on the phone a few minutes ago,' he said flatly. 'He's accepted my resignation. I'm on retirement as from next week.'

'I'm pleased for you, guv. You've well and truly earned it,' Ashley replied, standing up quickly and holding out his hand.

'There's something else,' the inspector said, eyeing his sergeant closely as they shook hands. 'You and the other police officers involved in the apprehension of Murray have been recommended for an official commendation. Congratulations.'

Ashley sat down again. 'I'd just like to say that I appreciate you covering for me, sir,' he said quietly. 'It could have been a bit tricky without your help.'

Ben Walsh nodded. 'After all that's happened on the manor recently, I'm glad to go. I'll enjoy the peace and quiet of my garden, and maybe I'll find time to go to the Old Vic. The Shakespeare season starts next month.' He smiled slyly at Ashley. 'By the way, I got some photos through the post this morning. You might like to know that I intend to put them with the rest of the rubbish I've accumulated over the years. There'll be one big bonfire in my garden next week.'

Ashley flushed slightly. 'I'm indebted. I'm going to miss working with you, sir. I just hope the next guv'nor measures up.'

Ben Walsh nodded appreciatively. 'One other thing. I took another look at those incident photos this morning. I was rather hoping to find out that Jack Murray was left-handed.'

Albert Prior whistled happily as he swirled the soft-bristled brush round the cake of soap in the shaving mug and surveyed his stubbly chin. Last weekend Annie Stebbings had actually taken his arm as they walked out of Pedlar's Row to go to the Sultan. Today he was taking her for a lunchtime drink and he was going to have a serious talk with her. She had been upset when Wally told her that he and his lady friend had set the day, but Albert had been quick to reassure her with the thought that now she would be able to spend more time enjoying herself. He had told her in no uncertain terms that she was a very smart and attractive lady who could still cut a dash. She had responded that Sunday noon by putting on her best bonnet and applying a touch of powder to her face. What was more, she had told him that she found him to be a nice, friendly man who obviously appreciated a good woman. The conversation had lifted his spirits to a magical degree, and as Albert applied a liberal amount of shaving foam to his whiskers he felt confident that he and Annie would soon be enjoying a much closer relationship.

Laura busied herself with the ironing, occasionally glancing at her father as he carefully ran the safety razor over his bristles. Thoughts of the weekend she had spent with Eddie at Brighton made her glow inside and she tried to concentrate her mind on their time together, not wanting to dwell on the sinister matter at home that was hovering like a dark cloud and threatening to spoil her happiness.

'There's a new bloke in the Sultan,' Albert said as he rinsed the soapy razor in the sink. 'I didn't fink that ovver dopey git would reign long. Too full of 'imself 'e was.'

Laura smiled briefly as she took the fresh iron from the gas flame and ran it over the coconut matting.

Albert looked at his daughter with concern. 'You all right?' he asked. 'Yer very quiet.'

Laura spat on the bottom of the iron to test the heat and ran the back of her hand over her hot forehead. 'Just finkin', Pops,' she said lightly as she set about ironing the collar of his best white shirt.

Albert hummed to himself as he strolled out of the

scullery and Laura instinctively glanced up again at the top of the Welsh dresser. The previous week she had climbed up on to a chair on a few occasions, feeling for the knife resting behind the shaped beading, hoping, willing it to have disappeared, but her searching fingers invariably touched its cold surface. As long as the weapon lay there, Roy was in danger, but there was nothing she could do; she could not let on that she knew about it. Early this morning she had climbed up once more and run her fingers along the dusty wood to discover with a sudden feeling of relief that the knife was no longer there. He must have disposed of it that weekend, she thought. But why take so long to get rid of it? He must have known the risk he was taking by leaving it there on top of the dresser.

An hour later, with the last of the ironing finished, Laura went out into the back yard and began to beat the large mat she had hung over the clothes line earlier. Suddenly Queenie's head came into view over the low brick wall between the houses. She was singing softly to herself. The robust woman saw Laura and stepped up on to an overturned beer crate, resting her arms on the top of the wall. ' 'Ello, gel,' she said pleasantly. ' 'Ow was the weekend? Lucy told me yer went down ter Brighton.'

'It was lovely,' Laura replied, blushing a little as she caught the knowing look on Queenie's round face.

'I saw yer sister's 'usband goin' off ter work this mornin',' she said. ' 'E's lookin' better.'

Laura nodded, realising why Queenie should say that. She had found Roy in a drunken state outside her front door on the night of Westlake's murder and she had helped him home, most probably noticing that his clothes were bloodstained. 'I fink Roy's beginnin' ter settle down now,' she replied.

Queenie nodded back at her. 'Yeah, an' 'e shouldn't

lose no sleep over what's 'appened,' she said firmly. 'What's past is past.'

Laura looked closely at her next-door neighbour. She and Queenie had never exchanged more than a few passing words and now the woman was being strangely friendly. She was fishing, Laura felt certain. 'I just 'ope so,' she replied.

Queenie's eyes seemed to be probing hers. 'The kettle's boilin'. C'mon in fer a cuppa,' she said quickly, getting down from the crate before Laura had time to refuse.

The parlour of number one was clean and tidy, not a thing out of place. As Laura sat sipping her tea, Queenie went on for a few minutes about her husband's difficulty in getting regular work at the wharf and about her four sons. Suddenly she put down her empty cup and leaned forward in her chair. 'I bet it was a shock that night when I knocked on yer door,' she said. ' 'E was in a state, that bruvver-in-law o' yours. What wiv that blood all over 'is trousers. At least that's what it looked like.'

'Lucy never noticed the bloodstains,' Laura replied quickly. 'Eddie carried 'im up ter bed an' took 'is trousers off. I cleaned an' pressed 'em before Roy an' Lucy got up next mornin'. Then when the news spread about that villain bein' found on the bomb site I was terrified in case Roy 'ad anyfing ter do wiv it.'

'Yer thought 'e might 'ave done it 'cos o' your Lucy goin' ter that club wiv Westlake?' Queenie queried.

Laura looked shocked. ' 'Ow did yer know about Westlake an' Lucy?' she asked quickly.

Queenie smiled. 'As a matter o' fact young John Bannerman told me.'

'John Bannerman?'

'Yeah, the bloke who used ter nark out fer the bookie,' Queenie explained. 'Yer must 'ave seen 'im standin' on the corner. 'E used ter find out all the news an' gossip. Bloody fool.'

Laura put her cup down on the fresh white linen cloth covering the table, realising that Queenie had put two and two together. The secret would be safe with her, though. The woman had made it clear early on that she hated the very name Westlake and so she would be no danger to Roy, but what if someone else had seen the state he was in that night and got talking? It could all come out, and someone might even decide to inform the police.

Queenie saw the anguish on Laura's face and she suddenly reached out and touched her arm in a friendly gesture. 'There's no need ter worry about it,' she said. 'Yer bruvver-in-law didn't kill Westlake.'

'I wish I could believe it,' Laura replied sadly. 'The thought of Roy goin' ter prison terrifies me. I've bin 'avin' nightmares over it. It would kill Lucy, an' those two boys o' theirs would be 'eartbroken.'

Queenie looked hard at the young woman for a few moments, seeing the tears forming in her eyes, then she studied her hands before speaking. 'I know Roy didn't kill Westlake,' she told her. ' 'Cos I know who did.'

'Yer know?' Laura said incredulously.

Queenie nodded slowly. 'I'm gonna get us anuvver cup o' tea first, then I'll tell yer everyfing,' she replied. 'It goes wivout sayin' o' course that what I'm gonna tell yer goes no furvver than these four walls.'

Rays of spring sunlight shone through the lace curtains and slanted across the small room as Queenie took a sip from her freshly brewed tea. 'Some years ago John Bannerman, the fella I was tellin' yer about, took a shine ter my young sister, Mary,' she began. 'They'd known each ovver since their school days. They were both in their teens. Mary was a really pretty girl, wiv long blonde 'air, just like yours. She liked 'im too an' they started walkin' out tergevver. They seemed ter get very close an' we all thought they'd end up gettin' married. Then that no-good whoreson Westlake came on the scene. 'E was a young villain, full of 'imself an' out to impress everybody. 'E turned our Mary's 'ead wiv 'is big talk an' she ended up wiv 'im. Poor John Bannerman was 'eartbroken. Anyway, Westlake promised Mary the moon an' she fell fer 'is big talk o' good times an' a glamorous life. The whoreson set 'er up in a flat an' promised ter marry 'er; but all the time 'e was playin' around wiv ovver women. Mary found out eventually an' she left 'im after a big bust-up. Westlake give 'er a good 'idin' and she was so bad she couldn't go outside the door fer a week.'

Laura sat transfixed as she listened and Queenie drained her cup before going on. 'John Bannerman 'ad found someone else in the meantime an' 'e was gettin' married. Poor Mary realised too late it was 'im she really loved an' she seemed ter go down 'ill fast. At first it was the drink. She got in bad company an' she flitted from one fella to anuvver. I tried ter warn 'er, we all did, but it was no good. Anyway, she finally left 'ome an' nobody seemed ter know where she'd gone. Some time later John Bannerman saw 'er. She was on the game down in Rovver'ive. 'E was too shocked to even talk to 'er. Two years ago Mary took an overdose an' she lay in 'er flat fer three days before someone found 'er. I blamed meself fer lettin' 'er get so desperate, but when I look back I realise there was little anyone could 'ave done. It was the life she chose, an' that bastard Westlake was the cause o' the poor cow takin' 'er own life.'

'That's terrible,' Laura said sadly as she saw the tears brimming in Queenie's eyes.

'A few weeks ago John Bannerman came ter see me,' Queenie continued, wiping her hand across her cheek. ' 'E told me that a pal of 'is 'ad got friendly wiv a young woman who knew Mary. This girl was on the game 'erself an' she 'ad a story ter tell. I went down ter Rovver'ive ter see 'er an' I found out from 'er that Westlake was very friendly wiv the girls' pimp. 'E used ter send clients ter the girls, it was common knowledge. In fact the pimp used ter tell the girls ter be extra nice ter Westlake's clients. One night the whoreson sent a bloke along who turned out ter be a nonsense-case. D'yer know what 'e did?' Laura remained silent, her eyes wide. ' 'E sliced Mary's face,' Queenie told her. ' 'E actually carved the letter "W" on 'er cheek. It was the beginnin' o' the end fer Mary. She was permanently disfigured. One month later she swallered a full bottle o' sleepin' pills. I just can't tell yer what it did ter me.' She paused for a moment and closed her eyes. 'Fer a long time I used ter go ter Mary's grave on a Sunday an' I'd tidy it up a bit. I used ter talk to 'er about all sorts of everyday fings, 'opin' that wherever she was she could 'ear me. It's strange, but I really felt in my 'eart that she could. I made 'er a promise. I swore I'd get my revenge on that evil bastard Westlake fer what 'e'd done to 'er, an' I did.'

'You did?' Laura said, dry-mouthed.

Queenie's face creased in a bitter smile that sent a shiver down Laura's spine. 'Wednesday before last, John Bannerman came ter see me again,' she went on quietly. ' 'E was in a terrible state. It turns out 'e'd bin grassin' on Westlake's mob. Some'ow they'd found out an' they were after 'im. I suspect it was the coppers who told Westlake. Anyway, I said 'e could 'ide out at my place fer a while. I suddenly got ter finkin' an' it all came ter me in a flash. I sent my young lad ter Westlake wiv a message sayin' I wanted ter meet 'im. Yer see, when Jack Murray killed the bookie and the ovver bloke 'e was runnin' off wiv counterfeit money an' the printin' plates. I got all this from John. I met

561

Westlake an' told 'im that my lads 'ad found the plates where Murray must 'ave buried 'em on the bomb site in Cooper Street, an' I'd told 'em ter leave 'em there. Westlake fell fer the story an' I said I'd show 'im where they were 'idden if 'e'd agree ter let Bannerman go free. 'E said 'e would but I knew 'e wouldn't keep 'is word. It made no difference though, 'cos while Westlake was bendin' over this piece o' pavin' stone I took out the carvin' knife from up me coat sleeve an' slit 'is froat.'

'Oh my Gawd!' Laura gasped, her hand at her mouth.

Queenie was impassive as she sat upright in her chair. 'I 'ad no compunction about doin' it, believe me. In fact it was just like slittin' a fowl's neck, an' I used ter do that every Christmas at one time,' she said with a distant gaze. 'I remember lookin' down on those starin', dead eyes an' I cursed 'is soul. Then I carved the initials W.S. on 'is cheek. Westlake was a whoreson while 'e lived an' I made sure that 'e's took that message to 'ell wiv 'im. I know I've gotta answer for it one day, but I'm sure the Lord'll take everyfing inter consideration. If I 'ave ter burn in 'ell, at least I know that I've paid Westlake back fer what 'e did ter my Mary.'

Laura sat dumb with shock as Queenie took a handkerchief from her apron pocket and dabbed at her eyes. Suddenly the big woman broke down sobbing, and Laura got up quickly and put her arm round her heaving shoulders. 'I'm sure yer'll be forgiven,' she told her, at a loss for anything else to say.

For a while Queenie sat silent, emotionally spent after her confession. Eventually she looked up at Laura with dry eyes. 'Roy came on ter the bomb site ter relieve 'imself just as I was leavin',' she explained. ' 'E was very drunk an' 'e fell over on the rubble. 'E didn't know where 'e was. I waited till 'e stumbled back ter the road then I follered 'im. 'E was staggerin' all over the place an' I took 'is arm. That's 'ow I come ter bring 'im ter yer door.'

Laura wiped a tear away from her cheek and smiled fondly at Queenie. 'I'm really very grateful that yer told me,' she said quietly. 'I know 'ow 'ard it must 'ave bin.'

'I feel much better now,' Queenie replied. ' 'Ave yer got five minutes if I put the kettle on again?'

Epilogue

Charlie Bromley and his young brother Frankie were standing together with Terry Grant outside the front door of number one, and their grubby, innocent faces turned to watch Wally Stebbings and Molly French walking along the paved area.

'That's Wally's gelfriend,' Charlie whispered to Terry.

'She's very old ter be a gelfriend,' Frankie butted in. 'I fink she must be seventy-five years old, or even ninety.'

'Nah, she only looks as old as Mum, an' Mum's not very old,' Charlie replied.

'Mum's pretty old,' Frankie argued.

'Hello, boys,' Wally said in a deep voice as he passed by.

' 'Ello, Mr Stebbin's,' Charlie and Terry answered him in unison, praying he wouldn't ask about the model fort.

Molly smiled sweetly at them and turned to Wally. 'They seem nice young lads,' she said. 'Were they the boys you made the fort for?'

Wally nodded. 'I don't suppose there'll be much time for model-making from now on,' he said matter-of-factly. 'There's a lot of work needed in the flat to get it up to scratch.'

Molly sighed happily. 'Ooh, Wally, I must tell you,' she said suddenly as they strolled along Weston Street. 'You remember that nasty Mr Lancing, the office manager?

Well, between you and me, I think he's going a bit senile. For the past week he's been in and out of his office like a cat on hot bricks, and yesterday I heard him say to one of the typists that the phone calls are driving him to distraction. Apparently someone keeps phoning him up asking about these Pekinese puppies for sale. I think he's just imagining it. Anyway, it serves him right, the way he treated you.'

Back in the Row Charlie shuffled his playing cards. 'We've gotta win our fort back off o' those Buildin's kids, Tel,' he said firmly. 'An' this time we're gonna play wiv my cards.'

Lucy and Roy were standing close together in the scullery when Laura walked in, and they smiled in embarrassment. 'Well, go on then, show us yer engagement ring,' Lucy said excitedly.

Laura displayed it proudly and Lucy gasped as she looked at her sister's outstretched finger. 'Cor! That must 'ave cost a bomb.'

Roy gave Laura a peck on the cheek. 'Congratulations,' he said fondly. 'I'm sure it'll all work out really well fer the two of yer. You deserve it, Laura.'

Laura smiled her thanks. She had decided earlier to approach Roy about the hidden knife and now, while he was looking very relaxed, seemed the perfect time. 'By the way,' she said casually, 'I was meaning to ask yer, Roy. When I was cleanin' the top o' the dresser the ovver day I found an' old knife. I left it where it was. Is it yours?'

Roy nodded. 'Yeah, it's me work-knife. I use it fer scrapin' old varnish off the cabinets we do up. I brought it 'ome the ovver weekend ter sharpen it an' Lucy told me ter keep it out o' the boys' way in case there was an accident. It seemed the best place on top o' the dresser. As a matter o' fact I took it back ter work this mornin'.'

Ernie Jackson had decided that the gods were smiling on
him and he was determined that it should remain that
way. On a dark night he took a taxi to Wapping High
Street, and as he walked over the swing bridge he looked
around furtively before taking the weighty parcel from
under his coat and dropping it, with a deep sigh of relief,
into the murky water below him. The water at that point
was kept at a high level by the lock gates, and he felt
confident that the printing plates would remain hidden in
the mud for the foreseeable future. One day some
excavating team might well uncover the copper plates
and no doubt feel that they had made a startling discovery. He should worry, he told himself. By that time his
head would not be aching.

Ira Stanley bent down with a grunt and picked up his
Saturday-morning mail. There was the usual pile of bills
and receipts, but one letter caught his eye. It bore a
Canadian stamp and Ira immediately tore the envelope
open. Inside there was a long letter written in a familiar
scrawl, and a photograph of a smartly dressed man
sporting a Van Dyke beard and standing beside a large
smiling woman. There were also two tickets for sea
passage to Halifax, Nova Scotia, and tickets for Toronto
via the Canadian Pacific railway. Marcus Levy, alias
Hiram Stanley, was planning a wedding to remember
and he wanted his old friend Ira and his wife to be there
for the ceremony when he married the widowed
Magdalena Thorpe.

'Is my best suit still a good fit?' Ira asked his wife.

'It fits as well as my best dress fits me,' Gilda told him
sarcastically.

'Then we'd better invite Manny Silverman round for
drinks,' Ira said, sighing. 'We'll need new rig-outs for the
wedding, and Manny might be able to do us a good deal.'

The families were gathering in the Bermondsey Town Hall committee room, which had been set aside for the meeting. Clara Hilton-Snape, the architect's assistant, busied herself with various papers, hoping that things would not become too noisy and unruly, and she smiled at Annie Stebbings who had just walked in holding on to Albert Prior's arm. They were followed by Joe and Bridie Molloy. A few minutes later Elsie and Len Carmichael came in, Elsie looking very angry and Len trying to act as though all was well. Eddie and Laura entered the large, lofty chamber along with Lizzie Cassidy and her husband Eric. Last of all was Queenie, who was clutching George's arm and looking very suspicious as she glanced around the room.

The architect's assistant seated herself at the long, highly polished table, her head bowed over the mound of documents in front of her. A tall young man suddenly came into the chamber from a side door and smiled nervously at the gathering as he took his place at the table facing them.

'I know you'll all be wondering and worrying about what I have to say,' he began, 'so I'll try to be as informative and helpful as I can. Firstly let me introduce myself. My name is Joseph Lee and I'm the Borough Architect. This young lady is Clara Hilton-Snape, my personal assistant.'

Clara smiled sweetly as she looked around the assembly.

'Now you all know that there's been an inspection carried out recently on your houses in Pedlar's Row,' the architect went on. 'I have to tell you that the inspection confirmed our fears that we have a major problem, due to the deterioration of the main sewage system and a gradual subsidence that has affected the foundations. In short, it means that the houses in the Row will have to be pulled down.'

There was a sudden murmur which increased in volume as everybody started talking together, and the architect raised his hands for silence.

'Now I know this has come as a shock to you all,' he said, 'but I can offer some good news. We have decided to bring our redevelopment plan forward with the aid of the government housing grant. Clara, will you put this up, please?'

The Pedlar's Row folk sat in stunned silence, eyeing the architect as he went over to the blackboard and stabbed at the plan with his forefinger.

'Here you can see the new blocks of buildings that will form three sides of a square,' he began, 'taking in Garfield's leather factory which adjoins Pedlar's Row, Cooper Street and the land along Weston Street as far down as the Bolton tanning factory. Pedlar's Row will become a partially raised grassed area inside the building complex, complete with trees. The outlook will be very pleasant and I have to say that I was determined some greenery should be included in the new building plans. I'm a Bermondsey lad myself; my father and grandfather lived in the borough too, and I feel it's very important that we develop pleasant dwellings with a good environment for all the people of Bermondsey. As a matter of fact my great-grandfather Joe was a pedlar who sold his wares in the borough.'

'Ashes to ashes,' Eric Cassidy whispered to Lizzie.

Lizzie nudged him. 'I s'pose yer 'appy now,' she hissed.

'As soon as the first stage of the building work is complete you will all be rehoused in the new block,' the architect went on. 'The last phase will be the demolition of Pedlar's Row and the grassing over of the site. Now, I'll be glad to answer any questions.'

'It's bloody weird,' Eric said to Len Carmichael later

that evening as they sat together in the Sultan. 'Did yer 'ear that architect feller say about 'is great-gran'farvver? I'd bet a pound to a pinch o' shit 'e was Gypsy Joe. It's really bloody weird.'

Len nodded sympathetically and finished his pint. 'I s'pose I'd better get back. Elsie ain't in a very good mood,' he said in a mournful voice.

'Why's that then, Len?'

'Those bloody soldiers, that's why.'

'She ain't got you paintin' 'em, 'as she?'

'Nah, but I tried to 'elp 'er out by puttin' the eyes on 'em,' Len went on. 'When Elsie come back wiv fresh boxes yesterday she was fumin'. Apparently the bloke at the firm told 'er she'd given 'im back two battalions o' boss-eyed troops. Mind yer, I'd just come off o' night shift when I done 'em.'

Laura strolled along the Row hand in hand with Eddie in the spring sunshine. 'Just fink. By the time those build-in's are finished we'll be married an' eligible fer a new flat,' she said, smiling happily.

A dull, clanking sound made her start and she looked up to see a small piece of guttering hanging down from the front of the Row. A metal rivet rolled against the wall and came to rest.

Eddie grinned and squeezed her hand. 'Yer'd better keep yer voice down, darlin',' he warned her. 'The ghost o' Gypsy Joe might get impatient an' decide ter bring the demolition date forward.'

A selection of bestsellers from Headline

LIVERPOOL LAMPLIGHT	Lyn Andrews	£5.99 ☐
A MERSEY DUET	Anne Baker	£5.99 ☐
THE SATURDAY GIRL	Tessa Barclay	£5.99 ☐
DOWN MILLDYKE WAY	Harry Bowling	£5.99 ☐
PORTHELLIS	Gloria Cook	£5.99 ☐
A TIME FOR US	Josephine Cox	£5.99 ☐
YESTERDAY'S FRIENDS	Pamela Evans	£5.99 ☐
RETURN TO MOONDANCE	Anne Goring	£5.99 ☐
SWEET ROSIE O'GRADY	Joan Jonker	£5.99 ☐
THE SILENT WAR	Victor Pemberton	£5.99 ☐
KITTY RAINBOW	Wendy Robertson	£5.99 ☐
ELLIE OF ELMLEIGH SQUARE	Dee Williams	£5.99 ☐

All Headline books are available at your local bookshop or newsagent, or can be ordered direct from the publisher. Just tick the titles you want and fill in the form below. Prices and availability subject to change without notice.

Headline Book Publishing, Cash Sales Department, Bookpoint, 39 Milton Park, Abingdon, OXON, OX14 4TD, UK. If you have a credit card you may order by telephone – 01235 400400.

Please enclose a cheque or postal order made payable to Bookpoint Ltd to the value of the cover price and allow the following for postage and packing:

UK & BFPO: £1.00 for the first book, 50p for the second book and 30p for each additional book ordered up to a maximum charge of £3.00.
OVERSEAS & EIRE: £2.00 for the first book, £1.00 for the second book and 50p for each additional book.

Name ....

Address ....

....

....

If you would prefer to pay by credit card, please complete:
Please debit my Visa/Access/Diner's Card/American Express (delete as applicable) card no:

Signature .... Expiry Date..............